Merry Christmas, Bertha

with appreciation for your great patience and help!

Tod

1979

SHADOW OF THE MOON

Also by M. M. Kaye

THE FAR PAVILIONS

Trade Wind

SHADOW OF THE MOON

M.M. KAYE

ST. MARTIN'S PRESS/NEW YORK

To
Sir John William Kaye
who wrote a history of the Indian Mutiny,
Major-General Edward Kaye
who commanded a battery at the Siege of Delhi,
my grandfather, William Kaye of the Indian Civil Service,
my father, Sir Cecil Kaye,
my brother, Colonel William Kaye,
and to all other men and women of my family
and of so many other British families who
served, lived in and loved India.
And to
that lovely land
and all her peoples,
with admiration, affection and gratitude.

 For information, write:
St. Martin's Press, Inc., 175 Fifth Avenue, New York, N.Y. 10010.
Manufactured in the United States of America

Library of Congress Cataloging in Publication Data

Kaye, Mary Margaret, 1911-
Shadow of the moon.

1. India—History—Sepoy Rebellion, 1857-1858—
Fiction. I. Title.
PZ4.K233Sh 1979 [PR6061.A945] 823'.9'14 79-5033
ISBN 0-312-71410-6

. . . and there you can see
Our English sun, convalescent after passing
Through the valley of the shadow of the moon.

Christopher Fry, *Venus Observed*

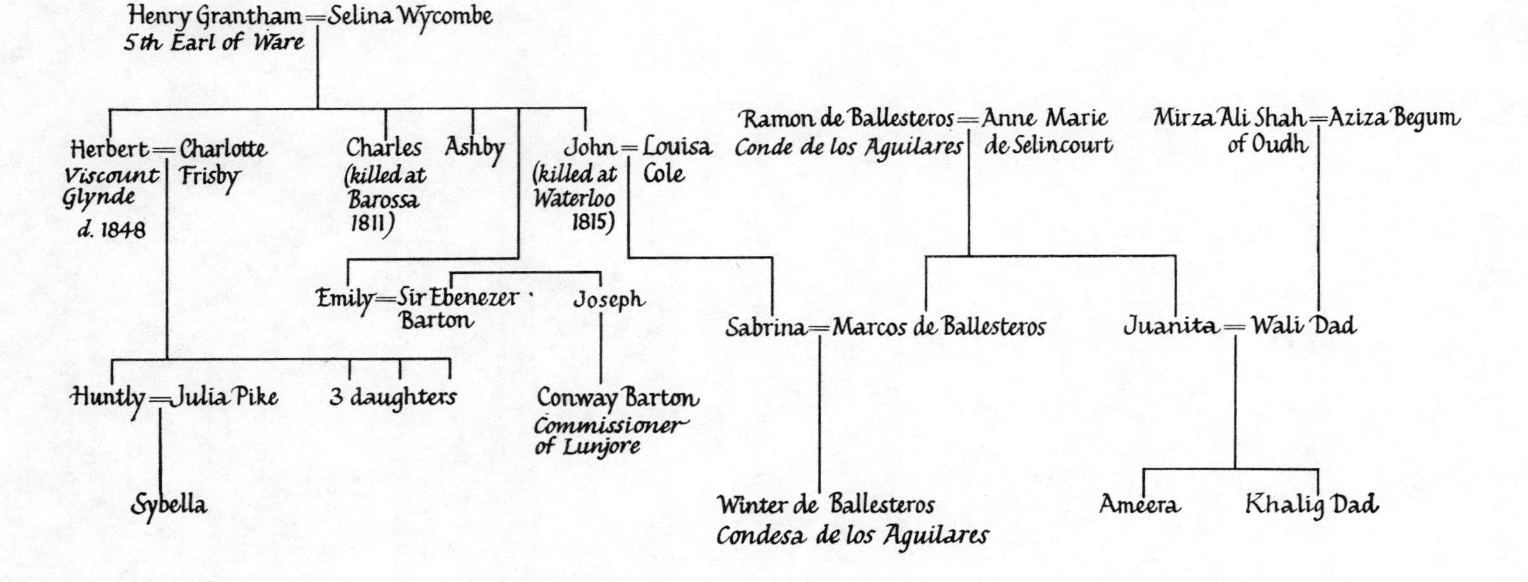
Henry Grantham = Selina Wycombe
5th Earl of Ware
Herbert = Charlotte
Viscount Glynde
d. 1848
Frisby
Charles
(killed at Barossa 1811)
Ashby
John = Louisa
(killed at Waterloo 1815)
Cole
Ramon de Ballesteros = Anne Marie
Conde de los Aguilares
de Selincourt
Mirza Ali Shah = Aziza Begum
of Oudh
Emily = Sir Ebenezer Barton
Joseph
Sabrina = Marcos de Ballesteros
Juanita = Wali Dad
Huntly = Julia Pike
3 daughters
Conway Barton
Commissioner of Lunjore
Sybella
Winter de Ballesteros
Condesa de los Aguilares
Ameera
Khalig Dad

BOOK ONE

THE SHADOW BEFORE

A glossary of Indian words appears on page 613.

I

'"*Winter*"! Who ever heard of such a name? It is not a name at all! Do pray be sensible, my dear Marcos. You *cannot* call the poor mite anything so absurd.'

'She will be christened Winter.'

'Then at least let her have some suitable second name. There are so many pretty and unexceptionable names to choose from.'

'No. Only Winter.'

Kindly Mrs Grantham threw up her arms in a gesture of exasperation. 'But my dear boy, only think how absurd it will sound! – Winter de Ballesteros de los Aguilares.'

'Sabrina wished it,' insisted the distraught young father stubbornly.

Mrs Grantham knew when she was defeated. There was no arguing with Marcos in his present frame of mind. If only the christening could be postponed he might yet be brought to see reason. But the baby was a sickly infant whose chances of survival appeared to be so slight that it had been considered expedient to baptize her without delay, and Marcos, who was a Spaniard and a Catholic, had even agreed to allow the ceremony to be performed by an Anglican parson; cholera having struck down the only available priest, and the child's mother having belonged to the Anglican Church. Marcos had been sufficiently distraught to agree to almost anything, but he remained adamant in the matter of his daughter's baptismal name.

'*Winter*!' repeated Mrs Grantham, dabbing ineffectually at her swollen eyes. 'Poor 'Reena must have been out of her mind.'

But Sabrina – poor pretty Sabrina – dying in childbirth in the merciless heat of an Indian May, had not been out of her mind. She had been thinking of Ware . . .

Sabrina's paternal grandfather, Henry John Huntly William, Fifth Earl of Ware, had married Selina Emily, youngest daughter of Sir Arthur Wycombe, Baronet, in the early summer of 1788: the year in which the Young Pretender – 'Bonnie Prince Charlie' of song and legend – died miserably in exile.

Their union had been a fruitful one, and punctually each spring for five successive years the dutiful Selina had presented her husband with a lace-swaddled bundle of squalling humanity. Herbert, Charles, Ashby, Emily and John had followed each other into the world in swift succession. But their mother's constitution, never robust, had proved unequal to the strain, and shortly after the birth of the last-named she had fallen into a decline and died.

The Earl, a hasty-tempered and autocratic man, had been sincerely attached to her, and though still not thirty at the time of her death he did not remarry; announcing instead that his daughter Emily could take over the management of his household as soon as she was old enough to leave the schoolroom. That day being a long way off, he installed an elderly female relative to see to his offspring's welfare and engage such nurses, tutors and governesses as she considered necessary to deal with their upbringing and education. Children, decided the Earl, were not only a dead bore but a confounded nuisance, and as his own grew up he saw no reason to revise that opinion; with one notable exception. His youngest son, John.

His first-born, Herbert, Viscount Glynde, had been a stolid child both in build and temperament, and grew up to be a stolid and silent young man. Charles early displayed a taste for cards, horseflesh and the society of opera dancers, and Ashby – bookish, nearsighted and interested only in the vanished civilizations of Greece and Rome – bored and irritated his father. Emily was more to his taste: she had failed to inherit her mother's beauty, but that she possessed more than a dash of his own firmness and character was proved by the fact that she left the schoolroom while still only fifteen, and having consigned the elderly relative to a position of comfortable obscurity, took over as chatelaine of Ware. She was a plain girl, kind-hearted and capable, but lacking in the charm that might have earned her a higher place in her father's regard; and like her three elder brothers she had always been more than a little afraid of him. It was only John who was not afraid.

Only John – Selina's last child, who had cost her her life – had inherited both his mother's beauty and his father's spirit, and the Earl loved him as Jacob loved Benjamin.

Johnny was everybody's favourite. A beautiful boy. Bold, bright and filled to the brim with the joy of living. Almost any other child would inevitably have been ruined by the spoiling he received, but there was something in Johnny's character that was pure gold without a trace of alloy. In him his father's quick temper and tyrannical disposition were transmuted to a high spirit and complete fearlessness, and though his less favoured brothers and sister might have been expected to resent the open and unblushing favouritism shown him, he was their darling.

'"*The dearest of them all, my handsome, winsome Johnny,*"' their old nurse would sing. And it was true. There was never such a boy. By the time he was fifteen he could out-ride, out-shoot, out-fence and out-box any young man in the county under twenty, and his father frequently found himself regretting, with a shamed feeling of baffled resentment, that Herbert and not Johnny was the heir.

Johnny, had he thought about it, would probably have chosen the younger of his two elder brothers for that role, for the dashing Charles had always been his hero, and when Charles received a Commission in a famous regiment, and rode to Ware for the first time in all the bravery of scarlet, gold-lace and a clanking sword, Johnny felt that he could hardly wait until he too would be old enough to hold the King's Commission.

But Charles rode away to the war, and to his death on a bare, stony Spanish hillside at the battle of Barossa.

Two years later, in 1813, Herbert, with an unhumorous recognition of his duty as the heir, married Lady Charlotte Frisby, a distant cousin of his mother's. The young couple did not set up a separate establishment, but remained at Ware, and it was here that the Earl's first grandchild, a boy, was born in the following year: an event somewhat overshadowed by the fact that Johnny had obtained the coveted Commission, and been gazetted a cornet of horse.

A year later, writing from Brussels less than three weeks after his twenty-first birthday, Johnny had announced his marriage to Louisa Cole:

'You must not think,' wrote John to his father, 'that because this news is unexpected, and comes to you in this manner, there has been anything clandestine about my marriage. But Louisa's father died very suddenly last week, and since her mother wished to leave Brussels immediately, there was nothing for it but to marry her out of hand.'

The Earl could not be expected to feel anything but dismay at the news, but his wrath was somewhat mitigated by the fact that he knew the bride's father by reputation. Mr William Cole was on the Board of Directors of the Honourable the East India Company, of which the Earl was a shareholder, and Louisa, being his only child, was a considerable heiress.

'I know you will love her,' wrote Johnny to his sister Emily, 'for she is everything that is sweet and gentle. You do not know what a lucky fellow I am. I can hardly wait to bring her home and show her to you all – and you to her. What a day that will be!'

But it was a day that was destined never to be realized.

Perhaps there is some truth in the saying that those whom the gods love die young, for certainly Fortune had done nothing but smile upon Johnny Grantham. But now the sands had run out. At the Duchess of Richmond's ball in Brussels he danced for the last time; tall and gay and laughing, outrageously handsome in his scarlet and gold uniform as he moved through the quadrille with his pretty young bride. Two days later he was dead, killed in the bloody shambles of Hougoumont on the field of Waterloo.

For a time life lost all meaning for the Earl of Ware.

When he had first heard the news he had raged furiously and futilely against fate. Why Johnny? Any one of his children – all of his children – but not John! He had turned his face to the wall and cursed God. But the days passed and the weeks lengthened into months, and the first frenzy of grief gave place to a dull resentment and then to numb acceptance. No one could ever take Johnny's place in his heart, but life had to go on and there was work to be done.

But there was one who lacked the Earl's resilience, and for whom the mainspring of life had been irreparably broken – Johnny's wife, Louisa, who had come to live at Ware: a shadow of the pretty young creature who had danced with her handsome husband at the Duchess of Richmond's ball.

Johnny's daughter, Sabrina, was born on the first day of the New Year, 1816, and by the evening of the same day Louisa had gone to join her young husband. There had been no particular reason why she should have died; except perhaps, quite simply, that she did not wish to live. And now that she had gone her sister-in-law, Emily, constituted herself foster-mother, guardian and protector in her stead to the baby Sabrina.

'Why Sabrina?' inquired the relations and connections. 'There has never been a Sabrina in the family before. Not one of *our* names at all.'

But it was Ashby who was responsible for that. Ashby the bookish, standing awkward and embarrassed by the lavishly trimmed cradle in the green dusk of a January evening. The tiny creature, not yet a week old, had already lost the crumpled redness of birth, and in the cold dusk she appeared unbelievably fair. Milk-white skin and hair the pale gold of early primroses – her father's hair. Grey eyes the colour of water on a winter's day – Johnny's eyes . . .

Ashby, his awkwardness changing to half-awed admiration, had quoted a line of Milton: '"*Sabrina fair – listen where thou art sitting, under the glassy, cool translucent wave.*" We ought to call her Sabrina.'

Sabrina grew quickly. Too quickly, mourned Emily. And every day she grew more like Johnny. Her grandfather, who had imagined that no one could ever take his youngest son's place in his heart, discovered that his son's child occupied it as if by right. All the love and pride and affection that he had lavished on her father he transferred to Johnny's daughter: to the unconcealed resentment of Herbert's wife, Charlotte, who considered it a piece of shocking injustice on the part of Providence that the good looks of the Granthams and the Wycombes should have passed her own children by, only to be lavished upon the daughter of the youngest, and therefore (in Charlotte's view) the least important son of the house.

Sabrina had been nine years old when she was taken on a lengthy visit to her mother's relations. Emily took her, and it proved to be the turning-point of both their lives.

England was changing. George III, the old mad King who had lingered on so long, a living ghost in a wing of Windsor Castle, had died at last, and the gross and scandalous 'Prinny' was King. The Regency was over, and Regency England with its bucks and beaux, Corinthians and Macaronis already fading into history and legend.

Emily was thirty-three, and by the standards of the day, middle-aged and doomed to perpetual spinsterhood. 'Such a pity dear Emily never married,' said the various aunts, uncles and cousins: 'She could have made some man an excellent wife. Of course she will never marry now.' But Emily surprised them all.

Louisa's father, Johnny's Louisa, and his father and his grandfather before him, had been rich merchants, engaged in trade with the Far East – 'nabobs' the popular press termed them. And it was at the house of Louisa's Aunt Harriet Cole that Emily met Sir Ebenezer Barton of the Honourable the East India Company, home on leave from his vast palace on the banks of the Hooghly.

Sir Ebenezer was then forty-five. A tubby little man with a choleric blue eye, mutton-chop whiskers and a face tanned by the suns of the East to a rich shade of mahogany. No one could imagine what Emily saw in him or he in her, but see something they did. Something that was hidden from other eyes. Emily the cool, the efficient, the dependable, blushed under his gaze like a girl fresh from the schoolroom, and Ebenezer, a singularly untalkative man, took her for walks in the park and found himself talking to her of India and his work; of the strange, brown, treacherous river beside which he lived. Of tiger hunts and elephants, and oriental princes and potentates, glittering with fabulous jewels, who lived in medieval state in fantastic marble palaces.

Emily was no Desdemona. It would not have made the smallest difference to her had he talked instead of stocks and shares or indoor plumbing. She was not interested in the East; only in Ebenezer. She found him lovable and dependable and knew that she could love him and mother him and lean upon him. She even thought him handsome.

Ebenezer, twelve years her senior and recently returned from a considerable spell in India, found in her his ideal woman. To him she appeared young without being 'missish': a poised, serene Englishwoman. He had always been ill at ease with women, but not with Emily. With her he was at home and at rest. He actually thought her beautiful.

They were married from Ware in the autumn of 1825, and Emily drove away with her Ebenezer to a honeymoon tour of the Lake District, leaving Charlotte to take over the duties of hostess and chatelaine of Ware, and charge of Sabrina's education and upbringing.

Sabrina did not welcome the change. True, her grandfather continued to pet and spoil her, but she was unable to spend more than a small portion of her time in his company, since the larger part of her days was spent, of necessity, in the schoolroom and under the eye of nurses and governesses selected by her Aunt Charlotte.

In 1830 'Prinny' died; unregretted by his people and unmourned save by his stout and grasping inamorata, Lady Conyngham. William IV, 'Sailor Bill', became King. And in the draughty Palace of Kensington a small, prim, composed little girl played with her dolls and went for walks with her German governess, still unaware that she was heiress-presumptive of England and destined to lift the Monarchy out of the mud and ridicule to which her uncles had reduced it, to unbelievable heights of popularity and prestige . . .

When Sabrina was seventeen her grandfather gave a ball to mark her début, and immediately Ware became the lodestone for every young gallant in five counties. Sabrina could have taken her choice of a dozen eligible offers, and Charlotte was not pleased.

Charlotte had seldom been pleased with Sabrina, and now she found it intolerable that her own plain, prim, well-mannered daughters should be entirely cast into the shade by her niece's golden loveliness and gay, inconsequent charm. To make matters worse the girl refused every offer made her in the course of the next two years; though this was not because she had never fallen in love. Indeed she fell in love only too often, but to her aunt's indignation and her grandfather's relief, she appeared incapable of remaining in love with the same man for longer than a week or so at the most.

To get Sabrina married and removed from Ware became Charlotte's relentless objective, and in the end it was Emily who unconsciously assisted her to attain it. Emily and the Earl and a certain Captain of Hussars . . .

The Lady Emily Barton, home on a visit to her father's house, was about to return to India to rejoin her Ebenezer – now a baronet and appointed to the Governor-General's Council. She had begged to take Sabrina with her for a year, and though at any other time the Earl would undoubtedly have refused, it so happened Emily's request had coincided with the appearance upon the scene of the first man in whom Sabrina had taken an interest that outlasted three weeks.

Captain Dennis Allington of the Hussars was handsome, dashing and experienced in the matter of women, and Sabrina, who found him dangerously fascinating, continued to allow him to dance attendance upon her, and treated him with more favour than she had previously shown to any of her suitors.

The Earl had become seriously alarmed. He knew Captain Allington to be a gambler and a spendthrift, with a reputation, where women were concerned, that would not bear investigation, and such a man was no suitable husband for his favourite grandchild. But when he attempted to take Sabrina to task she had been pert and saucy. Emily's invitation had therefore come at a propitious moment and the Earl grasped at it as a way out of his difficulties. He would send Sabrina away for at least a year: Emily could be trusted to take the greatest care of his darling, and Captain Allington out of sight would soon be out of mind.

Charlotte gave the project her enthusiastic support, but Sabrina herself was in two minds upon the matter. She was devoted to her Aunt Emily and found the prospect of a voyage to India both exciting and agreeable; on the other hand, there was Dennis Allington. She was not at all sure that she was not in love with Dennis, and she suspected that the whole idea of a year's stay in India was solely designed to part her from him.

While she wavered, Captain Allington himself decided the matter; and with it her future . . .

It had happened at a ball at Ormesley Court where Sabrina, having torn the lace flouncing of her dress during a country dance, had retired to get it repaired. Hurrying back to the ballroom she had taken a short cut through a side corridor and come suddenly upon Captain Dennis Allington kissing Mrs Jack Ormesley.

To do the Captain justice he had not intended to kiss Mrs Ormesley, whom he had been conducting to a salon where refreshments were being served. But as they passed through a small corridor which happened at the moment to be deserted, Mrs Ormesley had tripped on the trailing end of her long lace scarf, and would have fallen had Captain Allington not caught her. Not being a man to waste such an opportunity he kissed the lady, who returned his embrace with every appearance of enjoyment, and he would have thought no more of the incident had he not lifted his head to encounter the frozen gaze of the Honourable Sabrina Grantham.

On such small trifles do fate and the future depend. If Sabrina had not torn six inches of flouncing from the hem of her dress, or if Mrs Jack Ormesley's scarf had been six inches shorter, Emily would have sailed for India alone instead of being accompanied by her favourite niece.

Sabrina had been enchanted with India. She possessed a gay and uncritical nature, and everything, from the long and tedious voyage round the Cape to their arrival in the teeming port of Calcutta, delighted her. Dennis Allington and his perfidy were soon forgotten, and long before the end of the journey was reached Sabrina would have found it difficult to recall his features in any detail.

She enjoyed her customary success in Anglo-Indian society, but did not find herself in love again with any of the officers and officials who danced attendance upon her.

'I must be getting old, Aunt Emily,' said Sabrina in a panic. 'I haven't been in love for a year!'

It was 1837, and she was twenty-one.

Her grandfather had already written demanding her return, but since Emily's health had not been too good of late, Sabrina did not feel that she could leave her. Nor, in fact, did she wish to leave, for India still held a potent charm for her. Her Uncle Ebenezer, as a prominent member of the Governor-General's Council, would go on stately tours during the cold season, accompanied by his wife and her niece, and it was during an official visit to the court of the King of Oudh that Sabrina had met Juanita de Ballesteros.

Juanita's father, the Conde de los Aguilares, was a wealthy and eccentric Spanish nobleman who as a young man had travelled much in the East. Arriving in Oudh almost half a century earlier he had been greatly attracted to the country and the people, and in particular to a nephew of the ruling King. The two young men, Spaniard and Mussulman, had become fast friends. They were curiously alike in both features and temperament. Perhaps because the blood of a dark-eyed daughter of Islam, from the days of the Moorish conquest of Spain, had been transmitted down the ages to this son of Castille and Aragon.

Ramon de Ballesteros, Conde de los Aguilares, never returned to Spain. Oudh became his home, and the rich, barbaric, colourful kingdom his country. The King of Oudh made him a grant of land on the banks of the River Goomti, and there, surrounded by groves of orange and lemon trees and green, formal gardens, he built a house; a vast Spanish *castello* in the heart of India.

The Casa de los Pavos Reales, the House of the Peacocks, merged into the Eastern scene with the same ease and grace as its owner – Spanish architecture, with its cool open courtyards and splashing fountains, its high rooms and secretive balconied windows, being to a large extent the legacy of a conqueror from the East.

In due course the Conde married; not, as might have been predicted, a daughter of the royal house of Oudh, but the only child of a French *émigré* who had fled with his family from the bloody holocaust of the Revolution, and had subsequently taken service in the Army of the East India Company.

Anne Marie de Selincourt was a gentle dark-eyed creature who could not remember the country of her birth. She had been barely a year old when her parents had fled with her from France, and having lived ever since in the East, the Hindustani and court Persian of Oudh were as familiar to her as the Tamil and Telegu of the south, or the English tongue and her own native French. She settled into the colourful polyglot life of her husband's great house on the Goomti and never realized its strangeness. Her friends were the slender, olive-skinned, dark-eyed wives of the princes and nobles of Oudh, and her fourth child, Juanita, was born in the house of Aziza Begum, wife of her husband's great friend, Mirza Ali Shah.

'She shall marry the son of an Emperor and wear pearls on her head, and ride on an elephant in a golden howdah,' said Aziza Begum to Anne Marie, rocking her own small son in her arms; and the two young mothers had laughed together over the heads of their sleeping children.

Only two of Anne Marie's seven children survived their infancy; her son Marcos and her daughter Juanita. The others fell early victims to cholera and typhus, those two deadly plagues of the East. When Marcos was fourteen years old his father dispatched him to Spain in order that his son might complete his education in his native land, and Marcos did not return for nine years. By then he was a slim young man with the dark, hawk-like handsomeness that is so frequently seen among the great families of Aragon and Castille, and his sister Juanita had married her childhood playmate, Wali Dad, son of Ali Shah and Aziza Begum.

The marriage had aroused considerable opposition from both Christian priests and Mohammedan maulvis, but had in the end received the consent and approval of both families. Aziza Begum's slender figure had grown corpulent and unwieldy with the advancing years and her blue-black hair was streaked with grey, while the unrelenting heat of the Indian summers had shrivelled the young Anne Marie to a thin little woman with a nutcracker face and prematurely white hair. Their husbands were elderly grey-beards, their children grown men and women, and Aziza Begum was already grandmother to half a dozen plump brown babies. But though they and the world had changed, the old friendship between the two families had not. Handsome young Wali Dad, Aziza's first-born, fell in love with Anne Marie's gentle dark-eyed daughter: his parents had never denied him anything, and why should they deny him this? 'There is no God but God,' said Ali Shah to the maulvis, 'but is not Hasrat Isa (Jesus Christ) also numbered among the Prophets? And are not Christians also "Children of the Book"?'

'One of our own line was a Moorish maiden,' said the Conde Ramon. 'And Ali Shah is my oldest friend and Oudh the country of my adoption. If the young people desire it, I will not refuse my consent.'

Sabrina Grantham, visiting Oudh with her aunt and uncle in the spring of 1837, met Juanita de Ballesteros, wife of Wali Dad, at a banquet in the women's quarters of the Chutter Manzil Palace in Lucknow.

It was strange that two women of such dissimilar background and temperament should have found so much in common, but between Sabrina and Juanita there sprang up and flourished an instant and deep affection. They were young and of an age; each found the other different and stimulating and romantic, and they were friends from the first moment of their meeting: Sabrina, blonde and grey-eyed, with a skin like milk, wearing the trim-waisted, full-skirted fashions of the day with their absurd flower and ribbon and feather-decked hats as if they had been designed solely to accentuate her beauty, and Juanita, whose creamy magnolia-petal skin and large brown eyes lent a piquant touch of European charm to the graceful Eastern costume that she habitually wore.

Emily, who had remained staunchly insular, was at first both shocked and disgusted at the idea of a 'white woman' married to an Indian and living in what she persisted in referring to as a 'harem'. But she could not help being charmed by Juanita and her handsome gay young husband, her elderly and eccentric father and her gentle little mother; and as the long warm days of March merged into the heat of April, she allowed Sabrina to spend more and more time at the Casa de los Pavos Reales or in the Gulab Mahal* – the little pink stucco palace in a quiet corner of the city, where Juanita lived.

* Gul (rhymes with 'pull')-*arb* Ma-*harl*.

When April gave place to May and the heat danced and shivered on the walls and domes and minarets of Lucknow, Sir Ebenezer with his wife and niece retreated to the hills, taking Juanita with them: not because the heat held any terrors for her, but because she was expecting her first child, who would be born in the autumn, and as her health had not been too good of late it was felt advisable to send her to the cool of the hills. There was also an additional consideration. Trouble was brewing in the city.

The rulers of Oudh had been among the most corrupt of Eastern potentates – though this had not deterred the East India Company from lending troops to the King, in return for a large subsidy, in order to help him keep his dissatisfied subjects in a proper state of subjection. The present ruler, Nasser-ood-din Hyder, was easily the worst of a long line of evil men, and he had already been exhorted by Sir William Bentinck to mend his ways. But neither warnings nor threats had weighed with the King, and at long last the Court of Directors of the East India Company had taken action. They had sent a dispatch to Colonel John Low, the Resident of Lucknow, authorizing the temporary assumption of government in Oudh by the Company. But Colonel Low, certain that such a move would be misunderstood and bitterly resented throughout India, had begged instead that Nasser-ood-din should be deposed and replaced by another ruler selected from among the royal line. The strictest secrecy had been preserved, but the East has a sixth sense in such matters. Suspicion and speculation were rife, and all Oudh seethed with rumour and counter-rumour . . .

The Conde Ramon had of recent years withdrawn himself more and more from the world outside the high white walls that bordered his estate, and save for a handful of old friends, of whom only a few were European, he lived a life of retirement and seclusion. But even into this quiet backwater there crept ripples of fear and unease, so that when Lady Emily Barton had suggested that his daughter accompany their party to the hills, he had accepted the invitation with gratitude and urged his young son-in-law to agree to Juanita's departure.

It was cool among the pine trees and rhododendron forests of the hills, and here life appeared to move at a more peaceful and leisurely pace than in the teeming plains. Beyond the folds of the foothills rose the higher ranges; line upon line of wild, jungle-clad hills with behind and above them the changeless snows, their white, ethereal peaks unmoved by Time or the hurrying feet of History. Yet history was being made and the times were changing.

Far away in a small rainy island at the other side of the world a King died, and a young girl scarcely out of the schoolroom, who was to give her name to one of the greatest periods of British history and in time to be proclaimed Empress of all India, ascended the throne of Great Britain. The Victorian age had begun.

* * *

When the monsoon rains broke over the burning plains of India, Juanita would have returned to Lucknow. But Wali Dad and her mother-in-law Aziza Begum forbade it. 'Stay yet awhile, beloved,' wrote Wali Dad, 'for there is evil work afoot in this city and I am uneasy as to what is toward. Though my house is dark without the light of thy presence, nevertheless the thought that thou, my Heart and my Life, art safe from all danger, is of great comfort to me. When this evil is past I will come and fetch thee away.'

So Juanita stayed in the hills while far below, in the hot, humid capital of Oudh, Colonel John Low pleaded by dispatch and letter for the replacement of Nasser-ood-din by another of the royal house, rather than the annexation of his kingdom by the Company.

Colonel Low, like many of his contemporaries in the ranks of 'John Company', was alarmed and dismayed at the direction the affairs of the Company had taken. The Honourable the East India Company – 'John Company' – was a company of merchants and traders. They had come to India to buy and sell, and trade and profits were what they desired. They did not want an Empire. Yet slowly and insidiously, or so it seemed, an Empire was being thrust upon them.

In the days of the Great Moguls a British ship's surgeon had successfully treated the badly burned and beloved daughter of the Emperor Shahjahan, and when asked what he wished for in reward, had requested permission for the British to trade in Bengal. Those first small trading posts had flourished and paid rich dividends, but in their very success they had aroused the envy and resentment of other traders from beyond the seas.

The French, the Arabs, the Dutch and the Portuguese were also rivals for the golden prizes of Indian trade, and the British merchants, in order to protect their factories and their lives, had been forced to arm themselves and to hire mercenaries. They had in time succeeded in defeating their rivals and in establishing a monopoly of trade, but as their interests grew and expanded, and more and yet more factories and warehouses were built, the need for larger forces for their protection grew also; for the times were troublous ones, and India a medieval medley of small and warring states riddled with corruption, trickery and intrigue. The 'Company of Merchants' made treaties with many of these petty kings, and on behalf of their allies fought with others, while their arms, of necessity, kept pace with their profits. The Genie of Force had been let out of the bottle and it became impossible to replace it. Instead of reaping a harvest of gold, as they had in the early years, the Directors of the East India Company found themselves pouring out treasure upon what had become no less than a vast private army, and acquiring, in order to protect their trade, a huge and ever-enlarging Empire.

It was Robert Clive, one-time clerk in the service of the Company, who conquered India and propounded the revolutionary theory that if a country is taken over from its rightful owners, then it must be governed for the greater benefit of those owners and not merely to the advantage of the conquerors; and the erstwhile merchant adventurers found themselves, to the dismay of many of their members, dealing more and more in territorial administration and less and less in trade. Their armies policed the land and they appointed Governors and Residents and Political Agents to dispense law and justice to this vast country to which they had come to barter and remained to conquer, and their profits dwindled away.

'No man goes so far as he who knows not where he is going,' said Oliver Cromwell. The men of 'John Company' had not known where they were going, and they had travelled a long and far road from the days of the seventeenth century and those first small trading settlements on the coast of Coromandel. They had defeated Tippu Sultan, ruler of Mysore, and divided and apportioned his territory. They had defeated the Mahrattas and the Gurkhas, and deposed the Peishwa and added his lands to the Presidency of Bombay. Was the ancient Kingdom of Oudh now to go the same way, and its rule pass from the hands of its royal house into those of the Company? Colonel Low, for one, was resolved to do all he could to prevent it.

The whole question of India, he considered, was getting out of hand, for the greater the Company's territorial power and possessions, the less profit in terms of trade. 'John Company' was not only losing money, but was heavily in debt, and it was out of the question that they should take over the sole government of Oudh. Besides, he did not believe that the people of Oudh, though they had little love for their vicious kings and would welcome the fall of Nasser-ood-din, would approve of the rule of a foreign company in his stead. They would only see it as another example of Western aggression and the barefaced theft of more territory, and there would be riots and uprisings – and once more the profits of trade would be swallowed up in unprofitable wars. Yet Nasser-ood-din must be deposed.

But even as Colonel Low pondered the question, one aspect of his problem was solved for him. On a hot night in July Nasser-ood-din Hyder died by poison; and immediately all Oudh was in a ferment. The succession was in dispute and the streets of Lucknow surged with gangs of lawless troops ready to strike in support of their particular nominee, and only the firmness and courage of Low and a handful of British assistants saved the seething city from a bath of violence and blood. Eventually, with the consent of Lord Auckland the Governor-General, an aged and crippled uncle of the late King ascended the throne of Oudh. The city quietened, and Juanita returned to the pink stucco palace in Lucknow.

Juanita's brother was back from Spain: a tall stranger whose gay laughter awoke unaccustomed echoes in the quiet of the Casa de los Pavos Reales.

The warm, drenching rains of September washed the city clean, and October brought in the brilliant days and cool nights of the Indian cold weather. The Bartons returned to Lucknow where they were to spend a month with the Resident, and Sabrina, paying a call at the House of the Peacocks with her Aunt Emily, met Marcos de Ballesteros.

It was of course inevitable that they should fall in love. Marcos, dark-haired and romantically handsome, with his gay laugh and the novelty and charm of one newly come from that most charming of countries, Spain, and Sabrina Grantham who had, surprisingly enough, not been in love for over a year, and who was so small and slim and blondly beautiful.

'My niece, Sabrina——'

'My son, Marcos——'

They had stood looking at each other in the cool white hall of the Casa de los Pavos Reales where the orange trees grew in tubs as they do in Spain, and where the sunlight, filtering through the lemon trees planted about the house, filled the hall with a green, aqueous light.

Marcos too had read Milton, and the same lines that Ashby had quoted so many years ago at the cradle of the infant Sabrina rose now in the mind of the young grandee of Spain:

'*Sabrina*!' thought Marcos, staring at her entranced. ' "*Sabrina fair – listen where thou art sitting, under the glassy, cool translucent wave.*" Yes, she is like a mermaid. A water nymph.'

'He is like a Knight of the Round Table,' thought Sabrina. 'Like the picture of Sir Tristram in that book in Grandpapa's library.'

They stood and looked at each other and fell in love.

2

Juanita's daughter was born, and the old, old lullabies of Spain and France and Hindustan were sung above her cradle.

'*Hai mai!*' sighed Aziza Begum to her friend Anne Marie, 'rememberest thou the day thy daughter was born? So also do I. I am now an old woman, very fat and slothful, but it is as though it were yesterday. The years go swiftly: too swiftly. But there will be many more grandchildren for thee and me, and surely the next will be a son . . .'

For Sabrina it was a time of enchantment: a page cut from a fairy-story. But Emily was full of anxiety and foreboding. Emily was staunchly and stubbornly British; possessed of all the ingrained insularity of her race. Her two children had both been born, lived their brief days and died in this hostile foreign land, and had been laid to rest in this alien soil. She did not find India beautiful or exciting. She saw it only as the graveyard of her children; an uncivilized and barbaric country with a medieval standard of morality, sanitation and squalor that it was the divinely appointed but distasteful task of men like Ebenezer to govern and control and lead into the path of enlightened Western living. It was therefore not surprising that she viewed the attachment between her niece Sabrina and Marcos de Ballesteros with disapproval, and persuaded herself that it was no more than a passing infatuation that would fade as others had faded.

But this time Sabrina was in love: in love for the first time in her life. No one looking at her could doubt it for a moment. She walked as though her small feet barely touched the ground and it was as though an almost visible aura of happiness surrounded her. To Marcos, accustomed to the dark-haired women of Spain and France and his father's adoptive country, Sabrina's golden loveliness seemed like something out of this world – rare, fragile and exquisite. When they were together, in whatever company of people, it was as if they saw only each other; heard no other voices speak.

Emily awoke to the dangers of the situation too late (though had she but known it, even one moment after their meeting would still have been too late), and she prevailed upon Ebenezer to put forward the date of their departure from Lucknow. The Bartons had planned to visit the old Mogul capital of Delhi before proceeding to Calcutta, where they would remain until the spring, when Sabrina was to return to England. But Sabrina, who had once been delighted at the prospect, now viewed their impending departure with blank dismay and pleaded to be allowed to remain in Lucknow.

Emily had remained firm and Sabrina had wept stormily. And four hours later Marcos had asked for an interview with Sir Ebenezer Barton and had requested his permission to ask his niece for her hand in marriage.

Sir Ebenezer was for once at a loss. He both liked and respected the Conde de los Aguilares, and thought his son a very pleasant and well-mannered young man. He also knew the Conde to be immensely rich and of the best blood of Spain, and his wife Anne Marie to be descended from the old nobility of France. In many ways Marcos must be considered a most eligible match. But there were drawbacks; the greatest of which, in Sir Ebenezer's eyes, being that Marcos was what Sir Ebenezer termed to himself 'a foreigner' – by which he did not mean so much the young man's French and Spanish ancestry, but his mode of life, which was foreign to the English point of view. Many men like Sir Ebenezer Barton lived and worked and often died in this country that the 'Merchants of London trading to the East Indies' had conquered. But they never thought of it as 'Home'. To Marcos however, and to his father, mother and sister, India, and in particular the Kingdom of Oudh, was home. Marcos had returned to it from nine years spent in Spain and Europe, and it had been for him a home-coming. And his sister had married an Indian – a man of an alien faith.

'You desire my permission to ask my niece for her hand in marriage,' said Sir Ebenezer heavily, 'but have you not already asked her without that permission?'

'No,' said Marcos, very white about the mouth. 'I had not thought of it. I mean – I could not have done so without speaking first to you, but it seemed a thing that need not be said. I have known it from the first moment I saw her. I had meant to speak to you, but . . .'

Marcos could not explain even to himself, much less to Sir Ebenezer, the remote and enchanted world in which he and Sabrina had seemed to move ever since that first moment of their meeting. Of *course* they would one day marry and live happily ever after – what a foolish question! And because Marcos was his father's son, he would not say the formal and unnecessary words until he had duly asked the formal and necessary permission to speak them. Meanwhile it was enough for both of them to realize that they had found each other. It was from this dream-like state that Emily's decision to remove instantly to Delhi had aroused them.

Sir Ebenezer hedged, playing for time. He was in no position, he said, to grant or withhold permission for his niece's marriage: that responsibility rested with her grandfather, Lord Ware. Marcos must wait until such time as the Earl's views could be made known, which would be of necessity a matter of a few months.

'But Sabrina is twenty-one,' said Marcos. 'She is of age. I have requested this interview with you only because it is correct that I should do so. If it is true that you cannot grant or withhold consent, neither can Lord Ware. Only Sabrina can do that.'

‘He can disinherit her,’ said Sir Ebenezer drily. ‘The bulk of his property that is not entailed is to come to Sabrina.’

‘She will not need it,’ said Marcos. ‘You know that my father is rich and that I am his heir. Sir Ebenezer, I beg you to permit me to address her.’

‘And if I refuse?’

Marcos’s gay laugh rang out suddenly. ‘Then I ask her without it. I am sorry, but I cannot help myself. When you wished to espouse the Lady Emily, if permission to address her had been refused, what would you have done?’

Sir Ebenezer cast a reminiscent eye over that long-ago summer in Hampshire when he had fallen in love with his Emily, and was betrayed into a smile.

‘Never did ask for it, my boy. Asked her straight out. But then that was quite a different thing, you know. Emily wasn’t a chit from the schoolroom. She was of age.’

‘So is Sabrina.’

‘There is a vast difference between twenty-one and thirty-three!’ retorted Sir Ebenezer with an unconscious lack of gallantry.

‘Not in the eyes of the law,’ said Marcos.

‘Lady Emily will not hear of it,’ said Sir Ebenezer, cravenly shifting his ground. ‘She has set her heart on removing to Delhi immediately. She had hoped by doing so to avoid a declaration.’

‘Am I then so undesirable a *parti*?’ demanded Marcos bitterly.

‘No, no,’ said Sir Ebenezer unhappily, ‘it is not that. It is that she would have wished . . . Sabrina’s grandfather would have wished the child to marry someone who resided in England. Your home is here, and if she marries you it is here that she will live her life. That will seem a sad loss to those of her family who love her most dearly. You do not realize how great an affection my father-in-law has for Sabrina. It would be a cruel blow to him if she should remain in this country.’

‘There is no reason why we should not visit England on occasions,’ said Marcos with the buoyancy of youth.

‘That is not at all the same thing. To see someone you love once in six or eight years, and then only for a few brief months, is not enough.’

‘But I too love her!’ said Marcos passionately. ‘Am I to sacrifice my happiness and hers so that her grandfather may be made happy?’

‘Oh, well,’ said Sir Ebenezer, giving the matter up. ‘I cannot think what my father-in-law will say to all this. What a plague and a problem women are!’

He wondered what he was to say to Emily: Emily was going to be difficult.

Emily was more than difficult. She was distraught. ‘You should have made him see how impossible it is – how unthinkable! Oh, what will Papa say? How could you consent to such a thing?’

‘But my dear, I have not given my consent. I could not do so even if I wished. I am not Sabrina's guardian, I am only her uncle by marriage. Besides, the girl is of age, so we can only hope that your father's wishes may count with her. She must at least wait until his views are made known.'

'We will remove to Delhi immediately,' said Lady Emily. 'And if Marcos attempts to follow us I shall send Sabrina home to Papa, even if I have to take her myself.'

'But I cannot go with you,' said Sabrina, starry-eyed with happiness. 'I am going to marry Marcos.'

'You are going to do no such thing! I refuse to allow it.'

'You cannot stop me. Darling, darling Aunt Emily – do not be unkind. I am so happy. I never knew that anyone could be so happy. Do you not wish me to be happy?'

Emily wrung her hands and wept.

Sabrina would not leave Lucknow and Emily could not remove her by force, since as Marcos had already pointed out, she was of age and could therefore marry whom and when she wished. She had agreed, however, to make no plans until her grandfather's wishes were made known.

Emily, Sir Ebenezer, Marcos, Conde Ramon and Sabrina all wrote to the Earl of Ware, and Marcos wrote to Rome for a dispensation for his marriage. Emily cancelled her visits to Delhi and Calcutta and remained in Oudh. Her husband went, but he went alone.

The Christmas mails from England brought with them the news that Huntly – Herbert and Charlotte's only son – was to marry Julia Pike, the daughter of one of Charlotte's oldest friends. The wedding would take place in the spring and the Earl wrote to urge the immediate return of both daughter and grand-daughter so that they should be at Ware for the wedding of his only grandson. Sabrina, said the Earl, had stayed quite long enough in the East and it was high time she returned home. He added a postscript to the effect that Captain Dennis Allington had recently married the daughter of a wealthy cotton-manufacturer from Manchester.

Although Emily had known that these letters could not possibly contain the answers to those that had been dispatched homeward less than two months ago, guilt had made her eye the packet that bore her father's handwriting with considerable apprehension. But now she stood for a long time holding the pages in her hand and looking out of the window through a screen of blazing bougainvillea to where the distant domes and minarets and jostling roof-tops of the Indian city met the intense blue of the Indian sky, her thoughts four thousand miles away . . .

Huntly! That fat, solemn silent baby, Herbert's son who had been born the year before Waterloo . . . the year before Johnny died . . . And now Huntly was to marry Julia Pike. 'Well, if she is anything like her mother, I am sorry for Huntly,' said Emily. 'Sabrina, dear child, *could* you not consent to go home in the spring? Just for the wedding? It will look so particular if you are not there. And then you could discuss your own affairs with Papa at the same time. So much more suitable in every way. You and Marcos are both young. You can afford to wait for a few months, and it would mean so much to your grandfather . . . and to Huntly, of course.'

'Huntly? Pooh! Huntly does not care a fig for me or I for him. Uncle Ashby once said that Huntly was a cold fish, and he was right. No, Aunt Emily. If I go to Ware it will be as Marcos's wife. I love Grandpapa. He is a darling. But he is an old tyrant too, and I don't trust him.'

'Sabrina! What a dreadful thing to say.' Emily was genuinely shocked.

'But I mean it. Look how he behaved over Dennis Allington. Oh, he was right about Dennis, I know. But do you not see, Aunt Emily, even though he was so fond of me, he could send me away to India just to get his own way?'

'That is not fair, Sabrina,' said Emily. 'He did it only to prevent you from making a very great mistake. He wished to save you from unhappiness.'

'Oh, I know, Aunt. But it was not only my happiness he was thinking of. Supposing I had been really in love with Dennis? I was not, but suppose that I had been? He would not have cared. I was only to marry when he decided and whom he decided, and he was prepared to do anything to get his own way. If I went back to England now he'd try to stop me from marrying Marcos. He is a darling old tyrant from the Middle Ages, and I am afraid of him.'

'Oh dear,' sighed Emily, 'it is all going to be very difficult. I hope you may not find that you have made a sad mistake. You think now that this country is beautiful and romantic. But how are you going to like living all your days here? Heat, disease, wars, famines . . .'

'I shall have Marcos,' said Sabrina.

Emily gave it up and waited with as much resignation as she could muster for the arrival of the mails from England that would bring her father's answer to the request for his blessing upon the marriage of his granddaughter to Marcos de Ballesteros.

The new year dawned over Oudh in a blaze of saffron-yellow light. A new year that was to see the coronation of the young Queen Victoria, the Austrian evacuation of the Papal States, France declare war on Mexico, the abolition of slavery in India and the start of the disastrous Afghan War.

Beyond the borders of Oudh, in the Land of the Five Rivers, Ranjit Singh, the fabulous 'Lion of the Punjab', held dissolute court in Lahore; plundering the hapless peasantry, meting out savage punishment to those who angered him and heaping wealth upon those who pleased, intriguing with the British and driving himself towards an early grave by a deliberate indulgence in drink and debauchery.

To the north, among the barren hills of Afghanistan, Dost Mohammed the Amir, disappointed in his hopes of a treaty with the British, began to turn his thoughts towards Russia, while the British Emissary, Alexander Burns, defeated by the stubborn stupidity of Lord Auckland from making an ally of Afghanistan, prepared to return empty-handed to India.

In the capital city of Oudh, Sabrina Grantham celebrated her twenty-second birthday with a picnic in a grove of trees upon the river bank, and a ball at the Casa de los Pavos Reales.

The gardens were hung with lanterns on the night of Sabrina's Birthday Ball and the great house was gay with music and laughter, a flutter of fans, the glitter of jewels and the clink of dress-swords. Sabrina wore a dress of white crêpe trimmed with gold embroidery, and a magnificent triple row of pearls that were a birthday gift from Anne Marie to her future daughter-in-law.

'They were my mother's,' said Anne Marie, clasping the lustrous strands about Sabrina's white throat. 'She had them from her mother on her wedding day, who had worn them at the marriage of Louis XVI and Marie Antoinette. I have always meant them for Marcos's betrothed as a wedding gift, but I felt that I should like you to have them now – for your birth-night ball. You shall wear them at your wedding also, is it not so?'

But the year that had dawned for Sabrina with so much sunshine and happiness darkened swiftly. Anne Marie died in the first week of February. Perhaps it had been some premonition of the future that had decided her to give the pearls to Sabrina on her birthday instead of waiting until her wedding day.

As it must be in the East, the funeral took place within a few hours of Anne Marie's death; but to the Conde, although he was familiar with this abrupt disposal of the dead, the short space of time between his wife's death and her interment was particularly shocking. In Spain her body would have lain in state in the family chapel with candles flaring at the head and foot of the coffin while weeping mourners passed by, incense burned and priests sang masses for her soul, and only after several days would she have been carried in procession to her last resting-place in the family vault.

It did not seem right to Don Ramon that Anne Marie should be hurried thus to her grave, and when the rest of the household had retired to bed he took candles and flint and went by night to the little marble mausoleum he had built so many years ago to house the bodies of himself and his family. Five of his children already lay within it, and now Anne Marie had gone to join them.

No one heard him go save the night-watchman on guard outside the house, and him the Count beckoned to follow him, for he knew that he could not of his own frail strength open the heavy doors of the vault. The watchman, who saw nothing strange in this reverence to the dead, did not think to report it, and the ageing Count lit his candles and kept vigil all night beside the cumbersome lead coffin that contained the body of his wife. The night air had been warm and gentle, but the marble vault still held the chill of winter, and by morning he was shivering with cold and fatigue and unable to walk the short distance that lay between the mausoleum and the house. He was carried to his bed and did not leave it again. The chill reached his lungs and he died on the third day, and by the same evening his body lay beside that of Anne Marie's in the marble mausoleum of the Casa de los Pavos Reales.

'Now they are together again,' said Sabrina. She had wept for Anne Marie as though it had been her own and greatly beloved mother who had died. But her grief had been in part for the Count, lonely and bereft. Now that he too was dead she could not weep for him. She could only feel comforted. Somewhere, they were together again; not in the cold vault where the heaped flowers were already turning brown, but in some far and happy country of the spirit.

The brilliant days and cool nights of the late winter gave place to the warmer days of the Indian spring, and the days were hot and the nights pleasantly mild. It was more comfortable now to remain indoors, with the shutters closed against the glare, during the greater part of the day, and to go abroad only in the early mornings and the late afternoon.

The new fashions with their tight-fitting longer bodices, modest collars and full wide skirts suited Emily's taste, but with the approach of the hot weather she regretted the cooler and less formal draperies of the Directoire mode. Victorian England, in reaction from the laxity and licence of the preceding reigns, was already moving rapidly towards primness, and the gay high-waisted gowns and diaphanous materials of the earlier years of the century were giving place to more solid fabrics and a greater degree of sober respectability. Sir Ebenezer was still absent in Calcutta and the mails from England, though infrequent, never failed to bring a peremptory missive from the Earl of Ware commanding his grand-daughter's immediate return.

March brought with it a steadily rising temperature, dust-storms, and the monotonous, maddening call of the *köil*, whom the British had nicknamed the 'brain-fever bird'. It also brought Sir Ebenezer Barton and the dispensation that Marcos had written for to Rome.

Sir Ebenezer found his wife looking sallow and careworn after the sorrows and anxieties of the past two months, and much in need of a change of air. Emily, he thought, not only appeared tired and ill but as though she had suddenly aged ten years. He was both alarmed and angry, and spoke sharply to Sabrina, whom he held solely responsible for her aunt's anxieties and indifferent health. He would, he said, arrange for an immediate removal to the cooler air of the hills, and this time there would be no nonsense as to Sabrina refusing to accompany them.

Sabrina, thus rudely awakened from her absorption in Marcos and his affairs, was stricken with remorse, for with the selfishness of those who are young and in love she had given little attention to her aunt's state of mind and health during the past months. Aunt Emily certainly did not look well;

the heat was making her unusually listless and a few months spent in the pine-scented air of the hills would undoubtedly improve her health and spirits. But Emily would not consent to leave Sabrina behind in Lucknow.

If Anne Marie had still been alive it would have been a different matter, as it would have been entirely suitable for Sabrina to stay in the house of her future mother-in-law. But now she could not stay at the Casa de los Pavos Reales, and Emily refused to consider Juanita's house as a suitable place for a young unmarried girl to remain for a visit of more than a few days at the most: 'No, I have not forgotten that Juanita is Marcos's sister, and should you ever marry him' (Emily persisted in regarding it as a matter of doubt) 'you will of course be able to make your own decisions on that score. But at present you are under my care and your uncle's protection and you must be guided by us.'

In this Juanita had unexpectedly – and most unfairly, thought Sabrina – supported Lady Emily.

'You do not understand, *cariño*. Our menfolk do not think as yours on these matters. No, no – it is different for me. My mother and my husband's mother were friends before we were born, and my husband and I played together as children. I am of two worlds, but you are only of one.'

'When I marry Marcos I shall be of two also,' said Sabrina, 'England and Spain.'

Juanita shook her head. 'When you marry Marcos you will still belong only to one: to the West. To Europe. I belong to the East also, for I was born in the women's quarters of an Indian palace – in this house of Aziza Begum's who was my mother's dear friend and is my husband's mother. But even were I to agree to your remaining here with me, my husband's mother would not permit it. Already she is troubled because my husband's uncle, Dasim Ali, follows you with his eyes and makes excuses to call upon his nephew my husband when he knows that you will be visiting here at the Gulab Mahal. Go to the hills, Sabrina *chérie*, and Marcos can visit you there. Soon a letter from the grandfather will come, and you will be married and all will be well.'

'But Marcos cannot leave Lucknow,' said Sabrina forlornly. 'There are so many things to be seen to. So much to be done. He could only get away for a few days, and I cannot bear to leave him.'

'It will only be for a little while,' comforted Juanita. 'Time goes swiftly.'

'Not when you are unhappy,' said Sabrina, voicing the age-old discovery as though it were new.

A kinswoman residing in Lucknow, a Mrs Grantham, had already left for the cool of Simla, and although there were other British women in the city, Sabrina had never been intimate with any of them. They thought her charming, but were uneasy as to her association with the young Count from the Casa de los Pavos Reales, who was, after all was said and done, a Spaniard – a 'foreigner', whose sister had married an Indian.

Many of the Company's men, exiled from their homeland for long years at a time, had admittedly taken Indian brides, and many more had contracted less permanent alliances. But the reverse was of rare occurrence and therefore tended to arouse considerable comment and hostility. The British matrons who, with their daughters, dined and danced and drank tea in company with Lady Emily Barton, would not be likely to welcome her niece for a prolonged visit, so it seemed that Sabrina would have no recourse but to leave for the hills with her aunt. But even as preparations for their departure were made, the question was decided otherwise.

On a hot evening towards the end of March, while a dry wind rattled the dying leaves of the bamboos and *neem* trees, and the pariah dogs of the city bayed a sultry yellow moon rising through the hot dusk, the letter they had been awaiting for so long arrived from England.

It was short and to the point. On no account whatsoever would the Earl of Ware consent to the marriage of his grand-daughter to this expatriate Spaniard who had settled in the East. He had no intention of allowing Sabrina to throw herself away on any man, however wealthy or well born, who was not only a foreigner but had made his home in such a barbarous and uncivilized spot. As for Emily and his son-in-law, to whose care he had entrusted his grand-daughter, the Earl could only think that they had gone out of their minds to entertain any thought of such a preposterous marriage Sabrina would return home instantly. In the event of her refusing to do so and of persisting in this outrageous folly, she would be cut out of his will and cut off from all future contact with him or his family. This was his final word upon the subject.

'Well, that settles it I am afraid,' said Sir Ebenezer to his wife. 'We will have to cancel our plans for your stay in the hills, and you, my love, will have instead to take Sabrina home: at least the voyage will benefit your health. I only wish that I could accompany you myself, but I am afraid that pressure of work forbids it.'

Emily, exhausted by the heat, the problems of packing and moving to the hills, anxiety on Sabrina's behalf and awe of her father, gave way to an unexpected attack of hysteria and took to her bed – she would not leave Ebenezer! Sabrina must of course return to Ware – had she not said so from the first? – but she herself refused to desert her husband in order to act as escort to her niece. Both Mrs Tolbooth and her daughter, and Sir Hugh and Lady Bryan, were shortly leaving for England, and she was persuaded that either family would be only too happy to undertake the care of Sabrina.

But Sabrina had no intention of being sent home to England in the care of Mrs Tolbooth, Sir Hugh and Lady Bryan, or indeed of anyone else. She had promised her aunt and uncle that she would wait until her grandfather's views on her marriage to Marcos de Ballesteros were made known, but she had not promised to abide by those views. Now that her grandfather's letter had arrived, offering her the choice of giving up Marcos or being cast off and disinherited, there was no further need for delay. She could not stay with Juanita, and as Aunt Emily's health necessitated her removing to the cool of the hills, Sabrina solved the problem quite simply by marrying Marcos.

She would have liked Aunt Emily to be at her wedding, and dear Uncle Ebenezer too, but since she did not wish to involve them in any unpleasantness with her grandfather, she left a note pinned to her pincushion in the traditional manner, and slipping out of the house had her horse saddled and rode away to Marcos.

They were married in the little chapel of the Casa de los Pavos Reales in the presence of two young officers of the 41st Bengal Cavalry, friends of Marcos's on their way to rejoin their Regiment after a leave spent shooting in the *terai*, and of Juanita, who had been hurriedly summoned from her home in the city.

Sabrina wore a dress of Anne Marie's that she and Juanita had found stored away in a camphor-wood chest in Anne Marie's rooms, for she had brought nothing with her except the clothes she stood up in and the pearls that Marcos's mother had given her on the night of her Birthday Ball.

'I cannot be married in a riding-habit,' said Sabrina with a light laugh. 'It looks too – too urgent. As if we had suddenly decided to be married, in a great hurry. But we have known from the beginning that we would get married one day, and it is only the circumstances that have made it appear sudden and hurried.'

The dress was of a cut and fashion of over a quarter of a century earlier. The white satin of which it was made had yellowed with age, and the lace overskirt with its knots of pearls was as fragile as skeleton leaves. They had found it laid away among a dozen or more outmoded gowns of a similar cut, and did not know that it had been Anne Marie's wedding-dress. Juanita added a white lace mantilla that Marcos had brought back from Spain as a gift to his mother, and clasped the triple row of pearls about Sabrina's throat.

'Now you look like a bride, and very beautiful. I know that it should not be a white dress, because of Mama and Papa. But I am so sure that they would not have had you wear mourning for them when you marry Marcos. We cannot be sorrowful on such a day. The *cura* is waiting. Come and get married.'

Someone had put jasmine and white roses in the chapel, and the *cura* had lighted candles on the altar. The ring that had also been one of Anne Marie's slipped onto Sabrina's finger; a broad gold band set round with small pearls. Anne Marie's fingers had been plumper than Sabrina's and the ring was heavy and a little loose. Sabrina looked down at it – this symbol of her marriage to Marcos that had belonged to Marcos's mother – and as she looked at it she was aware of a strange feeling of timelessness and of the continuity of life. It was as if she realized for the first time that she and Marcos, who were young and gay and with all their life before them, must one day die as her own father and mother and Anne Marie and Don Ramon had died. That life was not long at all, as it appeared when one was young and impatient, but very short and very swift, like the shadows of the clouds racing silently over the unheeding earth. But that this was not a sad thing, because all time was one. She seemed to see it stretching back behind her and away ahead of her. Anne Marie who had been young once had worn this ring, and now she was dead and her son's wife wore it; as one day a daughter of Sabrina's would wear it in her turn. Anne Marie was still here in Marcos and Juanita, as she would be in their children and grandchildren . . .

Henry and Selina – Johnny and Louisa – Sabrina and Marcos . . . All time was one, and Sabrina was suddenly filled with a warm, shining happiness and an assurance of immortality.

'*Jesu dominus ora pro nobis.*' The words of the blessing echoed softly under the domed roof of the small chapel, and then Sabrina was signing her name on a paper that she could not read in the pale candlelight. There was dust upon the paper, the drifting all-pervading dust of the Indian plains, and the quill-pen scratched harshly in the stillness. Marcos also wrote his name, and the two young officers and the *cura*, and Juanita.

'Now you are really my sister,' said Juanita.

'The Condesa Sabrina de los Aguilares: my wife, *mía esposa*,' said Marcos, and kissed her, laughing.

They drank wine in the great drawing-room where the portraits of dead and gone Condes and Condesas, brought from Spain, looked down upon that light-hearted bride and the few guests who had attended her wedding. The two young officers toasted the bride and groom, and Wali Dad, who had brought Juanita from the city but had not attended the ceremony in the chapel, made a speech in flowery court Persian which only his wife and the *cura* understood, but which everyone applauded.

Sabrina and Marcos walked through the patio and stood on the wide terrace in the warm moonlight among the shadows of the lemon trees, watching the wedding guests ride away. The moon that had been rising above the mango-topes when Sabrina had ridden to the Casa de los Pavos Reales was already low in the western sky, and despite a first hint of the faraway dawn the air was cool, and sweet with the scent of orange blossom. And once again that strange sense of being one with all time and all living swept over Sabrina. One day this great house would crumble into ruin and be no more than the little heaps of timeworn stones that marked where some forgotten city had stood, like those among which her horse would sometimes stumble when she rode out over the plains or along the river bank. But she, Sabrina, would go on into time, as through Johnny and Louisa she went back into time . . .

'I shall live for ever and ever,' thought Sabrina, exalted. 'But however long I live I shall never again be as happy as I am now.'

* * *

Wali Dad's father, who had been Conde Ramon's friend, died that spring, and Sir Ebenezer and Lady Emily left for the cool air of Simla where Emily's health improved and Sir Ebenezer attended those endless conferences that were to result in the disaster of the first Afghan War.

In England, at Ware, the primroses that had barely come into bud at the time of Sabrina's wedding gave place to crocuses and daffodils and tulips. Hawthorn whitened the hedges, and the chestnut trees in the park were bright with spires of blossom that vied with the bunting and streamers that decorated the approaches to the castle in honour of Huntly's wedding. Huntly's bride Julia looked classically beautiful upon her wedding-day, and Huntly appeared adequately happy. Charlotte, for her part, felt smugly satisfied: Huntly was safely married to the bride of her choice, while Sabrina, that constant thorn in Charlotte's flesh, had contracted a *mésalliance* with a young Spaniard and been disinherited by her grandfather. There was only one thorn left in Charlotte's bed of roses; the fact that her three daughters were still unmarried. And judging from their looks, thought their grandfather, likely to remain so.

The Earl had aged considerably of late. Emily's letter, informing him that Sabrina had taken matters into her own hands and contracted a runaway match without his approval and against his express wishes and commands, had dealt him a cruel blow. He had been an autocrat all his days, and with the exception of his son John and his grand-daughter Sabrina, no one had ever seriously taken issue with him – with the result that it never occurred to him that anyone would ever do so.

Emily's letter had come overland via Egypt and had reached him in less than eight weeks, and only a few days before Huntly's wedding. It was followed shortly afterwards by one from Sabrina, but his rage and grief were still at white-heat, and he had enclosed her letter in another covering and returned it to her with the seal unbroken.

The furnace heat of the Indian summer closed upon Oudh like a steel trap from which there was no escape. But the high white rooms of the Casa de los Pavos Reales, with their thick walls and shuttered windows and the patios with their fountains and orange trees, had been built for coolness, and Sabrina did not suffer too greatly from the heat that first summer; though she grew pale from the enforced inaction of the long months.

In the early morning before the sun rose, or in the late evening after it had set, she would walk in the gardens with Marcos or ride with him in the park-like grounds that surrounded the house. But even at those hours of the day the stifling heat was almost unbearable and she was thankful to return to the dim, shuttered rooms where the swinging punkahs and the tinkling splash of the fountains at least gave an illusion of coolness.

Marcos, born in the East and educated among the sun-baked plains and fierce heats of Aragon, remained to a large extent impervious to the rising temperature. His father had left vast estates, for the Count had from time to time acquired land in outlying parts of Oudh, and as Marcos spent the greater part of each day in the saddle, Sabrina would often have been lonely that summer had it not been for Juanita.

Juanita and her baby daughter, and her husband Wali Dad, were frequent visitors at the Casa Ballesteros; but Aziza Begum never came. 'I am too old and too fat to go abroad,' said the Begum to her daughter-in-law, 'and your brother's wife speaks our tongue but haltingly. Also it fills my heart with sorrow to walk in the house of the friend of my youth who is dead – as my youth also is dead.' But often during the long hot evenings, if Marcos were away for the night, Sabrina would visit the Gulab Mahal, and as the moon rose into the dusty twilight the women would sit out on the flat roofs of the zenana quarter looking out across the minarets and white roof-tops, the green trees and gilded cupolas of the evil, beautiful, fantastic city of Lucknow, while Aziza Begum cracked jokes and shook with silent laughter, stuffed her mouth with strange sweetmeats from a silver platter, or told long, long stories of her youth and of kings and princes and nobles of Oudh these many years in their graves.

At first Sabrina did not understand more than one word in ten of the old lady's conversation, but she had a quick ear and a lively intelligence and would spend hours of the long sweltering days lying on a couch under a swaying punkah at Pavos Reales, learning the language from Juanita or Wali Dad or the wizened old *munshi* whom Marcos had engaged to teach her. Aziza Begum complimented her upon her progress, and as a mark of her favour sent a woman of her household, Zobeida, to be Sabrina's personal servant.

Zobeida was the daughter of a zenana slave; dark-skinned and sturdily built, with a quick brain, light deft hands, willing feet and a steadfast heart; and Sabrina grew to love her and to depend upon her as though she had been some faithful nurse from the days of her childhood. A love that Zobeida reciprocated with the protective devotion of a mother for her child.

With the arrival of the monsoon rains the deadly grip of the hot weather relaxed its hold a little. The warm rain fell from a dun-coloured sky in sheets of water that turned the parched dust to rivers of mud, and brought a fantastic wave of green, growing things where only yesterday there had been nothing but burnt grass. Then the hot winds would blow again and the mud cake over, and the sun blaze savagely down, turning the caked mud to iron and covering it again with a thick layer of dust that would whirl up into the dust-devils that danced across the scorching plains – until the next rain would fall and turn it back once more into liquid mud and green, steaming jungle.

But while the plains gasped in the grip of the hot weather, in the hills, among the pines and deodars of Simla, the Governor-General, encouraged by the irresponsible advice of men whose lust for power and conquest had made them deaf to the dictates of prudence, justice or common sense, had decided to declare war on Afghanistan.

It mattered little to Lord Auckland and his favoured advisers that Dost Mohammed, the Amir of Afghanistan, was the chosen ruler of a people who infinitely preferred him to that elderly weakling, Shah Shuja – the ex-ruler whom they had driven from his kingdom many years before. The Governor-General's advisers distrusted a man of the Amir's ability, who had proved that he could both think and act for himself. They considered it a vital matter of policy that Afghanistan should be an ally of Britain, and suspecting that Dost Mohammed might intrigue with Russia, decided to force the rejected Shah Shuja back on his unwilling people, in the belief that gratitude and self-interest would bind him to the British. With the object of making an ally of Afghanistan they began by making her a foe, and went to war with the Amir in order to avoid the remote possibility of his declaring war on the British. With this end in view they concluded a treaty that amounted to nothing less than a pact of mutual aggression with the dying Ranjit Singh, 'Lion of the Punjab' and ruler of the Sikhs.

In November, with the onset of the cold weather, the grandiloquently named 'Army of the Indus' assembled at Ferozepore before marching on Afghanistan, and Sir Ebenezer Barton, sick at heart at what he considered to be a war of unparalleled injustice and stupidity, resigned his seat upon the Council and retired to Lunjore, a small state upon the western borders of Oudh, to spend the winter months as the guest of the Resident, who was an old and valued friend.

Business connected with his mother's family called Marcos south that winter, and as the roads were rough and travel both difficult and uncomfortable, he went alone.

At any other time Sabrina would have insisted on accompanying him, but she was pregnant and subject to frequent attacks of nausea. And realizing that should she insist on going she would not only cause him considerable worry and alarm, but perhaps jeopardize the life of the unborn child, she gave way with as good a grace as she could muster, and agreed to spend the intervening weeks until Marcos's return with her Aunt Emily and her uncle at the Residency at Lunjore.

The Residency was a rambling house that had once been part of a much larger building; the summer residence of a local princeling. A former 'John Company' official had altered it to a great extent, pulling down those parts of it that had formed the zenana quarters and retaining only the larger reception rooms to which he had added considerably. The house stood in extensive grounds on the edge of the jungle from which it was separated by a deep nullah that formed a natural barrier and defence on one side, while on the other three the original fort-like ramparts had been replaced by a high wall of whitewashed stone in which only the massive gateway still remained to mark the fact that this had once been a semi-royal residence.

Despite her grief at being separated from Marcos, Sabrina was delighted to see her aunt and uncle again. They had parted from her in some anger after a brief interview following her wedding, but had made their peace by letter when the cool airs and quiet of Simla had restored Lady Emily to better health and a more tolerant frame of mind. 'After all, it is the child's own life,' decided Emily. 'She has the right to choose her own path. Papa is not God, and he cannot expect to alter the course of people's lives just to suit himself.' And she had sat down and written an affectionate letter to Sabrina that had gone a long way towards healing the hurt caused by the return of her own letter, unopened, by her grandfather.

'He does not really mean it, Aunt Emily,' explained Sabrina, discussing her grandfather's conduct with his only daughter. 'He hates not getting his own way. Well so do I, so I can sympathize with him a great deal. I got my way about Marcos and Grandpapa did not, and so he is in a rage about it. But one day I shall go back to Ware and, you will see, everything will be all right again. I am so fond of him, and I know that he cannot stop loving me just because I have disobeyed him.'

Emily was not so sure, but she kept silent. She was considerably disturbed by her niece's appearance. Sabrina was painfully thin and there were faint hollows in her cheeks and under her grey eyes, and no colour in her face. Her white skin had a strange look of transparency which reminded Emily uncomfortably of a story that she had once heard about Mary Stuart, the ill-fated Queen of Scots. Legend had it that when the Queen drank wine it could be seen passing down her throat, and though Emily, an eminently sensible woman, had always considered the story ridiculous, now she was not so sure. Sabrina's little neck and her white, thin arms and shoulders had a curiously delicate and transparent look that her aunt did not like.

'We must feed her up,' said Sir Ebenezer robustly when Emily spoke of her niece's appearance. 'Plenty of good food and rest; that is what she needs. She'll get both in this house and soon be as right as a trivet.'

Emily duly set about tempting her niece's appetite with the connivance of the Resident's Goanese cook, but the early days of Sabrina's pregnancy were proving troublesome ones, and she could eat little. The baby was not expected until late in June, and it was as yet only December; but Sabrina was racked by constant bouts of nausea and weakness which the doctor could do little to alleviate. And she did not like the Lunjore Residency.

This dislike was presumably only another manifestation of her condition, but the big house with its wide verandahs and high, echoing rooms seemed to her not only unfriendly, but in some inexplicable way actually hostile. It was different from other houses, but she could not tell why.

From the first moment that she had stepped over the threshold of the Casa de los Pavos Reales, Marcos's house had seemed to welcome her, and the feeling of a personal identity that almost every house possesses in some degree had been, in Pavos Reales, a friendly one. But it was not so in the Residency of Lunjore.

Perhaps her nerves were on edge. Perhaps it was because she was missing Marcos, or because of the baby; but she not only disliked the house, but was at times even afraid of it. While there were lights in the rooms, and her host the Resident, her aunt and uncle or the servants or any guests moved about them, they were just rooms: a background for the people who occupied them. But on the few occasions when she had been alone in them it was different, for then the empty rooms would seem to her to be full of whispers – and of dead people.

The garden was no better, for the dead were there too. And once, riding home in the bright morning sunlight from the open plain and the distant river, she thought that she saw the figure of a girl running swiftly towards her across the narrow wooden bridge that spanned the nullah behind the house; a girl in a strange hooped dress. Peri, the gentle chestnut mare, saw her too and shied violently, nearly throwing Sabrina. But it was only a trick of the sunlight and the wind-blown shadow thrown by a tall cluster of bamboos . . .

Zobeida, sensing her young mistress's unease, took to sleeping on a palliasse at the foot of her bed, and though Sabrina was ashamed of her fears she found Zobeida's presence comforting and did not dissuade her. To Emily, who had caught her once standing stiff and frightened in the dusk, she had said confusedly: 'There is someone who is very unhappy here. As if – as if it were *me*!'

Early in January Marcos returned from the south and took Sabrina home to the Casa de los Pavos Reales. He too, as Emily had been, was startled by Sabrina's thinness and pallor. Until this visit to the south he had never been away from her for longer than forty-eight hours since their marriage, and so had not noticed the change in her, for it had come about by imperceptible degrees. Now, seeing her again after an absence of several weeks, it struck him forcibly and with alarm.

'It is only the baby,' Sabrina assured him. 'I am really quite well, I promise you. And the sickness is so much better. The doctor says it is only natural, so you must not be alarmed. Once I am home again in dear Pavos Reales I shall be quite well again – you will see. It is only because I have missed you both so much.' And certainly once she was back in the House of the Peacocks her spirits rose and some of the lovely colour returned to her cheeks.

Juanita did not come so often to visit her these days, for the birth of her own second child was imminent and she preferred to remain within the seclusion of her own house. But when Marcos was absent Sabrina spent much of her time at the Gulab Mahal, talking and laughing with Juanita and Aziza Begum and playing with her niece, Juanita's black-eyed, dimpled first-born.

She was there on a golden morning in early February when Juanita's pains began, and would have stayed with her but that Aziza Begum and Juanita herself would not permit it.

'Send her away, my mother,' whispered Juanita urgently, the sweat already pearling on her brow. 'The English are not as we. They tell their maidens nothing of these things, and because it will go hard with her when her time comes, it were better she were not now made afraid.'

'*Arré*! and who should know better than I?' nodded the Begum. 'Her time will indeed be hard. She is not made for the bearing of children. *Hai mai*! I will send her away, do not fear. Rest now, my daughter, and in a little while my son's son lies in thy arms.'

Aziza Begum stuffed her mouth with *pan* leaves and waddled out to summon the carriage and reassure the anxious Sabrina. 'Do not fear: it is but a time that comes to all women. And what woman amongst us all would forgo it had she the choice? Not one, my bird! – not one. For is not this the end for which we were born? All will be well here. I, who have borne many children, tell you so.'

To Sabrina the obese old woman who was Juanita's mother-in-law had always seemed a grotesque figure; but now, suddenly, she saw her with new eyes. Saw the kindness and the shrewd wisdom in the bright eyes that peered out of that fat, wrinkled mask; the firmness and character that lay in those small plump hands; and, all at once, the vanished beauty and charm that had once been possessed by this corpulent and shapeless old woman who had been Anne Marie's life-long friend.

Moved by a sudden impulse Sabrina put out her hand, and groping for those beringed fingers, clung to them tightly. The Begum embraced her. It was surprising how comforting that plump sandalwood-scented shoulder was to lay one's head against. 'Haste now, little daughter, and return to thy husband's house, and I will send word when my son's son is born.' The old woman patted Sabrina's shoulder and whisked away a sudden tear with the corner of her veil.

Juanita's son was born before moonrise. A lusty, dark-haired creature with his mother's fair skin and his father's black eyes. 'He is born in an auspicious hour,' said the Begum. '*Arré*, *arré*, do not cry, thumbling! Thou shalt be a great king and have seven sons.'

As the cold weather neared its end and once again the days began to take on an uncomfortable warmth, Sabrina moved abroad less and less. Her slight figure was heavy now and distorted by the coming child, and she had suffered considerable unnecessary discomfort from the new tightly laced, small-waisted fashions of the day, until Juanita had persuaded her to adopt the Mohammedan form of dress for wear inside her own house. Lady Emily had been deeply shocked by the news of this innovation, but with the arrival of the hot weather Sabrina found the loose light silks of the Eastern garb unbelievably comfortable after the high, close-fitting bodices and innumerable petticoats demanded by the European mode.

The Bartons were moving to Simla once more, and Emily was anxious that Sabrina should accompany them. But Sabrina would not leave Pavos Reales, despite the fact that Marcos supported her aunt's plan.

'It is not good for you to remain here in the heat, *querida*,' said Marcos. 'Already the nights grow hot, and this is only the first week of March. April is a bad month in the plains, and May is worse. Go now with your aunt to the hills and I will join you there at the end of May. *Se lo prometo*!'

But Sabrina was obstinate. 'Your mother did not go to the hills when her children were born, and neither did Juanita. Besides, my son will spend his childhood in this country as you did, so he must get used to such things as heat. It does not trouble you, and it is only because I was born and brought up in a cold country that I feel it. This is your home and mine, and I want my children to be born here.' Yet in the end she had agreed to go: though not in March. Marcos had affairs that would keep him in Oudh until May, and she would remain at Pavos Reales until these were completed, and then remove to the hills with him.

So it was arranged, and the Bartons, who had been staying at Pavos Reales on their way to the hills, bade her an affectionate if anxious farewell and left for Simla.

It was often lonely at the Casa de los Pavos Reales during the early weeks of the hot weather, for Sabrina could no longer go riding with Marcos; and with Emily in Simla and Juanita unable to leave the Gulab Mahal, there were few visitors at the great house on the banks of the Goomti. Yet Sabrina did not find her solitude irksome. She loved the high, white-walled rooms, the beautiful portraits and carvings and tapestries that the old Conde had brought from Spain; the dark, glowing devildom of the magnificent Velasquez that hung on one wall of the vast drawing-room, and the scent of orange blossom and water on parched ground that drifted in from the patios. She loved the sound of horses' hooves that told her that Marcos had returned, and their walks together in the late evening along the stone-paved river terrace.

She was very happy, with a quiet serene happiness that nothing could touch or spoil. It was as though there was a wall around her; a shining transparent wall through which she could see the outside world, but which protected her from its harshness as the glass of a greenhouse protects a rare and delicate plant from the cold east wind. She loved and was loved. She was adored, cherished and protected. The whole world, it seemed to her, was beautiful, and life stretched ahead of her like a green path bordered with flowers along which she and Marcos would wander hand in hand, gently, happily and without haste . . .

Far to the north, as April drew to a close, Shah Shuja with the British Envoy, Macnaghten, riding behind him, entered Kandahar. Dost Mohammed's brother and his men had fled before the ponderous advance of the Army of the Indus, and the population of Kandahar gave the ageing Shah Shuja a riotous welcome that deceived Macnaghten into thinking that all Afghanistan was ready to welcome the puppet Amir and to depose Dost Mohammed – a conviction that the complete failure of a mammoth 'Demonstration of Welcome', staged two weeks later and virtually unattended by the disgusted Afghan population, apparently did little or nothing to erase.

In the last week of April Marcos had once more to leave for the south. Anne Marie's father, on his retirement from the service of the East India Company's army, had acquired land on the Malabar coast and settled down to the life of a planter. His estate had prospered and he had died a rich man. Anne Marie had been his sole heiress and the property had passed on her death to her children, Marcos and Juanita, but their grandfather's old overseer, who had managed the estate for many years, had died the previous autumn, and it was this that had necessitated Marcos's visit to the estate during the early part of the cold weather. He had installed a new overseer and had returned satisfied that the property would continue to be efficiently managed, but now news had been received of the new overseer's death from snake-bite, and also of disaffection among the coolies employed on the estate.

Marcos and Wali Dad, discussing the matter, decided that their best plan would be to sell the Malabar estates and re-invest the money in Oudh, since the property was too far away to be administered except at second-hand and at long range (an arrangement which the present news had proved to be unsatisfactory), and the two rode south in the last week of April, promising to return by the end of May.

'It will not be for long, *querida*,' said Marcos, comforting Sabrina. 'I shall be back before May is out, I promise you.'

But Sabrina would not be comforted. 'Why must you go? Why cannot Wali Dad go alone? Marcos, you cannot leave me now! I could not bear it. I am afraid!'

'*Qué pasa*? Afraid of what, my heart?'

'I do not know. I only know that I cannot bear to let you go. Let Wali Dad go.'

'We must both go, *cara mía*,' said Marcos, his arms about her. 'If only one were to go, it would have to be I. Wali Dad comes to help me. If he went alone the local officials and administrators might cause him trouble, for he is not of the south, but of Oudh. But once we have disposed of the estates we need never be worried by business in the south again. Does that not please you? I shall never again have the need to go more than a night's journey away from you.'

'You think more of the money than of me,' wept Sabrina.

'That is not true, *querida*. The property should indeed fetch a high price. But half of it is Juanita's, and if we delay, troubles and bad management may destroy its value. Would you have me rob Juanita of a large portion of the inheritance our mother left her, because I would prefer to remain with my wife instead of taking an uncomfortable and tedious journey on a business matter? I cannot believe it!'

Marcos had intended to send Sabrina to the care of her aunt before he rode south, since there was now no reason for her to delay her departure to the hills. But Sir Ebenezer had written from Simla to say that Lady Emily had suffered a severe attack of malarial fever, and though now convalescent, the state of her health was still causing anxiety. Reading that letter, Marcos realized that there would be little use in sending his wife to the care of a sick woman, since Lady Emily would be in no case to look after her, and Sabrina herself in no condition to administer to the needs of an ailing aunt.

'She must come to me,' said Juanita. 'I know she does not wish to leave Pavos Reales, and that it is cooler there. But it is not right that she should be alone just now. Loneliness is not good for her at such a time. Send her to me, Marcos. It will only be for a few weeks, and as soon as you return we will start for the hills. The child will not be born until late in June, and we shall be in the cool air many days before then. Have a care to my husband and return swiftly.'

So Sabrina moved from the Casa de los Pavos Reales to the pink stucco palace in Lucknow city, and watched Marcos and Wali Dad ride away under the flaming glory of the gold-mohur trees in Juanita's garden, her eyes misted with tears.

Marcos, turning in his saddle for a last look as he rode under the arch of the gateway, saw her standing among the hard, fretted shadows of the garden, an incongruous little figure with her white skin and soft blonde curls in that flamboyant oriental setting, and wished with all his heart that he were not leaving her. But it would not be for long . . .

With his departure it was as if the shining world of beauty and contentment in which Sabrina had walked had shattered like some fragile and iridescent soap bubble at the touch of a rough hand. She missed him with an intensity that grew rather than diminished as the days wore on. She missed, too, the cool stately rooms of Pavos Reales and the quiet of the vast park-like grounds that surrounded it.

The Gulab Mahal – the 'Rose Palace' – was full of noise, and the rooms with their walls painted and carved or inlaid with vari-coloured marbles and shining pieces of mother-of-pearl, and their windows screened with stone tracery, were stiflingly hot. Below the innumerable carved balconies lay paved courtyards and gardens thick with mango and orange and gold-mohur trees, while beyond and all about the high wall that hemmed them in pressed the teeming city with its crowded bazaars and gilded mosques, green gardens and fantastic palaces.

The noise of the city beat about the pink walls of the Rose Palace night and day, filling the small, hot, stifling rooms with sound, as the unguents and essences used by Aziza Begum and the zenana women filled them with the heavy scent of sandalwood and attar-of-roses, and the cooking-pots of the kitchen courtyards filled them with the smell of the boiling *ghee*, curry and asafoetida.

Even the nights brought only a diminution of the noise; never silence. Tom-toms throbbed in the crowded mazes of the city, beating in counterpoint to the piping of flutes and the tinkle of sitars, the barking of pariah dogs, the crying of children, the clatter of armed horsemen riding through the narrow streets, or the drunken shouts of revellers returning from some debauch at the King's palace.

With the passing of each slow day the heat became greater, and during the hours of daylight the walls and the roofs of the houses and the stone paving of the courtyards would steadily absorb the fierce rays of the sun, so that when night fell it seemed as though every stone and brick in the city gave off the stored heat in waves, as from the open door of a potter's kiln.

Sabrina found it possible to sleep a little during the day, for a hot, dry wind frequently blew during the day-time, and then the doors and windows would be opened and hung with curious thick matted curtains made of woven roots, which were kept soaked with water. The hot winds blowing through the damp roots cooled the rooms and filled them with a not unpleasant aromatic odour. But often the wind did not blow; and always it died at sunset.

Sabrina's thin body felt hot and dry and shrivelled with heat, and she began to long for the cool pine-scented air of the hills as a man parched with thirst longs for a draught of cold water, and to regret that she had not gone to the hills with Emily in March as Marcos had wished her to do. But she would never again go to the hills with Emily. Marcos had been absent just over three weeks, and May was half-way over when a brief letter arrived from

Sir Ebenezer Barton. Emily was dead. She had suffered a return of the fever, wrote Sir Ebenezer, and had died two days later. Her distant relative, Mrs Grantham, had been with her. Sir Ebenezer's handwriting, normally so clear and firm, wavered like that of an old man far gone in years.

Sabrina sat holding the letter in her hand and staring dry-eyed before her. She was looking back down the years to Ware and seeing Aunt Emily's face in the candle-lit nursery, teaching a three-year-old Sabrina her first prayers. At Aunt Emily tying her sash for her first party; protecting her from Aunt Charlotte's incessant nagging; reading her fairy-stories and telling her tales of her father's youth . . . A whole vista of Aunt Emilys like figures reflected in opposing sheets of looking-glass, stretching away and away, endlessly repeated in an endless corridor. All of them kind; all of them loving . . .

And suddenly Sabrina was afraid, with the fear that grips a sleeper when he dreams that he walks through the door of a familiar house and finds that the rooms are changed and strange and deserted, and that his dream has turned into a nightmare.

There had been no news of Marcos or Wali Dad beyond a brief note dispatched from the village where they had spent the first night of their journey. The lack of news did not worry Juanita or the Begum, who knew only too well the state of the roads and the difficulties of sending word through the dâk from out-of-the-way stations. But it worried Sabrina, and during the long hot hours of the sleepless nights her imagination would conjure up pictures of horror and calamity, and she would remember the overseer who had died of snake-bite. Marcos too might be bitten by a snake – attacked by a tiger – murdered by the wandering devotees of Thugee – fall a victim to fever or cholera or the plague, or die terribly of hydrophobia. The India that had once seemed to her so glamorous and beautiful a country began to wear a different aspect, for she knew by now that underneath that glamour and beauty lurked undreamed-of depths of cruelty and terror, just as the graceful minarets and gilded domes of the palaces rose above narrow, filthy streets and the squalid hovels of the poor.

On the far side of the high wall that bounded the garden of the Gulab Mahal, and immediately fronting her window, stood a mosque. It was an unpretentious little mosque built of whitewashed brick and plaster, its bulb-like dome crowned by an iron horned moon that is the symbol of Islam. The sun rose directly behind it, and with every dawn, while the air was still faintly cool from the long hours of darkness, Sabrina would see it framed by the curve of the open window and silhouetted darkly against the saffron sky. And when, too soon, the sun rose, it would cast the curved shadow of that horned moon across the floor of her room.

The shadow would creep slowly across the matting as the sun rose into a brassy sky, and sometimes at night Sabrina would awake to find it lying black in the moonlight. It came to symbolize for her all the fear and loneliness of those long days, and that growing sense of being alone in an alien country and surrounded by people of an alien race. It was a threat and a warning. A token of the inescapable and grinding heat of the coming day. Heat that sapped the strength from Sabrina's body and the power of connected thought from her brain.

She had not visited the Casa de los Pavos Reales since Marcos had left, but one breathless evening, after a day in which no wind had blown and the heavy curtains of wet *kus-kus* roots had only served to make the hot rooms of the Gulab Mahal more stifling, she was seized by a sudden desire to see it again and to walk through the gardens and along the river terrace. May was at best a burning month in the plains, but now a heat-wave held all Oudh in its grip and the mercury mounted steadily. But out at Pavos Reales it would be cooler. The trees and the open spaces and the terrace by the river would not hold this sweltering, remorseless heat as the city did.

Juanita offered to accompany her, but Sabrina preferred to go alone. Marcos had left a carriage for her use at the Gulab Mahal, and attended by Zobeida she was driven through the narrow, burning streets where the heat appeared to be imprisoned between the houses as water between the banks of a river, and out to the open country where the House of the Peacocks lay surrounded by acres of parkland and groves of trees.

The grass was burned brown and the *neem* trees were shedding their dying leaves over the pathways, but the orange and lemon and mango trees were still richly green, and the scent of late-flowering oleanders mingled with the heavy incense of the hot dust. The dim, shuttered rooms were close and stuffy and the patio fountains were silent, but after the noise and heat and colour of the Gulab Mahal it seemed to Sabrina incredibly cool and peaceful, and she wandered through the quiet, darkening rooms, touching the heavy Spanish furniture and the fragile French ornaments with a caressing hand, as though they were friends whom she was greeting – or bidding farewell.

There were still a few late roses by the river terrace, and fallen petals lay among the parched grasses and made small splashes of colour on the hot stone paving. The river was low and barred with the faint silver ripples of shoal water, and white, long-legged birds like a species of small heron picked their way along the warm shallows, ghost-like in the dusk. A peacock called harshly from among the bamboo thickets, its cry catching the echo from the curved wall at the far end of the terrace: Pea-oor! . . . *Pea-oor!* . . . *Pea-oor!* Sabrina had always loved to hear the peacocks cry at dusk and dawn at the Casa de los Pavos Reales, but tonight it seemed to her that the harsh call held a strange aching note of sadness.

From somewhere out on the plains beyond the darkening river the sound was taken up by the faraway long-drawn howl of a jackal: wild, wailing and unutterably lonely, and Sabrina was seized once more by the sudden uncontrollable spasm of fear that she had experienced when she had read the news of Emily's death. A fear of India. Of the savage alien lands that lay all about her, stretching away for thousands of miles and yet hemming her in. Of the dark, secretive, sideways-looking eyes; the tortuous unreadable minds behind those bland expressionless faces. The incredible cruelties that were practised within the King's palaces, of which the zenana women whispered. The stories that Aziza Begum would tell by starlight, sitting on the flat roof-top overlooking the crowded city – stories of battle and intrigue and murder. Of queens and dancing-girls and zenana favourites burnt alive on the funeral pyres of their lords. Tales of the savage sack of great cities:

'*. . . then went the Queens and the wives and the women to an underground chamber to make the* Johar*: dressed as though for a marriage feast and bearing with them their gold and jewels and all the treasure of the city. And the vaults were sealed, and they made therein a great pyre and were destroyed there: and the treasure also. Then those of their men who were left armed themselves and threw wide the gates and went out to do battle; and were slain, every one. Thus when Salah-un-din the Conqueror rode with his warriors into the city, Lo! it was a city of the dead, and hollow as the palm of my hand . . .*'

And yet again:

'*The son of Mahmoud took Fateh Khan prisoner and put out his eyes with a jewelled dagger; but still he refused to betray the hiding-place of his brother. Then Mahmoud and his family cut him in pieces, first an ear and then his nose; his right and then his left hand; but Fateh Khan said naught except to ask that they should speed his death. Only when his beard, which is sacred to a follower of the Prophet, was cut off did he shed tears. Then did they cut off his feet, the one after the other, but still he would not betray his brother, and at long last they cut his throat and death released him . . .*'

Thus Aziza Begum, telling the stories that made up the blood-stained history of the land. But though the one was a story several centuries old, the other was a tale of Sabrina's own lifetime – of the slaying of the elder brother of that very Dost Mohammed against whom Lord Auckland's Army of the Indus was advancing in the hills beyond Kandahar. India had not changed greatly because a handful of London merchants had brought much of her territory under subjection. She had been conquered before, many times, since the days when Sikander Dulkhan (Alexander the Great) had fought his battles on her soil and built his roads and tanks and left behind his nameless viceroys. Greeks, Huns, Arabs, Tartars, Pathans, Persians, Moguls – India had seen them come and had watched the fires of their power blaze bright and die again leaving nothing but ashes; and had gone on her way . . .

Some of all this was in Sabrina's mind as she stood on the river terrace of the Casa de los Pavos Reales and watched a vast yellow moon rise through the hot dusty twilight.

Daylight does not linger in the East as it does in cooler lands, and the Eastern twilight is barely a breath drawn between day and night. One moment the river ran gold in the last reflected glow of the sunset, and in the next the moon had laid a shining pathway across its dark surface and Sabrina's shadow lay black on the moonlit terrace. A jackal howled again, nearer this time, and although nightfall had brought little or no alleviation of the oppressive heat, Sabrina shivered as though with a sudden chill, and drawing the light scarf of Indian gauze closer about her, she turned back to the house.

The familiar white walls with their wrought-iron balconies and deep window embrasures looked as friendly and as peaceful as they had on that other night when she and Marcos, newly wedded, had stood on the terrace among the lemon trees to see their guests ride away across the moonlit park. But it was hotter here than it had been down by the river. The stone flags of the terrace burnt under Sabrina's thin, flat-soled slippers, and she could hear the old coachman's dry little cough and the restless stamp and click of the horse's hooves on the hard ground, and realized that it was getting late and that they wished to return. But the thought of the small hot rooms of the women's quarter at the Gulab Mahal filled her with revulsion and she lingered among the trees, reluctant to leave.

A shadow moved on the ground beside her and Zobeida touched her arm, and presently they were driving away down the long moonlit avenue, and the white walls of Pavos Reales were swallowed up by the trees.

'Perhaps I shall never see it again,' said Sabrina slowly, and did not know that she had spoken aloud.

The heat of the city met them like a blast from a furnace, but the streets and bazaars were uncannily quiet. It was too hot for speech or movement and men had dragged their string cots into the roadways and lay in the hard moonlight, sprawled and silent like the victims of some medieval pestilence.

There was a riderless horse standing just within the gateway of the Gulab Mahal. A tired horse, lathered with sweat, its head drooping and the white dust of the roads thick on its heaving flanks. It stood among the dappled shadows of the flame trees, but Sabrina knew it. She knew all the Pavos Reales horses, and this was Suliman, who had been ridden by one of the servants who had accompanied Marcos to the south.

Her heart leapt with a sudden wild joy and she stood up, swaying to the movement of the carriage as it jolted over the uneven paving of the courtyard.

But it was not Marcos. A messenger only, bearing letters, said the servant who opened the carriage door. Sabrina brushed aside Zobeida's hand and sprang to the ground. A letter from Marcos at last! Perhaps to say that he would be back in a few days. Only a few more days to wait. She ran down the short passage and up the two steep flights of narrow ill-lighted stairs that led to Juanita's rooms, laughing as she ran.

After the dimly lit stairways, Juanita's room seemed to blaze with light and it was full of people. Aziza Begum was there with two of her daughters and several serving-women. Juanita herself was holding a letter in her hand, and her face was white and frightened.

Sabrina stopped on the threshold and stood quite still. Her mouth was still curved with laughter and for a moment it stayed that way, as if Juanita's face had been Medusa's head and had turned her to stone. Then her lips closed stiffly and she said: 'Marcos——?'

Juanita ran to her, putting her arms about her and holding her close.

'Do not look like that, *querida*. He will not die. Many recover. Do not look so!'

Sabrina put her aside, pulling herself free of the clinging arms, and spoke across the small, hot, crowded room to Aziza Begum:

'What is it? Tell me.'

'It is the cholera, my daughter. One of thy husband's servants brought a letter from my son. He thought it best that we should know, so that——' The Begum checked herself and then said: 'But thy husband is a young man and strong. He will recover, never fear. There is no need for thee to be over-anxious, little heart. In a few days he will be well again. Many recover from the cholera who are not as young and as strong as he.'

But Sabrina did not hear her. She had heard only the one word – cholera! The swift, dreaded plague of the East. Marcos had cholera. Even now he might be dying – dead. She must go to him. She must go at once . . .

The heat of the small room pressed upon her with an almost tangible weight, but it seemed to her that her brain was suddenly very clear and cold. The only clear thing in this queer hot room full of oddly hazy faces and bright spinning colours. The only cold thing in this furnace-like city. She looked at the faces around her, trying to focus them. Dark anxious faces. Dark anxious eyes. Juanita's blanched cheeks. They were kind. She knew that. But they would try and stop her. They would prevent her going to Marcos. But Suliman was tethered by the gate. If she could only reach him she could ride away to Marcos and they could not catch her.

She backed away from them very slowly. Juanita took a swift step towards her, her hand outstretched, and the roomful of faces seemed to surge up and forwards. Sabrina whirled round and ran towards the stairs. The steep dark stairway yawned below her feet and she heard footsteps running behind her and glanced over her shoulder. And then she was falling, falling – falling into a hot spinning darkness that reached up and engulfed her.

Sabrina's daughter was born as the sun rose, after a night of agonizing labour, and Juanita, watching the white lips move, bent close to catch the whispered words:

'Don't . . . let . . . it . . . touch——'

'No, no,' comforted Juanita, not knowing of what she spoke.

'The shadow——' persisted Sabrina. She was too exhausted to turn her head, but her eyes turned, and Juanita following their gaze saw them rest on the curious curved shadow of the crescent moon that the early morning sun threw across the wall, and she rose quickly and drew close the heavy wooden shutters that should have been closed an hour earlier to conserve what little coolness the night had brought into the room.

Sabrina closed her eyes and lapsed into a coma, and Zobeida crouched beside her fanning her tirelessly all the long hot day. Late in the afternoon she moved her head and said one word: 'Water.' She drank thirstily but with difficulty. Aziza Begum brought her a tiny, swaddled bundle and laid it beside her, but Sabrina's eyes were closed and she paid no heed.

She lay motionless on the low Indian bedstead and her mind wandered back to Ware in winter-time; to keen biting winds and a white expanse of snow against which the yew trees and the leafless woods cut sharp black silhouettes; to icicles fringing the leaden gutters at a roof's edge, and to frost patterns on a window-pane; to grey skies and softly falling snow. In imagination she touched the snow and felt its crisp coldness; plunged her arms in it and held handfuls of it to her burning cheeks. If only she could lie quite, quite still – if she did not move or breathe – perhaps she could will it to be true.

The tiny creature beside her moved and uttered a thin cry, and the weak sound seemed to penetrate through the mists that were clouding her brain. She turned her head, forcing open her heavy eyelids, and looked at the child who lay beside her.

It was so small that it seemed more like a doll than a living infant, and it was not red as most new-born babies, but milk-white, with hair like curling black silk. Sabrina's arm tightened weakly about the small bundle, and the shadow of a smile curved her mouth.

'Is she not beautiful, your daughter?' said Juanita.

'Like winter——' whispered Sabrina.

'Like what, *querida*?'

'Winter. At Ware. Snow and dark trees . . . winter . . .' Her voice failed and her eyes closed again; but she was not asleep.

The heat of the small room played upon her exhausted body like an invisible flame. Outside the shuttered window the sun beat down upon the city like a giant hammer, and beyond and around the city walls lay the scorching plains, stretching endlessly away to the burning horizon. Somewhere out there lay Marcos. *Marcos – Marcos*! Was he dead already? Perhaps he would never know that he had a daughter . . . a baby who looked as white and as small as a snowflake.

A sudden sharp fear – a purely maternal fear – took possession of Sabrina. If Marcos were to die – if she herself were to die – what would become of the child? Emily will take care of it! . . . But Emily was dead. Juanita? *No – No*! thought Sabrina, agonized. Not this life for my baby!

Grandpapa! He would take care of her child. He loved her. Those angry letters meant nothing; it was only Grandpapa in a rage. Sabrina was aware of a quivering sense of urgency. Of time running out like sand between her fingers. She must send a letter to Ware, at once, before it was too late. She set her teeth and summoning up all her will-power, dragged herself up onto the pillow. There was a quick rustle of silk and Juanita was beside her.

'What is it, *cara mía*? Lie still.'

'I must write a letter,' whispered Sabrina. 'A letter to Ware . . . I must write at once.'

'Tomorrow, *hija* – tomorrow——'

'No,' said Sabrina desperately, struggling feebly against the restraining hands. 'Now. At once.'

'Then I shall write it for you,' said Juanita soothingly. 'You shall tell me what to say. See, I will sit beside you and write.'

So Juanita wrote at Sabrina's dictation; writing down the words that came so slowly and with such difficulty in that soft gasping whisper. She wrote in French, for although she spoke English well and fluently, she could not write it with ease. And looking at Sabrina's face, and the faces of Aziza Begum and Zobeida, she was afraid, and the tears that she would not let Sabrina see fell and blotted the written words.

'Look after her,' begged Sabrina of her grandfather. 'If anything happens to me or to Marcos – if we are not here to care for her – I leave her to you. Dearest Grandpapa, look after her for me. I do not know how to write a will, but this letter is my will. If Marcos dies I leave everything to my daughter, and I leave my daughter to you.'

When she had finished, the Begum and Zobeida lifted her, and with Juanita steadying her hand she signed her name to it. Juanita folded the paper and addressed it and put it away, and Sabrina smiled at her. It was as if a great weight had been lifted off her mind, and she closed her eyes and slept.

At sundown Zobeida opened the shutters and sprinkled water on the stone balcony outside the window, and Sabrina, waking, heard the water hiss upon the hot stone. The sky beyond the window was already green and a star hung low over the roof-tops. But the air was no cooler and she gasped for breath. As the room darkened Juanita lit a small oil-lamp. The shadows made a mist under the curved ceiling so that it was difficult to tell how high it was, and the moulded reliefs of trees and birds and flowers which decorated the walls appeared to move in an unfelt breeze. Aziza Begum, seeing that she was awake, brought her the child once more.

'What shall you call her?' asked Juanita. 'She is half a day old and should have a name.'

Sabrina looked at the tiny, white-skinned creature that lay beside her, and was suddenly reminded of a fairy-story that someone – was it Aunt Emily? – had told her one winter's day at Ware. A story about a queen who had sat at the window on a snowy day, spinning with an ebony spinning wheel, and had wished for a daughter with skin as white as snow and hair as black as ebony.

'Winter,' whispered Sabrina.

'*Winter*? But that is not a name, *cara mía*. She must have a beautiful name.'

'It is a beautiful name . . .' Juanita did not realize how beautiful! She had never seen the snow and the dark December woods. She only knew the harsh, flaming colours of this sun-scorched country, and the heat was not an intolerable burden to her as it was to Sabrina, pressing her out of life. She did not know what it was to long for grey skies and fresh winds and the cold touch of falling snowflakes.

Sabrina turned her head on the hot pillow and looked out at the moonlight beyond the open window, and as she looked it seemed to her that the white dome of the mosque and the moonlit walls and the black shadows of the orange trees were snow-covered fields and winter woods, and she began to talk in a clear light voice.

It was winter and the snow was falling, and Sabrina wept because Charlotte had locked her into the hot schoolroom and she could only see through the barred windows the white park where she was forbidden to play. She could see it so clearly: the snowy levels dotted with leafless trees, sloping up to the barrier of the dark woods that ringed the park. She struggled to reach it, but hands held her back. And then all at once the hands fell away and the door was open. She ran out of the room and along the familiar passages and down the wide staircase. The wind blew about her, smelling of the winter woods, and now she had reached the snow and it was cold and shining and wonderful, and she was not hot any more but cold, cold, cold.

Zobeida and the Begum fetched padded quilts and tucked them about her shivering figure as the fever mounted, but Sabrina did not feel them, and towards morning she died.

The sky beyond the balcony paled with the dawn, and presently the sun rose, filling the quiet airless room with harsh light and throwing a curved shadow across the wall from the mosque outside the gardens of the Gulab Mahal.

Juanita, remembering how Sabrina had feared that shadow, rose from her knees, and crossing softly to the window, closed the heavy shutters against the burning day.

Marcos did not die of the cholera. He was, as Aziza Begum had said, both young and strong. He returned home, but by that time Sabrina had been two weeks in her grave, and Sir Ebenezer Barton, who accompanied by Mrs Grantham had hurried to Lucknow on receiving the news of his niece's death, had arrived at the Casa de los Pavos Reales.

Sir Ebenezer, also widowed, had grown suddenly old. Stricken by the loss of his Emily, and disheartened by the policy of the Governor-General and the Court of Directors, of which he could not approve, he had decided to return to Calcutta to wind up his affairs before finally retiring to England. He was sorry for Marcos, who had lost father, mother and wife in so short a space of time, and was now left with an infant daughter to care for, but his own grief for Emily left him with little sorrow to spare for others, and he did not even wonder what Marcos would do with the child. He offered to do anything he could to help, but the words were purely automatic and he was surprised when Marcos took him seriously.

But there was something that Marcos wanted – a Commission in the Company's army.

To remain in Lucknow, at Pavos Reales where he had spent his brief year of happiness, was suddenly intolerable to him, and he wished to get away from Oudh at least for some years. There was always work for the Army, and Marcos yearned for change and hard work and, if possible, hard fighting. Anything – anything but the torment of staying here at Pavos Reales where, for him, Sabrina's lost, lovely ghost haunted every room and corridor and courtyard of the great house.

Sir Ebenezer did not question this decision, and since he still had considerable influence in the Company and with the Governor-General, he promised to arrange matters. Before he left he witnessed Marcos's will, which he took away with him, together with a brocade-enclosed packet that Juanita had given to Marcos and which contained Sabrina's last message to her grandfather.

'If anything happens to me,' said Marcos, 'I would beg you to see that both documents are delivered to Lord Ware.'

Sir Ebenezer nodded. Except with Emily he had always been a man of few words. But he was also a man of his word. He did not forget his promise to Marcos, and not long afterwards Marcos found himself gazetted honorary Aide-de-Camp to General Sir Willoughby Cotten, the officer in command of troops advancing upon Kabul.

Away to the north of Oudh, in the Land of the Five Rivers, Ranjit Singh,

Lion of the Punjab, lay dying. He had burnt the candle of his life at both ends, and in its bright flame had welded the Sikhs into a nation and carved out an Empire that stretched from the Holy City of Amritsar to Peshawar in the shadow of the Khyber Pass. But in the last week of June he died. His prematurely senile body was burned on a pyre of rare woods, and four queens and seven of his most beautiful slave girls followed him into the flames. And with him perished Lord Auckland's treaty with the Sikhs, for with his passing there was not one left among them who cared what became of the Army of the Indus . . .

Marcos placed his daughter in the care of his sister Juanita. Zobeida had already taken on the duties of nurse, and a wet-nurse, Hamida, a strong and healthy slave-woman whose latest infant had been still-born, had been engaged to feed the child. Marcos installed a reliable caretaker and overseer at the Casa de los Pavos Reales, put his affairs in order and rode north to join the Army of the Indus. And in that same month of July there landed in Calcutta, from the *Camden*, a tall, black-haired cadet of Bengal Infantry, not yet seventeen; John Nicholson, who was destined to be worshipped as a god and become a legend in his own lifetime.

Early in August the Army of the Indus reached Kabul, and after thirty years of exile Lord Auckland's aged puppet, Shah Shuja, rode into the capital city of Afghanistan while his people stood in sullen silence. Marcos reached Kabul by way of the Khyber Pass with the advance guard of a motley army under the leadership of Shah Shuja's son, and on arrival asked permission to resign his duties as an Aide-de-Camp in favour of more active employment. This was instantly obtained, for all through that year and the next Dost Mohammed conducted a series of guerrilla forays, and endless punitive expeditions were sent against him, and against those chiefs who had refused to accept the sovereignty of Shah Shuja. But the death that Marcos courted avoided him, though fatigue and cold and the fever of fighting often provided temporary anodynes to ease the pain of loss.

In the pink stucco palace in Lucknow city Sabrina's daughter grew and thrived. Her nickname among the household was *Chota Moti* – 'Little Pearl' – because of her whiteness and because Winter, her given name, had no meaning for them and its syllables were harsh to their ears.

The child would lie in the room that had been Sabrina's, her eyes on the colourful walls where formalized trees and flowers in the Persian style were moulded in high relief in *chunam*, a polished cement that had the appearance of coloured marble. As soon as she could crawl she would spend hours running her small hands over the flower designs, tracing their stylized curves with a tiny finger. They were her first toys and her first memory, so that in later years her recollection of her earliest days was that they had been spent in a fantastic garden in which she had played and eaten and slept surrounded by wonderful flowers and curious, beautiful birds that were so tame that she could touch them and stroke them.

Every animal and every bird in those colourful friezes had had its own name, and there had been one that was her especial favourite – the first within reach of her small clutching hands. A stylized parrot with a wise expression, who held one claw upraised as though he were commanding attention. He was called Firishta, after a celebrated Muslim historian who had lived in the days of Akbar and Jehangir, and the Begum would pretend that it was Firishta who told many of the tales of dead Moguls and heroes that the children loved to hear, prefacing them with 'Firishta says——' so that always, to Sabrina's daughter, Firishta was alive and could speak. When she was older, and the days were hot, she would stand by the pink plaster wall, pressing her small cheek against Firishta's cool smooth greenness, and talk to him as though he were a friend and a playmate.

Juanita made some attempt to dress her niece in European clothes, but in comparison with the loose silk and muslin garments worn by the other children of the Gulab Mahal, these appeared so stiff and uncomfortable that the Begum roundly told her that since the child was treated in every way as Juanita's own daughter, it was absurd to swaddle her small limbs in this foreign fashion. Time enough for that when her father removed her from their care and she went to live at the Casa de los Pavos Reales. The attempt to dress Sabrina's daughter in European style was therefore abandoned, and she wore instead the loose silken trousers, thin, short-sleeved, knee-length tunic and gauzy *deputtah* that was a replica of the Begum's own costume, to which Zobeida added tiny bangles of silver that were the delight of the child's life.

Zobeida adored her. Her own children, the fruits of an early marriage to one of the manservants in attendance upon the Begum's husband, had both been still-born, and their ne'er-do-well father had been killed in a street brawl. She looked upon Sabrina's child as though it had been her own, and transferred to it all the loving devotion she had given to its mother. The Little Pearl became the petted darling of the Gulab Mahal, but it was 'Beda' whom she loved most dearly, and 'Beda' to whom she ran when hurt or in need of comfort.

Her playmates were Juanita's two children, Khalig Dad and the little Anne Marie who was a year and a half her senior and had been named after Juanita's mother. Anne Marie the Second, despite her name, had not inherited her looks from her mother's side of the family. She was all Wali Dad: golden skin and eyes like sloes, a mouth like a curled rose-petal and hair as black as jet. 'She is her father again – and as I also, when I was but a child,' said the Begum complacently. 'My son had great beauty, as also had I, his mother, when I was in the bloom of my youth. *Hai mai*! but that was long since, and I grow old. It is good to see my children's children growing up about me. As for thee, Little Pearl, thou also art a grandchild of my heart, and were it not inauspicious I would tell thee that when thou art grown thou wilt be a very moon of beauty!'

The Begum would take the two small girls into her capacious lap and sing them songs and feed them with unsuitable fruits and sweetmeats, whereby they suffered frequent pangs of colic and indigestion to the no small alarm of Juanita and Zobeida. But while life in the Rose Palace went its peaceful way, the storm clouds gathered over far-off Afghanistan.

Dost Mohammed had fought a victorious battle and followed it up by voluntarily surrendering himself to Sir William Macnaghten, the British Envoy, who sent him under strong escort to India. Here he was received with the Honours of War and granted a substantial pension, and the Directors of the East India Company, convinced that now the ex-Amir was in their hands his country would be less unsettled, and disliking the prospect of continuing to lavish a million sterling a year on bribing the allegiance of the Afghan people, decided upon retrenchment. Sir William was forced to economize in the only possible way – the cutting off or curtailing of the subsidies that alone had kept the tribes quiet – and as a result of this policy in the space of a few months the entire country was hostile, and urgent warnings of ill-feeling among the tribes came in from every outpost.

Early in November the storm broke. Alexander Burns and his brother were hacked to pieces by a screaming mob, and soon all Afghanistan was aflame. The distant outposts were attacked and their defenders massacred. General Sale was besieged in Jalalabad and Colonel Palmer in Ghazi. Food became short, there was no hope of relief, and Lord Elphinstone, the senile and incompetent Commander who on Lord Auckland's insistence had replaced Sir Willoughby Cotten, was totally incapable of the prompt and daring action that alone might have saved the doomed Army. Akbar Khan, son of the Dost, murdered Sir William Macnaghten, and General Elphinstone remained supine and took no action to avenge the Envoy's death. Instead, a treaty was made with the chiefs by which the British forces were to be allowed to leave the country under a guarantee of safe conduct, Akbar Khan promising to send a strong Afghan escort to see them safely through the passes.

The retreat began early in the New Year, and more than four thousand fighting men, with twelve thousand camp-followers including many women and children, trudged wearily out of the cantonments towards the snow and the bitter cold of the barren hills that lay between them and the fortress of Jalalabad where General Sale still held his besiegers at bay. But once among the steep defiles of the passes Akbar Khan's escort deserted them, leaving them to the vengeance of the hostile tribes.

Hundreds died of exposure in the intense cold, and those who dropped by the way and did not die met a less merciful death from mutilation at the hands of the tribesmen. At some time during that long martyrdom Akbar Khan, with an eye to the future, offered his protection to those few Englishwomen who were still alive, together with their husbands and General Elphinstone. They had no option but to accept, and they turned back with him. The remainder fought their way forward against the snowdrifts and the murderous tribes, and on the thirteenth day of January a sentry on the ramparts of Jalalabad saw a solitary rider, emaciated, ragged, blood-stained, drooping with exhaustion on a starved and exhausted horse. It was Dr Brydon – the sole survivor of the sixteen thousand souls who had set out from Kabul on that tragic retreat.

Somewhere back in those terrible passes, among the butchered thousands who had paid the price of Lord Auckland's folly, Marcos de Ballesteros had died as Sabrina had imagined herself in her last hours – face downward in the cold and glittering snow. And his corpse, with those other thousands of mutilated corpses that rotted in the passes, were the seeds from which sprang the rank growth of rebellion that was in time to deluge all India in blood. For the power and the prestige of the Company had been humbled to the dust. Their troops had been defeated in battle and herded and butchered like sheep, and their bones lay bleaching in the sun and wind to bear witness that the mighty 'John Company' was mortal. All along the Border and throughout the length and breadth of India the news spread swiftly, and many men sharpened their swords in secret – and waited.

In the little pink palace in Lucknow Juanita wept for her brother, clutching his orphaned daughter in her arms until the child too wept aloud in bewilderment and alarm.

When her first grief had spent itself she wrote to Sir Ebenezer, addressing the letter to his house at Garden Reach near Calcutta because she did not know his address in England, and enclosing papers relating to the de Ballesteros estates that Marcos had left with her, instructing her to send them to Sir Ebenezer should anything happen to him. She wrote in March, but Sir Ebenezer had sold his house and sailed for England nearly two years previously, and summer had gone and the leaves were falling by the time the letter reached him.

He read it with difficulty, for his sight was failing and his knowledge of the French language was limited. And when he had finished it he rose stiffly and went to a heavy mahogany desk that stood against one wall of his study, and unlocking a small drawer, removed the packet that it contained and stood weighing it in his hand. It was the same packet that Marcos de Ballesteros had given him two and a half years ago at Pavos Reales, and it contained Marcos's will and Sabrina's last letter. He had hoped that the necessity of delivering them to his father-in-law would not arise, because he had his doubts as to the Earl's reception of the news that his grand-daughter's only child had been orphaned and that he was expected to take her in charge.

Sir Ebenezer had seen Emily's father only once since his return from India, and the old Earl had made no mention of Sabrina, and had been taciturn to the point of rudeness. But Sir Ebenezer did not know his father-in-law as well as Sabrina knew her grandfather, and Sabrina had been right when she had told Emily that whatever she did and however angry he might be with her, he could not stop loving her.

The Earl was well into his seventies, but he did not look his age. He read Sir Ebenezer's brief covering note at the dinner-table where the package had been delivered to him, and his face hardened. Sabrina's marriage had infuriated him, but though he had raged and threatened and vowed never to see or speak to her again, at the back of his mind there had lurked the thought that one day she would return and beg his forgiveness, and that all would be well again.

The news of her death had come as a crippling blow. It was as if, in some strange fashion, Johnny too had died again, but this time in some final and irrevocable way. The fact that Sabrina had borne a child meant nothing to him, except inasmuch as it had increased his bitterness and resentment. The child was his great-grand-daughter, but it was in no way his or Sabrina's: it belonged to this unknown foreigner whom Sabrina had married against his express command, and he was unlikely to see it or hear of it again.

He read Juanita's letter to Sir Ebenezer telling of her brother's death in the Afghan passes, and the will that Marcos had made in favour of his only child, in which he had concurred, in the tortuous legal phrases required by the law, with his wife's desire that the child should become the ward of her grandfather.

The Earl untied the strings of the small brocaded bag that still smelt faintly of sandalwood, and his lip curled with distaste. The letter within it was sealed with a large circle of wax and impressed with curving Sanskrit characters, and he broke it with a silver fruit knife, flicking the broken pieces away as though they were unclean.

The letter was written in French, and the ink was blotted in places as though the writer had been crying and the tears had fallen upon the paper. The Earl read it once slowly, and then again. And suddenly there were tears on his own cheeks.

He sat there oblivious of them. Oblivious too of the startled and embarrassed glances of his family and the servants waiting at the table.

The Earl's immediate reaction was that someone – preferably his daughter-in-law – must leave at once for India and fetch Sabrina's child. But in this he had encountered unexpected opposition. Charlotte had not the least intention of undertaking such a journey, and said so categorically.

Very well then, Huntly and Julia should go. They were young and would enjoy the voyage and the chance of seeing new countries. But Sybella, daughter of Huntly and Julia, had been born only a month or two before Sabrina's child, and her parents refused to leave her in order to embark on any wild-goose chase to the East.

The Earl, thwarted by his family and convinced by his doctors of the inadvisability of undertaking the voyage himself, was forced to appeal to his son-in-law Ebenezer for assistance in the matter, and Sir Ebenezer had been prompt and helpful. He had many friends in India and was sure that he could arrange for some suitable gentlewoman returning from that country to escort the child. He was as good as his word, but mails were slow and travel slower. The loss at sea of the first letters, followed by the death from typhus of a lady who had agreed to bring the child home, delayed matters considerably, and so it was not until the autumn of 1845 that Sabrina's daughter, Winter de Ballesteros, Condesa de los Aguilares, arrived at Ware.

She was six and a half years old. And with her, to the mingled curiosity and consternation of Charlotte, Julia and the servants' hall, came a dark-skinned attendant: Zobeida.

Save for one notable exception the small Condesa made an unfavourable first impression. She was a tiny creature, small-boned and, according to Lady Julia, sickly-looking. The white skin that had reminded the dying Sabrina of snow at Ware had ripened with time and the suns of the East to a warm ivory that her newly found relatives described as 'yellow'. Her enormous eyes, the dark velvet-brown of pansies and over-large for her small face, and the rippling blue-black hair that already fell below her waist, were pronounced 'foreign', and they resented her sonorous Spanish title.

She was a silent child who spoke English haltingly and with a pronounced accent. The complete change of scene and environment, the contrast between the warm, colourful, casual life of the Gulab Mahal and the cold, gloomy rooms, Victorian discipline and stately routine of Ware, coupled with the bitter pangs of homesickness for the loving friends and the only home she had as yet known, reduced her to a state of dumb misery. Had she wept and displayed her fear and loneliness it might have aroused compassion and understanding even in the breast of so unimaginative a person as Lady Julia. But the child possessed a dignity and reserve beyond her years, and she would not weep and cling to these foreign strangers. Her silent, dry-eyed misery was taken for sullenness and her slow speech for stupidity, for her relatives were not as yet aware that the child spoke four languages, of which English, owing to the fact that it had been taught her by a woman of Franco-Spanish ancestry, was the least fluent.

To Charlotte and Julia the fact that Sabrina's daughter was a plain, sallow and silent child proved a relief, for Charlotte had never outgrown the jealous dislike she had felt for Sabrina, and consciously or unconsciously she had communicated a considerable proportion of that dislike to her daughter-in-law. Neither woman had been unduly distressed by Sabrina's fall from grace, or, later, by the news of her untimely death, but when they learned that the girl's daughter was to come to Ware, both viewed her arrival with some anxiety.

Julia, like her mother-in-law, had a jealous nature, and her small daughter Sybella was the apple of her eye. Sybella was a beautiful child, and as it seemed that she would be an only child, her mother's ambitions for her were already unbounded. She did not relish the appearance of a rival, and from what she remembered of Sabrina, Sabrina's daughter might well prove to be a formidable one. The subsequent arrival of such a notably unattractive child therefore relieved her anxiety. But her relief was of short duration, for the single exception to the disparaging view that her noble relations had taken of Sabrina's daughter was provided by the Earl himself.

Between the old man and the small silent child there sprang up a strong bond of sympathy and understanding. He alone came to realize what the child must be suffering in heartache and homesickness, and young as she was she sensed the loneliness and need for affection that lay behind the old man's forbidding exterior and irascible manner.

Johnny, Sabrina, Winter . . . Each in their turn had been the only one of the family who had never feared him, and here once again, in the third generation, he had found something to love, and Charlotte and Julia saw their worst fears realized.

Zobeida was yet another thorn in their flesh and they had done their best to get her sent back to her native country. Her outlandish appearance, her foreign speech, her silence and her single-minded devotion to Sabrina's daughter galled Charlotte unbearably. 'To be waited on hand and foot only tends to give the child an air of consequence that is unsuitable to one so young. What she stands in need of is an English governess who will be firm with her,' Charlotte told her father-in-law. The servants' hall too mistrusted the silent, dark-skinned foreign woman and complained that she 'gave them the grue'.

But the Earl could not be persuaded to send her away. Her love for his small great-grand-daughter had been sufficiently deep and strong to enable her to face voluntary exile from her native land and her own people, and he could not but admire that. In any case, said the Earl, Winter would need a personal maid, and in his opinion one volunteer was worth three pressed men. So Zobeida stayed; growing more and more silent with each passing year and ageing with the strange rapidity of Eastern women. But though silent with others, she talked often to Winter in her own tongue, and always of the Gulab Mahal: 'Some day,' promised Zobeida, comforting the lonely and homesick child, 'we will go back to the Gulab Mahal, and then all will be well with us.'

The next few years of Winter's life were not entirely unhappy ones, though except from her great-grandfather and Zobeida, she received little affection or attention. But then she did nothing to merit it, for only when she was in the company of the two people who loved her did she display any qualities worthy of affection or attention. To everyone else she remained a plain and silent child, so unobtrusive as to be almost unnoticed.

Her Great-Uncle Ashby, that kindly and studious man, discovering that she had some knowledge of French and Spanish, encouraged her in the study of these languages, but since his choice of literature was frequently above the child's head, she derived small amusement from it.

Herbert, Viscount Glynde, died when Winter was nine years old. He had been ailing for some years, although few people realized it, and when Charlotte at last awoke to the fact that her husband was seriously ill, the cancerous growth that had been the cause of his ill-health had gone beyond the reach of medical skill.

In her domineering fashion Charlotte had been very fond of Herbert, and his death came as a double blow; to her heart and to her ambitions. It had never occurred to her that she would not one day be Countess of Ware, and though she would have been genuinely horrified if anyone had accused her of desiring her father-in-law's death, she had for many years looked forward with feelings of pleasurable anticipation to the day when her husband would inherit the title and estates. But now that day would never come. She would never be Countess of Ware: it would be Julia, now Viscountess Glynde, who would be that.

Bewildered and distraught by the death of her husband and her hopes, Charlotte's health gave way and the doctors ordered her to Baden for a cure. She left for the Continent accompanied by her three plain daughters and did not return. Huntly, hurriedly summoned from Ware, arrived too late to see his mother alive and remained to attend her funeral, and on returning with his sisters, moved from the Dower House, which he and his wife and daughter had been occupying, to the castle, so that Julia could take up the reins that Charlotte had let fall.

For a few months after Charlotte's death life seemed a little easier for the child Winter. No one worried her now or took the trouble to nag or lecture her for her own good. But her period of peace was short-lived, for the greater part of Charlotte's hostility towards Sabrina had sprung from maternal jealousy, and now the same feelings began to animate Julia.

The fact that the Earl had shown no interest whatsoever in her daughter, apart from expressing disappointment on the score of the child's sex, had not worried her unduly, since he was, as every member of his family was fully aware, embittered by what he regarded as Sabrina's betrayal of him, and later profoundly shaken by the news of her death. But Julia had been confident that once his first grief and bitterness had passed he would awake to the realization that her sweet Sybella possessed all and more of the beauty he had so idolized in his son John and his grand-daughter Sabrina.

Julia herself idolized her only child. Had there been other children it is probable that her love would have remained within the normal bounds of maternal affection, but Sybella's birth had been protracted and difficult and Julia had made a slow recovery only to learn that she would be unable to bear any more children. Like her mother-in-law Charlotte, she was ambitious, and it had been a bitter blow to learn that she would never be able to provide her husband with an heir, and that one day the title and estates would pass to some child of her husband's uncle, Ashby. But Ashby showed no signs of marrying, and should he fail to do so the title and the entailed portion of the estate would pass out of the direct line, though there was a good deal of unentailed property which Julia was convinced must descend to Sybella. She was therefore unprepared for the strong bond of affection that developed between the aged Earl and Sabrina's daughter, and it seemed to her nothing less than a deliberate affront that her own beautiful child should fail to hold first place in Ware's affections, owing to the presence of this pallid, silent, Anglo-Spanish brat.

Anything that hurt Sybella hurt Julia, and a slight to Sybella was a slight to herself. She could not forgive Sabrina's child for stealing what she considered to be her daughter's birthright, and her resentment began to make itself felt in numerous small ways.

The child herself did not know what she had done to earn the new Viscountess's dislike. She was merely aware of it and did her best to keep out of her way; though this was no easy matter, as she and Sybella shared schoolroom and governess, music and dancing lessons and the weekly visit of the drawing master.

Winter possessed a quicker brain and a livelier intelligence than Julia's daughter, but she learned early that for some reason it annoyed Lady Glynde if she did her lessons quicker or better than Sybella, and so she deliberately lagged behind her slower-witted cousin, until the governess and tutors, who had at first been delighted with the precocious quickness of the child, felt disappointed with her and decided that she was, after all, somewhat stupid.

She was a lonely child, driven in upon herself by the circumstances of this new life; her only companions the silent Indian woman and the old man crippled by years and gout. It was therefore not surprising that her memory painted India as a place of wonder and beauty where the sun always shone and where people did not live in vast chilly rooms full of ugly dark furniture, but in gardens full of strange and beautiful flowers and tame birds. 'One day,' Aziza Begum had said, taking tender farewell of the weeping child, 'you will come back to the Gulab Mahal and we shall all be happy again.' Zobeida too longed for her homeland, and kept it alive in Winter's memory, re-telling the tales that Aziza Begum had been wont to tell of an evening seated on the flat roof-top of the zenana quarters and looking out across the beautiful, garish city of Lucknow.

These tales Winter would relate to the old Earl, sitting opposite him in a tall oak-backed chair, her small feet dangling well clear of the floor, and translating direct from the language of Zobeida and Aziza Begum so that they assumed a strongly Biblical flavour. Her eyes would grow enormous and her small pointed face glow with colour, and her warm, hoarse little voice become a slow chant:

'*. . . so he built him a great City all of red sandstone and white marble from*

Jaipur, with palaces and towers and courtyards; and around it a great wall higher than many palm trees. But the Gods turned their faces from him, for the rains failed and the wells ran dry and the river lay many koss *away, so that the cattle died of thirst and the crops withered in the fields. Then said the people: "Let us go from here. The City is accursed." And they went away. And the sand crept in upon the City and buried it, and it became as though it had never been——'*

Once Julia had interrupted one of these sessions, and the old Earl, nodding towards the small figure in the great chair, had remarked unexpectedly: 'Going to be a beauty one day: like her mother.'

Julia had turned swiftly, conscious of a sudden pang at her heart. But the colour had faded from Winter's face and the glow from her eyes, and all that Julia saw was a plain, sallow-skinned child sitting very still with the stillness of a hedge-bird when a hawk hovers overhead. A feeling of intense relief that she did not pause to analyse flooded Julia, and she laughed her brittle tinkling laugh that always reminded Winter of icicles falling onto frozen ground, and said, 'What nonsense, Grandpapa! She is not in the least like Sabrina.'

'Beauty is not only a matter of colouring and regular features,' said the old man sharply. 'You will find that out some day, Julia.'

He chuckled maliciously, regarding his grandson's wife with a disconcertingly shrewd eye. He had no illusions about Julia and was fully aware of her antagonism towards Sabrina's child, as well as the reason for it.

During those early years at Ware Winter and her cousin Sybella saw a great deal of each other; they played and rode and had lessons together, quarrelled and made up. Winter unreservedly admired her cousin's beauty, for Sybella seemed to her the very embodiment of the Princess of a fairy-tale; her pink and white complexion, large forget-me-not blue eyes, yellow curls and fascinating pale-coloured frilled and lacy satin-sashed dresses (so different from the dark stuffs that Julia considered suitable to Winter's sallow colouring and orphaned state) were the objects of her unfeigned admiration. It seemed only right and proper that such a dazzling creature should receive preferential treatment from all who came into contact with her, and it did not occur to Winter to consider it unfair when she herself was punished for some fault that when committed by Sybella went unrebuked.

It was not that she was a dull or spiritless child. She was the daughter of Marcos and Sabrina, who had neither of them ever lacked the courage of their convictions. But she had come into conflict with Sybella on several occasions during the first year at Ware, and discovered that when Sybella did not get her own way she would immediately appeal to some grown-up, who would as invariably take her part. Winter could have held her own against Sybella, but she could not prevail against Sybella's mother, grandmother, nurse and governess. Had she complained to her great-grandfather there is no doubt that the scales would have been more fairly adjusted, but she despised her cousin for running to the skirts of Authority with every complaint, and would have scorned to imitate these tactics.

Sybella knew that she was beautiful and talented and an heiress because she had often been told or overheard these things. And for the same reason Winter knew that she was plain and dull and 'foreign'. She had no idea that she was a considerable heiress and bore a Spanish title, since no one had thought to tell her so. Her Great-Aunt Charlotte had originally given orders that she was to be known as 'Miss Winter', and 'Miss Winter' she remained. Zobeida would talk to her of the Casa de los Pavos Reales, the great house standing among its park-like grounds on the banks of the Goomti, but without being aware that it now belonged to Winter – together with all her father's very considerable property and Sabrina's own fortune left her by her mother Louisa who had been Louisa Cole, only daughter of an East India Company 'nabob'.

At first Juanita had written two or three times a year, sending news of all at the Gulab Mahal and messages to Zobeida, who could not read. But one year the letters ceased, and there was no one to tell them that the cholera had swept like a forest-fire through the packed mazes of Lucknow and had claimed ten victims from the pink stucco palace: among them Juanita, her husband Wali Dad and old Aziza Begum. In time the past became shadowy and a little unreal to Winter, as though it were only a magical story told in childhood. Yet always there remained, hidden at the bottom of her heart, the hope and the promise that some day, somehow, she would reach the Gulab Mahal again – and then, as had been promised, all would be well with her.

As the years went by Zobeida came to talk less and less of her own country, and Winter's days were fully occupied with lessons in the schoolroom. India retreated into a golden haze and she began to forget many things, until at last only that impression of rose pink walls, sunshine, flowers and brightly coloured birds – and happiness – remained. As lovely and as lost and as far out of reach as the moon.

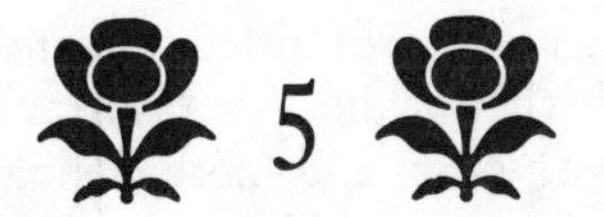

Winter was eleven years old when her distant cousin, Conway Barton, accompanied Great-Uncle Ebenezer on a visit to Ware.

Sir Ebenezer was getting old and his contacts with India, together with his interest in it, had shrunk with the years. But his influence had been sufficient to assist the advancement of his nephew in that country, and old Lord Ware, learning that the younger man had obtained a well-paid administrative post in a newly annexed district that bordered on Oudh, had expressed a wish to meet him with a view to asking him to see to certain matters connected with the de Ballesteros estates that could only be dealt with by someone in India.

Conway Barton was at that time in his thirty-seventh year, and still a personable enough figure of a man. Already moving towards stoutness, he was of sufficient height to make it appear that he was powerfully built rather than overweight, and his blond hair and blue eyes appeared lighter in colour than they actually were, owing to the sun-tanned skin of one newly arrived from the East. He was an ambitious man, not too scrupulous where his ambitions were concerned, with an easy address and an excellent opinion of his own capabilities.

The Earl of Ware had always considered himself to be a good judge of character, but he was old and tired, and in this instance his judgement was at fault. His eyesight too had dimmed, and so he not only failed to mark the signs of weakness and dissipation that were already written clear on Conway Barton's face, but he had been reminded, fatally, of Johnny. Perhaps memory or failing eyesight had played some trick upon him; or perhaps it was the blond hair, or light-coloured eyes in a tanned face. Whatever the reason, the impression remained, and it warped the old Earl's judgement. He took a great fancy to his son-in-law's nephew, entrusted him with much of Winter's affairs, and when Sir Ebenezer left, pressed the younger man to extend his stay.

It was at some time during this visit that the idea occurred to Mr Barton, who was already familiar with Winter's story and now heard for the first time the full tale of her possessions and estates, that this sallow and unprepossessing child would one day make a most eligible wife for some ambitious man. From here it was but a short step to substituting Conway Barton for this anonymous future husband. The more he thought about it the better it appeared. He was only thirty-six and could afford to wait for six years – or ten if need be. But only if he were assured of the outcome.

Mr Barton reviewed the problem carefully. At the moment few people were likely to take much interest in the Anglo-Spanish orphan, but a time would surely come when a succession of titled fortune-hunters would present themselves at Ware, and when it did, Mr Conway Barton would have little to offer in competition with other and more eligible applicants for the hand of such an heiress. Therefore, it would be as well to consolidate his position in advance. It had not taken Mr Barton long to gain a fair knowledge of Winter's position at Ware, and now he made the best possible use of it.

Fortune favoured him, for he had come from the East – from India, the Enchanted Land that was a fast-fading memory in Winter's mind. He had talked of that country once, in tones not untinged with distaste, in the presence of the child, and had been aware of her sudden avid attention. Thereafter he changed his tone and spoke of India as he himself had never seen it. His personal opinion of the country and its inhabitants was not a high one (he considered the former insanitary and barbaric and the latter uncivilized and contemptible), but having realized that there were fortunes to be made in India he had had every intention of making one. Now, however, Fate appeared to have presented him with a yet easier way of acquiring riches, and one which, if he were not mistaken, would entail the exercise of considerably less effort.

Mr Conway Barton began to speak to the eleven-year-old Winter of life in India, describing fantastic beauties of scene which were for the most part purely imaginary. The India he created for her was apparently entirely populated by oriental kings and queens who rode on white elephants decked with golden trappings, and lived in glittering fairy-tale palaces of white marble in a land where the sun always shone and the gardens were full of flowers and fountains and exotic fruits: all of which was so much in tune with the shadowy country of Winter's memory and imagination that she listened with rapture.

Apart from her great-grandfather and Beda, no one at Ware had ever troubled to single her out for attention or kindness. But this tall, yellow-haired man was kind to her, noticed her, talked to her, flattered her. She thought him wonderful, and the Earl, pleased that his favourite should show such partiality for a man who had taken his fancy, put it down to an unconscious endorsement of the soundness of his own judgement. 'Children and dogs,' said the old man, producing the platitude as though he himself had originated it, 'they always know. Can't fool a dog. Can't fool a child.'

Conway Barton left Ware with a pressing invitation to return, and it was during his last visit, when less than two weeks of his furlough remained, that he spoke of Winter to the Earl. He had given the matter considerable thought, and chose his words with care. He had, he told the Earl, become greatly attached to the girl, but he would now be going back to India for a further period of some eight to ten years, and before there was any likelihood of his returning, Winter would be a young woman. He suggested, delicately, that the Earl's expectations of life could not be great and should anything – er – unforeseen occur, Winter would be left to the care of Lady Julia, with whom the child did not appear to be entirely in sympathy. He realized, of course, that no such thing as a formal engagement could be entered into with a girl in the schoolroom, but he would like to feel that when he returned from the East he might, with the permission and approval of Lord Ware, approach her as a possible suitor for her hand.

Mr Barton had a great deal more to say on the subject – all of it well phrased and calculated to make the best possible impression – and the aged Earl was much moved. He had always known that Julia disliked Sabrina's daughter, and he placed no reliance upon her being either kind or considerate towards the child once he himself were dead. He was already eighty-six and that – although he had every intention of reaching his century – was an over-ripe age for a man, and few having reached it could do more than count on each passing month of life as a favour granted by time, and not as a right.

Lord Ware had worried sometimes, when waking from the light sleep of old age, about Winter's future. When he was no longer here, could he trust Julia to care for her? He very much doubted it. All that Julia cared for in this world was her vain, pretty daughter and her cold, ambitious self, and she could not be counted upon to protect Winter from fortune-hunters and men of the stamp of Dennis Allington – spendthrifts, rakes and gamblers. But now here was a way out of all his difficulties. This admirable young man who reminded him of his own long-lost Johnny, and who was so sensible and steady, and whom Winter herself was so fond of, was surely a right and proper person to care for his little ward. Married to him she would be secure, and with her affection for him she would also be happy, since it was safe to assume that her childish attachment would grow and not diminish with the years.

As for the idea that Barton should wait until he was next in England before the subject was broached, the Earl would have none of it – he himself could well be dead before then. In his own long-vanished youth, as it was still on the Continent and in the land of Winter's own father, children were frequently promised in matrimony at a very early age. And since he himself was an old man who could not expect to live much longer, Winter's future must be safe-guarded now.

Fired with this idea the Earl sent for Huntly and explained his wishes. Huntly was dubious, but the proposition received the instant and unqualified support of Julia, and urged by his wife he gave his support to the suggestion that a betrothal between Winter and Conway Barton should be recognized by the family; although it would naturally remain a purely private matter for some years to come.

Winter was summoned to her great-grandfather's room, the situation explained to her, and her future decided. It seemed to her the most delightful thing in the world, for to the eleven-year-old child her great-grandfather's age was terrifying. Ever since the deaths of her Great-Uncle Herbert and Great-Aunt Charlotte she had lived in daily dread that he too might die, because when he did, she and Beda would be alone and friendless. But now dear Mr Barton, who was so kind – almost as kind as Great-Grandfather himself – would take care of them and they would not be left alone at Ware. He would come for them and take them away, back to that golden, enchanted land whose memories he had reawakened for her. Away from the cold-eyed and cold-hearted dragon that was Cousin Julia.

At the Earl's desire a formal contract of betrothal was drawn up in which he, as the girl's legal guardian, gave his consent to the eventual marriage of his ward to Conway Barton, and Mr Barton signed his name to it in a bold flowing hand beneath Winter's childish signature. This contract the old Earl had insisted upon, it being his wish that in the event of his death Conway Barton should immediately claim his bride, provided she had reached marriageable age.

Later that week the Earl's solicitors called at Ware and drew up various legal documents with which Winter, as a minor, had no concern; her great-grandfather signing on her behalf. And on the day he left Ware, Conway presented her with a ring.

It was a small thing, made to fit a slim finger, yet still too large for Winter's childish hand. An unpretentious little trinket (Mr Barton knew that Lady Julia would take strong exception to any more ostentatious piece of jewellery) consisting of a small pearl set in a plain gold band. 'You cannot wear it on the correct finger yet,' said Conway Barton, slipping it onto the third finger of Winter's right hand, 'but it is only a token. One day, when you are grown up, I shall put another one there – the brightest diamond I can find for you in India. You must grow up quickly, and you must not forget me while you are doing so.'

The child flung her thin arms about his neck in a strangling hug: 'Forget you? As if I would! I love you better than anyone except Great-Grandfather and Beda. You are so good and so kind, and I will try and grow up as quickly as ever I can.'

Conway Barton patted her head encouragingly, disengaged himself and rode away.

He looked smug and well satisfied with himself. He had always known that he would do well, but what luck – what incredible luck – that fate should have thrown this chance of acquiring a vast fortune in his way, and given him the brains to profit by it. His satisfied smile changed to a frown . . . there was a stain on the breast of his impeccable riding coat – jam. Disgusting! The child must have been eating bread and jam. He took a handkerchief out of his breeches pocket and dabbed at it, wearing an expression of acute distaste. It was a pity she was such a skinny and unattractive little creature: he himself preferred buxom beauties, and his betrothed did not look as though she would grow into anything but a plain and skinny young woman. However, one could not have everything in this life. As for taking her out to India, he had no intention of doing any such thing. In six years' time, seven at most, he would resign his post and return and marry her. Once her fortune was in his hands there would be no need for him to do anything but live a life of ease and luxury, and he saw no reason why a wealthy and discreet man, even though married to a plain wife, should not continue to enjoy the favours of other and more beautiful women. Conway Barton broke into a snatch of song: he had every reason to feel pleased with himself.

Winter wore his ring for exactly two days. During which time it fell from her finger some twenty times, and Sybella remarked crushingly that it was a trumpery thing and that she herself would never consent to wear such poor stuff. Their governess refused to allow it to be worn during school hours, and when worn out riding under a leather gauntlet it cut into her finger. Winter gave up the attempt, and threading it on a narrow ribbon wore it thereafter around her neck, hidden beneath her bodice.

The years that followed Conway Barton's departure from Ware dragged by very slowly for Winter, and as she grew older she discovered that her cousin Sybella had less and less time for her outside their hours in the schoolroom.

Sybella was for ever driving out with her mother to visit friends in the neighbourhood, or taking tea in her mother's drawing-room at parties to which Winter was not invited. At thirteen Sybella put on all the airs and graces of a young lady of fashion, and her sole interest apparently lay in her own appearance and its effect upon the young sons and daughters of her mother's friends.

The old Earl now seldom moved from his room, and his hearing as well as his eyesight deteriorated daily. Winter still spent as much time as she was permitted in his company, but he tired very easily. Conversing with him became more and more difficult, and the lonely child, left largely to her own devices, drew what comfort she could from weaving stories to herself about the future: with the result that as the years crawled by her memory of Conway Barton became more and more romanticized and unreal. He became to her a tall, broad-shouldered, golden-haired knight, handsome, kind and endowed with all the virtues, who would one day come riding up the long oak avenue with the sun glittering on his blond head, and carry her and Beda away far over the seas to the lovely land of her birth where, like the princess in a fairy-story, she would live happily ever after.

She was fourteen when Zobeida died.

The damp cold and the fogs and frosts of the English winters had always been a torment to Zobeida, and of late years her once sturdy frame had seemed to shrink and shrivel until she was barely more than skin and bone. But she had never complained and never once suggested – or dreamed of suggesting – that she should be allowed to return to her own land. Sabrina's child, from the moment of its birth, had possessed her whole faithful loving heart, and wherever that child went, there would Zobeida have gone.

She had been much troubled by a dry cough that assailed her during the cold months, and going for a walk with her charge to pick cowslips in the fields beyond the Home Park they had been caught in a sudden rainstorm, and by the time they reached home were both wet through. Winter escaped with a chill, but Zobeida developed pneumonia and died within three days; babbling in her native tongue words that only Winter understood.

For a time it seemed as though the shock of Zobeida's death had seriously affected the child's health. She crept about the castle, white-faced and shivering, and spent long hours in her great-grandfather's room, sitting on a low stool beside him, but seldom speaking. The old man's heart ached for his darling, but he knew that this sort of sorrow has to be endured, and that in the end the sharpness of even the greatest grief becomes blunted. Had he not proved this himself? When the news had come that Johnny was dead he had thought himself an old man prematurely aged by grief, who would never care deeply for anyone or anything again. And yet Johnny had died . . . how many years ago? He could not remember – a lifetime ago it seemed – and he had loved Johnny's daughter, Sabrina; and now he could do nothing to assuage the grief of her child, sorrowing for the loss of a foster-mother and friend.

After Zobeida's death Winter turned more and more to her make-believe world of the future. The years might be passing slowly, but at least they were passing: only a few more of them and Conway would come home and marry her. She would pull out the little ring on its worn loop of ribbon and look at it and feel comforted. It was her talisman and her magic lamp; as was the thought of the Gulab Mahal of which Beda had so often spoken, where one day they were to return so that they might live happily ever after. But Beda would never go there now, and Winter grew afraid that now Beda was dead she might forget the language that had been as a mother-tongue to her. As Conway's wife she must be able to speak it so that she could be of help to him in his work, and so that she would not be a stranger in the Gulab Mahal. Thereafter she spoke it to herself daily, translating into it whole chapters from her school books.

She wrote long letters to Conway Barton, telling him of her small doings and asking news of him and his work, but Mr Barton's replies were disappointing. They were apt to be full of complaints about his superiors, and Winter would burn with resentment against these stubborn and mean-minded officials who could oppose so good and kind a man. Conway's superiors were, it appeared, an envious lot who were jealous of his outstanding talents and judgement and did their best to keep him from preferment.

Mr Barton was still occupying the post of Commissioner of Lunjore, a district bordering on Oudh, which he had originally obtained through the influence and reputation of his Uncle Ebenezer. He had expected to be promoted before now to some more prominent position, and did not hesitate to accuse several senior political officers and various members of Council of envy, malice and all uncharitableness in that he had not.

It was a day in which influence in high places formed an excellent substitute for talent. But Sir Ebenezer neither could nor would do anything more for his nephew, since Conway Barton possessed a love of two things that have never yet failed to ruin those devotees who have worshipped them to excess. Drink and Women.

For a time his strength of body and natural health stood him in good stead, but eventually indulgence and dissipation began to take their toll, aided and abetted by climate and the conditions of life in the East. The prospect of being able to retire to England and enjoy a vast fortune did nothing to assist him, for his ambition had been solely confined to amassing riches, and this was now within his grasp. He would gain what he wanted by the easier route of marriage, and so need no longer trouble himself with work. Time was all that now lay between him and the fulfilment of his ambition, and he intended to see that it passed as pleasantly as possible.

Conway Barton despised all coloured races and was wont to refer to them impartially as 'niggers'. But his distaste for a brown skin did not appear to extend itself to those women of the country who in turn occupied the small *bibi-gurh*, or women's house, that he had built behind the Residency, and he did not realize that with every day that passed his body came to mirror more clearly his many debaucheries. He put on weight and became fat and slothful, and because he abandoned the practice of taking active exercise in the open air, his once tanned skin became pale and puffy and his yellow hair thinned.

He would squint down at his spreading stomach and say that he feared he had put on a little weight, but that it was nothing that the cold weather, a few hours in the saddle and a cut in diet would not cure, and that he would take himself in hand and start getting back into good shape next week. But the first steps were never taken and the unhealthy fat accumulated on shoulders, stomach and jowl like snow drifting down upon the sharp angles of roof-top and gable, padding them out into gross curves.

His work deteriorated with his figure, but the fact that he was Sir Ebenezer's nephew saved him from much interference. And Fortune was kind to him in that it sent him as an assistant Alex Randall, one of those younger men, protégés and pupils of Sir Henry Lawrence; soldiers who had perforce become administrators – some of them the best administrators the world has ever seen.

Randall was content to do the work and let his chief take the credit: an arrangement that suited Mr Barton admirably. The Commissioner relapsed deeper into sloth and dissipation, and with it his delusions of grandeur and the power and position that wealth would bring him grew daily greater; nourished by the unwholesome drugs, opium and hashish, that he had begun to toy with. It was from this dream world that he was abruptly brought back to reality by the arrival of a letter from the Earl of Ware.

Winter would be seventeen in the following spring, wrote the Earl in a wavering senile hand, and although he had not intended that she should marry for some years to come, he felt himself to be failing fast. The doctors held out small hopes of his surviving for another year, and he wished Conway to return as soon as possible so that he might have the happiness of seeing his dear child safely married before he died.

So the day had come! Fortune lay at last within Mr Barton's grasp and all that he needed to do was to send in his resignation or, to hasten matters, demand sick-leave on the score of ill-health (and indeed he did not feel at all the thing these days), and as soon as it could be arranged, which would probably not be before the cold season, he would take ship for England.

The Commissioner heaved himself out of his chair and rolled across the living-room towards his office. And as he neared the door he saw a face . . .

It was a fat face, sallow and puffy, with pendulous jowls and heavy dark pouches under pale, protuberant eyes; the hair above it was thin and straggling, as was the long ragged moustache, much stained with nicotine. His own face, looking back at him from a glass-fronted cabinet that a trick of the light had turned into a looking-glass.

Mr Barton stopped dead, staring at that reflected face with a sort of horror. It was rarely that he saw himself in a looking-glass – the idle luxurious life of the East having made it virtually unnecessary for him to do so, since he was shaved, bathed and dressed, his hair combed and his nails cut by soft-footed, deft-handed servants. On those few occasions when he did glance at himself in a glass, he saw only the reflection of what he expected to see there. The Conway Barton of a dozen, or even four years ago: a little older perhaps – that was not to be wondered at – but still, not too bad. Not too bad. But now he had been taken off guard, and because he had not expected to see his own reflection he had thought for a moment that it was some stranger that he saw, and had not immediately realized that what he was looking at was his own face.

He stood where he was, swaying a little and breathing heavily, staring at the glass-fronted cabinet. After a full five minutes he walked unsteadily across the room and into his bedroom, and unhooking the looking-glass that hung on the wall above his dressing table, carried it over to the window and stared down into it.

Thoughts were churning round in his head. Some of them familiar ones. 'If I give up drink and all this rich greasy food, and take cold baths and walk and ride every day, I could get fit again by the cold weather. I could do it.' But he knew he could not. He knew that he no longer possessed the will-power. He knew too, as he stared down at his reflection in the glass, that if he were to present himself as he now was to his betrothed and her guardian, they would almost certainly show him the door. He was seeing himself for the first time as others saw him; as the seventeen-year-old Winter would see him, and even the senile, half-blind Earl of Ware.

What a fool he had been! What an unutterable fool to take chances when such a dazzling future was at stake. If he were to return to England now he might lose it all. And yet if he did not go—— Conway Barton flung the looking-glass from him in a spasm of futile rage and it smashed against the wall and strewed the carpet with a score of glinting fragments that winked up at him, reflecting a score of gross, middle-aged men with fat white faces and bulbous red-rimmed eyes.

He could not go to England! To go would mean losing the fortune that he had come to look upon as already his own. Yet how could he possibly ignore the Earl's summons? Then all at once a solution presented itself and he laughed aloud. A cackling, half-hysterical laugh of relief. Of course! – if the mountain cannot come to Mahomet, Mahomet must come to the mountain. He laughed again, and uproariously, at the pleasantry.

The girl must come out and marry him here. He would write to Ware. He would think of some plausible excuse. Once let her arrive in Lunjore, alone and without friends, and the marriage could be hurried through before she had time for thought. She would be far from Ware and with no one to turn to except possible shipboard acquaintances. It would be easy. She was young – she would barely be seventeen – and to return alone to Ware, unmarried, when she had left it with her bridal clothes and her trousseau, *en route* to her wedding, would be unthinkable. He would write at once. Letters to Ware and to his solicitors. Alex Randall should take them. And, better still, Captain Randall should escort the bride back to Lunjore, for although some respectable female returning to the East would be found to act as chaperon, a male escort to protect her would establish confidence. And who better than his trusted personal assistant?

Mr Commissioner Barton repaired to his office, and having stimulated himself to the effort by a large glass of rum and brandy, wrote steadily. A terse letter to his solicitors; a more lengthy and explanatory one to Lord Ware; another, requesting her assistance and relying on her good offices, to Lady Julia, and finally an affectionate and affecting letter to Winter herself, hinting at ill-health incurred through zeal towards duty, and the patriotic necessity of remaining at his post in anxious and troublous times when it would be inadvisable for the guiding hand to be summarily removed from the helm.

Mr Barton regarded this last epistle with considerable satisfaction. It conveyed just the right note of pathos and manly devotion to duty, and should serve to remind his betrothed that womanly duty as well as inclination should send her flying to his side.

It was late by the time the letters were finished and sealed, and the Commissioner summoned the attendant who squatted native-fashion just outside the door and bade him send a messenger to Captain Randall's bungalow requesting that officer's immediate presence. After which, well pleased with his handling of a difficult situation, he called for more brandy and drank deeply, congratulating himself upon the fact that although his outward appearance might have suffered some temporary change for the worse during the past five years there was still, thank heaven! nothing wrong with his brain.

The chill wind that was driving tattered regiments of cloud across a watery moon brought with it a sudden and vicious spatter of raindrops and a hint of snow. It jerked unexpectedly at the folds of a long military cloak that wrapped the solitary rider on the moor road, and wrenching it back sent it flapping out behind him like the wings of some monstrous bat.

Captain Alex Randall swore into the cold night and reining in his horse gathered the heavy folds about him again, gripping the slack beneath his arm. He rose in his stirrups and peered ahead into the wind-torn darkness, but could see no sign of light or human habitation. The moon, momentarily shaking itself free from the millrace of the clouds, showed nothing but a desolation of moorland across which the lonely road cut a pale track like the wake of a ship running before the wind.

A fresh gust of rain whipped out of the darkness and set Medusa jerking at her bit and sliding on the rough roadway, impatient to be off. Randall gave the mare her head and rode forward into the driving wind.

It was on Medusa's account that the Captain was on the road at this late hour. He had hoped to reach Ware before dark, but just beyond Highelm the mare had cast a shoe, and a passing yokel having informed him that the next smithy lay over ten miles ahead, he had had no choice but to turn back and get the damage repaired by a smith in Highelm.

There had been a considerable delay before a new shoe could be fitted and Medusa ready for the road again, and the smith, inquiring as to Captain Randall's destination, had advised against a resumption of his journey that day. There was, he affirmed, an excellent coaching inn in Highelm, and the road to Ware lay over a lonely stretch of moor, unpleasant enough by daylight in bad weather, but certainly to be avoided by night, with the sky darkening to storm clouds, a rising wind, and the threat of snow before morning. Only last week, said the smith, a London doctor, hastening to his Lordship, had been overtaken by darkness on the moorland road and had perforce to spend the night in his stationary coach owing to the loss of a wheel – his coachman having mistaken the lie of the road in the darkness: 'An' 'e might 'av' saved hisself the journey. It's for Thursday we hears. There's bin many goin' past this day.'

The smith, a well-meaning man, had urged Captain Randall to spend the night at 'The George' and resume his journey on the morrow, but Randall was not to be persuaded. His distaste for his errand was sufficiently great for the prospect of further delay to be unpalatable, and the sooner he was finished and done with it, and away again, the better. He thanked the smith for his well-meant advice but persisted in his intention of continuing on his way, and night had overtaken him while some eight to ten miles still lay between him and the tall towers and florid battlements of Ware.

The rain that drove under Captain Randall's hat-brim and trickled icily down his neck was turning to snow. Intermittent gusts of gradually thickening flakes streamed out of the darkness, touching his face with a thousand soft, furtive fingers and clotting in the folds of his cloak, and he began to think regretfully of the warm beds and roaring fires of 'The George Inn', and to regard his chances of reaching Ware that night with a less optimistic eye. His hands, encased in heavy gauntlets, were so frozen that he could barely feel the reins, and his booted feet ached with cold. He flexed his numbed fingers and smiled wrily into the darkness.

How many times during the last ten or eleven years had he not longed for the sight of grey skies and the smell and bite of east winds blowing across English soil? How many times, in the merciless grinding heat of an Indian summer, lying panting under a flapping punkah that merely disturbed but could not cool the molten air, had he not yearned in imagination for the ice and frost and snow of an English winter? Well he had them now, and he should be satisfied. But perhaps the blazing suns of the last twelve years had thinned his blood, for the icy wind that disputed his passage chilled him to the bone and his whole body ached with cold and fatigue.

To distract his thoughts from his physical discomforts he turned them to the counter-irritant of his present mission, and for perhaps the hundredth time, and with a deepening sense of exasperation and distaste, mentally reviewed the events that had led to his riding along this moorland road by night and in the teeth of a rising gale towards the great house of Ware.

Almost twelve years ago, in the autumn of 1844, Alex Mallory Randall, having completed his training at the Honourable the East India Company's Military College at Addiscombe and celebrated his eighteenth birthday, had embarked for the shores of India. He had served with distinction in that vast and turbulent land, and it was a day in which young men possessed of ability and ambition could find ample scope for their talents and energy in the colourful cauldron of 'John Company's' rapidly expanding Empire.

Alex had fought at Ferozeshah and Sobraon and at Chillianwallah – that disastrous shambles that had cost Lord Gough over two thousand four hundred lives and had been claimed as a victory by both Sikhs and British. He had been fortunate enough to catch the eye of the irascible Commander-in-Chief himself, and had been rewarded by a brevet to the rank of Lieutenant. As a result, he was removed almost immediately from regimental duty and set to work in an administrative capacity under the eye of that great administrator, Henry Lawrence.

Lawrence's passionate love and understanding of the country and its peoples was untainted by the lust for conquest, and he expected – and got –

as gruelling a standard of work from his subordinates as he himself gave to the task before him. Under his tutelage Alex had been in turn surveyor, road-builder, and magistrate, and had helped to govern and control vast expanses of lawless territory at an age when many a man is licking stamps or running errands. His handling of a swift and ugly crisis on the North-West Frontier had led to a second brevet, but he had not been permitted to return to his Regiment, and had once more found himself employed in a capacity that was more political than military.

His immediate superior in his present appointment was Mr Conway Barton, Commissioner of Lunjore, and Alex Randall had not taken to his chief. There were too many aspects of Mr Barton's character and habits that failed to commend themselves to him, but the two men had worked together reasonably amicably. Alex avoided his chief's company as far as possible and, as that gentleman was only too willing to transfer the bulk of the work to his junior's shoulders, went his own way to a large extent, unhampered by much interference.

It was on the eve of his departure on a year's furlough that Mr Barton had thrust an unwelcome commission upon him, and looking back on it Alex was surprised to find how clearly he remembered the events of that evening. He had seen that the last of his packing was completed, and in response to an unexpected summons from Mr Barton had walked over in the hot, harsh moonlight to the Residency; conscious of a twinge of anxiety as to what the sudden summons might portend. He had already paid his formal farewell visit, and as far as he knew all official matters had been handed over in good order to his successor. He could think of nothing that had not already received his attention; but supposing some sudden crisis had arisen at the last moment to delay his departure? It did not bear thinking of.

He was to leave the next day for Calcutta, and from there, via the overland route, for England. What would England look like? . . . feel like? . . . smell like? Would it really be as cool and green and fragrant as his memory had painted it for him during the last hot and crowded and eventful years? Could two such places as the England of his imaginings and the India of the stifling present really exist in one and the same world?

His footsteps made no sound on the thick dust that blanketed the ground between the avenue of shade trees, and overhead a bone-white moon blazed in a sky that seemed almost iron-grey. The air under the great gateway of the Residency was cooler than that of the hot night outside, and Alex lingered there, grateful for the small relief of that coolness.

Standing in the shadow of the thick archway he was struck by the uncanny stillness of the night, but presently he became aware of a faint sound that came from somewhere deep in the black shadows of a banyan tree that grew to the left of the gateway and just inside the Residency walls.

From an angle of the archway, where the shadow cut across the white, moonlit drive, Alex could see the dark mass of the banyan. There was a stone idol among the roots of the great tree; the symbol of virility roughly carved on an upright slab of stone, garishly bedaubed with orange paint and, on feast days, wreathed with garlands of fading marigold flowers. As his eyes became accustomed to the shadows he could make out figures crouched about the main trunk where the idol stood. One of them was speaking in a voice that was barely a whisper, for only the sibilance of the sound reached his ears. But the whispering voice was quick and urgent, and somehow conveyed an indefinable impression of authority.

Alex's first and instant suspicion was that he had stumbled on a gang of dacoits intent on robbery; but as he watched he abandoned it, for the group among the roots of the banyan tree was becoming more distinct and one of them, surely, was Akbar Khan, the gatekeeper, while another was the oily down-country *khansamah*, cook to the Commissioner. He caught a momentary glimpse of a third profile as it turned against a narrow bar of moonlight that struggled between the hanging fringe of banyan roots, and recognized the havildar of one of the native infantry regiments stationed in Lunjore.

There were at least a dozen men in the shadow of the great tree, and Alex came to the conclusion that they were for the most part Residency servants. These were largely Mohammedan with a sprinkling of low-caste Hindus; but the havildar was a Brahmin. What, then, were they all doing, meeting in secret conclave at this hour at the feet of a Hindu idol? And why did they consider it necessary to speak in whispers?

As he listened the speaker ceased and a low-toned murmur of conversation broke out, and presently a lone figure detached itself from the group among the tree roots and moved out into the moonlight. Alex saw with surprise that it was a sadhu, a Hindu holy man. The tall, spare figure was naked except for an intricately tied loin-cloth, and in the clear moonlight the man's ash-smeared body and long rope-like locks of ash-covered, uncombed hair appeared grey and ghost-like.

The sadhu reached the path before the gateway and without pausing walked directly towards Alex, his naked feet making no sound on the baked earth. The long, carved rosary he wore about his neck swung and clicked in the silence and Alex waited, expecting the man to check at the sight of him. He had a momentary glimpse of a grey, skull-like face blotted with a dark caste mark, in which a pair of glittering eyes showed astonishingly alive; and then, before he had quite realized it, the man had walked swiftly past him and through the dark arch of the gateway.

Alex swung round and ran after him, but the road beyond the gateway was empty, and the sadhu had vanished as completely as though he had indeed been a ghost.

Alex stared unbelievingly at the long expanse of roadway, white in the moonlight, that stretched away to the left and right past the Residency gateway. But the road was lined with shade trees that were grey with the dust of breathless days, and the sharp-edged shadows of any one of them might have swallowed up the figure of the sadhu. It was only then that Alex realized that the man had probably not been aware of his presence, for the sadhu had come from the deep shadow of the banyan out into the bright moonlight, while Alex had been standing in the shadow near the mouth of the gateway, his white drill backed by the whitewashed stone. He must have been as nearly invisible in that setting as the sadhu's ash-smeared greyness among the moonlight and shadows of the long cantonment road.

He heard a slight sound behind him and turned quickly. Akbar Khan, the gatekeeper, a shadow among the shadows, stood salaaming under the archway.

'Where hast thou been?' demanded Alex harshly in the vernacular, 'and what hast thou and the others to do with a sadhu? What evil is toward?'

'No evil, Huzoor,' said Akbar Khan tranquilly. 'We do but make prayer for rain.'

'What child's talk! Thou art a follower of the Prophet. Imal Din also; and Ustad Ali. Since when have Mussulmans made prayer to the gods of the Hindus, or consorted with their holy men? And what has Havildar Jodah Ram to do with such as Bulaki of the sweeper-*log*?'

'Huzoor,' said Akbar Khan, 'in evil times, when the rains fail, we suffer as one. The monsoon tarries and the crops die. Soon, if the rains delay overlong, there will come a great famine and many will die – Mussulman and Hindu, Sikh and Bengali together. Yonder fakir makes petition to his gods for rain. While we Muslims call upon Allah for rain, the Hindus of the city call also upon their gods. That is all.'

'Hmm,' said Alex. 'In the circumstances it is almost conceivable that you might be speaking the truth. But I don't believe it, and I don't like it. And don't leave the gate unattended again, you old reprobate.'

Akbar Khan, to whom these last remarks, spoken in English, were unintelligible, salaamed deeply and drew back against the wall as Alex walked past him and up the long, curving drive towards the big white single-storeyed house among the flame trees.

From a courtyard behind the house a woman's voice could be heard singing a shrill, quavering Indian song to the accompaniment of a sitar. It stopped suddenly, as though checked by an order, as Captain Randall mounted the verandah steps, his boots ringing loud on the stone. A white-clad figure rose with a rustle from the matting and, salaaming low, pattered away to a lighted doorway screened by a *chik* – a curtain of split cane – that led into the Commissioner's drawing-room. Alex could see the crouching figure of a punkah-coolie seated cross-legged in the shadows, his body bowing to the rhythmic tug and release of the rope, and from inside the room came the familiar flap and fall of the punkah cloth, a clink of bottles and glasses and the murmured Hindustani of the native servant.

'What's that? What's that?'

The Commissioner's voice was thick and blurred and Captain Randall's mouth twisted in a fleeting grimace of impatience and contempt.

The servant lifted the split-cane curtain and the Commissioner's bulky figure appeared in the doorway, black against the yellow lamplight.

'That you, Alex? Come in. Come in. Just the man I wanted t'see. Siddown. Have a drink. Know why I sent f' yer?'

'No, sir. Nothing gone wrong with my furlough, I hope?'

'No, no. That's all right. It's just that I want you t'do something fer me. Favour. Long story. It's m' future wife . . .'

He took a deep pull at the glass in his hand while the sweat trickled down his pale, puffy features and soaked into the thin Indian-style garment he wore in lieu of more formal attire.

Alex sat down and resigned himself to listen. He knew the Commissioner for a bore and a snob, and both attributes were apt to colour his conversation to an intolerable degree. He was also aware – as who was not? – that Mr Barton was affianced to a distant cousin; a great-grand-daughter of the Earl of Ware.

Conway Barton was proud of his connection with Lord Ware and lost no opportunity of mentioning the relationship, though in actual fact the connection was of the slightest; the Earl's only daughter having married an elderly nabob whose youngest brother was Conway Barton's father. The lady's niece had apparently married a Spanish nobleman, and it was to this niece's daughter that Mr Barton was affianced. The match had been arranged some five or six years previously, during the Commissioner's last furlough in England, and it had been intended, explained Mr Barton, that there should be a long engagement – no unusual thing in the circumstances – and that the marriage should take place during his next home leave. But now the Earl of Ware, who was her great-grandfather and guardian, had written to urge the return of Mr Barton and his immediate marriage to his betrothed. This course, however, was impracticable, and therefore he had decided upon an alternative arrangement . . .

Captain Randall smothered a yawn and shifted uncomfortably in his chair. He could feel the sweat trickling down between his shoulder-blades, and his body itched with prickly heat. The punkah flapping gently to and fro above their heads had drifted to a stop as the weary punkah-coolie dozed at his post, and Alex wondered tiredly why the Commissioner had found himself unable to go home. For one of his seniority it should have been easy enough to arrange. The districts were always intolerably short of officers, but Conway Barton's reputation did not stand so high as to class him among the irreplaceables. And why should the Commissioner have sent for him, Alex, at this hour, merely in order to discuss his projected marriage?

'The mountain must come t' Mahomet,' said Mr Barton, and laughed heartily at his own wit. 'An' thish, m'dear Alex, is where you come in——'

'I, sir?' Alex sat up with a jerk, roused from his bored lethargy into apprehensive attention.

'Yesh, you, m'dear fellow. Wouldn't trust anyone else. But you're a genel'man. Can't shay the same of some others. An' though you're a sight too good-looking for a man, or would be if y'd only grow some hair on y'lip . . . wasser marrer with you anyway? it ain't decent at your age, shavin' your face like a demned nigger! . . . you don't go much with women. Never known you tie up with a petticoat yet. Can't shay the same of some others. 'Tisn't normal, but there it ish. Sho when I had to decide, I said "Randall! Just the f'llow. He'll do!" '

The Commissioner stopped as though he had fully explained himself, and lay back in his long cane chair and drank deeply.

'Do what, sir?'

'What? Wha's that? Oh; fetch her of course, m'boy. Bring her out here. Mountain t'Mahomet. Hope she ain't a mountain. Half Spanish y'know. They can run to fat. Mountain t'Mahomet.'

For a few minutes Alex had thought that the Commissioner could not possibly be serious, but he was speedily disabused: the Commissioner was perfectly serious. He had given prolonged thought to the problem and had spent the greater part of the day in writing letters. They lay on an inlaid ivory and sandalwood table beside him as he spoke. His plans were all made. Captain Randall was to carry letters to the Earl of Ware, to Mr Barton's betrothed, to Mr Barton's solicitors, Mr Barton's uncle and Mr Barton's bankers. He was, in addition, to explain the whole matter in person to the Earl, and add his entreaties to those of the Commissioner that the Condesa de los Aguilares should set sail for India in the following year, under the charge of Captain Alex Randall and of any suitable chaperon that could be provided, when Captain Randall returned from furlough.

'I leave it to you,' said the Commissioner expansively. 'Very capable f'llow. Always said so. "Randall's the man for this," I said. "Once they shee him they'll realize it's safe enough to shend – send 'er out." Genel'man to protect her. Makesh a difference.'

Alex had argued and protested, but to no purpose. The Commissioner was not a man to be deflected from any course of action which he had once decided to follow, and short of a flat refusal – and the incurring of the Commissioner's enmity thereby – there was nothing he could do about it. To make an enemy of his chief over such a matter seemed absurdly quixotic, for after all, he had to return and work with the man. That work must come first, and it could be made difficult, if not impossible, if Mr Barton's antagonism was aroused against him.

Alex fought a perpetual battle with the daily problem of how to do what appeared to him as obviously right, sensible and just, while at the same time steering clear of a direct collision with some senior official who resented his early promotion and his impatience with bumbling ineptitude. He had learned long ago the necessity of riding his temper and his impatience on a curb, but he still found it the hardest part of his work. He could not afford to quarrel with Mr Barton, and so it had ended with his accepting the distasteful commission that had been thrust upon him by his superior. But with certain inward reservations.

Alex had considered those reservations often since that hot night at the Lunjore Residency, but had been unable to come to any definite decision. There were two alternatives before him, and both were distasteful. On the one hand he was to make himself responsible for conveying a gently nurtured woman to an unknown land seething with sedition and unrest – to say nothing of the dangers and discomforts of such things as disease, intolerable heat and an almost total lack of sanitation – and eventually hand this fellow-creature into the care of a man whom he knew to be both a drunkard and a libertine. On the other hand, should he warn Lord Ware of these aspects of the affair, he would be betraying the trust of his superior officer, and stand guilty of disloyalty.

It was always possible, of course, that the Commissioner's betrothed was well aware of the disadvantages of the match, for according to Conway Barton the marriage had been arranged some five years previously, and since the earliest that a young lady of rank would be likely to be affianced was seventeen, that would make her at least of age. But possibly she was a good deal older than that, and plain into the bargain; which would account for the aged Earl's anxiety to get her suitably bestowed. If so, it was likely that the lady herself was fully prepared to accept the prospect of life in the East and a drunken husband of loose morals, as an escape from spinsterhood. Women were unpredictable in such matters. The solution of the problem would have to rest on the outcome of his visit to Ware, and the character and understanding of the aged and possibly senile Earl. Nothing of course could be said to Mr Barton's betrothed, but if her guardian was a sensible man, Captain Randall had little doubt that the Commissioner of Lunjore would wait in vain for the arrival of his bride.

Medusa stumbled and recovered herself, and Captain Randall's tired brain jerked itself back from the past and into the immediate and uncomfortable present.

The snow had turned back to sleet, and now it was raining again. No heavy, tropical, lukewarm downpour this time, but the icy, stinging sleet of the northern latitudes, that lashed at him as the wind blew in uneven gusts. For the last mile or so Medusa had been moving at a walk, picking her way uncertainly in the darkness and confused by the whirling snowflakes. But now all at once she lengthened her stride and began to trot.

Alex roused himself from his stupor of cold and fatigue and peered ahead. There were trees near by. And surely that was a glimmer of light? They were leaving the moors behind them and entering a more hospitable country of fields and hedges and woodland, and Medusa shook her head and snorted as though she knew that a warm stable and a feed of oats lay not far ahead.

The road dipped downwards, sheltered now by trees, and the whine of the gale over the moorland changed to the surf-like croon of wind among branches. A high wall loomed up out of the darkness; sensed rather than seen, for the wind was cut off abruptly and the sound of Medusa's hooves rang hollowly on the roadway. The wall followed the line of the road for a mile or so and then turned away almost at right angles in front of a vast stone gateway topped by the heraldic wolves of Ware.

Lights glowed behind the windows of the lodge-keeper's cottage and it seemed that Captain Randall was expected, for the heavy wrought-iron gates stood open. Beyond these lay a long avenue of oak trees rising out of a sea of dead bracken, and on either side stretched the open spaces of a park across which the wind, unhampered now by the high stone wall that had sheltered the road, blew in savage gusts between the tree-trunks.

Medusa broke into a gallop, and ten minutes later the park and the avenue ended in a wide sweep of gravel before the towering bulk of a great house, half-castle, half-mansion. A faint gleam of light showed from a high window, but except for that the place was in darkness.

Captain Randall dismounted stiffly, and knotting the sodden reins, looped them about the neck of a dimly seen griffin carved in weather-worn stone, and mounted the wide steps that led up to the front door. He tugged at the iron bell-chain and waited, stamping his feet on the wet stone to restore the circulation to them. After what seemed an unconscionably long wait he heard a sound of slow footsteps, and the great door creaked open. An aged man, bent and wrinkled, his white hair dressed in the manner of an earlier day, peered out at him, and then setting the door a little wider drew back to let him pass.

Captain Randall found himself standing in a vast hall that appeared even vaster in the dim light of the single branch of candles that formed the only illumination in all that wide place of shadows. He looked about him in some surprise. In such a hall one might have expected to see family portraits, weapons or trophies adorning the enormous expanse of wall. Yet here there was nothing. Nothing but a blackness that seemed to move and sway and shiver as the draught blew in through the half-open door and eddied about the hall.

The candle-flames flickered wildly in the rush of cold air, to flare up again as a tall footman in black livery leant his weight against the door, shutting it upon the wild night. Captain Randall stared about him in the grip of an odd sense of unreality. Weariness appeared to be playing tricks with his eyesight. Was it only imagination or the effects of cold and fatigue that made the shadowy walls about him seem to move and tremble?

The ancient steward who had peered at him through the half-open door tottered across the hall and lifted the branched candlestick, holding it high, and Alex saw with a sense of shock that the walls of the vast hall were hung from ceiling to floor with black curtains that still swayed and shifted uneasily from the wind that had blown in from the night.

The old man tapped on the stone floor with the long steward's wand he held in one shrivelled hand, and two more sombre-liveried flunkeys materialized out of the shadows. 'Your horse shall be attended to, sir, and Thomas will see that you have all you require. You will be one of the family? I do not for the moment recall the name. Forgive me, sir – your Lordship – we were not expecting——' The old man's voice quavered to a stop and Alex spoke curtly:

'You mistake me. I am Captain Alex Randall. Lord Ware requested me to wait upon him on this date. I was delayed upon the road, or I should have reached here before dark. You will find my valise strapped to the saddle.'

'His Lordship requested you . . . ?' The words appeared to carry a note of disbelief, and Alex thrust a hand into the bosom of his coat and drew out a folded sheet of paper that bore a few lines written in a wavering, spidery hand. 'I received this a week ago, and sent a letter in reply, informing Lord Ware that I would do myself the honour of waiting upon him. Was my letter not received?'

'I – we – there have been so many letters,' said the aged steward uncertainly. 'Perhaps it was overlooked. A week ago, you say——'

To Alex's puzzled amazement he saw that tears were standing in the old man's eyes, the feeble tears of old age that brimmed over and trickled down the furrowed, parchment-like face and flashed in the candlelight. And suddenly several things that had meant nothing to him a moment before took on shape and meaning. The smith at Highelm who had said: 'It's for Thursday we hears. There's bin many goin' past this day.' The London doctor who might have saved himself a journey. The open gates at the entrance of the oak avenue; the black liveries of the servants and the funereal hangings that draped the walls of the great hall. He said suddenly, sharply: 'The Earl——?'

'His Lordship died five days ago,' said the old steward.

The morning dawned wet and cold. It had snowed again during the night, and although the snow had once more turned to sleet, patches of it still lay in the hollows of the park and along the margins of the long oak avenue. The wind moaned among the dark corridors of the great house and bellied the funereal hangings that draped the walls.

Captain Alex Randall awoke with a headache and a sense of acute irritation. He had slept little, and that uneasily, for the problem that he had intended to transfer to the Earl of Ware was once more back upon his own shoulders. Lord Ware, thought Alex crossly, had no right to die before settling his ward's affairs. Now what was to be done? It was one thing to explain the true state of affairs to an elderly man of the world, but quite another to interview Mr Conway Barton's betrothed herself. What the devil was he to do now?

Simply deliver the letters, discharge his duty as courier, and let the woman go hang? After all, it was no concern of his whom she married or did not marry. Who was he to play Providence? And yet—— Here he found himself back once more at the interminable argument.

He breakfasted alone in a small panelled room warmed by a blazing log fire, and an elderly and sedate secretary waited upon him with a message from the new Earl. Lord Ware, owing to pressure of work, found himself unable to see Captain Randall until late in the day. He trusted that it would be convenient for Captain Randall to spend another night or so at Ware, since the business he had come upon was not one to be dealt with in haste.

'It is most damnably inconvenient,' said Captain Randall sourly. 'But I suppose there is no help for it.'

Left to his own devices he passed a tedious morning, and the company at luncheon proved unenlivening. They were all, with the sole exception of himself, relatives or connections of the family who had assembled for the funeral of the late head of their house, which was to take place the following day. They were dressed in deep black and conversed in the hushed undertones deemed suitable in a house of mourning, but bereavement had evidently not impaired their appetites. The meal was rich, indigestible and interminable, and the conversation, of necessity, lacking in sparkle.

Alex spent the greater part of the afternoon moodily watching a stream of black-clad tenants and their families who, despite the inclemency of the weather, were moving slowly up the oak avenue to pass through the guardroom where the late Earl's coffin lay in state. Eventually, more for lack of other occupation than from any desire to pay his respects to the unknown dead, he abandoned his post at the window and went down to join that sombre procession.

They moved forward slowly and in silence through a low stone porch in the oldest part of the castle and entered a long passage leading to the guardroom. The air was heavy and cold and the walls were hung with black drapery that billowed continuously in the draught. A short flight of stone steps led down into the guardroom, and at the foot of them stood the catafalque.

Alex drew to one side and stood looking down on a strangely impressive scene. The walls were draped in the same unrelieved black, and the catafalque itself and the floor about it was covered with heavy black cloth and lit by four massive candles in iron sconces. But the rest was colour and glitter and magnificence; a magnificence made even more startling by very contrast with its funereal setting. A defiance and a boast in the face of death.

The ornate hatchment suspended above the coffin-head gleamed with all the colour and gilding and pride of heraldry, and below it crimson velvet drapery covered the heavy oak of the coffin, on which, placed upon a velvet cushion, stood the Earl's coronet and the Star and Garter. The diamonds flashed and blazed as the candle-flames wavered in the draught, sending out splinters of brilliant light – violet and green and blue, scarlet and white. The breastplate, surrounded by various orders and badges of honour, was surmounted by the Earl's own arms, while below them, together with the gilt spurs of Knighthood, lay two crossed swords; the dress-sword of a Knight of the Garter and one which Alex took to be the sword of some Militia regiment.

At the foot of the coffin hung a Knight's gold collar, and beneath it were grouped on either side of the bier the Earl's mantle and the velvet and ermine of a Knight of the Garter, the hat of a Colonel of Militia and a military scarf. Servants dressed in black livery stood guard at each side of the coffin, and as the silent procession of mourners passed slowly by the bier and out through the low stone arch at the far side of the room, Alex found his lips moving in scraps of remembered poetry: '*The boast of heraldry, the pomp of power, and all that Beauty, all that wealth e'er gave, await alike the inevitable hour. The paths of glory lead but to the grave.*' A sobering reflection. Yet there was no meek acceptance of the latter end here. His aged Lordship was moving to the grave with all the pomp and ceremony that had attended him in life.

The steady stream of mourners thinned gradually to a mere trickle, and beyond the narrow stone embrasures of the guardroom windows the grey daylight took on the purple hue of dusk.

A woman, veiled and in heavy mourning, brushed past Captain Randall and went swiftly down the steps to pause beside the resplendent bier, her clothing outlined with a faint nimbus of gold from the candlelight beyond.

The thick veil that fell from her bonnet's edge almost to her feet permitted no glimpse of her features and did not betray even the colour of her hair. But the vast hooped crinoline, the heavy crêpe veil and a deeply fringed pelisse, unwieldy as they were, failed to conceal the wearer's youth. They failed, too, to conceal something else. Despite its rigidity there was about the slight figure in its cumbersome mourning a poignant impression of intense and hopeless grief. Alex could not have explained even to himself why this should be so, for the girl stood stiffly; head erect and black-gloved hands pressed back the spreading skirts of her dress. But he was aware of a sudden sense of guilt, as though he were eavesdropping on some private and very personal conversation, and turning abruptly he walked quickly away.

Darkness had fallen by the time the secretary appeared to request Captain Randall's presence in his Lordship's private apartments, and to lead the way along interminable corridors to a more recently constructed wing. Turning the handle of an ornate white and gold door, he ushered Captain Randall into a large high-ceilinged room whose original Regency character had been successfully submerged in a wave of taste generated by the Great Exhibition of 1851. But it was the Countess, and not the Earl, who waited to receive him.

Lady Ware rose with a rustle of heavy silks. Julia, lately Viscountess

Glynde and now Countess of Ware, was a tall woman, verging on middle age, with a coldly handsome face and smooth loops of light brown hair already streaked with grey. She held out a white hand with a gesture that was almost royal, and Alex Randall bowed over it and straightened up to meet the critical gaze of a pair of slightly prominent blue eyes, cold, pale and calculating. She studied him for a moment in silence and apparently liked what she saw, for her somewhat thin-lipped mouth relaxed in a faint smile.

'My dear Captain Randall,' said the Countess of Ware, 'you must forgive me for being unable to receive you earlier, but under the present sad circumstances – well, I am sure that you will understand how difficult it has been for us. Pray be seated. My husband has asked me to convey to you his regrets that he cannot, after all, find the time to see you today. He hopes that he will be able to do so later.'

The Countess seated herself again, the vast expanse of her black silk mourning billowing about her in impressive folds, and waved Captain Randall to a chair beside her. Captain Randall sat down warily. He had never had much to do with women, and apart from several light and lovely ladies who had provided him with amusement and a substitute for love, had met singularly few of them. This, it may be added, was not from lack of opportunity. Alex Randall was no celibate, but two things obsessed him to the exclusion of all others: India and 'John Company'. The glamour of India – the vast, glittering, cruel, mysterious land teeming with violence and beauty – and the romance of 'John Company', that prosaic collection of merchant-traders from London who had conquered a sub-continent and now maintained their own armies and administered justice and law to sixty million Indians. These were the things that held his heart and his imagination and his loyalty, and he had little time for other matters.

Now, facing the imposing figure of the Countess of Ware, he knew himself to be at a disadvantage. He could have dealt with a man. He disliked having to deal with a woman.

'I must apologize for my inopportune arrival,' he said stiffly. 'I had of course no idea——'

Lady Ware cut him short in her clear, incisive voice.

'My dear Captain Randall, no apology is necessary, I assure you. We are exceedingly grateful to you for all your trouble in being the bearer of these letters. We have heard of you from Mr Barton of course. He sent other letters through the post, apprising us of your arrival and giving us some indication of the nature of your mission, although naturally he did not write so fully as in the letters he entrusted to your personal care. You must know that we had expected to see you some months earlier.'

'Yes. I am sorry. I had myself expected to arrive a good deal earlier, but I visited the Crimea *en route*, and was delayed. I wrote to Mr Barton and the late Lord Ware to explain matters.'

'We quite understand. You were wounded, were you not. Did you see much fighting?'

'A certain amount,' said Alex uncommunicatively.

Lady Ware lost interest in the Crimea and returned to Mr Barton.

'... and now that we have had the opportunity of meeting you, and of reading the letters you brought with you,' she concluded, 'the position is of course quite clear.'

She lifted one of the letters under discussion from an ormolu table at her side, and the thin sheets of paper, covered with the familiar erratic handwriting in heavy black ink, crackled sharply in the stillness, echoing the sound of the burning logs in the wide hearth. One letter was still unopened and the seal intact: 'We have not,' said Lady Ware, 'given Winter her letter as yet. I shall now do so at the earliest opportunity.' The shadow of a frown passed over her face and her narrow mouth drew itself into a tighter line.

'Winter?' Captain Randall's voice was puzzled.

'My cousin. The – Condesa,' explained Lady Ware, pronouncing the title with palpable distaste. 'Naturally she will be allowed to express her views. But I am convinced that she will consent to dear Conway's plan. It is unfortunate that he cannot come home, but in the circumstances I feel that to delay the marriage for a further, and possibly indefinite, period, would be unnecessarily harsh. Both on dear Conway and on Winter herself.'

Winter! thought Alex Randall. What an impossible name. Probably the diminutive of some more lengthy Spanish one.

'There are times,' said Lady Ware with the air of one who is prepared to be both broad-minded and magnanimous, 'when one must sacrifice one's own wishes in order to forward the happiness of others. I am sure that you will agree with me.'

Captain Randall was far from being in agreement with her, since he felt tolerably certain that the dear Conway of five years ago bore little resemblance to the Commissioner of Lunjore as he had last seen him. Five years in the East were apt to leave their mark on most men, and with a man of Conway Barton's character and habits the change was not for the better.

'Have you any knowledge of the East?' inquired Alex abruptly.

Lady Ware looked a little taken aback. 'If you mean, have I ever been there, I have not. Why do you ask?'

'I only wondered if you have any idea as to what life, and to what conditions of life, you are sending your cousin? It is no country for a young lady who has been brought up in such surroundings as these.'

'Nonsense!' said the Countess crisply. 'Thousands of Englishwomen – many of them well bred – have managed admirably out there. I myself am acquainted with some of them. Lady Lawrence, Sir Henry's wife——'

'She is dead,' interrupted Alex curtly. 'Did you not know?' It seemed to him incredible that anyone who had known Honoria Lawrence should not know that she was dead.

'Dear me,' said the Countess inadequately. 'I had not heard. Poor Sir Henry. Of what did she die?'

'India,' said Alex laconically.

The Countess stiffened indignantly. 'I do not understand you, Captain Randall. You yourself have spent some years in that country——'

'Twelve,' interjected Captain Randall.

'Then surely you have met many of your fellow-countrywomen out there? Are you trying to tell me that none of them finds life supportable? I cannot believe that you are serious.'

'No,' said Alex slowly. 'Many of them would be nowhere else if given the choice. But as a general rule these fall into two categories: those who remain, and endure every hardship that heat and disease and exile can bring, for love of husband or father. And those whose social status in this country is such that India gives them a sense of position and importance that they cannot obtain here. The rest hate it. The latter consideration will hardly apply to the Condesa, but can you be sure of the first one? I understand that it is five years and more since she last saw Mr Barton.'

'That is a matter that must be left to my cousin,' said the Countess frostily. 'It is no concern of ours. No doubt she will decide for herself.'

She rose with an impressive rustle of silk and held out her hand. Captain Randall stood up and bowed over it.

'I hope,' said the Countess with a return to graciousness, 'that you will not mind extending your stay for another two days? My husband hopes to be able to see you tomorrow afternoon. Most of our guests will be leaving after the funeral, and he will then be able to give you his undivided attention.'

Captain Randall murmured his thanks and turned to go, and as he did so he noticed for the first time a large portrait that hung above the clutter of a velvet-draped overmantel. It depicted a young girl in a white crinoline and a blue sash. A pretty creature, barely more than a child, with pale gold ringlets falling onto sloping shoulders, and one small hand holding a single rose. He had observed the original of the portrait at luncheon that day, and looking at the painted likeness he had a sudden and disturbing vision of what a few years of scorching heat, difficult childbirths, cholera, typhus, dysentery, and the society of a dissolute and drunken husband would do to that face. It did not seem made of the stuff of endurance. 'No stamina,' thought Alex with a stab of anger and frustration. It would be unthinkable to have a hand in condemning such a defenceless creature to the life that awaited any wife of Conway Barton, Commissioner of Lunjore.

'My daughter, Sybella,' said the Countess complacently, and Alex drew a quick breath of relief. At least the future of that fragile-looking child need not be on his conscience. He turned and smiled at the Countess. Few women were proof against Alex Randall's smile, and Julia Ware proved no exception. She thawed visibly. 'Such a dear child. You must meet her, Captain Randall. Herr Winterhalter informed me that of all his subjects Sybella was——'

The discreet entrance of an elderly lady, evidently a companion, interrupted her: 'What is it, Mrs Barlow?'

'Lady Augusta. You asked that she——'

'Yes, yes. I shall not be a moment. Good night, Captain Randall. I have so enjoyed our little talk.'

She inclined her head in a slight but gracious nod of dismissal and turned her attention to the elderly companion.

There was no sign of the young lady of the portrait at dinner that night, and Alex concluded that she must be dining with her parents. He found himself seated between a portly clergyman, and a Lady Wycombe who, having demanded an explanation of his presence at Ware, remarked: 'For one can see that you are not one of the family.'

'How?' inquired Alex, interested.

'The family favours fair hair. Have you not noticed? Yours is dark. And you are burnt so exceedingly brown. India, I presume?'

Alex introduced himself and explained his presence in the house. He did not go into the details of his errand, merely allowing it to be inferred that he had had business to transact with the late Earl.

'Yes, of course. He was a shareholder, was he not? Of the East India Company, I mean. A very interesting country, India, I feel sure. But too hot. You were looking for someone, were you not? Who did you expect to see here?'

'No one, I assure you,' said Alex with a smile. 'But there was a young lady sitting opposite me at luncheon. I noticed that she is not here tonight.'

'Ah, you must mean Sybella,' said Lady Wycombe. 'She is having a light supper in her room. Do not tell me that you too have fallen a victim to her charms! If so I must hasten to warn you that you stand no chance; no chance at all. When Bella marries it will be to the heir of a great name or a great fortune. Probably both.'

'I have met Lady Ware,' said Alex gravely.

His companion laughed. 'Oh, I was not referring to Julia. Naturally *she* thinks that no one under a Prince of the Blood is good enough for her dazzling daughter, but she could be brought to consent to anything that her child demanded. No, it is Sybella herself who sets the mark high. And she will hit it, of that I have no doubt. That is, if she can rid herself of her cousin. Winter may yet spoil her aim. It is a way she has.'

'Winter. That is a curious name. Does it derive from the Spanish? It sounds a trifle bleak.'

'You have not met her yet?'

'No. What is she like?'

Lady Wycombe laughed on rather an odd note.

'No woman can describe her to you without injustice. But I am sorry for Julia – and Sybella. Sybella is a spoilt, selfish chit who will grow up into a spoilt, selfish woman. Nevertheless one cannot help feeling for her. Do you see that young man over there? On the far side of that candelabrum; sitting between old Lady Parbury and Camilla Grantham – the girl with the red hair. That is Amberley's heir, and the greatest *parti* in Europe. He is also Sybella's first cousin, though that will not stop them. There is only one thing that may stand in the way of a satisfactory conclusion, but now that Henry is dead I am quite sure that suitable steps will be taken. Yes, they will certainly get rid of Winter.'

Alex said: 'I am sorry to appear so dull-witted, but you forget that I am a stranger here. I have never met any of these people before, and I must confess that I have not the least idea what you are talking about.'

'And why should you, indeed?' said Lady Wycombe.

'Enlighten me, please.'

'You will find it very tedious stuff. What is it you wish to know?'

'About the Condesa with the chilly name. And Lady Sybella. What was it that she could do nothing about while Henry – the late Earl I collect? – was alive, and why will she get rid of this Winter now that he is dead? You perceive that you have aroused my curiosity.'

'Wait until you know them better, and then you will see for yourself.'

Lady Wycombe had clearly lost interest in the subject. She turned her shoulder upon him, and Captain Randall found himself engaged to listen to a long monologue from his right-hand neighbour, a portly ornament of the church, anent the disgraceful advance of the railroads, which were spreading a pernicious network all over the country to the great detriment of the natural scene and a decline in the use of that noble animal, the horse.

There had been no gathering of the assembled guests at the conclusion of the meal, for the ladies withdrew to their several rooms immediately upon leaving the table. After an unusually brief interval with the port the gentlemen followed their example, and Captain Randall, making his way back to his room, took a wrong turning and so came upon a curious scene.

He found himself at the entrance of a long, unlighted gallery hung with tapestries and family portraits, at the far end of which, blackly silhouetted against a lighted hall beyond, stood two closely embraced figures. He was preparing to retreat hastily when it was borne in upon him that what he was witnessing was not a love scene, for the woman at the far end of the gallery was being held against her will. Her captor held her with her arms closely pinioned to her sides, and so hard against him that she could move nothing but her head as she strove frantically to avoid his avid kisses. She did not cry out, but struggled silently, and in the stillness of the quiet gallery Alex could hear her short, panting breaths. He started forward at a run.

The floor of the gallery was thickly carpeted and the two at the far end of it too engrossed in their struggle to be aware of his approach.

'Just a moment,' said Alex crisply. He caught the gentleman's shoulder in an ungentle grip and jerked him round, and the lady, freed, drew back with a gasp of relief and leant panting against the wall, her hands at her throat. The wide black skirts of her crinoline merged with the shadows of the gallery, and only her face and her small hands made white blurs in the dim light.

Alex turned his attention to the gentleman, but before he could speak, yet another figure appeared upon the scene; someone who must have started to run across the wide hall towards the struggling figures at almost the same instant that Alex had started towards them from the far end of the gallery, but who, hampered by a trailing cashmere shawl, had arrived there a close second.

'*Edmund!*' The word was a gasp of fury.

Captain Randall released his captive who took a hurried step backward, bringing his face into the subdued light of the hall. It was the young gentleman whom Lady Wycombe had referred to as the most eligible *parti* in Europe.

The new arrival stared up at him for a moment, her breath coming short. Then suddenly, swiftly, she brushed past him, ignoring Captain Randall as though she were unaware of his presence, and confronted the panting figure in the shadows.

'*You!*' The single syllable was scarcely more than a breath of rage in the silence. It was followed by another sound, equally shocking in its unexpectedness: the crisp, sharp sound of a slap delivered with the full force of an open palm.

The woman in the shadows threw up an arm as though to protect herself from further attack, and then picking up her wide skirts, whirled about and ran down the length of the dark gallery, the heavy silk of her dress rustling in the silence like a rush of wind through dead leaves. In the same instant the eligible Edmund turned on his heel and disappeared with startling suddenness through a door that led out of the circular hall a few paces from the entrance to the gallery, and Captain Randall was left alone with the lady in the cashmere shawl.

She turned slowly, and apparently for the first time became aware of the presence of a stranger, for he heard her startled gasp. The warm light from the hall fell full on the white face and tumbled blonde curls of the girl of the dining-room and the Winterhalter portrait. The Lady Sybella Grantham. The next moment she had swept past him and run lightly across the hall to vanish down a dimly lit corridor beyond.

The whole curious incident had occupied less than two minutes of time, and Captain Randall, unexpectedly involved in the brief drama and left in sole possession of the scene, retraced his steps, and coming upon a hurrying flunkey was redirected to his own part of the house.

The morning of the funeral dawned cold and windy. Hurrying ranks of clouds streamed endlessly overhead against a lowering background of grey skies that failed to show a glimpse of blue, and patches of discoloured snow still lay about unmelted among the roots of the oaks and the beech trees in the park.

The body of the late Earl had been laid to rest in the ancestral mausoleum attached to a chapel in the grounds of the castle, and when the service was over Captain Randall found himself standing next to his neighbour of the previous evening, Lady Wycombe.

'Let us wait in the porch until the crowd thins,' said Lady Wycombe. 'At least it is out of the wind. It will take some time to get the carriages away, and I do not intend to walk.'

The crowd about the mausoleum was thinning rapidly, for the keen wind did not encourage loitering. Those who had come or were returning on foot had already set off at a brisk pace, and the carriages that waited to one side of the yew-lined avenue were being filled and driven away.

A lone woman was standing apart by the nearest yew tree, using the thick trunk as a shelter against the wind and evidently waiting, as were Alex and Lady Wycombe, until the major portion of the crowd had left the avenue. Something about her, something vaguely familiar, attracted Captain Randall's attention. Despite the heavy veil that obscured her features he had the impression that he knew her or had seen her before. Yet it was not the Lady Sybella; of that he was certain. This woman was not so tall and her hair was dark, not fair, for in the cold light of the windy morning even a heavy black mourning veil could not have entirely disguised the pale gold glint of Lady Sybella's curls.

She stood quite still; so still that Captain Randall suddenly realized where it was that he had seen her before. It was the woman who had entered the guardroom yesterday and had stood in that same rigid attitude before the old Earl's coffin.

He watched her idly, wondering how it was that such complete immobility could yet manage to convey such a vivid and unmistakable impression of grief. And as he watched, a freakish gust of wind, sweeping about the trunk of the aged yew tree, snatched at the long black veil and whipped it out and above her head, revealing a young, unguarded face.

It was a small face, the colour of warm ivory. Wide at the brow and pointed at the chin, with enormous dark eyes under delicate black brows that curved like a swallow's wings. The thick waves of hair that sprang from a deep widow's peak on her forehead held the blue, burnished gleam of a raven's plumage and made the mourning hue of bonnet and gown appear dull and rusty by comparison; and though her mouth was too wide and too full to suit the accepted standards of beauty in that age, it was a mouth, all the same, to set a man's pulses beating.

The girl reached up an arm to recapture her veil, and as she did so she turned her head more fully towards the two in the porch. Upon her left cheek, and sharply visible against the ivory skin, was an irregular blotch that might have been a birthmark – or the mark left by a vicious blow given with an open hand.

Alex's eyes narrowed. So this was the girl who had been in the gallery last night and whom he had rescued from the unwelcome attentions of the Honourable Edmund Rathley. It was evident, too, that the white hand of Lady Sybella, which Herr Winterhalter had depicted as gracefully holding a rose, was possessed of surprising strength.

'Who is that?' inquired Captain Randall of his companion. 'The young lady over there by the yew tree?'

Lady Wycombe turned. 'That? We were discussing her last night – the Condesa de los Aguilares. That is Winter.'

If Alex was surprised, it was because he did not know that Mr Barton was not the only person whose appearance had altered drastically during the past few years. Winter too had changed.

In the months following Zobeida's death she had grown paler and thinner and more silent than ever. Her skin appeared to be stretched too tightly over the fine bones of her skull, making her mouth seem even wider than its wont and her eyes far too large for her small sallow face.

Her Spanish blood might have been expected to lead to an earlier maturity than is found in women of purely northern and Anglo-Saxon descent, but the shock and sorrow of Zobeida's death had affected her both physically and mentally, and although Sybella at fifteen had the appearance of a petted and poised young woman, Winter, her junior by less than three months, seemed only a skinny child with several years in the schoolroom still ahead of her.

But even the deepest sorrows outwear their first bitterness, and although the cruel void left by Zobeida's death remained unfilled, the natural health and resilience of youth eventually reasserted itself and a change came over her. Almost overnight – or so it seemed – Sabrina's daughter grew from a plain child into a young woman of strange and disturbing beauty. It was a beauty that many (and they were all women) could neither appreciate nor understand, for England was in the throes of a sentimental age: an era where the ideal of feminine beauty consisted of a smoothly oval face of a stereotyped pink and whiteness, a small rosebud mouth, limpid eyes – preferably blue – and long sleek curls *à la* Stuart caressing the cheeks and dressed so as to accentuate the oval of the face, or at least to give that effect to those unlucky enough not to possess the fashionable features.

Sybella was the very embodiment of the Victorian ideal of beauty. But Winter possessed none of these attributes, and it was therefore not altogether surprising that to the majority of feminine beholders she should still appear entirely unremarkable, if not actually plain. But it was quite otherwise with their men. By the time she reached her sixteenth birthday, masculine heads began to turn when she passed by, and masculine eyes followed her whenever she entered a room.

The scrawny angular child had grown into a slender girl whose slim seductive shape even the overblown hoops of the newly-fashionable crinolines could not entirely disguise. Her thin little face had filled out, setting her features in proportion at last, and the wide mouth was seen to be curved with beauty and of a rich and lovely redness. The sallow skin had warmed to ivory and the sweet curve of her young breasts owed nothing to the ruffles and padding so often resorted to by Victorian maidens. Winter's expressive dark eyes tilted slightly upwards at the outer corners, which women pronounced unbecoming and men found irresistible. But even the sternest of feminine critics were obliged to allow that her long slender neck and the thick sweep of her silky black lashes were both exceptional beauties.

The girl appeared to have acquired, too, the graceful carriage that is possessed by so many Spanish women. Perhaps, like her colouring, it was a legacy from Marcos; and possibly she had always possessed it, only no one had troubled to notice it until now.

It was not until the summer of 1855, when Winter was sixteen, that Lady Glynde awoke to the fact that the ugly Anglo-Spanish duckling had turned into a swan. Julia had given a young people's party for Sybella: a summer dance (it was not to be termed a ball, because Sybella would not make her official début until the following spring, but was a ball in all but name). Ware was filled with young ladies and gentlemen of quality and wealth, and the guests had been most carefully chosen. The gentlemen were not all so young, and those young ladies who had been invited had been the subject of much thought, for Julia was nothing if not thorough and none was asked who could rival Sybella in looks – though she was far too astute to invite only the plain.

For some years past Julia had kept a secret list locked away in a drawer of her escritoire. It bore the names of those few eligible men who in her opinion would be acceptable as suitors for the hand of her peerless Sybella; young men who had inherited or would inherit both titles and riches. There were other names on a second list. Their owners were none of them possessed of sufficiently spectacular wealth or title to make them eligible as a husband for Julia's daughter, but it did no girl any harm to be surrounded by admirers, and provided that they were kept at a suitable distance by a vigilant mama, they enhanced a girl's value and desirability in the eyes of the more favoured few.

During the past year several names had been removed from these lists, their owners having contracted alliances with other young ladies who had already made their débuts. The party for Sybella might therefore with more truth have been termed a Private View, for whatever glamour might attend her future début, this comparatively small assembly constituted her real introduction to the social world in which her mother intended that she should be queen. And certainly Julia had every reason to feel proud of her child as Sybella stood before the long pier-glass in her mother's bed-chamber, complacently admiring her enchanting reflection.

Sybella's white satin bodice, tiny waist and soft, sloping, flower-wreathed shoulders rose out of a wide crinolined ball-gown of white *gros de Naples* with an overskirt of satin-striped gauze trimmed with blonde and looped up at intervals with bouquets of white primroses, heath and lily-of-the-valley. Her golden curls were adorned by a wreath of the same flowers, and in deference to her youth she wore only a simple necklace and bracelet of seed pearls.

Winter's dress had received considerably less attention. It had in fact, been selected by the housekeeper, Mrs Flecker, who had been told by Lady Julia to see that Miss Winter had a suitable gown: it would have to be white, and as simple as possible, since Miss Winter was younger than Lady Sybella and therefore must consider herself fortunate in being permitted to attend at all.

Mrs Flecker procured a sufficient quantity of white Indian muslin and the services of an elderly dressmaker from the market town of Wareburn, and the result was a gown that met with Lady Glynde's approval. But the effect of the same garment when worn by Winter was entirely unexpected. The blood of her grandmother, Anne Marie de Selincourt, may have had something to do with it, but the fact remained that the simple and unadorned muslin gown acquired from its wearer that look of rare distinction that many Frenchwomen and few Englishwomen can give to an otherwise unremarkable dress.

Winter's wealth of blue-black hair had been drawn straight back and confined in a net of white silk, so that its shining weight tilted her little pointed chin as though with pride, and she wore no jewels – she was as yet unaware that she possessed any. But Mrs Flecker, tying the wide white taffeta sash about her slender waist and turning the girl about to see that she was ready to be sent downstairs, had reached out of the window to where the climbing roses nodded just below the sill, and breaking off a white rosebud had tucked it into the dark sweep of hair above one small ear.

Winter had had an astonishing success, and Julia was both angry and bewildered. She could not understand why the girl received so much attention from men whom she had confidently expected to have eyes for no one but Sybella. It was not that Winter had outshone her cousin; she could not do that. Sybella had attracted the lion's share of attention, but Julia was not slow to note how the older and more eligible men turned to look again and yet again at Sabrina's daughter. Lord Carlyon, handsome, wealthy, bored, thirty-five and still a bachelor, had inquired of Sybella who the beautiful creature in white might be. Sybella had not recognized her cousin by this description, and Lord Carlyon had been more specific.

'You mean *Winter*?' demanded Sybella, astounded.

'Winter?'

'My cousin Winter. Such a peculiar name, is it not?'

'*Winter*!' He repeated the word almost with awe. 'But how perfect.'

'What *do* you mean?' Sybella's fluting voice had a sudden sharp edge to it.

'I mean that it suits so admirably. She is like snow and black shadows: cool and mysterious and yet——' He laughed on an odd note. 'So this is the plain cousin from the East. I have heard of her. The ugly duckling in person. Pray introduce me, Lady Sybella.'

Arthur Carlyon was no impressionable youth but a coldly handsome rake with a considerable experience of women. Match-making mamas, attracted by his fortune and undeterred by his reputation, had cast hopeful eyes in his direction for well over a dozen seasons past, but Carlyon had remained languidly aloof and more interested in mistresses than marriage. He had attended Lady Julia's ball expecting to be bored, but with a mild feeling of curiosity as to the appearance of the heiress of Ware whom report had rumoured to be outstandingly beautiful. He had been bored. Surveying Sybella with an indolent and experienced eye, he had summed her up as spoilt and insipid. Blondes, though fashionable, were not in his line; he considered that they lacked fire. In the rôle of eligible bachelor he had had occasion to meet most of the other young ladies present, and had found nothing to interest him, and he was considering an early retreat from the festivities when his eye had alighted on Winter de Ballesteros.

Carlyon's confident approach and suavely experienced manner had, however, made no impression on Sybella's young cousin: Winter had not been in the least sensible of the honour implied by his interest, and Carlyon, who had imagined that such a youthful creature would be easy game, found himself being put in his place and dismissed with a cool grace that would have done credit to an experienced London hostess. He was unwise enough to treat her dismissal of him as a piece of girlish coquetry, and Winter had been driven to administer a snub that left no room for doubt as to her opinion of him. It was an entirely new and salutary experience to Lord Carlyon, and an unpleasant one.

But he had by no means been the only one to comment on Winter's unusual style of looks. 'Striking gel,' cackled old Lady Grantham, who was playing chaperon to her grand-daughter Camilla. 'I don't recollect seeing her before. Who is she, Julia? What? What? *Who*? Dear me – you don't say so! Sabrina's daughter. Well, well! Yes, of course I have seen her before. Hideous little thing she was. Skinny. Like an owlet – all eyes. And look at her now. Well, her mother was a beauty too. The girl is really quite remarkable. Such a welcome change from all these insipid die-away creatures. And presumably inherits her mother's fortune . . . I must see that Harry meets her.'

No, the evening could not be considered an unqualified success from Julia's point of view, and she did not repeat her mistake. Winter attended no more balls, but it was surprising how many young men, calling at Ware ostensibly to see Sybella, contrived at the same time to see her cousin Winter. Even Lord Carlyon had called; though he had made no pretence of wishing to see Sybella and inquired after the Condesa; only to be frostily informed by Lady Glynde that Winter was still in the schoolroom and too young to receive visitors: her appearance at Sybella's party, explained the Viscountess, had been only in the nature of a special treat for the child. Carlyon had not been sufficiently interested to pursue the matter further, but others had.

Sybella had admirers in plenty, but Julia was quick to notice that these were for the most part the younger and less eligible men. The select few whom she had considered as possible husbands for her peerless daughter showed more interest in the young Condesa – who did not conform to the prevailing fashion in looks and was not in the least interested in any of these excessively eligible gentlemen. A combination that had the merit of novelty, which has always had its own attraction. But the girl possessed something more: that indefinable something that for lack of a better word is known as 'allure', and when several titled heirs to great estates who had initially been intrigued by novelty fell victims to it, Sybella was at first astounded and then outraged, and her mother coldly furious.

There was only one thing to be done. Conway Barton must come home and marry the girl as soon as possible. She would be seventeen in the following spring and quite old enough to be married.

'I have already written,' said the old Earl.

He had not meant to write. He had not wished Winter to marry until she was eighteen or nineteen – or even twenty. He had celebrated his ninetieth birthday the previous year and felt unusually well . . . better than he had felt for a long time. He would see a hundred yet! There was no hurry . . .

But the snow had lain late into the year, and spring had been tardy and wet. The damp cold to which he had been impervious for so long seemed to seep into the old man's very bones and he could not keep warm. He felt the tide of his life running out and drawing away from him, driven by that driving rain, and he had written to Conway Barton.

It was, all at once, not enough for old Lord Ware to know that when he was dead Winter would be taken care of by the husband he had chosen for her. He wanted to see her married before he went, and to know that she was safe, so that he would be able to face Johnny again, and Sabrina, and tell them that all was well with the child. The Earl would not have considered himself in any way a religious man, and his beliefs – or lack of them – had frequently shocked his chaplain. But he believed profoundly in an after-life. When he died he would meet again, instantly and in the earthly form in which he remembered them, those few people whom he had loved: Selina, his wife. Johnny, his pride. Sabrina, his darling . . .

With the coming of the warm summer weather the Earl's health improved and he almost regretted his letter to Conway Barton, but he began to make plans for the wedding. The letter would have reached Conway before the end of June, and it would of course take some little time for him to arrange for his resignation and replacement (it was no part of the Earl's plan that Winter should return to India, Conway must of course retire to England and devote himself to the care of his wife and the management of her fortune), but even allowing for every contingency the groom should be able to reach England not too late in the New Year. Time enough to announce the betrothal then and to arrange for the wedding to take place at the end of May, when Winter would be seventeen. The doctors must patch him up so that he would last until then.

In the early autumn a letter arrived from India. Mr Barton had received Lord Ware's communication and was deeply grieved to hear of his failing health. He could only hope that Lord Ware was by now fully recovered. Naturally it was the dearest wish of his heart to marry the Earl's ward, but various unforeseen difficulties had arisen which necessitated his remaining at his post for the present. However, he had a suggestion to make that he hoped might meet with the Earl's approval: he had written at some length on the matter, and was sending that letter by the hand of a trusted subordinate, Captain Alex Randall, who should reach England some time in the autumn. Owing to the unreliability of the mails he had thought it better to make Captain Randall his courier, despite the fact that this would cause some delay, and the Captain, being in his confidence, was empowered by him to discuss the matter with Lord Ware.

But Captain Randall, as it happened, was considerably delayed. He had met with friends at Alexandria, and instead of continuing on his way had turned aside with them and gone instead to the Crimea, where he had managed, entirely illegally, to get himself attached to General Windham's Staff, had fought at the taking of Sebastopol and been wounded in the bloody battle for the Redan. He had not reached England until late in February, and it was not until the second week of March that he arrived at Ware.

BOOK TWO

KISHAN PRASAD

The majority of the guests who had stayed at Ware for the funeral left the same afternoon, and those few who remained kept to their rooms. Towards dusk on that cold and windy day the sixth Earl sent a footman to find Captain Randall, and once again Alex was led through the corridors and galleries of the west wing. But this time he was not taken to Lady Ware's drawing-room, but ushered instead into a small panelled room where a fire crackled in the hearth and the new Earl sat warming himself at the blaze.

Huntly, Lord Ware, was a stout and undistinguished man who disguised his lack of character behind an impassive and somewhat pompous manner. He greeted Captain Randall graciously enough, regretting his inability to see him earlier and hoping that he had not been put to too much trouble in coming to Ware. After which he spoke at some length on the subject of Mr Barton and his young cousin's approaching marriage, and concluded by saying that he understood that the Captain was returning to the East in June, and that he would make arrangements for the Condesa to travel on the same packet.

Alex's hard grey eyes ran over him in a comprehensive glance and summed him up dispassionately as a nonentity. The last of the Wares! The old man whose funeral he had attended that morning must have had more hot blood in him than this, if all accounts were true.

'I have heard of you, Captain Randall,' said Huntly graciously. 'I understand that you obtained a brevet for conspicuous gallantry at Chillianwallah, and a similar promotion only a few years later. Quite a remarkable achievement.'

A faint tinge of red deepened the dark sun-tan of Alex's face and he said expressionlessly: 'There are many opportunities for such advancement in India, sir. It was kind of Mr Barton to speak well of me.'

'Oh, it was not Barton. A gentleman I met at the Granchesters', who was lately from the Punjab. We have always, as a family, been greatly interested in India on account of our connection with the East India Company. I regret that I have had no opportunity for discussion with you on a subject of such interest, but my time is lamentably occupied. You will be leaving in the morning? I hope I may see you again before you go.'

It was evidently a dismissal but Alex disregarded it. He had been unable to speak plainly to the Countess but no such scruples need weigh with him now. This plump, pallid man with his air of consequence had presumably inherited the guardianship of the young Condesa and should therefore be apprised of the truth. But there was a faint chance that he might be dissuaded from sending the girl to India without being informed of the facts about Mr Conway Barton. It was at least worth trying and Alex tried it:

'Might I suggest, sir, that it would be advisable to postpone the Condesa's departure for – for a few years? Until the country is in a less unsettled condition? You cannot, I think, fully appreciate the present state of unrest that prevails in India. I am aware that I hold what is perhaps a minority view, but it is one that is also held by such men as Sir Henry Lawrence and General Jacob. There have been disturbing signs of late, and Sir Henry and many others have warned of the possibility of grave troubles arising out of the policy of annexation of sovereign states, in particular if it is pressed over the matter of Oudh. India and the Bengal Army are far from being in the condition of tranquillity that some would have us suppose, and I would urge on you most strongly, sir, that this is no time to send any woman to that country – let alone a young girl.'

Huntly raised his eyebrows and observed coldly that Captain Randall was mistaken in supposing that he had no knowledge of the situation prevailing in India. He had had occasion to attend, only the previous August, the banquet given at the London Tavern by the East India Company in honour of Lord Canning the Governor-General designate, where he had been assured, through the medium of public speeches and private discussions, that our Indian dependency had never before been so peaceful or so prosperous. He ventured to think that the speakers on that occasion had at least as much knowledge of the conditions pertaining to that country as had Captain Randall.

Alex said, 'If I cannot speak with their authority, sir, I can at least speak from experience, since I have of necessity come into far closer contact with the natives of the country than many senior officials, whose very seniority debars them from a too intimate approach. But Lord Dalhousie's policy of Annexation and Lapse, though it has added immeasurably to our territories, has aroused the bitterest enmity among those nobles whom we have dispossessed. They, or their agents, are engaging in active intrigue against us, and their numbers increase yearly. It is known that Lord Dalhousie and the Directors of Leadenhall Street favour the annexation of Oudh, but if Oudh too passes into the Company's possession, the danger will become gravely aggravated.'

'I think that you exaggerate,' said Huntly, bored. 'Several of the Directors are well known to me, and my cousin Grantham has informed me that a gratifying number of sons and relatives of the princely houses have gone so far as to enlist in the ranks of the Bengal Army.'

'That is true,' said Alex grimly. 'But what your cousin Grantham and others like him fail to see is that many of these men have a particular reason for accepting such employment. It gives them unparalleled opportunities for spreading sedition and disaffection in a quarter where it can do us the most harm: among the sepoys – the Indian soldiers. A large-scale revolt on the part of the Bengal Army would be a difficult thing to deal with, and it may yet come to that.'

'I should be sorry to think that you are serious, Captain Randall,' said Huntly frigidly. 'Such faint-hearted and alarmist views are hardly what I should have expected from one of your reputation, and I can only suppose that overwork and the rigours of the climate have affected your spirits.'

Alex smiled. It was an unpleasant smile, but his voice remained level, though the faint drawl in it was suddenly more pronounced:

'Possibly, sir. But not my wits. There is such a thing as overplaying one's hand, and the arbitrary acquisition of Oudh would mean, once again, a province almost the size of England awash with disbanded soldiery and embittered nobles to whom annexation will have meant the loss of power and privilege and, in many cases, of even the bare means of existence. In addition to which, Oudh – although its people are largely Hindu – is one of the last remaining Mohammedan states, so that its annexation would not only antagonize all Mohammedans, but give rise to the fear that we intend to swallow the rest of India, and that no state is safe from us. Besides, since at present we have not sufficient British troops at our disposal with which to garrison newly acquired territory, it would have to be done, if at all, by native regiments who are bound in the nature of things to resent such an annexation.'

Huntly said pompously: 'All these aspects of the situation must have occurred to those in authority. And you forget, I think, that the bulk of the population cannot but look upon us as their deliverers from the long reign of oppression, torture and extortion inflicted upon them by their native rulers. We are not only giving them better government, but bestowing upon them the blessings of progress and civilization, for which they are bound to be grateful.'

'That is a view only too commonly held by our race,' said Alex drily. 'It is a comforting one with which to justify conquest, but unhappily, entirely untrue. The blessings of civilization are seldom appreciated by the conquered; especially when rammed down their gullets with a musket. I would assure you, sir, that I am no alarmist. And neither has my nerve failed me. We shall hold India. But all that I have heard and seen and felt during the past few years has served to convince me that we are moving blindly towards disaster. I am entirely sure of that. No less sure than I am that we shall survive it. But this is no time to cumber ourselves with women, or to send out a young girl who knows nothing of the East.'

Huntly drew himself to his full height and looked haughtily down his somewhat fleshy nose. 'My dear Captain Randall,' he observed in chilling tones, 'had there been any risk attached to sending my cousin to India, you may be assured that Mr Barton would never have suggested such a thing. As your superior officer his knowledge as to the true state of affairs is bound to exceed yours. In the circumstances I cannot but feel that you are needlessly alarmed.'

Alex said ruefully: 'I can see that I shall have to speak plainly, sir. I am well aware that in doing so I am open to a charge of disloyalty to my superior officer, but the occasion appears to me serious enough to warrant plain speaking. What I have to say is naturally in confidence, but as the Condesa's relative and guardian it is a thing that you should know.' And he spoke clearly and dispassionately on the subject of Mr Barton . . .

Lord Ware's prominent eyes bulged palely in the firelight and he remarked a little nervously that of course he had no idea . . . What Captain Randall had divulged was most disturbing . . . Surely he exaggerated? He could not bring himself to believe——

Captain Randall cut him short: 'I must ask you to believe, sir, that what I have told you of the Commissioner is less than the truth. I could not reconcile it with my conscience to escort your young cousin to India without first acquainting you with these unpleasant facts, but having done so I have no further obligation in the matter, since it will now be for you to decide whether she goes or not. Your servant, sir.' He bowed curtly and withdrew.

Once again, as on the evening of his arrival, Captain Randall dined alone, but at the conclusion of the meal the secretary made his appearance with a message from Lady Ware. The Countess wished to see Captain Randall at his earliest convenience in order to make him known to Miss – er – that is, to the Condesa. Captain Randall heaved a resigned sigh, and pausing only to possess himself of a small package that had been entrusted to him for personal delivery into the hands of the Commissioner's betrothed, followed the secretary to Lady Ware's apartments.

'Captain Randall, your Ladyship,' murmured the secretary, ushering him in and closing the door softly behind him. The Countess turned with a rustle of silk. 'So good of you to come, Captain Randall. I trust you have been well looked after? You will forgive us, I know, for dining *en famille* on this sad occasion. You have met my husband, have you not? This is my daughter, Sybella. And this is dear Conway's future wife – Winter de Ballesteros. Winter, this is Captain Randall——'

Alex bowed stiffly. Lord Ware did not meet his gaze, but Lady Ware returned it with a coldly smiling blandness that told its own story. 'So her husband has told her,' thought Alex, 'and she means to ignore it. She will tell that child nothing, and neither will she do anything to prevent the marriage. That Wycombe woman was right!' He became aware that Sybella was smiling at him and was abruptly recalled to a sense of his social obligations. He murmured a few words of conventional greeting and looked past her into the wide, wary eyes of the Commissioner's betrothed. He looked long and deliberately, studying that young and guarded face; noting the wariness and schooled immobility with cool interest.

A faint flush of colour rose into the pale cheeks, and Alex put his hand into his pocket and drew out a small sealed packet that the Commissioner had given him. He said briefly and without preamble: 'Mr Barton requested me to give this to you.'

The girl's fingers closed about it, holding it tightly, and colour and life flamed up into her face so that she was suddenly beautiful. She made a small swift gesture with the clenched hand as though she would have hidden it among her billowing skirts, but Lady Ware spoke with calm authority:

'You may open it, my dear. It will be your betrothal gift.'

Winter looked down at the small packet in her hand. She knew without opening it what it contained. She had never forgotten anything that Conway had said to her, and had he not said that he would one day give her a diamond – 'the brightest diamond I can find for you in India' – to wear on her finger instead of the little gold and pearl ring that she had worn for so long on a ribbon about her neck? He had sent for her, and he had sent the diamond. All her dreams were coming true at last. She did not want to open Conway's gift in the presence of Cousin Julia and this stranger who studied her with such cool and speculative interest. This was not something for critical and unsympathetic eyes to appraise. It was something intensely personal to herself.

'We are waiting,' said Cousin Julia.

The lovely colour faded from Winter's cheeks and she broke the seal with cold, unsteady fingers.

The firelight gleamed on an enormous carved emerald in a curiously wrought setting of Indian gold, and Alex, recognizing it, was unprepared for the sudden shock of anger and disgust that the sight of it gave him. He had seen that stone before, many times. Three years ago it had adorned the hand of a member of a princely house, by name Rao Kishan Prasad.* Alex knew a good deal about Kishan Prasad, for the man had aroused his interest. There had been odd whispers about him, and the subsequent appearance of that ring in the possession of the Commissioner of Lunjore had caused Alex to wonder more than once just what piece of bribery the fabulous stone had represented. It had been flaunted thereafter by the Indian woman, a dancing girl from the city, who was the latest occupant of the *bibi-gurh* attached to the Lunjore Residency, and she had worn it as she gyrated for the amusement of the guests at one of the Commissioner's more questionable parties which Alex had reluctantly attended. Alex had also seen Kishan Prasad comparatively recently and in unexpected surroundings, and he scowled down at the great carved jewel with incredulous distaste.

Sybella gave an audible gasp of envy and admiration and even Lady Ware's cold eyes widened in involuntary astonishment, but to Winter it was as though a small chill wind had momentarily breathed upon the shining warmth that Conway's letter had lit in her breast. He had forgotten! The next second she had taken herself to task. Why should he take literally a sentence

* Pra-*shād*.

spoken to a child? He had meant only that he would one day send her a jewel of beauty and price to wear on her finger in place of the modest trinket he had given her at parting. And he had remembered, and sent it.

She slipped the barbaric thing onto the third finger of her left hand where it hung as loosely as that other ring had done five years before, and thought as she did so that soon Conway would put a wedding ring on that same finger, and after that she would be safe and protected and loved, and free from loneliness for ever and ever. She smiled down at it; a little secret smile; and looked up to meet the anger and disgust in Captain Randall's eyes.

For a moment the intensity of that cold disgust startled her. This man was for some unknown reason hostile to her. No. Not to her – to Conway. Yet that was surely impossible, for Conway himself had sent this man, his trusted subordinate, to be his emissary and escort his future wife to India. If Conway trusted him he could not be an enemy. She must have mistaken that expression: and indeed it was there no longer. The face that looked back at her was blankly impersonal; the grey eyes remote and expressionless.

The brief moment of silence was broken by Lady Ware, who begged Captain Randall to be seated and embarked on a recital of the arrangements for her young relative's departure. Evidently there was to be no question of discussion or delay, and it was equally evident that neither the new Earl nor his wife had any intention of indulging in any further private conversation with Mr Barton's courier. The matter was considered as settled and all that now remained was to thank Captain Randall for his good offices, and assure him that the young Condesa and a suitable chaperon would be only too happy to avail themselves of his escort and protection on the journey.

'You will forgive me if I say good-bye to you now,' said Lady Ware, dismissing him. 'I fear I am not an early riser, and you will, I feel sure, be anxious to be on your way. You sail on the *Sirius,* I believe? I shall of course inform you by letter of the arrangements I have made for dear Winter.' It was plain that he was to be given no opportunity for private conversation with the Condesa herself.

The entire affair had filled Alex with boredom and irritation and, finally, disgust; but he had never had any intention of exerting himself in the matter, beyond informing the Condesa's guardian of certain aspects of the Commissioner's character and mode of living of which he believed her relatives to be ignorant. He had discharged this office and his conscience was clear. But now, unaccountably, he found himself angry.

This was no poised and mature woman who was to be tied in matrimony to the obese *roué* who was Commissioner of Lunjore. This was a girl – a child. Yet for reasons that the gossiping Lady Wycombe had made abundantly clear, her august relatives, far from pausing before consigning her to the fate that must inevitably overtake any wife of Conway Barton, had every intention of hurrying her towards it without uttering one word of warning.

All the impropriety of bluntly informing her himself of the true state of affairs occurred most forcibly to Captain Randall. The robust outspokenness of the Regency had given place to an age of extreme and mealy-mouthed prudery, in which young girls were sedulously guarded from the facts of life and expected to have no inkling of the coarser aspects of masculine amusements. But twelve years in the East had robbed Alex Randall of any particular respect for the polite conventions, and he was suddenly and stubbornly resolved that the Commissioner's betrothed should not walk blindly upon her fate if he could prevent it. Once back in his room he found letter paper, a quill-pen and a standish, and having written a brief note, folded the paper, sealed it and tugged at the bell-pull.

It was answered by a maidservant in a neat print dress; young and presumably romantic, noted Alex; relieved that some more elderly and conservative retainer had not answered his summons. The note and a gold coin changed hands and the girl, her eyes round with pleasurable interest, assured him in a conspiratorial whisper that Miss Winter would receive his communication without fail. Alex yawned largely, scowled at his reflection in the vast oval looking-glass that adorned one wall of the room, and retired to bed.

The morning dawned cold and grey, and a white layer of mist lay over the park and pressed against the wet window-panes. In the great hall a covey of servants were busied with removing the funereal trappings from the walls under the eye of the aged major-domo, and on the wide sweep before the main door Medusa sidled and snorted in charge of a groom. Captain Randall swung himself thankfully into the saddle. In some obscure fashion Medusa typified action as opposed to intrigue, and he was grateful to see the last of Ware.

The mist lay thicker under the over-arching boughs of the oak trees that lined the long avenue, and the trees themselves appeared pale and ghostly. For a mile or more Alex gave the mare her head, exhilarated by the speed, the rush of the cold misty air and the swift hollow drum-beat of Medusa's flying hooves, but presently his ear caught what at first seemed an echo of that sound, and he slowed his mount to a trot and then to a walk. There was another rider in the long oak avenue, and Alex, listening, made a wry grimace in which distaste and relief were oddly mingled, and reined to a stop. Medusa's ears pricked and she whinnied softly as a moment later a horse and rider materialized out of the mist and drew level with them.

There were raindrops like a spangle of moonstones on Winter's dark hair, and the cold air and exercise had whipped a glow of colour into her pale cheeks. Those enormous dark eyes – the eyes of her father Marcos de Ballesteros, who in turn had inherited them from some long-forgotten Moorish ancestress – were wide and young and wary, and looking at her Alex was conscious once again of that unexpected flood of anger and exasperation. It must have shown briefly in his face, for some of the colour faded from her cheeks and her voice was breathless and a little uncertain:

'You – you have a message for me, Captain Randall? – from Conway – Mr Barton?'

Alex shook his head.

'But . . . you wrote——'

'You must forgive me for the subterfuge,' said Alex curtly, 'but I wished to see you privately. I have something to say to you that your relatives would apparently prefer to remain unsaid, so I took this method of ensuring that you would see me.'

He saw the slender figure stiffen and draw itself erect, and the dark eyes became guarded. 'What is it you wish to tell me?'

Alex studied her for a moment, frowning. 'How old are you?' he inquired abruptly.

The unexpectedness of the question appeared to take her by surprise, and she answered in unconscious obedience to the authority in his voice. 'Sixteen. But I shall soon——'

'*Sixteen!*' said Alex, exasperated. 'It's not decent! Have you any conception as to what you are going to? Of the life you will be expected to lead? Of the country in which you will live?'

Winter looked at him in surprise. 'Why – you are kind,' she said. Her voice held a note of wonder and Alex realized with a sudden stirring of pity that kindness had been a rare thing in this young creature's life. She leant forward with a little confiding gesture and said: 'You think that I am going to a foreign land and that I might be unhappy there. But you are wrong. I am going home. Did you not know that my father was a Spaniard who lived and was born in Oudh, and that I was born there too? India is more my home than this country could ever be, for I was born in an Indian palace in Lucknow city, and my foster-mother was a *pahari* – a hill-woman, from Kufri. I spoke their tongue before I spoke my own, and I can speak it still. Shall I show you?' She turned from English and said in liquid Hindustani: 'How should I fear when I do but return to mine own people and to my father's house?'

Alex heard the familiar tongue with a renewal of his previous anger, and seeing it she said breathlessly, watching his face: 'What is it? Is Conway ill? Is that what you meant to tell me? Is he——'

'No.' Alex's voice was hard and expressionless. 'He is not ill. Not in the way that you mean. But I imagine that he has changed considerably since you last saw him.'

'Of course he has changed,' said Winter quickly. 'I have changed too. I was only a child then, and now I have grown up. He has had years more of hard work and sickness and heavy responsibility. I know all that. He has written to me of his difficulties. He will look older, but it will not matter.'

'You do not understand,' said Alex curtly. 'I felt it my duty to explain something of the true state of affairs to your cousin Lord Ware, but he apparently did not think fit to inform you of the facts, or indeed to take any action to prevent your marriage.'

'To *prevent*?' Winter stared at him, white and rigid.

'Yes. To prevent it. I cannot say what Mr Barton may have been five or six years ago. But I know what he is now, and I can do no more than to urge you, in your own interests, to abandon your journey to India and postpone your wedding until such time as he can return to this country, so that you may have the opportunity of judging for yourself.'

Winter's eyes were suddenly bright with anger and her voice shook. '*You* say this? You – his trusted subordinate?' She saw the sudden flush on Alex's brown cheeks and her voice sharpened to scorn. 'So I *was* right! You are one of them. One of his enemies who scheme against him behind his back because you are envious of him. And you dare to speak against him to me – to *me*!' Her chin lifted haughtily: 'Well, have you nothing else to say?'

'Yes,' said Alex, unmoved. 'I cannot expect you to accept the word of a stranger – even a "trusted subordinate" – who speaks against his chief. I can only repeat that you would be well advised to wait here with your relatives until Mr Barton can come home and claim you. You will then have the evidence of your own eyes.'

'That is not enough,' said Winter steadily. 'I must ask you to be plain, sir. You cannot make veiled accusations and not qualify them. Or do you prefer imputation to plain speaking?'

'No,' said Alex slowly, 'but I do not wish to offend your ears with matters that cannot be within your comprehension. However, if you will have it, your betrothed is no fit husband for any young or decently bred woman, and——'

He saw the young face turn as white as the mist around it and the gloved fingers clench on the riding-whip they held, and knew a fraction of a second before she raised her hand what she would do. But for some reason that he could not have explained he made no attempt to avoid the blow. The lash of the whip cut savagely across his face and he felt a thin trickle of blood run warmly down his chin from a corner of his mouth, and suddenly and unexpectedly he laughed.

'The Ware women,' said Captain Randall, 'would appear to be remarkably quick with their hands. I see I have misjudged you. You may well be a match for him after all.'

The bright colour flamed up into the girl's face once more, and she brought the whip down again, but this time on her horse who sprang forward and galloped away down the long avenue to disappear into the mist.

Captain Randall lifted his hand to brush the blood from his chin and laughed again. So much for the popular conception of gently bred young ladies as frail and tender plants given to swooning and the vapours! He wondered if he had seen the last of Winter de Ballesteros? It seemed likely, since he could not believe that after what had just occurred she would avail herself of his escort to India. She would now take a passage on some other ship and dispense with his services, and she would undoubtedly warn her betrothed against him. In that case the Commissioner could be counted upon to effect his removal from Lunjore. He had, in fact, bungled the whole affair; branded himself as disloyal to his chief, incurred the enmity of the young Condesa and her influential relations, and probably brought about his own dismissal – and all for nothing. The weal that the Condesa's whip had raised across his face throbbed painfully: 'My just deserts,' said Captain Randall philosophically, and gave Medusa her head.

Firm in the belief that he would not now receive any further communication from Ware (and having, if the truth be known, succeeded in dismissing the whole matter from his mind), Alex was surprised and more than a little annoyed by the arrival, some three months later, of a letter from the Countess. A passage had been procured, wrote Lady Ware, for her young cousin on board the steamship *Sirius* sailing from London to Alexandria on the twenty-first of June. Mr Barton would be meeting his betrothed in Calcutta, and the marriage would take place almost immediately following her arrival at that port. She would be travelling in the company of a Mrs Abuthnot, who with her two daughters was proceeding to India in order to rejoin her husband who commanded a regiment of Bengal Infantry at Delhi. The ladies would be pleased to avail themselves of Captain Randall's protection and assistance on the voyage. The Countess trusted that Captain Randall was in good health, and was confident that under his escort her young relative could come to no harm.

Captain Randall scowled at the single sheet of paper with its thinly elegant handwriting and florid seal, and crumpling it in his hand tossed it impatiently into the waste-paper basket; mentally consigning all women (with the possible exception of a certain charming and accommodating *première danseuse*) to the same receptacle.

He had more important things to think about than the doings of the Granthams, for on the thirtieth of March the news had spread slowly that the Great Powers of Europe, together with Turkey and Sardinia, were at last at peace after one of the most futile and wasteful of wars. It was Sunday, and in order not to interrupt the evening services the salute of a hundred and one guns was fired at ten o'clock that night. Alex had gone out into the cold starry night and listened to the crash of the guns in St James's Park, the blare of military bands playing the national anthem, and the answering salvos from the Tower of London. And as he listened he thought of the dead who rotted on the heights of Sebastopol – and of the smiling face of Kishan Prasad taking gloating note of the ragged and demoralized British Army as they fell back after their failure to capture the Redan. He did not know why such men as Kishan Prasad had ever been permitted to visit the Crimea.

But they had done so, and Alex was sure that no good would come of it.

Earlier in March he had seen a brief notice in the press, sandwiched casually in between the arrival of the Far Eastern mails and a paragraph relating to Lord Canning's arrival in India, which had stated baldly: '*Oudh is to be annexed, with General Outram as Chief Commissioner.*' There had been a longer one a week later: '*An army of 16,000 men is now collected at Cawnpore, and in a few days will be pouring towards Lucknow. No resistance is expected, but Lord Dalhousie never leaves opportunities to the disaffected by any mistimed affectation of security. The King will be dismissed with a pension of a lac* of rupees a month.*'

The Marquis of Dalhousie, Governor-General in India, had every reason to feel pleased with his achievements. He had added the Punjab and lower Burma to the British Empire, the Koh-i-noor diamond to the British crown, secured the western frontiers of India and brought to the country the blessings of civilization in the form of the railway and the telegraph. He had been succeeded in office by Lord Canning, who before he sailed had reminded the complacent Court of Directors of the East India Company that 'in the sky of India, serene as it is, a small cloud may arise, at first no bigger than a man's hand, but which growing larger and larger may at last threaten to burst and overwhelm us with ruin.'

But that cloud, thought Alex uneasily, listening to the guns that celebrated the Peace Treaty and broke the Sabbath silence of the cold March night, had already arisen. He and many like him had been aware of it for some considerable time – a small, ominous stain on the clear blue sky of the East India Company.

Only two years previously Sir Henry Lawrence had written to Lord Stanley:

'*You ask me how long Oudh and Hyderabad are to last? It is the fashion to cry out for their annexation . . . and bad as we are I believe that we are better than any native ruler of the present age; but that does not justify us in picking their pockets. The Oudh treaty permits us to take over the management of their country, if necessary. We can protect and help the peasants without putting their rents in our pockets . . . I am however in a terrible minority. The Army, Civil Service, Press and Governor-General are all against me. I still say – look at our treaties. We have no right to make one day and break the next.*'

Alex Randall, walking through the crowded, gas-lit streets where the people had gathered to cheer a Peace Treaty and the end of the long and costly Crimean War, thought of the words of Henry Lawrence and of the knot of servants and sepoys who had whispered together in the shadow of the banyan tree by the gate of the Residency at Lunjore: and was afraid.

As March gave way to April and spring warmed to summer, the problems and policies of the land that he loved continued to obsess him, and he became

* A hundred thousand.

impatient to return. Lunjore touched the very borders of the newly annexed province, and there would be work to do: work that Mr Commissioner Barton was entirely incapable of performing, since his district, which took its name from its capital city, was largely inhabited by petty chiefs who had been involved in a rebellion some twelve years previously. The rebellion had been put down and the district brought under the control of the Company's government, whose policy it was to discourage large landowners. It was a policy that had the full approval of Mr Conway Barton, and Captain Randall had done what he could to mitigate the hardships and injustices that the purblind pursuance of it had so often involved. With these and other things on his mind he had had no time to think about the problem of the Commissioner's bride, and when reminded of it his only feeling had been one of impatience as he consigned Lady Ware's letter to the waste-paper basket.

He himself had been equally dismissed from Winter's mind. Conway's promised bride entertained no doubts or forebodings as to the future. The long waiting was over. She had grown up at last and Conway had sent for her. She was to see India again – the enchanted country – and leave behind her the cold walls of Ware and the cold eyes of Sybella and Cousin Julia. Ware held nothing for her now that the only two people she had loved were dead. The old Earl lay in a marble vault below the mausoleum, while Zobeida, denied burial in consecrated ground by a bigoted clergyman, lay in a quiet corner of the park with only the wind in the alien yews to sing her lament.

Cousin Julia, with unexpected kindness, had sent Winter to the care of a relative in London who had been charged with the agreeable task of selecting the young bride's trousseau. Lady Adelaide Pike, though elderly, was also sprightly, kind-hearted and excessively social, and Winter did not suspect that Julia's decision to send her to London was prompted less by a desire to see her suitably provided with bride-clothes, than to remove her as speedily as possible from Ware.

Winter was still in mourning for her great-grandfather, but Lady Adelaide refused to allow such a circumstance to interfere with the round of social engagements: 'After all, my dear, it is not as though you were a Grantham. And as you are shortly to be married, and we cannot purchase a trousseau in black, there is no reason why we should not be gay. You will find no such amusements in the East.'

She took Winter to hear Grise sing in *Norma* at the Royal Italian Opera House, Mrs Fanny Kemble give readings from *Othello* at Willis's Rooms, and Marietta Alboni perform in Italian opera at Her Majesty's Theatre. They attended balls and 'musicals', dinner-parties and luncheons, and drove in the Park. Dressed in forty yards of white tulle supported by a vast crinoline, and wearing a train of moiré gothique, sixteen-button gloves and three curled ostrich feathers in her hair, Winter drove to St James's Palace to make her curtsey to the plain, dowdy, dumpy little woman who was Victoria, by the Grace of God Queen of Great Britain and the Dominions overseas.

England was gay that year. The war was over. The Treaty of Paris was celebrated with illuminations and fireworks, and the Queen reviewed her Fleet on the Solent and her Army at Aldershot. William Palmer, the Rugeley poisoner, was publicly hanged at Stafford before a packed crowd of thousands who had poured into the town to see a fellow-creature die, and the wearing of crinolines was attacked by the clergy, who pointed out that women 'forgot, in loading themselves with such voluminous garments, that the gates of Heaven were narrow'.

Lady Adelaide Pike, undeterred by the straitness of that Gate, selected Winter's trousseau with wide and ever wider-spreading skirts. Ball-dresses of tarlatan with five flounces edged with silk fringe and banded with velvet ribbons; of white tulle over white glacé, the tulle gathered up in festoons by chains of pearls and bouquets of white camellias; of white muslin barred with silver basket-work; of moiré antique in tea-rose yellow. Day-dresses in muslins, merinos, taffetas and light French *barèges* in delicate hues. Morning-dresses of grey cashmere, batiste, poplin and figured jaconet. Gloves of every shade and hue, mittens of black *filet*, absurd evening head-dresses of lace, flowers, pearls or ribbon. Ravishing chip bonnets of straw or terry velvet trimmed with feathers or blonde, and dozens upon awe-inspiring dozens of petticoats and pantalettes and other articles of feminine underwear.

It was an age of lavishness. Of enormous meals, enormous families, enormous, spreading skirts and an enormous, spreading Empire. An age of gross living, grinding poverty, inconceivable prudery, insufferable complacency and incomparable enterprise. Those dozens of petticoats and pantalettes deemed necessary to the feminine wardrobe were both a symbol of that lavishness and of the sweated labour in the crowded slums, where women wore away their fingers and their eyesight and their youth sewing such furbelows for a wage of a few ha'pence.

Early in June Winter journeyed to Suffolk under the care of Mrs Barlow, the distressed gentlewoman who occupied the post of companion to the new Countess of Ware, in order to pay a farewell visit to Conway's uncle, old Sir Ebenezer Barton.

Sir Ebenezer would be seventy-seven that year, and his hearing and eyesight were failing. After a lifetime spent largely in the East, the winds and frosts and the long wet winters of England had shrivelled his once burly frame and racked it with rheumatism and sciatica. He kept to one room of the sprawling draughty Suffolk mansion to which he had brought Emily as a bride over a quarter of a century ago, and seldom left it. His mind too was wandering and he dwelt much in the past. Winter meant nothing to him, and when reminded of his nephew Conway he had remarked in a high cracked voice and with sudden energy: 'Bad blood there. Bad blood. Takes after his mother's side of the family. Thought the boy might avoid it – Joseph's son you know – but what's bred in the bone . . . What's bred in the bone . . .'

His voice sank to a mumble and he did not mention his nephew again, but talked instead in a staccato mutter, difficult to understand, of the India of his youth and of friends and enemies and builders of Empire dead these many years. Once, in the twilight, he had addressed Winter as Marcos; seeing in those dark eyes and clean-cut features some echo of a face that had laughed at him in the hot dusk of a forgotten evening . . .

'You know, Marcos,' said old Sir Ebenezer, 'Emily isn't going to like this. No, she ain't going to like it at all. And if you think that Sabrina's grandfather will give his consent, you're wrong, my boy. Quite wrong – eh, eh? To see someone you love only once in every six or seven years is not enough. There's going to be trouble. A peck o' trouble.'

On the night before she left, Sir Ebenezer had presented Winter with a square and much-worn morocco case that contained Emily's jewellery. 'She meant it for Sabrina,' said Sir Ebenezer, lifting the lid with a trembling hand and stirring the glittering contents with one bony finger: ' "Give 'em to my girl," she said. But Sabrina died too.'

The slow easy tears of old age crept down Sir Ebenezer's withered cheek: for Emily? – for Sabrina? He screwed up his eyes and peered at Winter like an elderly tortoise: 'They tell me you're her daughter. You ain't like your mother. A golden girl, she was. Take after y'father's side of the family I suppose. So you're going to marry Conway. Eh? – eh? You'll need some gew-gaws when you're married. I kept 'em for you: didn't trust that hard-faced harridan, Julia. Better to keep 'em until the girl's of age, I said. Eh? – eh? Emily never thought much of jewellery, but I liked giving 'em to her. She wanted Sabrina to have them. Sabrina never wore 'em, but you will. You will.'

He pushed the box towards Winter and said wistfully: 'If I were ten years younger, I'd sail with you. I'd like to heave-to off the Sandheads again, and see the Hooghly once more and the houses by Garden Reach – and the fireflies and the fruit bats – eh? – eh? A wonderful country. A rich and wonderful country. Ring for Pir Khan, Marcos . . . I'm tired.'

The jewels in their heavy old-fashioned setting were magnificent: *parures* of emeralds and diamonds, necklaces, bracelets, rings, brooches, jewelled combs and buckles. Flaunting and almost barbaric things that Ebenezer had loved to buy for his Emily, and which Emily had so rarely worn.

Julia had looked at them with frigid disapproval and Sybella with unconcealed envy. 'Entirely unsuitable for a young girl,' pronounced Julia coldly. 'You had best send them to the bank for safe-keeping. It would be most unwise to take them with you. Such valuables are an invitation to robbery and violence.'

But Winter had taken them: Emily's jewels, and the triple strand of pearls that Marcos's mother, Anne Marie, had given to Sabrina over eighteen years ago on the night of her Birthday Ball. The pearls that a Vicomtesse de Selincourt had worn at the wedding of Louis XVI and Marie Antoinette.

Julia herself had taken the unprecedented step of travelling to London in order to see her young relative safely bestowed into the care of Mrs Abuthnot. She had stayed only one night, putting up at the Pulteney Hotel, and left the following morning to visit friends in Surrey. But she had stayed long enough to see the cab containing Sabrina's daughter drive away in the rain towards the docks and the steam-packet *Sirius* that was to take her to Alexandria on the first half of her journey towards India.

Mrs Abuthnot was kind, stout and talkative. She had been barely Winter's age when she had married her George and first set sail for the East, and she was not yet forty. But the long years spent in India, the birth of seven children and death in infancy of five of them, had left their mark on her, and she might well have been ten or even twenty years older.

'Ninety days dear,' said Mrs Abuthnot describing that first voyage to Winter. 'We sailed round by the Cape. It does not seem so very long ago, but I well remember that there was a Miss Marshall on board. She was going out to marry a young man called Lawrence . . . Sir Henry now. She died a year or so ago . . . such a loss . . . And now here am I going out yet again, and this time with two grown-up daughters. How time does fly!'

Lottie and Sophia Abuthnot, in contrast to their stout and voluble mama, were slim and shy and silent and, it was to be presumed, took after their papa, for they in no way resembled their mother; being small and fair where Mrs Abuthnot was an ample, though greying, brunette.

Sophie, the younger by three years, shared a cabin with her mother, while the eighteen-year-old Lottie was to share an adjoining one with Winter. The cabins were small and cramped and sparsely furnished, and the first days of the voyage had been anything but pleasant.

The early summer had been wet and cold, and the rain that had been falling as they drove to the docks had later given place to blustering gusts of wind that drove the dark banks of cloud before them and whipped the water of the Thames Estuary to a white froth of broken wave-tops. Lottie, Sophie and Mrs Abuthnot had retired to their berths while the ship was still in sight of Sheerness, but Winter had returned to the deck to watch the coast of England fade into the wet greyness of the evening.

Seagulls screamed and wheeled above the churning wake, and the acres of straining canvas overhead roared and sang to the rush of the wind, while spray drove over the bows in a fine, stinging veil of mist. It had been raining, thought Winter, on that long-ago day when she and Zobeida, cold, wet, and shuddering with sea-sickness, had landed at Southampton. She had not been seven years old . . . and now she was seventeen and sailing away again – sailing away to be married and to live happily ever after . . .

The ship rolled and pitched and a hissing spatter of spray stung Winter's cheek, and she began to feel distinctly queasy. But she could not face the prospect of descending once more to the cramped cabin where Lottie Abuthnot, prone upon her berth, had already succumbed to the pangs of sea-sickness. The fresh air, despite the drenching spray, was preferable to the narrow reeking cabin, and clenching her teeth she turned instead to pacing to and fro.

The deserted deck heaved up and sank away again beneath her feet, and presently she began to regret her decision not to go below. She should have retired to her cabin while she still had the strength to do so, because now, quite suddenly, it was impossible to move. Impossible to do anything but cling to the wet rail, oblivious of the driving spray and the fact that the wind had whipped her cloak from her grasp and was billowing it out in imitation of the straining sails above her, or that her bonnet had fallen off and was now only attached to her by its ribbons.

Her head appeared to have swollen and to be full of whirling sparks, and she leant on the rail, wet, chilled and racked with nausea. She did not hear the footsteps behind her, and she would not have cared if she had. She was beyond caring. She only knew that arms were around her, holding her, and that she need no longer cling to the rail.

Someone lifted her as easily as though she had been a small child, and a man's voice with a hint of a laugh in it said: 'I suppose this is included in the duties of a courier?' And then she was being carried down into heaving darkness to her cabin.

She was aware of the cabin door being thrown open, and above the creaking pandemonium of the labouring ship she could hear the alternate moans and retching of Lottie Abuthnot. Winter turned her head feebly away from the sound and buried her face against the shoulder of the man who carried her. She heard him say 'Good God!' in tones of half-humorous resignation, and then he had closed the door on Lottie's woe and turned abruptly away.

A moment or two later he laid her down and Winter opened her eyes and looked up into Captain Randall's face. He appeared to be amused, and she closed them again, and pressing a hand over her mouth managed with an enormous effort to say in muffled tones: 'Please go away. I – I fear I am going to be very unwell.'

'I've seen worse things,' remarked Captain Randall philosophically, reaching for a basin. And presently it ceased to matter to Winter whether he went or stayed.

It had not, in fact, occurred to Captain Randall to abandon her at this juncture, for if the truth were known he did not look upon her as an adult. He had not stopped to think that she was now seventeen and on her way out to India to be married to the Commissioner of Lunjore, for Winter, small and wet and sea-sick, had looked nearer seven than seventeen.

It had been morning when she had awakened. A cold wet morning in which rain fell steadily and the ship creaked and shuddered and groaned as it thrust its way through the steep choppy seas, driven onward by a shrill wind.

The small cabin rose and fell alarmingly before Winter's eyes and she shuddered and closed them again quickly. Presently, struck by a sudden thought, she opened them once again. This was not the cabin that she was to share with Lottie Abuthnot. She was in a strange cabin. Captain Randall's, of course. He had brought her there yesterday evening because Lottie had been so ill, and he must have slept elsewhere; probably in the saloon. She could only be surprised that he had bothered to remove!

Winter lay still, remembering the details of yesterday's deplorable collapse with horrified dismay. How could she have behaved so? Instead of insisting on decent privacy she had done nothing to prevent Captain Randall from remaining in the cabin and rendering aid, but, if she remembered rightly, had actually welcomed his assistance! She had a distinct recollection of him holding her head over a basin when she no longer retained the strength to perform that necessary office for herself. He had laid her back on the pillows and washed her face in cold water, removed her spray-sodden cloak and bonnet and forced brandy down her throat with a matter-of-fact competence and a total lack of embarrassment that surprised her.

Winter did not realize that the life of a political officer in the India of that day called for a far greater degree of proficiency in dealing with the unexpected than was required of the average man. Alex Randall had in his time been called upon to perform a variety of actions in excess of his official duties, including amputating the leg of a man who had been mauled by a wounded tiger, hanging a murderer, housing and feeding thirty-seven small children ranging in age from one month to approximately eight years in a year of plague and famine, acting as midwife to a woman in childbirth and dragging another one screaming from the pyre that consumed her husband's corpse, and on which she had intended, following the custom of her people and in defiance of the Company's new law, to immolate herself.

In the circumstances it was hardly surprising that he had behaved as though dealing with a young woman in the throes of sea-sickness was nothing so unusual. Winter could only be surprised that he had not also thought fit to remove her dress. She moved cautiously, aware that her head was aching badly, and discovered that he had in fact done so. The voluminous folds of her black batiste travelling-dress and the whalebone hoops of her crinoline were flung over a chair-back, and the blankets that had been drawn up over her concealed only petticoats and pantalettes. Further investigation revealed the horrifying fact that Captain Randall had also unlaced her stays.

The indignity of this discovery impelled her to sit upright, but it proved an unwise move. The cabin swam unpleasantly before her eyes and she was forced to lean her aching head against the polished wooden boards that formed the wall of the berth.

Someone rapped on the panels of the door and after a momentary pause it opened to disclose Captain Randall himself, looking, thought Winter resentfully, almost offensively well. He encountered her hostile gaze and smiled.

It was a disconcertingly pleasant smile, and the fact that even through a haze of acute physical misery and social embarrassment she could recognize it as such, increased rather than diminished her hostility.

'I've brought you some food,' said Captain Randall. 'May I come in?'

'It's your cabin,' said Winter bitterly, 'so I cannot prevent you coming in. But at least you might have sufficient consideration to avoid any mention of food.'

Alex laughed, and entering the cabin closed the door behind him and set down a small tray. 'You'll feel a great deal better when you have had something to eat,' he assured her. 'It's only hot soup and biscuits.'

Winter glanced at it and shuddered. The small cabin dipped and rose, tilted, sank and steadied again in an endless sickening rhythm, and the soup in the thick china mug slopped over the rim onto the tray. 'Go away!' said Winter in a gasping whisper. 'Take it away and go away.'

Alex sat down on the edge of the berth beside her. 'If you intend to go on being sea-sick, you will find it far better to have something to be sick with,' he remarked prosaically. And then, she did not quite know how it happened, he was holding her against his shoulder and feeding her with soup and dry biscuits as if she had been a sick child – and with much the same manner that old Nurse or Mrs Flecker the housekeeper might have employed in similar circumstances.

The soup was hot and sustaining and, unlikely though it had seemed, she managed to swallow a fair proportion of the biscuits he had brought, and felt considerably better for having done so. Captain Randall's shoulder was strangely comforting to lean an aching head against, and she tried to remind herself that this man was an enemy; a traitor to Conway. That she had once cut him across the face with her riding-whip – and deservedly. But it did not seem to matter any longer. She was conscious only of an unfamiliar and inexplicable feeling of being safe: a feeling she had been a stranger to ever since the day when a small, weeping and bewildered child had been torn from the comforting arms of Juanita and Aziza Begum and the safe familiar walls of the Gulab Mahal. She did not know why the presence and the touch of this man who was Conway's enemy – and therefore, surely, hers? – should give her this warm feeling of safety, and she was too physically exhausted to puzzle it out. It was enough to feel relaxed and protected. The uneasy motion of the ship seemed to be lessening, or perhaps it was true that the food had benefited her. She felt infinitely better, but strangely disinclined to move.

Alex put down the empty cup and said: 'It is just as well that your chaperon and every other woman on board is prostrated with sea-sickness, or I am afraid that I should have damaged your reputation beyond repair. As it is, the ladies have no attention to spare for anything but their own sufferings, so for the moment I think that you can safely stay here.'

'I can't do that,' said Winter drowsily. 'I must go back to my own cabin.'

'I wouldn't advise it,' said Alex. 'Your cabin-companion is showing no signs of recovery yet, and ten minutes in there will undo any good that a night's sleep and a meal have done you.'

'How do you know?' inquired Winter, interested. 'Have you been looking after them too?'

'I have,' admitted Alex with the ghost of a laugh. 'I must admit that had I realized earlier that the duties of escort would include those of sick-nurse, I might have declined the office. The stewards are doing their best, but they are only possessed of one pair of hands apiece, and as your chaperon and her daughters are also technically in my charge, I felt obliged to offer assistance. I have no doubt that when she is feeling better Mrs Abuthnot will find it hard to forgive me for it, but at present she is tolerably grateful.'

'If you unlaced her stays for her,' remarked Winter, 'I shouldn't think she would ever forgive you.'

She had spoken without thinking; a thing that she had schooled herself not to do for a third of her short life; and the moment the words were out she would have given anything to recall them. She jerked herself away from Captain Randall's supporting arm, her hand to her mouth and a hot wave of colour dyeing her throat and white face. How could she have said such a thing! Underclothes were considered an unmentionable subject, and she had spoken of them to a man – and to a strange man at that. A man who had had the incredible effrontery to act as lady's-maid to her. Cousin Julia would have swooned with horror. Captain Randall, however, remained unmoved. The enormity of her observation appeared to have escaped him and he replied to it in all seriousness:

'It wasn't necessary. She seemed to have managed it herself.'

His attitude, had she but known it, was entirely genuine, for owing to the nature of his work he had escaped to a large extent the corroding prudery of Victorian England that muffled and enshrouded almost every aspect of domestic life in layers of shibboleth and taboo. The fact that women wore undergarments did not seem to him a matter of any interest, let alone a subject for speculation and salaciousness. Nor did it strike him as outrageous that he should have taken it upon himself to remove this child's drenched outer garments and unwieldy crinoline: it appeared to him merely a matter of common sense. She was obviously incapable of doing it for herself, and he had removed them of necessity and without giving the matter a second thought. He could hardly be unaware of the practice of tight lacing, and as it happened the mechanics of the female corset were no mystery to him. It seemed to him a ridiculous and torturous garment, but possibly no more ridiculous than the close-fitting, high-stocked coat with its elaborate frogging and heavy epaulettes that he himself wore when in uniform, despite a temperature that frequently reached well over a hundred in the shade.

The sight of Winter's scarlet cheeks and wide horrified eyes brought home to him for the first time the fact that his proceedings might be considered shockingly unorthodox, and a muscle twitched at the corner of his mouth. He said gravely: 'May I give you a piece of advice, Condesa? Common sense will nearly always stand you in better stead than a slavish adherence to the conventions. If I had left you to spend the night in wet and uncomfortable clothing it might have saved you some temporary embarrassment, but it would have done no good at all to your health. And in the country to which you are going, health is an important thing. You cannot afford to be ill in India.'

The shamed colour faded from Winter's cheeks and the horror in her eyes was replaced by interest. That common sense was preferable to convention was a point of view so diametrically opposed to the teachings of Cousin Julia and the various governesses, nurses and under-nurses who had had charge of the education and upbringing of Sybella and herself, that for a moment it seemed almost to smack of heresy. Yet on consideration it was so obviously right that Winter was conscious of a sudden sense of release from bondage; as though some mental form of tight lacing had suddenly been unloosed.

She had never had a very high opinion of her Cousin Julia, but it had not occurred to her to question her authority and the rightness of her views in matters of behaviour and etiquette. But Cousin Julia, she knew, would not only have looked upon Captain Randall's eminently sensible proceedings as entirely scandalous, but have regarded Winter, as the recipient of them, as next door to a fallen woman. Cousin Julia's inflexible code would have visualized no alternative for Captain Randall but to have abandoned Winter to be sick in decent seclusion, and that such a course of action might well have resulted in a severe chill, or even pneumonia, would have carried no weight at all when placed in the balance against the strict preservation of the social conventions.

Winter considered the matter and came to the conclusion that Captain Randall's point of view was infinitely more practical. A dimple broke the smooth curve of her grave young cheek and she smiled.

It was the first time that Alex had seen her smile, but he did not return it. He sat quite still, looking down at her and no longer seeing her as a forlorn child, but as a young woman. The heart-shaped face was unusually pale, and the shadows under the wide dark eyes made them appear even larger. The crumpled whiteness of petticoat and corset-cover served to turn her bare arms and shoulders to a warm shade of ivory, and the loosened hair that tumbled about her in rippling profusion glinted with blue lights in the cold greyness of the small cabin.

Alex had a sudden and disturbing vision of the moist, unsteady hands of the Commissioner of Lunjore twining themselves in that soft darkness and sliding over those smooth ivory shoulders, and the lines of his face hardened and set. He stood up abruptly, and retrieving the tray said brusquely: 'The Captain appears to think that we shall run out of this bad weather by sunset. You had better stay where you are for today at least. I have this cabin to myself as far as Gibraltar.'

'But – what about you?' asked Winter hesitantly.

'I can manage,' said Captain Randall briefly.

The cabin door closed behind him and Winter did not see him again for some considerable time. It was a steward who knocked at her door with a tray of food at mid-day, and towards the late afternoon she felt sufficiently recovered to resume her discarded dress and find her way to her own cabin. But it proved to be an unwise move. In the peace and privacy of Captain Randall's cabin she had succeeded in throwing off the worst effects produced by the boisterous seas, but ten minutes in the company of Lottie Abuthnot sufficed to bring on a renewal of nausea. The cabin reeked of sickness and resounded with Lottie's lamentations, and Winter took to her berth where she remained for the next few days.

The Captain's optimistic assertion as to the weather proved incorrect, but a Mrs Martha Holly, who had recovered her sea-legs after a temporary set-back of twenty-four hours, had come to the rescue of the Abuthnot party.

Mrs Holly was stout, brisk and motherly, and had once been a nursemaid. She had borne and lost several children in India, but sorrow and adversity did not appear to have damped her invincible spirits, and after a year spent in England, to which she had returned in the capacity of nurse to an invalid wife and two small sons of a Colonel of Native Foot, she was returning to rejoin her husband.

'Not that I can stand the place, miss,' she confided. 'The 'eat kills me, and I don't 'old with foreigners – bein' British. But 'Olly's bin' a good 'usband to me and 'e's lost without me. Those blacks 'ave no idea 'ow to darn a man's socks and iron 'is nightshirt right. Like as not they'd use starch—I'd put nothin' beyond 'em! Yes, I've bin sixteen years in India. It's a long time. I suppose it 'as its points, but give me Islington any day. Now, Miss Lottie, just you swaller down that soup while I go and see to your poor ma. If you don't keep nothing down you'll keep on bringing nothing up, an' that's uncomfortable as well I knows. I made meself eat ship's biscuit, and in less than no time I was up and about again.'

Her energetic ministrations had the desired effect, and when four days later the *Sirius* finally ran out of bad weather and into sunshine and blue seas, even Mrs Abuthnot was able to appear on deck.

Their fellow-passengers included several other ladies, among them a Mrs Gardener-Smith and her daughter Delia who were also bound for Lunjore, in addition to two Generals and a Judge, a number of officers of all ranks – the majority of them returning from leave – and a sprinkling of civilians. There were also two persons who were well known to Captain Randall: a Colonel Moulson, who commanded one of the regiments of Bengal Infantry stationed at Lunjore and was a bosom friend of Mr Barton's, and a slim, pleasant-mannered Hindu who spoke excellent English and was accompanied by several Indian servants. That same Kishan Prasad whom Alex had last seen outside Sebastopol.

Kishan Prasad and his retinue had attracted Winter's immediate attention, for the sight of the brown-skinned faces and the sound of the swift familiar speech revived memories of her childhood and of Zobeida's dear dark face, and reminded her not of a foreign land, but of home.

Kishan Prasad had spoken to her one evening while she had been standing under the awning on the poop deck, watching the sun sink into the Atlantic while Cape Finisterre showed like a violet shadow on the horizon behind her. The evening breeze had tugged unexpectedly at the light shawl she wore and tangled its long silk fringe inextricably about a stanchion, and Kishan Prasad, who had been passing, had come to her assistance. She had thanked him prettily, and he had been about to turn away when his gaze had fallen upon her left hand. She had been wearing Conway's ring; the great carved emerald in the curiously wrought setting that Alex Randall had brought with him from Lunjore, and Kishan Prasad had checked at the sight of it. The pupils of his eyes had narrowed like a cat's in the light, and he said in his soft voice whose faintly sing-song intonation alone betrayed the fact that it was not an Englishman who spoke: 'That is a very unusual ring you are wearing. May I be permitted to ask where it came from? It looks as though it were a jewel from my own country – from Rohilkhand.'

'Perhaps it is,' said Winter holding it out for him to see. 'It was sent to me by the man I am going to marry. Mr Conway Barton.'

'Ah! – Mr Barton. That is very interesting. He is the Commissioner of Lunjore, is he not?'

'Yes. Do you know him?'

'I have some slight acquaintance with Mr Barton. I own land in Lunjore District.'

Kishan Prasad was an agreeable man and an entertaining conversationalist, and he was soon on good terms with the majority of his fellow-passengers. Even Mrs Gardener-Smith, who did not consider that it was at all the thing for an Indian gentleman to converse freely with young ladies of European birth, pronounced him to be a very pleasant-mannered man. 'Who is he?' she inquired of the ship's Captain.

'No one of any special importance, ma'am. He is merely a wealthy Indian who has been visiting Europe. Doing a Grand Tour of the Continent, I imagine.'

'One wonders what he made of it,' remarked Mrs Abuthnot. 'The contrast between our great cities and the squalor of the East must cause such visitors the greatest amazement. Lottie dear, pray move under the awning. The sun is so strong, and freckles are *so* unbecoming.'

'Yes, Mama,' murmured Lottie dutifully, her eyes under their soft lashes busy with a party of gay young officers who were lounging on the rail at the far side of the deck. Freckles might be considered unbecoming in a young lady, thought Lottie, but on a man they could be strangely endearing.

Lieutenant Edward English was a large young man who possessed a generous supply of freckles, red hair and charm. He also possessed a pair of deeply blue and openly admiring eyes, and Lottie's fairness and fragility had made an instant impression upon his susceptible heart. He had lost no time in making her acquaintance, but her mama did not mean to allow any young man to fix his interest with her daughter at such an early stage of the voyage, and she had contrived to keep Mr English at a safe distance. Mrs Abuthnot had every intention of marrying her sweet Lottie to the first really suitable *parti* who offered for her; marriage being in her opinion a woman's sole purpose in life. But was Edward English suitable? She would have to find out. Meanwhile there was plenty of time – and plenty of other men on board.

There were also, of course, several other young ladies. Notably Miss Delia Gardener-Smith. Miss Gardener-Smith possessed sufficient pretensions to beauty to cause some slight anxiety in the breast of any mother of other marriageable maidens, being tall, blue-eyed, and inclined to plumpness, and endowed with a spectacular wealth of chestnut curls. 'I have been told that even the Empress Eugénie has not such beautiful hair,' confided her mother complacently to Mrs Abuthnot.

Mrs Gardener-Smith, who was distantly related to a peer, had an inflated opinion of her own consequence; but on hearing that Mrs Abuthnot was acting as chaperon to a young lady of title, a cousin of the Earl of Ware and the affianced wife of the Commissioner of Lunjore, she had hastened to make her acquaintance. She pronounced Lottie to be a sweet girl and Sophie a charming child, but she had not known what to make of the young Condesa de los Aguilares, and like others before her, Mrs Gardener-Smith could see little to admire in the girl's unusual beauty.

'Her father was a Spaniard, you say? It is a pity that she should be so sallow – and have such *very* black hair. And those eyes! I fear such colouring will be misunderstood in the East. It is almost oriental, is it not? She looks to be very reserved.'

'I think she is shy,' said kindly Mrs Abuthnot. 'The poor little thing is an orphan, you know. But she is a dear child, and does not push herself forward at all. In my opinion Mr Barton is a singularly fortunate man.'

There were others who were of the same opinion, but they were exclusively male. Winter's unusual style of beauty might not appeal to Mrs Gardener-Smith, but it was very much to the taste of the male passengers on board the steamship *Sirius*, and in particular to Colonel Moulson.

Colonel Moulson was a bachelor and a lover of women, and he fancied himself as a connoisseur of female charms. He had been a rake in his youth, and had managed in later years to purchase what he could no longer obtain by his own merits – a fact that his vanity would not allow him to admit. Advancing years had given him a taste for youth, and no young girl was safe from his ogling gaze and the sly pattings and pressures of his sinewy hands. Lottie and Sophie, who were too shy and inexperienced to know how to avoid his amorously-avuncular advances, were terrified of him. But Winter's cool dark eyes had a way of looking through him that he found more than a little disconcerting, though as the affianced wife of one of his greatest friends he felt, he informed her, a special responsibility towards her.

Winter could only be surprised that such an unlikable man should be a friend of Conway's, but she concluded that Conway must of necessity, and in the course of his official duties, remain on friendly terms with many people whom he would not choose as friends in a private capacity. For Conway's sake she tried to be as polite as possible to Colonel Frederick Moulson, and it was an easy enough matter to avoid being left alone in his company, there being a great many other men on board who were only too ready to make themselves agreeable to the young Condesa.

There was, indeed, only one gentleman who appeared entirely uninterested in her. Captain Randall had not addressed more than a dozen words to her since her emergence from her cabin, and during the succeeding days, while the *Sirius* sailed southward through blue seas and the passengers spent the greater part of the day in sociable converse in the shade of the awnings, although he made himself pleasant to Mrs Abuthnot and won golden opinions from that warm-hearted lady, he never made one of the group who surrounded Mr Barton's betrothed, and Winter came to the conclusion that he was deliberately avoiding her.

The discovery filled her with a vague feeling of resentment, and she was forced to remind herself yet again that this man had spoken against Conway, and that had he not kept his distance she herself would have been compelled to avoid his society. The fact that he had come to her rescue during the early stages of the voygage, and had treated her with a casual familiarity that could only have been socially excusable had she been his sister, should not be allowed to weigh in the balance against his disloyalty. Captain Randall had obviously realized this, and therefore kept out of her way; which was understandable. What was not understandable was why she should resent it. She found herself covertly watching him and comparing him, to his disadvantage, with Conway.

Alex Randall was slim and deeply tanned and undeniably good-looking. His rather hard grey eyes were fringed with black lashes as long as her own, and though he was not much above medium height (while the Conway of her memories was exceptionally tall) his slimness and grace of carriage conveyed an impression of more inches than he possessed. But Conway – blue-eyed and blondly handsome – was of a size to make Alex Randall appear insignificant by contrast, and his luxuriant corn-gold moustache enhanced his masculine beauty and compared most favourably with Captain Randall's unfashionably clean-shaven countenance. Conway was also great-hearted and the soul of chivalry, and he would have scorned to speak against a man behind his back as Captain Randall had done.

Nevertheless, that irrational feeling of resentment remained. He might at least speak to her! After all, had he not been deputed to look to her comfort and safety? Mrs Abuthnot was more than kind, there was no Cousin Julia to criticize or correct her, and she should have been perfectly happy. But the fact remained that she was not. Despite the kindness of her new-found friends and the attentions of her fellow-passengers, she was troubled by vague and unformulated doubts and fears and a haunting sense of insecurity. She did not understand herself, despised herself for her inability to shake off the restlessness and uncertainty that possessed her, and continued to watch Captain Randall with feelings that wavered between resentment and unwilling curiosity.

She had encountered him one evening in the dark passageway that led to the cabins, and he had stood aside to let her pass. Winter drew back her hooped skirts, for the passage was narrow, and was about to pass him when she changed her mind and stopped. Her crinoline, released, brushed the walls of the passage on either side and effectually prevented Captain Randall from moving.

She said hesitantly: 'I – I never thanked you for – for your help. It was most kind of you, and – and I would not wish you to think me ungrateful.'

Alex bowed but he did not speak. A sudden colour tinged Winter's pale cheeks and she said abruptly, her voice unexpectedly breathless: 'I am sorry about – striking you with my whip. It was unforgivable of me.'

'But entirely understandable,' said Alex gravely.

She waited, expecting him to apologize for the words he had said that day: confident, now that she had given him the opening, that he would retract them, or at least admit that he should not have spoken as he had; but he remained silent.

The colour deepened in Winter's cheeks and her chin lifted haughtily. She gathered up her wide skirts, and as she did so the ship heeled to a sudden fresh breath of the evening wind that blew off Spain, and threw her against him. For a brief moment his arms held her, and once again she was conscious of that warm sense of safety that she had experienced before on the first morning of the voyage. She lifted her head from his shoulder and saw that his eyes held a glint of something that was uncommonly like anger. Then he had set her on her feet again and walked quickly away.

After that Winter made no further attempt to speak to him. She acknowledged his occasional brief civilities with even briefer replies, and found no difficulty in ignoring him.

The *Sirius* was to make a short stay at Malta, and the majority of the passengers had arranged to put up at hotels on shore as a welcome change from the cramped conditions on board. But engine-trouble having delayed their arrival by some hours, the moon had already risen by the time the *Sirius* steamed into the Quarantine Harbour.

Mrs Abuthnot had been inclined, owing to the lateness of the hour, to remain on board, but the earnest entreaties of her daughters had finally prevailed upon her to leave, and presently, in company with others from the ship, they were cautiously entering one of the gondola-like harbour boats and being rowed across the dark waters to the landing stage. Supper and rooms were in readiness for them at the Imperial Hotel, and at the conclusion of the meal Mrs Abuthnot had decreed an immediate withdrawal to bed.

Once again Winter found herself sharing a room with Lottie. But although it was late, she also found that she had no desire for sleep. It was wonderful to be on shore again and to feel solid ground under her feet in place of the uneasy decks of the *Sirius*; to smell the scent of flowers and earth instead of the salt winds and the mixed aromas of shipboard. The very air of the hot, semi-tropical night called to the Southern blood in her, and she made no attempt to prepare for bed.

Their room was stone-floored and bare of unnecessary furniture, and led out onto an arcade that surrounded an open courtyard where tropical plants grew in lush profusion. The outer door stood open onto the black shadow of the arcade and the moonlight beyond, and Winter pushed aside the heavy curtain that hung over it and looked out into the night.

On the far side of the courtyard an orange point of light and a faint smell of cigar smoke betrayed the presence of a tall young man who leant against a stone pillar. Winter studied him for a moment or two and then spoke softly over her shoulder:

'Lottie——'

'Yes?'

'How much do you like Mr English?'

There was a small gasp from Lottie. 'Winter! How can you? . . . Why, I—— Of course he is very agreeable, but Mama says——'

'He is out there now: in the courtyard. Watching this room.'

There was a swift rustle behind her and Lottie was at her elbow, breathing a little quickly.

Winter said: 'I do not think there could be any harm in your going out to . . . to look at the flowers? They are very beautiful.'

Lottie said breathlessly: 'Oh, no . . . I could not!'

'Why not? Your mother has nothing against Mr English, has she? I heard her telling Mrs Gardener-Smith that he was a very nice-mannered young man and a relation of the Grimwood-Tempests.'

'No,' said Lottie unhappily, 'Mama has nothing against him, only . . .'

'Only what?'

'She . . . Mama thinks that I am too young to know my own mind where – where gentlemen are concerned. She says that I shall have many opportunities of meeting other and – and more eligible gentlemen in the near future, and she does not wish me to fix my interest until . . . until I have had that opportunity.'

'And what do *you* think? Do you think that meeting other men will make you change your mind, Lottie?'

There was a brief silence. Then: '*No*!' said Lottie with soft vehemence. 'No. But Mama will not permit me to speak to him other than in her company, and – and I could not go out there. It would be shockingly forward and un-ladylike in me to do so.'

Winter did not reply for a moment or two. Then she said reflectively: 'Someone, only the other day, gave me a piece of advice. He – they – said that common sense was nearly always preferable to a slavish regard for the conventions. I have often thought about that since, and it seems to me a very sensible view. I am sure it would be most unconventional of you to walk in the courtyard.'

'Mama – Mama would see . . .'

'But her bedroom does not face this way,' pointed out Winter. She turned her head and looked at Lottie, and then quite suddenly she laughed; a soft gay laugh. 'No, Lottie, you are quite right of course. You ought not to go. I don't know what can have come over me tonight: I am trying to lead you into temptation, and you should say, "Get thee behind me, Satan," and say your prayers and go to bed. And one day you will marry some vastly eligible gentleman of immense fortune, and say to yourself, "Oh, what a narrow escape I had in Malta"! '

'Is that common sense?' inquired Lottie with an answering laugh.

'I think so,' said Winter soberly. 'I am not sure.'

'But I am,' said Lottie. 'Quite, *quite* sure.' She brushed Winter's cheek with swift warm lips and slipped past her and out into the darkness of the arcade.

Winter saw her move out of the shadows and into the bright moonlight, and saw the tall figure at the far side of the courtyard start forward: then a tangle of oleanders hid them from her view. Winter laughed again, but the laugh broke off in a sigh. She dropped the curtain and turned back into the room, but the sight of the plain iron bedstead with its shroud of mosquito-netting did not incline her to sleep, and the hot night and the white moonlight called to her with a restless urgency.

On a sudden impulse she pulled up her wide skirts and unfastened her hooped crinoline. It fell on the stone floor with a click of whalebone and she stepped out of it, and having fetched a black lace shawl from among the few belongings that she had brought with her from the ship, threw this over her head, and gathering up the trailing skirts of her mourning dress, tiptoed quietly out into the night.

The arcade was a tunnel of shadow broken at intervals by warm squares of light from other windows and doors that looked out onto it. There were several stone benches against the walls, one of which appeared to be occupied, and Winter trusted that Lieutenant English was making good use of his time. She herself did not intend to remain in the courtyard, and a few minutes later, having met no one except a few loitering and sleepy servants, she was clear of the hotel and hurrying down a narrow shadow-barred street.

There were not many people abroad on that hot night, and those who were did not turn their heads to see her pass. Once a roistering party of passengers off a ship from Southampton passed her singing: 'Polly, won't you try me, Oh!' in faulty harmony, and once a group of men in the uniform of the 47th Highland Regiment reeled down a side street, arms interlocked, roaring out the haunting, heart-tearing melody of the 'Skye Boat Song' – that lament for lost dreams and lost hopes and the lost cause of Charlie . . . Charlie the darling, the young Chevalier.

The narrow street gave place to a silent square dotted with trees and overlooked by secretive shuttered houses with covered balconies and flat stone roofs, and Winter crossed it keeping to the shadows and avoiding the occasional late idler, her thin slippers making no sound in the warm dust. A cascade of scented creeper, its colour indistinguishable in the moonlight, tumbled over a high wall beyond which the tops of orange trees and two tall cypresses showed dark against the moon-washed sky, and a twisted fig tree leaned against it in an angle of a buttress. Winter paused beside the tree, eyeing it speculatively. It made an admirable ladder, and a moment later, laughing and a little breathless, she had reached the broad top of the wall.

There was a garden on the other side, evidently belonging to a large private house that lay beyond a line of aloes and a cluster of orange trees on the far side of a wide lawn. The garden was full of trees, flowers and shadows, and the night was so quiet that Winter could still hear the faint sound of voices singing the 'Skye Boat Song', and from nearer at hand, in the house beyond the aloes, someone playing a plaintive melody full of odd, unexpected breaks and quavers on a guitar, and singing to its accompaniment in a language that was unknown to her.

Beyond the quiet garden the flat-topped houses fell away to the harbour, and between the tree-tops and the jostling roofs she could see the shining floor of the Mediterranean. The smells of the South rose up about her, and the hot night was still and white and wonderful, and mysterious with the mystery that permeates every Southern night.

Winter drew a long breath of rapture and settled herself in the shadows of the fig tree, leaning back against a convenient bough that stretched parallel to the top of the wall, and screened on three sides by broad leaves and a tangle of creeper. Something that had been closed and frozen inside her was awake and stirring, as though a tightly furled bud had felt the first warm breath of summer and was slowly unfurling. The ice of the cold years at Ware was melting from about her heart, and the blood of young Marcos de Ballesteros awoke and sang in his daughter's veins.

The lights in the houses were extinguished one by one, and as the moon sank the shadows in the garden lengthened and changed their shape, and a huge white moth, attracted by the scent of the flowering creeper, whirred out of the night and hovered within reach of Winter's hand.

The singer in the house behind the aloes and the orange trees had ceased his song and the night was strangely silent. So silent that Winter could hear the pattering of hooves of a small herd of goats that wandered across the deserted square, and the soft footsteps of someone who walked quietly towards her. She heard the footsteps come to a stop at the foot of the aged fig tree, and a moment later there was a scraping sound and the branch against which she leant shook slightly, sending a scatter of fading blossoms from the hanging masses of the creeper showering down onto her lap. Someone was climbing the fig tree as she herself had climbed it . . .

Winter shrank back into the shelter of the leaves and sat quite still, holding her breath. Her black dress with its powdering of fallen flowers merged with the shadows, and it was evident that the man who swung himself up onto the wall almost within reach of her hand had not seen her. He wore a dark shapeless garment that might have been a closely wrapped cloak, and though she could not see his face she could hear the sound of his quickened breathing. Through the thin screen of leaves that lay between them she saw him lean forward as though to look into the garden below, then he dropped lightly down into the shelter of a tangle of oleanders and geraniums that grew against the wall beneath him, moved to the left, and appeared to melt into the moonlight.

There was no further sound, but Winter was convinced that he was still somewhere close at hand. Was he a thief, intent on breaking into the house to which the garden belonged? Or was there perhaps some Maltese Juliet awaiting her Romeo among the shadows of the orange trees? This was certainly a night for love and lovers, yet there had been something about that silent, swiftly moving figure that had sent a cold tremor down Winter's spine, and she did not move hand or foot for fear that even the slightest movement might attract the hidden man's attention. Then a door opened in the house beyond the aloes and the orange trees, and a square of warm light glowed against the hard black and silver of the night.

Winter drew a breath of relief and was tempted to laugh at herself. The man who had come over the wall had obviously skirted the garden and knocked on the door of the house, and there could be nothing sinister about anyone who performed such an action. She could already hear a subdued murmur of voices from the direction of that open door, and presently she heard the sound of footsteps on a stone-flagged path. A moment or two later three men moved out of the sharp-pointed shadows of the aloes and advanced across the garden

They stopped in the full moonlight and spoke together in undertones, their voices pitched so low that despite the silence of the night Winter could hear only an occasional word. They were speaking in English, but there was something in the almost inaudible voices that was entirely un-English and suggested that they only spoke in that tongue from necessity, because it chanced to be the only language they had in common.

A single sentence separated itself from the murmur of speech. A strange sentence to hear on an island in the Mediterranean:

'. . . as before the rising of the Mahrattas. Only then it was millet. This time it shall be bread and *bakri*.'

One of the men laughed; a cold clear little chuckle.

'*Bakri*,' thought Winter, remembering the flock of goats who had pattered across the silent square behind her. Who was it who spoke of the Mahratta invasion and used the Hindustani word for 'goat'?

One of the men was smoking a cigar and the scent of the tobacco came clearly across the garden. He was a tall man, bearded and powerfully built, and he dwarfed his two companions; one of whom, a small stout gentleman who wore a long tight-fitting coat and what appeared to be a round cap, barely came up to his chest. The third man was slim and of medium height, and Winter presumed that it was he who had climbed the wall, for he wore a dark cloak: moreover the big man was too large and the fat man too small to have been the night prowler.

She became aware of the first twinges of cramp, but she did not move. She was not afraid, since it did not occur to her that there was anything to be afraid of. But she did not wish to be caught in the embarrassing position of a trespasser upon private property (though whether a seat on the top of a wall constituted trespass was a matter of doubt), for the stealth and caution of the man who had climbed the fig tree convinced her that he had made his entry into the garden by this unorthodox route because he wished his visit to be secret. Therefore, it followed that she was in the awkward position of eavesdropping on some more than usually private conference, and that being so her presence had better remain undiscovered.

The tall man said something in a voice that was no longer an undertone, and which sounded like '*Kogo zakhochet Bog pogubit, togo sperva lishit razuma*.' But the words made no sense to Winter, and she did not recognize the language in which they were spoken. She saw the three men turn and move across the open lawn, and thought for a moment that they had seen her, because they walked directly towards her, their figures dark against the white expanse of lawn and their black shadows preceding them, grotesquely elongated on the sun-dried turf. But they stopped not half a dozen yards from where she sat, and it was only then that she realized that there was a door in the wall, the far side of which must have been concealed by the shadow of the buttress.

She heard a key turn and the rasp of a bolt being drawn, and then hinges creaked as the unseen door was opened. She could see the faces of two of the men quite clearly in the moonlight, but the slim man in the cloak had his back to her, and it was he who spoke in a soft voice that seemed vaguely familiar:

'We shall want money,' said the man in the cloak. 'A great deal of money.'

The tall man laughed shortly. 'Money – always money! It is the same tale everywhere. We, a rich country, remain poor because we pour out our wealth on others.'

'In bribes, my friend,' said the fat man softly. 'In bribes. You cast your bread upon the waters, is it not so?'

'But of course,' said the big man with another laugh. 'We are not fools. A year – a hundred years – two hundred years. It is all one. We are patient. We too can wait. Our bread will return to us, it may be soon – it may be late.'

'But the price goes up,' murmured the slim man. 'Thirty pieces of silver are no longer considered sufficient. It is three hundred, and then three thousand – and then three-hundred thousand.'

Winter saw the big man scowl, and then he laughed again and said: 'Be content that it is paid. In four months' time then. *Do Svidānya.*'

The small fat man slipped through the gate, and as the man in the cloak sketched an oriental gesture of farewell and turned to follow him, the moonlight fell full on his face and Winter recognized a fellow-passenger from the steamship *Sirius*. It was Kishan Prasad.

The hinges creaked again and a moment later the bolts were shot home and the key turned in the lock. The big man waited until the soft sound of retreating footsteps had died away on the far side of the door, and the scowl was back on his forehead. He cleared his throat and spat on the ground in a violent gesture of contempt, and then turning away strode quickly back across the lawn and vanished among the shadows of the aloes and the orange trees. A minute or two later the square of yellow light from the open doorway of the house vanished, a chain rattled briefly, and then the night was silent again.

Winter drew a deep breath of relief and was about to move when a sound stopped her. It was a very small sound, but painfully audible in the stillness. A faint rustle of leaves and a sigh that seemed to echo her own. It came from almost immediately below her, and she realized with a sudden stab of horror that the man she had seen climb over the wall had not been Kishan Prasad – and he had not gone. He had been there all the time; standing motionless among the oleanders and so near her that she might almost have heard him breathing.

The bushes shook as though to a breath of wind and a figure detached itself from the shadows and moved into the open. It was a man, hatless and wearing some sort of wrap flung over one shoulder, oriental fashion – an unusual piece of apparel on so hot a night, but presumably intended to disguise the wearer's features, since a fold of the cloth had been pulled up over his chin.

'If he comes back over the wall,' thought Winter in alarm, 'he can't help seeing me.' The branches and leaves and the thick trails of creeper had served to conceal her from anyone coming from the far side of the wall, but if the man intended to return by the same route he would have to jump for the coping and pull himself up facing her. Perhaps if she could manage to edge round and face the other way without noise she could jump to the ground. It was not much more than an eight-foot drop, and once down she could run across the square and be out of sight before he could reach the top of the wall.

She moved one foot with extreme caution. But she had not calculated on the effects of cramp. An agonizing pain shot through her numbed foot, wrenching an involuntary gasp from her, and the man below her whirled like a flash and the moonlight glittered on the barrel of a pistol that was suddenly and surprisingly in his hand.

Winter did not wait for explanations. The sight of the weapon had startled her considerably, and for the first time that night she was frightened. She struggled to her feet, clutching at her skirts with one hand and the treacherous trails of creeper with the other, but her legs were numb with cramp and she was not quick enough. The man below her took a short run, leapt and grasped her ankle. The creeper ripped in her hand, and with a gasp of terror she tumbled headlong from the wall to be caught in a savage hold and fall full length with her captor into the thicket of oleander and geranium below.

The man twisted on top of her, holding her in a crushing grip that felt as though it must break her ribs, her face pressed hard against his shoulder so that the thick folds of cloth that wrapped him stifled her attempts to scream. She fought him frantically, writhing and twisting, but the weight of his body and the crushing clasp of his arms drove the breath from her lungs and she gave in suddenly and lay still. His grasp slacked a little and she managed to turn her head, gasping for air.

He did not move, and she became aware that he was listening intently to the small night noises. Perhaps the sound of their fall and the rustle and snap of branches had been audible in the house and the big man had returned. If she could only cry out, she might be able to attract his attention.

Winter lay quiet, husbanding her strength, and then summoning up all her forces she opened her mouth to scream. But the sound died unuttered, for suddenly and inexplicably, and despite the fact that she could not see his face, she knew who it was who held her, and she spoke his name instead, gasping and incredulous: 'Captain – Randall!'

She felt him start violently and he wrenched one arm free and brushed his hand swiftly over her face and the tumbled mass of her loosened hair.

'*Damnation*!' The expletive was barely more than a breath of sound.

'Why——'

'Be quiet!' whispered Captain Randall savagely.

There was a faint noise somewhere near them, but for a moment or two Winter could not place it because the sound of her own gasping breath was loud in the silence. Alex made no movement except to take his weight onto one elbow and lift his head a little, and Winter struggled to control her panting breath and to listen as he was listening.

And then she heard it. A faint pattering sound. So faint that it was less a sound than a vibration of the stillness, and quieter far than the beat of her own heart. She felt Alex's body stiffen and heard him draw his breath in between his teeth. The pattering sound seemed nearer, and she remembered the chink of that chain and realized suddenly that there was an animal in the garden. The big man with the beard had obviously released a watchdog and it must be its paws on the dry ground that pattered to and fro in the moonlight.

Presently she heard it snuff loudly and give vent to a small, excited whimper, and then all at once the silence was rent by a spitting feline yowl, a crash among the bushes and a hurricane of barks that retreated across the garden.

Almost in the same second Alex was on his feet and had swung Winter up in his arms and flung her up onto the wall. He did not waste breath on words – the situation did not call for any – and she grasped at an overhanging bough of the fig tree with one hand and the coping with the other, kicked violently, heard a smothered expletive behind her, and scrambled to safety.

10

Winter turned to see Alex back away, take a run at the wall and leap for the coping; and then she had grasped his shoulders and was pulling with all her strength. Half a minute later they had dropped to the ground on the far side, and Alex had gripped her arm and they were running swiftly, keeping to the shadow of the wall.

He dragged her across the square and dived down a narrow alleyway between two tall houses, and turning sharply to the right, came out on a smaller paved square that was dominated by the wide stone steps and ornately carved façade of a church. Here Winter's skirts escaped her frantic clutch at last and tangled about her feet, and she tripped and would have fallen but for Alex's hand on her arm.

He jerked her upright, and she put one hand to her side, painfully aware of the constriction of whale-boned stays that reduced her small waist to a bare eighteen inches, and said pantingly: 'It's no good – I can't run another step——' Pulling away from his grasp she walked unsteadily to the steps before the church and sank down upon the warm stone, her back to the carved balustrade.

Alex followed and stood above her, frowning down at her, and she looked up at him for a full minute with her mouth wide, drawing air into her lungs in deep gasps. Then suddenly and unexpectedly, she laughed.

It was a joyous sound, gay, courageous, and full of the magic of youth and moonlight. And hearing it, Alex was conscious of a swift flash of admiration. He had expected tears or hysteria and possibly both, but not laughter. It took him completely by surprise, and for a long moment he stared down at her incredulously. Then suddenly he was sitting down on the wide step below her and laughing too.

They sat there and laughed together, and the sleepy, secretive stonework threw back a chuckling echo of their mirth . . .

It was Alex who stopped first. The laughter died out of his eyes and he said abruptly: 'What were you doing there?'

'Looking at the moon,' said Winter.

Alex reached up and his fingers closed about her wrist in a hard grasp. 'I want the truth, please.'

'But it is the truth,' protested Winter, still laughing. 'It was the ship, I think – and sharing that cramped little cabin with Lottie. It was so lovely to be on land again and smell the dust and the trees. And – and it was such a beautiful night. I couldn't just go to bed. I wanted to go out, so I played truant. That wall was easy to climb because of the tree, and I only meant to sit there and look at the moon and smell the flowers. But then you came along, and at first I thought you were a burglar, and then I thought you were one of those three men.'

Alex's fingers tightened about her wrist and he looked at her long and intently, his face unexpectedly harsh in the white moonlight, and presently he said slowly: 'Is that really all?'

'Yes. I meant to run away when I saw you, but I got cramp. That's why you caught me.'

Alex released her wrist and the rigid lines of his face relaxed. He looked away from her and across at the black shadows of the houses that faced the church, and seeing that he was frowning again, she said curiously: 'Why were *you* there? Were you watching Kishan Prasad?'

Alex made no perceptible movement, but she was aware of an indefinable change in him, and he was silent for so long that she thought he did not mean to answer the question. But at last he turned his head and looked up at her, and said: 'Yes. I wanted to know who he had gone to meet. And now I know.'

Winter said: 'Who were they? What were they doing – those men?'

'Plotting devilry. One is a Russian and another is a Persian: the third is a man I have known for three years.'

'Who is he? Tell me about him.'

'Kishan Prasad? He is a member of one of the great families of Rohilkhand; an exceedingly clever man and an embittered one, which is always a dangerous combination. He went to one of the better India Colleges and took top honours in all English subjects. He studied engineering for the Company's service, and passed out as the senior student of his year with higher marks than any European there. But because he was *not* a European he was only nominated to the rank of jemadar, where he was actually subordinate to a European sergeant – a man who was his inferior in every way and was at the same time arrogant, insolent and stupid, and lost no chance to insult him. The Hindus have been civilized for over a thousand years – they were writing books when we in Europe were living in caves. And Kishan Prasad is a proud man and a descendant of princes. He found the position intolerable, and resigned from the Company's service. We lost a good man when we allowed that to happen; and gained a dangerous enemy . . .

'A year ago he went on a tour of Europe, which was a strange thing for a man of his position to have done, for he will have to pay his priests very heavily to regain the caste that he will have lost by doing so. I saw him last in the Crimea, where he saw us fail in the assault on the Redan at Sebastopol, and met Russian agents . . . and now he is returning to his own country. We should never have allowed any Indian to see the British Army in the Crimea. Or, having seen it, to return and tell of what he had seen——' Alex appeared to be talking to himself more than to Winter, for his voice had dropped as he spoke until it was almost inaudible.

A wandering breath of wind blew in from the sea and drove a little whirling cloud of dust across the square. It tugged at Winter's lace shawl and ruffled her hair, and she shivered. But it was not the warm wind that made her shiver, but the recollection of the weapon she had seen in Alex Randall's hand. She said with a catch in her voice: 'Were you – did you mean to kill him?'

'Kill him?' Alex laughed shortly. 'No. Unfortunately, assassination is alien to the British temperament – which must on occasion be a matter for regret.'

'*Regret*? But one cannot do murder!'

'Are you speaking as a Christian?' inquired Alex, 'or a humanitarian?'

'Surely they are the same thing?'

Alex shook his head. 'Oh, no, they are not. The sixth Commandment says, "Thou shalt not kill." But what if by obeying it one dooms to death a hundred or a thousand innocent people?'

'I don't think I understand,' said Winter slowly.

'Don't you? I have seen men – there are many in India and there were many in the Crimea – whose crass stupidity was only exceeded by their overweening conceit, but who had reached a position of power and authority owing to an accident of birth or the possession of wealth, or to a mere matter of seniority in years and service entirely unconnected with personal merit. The abysmal blunders of such men cannot only doom thousands to death, but pile up legacies of hatred and bitterness that will bear poisonous fruit for generations to come. If you saw a lunatic in possession of a lighted brand, and knew that he intended to set fire to a building containing a hundred helpless women and children, all of whom would inevitably be burnt to death, and if the only possible method of preventing it was to kill the lunatic, would you consider that murder, or humanity?'

Winter said slowly: 'You cannot justify murder.'

'I'm not. But whose murder are you talking about? The lunatic's or that of the people in the building?'

Alex looked up into Winter's troubled face and laughed. 'There is no answer to that one, is there? Possibly heaven has one, but we do not appear to have found a satisfactory one on earth: which is why I am at times inclined to regret that the British consider assassination to be socially indefensible.'

His mouth twisted a little wryly and he said with a note of surprise in his voice: 'I don't know why I should be talking to you like this – unless it is because I feel the need to justify an inability to commit murder.'

He came to his feet, and as he did so Winter saw the moonlight glint on the butt of the long-barrelled pistol that he carried tucked into the folds of a wide silk waistband. 'It is quite time you got back to the hotel,' said Alex. 'Miss Lottie has probably already raised the alarm, and I can see that I shall have some very complicated explaining to do to your chaperon.'

A dimple showed in Winter's cheek. 'I do not think that Lottie will have noticed my absence,' she observed demurely.

'In that case I can only hope that she will also fail to notice the black eye I shall undoubtedly have by the morning.'

'Oh!' said Winter on a gasp. 'Did I kick you? I was afraid I had. I am so very sorry.'

'Considering all things, I feel I have escaped lightly,' observed Alex with a grin. He leant down and pulled her to her feet, and they walked back through the quiet streets in companionable silence.

The hotel was in darkness and moonlight no longer flooded the courtyard. But though the arcade that surrounded it was a tunnel of black shadow, a lamp still burned in Winter and Lottie's bedroom and made a faint square of warm light in the blackness. Winter came to a stop by the entrance to the courtyard and turned to face the shadow that was Alex:

'Captain Randall——'

'Condesa?'

The unfamiliarity of the formal title took her aback and she was silent for a moment, trying to make out his features in the darkness. She thought that he was smiling, but she could not be sure, and she had forgotten what it was that she had meant to say.

The moon was nearing the horizon, and the pale stars were gaining strength as it waned: they glittered in the square of sky above the courtyard, and a falling star drew a brief, brilliant finger of fire across the velvet blue. The night was so still that Winter could hear the distant murmur of the sea, the sound of Alex's quiet breathing and the beat of her own heart, and she was aware of an odd breathlessness and a feeling of expectancy: as though she were waiting for something to happen.

The scent of jasmine and geraniums, parched earth and the salt smell of the sea, filled the shadows with a heavy fragrance that was as potent as the sound of distant music, and there was a strange magic in the hot night. A sparkle and an exhilaration; a narcotic and a spell. Quite suddenly, and with a queer stunned amazement, Winter was conscious of a fantastic, overwhelming impulse: an impulse to reach up in the dimness and take Alex Randall's dark head between her hands and draw it down to her own. For a long moment it was almost as though she could feel his thick hair under her fingers . . . the shape of his head and the touch of his warm mouth. Then a cock crowed shrilly from somewhere behind the hotel, and the unexpected sound shattered the spell of the silent night, bringing her back to reality as though from a drugged sleep. A hot tide of incredulous horror engulfed her mind and her body in a burning wave of shame, and she whirled round and fled down the dark arcade as though she were pursued by the Furies.

Lottie was asleep, and Winter blew out the lamp and undressed in the dark, shivering with shock and self-loathing.

She could not understand herself. She had no affection for Captain

Randall. She did not even like him! How could she possibly like anyone who had spoken against Conway as he had done? And yet a moment ago if he had made the slightest movement towards her she would have been in his arms. With a superstitious shudder she remembered that it was only the crowing of a cock, that age-old symbol of betrayal, that had saved her from translating thought into action, and betraying Conway. She was no better than Emma Bolton, a still-room maid whom Mrs Flecker had dismissed.

Winter and Sybella were not supposed to have known the reason for the girl's dismissal, but Sybella had been pulling roses outside Mrs Flecker's open window during a dramatic interview between the outraged housekeeper and the frantic Emma, and had retailed a garbled account of it to Winter: 'She's been kissing Thompson,' reported Sybella, 'and Mrs Flecker said she was a bad woman and no better than she should be.'

'I am no better than she was,' thought Winter, sick with shame and remorse. 'Only a bad woman would have wanted to do such a thing . . . would even have *thought* of such a thing!'

She buried her face in her pillow and wept.

Alex remained for some time where she had left him. He heard the sound of her light running feet and the swift rustle of her skirts die away in the darkness, and leant against the wall staring blindly into the shadows. His thoughts were not pleasant, but they did not include Winter de Ballesteros: and when at long last he returned to his own room, sleep eluded him.

He lay on his back in the hot darkness and thought of India and the unregarded warning of men like Sir Henry Lawrence. Of the gross stupidities of men like Conway Barton. Of the whispered warnings of spies, of the sadhu whom he had seen in the grounds of the Residency at Lunjore, and the face of Kishan Prasad watching, with eyes that were avid and intent, the shattered men of the British Army flung back from the Redan, stumbling and dying in the mud and blood before Sebastopol.

He thought too of the faces of the three men whom he had seen only that night in a moonlit garden, and realized that he would have to speak to the Governor in the morning. Though he knew just exactly how much good (or how little) that would do, for the Peace Treaty having been signed in Paris there was nothing to prevent Gregori Sparkov, merchant and non-combatant, from visiting the island of Malta, or Mohammed Rashid, son of a French governess and a Persian princeling, from staying at the house of a Maltese Jew. And no reason at all why Rao Kishan Prasad, native of India, gentleman of leisure and passenger on the steamship *Sirius*, should not be seen speaking to either or both of them.

There were many men in India, among them 'Lawrence's young men', who had learned to speak the languages and dialects of the country and to know and love and try to understand those of its people among whom they lived and worked, who sensed and smelt the approaching storm and saw the shadow of coming events crawl silently over the uneasy land, drawing closer and ever closer. But they were far outnumbered by the complacent, the smug, the conceited and the merely stupid. By senior officials in the service of the Company who pooh-poohed any talk of a general rising as either hysteria or the unfounded fears of a timorous and over-imaginative minority. By colonels of regiments, wedded to their men and their battalions through long years of service, who looked upon any such suggestions as grossly insulting to themselves and to the men under their command, and derided those who warned as cowards and agitators. Complacency reigned in high places and lay like a bandage over the eyes of those who did not wish to see.

Alex turned restlessly, as though by doing so he could turn his back on the thoughts that kept him from sleep. Kishan Prasad . . . Kishan Prasad was a victim of the Conway Barton mentality. A man of brains and breeding; imaginative, intelligent and sensitive, whose brilliance had gone for nothing because of the colour of his skin, and whose ambition and enthusiasm had been broken and corroded by a sadistic oaf who was his inferior in everything except mere brute strength.

Alex had suspected for a long time that Kishan Prasad was engaged in treasonable activities, and had reported as much to Mr Barton. The Commissioner had demanded proof, which Alex was unable to supply since it had been more a matter of instinct and rumour than of evidence. He had, however, suggested various measures that might serve to check any tendency towards subversive activity on the part of Kishan Prasad. But these had been ignored, and it was shortly afterwards that the fabulous emerald that Alex had last seen adorning Winter's slim hand had passed into the Commissioner's possession. Which might have been a coincidence, but was probably not.

Kishan Prasad had been permitted to come and go without hindrance, to visit the Crimea and to contact Russian and Persian *agents provocateurs*. And there was little or nothing that he, Alex, could do about it, unless he were prepared to commit murder. Why was it that a man could kill his fellow-men in the heat of battle or by the chill permission of the Law, and yet not be able to bring himself to shoot down in cold blood a single human being who was as dangerous and unpredictable as a loaded pistol in the hands of a child? Or as the lighted brand in the hand of a lunatic that he had used as an illustration to Winter?

Alex had heard something of Winter's story from the Commissioner, and he remembered now that her father had died on the disastrous retreat from Kabul. His death could be laid at the door of the irresponsible architects of the Afghan War, but also at the door of the senile weakling who had commanded the troops in Kabul. Lord Elphinstone's obstinate incapacity must have been obvious to most if not all of his Staff. But since there was no legal way of removing him from command or of over-ruling his feeble and vacillating decisions, might not a well-placed bullet perhaps have saved sixteen thousand people from an agonizing death in those cold passes?

'It is one of the things that one cannot do,' thought Alex, arguing with himself as he had argued with Winter. 'But why not?' Because it was the gospel of Violence, and as such it could lead to worse things than the death of the innocent. As for Kishan Prasad, his actions were treasonable or laudable only according to who was regarding them, and in either case entirely understandable. The Briton who plotted against the Roman invader was undoubtedly looked upon as a hero by his compatriots and hung as a rebel by the Romans, and the Cavalier who spied for King Charles was hunted as a traitor by Cromwell's men. If Kishan Prasad schemed for the overthrow of the Company's Raj, did that make him a traitor, or a patriot?

'And why in the name of hell,' thought Alex in tired exasperation, 'can't I stop seeing the other man's side of the question? Why can't I believe, as Lawrence and Nicholson and Herbert Edwards do, in the divine right of the British to govern?'

Henry Lawrence and John Nicholson occupied adjacent pedestals in Alex's private pantheon, but he could not believe what they believed. He worked for the same end, but for a different reason: because he believed, with a passionate sincerity, that it was better for England and for India and for the world that the British rather than the Russians should hold the land of the Moguls.

Contrary to general belief, Alex's given name was not Alexander. His father had visited St Petersburg as a young man and while there made a life-long friend of a young Russian officer, and many years later, on duty in India, he had named his son after that friend. Alexis Lanovitch had stood godfather by proxy to the child, but the parson who had officiated at the christening had either been unable or unwilling to get his tongue round such a foreign-sounding name, and the infant had been baptized 'Alex' and not 'Alexis' Mallory, and as such had been entered in the register of the English church in the small Indian station where he had been born.

Later, as a boy of fifteen, Alex had travelled in Russia with his father, and the vast, secretive land with its limitless horizons had left an indelible impression on his mind and his imagination. To him Russia was the Enemy. An enemy to be feared above all others because the very vastness of her territory made her invulnerable to attack, as Napoleon had found to his cost. Russia had only to retreat before an invading army – to withdraw into that silent, brooding land that stretched away and away in endless steppes, forests, forgotten lakes and uncharted mountain ranges, eastward to the Bering Straits and westward to the borders of Poland. Six seas washed her shores; the Bering Sea, the Arctic Ocean, the Baltic, the Black Sea, the Caspian and the Sea of Okhotsk. And within her confines Europe and Asia together could be placed and lost. Russia the cold-eyed, the patient: consumed by the hidden fires of her belief in her ultimate destiny as the ruler of the world . . .

Alex had never forgotten that year in Russia. Or that beyond the Khyber

Pass lay the Kingdom of the Cossacks. 'We have got to hold India,' thought Alex. 'We have got to hold it until it is strong enough to hold out by itself, and not for any of the reasons that gross fools like Barton will hold it for.'

Conway Barton—— How much damage would the Commissioner of Lunjore have done during the past year? Men like Barton, mercifully in a minority, imagined that the mere fact of their being a member of a conquering race entitled them to be treated with servile awe and admiration, and the fact that their debaucheries and brutality, and their capacity to absorb bribes, were regarded with rage and contempt by the local population did not occur to them, because the anger and scorn was hidden behind lowered eyelids and bland, unreadable Eastern faces.

For the first time since she had turned and run from him, Alex thought of Winter de Ballesteros who was to marry the Commissioner of Lunjore. A girl in a million, thought Alex with a reminiscent grin. She had neither shrieked nor fainted when he had dragged her head-first off that wall, but had fought him instead like a young tiger-cat, and lain still while that huge rough-haired hound had pattered to and fro in the moonlight. She had helped to drag him back over the wall, had run with him until she could run no longer, and then, instead of treating him to tears or an attack of the vapours, she had laughed. She was a thousand times too good for a gross debauchee like Conway Barton.

Not that Alex believed any longer that the marriage would take place. It was quite obvious that the girl cherished some glorified mental picture of the man, based on the memories of an impressionable child; and equally obvious that the Conway Barton of 1856 would bear so little resemblance to this picture that one look would be enough to produce complete and shattering disillusionment.

Alex had imagined, once, that having made a long voyage to a country in which she had no friends or relations, she would be left with no alternative but to go through with the marriage, however distasteful it might appear upon arrival. But he was no longer of that opinion, for the Commissioner's betrothed was plainly no milk-and-water miss. Despite her youth she clearly possessed both character and courage, and was probably quite capable of breaking off her engagement at the altar steps if necessary. He hoped so, for her sake.

Perhaps he should have kissed her tonight. Would it have made any difference if he had done so? There had been a brief moment in the darkness of the archway when he had known without any shadow of doubt that he had only to touch her to have her in his arms, and he did not know what had held him back. Certainly it had been no feeling of loyalty to the Commissioner of Lunjore, and that lovely, passionate mouth would have been sweet to kiss. Had it been some obscure instinct of self-preservation? A sudden fear of being caught up in some emotion from which there might be no escape?

Alex became aware that the square of sky beyond his window was no longer flecked with stars but paling to the clear light of a new day, and as the first faint murmurs of awakening life rose up from the harbour and the crowded city, he turned on his side and slept.

11

Winter awoke late on the following morning to find that Lottie was already up and dressed, flushed and shy and overcome with fluttering alarm at the recollection of her own temerity of the previous night.

'I cannot think how I could have – have behaved in so *un-ladylike* a manner,' gasped Lottie, pressing her hands to her burning cheeks. 'Oh Winter, do you think he knew? That I had gone out because – because I knew that he was there, and not to – to view the flowers?'

'Are you sorry that you went?' inquired Winter bluntly.

'Oh *no*!' breathed Lottie on a heartfelt sigh. 'He is all that is noble and good. I knew that I could not be mistaken. And—— Oh, Winter . . . he loves me! He told me so. He intends to speak to Mama at the earliest opportunity, and to Papa of course as soon as we reach Calcutta. Do you suppose that it can be right to be so happy when one knows that one has behaved in a bold and forward manner?'

'Lottie, you are a darling goose,' said Winter kissing her, 'but I fear I am the one to blame, and if you marry your Edward and live unhappily ever after, it will be all my fault. I behaved quite shockingly last night. I cannot understand it. I have heard tell of people going mad from sleeping in the moonlight. Do you think it can be true?'

'Perhaps,' said Lottie. 'I think we must both have been a little mad last night, for I do not know how you can have dared to walk in the streets unattended. You might have been molested. It does not bear thinking about! Did you meet with no adventures?'

'No,' said Winter briefly. She hoped that Lottie would not pursue the subject, and Lottie obliged her in this since she was far too taken up with her own affairs and the many perfections of Lieutenant Edward English: 'He is only a second son,' explained Lottie, 'but he has prospects, and a more than adequate competence in addition to his pay. It seems so mercenary to even *think* of money, but as I know that it will weigh with Mama and Papa, I cannot but feel glad that Edward is not without means. Edward says that he admired me from the very first moment that he saw me when we were embarking at the docks. It is strange to think that I did not even notice him. Oh, I do trust that Mama will not be difficult! Supposing I do not see him at all today?'

But Lieutenant English appeared to be possessed of the determination that so frequently accompanies red hair and freckles, and shortly after breakfast the Abuthnot party found themselves committed to a tour under his guidance.

Winter saw Captain Randall only twice that day. She had donned a wide-brimmed sun-hat and rejoined Mrs Abuthnot in the hall preparatory to setting out to see the town, and Mrs Abuthnot, similarly hatted and grasping a serviceable sunshade, her reticule and a palmetto fan, was talking to Captain Randall. Winter had checked for a fractional moment at the sight of him, and perhaps he observed that involuntary hesitation, for when she joined them he bowed unsmilingly, and after inquiring in a colourless voice but with a faintly derisive gleam in his eye if she had passed a comfortable night, excused himself and walked out into the hot sunlight.

The full daylight revealed a dark bruise on his cheekbone, and Mrs Abuthnot informed Winter that dear Alex had had the misfortune to collide with the open door of his bedroom cupboard in the dark, and that she had advised an instant application of arnica.

Later that morning they had caught another brief glimpse of him coming out of a side door of the Governor's Palace, accompanied by a portly and somewhat pompous looking individual who was wearing military uniform and sweating profusely in the heat. In the hard sunlight his face looked tired and grim, and he had been listening with obvious impatience to his companion's conversation. He had not seen the Abuthnot party, and having bowed curtly to the military gentleman, had turned and walked quickly away in the direction of the Strada Reale.

Mrs Abuthnot had made a few purchases – necessities they would need to tide them over until they reached Alexandria – and they had returned to the hotel for luncheon. The remainder of the day passed without incident, and when, that night, the moon rose pale and enormous to hang above the shining levels of the Mediterranean like some enchanted Chinese lantern, Winter resisted its lure and retired early to bed.

On the following morning they rose at daybreak, to partake of rolls and coffee under the beautiful vaulted ceiling of the Commercia before re-embarking on the *Sirius*. And presently the little island vanished into the heat-haze, and once more there was only the blue sky and the bluer sea above and around them, and the white wake of foam stretching away like a pathway behind.

The long, hot days dragged slowly for Winter, but Lottie and her Edward found the time passed all too quickly. Edward, true to his promise, had approached Mrs Abuthnot on the first day out from Malta to ask her permission, in the absence of Lottie's father, to pay his addresses to her daughter. He had added a diffident but satisfactory account of his financial situation, and had indeed been so earnest and engaging that Mrs Abuthnot's heart had quite melted, and she had ended by assuring him that although the last word must of course lie with Lottie's Papa, if Lottie reciprocated his feelings she herself would not stand in the way of her daughter's ultimate happiness.

And indeed, thought Mrs Abuthnot complacently, although dear Lottie might well have made a more dazzling match, Edward English was of good family and appeared to possess both prospects and adequate means. It might do very well.

As the ship neared the coast of Egypt the heat became more intense. The sea turned from blue to green and the eager passengers crowded onto the paddle-box or hung over the deck-rails to see the minarets and roof-tops of Alexandria apparently lifting out of the water. The pilot, a vast bearded Mussulman, was taken up, and an hour later a variety of Egyptian officials boarded the ship and the passengers went ashore to drive through the town and admire the palms, the giant cactuses, the white houses and the stylish carriages of Alexandria.

They were to leave the *Sirius* and go by train to Cairo on the following morning, and they returned to spend a last night on board. But few if any of them were able to sleep, for the air from off the sweltering land came out to them in wafts like the hot breath of some great animal, while the racket of the Arabs coaling the ship by torchlight went on hour after noisy hour.

Winter did not find the heat too unbearable, and she might have snatched some sleep if it had not been for the noise. But Lottie gasped for air, tossed restlessly on her berth or walked about the small cabin bathing her forehead and arms with water that was almost as warm as the night, until at last Winter could stand it no longer. 'I'm going on deck,' she announced. 'Why don't you come with me, Lottie? It will be cooler up there, and no one could be expected to sleep in this noise.' But Lottie only shook her head and flung herself once more upon her berth, and Winter reached for a large paisley shawl, and wrapping it about her left the cabin.

The deck was a patchwork of jet-black shadows and vivid orange-coloured light from the flaming torches and flickering oil-lamps of the coal-boats, but it appeared at first sight to be comparatively deserted, and Winter peered cautiously over the side from the shelter of a dense bar of shadow to look down upon the swarming coalers who, bathed in the lurid torchlight and with their bowed, almost naked bodies grimed with coal-dust and glistening with sweat, looked like some illustration to Dante's *Inferno*. Behind them the sea lay like a dark lake of oil with the mirrored lights of Alexandria barely moving on its sluggish surface, and the hot air stank of coal-dust and sweating bodies, engine-oil and the Middle East.

A burst of laughter added itself to the noises of the night and Winter turned quickly, to see a group of men come down from the poop deck, cutting off her retreat. They had evidently been dining and wining on shore and were in considerable spirits, and one of them embarked upon a story which, despite the fact that most of it was happily unintelligible to her, was still sufficiently racy to cause her cheeks to burn with startled horror. Yet another man – Winter recognized him as Major Rattray, an officer *en route* to China – joined the group.

The Major, a corpulent gentleman, was at the moment clad in nothing but a species of loin-cloth, and Winter became suddenly aware that other gentlemen, equally lightly clad, were lolling about in the hot starlight. With this discovery all the impropriety of her presence on deck at that hour came home to her, and filled with shame and dismay she began to edge her way through the shadows towards the further companionway, when she heard a swift step behind her. A hand grasped her arm and jerked her round, and Captain Randall's voice said: 'What in thunder are you doing on deck! Is anything the matter?'

'N – no,' said Winter breathlessly. 'It was so hot in the cabin, and I thought——'

'Have you taken leave of your senses?' demanded Alex in an exasperated undertone. 'This is no place for a woman. Half the men have been celebrating ashore and the rest are less than half-dressed, and the place is thick with Arab coolies. You're going back to your cabin at once. Now, march!'

He turned her about and propelled her firmly in the direction of the companionway, but just as they reached it a man came up it and blundered out onto the deck. It was Colonel Moulson; noticeably the worse for drink.

Colonel Moulson was not a particularly pleasant person when sober, and when under the influence of alcohol he was even less so. Alex thrust Winter behind him, interposing himself between her and the swaying figure that stood starkly outlined against the light that streamed up from the companionway. But he had not been quick enough. The Colonel, though drunk, was not sufficiently inebriated to be unobservant, and he gave vent to a raucous whoop.

'A petticoat, b'gad!' cried the Colonel. 'Brought a fancy piece on board with yer, have you, Randall? Le's have a look at her.'

'I am sorry to disappoint you, sir,' said Alex levelly, 'but this lady wishes to go below. Would you please allow us to pass?'

'*Lady*!' bellowed the Colonel, 'that's rich. 'Pon my soul that's rich. If she were a lady she wouldn't be up here. Don't be a dog-in-the-manger, m'boy. What is she? a Gyppy, or an Arab bint? Come on out, my pretty – le's all have a look at you!'

He made a clumsy dive, and Alex fended him off and repeated patiently enough: 'I must ask you to let us pass, sir.'

'Damned if I do!' retorted the Colonel. And staggering backwards a pace or two he barred the entrance to the companionway with outstretched arms and proceeded to utter a series of loud 'view halloos'. The revellers at the far side of the deck, their attention attracted by the noise, began to move towards them, and Alex addressed Winter without turning his head:

'You'll have to run for it,' he said briefly, and took a swift stride forward. His right hand shot out and grasped the Colonel's neckcloth, twisting it violently so that the raucous whoops were cut off in mid-breath, while his left came into abrupt contact with the Colonel's protuberant stomach. The next instant the Colonel had been heaved aside to collapse sprawling on the deck, Winter was down the stairs and out of sight, and Alex and the recumbent Moulson were the centre of an interested group of spectators.

'What's all the to-do?' demanded Major Rattray.

'Fisticuffs, b'gad!' announced Mr Commissioner Ferringdon buoyantly: 'Someone's given him a leveller.'

'Allow me, sir,' said Alex solicitously, assisting the gasping Colonel to rise.

Colonel Moulson staggered to his feet and threw off Alex's hand. He tore at his twisted neckcloth, his face purple with rage, choking between breathlessness and apoplectic fury: 'By God, Randall, you'll meet me for this!' spluttered the Colonel.

'I shall be delighted to,' said Alex with disconcerting promptness.

A considerable proportion of the Colonel's high colour faded and his ire diminished appreciably. He scowled at Alex, and his breathing became less stertorous.

'What's this? What's this?' demanded a thin grey-haired gentleman clad simply in a towel, a tasselled smoking-cap and a pair of embroidered slippers. 'Can't fight a junior officer; thing's absurd. Duelling illegal.'

'He struck me!' spluttered the Colonel. 'The young puppy struck me.'

'Good gad!' said Major Rattray blankly. 'Deuced serious offence strikin' a superior officer.'

'But he ain't in uniform, dear boy,' murmured a languid gentleman attired in nothing but a pair of Turkish-style trousers and an eyeglass. 'Can't call that uniform. Purely private matter when not in uniform. Personal disagreement between gen'l'men.'

'I must apologize for being a little hasty,' said Alex smoothly. 'One of the ladies, being of a nervous disposition and alarmed by the torchlight and the noise, fancied that – that the ship might be on fire and ran up on deck. I offered to escort her below, but as Colonel Moulson, imagining her to be a woman of a very different sort, disputed her passage, I was compelled to be a little rough. I trust that he will accept my apology for any hurt he may have suffered.'

The Colonel scowled blackly but there was a look in Alex's eyes that was considerably less conciliatory than his words had been, and as the fumes of brandy gradually lost their grip on Colonel Moulson's brain, it began to dawn on him that should Captain Randall's story be true, the lady in question could well have a husband awaiting her in Calcutta. In which case, his own part in the affair might be brought into question. He therefore growled a surly acknowledgement to the apology and lurched away.

Alex looked after him thoughtfully. It was a pity it had had to be Colonel Moulson . . . He had never liked the man and considered him, scornfully, a suitable companion for Conway Barton. But it had been necessary for the smooth running of affairs in Lunjore to keep on good terms with Moulson, and he regretted that necessity had compelled him to make an enemy of the man, since it would make things just that much more difficult in Lunjore. The task of seeing that the Condesa de los Aguilares came to no harm was proving no sinecure, thought Alex irritably.

Winter had reached the safety of her cabin without further mishap, and as it was in darkness, it was not until the following morning that a shriek from Lottie and a hurried inspection of herself in the looking-glass revealed the fact that her hands were grimed and her face liberally streaked with coal-dust.

'*Oh!*' said Winter on a gasp of fury. 'What can he have thought?'

It seemed to be her fate to appear before Captain Randall at a disadvantage: losing her temper and lashing at him with her riding-whip like a harpy – struggling in the arms of Edmund Rathley – being degradingly sea-sick – climbing walls and falling off them like a hoyden. And now appearing on deck at a most improper hour of night and being found there with her face streaked with soot like a nigger-minstrel's! Somehow (she did not quite know why) it was all Captain Randall's fault. And as she scrubbed her face furiously with soap and cold water she summarized the Captain's behaviour in trenchant Spanish, to the alarm of Lottie, and resolved to treat him in future with the greatest possible coolness – which was surely no more than he deserved. But there was scant opportunity to do so, for she saw very little of him in the succeeding days.

In his role of escort to Mrs Abuthnot's party Alex had arranged for the dispatch of their baggage and their own conveyance to the station, but he had not travelled in the same compartment on the train, and Winter had not seen him again until they left Cairo for Suez two nights later in a 'desert omnibus' drawn by mules and horses. Even then he had not spoken to her. He had sat opposite her, and Sophie had fallen asleep with her head on his shoulder.

Winter studied him by the bright starlight and the glow of the oil-lamp that swung by the driver's seat; aware that her own face was in deep shadow and that he could not return her scrutiny. In a day when luxuriant beards, lush moustaches and flowing Dundreary whiskers adorned almost every masculine countenance, Alex Randall's clean-shaven face had at first sight an alien and almost effeminate look. Yet in spite of the fact that his thick eyelashes would have compared favourably with any girl's, there was nothing in the least weak or effeminate in the hard planes of his face or the line of the obstinate chin. His skin was burnt as brown as an Arab's, but even by that dim light Winter could still see a faint trace of the bruise that her heel had made on that night in Malta. It seemed a very long time ago, yet it was less than ten days since she had helped to drag him over a wall and had run headlong with him through deserted streets, and sat in the moonlight talking to him as if he were someone whom she had known all her life.

Her gaze moved from Alex's face to Sophie's. Sophie was only fifteen, but already a woman: a pretty enough creature, small-boned and fragile with timid brown eyes and a shy, charming smile. She reminded Winter strongly of one of the white mice that Billy Wilkins, the bootboy, had kept in a box in the stableyard at Ware. The van lurched as the offside wheels went over a boulder or the bleached bones of a camel, and Sophie's small head slipped down from Alex's shoulder to his breast, but she did not wake.

Winter was conscious of an acute and entirely irrational feeling of annoyance. It was ridiculous that Sophie should fall asleep in this abandoned manner! though admittedly, most of the other occupants of the van were also slumbering soundly. But she, Winter, was not in the least sleepy, and how anyone of any sensibility could sleep in such a rattling, bumping, uncomfortable conveyance she did not know. Besides, if Sophie *must* sleep, surely it would have been more proper in her to have inclined the other way and allowed herself to be supported by Mrs Hillingworth, the comfortably upholstered wife of a Major of Bengal Artillery, instead of allowing herself to be embraced by Captain Randall? She saw Alex shift Sophie's weight and his face twitch in a faint grimace of discomfort, and realized that he was suffering from the twinges of cramp. 'Serve him right,' thought Winter crossly.

She shut her eyes with determination and thought of Conway. But for some unaccountable reason she found that she could not picture him clearly. Always before she had been able to conjure him up by a mere effort of will: the Conway who had given an eleven-year-old girl a gold and pearl ring, standing in the Long Walk at Ware with the sun shining on his blond head and his shadow stretching across the velvet turf. Tall, broad-shouldered, yellow-haired and handsome; a shining knight. Now, for the first time, the vision failed her, and it was no longer a living man that she saw, but a picture out of a child's book – a flat, two-dimensional representation, crudely drawn, wooden and unreal. A blank face whose blue eyes were as glassy and as empty of meaning as a doll's, and whose mouth was hidden by a drooping corn-coloured moustache so that she could not tell if it were firm or full or weak.

Winter opened her eyes and found herself looking once more at Alex Randall's relaxed, unguarded face in the pale light of the newly risen moon. Alex's mouth was firm enough, and unexpectedly sensitive. He was Conway's assistant and she supposed that she would see a great deal of him once she was Conway's wife. The reflection disturbed her, and the thought passed through her mind that it would be better – she was not sure for whom – if he were to be transferred to some other district.

Two days later the travellers embarked upon the *Glamorgan Castle* and sailed down the Red Sea, leaving the dust and glare of Suez behind them. And once more the days settled into a pattern of pleasant shipboard monotony.

Three days out of Aden they ran into a storm, but it blew itself out after twenty-four hours of tossing discomfort, and on the last evening before they sailed into fine weather again they passed the water-logged wreck of a dismasted ship, its decks swept by the heavy seas.

Captain Ross of the *Glamorgan Castle* had manoeuvred his ship as close to it as he dared, and launched a mail-boat, in charge of the first officer, with a boarding party. They returned wet and exhausted with the news that the vessel had apparently been a troopship bound for China, but that there was no one on board and few papers or particulars to be found on her. It was to be presumed that all on board had taken to the boats, for all the boats were gone. The bulkheads of her Captain's cabin had been carried away, the port anchor and the cathead had gone, and from the appearance of the tattered sails and broken spars it was obvious that a sudden squall of hurricane force had carried all away at once. It was unlikely that the men on board would have lived to reach any shore, but there was nothing that could be done about it now, and the *Glamorgan Castle* went on her way in the swiftly gathering twilight.

Winter, who had crept up onto the windy spray-swept deck, watched the abandoned wreck fade into the stormy dusk; a forlorn sight with jib and staysail hanging in shreds from bowsprit and jib-boom, her masts shattered and broken spars trailing over the side into the sullen seas that washed the deserted decks.

A cold shiver ran down Winter's spine as she looked. In spite of the wild weather the fact that she was actually in the Indian Ocean, and that India itself lay ahead of her at last, had filled her with a sense of glowing happiness. But the sight of that battered and broken ship, drifting and sinking in the lonely wastes of the sea, dimmed the glow and brought with it a chill breath of apprehension and foreboding.

She heard a sigh beside her that was not the wind, and turning quickly, saw Kishan Prasad standing near by, his eyes fixed on the fast-vanishing wreck. But for once his bland, inscrutable face had dropped its guard and it was as though a mask had been stripped from it, leaving it naked and exposed. He did not appear to be aware of Winter, and he did not move or speak. But quite suddenly, and as though he had shouted it aloud, she knew his thought with a complete and horrified certainty.

He was thinking, with a fierce, gloating pleasure, of the men who had been on that ship. Seeing them in his mind's eye swept away by the savage seas; sinking down into the hungry fathoms, dragged under by the weight of their sodden uniforms; choking and drowning, their struggling bodies torn and ripped by sharks and barracudas. He sighed again. The same long-drawn sigh of hatred and satisfaction, and Winter shrank away, and backing from him, turned and ran headlong, stumbling down the steep stairs and tripping on her full skirts.

Alex Randall was coming down the passage towards her, and he caught her arm and steadied her: 'What's the matter? Feeling ill again?'

'No,' said Winter on a gasp. She had forgotten that she had meant to avoid all conversation with Captain Randall outside of social necessity, and she clung to his arm, her eyes wide with shock. 'It was Kishan Prasad——'

She saw Alex's face change and his mouth tighten, and said breathlessly: 'He was looking at that ship. And he was *glad*! He hated them and he wanted them to drown . . . he was glad that they had been drowned . . . I could see that he was!'

Alex said: 'It isn't so surprising. They were soldiers – British troops. If he could have drowned them singly with his own hands he would probably have done so.'

'Why? Do they – do they hate us?'

Alex said impatiently: 'Did you suppose that they loved us? The benefits of Western civilization are not necessarily looked upon as an unmixed blessing when imposed upon the East by a foreign conqueror, you know.'

He looked down at Winter's white face and glimpsed something of the shock that this sudden revelation of hatred had dealt her. The girl had obviously never thought of India as a conquered country. She had imagined herself to be coming home, and the realization that many of the inhabitants of that land could hate all those of British blood with a savage and implacable hatred was like a blow in the face to a trusting child. He wanted to say: 'Don't look like that! It isn't safe to be so vulnerable – to expect too much of anything or anyone.'

He said instead, with a kind of exasperated anger: 'I warned your cousin Ware that this was no time to send any young woman out to India, but he would not listen. None of them will!' And turning from her abruptly he went on down the passage and up onto the wet deck.

But it was only two days later than Kishan Prasad fell overboard, and it was Alex who went after him.

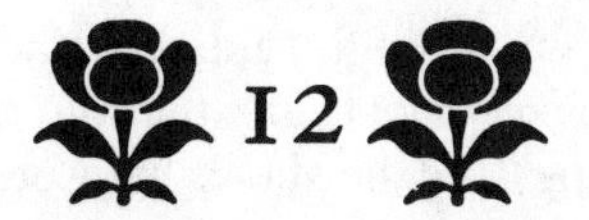

Alex had not known that it was Kishan Prasad who had fallen. Perhaps if he had it might have altered the course of a great many lives.

The day had been hot and still and all that remained of the storm was a long, heaving, barely perceptible swell that swung the cabin doors idly to and fro and made the line of the horizon lift up and fall again in a slow, leisurely rhythm. The sea was blue with the intense midnight blue of the Indian Ocean, and so clear that floating squadrons of jelly-fish far below the surface appeared as though embedded like bubbles in blue glass, and the sun that had blazed down all day from a cloudless sky had made the deck planks uncomfortably hot to the touch, even under the shade of the awnings.

It was after four o'clock and the decks were comparatively deserted while the passengers changed for dinner. Lottie had come up early, intending to meet her Edward, and she had looked up and seen Kishan Prasad standing on the paddle-box gazing out to sea. Even as she looked the ship rolled suddenly in the trough of an unexpectedly deep swell, and she saw Kishan Prasad, taken off guard, slip and fall and slide under the rail. The next moment he had vanished, and Lottie shrieked and ran.

Two of the lascars, together with a ship's officer and Colonel Moulson, had also seen someone fall, and they ran along the deck shouting. Colonel Moulson, with what he considered to be admirable presence of mind, picked up two deck-chairs and heaved them overboard into the creaming wake, and these were followed almost immediately by a hen-coop thrown after them by one of the lascars.

'*Man overboard*!' bellowed Colonel Moulson and the ship's officer.

Alex, who had been lying asleep face downward in a patch of shade with his head buried in his arms, woke at Lottie's shriek and came to his feet. She stumbled towards him, her face chalk-white, screaming and pointing, and he turned and raced aft along the deck and caught a brief glimpse of a despairing hand that reached up from the foaming wake.

'It's all right, Randall,' snapped Colonel Moulson. 'Only one of those blacks. He'll be drowned by now – they can't swim.'

A sudden flash of pure rage hit Alex with the force of a blow. He kicked off his shoes, and in the next second had vaulted over the rail and dropped feet first, and the rush of the sea closed over his head.

The water was unexpectedly cold and the churning wake sucked him down and down until the sea felt like a ton weight upon his shoulders. Just when it felt as though his lungs must burst, the weight lifted and he was being shot to the surface like a cork, and there was air again. He gulped deep draughts of it and struck out strongly, aided by the swirl of the wake. After the sweating heat of the *Glamorgan Castle* the cold rush of the foaming water was incredibly exhilarating, and he shook his wet hair out of his eyes and laughed.

It was, he presumed, one of Kishan Prasad's servants who had fallen overboard, for had it been a member of the crew Moulson would have said 'a lascar'. 'Of all the goddamned, bloody, idiotic things to do!' thought Alex, anathematizing his own conduct. 'What the hell is the life of one heathen lackey worth that I have to make a quixotic exhibition of myself trying to fish the man out? Why does common sense betray one in a crisis?'

He saw a dark struggling shape ahead of him and the next moment it had disappeared. Alex filled his lungs with air and dived. The man struggled feebly, and for a minute that seemed like an endless hour they sank down together through the blue water. And then Alex got a grip on him and kicked strongly and they were rising once more into light and air.

Even then he did not realize who it was that he held. He caught the half-drowned man under his arms and swam towards the heavy wooden hen-coop that was lifting to the swell not twenty yards away. After several fruitless efforts he managed to heave his limp burden face downwards across the stoutly built coop and hold him there while he trod water.

The swell that had been barely perceptible from the decks of the *Glamorgan Castle* was a very different thing when viewed from the level of the sea itself, and in the trough of it the ocean appeared to be empty and the *Glamorgan Castle* had vanished. The next swell swung them slowly upwards, and far away – miles away it seemed – the ship showed small against the blue. It would take a long time for them to heave-to and circle back, thought Alex. They would lower a boat as soon as possible but it would be a long wait. The distant ship vanished as the laden hen-coop slid once more into the glassy trough of the swell, and the Indian coughed, retched, lifted his head and moved feebly.

'Lie still, fool,' said Alex in the vernacular. The man obeyed, but presently he turned his head, and Alex saw for the first time who it was that he had rescued——

The two men stared at each other for a long moment and Alex was conscious of a queer twisting wrench at the pit of his stomach: a helpless, futile, sick anger against fate and himself and the fatuous foolish instinct of his kind and his creed that had driven him to leap unthinkingly to the rescue of a drowning man, and by so doing had betrayed him.

Winter had asked him once if he had meant to kill this man, and he had replied bitterly that assassination was unfortunately alien to the British character. He knew that he could not bring himself to murder Kishan Prasad in cold blood, although if he could have proved his suspicions and thereby brought him legally to the gallows, he would have done so without a second's hesitation. But he had been unable to do that, and owing to the smug blindness of those who did not wish to see, he knew that he might never obtain such proof as would satisfy them. And now Providence had stepped in and done its best to put an end to Kishan Prasad, and he, fool that he was, had risked his neck to save a man whom he regarded as among the most dangerous enemies to British supremacy in India.

If only he had waited! If only he had asked questions before he had jumped. It had been Moulson's remark that had undone him. Moulson had said: 'It's only one of those blacks——' and Alex had instantly lost his temper. With the result that he had fallen into a booby-trap, for it was Kishan Prasad whom he had saved. The salt sea-water was bitter in Alex's mouth and he looked into Kishan Prasad's grey face and laughed.

Kishan Prasad's lips drew back from his teeth in an exhausted grin that was a grimace of complete comprehension. He said in a hoarse voice between difficult breaths: 'Whom did you think you had saved . . . Sahib?' – the appellation was nearer an insult than a term of respect – 'One of your own kind? The General Sahib, belike?'

'No,' said Alex, treading water. 'I thought it was one of your *naukerlog*.'

He saw the flare of astonishment and disbelief in the dark eyes.

'My *servant*?'

'Yes,' said Alex shortly. 'Had I known it was you——'

'You would have let me drown,' finished Kishan Prasad, fighting for each breath.

'Yes,' said Alex bluntly. 'Do not talk. You will tire yourself and the boat will not reach us for some time yet.'

Kishan Prasad was silent for a long while. The slow swell lifted them up lazily so that at intervals they could see the distant ship and the small speck that was a boat rowing towards them, then it would slide them down into a long blue-black hollow and the ship would vanish and there were only two men and a wooden hen-coop alone in all those endless leagues of ocean.

Kishan Prasad looked down into the glassy water and thought of the unimaginable depths that lay beneath him: the cold fathoms that stretched downward and ever downward to the slimy darkness of the sea floor; and his fingers tightened convulsively on the rough wood that supported him.

He spoke at long last, and softly, in a voice that despite himself he could not keep quite steady: 'You say that had you known it were I who had fallen, you would have left me to my death. But it would seem that death is here now for one of us. Look there——'

Alex turned his head, and his diaphragm seemed to contract and turn to ice, for in the glassy swell beyond them lay a long silvery-brown body, the triangular dorsal fin just clear of the water. Shark! . . .

The sea was darkening below them and the low sun burned along the water, turning the surface of the swell to gold and outlining the creature with fire. It did not move, but hung motionless like a fly embedded in amber.

Alex seemed to have lost all power of movement. He held onto the edge of the hen-coop with one hand and stared back at that small cold eye. It had seen them and was watching them, idly curious.

Kishan Prasad said in a hoarse whisper: 'This wooden thing will not bear two upon its surface, and my life is forfeit to thee.' He had forgotten to speak in English. He began to slide softly from the coop and Alex said furiously: 'Don't be a fool! Get back onto that. You can't swim.'

At the first movement the shark had flicked away and now they saw its fin cut the water on the far side of them. The swell swung them up once more and they could see the boat, the low sun flashing along the oar-blades. But it was still a long way off.

Alex remembered having heard that sharks disliked noise and he beat the water with his cupped hand. The fin sheered away, circled and came back. Kishan Prasad was in the water holding on with only one hand, and Alex said again: 'Get back, you fool!' He grasped the Indian about the waist and heaved, and releasing him, caught his legs and thrust him onto the top of the hen-coop where he remained on all fours gripping the edge. It was a perilous and inadequate raft, and now that it bore Kishan Prasad's full weight it lay barely an inch or two out of the water. But at least it held his body clear of the surface.

The fin cut slowly through the water, cruising gently along the flank of a long glassy slope parallel to them, and Alex suffered a spasm of cold, crippling panic. 'Oh God, if only I had a knife,' he said in a whisper, unaware that he had spoken aloud.

'Here,' gasped Kishan Prasad: he fumbled among his wet clothes, the flimsy raft rocking dangerously, and drawing out a knife with a slim wicked eight-inch blade, thrust it into Alex's hand. It was an inadequate enough weapon to pit against the twelve-foot monster who circled warily about them, but the feel of it in his hand gave Alex a sudden surge of hope. It was something. He had read of pearl divers off the coast of Ceylon who fought off sharks with a knife.

He beat the water again and shouted and the creature shot away, hovered and returned. It seemed to hang in the water above him and he realized suddenly that if it came at him while he held to the hen-coop, the rush of its great body would overturn that makeshift raft and dislodge Kishan Prasad. He had forgotten that Kishan Prasad was an enemy whose death he would have welcomed and whom a few short minutes ago he had been passionately regretting that he had not left to die. The man on the raft was a fellow-human and as such they were leagued together against this finny cold-blooded killer from the deeps beneath them.

He released his hold and swam away at a tangent, his eyes on that cruising dorsal fin. The swell lifted it up and once again the creature seemed to hang in the water above him. It came at him quite slowly, and as it came it turned. Alex avoided it with a superhuman effort, kicking backward with all his strength and twisting again to face it. He heard a hoarse shout of warning from Kishan Prasad and the thought flashed through his mind that the boat had come.

'Just in time,' thought Alex grimly. And then he saw a flicker of movement to his left . . . another fin. There was a second shark – a third. They circled him as though merely curious, and he felt the heave of the water under him as the first shark returned to the attack, and somehow he avoided it. Now they would all rush in. He would not wait for them to come at him, and be torn to pieces without a fight. His fingers tightened hard on the haft of the knife and he swam towards the nearest shark.

It was apparently an unexpected movement, for the creature sheered off at lightning speed, and he turned quickly and saw in the slow swell that bore down upon him the swift shape of another coming in. For the flash of a second he saw too, with uncanny vividness, the tiny striped bodies of the pilot fish who raced before and beside it; and then he had dived to meet it and as it rolled to bring the wicked jaws into play he struck with all his strength.

The knife sliced through a foot of the creature's side and was wrenched from his grasp, and there was a cloud of blood in the water. For a moment the other sharks lay motionless and then suddenly the water boiled into foam as they rushed in upon their wounded companion, fighting, snapping and tearing like hounds upon a fox. The dark water was red with blood, and Alex turned and swam desperately away. He was still swimming when someone grabbed his shoulders and shouted above his head, and then hands were pulling at him and he was dragged over a gunwale to tumble gasping and helpless among the feet of the boat's crew.

'That was a near thing,' said the first mate, beating him on the back. 'Touch and go. Here! get down, Mr Prasad. Holy Moses! Look at the brutes, they'll have us over. Hit with oars – *sumjao*.' The boat rocked dangerously as a ten-foot blue shark, attracted by the taint of blood, rubbed along the keel, and the sea seemed alive with triangular fins and lithe rolling bodies. And then they were rowing back to the ship into the eye of the setting sun over a sea that was no longer blue, but black below them and bright gold beyond.

Alex sat up dizzily and grinned at Kishan Prasad, and Kishan Prasad laughed and lifted his head in a brief gesture of salute. For a moment they were no longer enemies, but men who had seen no escape from death and yet by some miracle had escaped it, and were whole and alive. They drank the fiery grog proffered by the first mate and grinned weakly at each other and looked with dazed thankfulness at the clear sky above them while the lascars chattered and tugged at their oars, and the *Glamorgan Castle*, its deck-rails lined with excited cheering passengers, grew larger and nearer and at last loomed solid and safe above them.

Alex was aware, as though through a thick fog, of noise and shouting voices and people who shook his hand and thumped his shoulders. He felt absurdly sleepy and rather as if he were very drunk. It was an effort to keep his head erect and his eyes from closing, and he yawned largely in the faces of the congratulatory passengers, and pushing his way through them, stumbled down to his cabin and collapsed onto his berth, where the ship's doctor, following him, found him so deeply asleep that he did not even wake when his wet clothes were removed and a blanket thrown over him.

He woke early the following morning, feeling refreshed and fitter than he had for many days. The long swim and the violent exertion of the previous evening, followed by almost twelve hours of uninterrupted sleep, had apparently proved more beneficial than the hot idle days and sweltering sleepless nights that had followed on their departure from Malta. His cabin companions had evidently slept on deck, and Alex lay looking about the small cramped space and the low ceiling above his head with a strange new appreciation of mundane things and the miraculous fact of being alive. He rolled out of his bunk, and pulling on a pair of trousers went up on deck to breathe the dawn air.

The sun had not yet risen, but the sky was already bright and the decks glittered with the night dew and the salt water with which a busy group of lascars were washing down the planks. The sea lay colourless in the dawn light except near the ship where it appeared coldly black and clear as glass. The whorls of foam and bubbles sank down into the blackness, still visible a fathom and more below the surface and turning from white to silver to grey until they vanished into nothingness. The deck hatches were strewn with the bodies of those who preferred a cool night under the stars to the close heat of the cabins, and only the lascars were as yet awake.

Alex went aft and leant against the rail, idly watching the long white track of the wake. He heard footsteps behind him and turned to see Kishan Prasad. The two men looked at each other for a moment or two in silence and with the cool, narrowed, calculating look of adversaries who measure swords, and then Kishan Prasad said slowly: 'I wish to thank you——'

'You have nothing to thank me for,' interrupted Alex curtly.

'You mean because had you known that it was I you would not have saved me? Is that indeed the truth? If you had known – and knowing that I could not swim, must drown – you would not have gone after me?'

Alex returned his look with eyes that were hard and level. 'No. I would not have lifted a hand to save you.'

Kishan Prasad bowed gravely as though he had received an answer that he both expected and understood. He said: 'It is for that reason that I come to thank you. Not for what you did for me, but for what you would have done for one of my servants. There are very few who would have risked their lives for . . . a black man and the servant of a black man.'

'You overrate me,' said Alex brusquely. 'There was no risk. I am a strong swimmer.'

'And the sharks?' asked Kishan Prasad gently.

'You force me to admit,' said Alex with a grin, 'that I had clean forgotten that there might be sharks. If I had remembered it, I give you my word that I should not have jumped. So you see, you owe me nothing.'

'Nevertheless,' said Kishan Prasad smiling, 'willingly or unwillingly, you gave me back the life that the Gods would have taken from me. In the past I have intrigued against your race——' He saw the sudden flare in Alex's eyes and laughed, lifting a protesting hand: 'Oh no! That is not evidence – I tell you nothing that you did not already know. And here there is no one to overhear. We two speak under the thorn tree. Your Commissioner will not move against me. That I know.'

'And I also,' said Alex bitterly. 'Are you by any chance telling me that you have suffered a change of heart because I risked my neck to pull you out of the sea?'

Kishan Prasad smiled and shook his head. 'Alas, no. I have suffered no change of heart. In the name of my country and my people and my Gods I will do all in my power to pull down your Company's Raj.'

'And I,' said Alex, 'will do all in my power to get you hanged or transported – for the sake of my countrymen who govern your country.'

'It is well,' said Kishan Prasad gravely. 'We understand one another, and we are not children.'

He twisted a small ring that he wore on his right hand and pulling it off held it out to Alex. It was a trumpery thing of little value, fashioned out of silver in a curious design set with three small red stones that might have been flawed rubies. An odd ornament for the hand of such a man as Kishan Prasad. He said: 'Will you wear this for me? As a token of my gratitude? It is worth less than ten rupees, but it is a talisman that may one day save you from much evil. If ever the day comes, as I pray it will, that the Company's Raj falls and its charter for robbery and confiscation is destroyed, look on that ring and remember Kishan Prasad. For in that day – who knows – it may repay a part of my debt.'

Alex looked at the outstretched hand with a frown in his eyes and made no attempt to disguise his hesitation. Then he reached out and taking it slid it onto the little finger of his right hand and said slowly: 'I did not remember that there might be sharks when I went over that rail yesterday. But you would have had me take your place on that damned hen-coop when you saw them come. I will wear this because it is the gift of a brave man.'

Kishan Prasad put his hands together, the finger-tips touching, bowed gravely above them and turned and walked away.

13

'We shall be in Calcutta tomorrow,' thought Winter. 'Only one more day – and then I shall see Conway!'

It did not seem possible that the long waiting that had begun six years ago in the Long Walk at Ware could be over at last, and that in only two days' time she would no longer be 'Miss Winter' or the Condesa de los Aguilares, but Mrs Conway Barton; driving away from the church with her handsome husband to live happily ever afterwards like a princess in a fairy-tale.

The *Glamorgan Castle* was anchored off the Sandheads awaiting the first light and the turn of the tide when, with the pilot on board, she would begin the slow journey up the Hooghly to Calcutta, and Winter, lying wakeful in her narrow bunk, wondered if Conway would meet her at the mouth of the river or board the ship on the way up – Colonel Moulson seemed to think it possible.

There had been a time during the voyage when she could not picture Conway clearly and his image had become unreal and lifeless – a shadow without substance. She could not explain why this should be so, and she had, obscurely, placed the blame for it on Captain Randall, though she could not have told herself in what way he was responsible. But at least it had been Captain Randall who had been responsible for reinvesting Conway with all his old glamour. The way in which he had brought this about was equally involved and quite as impossible of explanation. It had arisen out of his dramatic rescue of the Indian, Kishan Prasad . . .

Winter had been in her cabin when Lottie screamed, and the sound had been muffled and indistinct. She had heard the thud of running feet on the deck overhead and had been aware of uproar and confusion, and then, through the open port, she had heard the cry of 'man overboard!' and had run up on deck to find it crowded with excited passengers and noisy with bellowed orders to stop the ship – to lower a boat – to come about——

Whistles had shrilled, men had shouted, and Lottie had continued to scream. Winter had taken her by the shoulders and shaken her violently, which had proved instantly efficacious. Lottie had gulped, gasped, drawn breath and poured out the story. Kishan Prasad had fallen overboard – Lottie had seen it – and he could not swim, and Captain Randall had gone in after him.

Winter had been conscious of a sudden cold shock as though she had been hit by something frozen and solid: an icy fist that lashed at her and was gone. She had released Lottie and run to peer over the rails, but the crowd was too thick and she could not see, and she had waited with a strange sense of breathlessness for what seemed like hours while the ship had slowed and circled back.

'Just as well we ain't running under sail,' said Colonel Moulson. 'If there'd been a breath of wind and we'd been carryin' canvas we'd have left 'em miles behind before we could have heaved-to. Steam's a marvellous thing, by George!'

'Can you see them?' demanded Winter urgently.

'Not a sign. But we'll pick 'em up the moment we get a boat out. Sea's as calm as a billiard table; no danger at all, provided they keep afloat. Unless the sharks sight 'em of course. If that happens it will be all over with them. Saw a man fall overboard at Aden once. Sharks got him before we could lower a boat. Tore him to bits. Dreadful sight!'

Mrs Abuthnot screamed faintly and Winter turned so white that the Colonel, afraid that she was about to swoon, hastily excused himself and hurried off to watch the boat being lowered and pulled smartly away under the charge of the first mate.

The hour that followed seemed endless to Winter. The sun was moving down the sky and she watched the shadow of the wheelhouse stretch out across the deck and grow longer and longer. Then, from the mizzentop, a look-out with a telescope who had sighted the two men, and had been shouting at intervals that all was well, put his hands to his mouth and bellowed: '*Shark*!' And once more the deck was in an uproar.

Women screamed and wept and Sophie, who had conceived a passionate though secret admiration for Captain Randall, swooned and had to be carried below; followed by Mrs Abuthnot, whom affection for Alex, and the conviction that he was even now being torn limb from limb and devoured by sharks, had sent off into strong hysterics.

Lottie having collapsed into tears, it was left to Winter and the ever-helpful Mrs Holly to minister to Sophie and her mother. But when Lottie brought the news that both men had been rescued in time and were being rowed back to the ship, Mrs Abuthnot, pausing only to take another strong dose of *sal volatile* and grasp her smelling salts, had hurried up on deck. Winter had followed more slowly. She had heard the shouts and cheers as she left the cabin, and Alex had stumbled down the stairs and passed her without seeing her.

His face appeared drained of all colour and drawn with exhaustion, and he walked as though he were drunk or drugged. The ship's doctor hurried down after him, and Winter went up on deck where the first mate and various passengers were vying with each other to tell the story as Kishan Prasad had told it to them, with embroideries and embellishments of their own.

Winter sat down in a deck-chair, her knees feeling unaccountably weak, and remembering that Alex had once expressed regret that he could not bring himself to murder this man whose life he had just risked his own to save, she was filled with a warm, glowing flood of admiration that went a long way towards expunging the memory of his disloyal attack on Conway.

The admiration, however, had lasted considerably less than twenty-four hours.

She had had no opportunity of speaking to him until half-way through the following morning, when at Mrs Abuthnot's imperious bidding he had come to sit on the deck at her feet under the shade of the awning and to answer innumerable questions. 'Of course it was exceedingly noble of you, dear boy,' said Mrs Abuthnot, handing him a skein of embroidery silk to unravel, 'but quite inconceivably rash. You could well have drowned!'

'In a sea like a mill pond?' inquired Alex lazily. 'Nonsense. No one who could swim a stroke could have drowned in a sea like that, and I'm a strong swimmer. It was extremely pleasant after the heat of these decks, let me tell you.'

'I see that you are determined to make light of it,' said Mrs Abuthnot approvingly. 'But I shall not allow that. To jump unhesitatingly to the rescue of a drowning man in a shark-infested sea was a heroic deed and worthy of the highest praise.'

'Mrs Abuthnot,' said Alex, handing back the skein of silk and receiving another, 'I cannot masquerade as a hero to you, much as I should enjoy doing so. But as I have already been forced to point out to a good many people, I had entirely forgotten that there were such things as sharks. The possibility of meeting any had not so much as crossed my mind, and had it done so I do assure you that I should not have gone in after that man. I should have contented myself with throwing over another hen-coop, and prayer.'

'I do not believe it,' said Mrs Abuthnot with energy.

'Alas, it is only too true. The sight of that shark gave me the worst shock of my life and I hope I may never have another as bad.'

Winter looked up from the embroidery she held in her hands and spoke for the first time:

'Perhaps you had not thought of there being sharks, but you went to the rescue of a man whom you – you had no cause to think well of. That at least was noble.'

Alex regarded her with a distinctly ironical eye. 'I'm afraid not. You see I did not know who it was whom I had gone after.'

'You didn't know?'

'Not until I had reached him; no.'

Winter stared at him wide-eyed. 'But – but if you had known, you would not have left him to drown.'

'Oh yes, I would,' said Alex grimly. 'The gesture was a lamentable mistake on my part, and one which I deeply regret.' He came to his feet, and handing over the unravelled skein of silk to Mrs Abuthnot with a bow and a smile, turned away and left them.

'He does not mean a word of it,' said Mrs Abuthnot comfortably. 'He is just being modest. So truly heroic!'

'Oh, no, he is not,' said Winter scornfully, her eyes sparkling with anger. 'He means every word of it. And he is quite right – he did nothing in the *least* heroic, because he knew quite well that he himself would not drown and he had not even thought of there being sharks. He did not know who had fallen overboard, and may even have thought it was you or Sophie. If he *had* known, he would have let that man drown!'

'How can you say such a thing, Winter?' Sophie's soft voice quivered with indignation.

'Because it's true,' snapped Winter. The reflection that she herself had come close to regarding Captain Randall's exploit with as much admiration, if not more, as the hero-worshipping Sophie, filled her with fury, and the fact that she had been in a fair way to forgiving and forgetting Captain Randall's disloyalty to Conway added immeasurably to her anger.

Conway, she thought, would have sprung to the rescue of a drowning man even if he had known the risks – it would not have occurred to him to stand by and see even an enemy drown. And suddenly, with that conviction, Conway was alive and real again and no longer a thing of pasteboard and straw.

The remainder of the voyage had been uneventful. They had seen a school of whales off Colombo and passed an East Indiaman under full sail by moonlight, looking like some fabulous thing made of silver. They had braved the surf in cockle-shell boats to land at Madras, and had driven through the town in curious carriages shaped like oblong boxes made from Venetian blinds. And now at last they were almost at the end of their long journey.

The tide lapped and gurgled against the sides of the stationary ship, and through the open porthole Winter could see an enormous star, low above the the sea and swinging like a diamond on an invisible chain to the slow rocking movement of the anchored ship. One of the housemaids at Ware had told her that if you wished upon a star your wish would come true, and ever since then, on every clear night, Winter had wished on a star. Always the same wish. That the years would pass quickly until the day that Conway would come for her. Now there was no need to wish that wish any longer, and the blazing brilliance of the star that she could see beyond the cabin porthole seemed to point the difference between tonight and all those other nights, and to be a sparkling omen marking the start of a new life and of so much happiness that she would never need to wish upon a star again – unless, perhaps, it were to wish that Conway might never be disappointed in her.

As she watched, the sky turned to grey and a cock in the galley began to crow. Soon the sun would turn the silt-stained sea to gold, the boatswain's whistles would shrill and there would be a patter of feet on deck and the rattle of the anchor chain. The last day——!

Except for the last few necessities, Winter had completed her packing on the previous afternoon, for she could not bear to waste a moment of that wonderful day. Every foot of the way, the tangled thickets of bamboo, the thatch-roofed huts surrounded by groves of tamarind, jackfruit and custard apple, the low brown land, the temples and the wide, mud-coloured Hooghly with its treacherous shifting shoals and unpredictable currents, was wonderful and exciting to the girl who had passed that way as a child almost a dozen weary years ago, held in the arms of Zobeida who had wept as she looked her last on her homeland.

Every approaching craft, every carriage seen upon either bank, might be one that contained Conway. A horseman riding behind a far belt of trees or a figure carried in a rough palanquin might be he.

Alex Randall, seeing her run to lean over the deck-rail as a river launch approached the ship, felt again the same half-angry, half-exasperated desire to tell her that she must not look like that: she should not let such glowing expectation show on her face for all to see, for before the day was out she would have seen for herself what the years had done to Mr Commissioner Barton, and she would never wear that look again. Watching that young and vulnerable face, Alex thought entirely dispassionately that it would be a pleasure to choke the life out of Mr Barton.

The sky was ablaze with sunset by the time the *Glamorgan Castle* reached the Calcutta anchorage, and boat after boat shot out from the shore bringing relatives and friends of those on board, or coming to fetch the passengers away. Mrs Abuthnot, who had informed Lottie only the day before that any public display of affection was not only intolerable but indelicate, abandoned all reserve and cast herself into the arms of a tubby little gentleman with a cherubic face, silver-white hair and mild blue eyes, who proved to be Colonel Abuthnot, and the reunited family retired to shed happy tears in the privacy of their cabin.

Winter stood apart from the turmoil of welcome and departure, her eyes anxiously scanning every boat. But none contained a familiar face. She had seen Kishan Prasad leave, loaded with scented garlands of flowers and tinsel that had been brought by the friends who had welcomed him; and had watched a boat with two rowers bring an Indian wearing an odd, sandy-coloured uniform out to the ship, and seen Alex Randall go quickly to meet him.

The man had saluted stiffly as he reached the deck and then his brown face had creased into a grin of pure pleasure, and Winter saw Alex's hand go out and grip the man's shoulder, holding it hard, and saw that he was smiling the same smile. For a moment the two men had looked at each other without words, as brothers might look who meet again after a long separation, with affection and relief in each other's safety. Then Alex's hand had dropped and they had both laughed and turned away together, talking rapidly.

The crowded decks emptied and Winter watched anxiously as boat after boat drew away laden with passengers for the shore. At last someone touched her on the arm and she turned quickly. But it was only Captain Randall. There was a look on his face that was dangerously near pity and it stiffened Winter's slim shoulders and brought her chin up with a jerk. She looked very young, thought Alex, and despite the haughtiness of that lifted chin, very frightened and wary. He said bluntly: 'He has not been able to come. My orderly has brought letters from Lunjore.'

Winter took the proffered packet with a hand that was not quite steady. Her fingers closed on it so tightly that the stiff paper crackled and she could feel tears prickling behind her eyelids, but she forced them back. If she let Alex Randall see tears in her eyes she would never forgive herself. Or him. She said: 'Thank you,' in a small cold voice, and Alex turned away abruptly and left her.

Winter caught at the rail to steady herself. She found that she was trembling, and the tears that she would not let Alex see stood in her eyes so that she saw the river and the trees and the houses on the bank through a swimming mist. The disappointment was almost too bitter to be borne. Today was to have been the end of a long journey, but the journey had not ended after all. She looked down at the letter she held clenched in her hand, and after a moment broke the seal.

Pressure of work, wrote Conway, had made it impossible after all for him to meet her in Calcutta. She must know how great a disappointment this was to him. As great, he knew, as it would be to her. But duty must come first and he was persuaded that she would not have him neglect his duty even for her. He had written to Randall asking him to make all arrangements for her journey north, and as he had heard that the Abuthnots, who had so kindly escorted her out, were proceeding to Delhi, she had better remain under their protection and travel as far as Delhi with them. It was a little out of the way, but since he himself would have occasion to go there in the near future and would be staying with the Commissioner, Mr Simon Fraser, it would suit very well. They could be married in Delhi and spend their honeymoon in that historic city, visiting the various places of interest with which the ancient Mogul capital abounded. It would mean a delay of a few more weeks, but what were a few more weeks when they had the rest of their lives before them? He hoped that she had had a pleasant voyage and remained, as ever, her affectionate, devoted husband-to-be . . .

The writing was straggling and uneven and the lines ran crookedly across the page. He must have been very tired when he wrote it, thought Winter with loving compassion. Tired and disappointed. It made her own disappointment seem a selfish emotion. It was noble of Conway – and so like him! – to put duty before personal happiness. Dear, dear Conway!

She crushed his letter between her hands, pressing it to her breast and fighting a desire to put her head down on the top bar of the deck-rail and cry. But she must not cry here on the open deck, and there was no privacy anywhere on the ship that day. To let her bitter disappointment be seen might be taken by others to imply a criticism of Conway, and that would be unforgivable in her. She turned away from the rail and walked steadily down to her cabin with her head high, her face calm and composed and her eyes very dry and bright.

Mrs Abuthnot was motherly and sympathetic. Dear Alex had already informed her of the state of affairs and had handed her a most *charming* letter from Mr Barton. So disappointing! But then life in India was sadly full of such disappointments. One had to learn to bear them. Officers in the service of the Company were not their own masters, and India, said Mrs Abuthnot profoundly, was not England. Naturally, dear Winter would remain in her care; it would be delightful to have her! – although she feared that it would mean some delay, as Colonel Abuthnot had official business to transact in Calcutta and Barrackpore which might keep them here for a little time. He had arranged for them to stay with a friend – Mr Shadwell, a Calcutta merchant. The Shadwells, she knew, would be only too pleased to welcome Winter as an additional guest, for Horace Shadwell had known her Uncle Ebenezer well. And what could be more delightful than to travel to Delhi in company? Dear Lottie was overjoyed at the prospect!

The Shadwells' house proved to be a palatial two-storeyed mansion on Garden Reach surrounded by lawns and gardens that fronted the river, and to Winter's relief she was given a room to herself.

She shut the door behind her and leant tiredly against it, released at last from the necessity of keeping her features composed and her lips smiling. She could cry now that there was no one to see, and let tears relieve some of the strain and the pain of disappointment that the day had brought her.

But she did not cry. She looked about the huge, high-ceilinged room with its whitewashed walls and long french windows opening onto a deep verandah. A room that was as utterly unlike an English bedroom as the vast, slow-moving Hooghly was unlike an English stream. And as she looked, the tight band that had seemed to be tied about her heart relaxed, and the fever of excitement and the leaden weight of disappointed hope both faded.

She walked slowly across the room and out onto the verandah, her wide skirts rustling softly on the matting. Below her a long lawn sloped down between thick groves of trees to where the river ran gold in the brief twilight. The sky was a wash of clear pale green in which the first stars were already ghostly points of light, and the evening air was full of sounds: half-forgotten yet wholly familiar sounds. Conches blaring in a temple; a distant throb of tom-toms; peacocks calling and a jackal-pack wailing; the barking of pariah dogs, and all the many noises of an Indian city. The air smelt of sun-baked dust and cow-dung fires, of wood-smoke, marigolds and jasmine and the rank scent of the river, while in the gathering dusk a myriad faintly glinting pin-points of light spangled the bamboo-brakes, and overhead a line of dark shapes winged their way across the garden – the fireflies and the fruit bats that old Sir Ebenezer had wished that he might see once more . . .

Winter leaned on the broad verandah rail and drew a long, long breath of happiness. It did not matter any longer that Conway had been unable to come to Calcutta to meet her, or that tomorrow would not, after all, be her wedding-day. She could wait. She had come home.

The travellers awoke next morning to a babble of birdsong: crows, minas, jays, parrots, '*saht-bai*' and doves, whistling, screeching and cooing.

The sky was yellow with dawn and air still cool, and the fruit bats were coming home to roost as the birds awoke; hanging themselves up in the deepest shadows of the mango trees and quarrelling and flapping as they jostled for sleeping-space. The river too was already awake and noisy. A paddle-steamer churned past on its way to Allahabad, and skiffs, country boats and slender *dinghies* punted by boatmen wielding long bamboo poles drifted by. A small striped squirrel chattered indignantly from the scented masses of flowering creeper that clothed one of the verandah pillars, doves cooed upon the cornices and a flight of parrots flew screaming overhead.

Their scream was echoed by Lottie, whose room gave onto the same verandah, and a moment later Lottie herself, clad in a pink cotton peignoir over a cambric nightgown and with her soft fair curls in tangled disarray, appeared in Winter's bedroom. An Indian had walked into her room, she announced in trembling tones. 'A *man*, Winter! He did not even knock . . . he just walked in. I thought I should have swooned with fright.'

'What did he want?' inquired Winter.

'Oh, he did not want anything. He brought me tea and fruit. He just put them on a table beside my bed and went out again. Don't laugh, Winter! It is most unkind in you. I was never so frightened in my life.'

'That was only the bearer,' said Winter, continuing to laugh. 'He brought me some too. You will have to get used to it, Lottie darling. I do not think servants in India ever knock.'

'I shall *never* get used to it!' declared Lottie, shuddering.

'Oh yes, you will. I prophesy that within a year you will find yourself quite unable to support life or run the simplest *ménage* without the assistance of at least a dozen servants, with another ten for Edward. Mrs Shadwell informed me last night that they run a very modest establishment here – a mere thirty-five servants!'

But the mention of Edward had instantly diverted Lottie, who blushed pinkly and said with a small gasp: 'Oh Winter, Edward is to call on Papa today. Mama has told him all, and Papa has been so kind. And only think – he knows Edward's uncle! They were at school together. He would not commit himself, but – but he did not look at all displeased, and he said that it was hard for a father to find his daughter again after so many years only to lose her before he had time to know her. That does not sound as though he meant to refuse his consent, does it?'

'No, of course it does not. What possible objection could he have? Edward is most eligible. And so handsome,' added Winter with a twinkle.

'He is handsome, is he not?' sighed Lottie, accepting the tribute as a simple statement of fact. And indeed to her adoring eyes Edward's blunt-nosed, blue-eyed, freckled face and flaming red hair embodied all that was admirable in masculine good looks – although barely two months ago her mental vision of the ideal male would have been found to resemble the late Lord Byron; a gentleman who had borne no recognizable likeness to Lieutenant Edward English.

'You are so lucky, Winter,' sighed Lottie. 'I do not think that it is fair. You are a whole year younger than I am, and yet you are going to be married in a few weeks' time whereas I shall have to wait for at least half a year, and probably a great deal longer. Mama says that an engagement of only six months would be considered scandalously short, but Edward hopes to be able to persuade Papa to allow it so that we may be married in the spring. Do you think he will agree? It is delightful, of course, to be with Papa again, but—— Oh, I know that it sounds most undutiful in me, but he is not *Edward*!'

But as it happened, Lottie had not to wait for as long as that.

She was to be married within a few weeks of their arrival in Delhi, for Edward had received information – unofficial but believed to be reliable – that his Regiment, who were Queen's and not Company's troops, might be sent to augment Admiral Seymour's forces in China early in the New Year. In the light of this information he desired to get married as soon as possible, in case such a calamity occurred. He had, he said, already known Lottie for two months, during which time he had seen her daily, and this surely constituted a long acquaintance, for had they been in England he might well have seen her at the most once or twice a week even if they had been betrothed. There was little point, he argued, in being separated from her for the next few months, only to be married on the eve of his departure and when faced with the prospect of indefinite separation. Let them at least enjoy a short spell of happiness, and then if the worst occurred and he was indeed ordered to China in the following year, they could face it with more fortitude as husband and wife. While should he be killed, added Edward bluntly, his wife would be amply provided for, since all he possessed would revert to her.

From this last and strictly worldly point of view Edward's arguments carried considerable weight, and when reinforced by the appeals of sentiment and emotion they had carried the day, for Lottie, upon hearing of the possibility of her Edward being sent to China, had instantly swooned away, and only the promise of an early wedding had prevented her – upon being revived with the aid of burnt feathers and hartshorn – from repeating this affecting gesture.

Mrs Abuthnot, alarmed by her daughter's pallor and despair, had withdrawn all opposition, and the entire party had repaired to the drawing-room where Mr Shadwell, despite the unsuitability of hour, called for champagne so that all might drink to the health and happiness of the betrothed pair.

It was at this point that a servant announced Captain Randall, who was greeted affectionately by Mrs Abuthnot, introduced to the Shadwells and once again thanked for his assistance on the journey by Colonel Abuthnot. Informed of the betrothal and wedding plans of Lottie and Edward he congratulated them in a somewhat preoccupied voice, and announced that he had only called in order to make his adieux. He regretted that he could not accompany them to Delhi, but he could not delay his return to Lunjore any longer.

Winter had spoken a few stiffly formal words of thanks when he had shaken hands with her, to which Alex – his eyes on a massive clock at the far side of the room – had replied briefly that he was happy to have been of any assistance to her. He was quite obviously in a hurry and impatient to be off, and having swallowed half a glass of champagne with absent-minded haste had shaken hands with the assembled company and left. The rattle of his carriage wheels died away on the long drive, and Winter was astounded and disturbed to find that the sound brought her a sudden feeling of being alone and unprotected. Which was of course absurd, for was not Colonel Abuthnot here to take his place and see that she came to no harm?

But as the slow days dragged by she was surprised to find how much she missed him. Not the man himself, but the feeling he had given her that as long as he was there she was safe. She had not stopped to analyse it, and she would not do so now. But the fact that he had gone, and that it would never again be any part of his duty to see to her comfort and safety, did not bring her any feeling of relief, but rather a vague sensation of insecurity and loss. Which must, she decided, be because he had been a link with Conway.

Edward English left for Meerut on the day following his momentous interview with Colonel Abuthnot, and Lottie found what comfort she could in planning her wedding, which was to take place late in October. But their stay in Calcutta was by no means spent in idleness, for the kindly Shadwells arranged numerous entertainments for their guests, and cards of invitation for balls and assemblies, including a State Ball at Government House, arrived at the house on Garden Reach in an apparently never-ending stream.

Mrs Gardener-Smith and Delia were also in Calcutta, for Colonel Gardener-Smith having obtained three months' leave, they had decided to remain there for a week or two in order to rest and recuperate after the long voyage, and they had driven over several times to visit the Abuthnot ladies and accompany them on shopping expeditions to the city.

Calcutta, as the capital and headquarters of the Governor-General and the Council, and seat of the Supreme Government, had a reputation to keep up in the way of gaiety, and the State Ball had been a revelation to Lottie and Sophie, who had never attended such a function before. Even Winter, accustomed to the almost unrelieved black and white attire of the men who had danced at Ware and in the London ballrooms, had imagined for one dazzled instant that the Governor-General was giving a fancy-dress ball.

Men in the gorgeous dress-uniforms of regiments whose names were rarely heard outside India, regiments of Cavalry, of Irregular Horse, of Bengal Infantry and Artillery – men wearing the pale blue and gold of the Light Cavalry, the canary yellow of Skinner's Horse, the green of the Rifle companies and the scarlet of Infantry regiments – vied with the shimmering silks and frothing tarlatans of feminine ball-gowns in richness of colour and glitter of gold lace, and outnumbered the women by six to one.

Moving among them in more sober attire, crows among a flock of peacocks, were the rich Calcutta merchants – men such as Mr Shadwell – or, distinguished by ribbons and orders, the members of the Governor-General's Council and high officers of the East India Company. Indian guests, many of them ablaze with jewels and wearing brightly coloured brocades and muslins, their dark faces often no darker than the sun-burned skins above the high tight collars of dress uniforms, mingled with the company but did not dance, and Lottie commented with surprise on the fact that there were no Indian ladies present.

'In the East, women are kept in their proper places,' said Colonel Abuthnot with a twinkle. 'An Indian gentleman would consider it highly improper to allow his womenfolk to gallivant about in public semi-naked. As for permitting them to be clasped about the waist to prance to music in the arms of a strange man, such a thing would be unthinkable.'

'George, how *can* you speak like that!' – Mrs Abuthnot was genuinely shocked. 'Surely you do not disapprove of dancing? As for being semi-naked, that is the *grossest* exaggeration, and I wonder at you for saying such things before your daughters.'

'I did not say that I disapproved of dancing, my love,' retorted Colonel Abuthnot mildly. 'But I confess I have often thought that our Western dances must appear exceedingly abandoned when viewed by Eastern eyes. And you must admit that modern fashions display a great deal of the female form.'

'No such thing!' declared his wife indignantly. 'Why, when one considers that our grandmothers thought a mere slip of wetted muslin sufficient for evening wear, I cannot imagine how you can regard the present fashions as immodest.'

'Oh, I will concede that they are an improvement on the fashions of the Regency,' admitted the Colonel, 'but it never fails to surprise me that a woman who feels it necessary to conceal herself from the waist downwards in a vast cage of skirts and whalebone, should be able, without a blush, to make such a display of arms, shoulders and bosom. Not, as a European, that I have any complaint to make. I merely wonder what our oriental friends think of it.'

Mrs Abuthnot looked ruffled, but the retort that she had been about to utter died at the sight of Delia Gardener-Smith who happened to pass at that moment on the arm of a scarlet-coated officer, for Miss Gardener-Smith so amply bore out the truth of Colonel Abuthnot's statements. The hoops of Delia's crinoline supported at least twenty yards of lime-green taffeta trimmed with blonde, and her wide, swaying skirts permitted only the barest glimpse of small satin slippers; but the tight-fitting décolleté bodice allowed for a lavish display of plump white bosom and dimpled shoulders.

Mrs Abuthnot flushed uncomfortably, and furtively twitching her light lace shawl closer about her own ample shoulders, cast an anxious eye over her own two daughters. But neither Lottie nor Sophie, small-boned and fragile, could have lent even the most revealing of gowns a look of abandon, and the bodices of their modest pink and blue tarlatan dresses were provided, unlike Delia's, with discreet fichus and small puffed sleeves.

Winter's dress was a different matter, for she wore one of the trousseau ball-gowns selected by Lady Adelaide; a white moiré-antique of imperial magnificence, draped with flounces of Brussels lace looped up at intervals with pearls, and with a bodice cut every inch as low as that worn by Delia. But the carriage of her slim shoulders, and the tilt of her small head with its weight of smoothly netted black hair, had an unconscious dignity that forbade any comparison with Miss Gardener-Smith's lavish display of dimpled flesh.

Mrs Abuthnot, her stout and comfortable person suitably arrayed in *gros-vert* taffeta shot with black, confided in an uneasy whisper to Delia's mama that it was an odd circumstance that toilettes which had seemed unexceptional in England should appear almost daring when worn in the East: 'I suppose it is because there are so many Indian guests present tonight,' she concluded unhappily.

Mrs Gardener-Smith bristled slightly and observed that for her part she considered the present fashions quite *charming*, and that several people had complimented her upon Delia's appearance. Lady Canning indeed had been more than kind. *Such* a pleasant creature! – although to be sure it was a pity that she had elected to wear crimson, as it made her appear sadly pale. It was probable that she found the climate trying, this being her first visit to the East. As for the Governor-General, though Mrs Gardener-Smith had not yet spoken to him, she considered that he too did not look to be in the best of health.

Lord Canning's health, as it happened, was excellent; but he was having a troublesome time. He had hoped for a quiet term in office in succession to the dynamic Dalhousie whose reforms were said to have launched India on an era of enlightenment and progress, but India was proving a bed of thorns rather than roses.

The new Governor-General, a remarkably handsome man in his early forties with a noble brow and a somewhat womanish mouth, had taken over the reins from Lord Dalhousie less than eight months previously, and had early discovered that his predecessor's confident prediction that all was well with India was unfounded. Dalhousie had enlarged the bounds of Empire to a previously unthinkable degree, but there had been no corresponding enlargement of the number of Company's men needed to control and administer it. The Bengal Army had been stripped of officers, who had been sent on special service to administer newly acquired districts, act as judges, build roads and bridges or pacify revolting populations, and efficiency in the regiments had suffered in consequence. A situation to which the new Governor-General was not blind, but which he found himself unable to rectify.

The annexation of Oudh had been one of the last acts of Lord Dalhousie's reign, but the settling of the province had fallen to Lord Canning, whose appointment of Mr Coverley Jackson as Chief Commissioner of this newest of the Company's possessions had not proved a happy one. Mr Jackson appeared to be more interested in conducting a lively paper war with his subordinates, Gubbins and Ommaney, than in the affairs of Oudh. Mr Gubbins, equally irascible, had entered with enthusiasm into the combat, and the hapless province – the main recruiting ground for the Company's Sepoy Army – was left to limp along in chaos while its chief British administrators expended a large part of their time and energy in mutual recrimination and in formulating charges and counter-charges which they dispatched almost daily to Calcutta.

To add to Lord Canning's worries war clouds were massing over Persia, and he knew that if war were to be declared he would be required to send troops from India which could be ill spared. There was also the problem of Wajid Ali, the deposed King of Oudh, who had settled in Calcutta, bringing with him a large following of relatives and retainers who lived a life of idleness and occupied themselves with intrigue and the formulation of endless complaints against the British officers in Lucknow who, they alleged, were inflicting disgraceful suffering and indignities upon the dispossessed nobles of the state, plundering their possessions, turning their women into the streets, and using their palaces to house horses and dogs.

The Marquis of Dalhousie, sailing away from India towards an early death, imagined that he had left behind him peaceful agricultural acres reclaimed, in effect, from the savage forests of medievalism and barbarity. But the dragon's teeth that had been sown in them were springing up under the feet of his successor, and Lord Canning watched his carefree guests dancing the waltz in the ballroom of Government House with an abstracted eye and a mind that was on other matters.

Colonel Abuthnot, who was no dancer, left his wife to gossip among the older women and keep a watchful eye upon Lottie, Sophie and Winter, and removed himself to the more congenial company of several like-minded gentlemen who were smoking a quiet cigar in an ante-room some distance from the ballroom. His appearance was hailed by a portly civilian whose high stock seemed to be in some danger of choking him:

'Hullo, Abuthnot – you're just the man I wanted to see. Fallon here has been talkin' a lot of twaddle about disaffection among some of the regiments around Delhi way. That's your part of the world, ain't it? I've told him that he's too credulous by half. The Army's as sound as a bell!'

'Well . . . there have been rumours of course,' admitted Colonel Abuthnot cautiously, 'but I have certainly had no trouble with my own men. 'Evening, General. 'Evening, Fallon.'

'Pah – *rumours*!' snorted the stout civilian scornfully. 'There are always rumours. Wouldn't be India without 'em. But it's only the alarmists who go quackin' about, takin' them seriously.'

Colonel Fallon's bronzed countenance took on a distinct tinge of purple. 'I resent that aspersion, sir! I am no alarmist. But neither am I a Government ostrich burying my head in the sands of complacency. I tell you that there are dangerous ideas stirring among the sepoys. Ideas that we have fostered ourselves – or done nothing to prevent. Grievances that we have given insufficient attention to.'

'Such as what, sir?' demanded the first speaker bristling. 'The sepoy is better fed, better treated and better paid than ever before.'

'Ah, that's the trouble,' cut in an elderly man with fierce white moustaches, who wore the uniform of a famous Bengal infantry regiment. 'They used to be as tough as hickory sticks in my young days; but nowadays we pamper 'em. Yes, by God! we pamper and pet 'em as though we were running a demned girls' school instead of an army. The whole thing's going soft.'

'Not soft,' snapped Colonel Fallon. 'Rotten. Rotten from top to bottom. Half the younger officers don't even know their men, and the rest of them are for ever being removed from regimental duty on special appointment to civil posts – or the staff. Then there's all this damned Brahminism. We should have done something to limit it.'

A tall handsome man with cold eyes and a marked air of fashion added a languid voice to the discussion: 'Brahminism? Pray enlighten an ignorant globe-trotter, Colonel Fallon. I was not aware that there were political parties in this country.'

'It is not a political party, Lord Carlyon; it is an aspect of Hinduism. The Brahmins – the twice born – are the priestly caste of the Hindus and as such are held in great reverence by all other castes. There was at one time an attempt to limit the employment of Brahmins in the ranks, but they have enlisted as Rajpoots and Chutreeahs, yet kept their sacred rights and privileges – to the grave detriment of discipline.'

'How sir? Do you mean to tell me that the Company enlists priests as fighting men?'

'They are not priests in the ordinary sense,' explained Mr Halliwell, the portly civilian. 'They are the hereditary members of the highest of all castes. One can only be born a Brahmin, not become one. And no Hindu of a lower caste dare offend them, for fear of the fearful penalties that would fall upon him not only in this world but the next.'

'Which leads to endless trouble in the ranks,' put in Colonel Fallon, 'because they hang together like members of a secret society. One Brahmin will not report another, and it is no uncommon thing to see an Indian officer of a lower caste grovelling to a mere sepoy who happens to be a Brahmin. It rots discipline, and we should have put a stop to it long ago; clapped a limit onto the number we recruited, and kept the whole Army on a lower caste level. It is the Brahmins who are at the back of all this present trouble.'

'What trouble, sir?' inquired Lord Carlyon in a bored voice. 'I understood Mr Halliwell here to say that reports of trouble were entirely without foundation.'

'So they are,' snorted Mr Halliwell. 'No foundation. Lot of chicken-hearted flap-doodle.'

'Henry Lawrence ain't exactly my notion of a chicken-heart,' murmured a thin man with a brown, nutcracker face who wore the blue and silver of a Punjab cavalry regiment.

Mr Halliwell swung round on the speaker, his face above the high stock becoming dangerously empurpled: 'I have every respect for Sir Henry's capabilities as an administrator,' he said angrily, 'but the man's a demned nigger-lover! He was against the Oudh annexation, and made such a devil of a nuisance of himself that Dal' had to put him in his place pretty sharply.'

'Sir Henry was not the only one whom his Lordship put in his place,' said the thin man drily. 'Seem to remember him doin' the same to Napier in '50 – and for much the same reason.'

'Two of a kind,' retorted Mr Halliwell. 'Alarmists, both of 'em. Sir Charles would have it that the Bengal Army was on the verge of mutiny and the Empire in danger. Quite fantastic – and he was proved wrong!'

'If you mean that the danger was temporarily averted owing to the prompt action taken by Sir Charles, yes,' said Colonel Fallon with a snap. 'But the fact remains that the whole Army noted and discussed the disagreement between their Commander-in-Chief and the Governor-General. The matter became common talk in every bazaar, and did us a great disservice, for the men not only saw their Commander-in-Chief forced to resign, but realized that their conquerors were divided in their councils. They also learned something far more dangerous. I think that you must have forgotten, sir, that the disaffection that Sir Charles Napier feared might lead to mutiny arose out of disappointment over pay and allowances, which he attempted to remedy himself.'

'And wrongly! And wrongly!' blared Mr Halliwell. 'It is not the province of the Army to decide such matters. That rests upon the decision of the Civil Government, who——'

'Who do not know the mind of the sepoy!' countered Colonel Fallon angrily. 'Are we never to learn by our mistakes?'

He was interrupted by a large blond gentleman whose countenance was adorned by a magnificent set of Dundreary whiskers and whose manner suggested – correctly – the House of Commons. Mr Joseph Leger-Green, who had lost his seat in the last election, was but newly arrived in Calcutta. He intended to make a short stay in the Orient with the object of writing a book on the subject of 'Our Colonial Possessions', and had already compiled an impressive collection of notes. He turned now on Colonel Fallon and fixed him with a glittering eye:

'May I ask what mistakes you refer to, Colonel? I confess to being at sea.'

'I am sorry, sir,' apologized Colonel Fallon. 'This must be an exceedingly tedious discussion for you. Let us abandon it.'

'On the contrary, Colonel. I am intensely interested. I intend,' said Mr Leger-Green impressively, 'to study the whole question of our foreign possessions during my tour. What question of pay and allowances do you refer to?'

The Colonel took another deep draught from the glass in his hand and regarded his interlocutor critically. Like most of his kind he had little use for visiting writers and politicos who arrived in Calcutta for a brief stay in the cold weather and returned to pose as experts on all Eastern questions, but the subject under discussion was one on which he felt strongly. He said:

'The sepoys, sir, were granted special allowances for service outside British-held territory. We have used them to conquer vast new provinces which, once annexed, we have pronounced British and thereafter, with short-sighted parsimony, cancelled the "foreign" allowance of all sepoys serving there. The sepoys resent annexation at the best of times, but when it is followed by loss of allowances, that resentment is gravely aggravated. They resented it in Sind and later in the Punjab, and finally resorted to mutiny. The mutinies were put down. But concessions were made; and because they were made as the result of mutiny the sepoy gained the impression that they were made from fear, which has given him a sense of power . . .

'The disasters of the Afghan War shook his belief in the infallibility of the British, the open quarrel between the Commander-in-Chief and the Governor-General showed him that his British rulers were divided against each other, and the concessions that followed the outbreaks of '49 and '50 have fostered the belief that we fear his strength. Lord Dalhousie, in common with many others, imagined that because the surface appeared calm there were no strong or treacherous currents beneath it. But I venture to think that his Lordship had a less intimate knowledge of the sepoy than Sir Charles Napier – and less understanding of the Eastern mind than Sir Henry Lawrence!'

'*Pshaw*!' exclaimed Mr Halliwell vigorously. 'As Governor-General his Lordship had the benefit of the best-informed opinions in India. Besides, everyone knows that Sir Henry is a dreamer and an impractical idealist. His brother John is worth a dozen of him – more sense and less sentimentality. These people don't appreciate sentimentality. They take it for weakness, and by George, they're right. The strong hand, that's what they need.'

'Oh, I agree with you, sir,' said Colonel Fallon. 'The worst turn anyone ever did the Army was Bentinck's folly in abolishing corporal punishment. If anything encouraged weakened discipline, it was that. Our Indian officers were the strongest against it. I had a deputation of 'em who told me that if we abolished corporal punishment the bad elements in the Army would cease to fear and would one day turn upon us. Yet we continue to flog British troops, and what is more we permit our sepoy soldiers to witness such floggings. We must be mad. And now there is this final folly of Oudh——'

'Sir!' began Mr Halliwell hotly, but was unable to continue, for once again the smooth tones of Mr Leger-Green intervened:

'I am greatly interested in this question of Oudh,' said Mr Leger-Green. 'I have had several interviews with the ex-King. Pray, why do you consider it a folly? Taking the humanitarian view——'

'I was speaking from a purely military one,' said Colonel Fallon impatiently. 'We recruit the bulk of our sepoys from Oudh, and they had certain privileges in the state as servants of the Company. One of which was the right of appeal in cases of law to the British Resident, so that an Indian judge, if a sepoy was up before him, knew that, theoretically at least, the

Resident was that sepoy's advocate, and therefore walked warily. This privilege was so prized that almost every family in Oudh had at least one member serving in the Bengal Army. But now that every citizen of Oudh is equally under the Company's law, that privilege has gone, with many others, and there is no longer any special advantage in being in the service of the Company.'

Colonel Abuthnot, who had so far taken no part in the discussion, coughed gently and remarked in a diffident voice: 'I agree that the recent annexation has caused a good deal of ill-feeling, yet in my opinion it is this matter of foreign service and the General Services Enlistment Act that has given rise to any uneasiness that may prevail in some regiments. It will pass, of course. But they are bound to regard it with some suspicion to begin with.'

Mr Leger-Green turned to the speaker and produced a small notebook in which he jotted down a hurried line of script: 'The General Services Enlistment Act, did you say? And what is that?'

'Service overseas, sir. The Bengal sepoy enlisted on the understanding that he should not be required to cross the sea.'

'Caste again,' interpolated Colonel Fallon. 'The men believe that crossing the sea would deprive them of their caste, and they would have to pay heavily to the priests on their return to be cleansed of the defilement. But the Governor-General, with the approval of Mr Halliwell here and his friends in the Council, recently issued a General Order to the effect that no recruit would in future be accepted who would not undertake to go wherever his services might be required. And that means Burma, sir! – or Persia – or China. Is it not understandable that a caste-ridden, bigoted and superstitious people are willing to believe any agitator who whispers that the British plan to destroy their caste so that they may become willing tools of the Company, prepared to go anywhere and do anything we tell them in order to gratify our lust for conquest?'

'Rubbish!' exploded Mr Halliwell. 'You exaggerate grossly, Colonel.'

'I think not, sir. I think I may claim to have met and conversed with more of the people of this country than you gentlemen in Calcutta. Mohammedans and Hindus alike have regarded the advent of railways and telegraphs with the gravest suspicion, and when we permit the Missionary Societies to publish a manifesto to the effect that our trains and steamships, by facilitating the material union of all races of men, are to be the instruments for bringing about their spiritual union under one Faith – ours! – it is not to be wondered at that the wildest rumours are given credence.'

'Am I to take it, Colonel Fallon,' said Mr Halliwell contemptuously, 'that you consider your own Regiment to be a hotbed of sedition and unrest?'

A dark spot of colour burned beneath the brick-red of Colonel Fallon's sun-burnt cheeks and his hand made a small instinctive gesture towards his dress-sword, and fell again. He said hotly: 'No, sir. I thank God that my own men are loyal! But I am not blind to the attacks that are being made upon both their loyalty and their credulity by agitators and trouble-makers. Neither am I blind to the fact that we have done our best to give the sepoy an overweening sense of his own importance, while at the same time reducing his respect for authority. The commanding officer of his regiment, who should be the final arbiter of his fate, may neither reward nor punish him according to his deserts. I and my fellow colonels are reduced to impotence by red tape, and our decisions overruled by Headquarters. The only advancement an Indian may obtain is by seniority. Merit is apparently of no importance, and——'

A tall man with a thin grey beard and wearing the insignia of a Brigadier General said coldly: 'You forget yourself, Colonel.'

Colonel Fallon turned quickly and the flush faded from his cheeks as he became aware that he had permitted his temper to lead him into openly expressed criticism of military policy, but his indignation was supported by the wine he had drunk and he was in any event no coward. He returned the Brigadier's cold gaze with composure and said hardily: 'Perhaps, sir. But I do not forget that our native troops number two hundred and thirty-three thousand men, while the European soldiery totals barely more than forty-five thousand of all arms. Those are sobering figures, sir.'

'*I* do not find them so,' declared Mr Halliwell. 'It is well known that one Britisher is a match for fifty Asiatics any day. Are you not agreed, gentlemen?'

There was a chorus of assent and Colonel Fallon said sharply: 'That, if I may say so, is a remark that could only be made by a civilian and a politician! I will bid you good evening, sir.' He bowed stiffly and walked angrily away.

'Disgraceful!' puffed Mr Halliwell indignantly. 'Man's a menace! a rumour-monger. Taken to nerves and the vapours like some mewling female. He ain't fit to command troops if he's started listening to that sort of flap-doodle.'

'Two hundred and thirty-three thousand . . . !' It was the ex-Member for Chillbury and Howersford who spoke, and his mellifluous voice had a startled note in it. 'And how many British did he say? Forty-five thousand odd? It is indeed a sobering thought. You are quite sure that there is no danger to be apprehended? I had intended to pay a brief visit to Delhi and the interior but——'

'I assure you, sir,' said Mr Halliwell, 'there is no need for any anxiety. The country is pacified from end to end and basks, if I may say so, in the beneficial sunshine of our benevolent rule. As for the Bengal Army, it is loyal to the core – I am sure that all you gentlemen will agree with me.'

'Undoubtedly,' concurred the grey-bearded Brigadier. 'The finest army in the world! Naturally, when one reflects that they have served us for a century, there are bound to have been a few unpleasant incidents from time to time. But they mean nothing. Mere ripples. The vast mass of the country and the Army are well content. In fact I can safely say they have never been more so. Those who prate of disaffection are cranks and alarmists, but fortunately they are few in number. If you intend to visit Delhi, sir, Colonel Abuthnot here can tell you more about it than I can. His Regiment is stationed there, and I am quite sure that he does not consider them to be on the verge of revolt.'

'Hardly, sir,' said Colonel Abuthnot with a smile, 'or I should not be taking my wife and daughters to Delhi.'

'Indeed? That is most reassuring.' The ex-Member of Parliament appeared relieved. 'I cannot suppose that you would contemplate putting your wife and daughters in any danger, and if the ladies can proceed in safety, there can be no cause for anxiety. I had intended to venture into Oudh, should time permit, in order that I might be able to gain first-hand information on this newest addition to our territorial possessions. I have been given a letter of introduction to a Mr Coverley Jackson——'

'What is that about Coverley Jackson?' inquired a new voice, and the group turned as one to see their host advancing upon them. 'Are you contemplating a visit to Lucknow, Mr Leger-Green?'

'Only if time permits, your Excellency. I have an introduction to Mr Coverley Jackson from a mutual friend.'

'Ah yes,' said Lord Canning. 'Competent fellow Jackson – if only he were not so quarrelsome.'

'You're looking fagged, Charles,' remarked Lord Carlyon. 'India don't appear to agree with you. Too many social functions and too much heat.'

'And too much work,' said the Governor-General with a smile. 'You should try it, Arthur. It would at least have the charm of novelty.'

'Now that is too bad of you, Charles,' protested his Lordship indolently. 'I work like a demned nigger.'

'You surprise me. At what, may I ask?'

'Keeping boredom at bay. And here I am flogging round the globe in proof of it.'

'Stay here awhile and try some real work instead,' advised Lord Canning. 'We can use even someone as ornamentally useless as yourself.'

'Then you must be devilish hard up for hands, Charles.'

'We are; or we shall be if this Persian business blows up into anything. The annexation of Oudh has stretched our resources to the limit. But this is no time for such dull talk. You gentlemen are neglecting your duty; you should be dancing.'

'We leave that to our juniors, your Excellency,' said Mr Halliwell. 'Every lady is at least three-deep in would-be partners already, and such old fogeys as ourselves would receive short shrift from them.'

'Speak for yourself, Halliwell,' said the Brigadier, straightening his befrogged tunic. 'I intend to dance the lancers with my wife – if I can persuade her from the whist table.'

'Bravo, General!' approved Lord Canning. 'I trust that the rest of you intend to follow such an intrepid lead. A word with you, Arthur——' The Governor-General took Lord Carlyon's arm and moved away in the direction of the ballroom.

'What's on your Excellency's mind?' inquired Carlyon, his lazy-lidded eyes unexpectedly observant. 'You were not by any chance serious just now?'

'When I suggested that I could use your services? Certainly.'

'My dear Charles! In what capacity? To dance with the ladies who attend your crushes? It is the most that I am capable of – and then only providing they are pretty. I cannot dance with a plain woman. I lose all sense of rhythm and am instantly abroad.'

'You underrate yourself, Arthur. I know you to be a superlative horseman and a first-class shot.'

The younger man stopped suddenly and turned to regard his host narrowly. He said slowly: 'What exactly do you mean by that? Do you too think as that Colonel in there – that there is going to be trouble?'

'What Colonel? Was someone prophesying trouble?'

'Fallon, I believe the name was. Elderly little man with a face the colour of a brick wall. Tell me, Charles, is it one of the rules of the Indian Army that a man must be at least a grandfather before he is considered fit for command? Damme if I've ever seen such a gaggle of grey-beards. Your colonels are all tottering on the brink of gout and the grave, while your generals would appear to have both feet already in it. And they told me that this was a young man's country!'

'So it is – for those who make the most of their opportunities.'

'Not if they stay in the Army, I collect! I am no military strategist, but isn't it time that the Company overhauled its policy of promoting by seniority? I gather that no one can become a senior officer in the Bengal Army until they are senile and consequently useless. No wonder some of the less moribund go around croaking of impending disaster.'

'Was Fallon croaking of impending disaster?'

'Like a raven,' said Carlyon lightly. 'But he appeared to be in the minority. What are your own views? Do you too anticipate the deluge?'

'No, of course not. Nothing wrong with the country. Some people enjoy croaking of doom. The effects of this prophecy, I suppose. It is quite astonishing how superstitious even the most level-headed can become.'

'What prophecy?' inquired Carlyon, interested.

'Oh, it's an old tale now. It cropped up after Plassey. The Company's Raj – rule – was to last for a hundred years after the battle that established it. And Plassey was fought in 1757.'

'So the hundred years are up next year,' commented Carlyon. 'Very interesting. But surely you cannot take this seriously?'

'Naturally not. I wish you will not be ridiculous, Arthur.'

'Then what is worrying you?'

'Nothing. Nothing. It is just that . . . Well, I would like you to extend your visit if that is possible. Will you do that?'

'Why?'

The Governor-General looked down upon the crowded ballroom and spoke in an undertone that was barely audible above the chatter of voices and the gay music of the fiddles: 'It would be of use to me if you were to decide to go on an extended tour of this country – in an entirely private capacity, of course, as a casual sightseer only – and give me your impressions. I find that too many people tell the Governor-General only what they think will please the Governor-General. It is this question of Oudh. The ex-King and his swarm of hangers-on are here in Calcutta, and they deafen me with their complaints as to the behaviour of our people in Lucknow. I have sent the strongest representations to the Commissioner, Coverley Jackson, but his replies have been evasive.'

'Sack him,' recommended Carlyon, bored.

'I can hardly do so without hurting his feelings,' said Lord Canning unhappily. 'The charges are quite possibly without foundation, and are certain, at worst, to be grossly exaggerated. But they are doing our reputation a great deal of harm and providing fuel for the malcontents. If only I could have effected the Commissioner's removal without the necessity of direct dismissal . . . I had hoped——'

He paused, frowning, and Carlyon threw him a glance of friendly contempt. He was aware of Canning's tendency to avoid harsh measures, and of the conscientiousness that would not allow him to give an arbitrary decision on any matter that he had not thoroughly and personally sifted to the bottom. Carlyon, less patient, had little sympathy with such an attitude, and no intention of prolonging his stay in the East. He intended to reach England by the New Year, and he would not have considered visiting India in the first place had it not been that his skill in managing his *amours* had temporarily deserted him, and a situation had arisen which had made it seem advisable to pay a protracted visit to foreign parts. An invitation from the Cannings to visit them in Calcutta had arrived at this opportune moment and been accepted. But he considered that he had been abroad for quite long enough, and the prospect of proceeding to Lucknow in order to test the accuracy of charges brought against the British administration of the newly acquired province by its deposed King, did not appeal to him. His languid gaze rested without interest on the dancers, and his attention wandered.

'You could not of course proceed direct from here,' said Lord Canning, 'but were you to go first to Delhi and return via Lucknow, it would give the appearance of a sightseeing tour, and——'

He became aware that Carlyon had ceased to lounge and was gripping the balustrade with both hands and watching someone in the ballroom below with every appearance of lively interest.

'By Jove!' said Lord Carlyon under his breath, 'it *is* the ugly duckling!'

He turned to his host with an unwonted gleam of animation in his bored eyes. 'Forgive me, Charles. I see an acquaintance of mine below. Perhaps we may continue this conversation some other time.' He turned to descend the flower-decked staircase and was lost to view.

Lord Canning sighed a little tiredly. It was true that he wished for an accurate and unbiased report on the state of affairs in Lucknow, without the necessity of any official inquiry that might force him to remove the Commissioner from office. But quite apart from that he was conscious of a strong reluctance to see any able-bodied Englishman leave the country. He was not a particularly imaginative man and he had no patience with those who prated of disaster. But there were times when the enormous extent of this strange subcontinent that had passed into his charge oppressed him with the thought of its size and its dark, teeming millions. So vast – and held by so few . . .

He looked down upon the shifting colour of the ballroom with its glittering uniforms and swirling crinolines, and as he listened to the bright web of music and laughter that wove an almost tangible pattern above it, he caught sight of Carlyon's tall figure shouldering its way through the press of dowagers and spectators at the ballroom's edge, and saw him accost a slim, dark-haired girl in a white ball-dress who appeared to be surrounded by young officers.

The Governor-General turned and retreated to his study to wrestle with the contents of a dispatch box, leaving his wife to do the honours. He had emerged in the grey dawn, when the lamps and the candles were burning low and carriages drawing away laden with yawning men, sleepy dowagers and excited laughing girls, to find Carlyon escorting a stout matron in a crimson opera mantle across the hall and into a closed carriage. The lady's face was unfamiliar to him and she did not look to be at all in Carlyon's style – both her dress and her *coiffure*, even to the Governor-General's disinterested eye, being far from in the first rank of fashion.

Lord Carlyon, however, handed her into the carriage with a display of affability that was most unusual in him, bowed over her hand and expressed his intention of calling upon her at the earliest opportunity, and stood back to allow a tubby gentleman in the uniform of a Colonel of Native Infantry, presumably the lady's husband, to enter the carriage. There were half a dozen young officers grouped upon the steps, and they dispersed as the carriage drove off.

Lord Carlyon turned and made his way slowly back across the hall between the crowd of gorgeously uniformed servants and stopped at the unexpected sight of his host.

'Ah, Charles – I imagined that you had very sensibly decided to retire to bed.'

'Who was that?' inquired Canning without much curiosity.

'No one of interest. A Mrs Abuthnot.' Lord Carlyon glanced down at the wilting flower in his buttonhole, removed it and dropped it onto the polished marble floor. 'By the way, Charles,' he said softly, 'you will be interested to hear that I have decided to take your advice and extend my stay in India. I shall visit Delhi, and I may even return by way of Oudh.'

15

'Can we take our own road from here?' asked Niaz* Mohammed.

Alex turned away from the window of the sparsely furnished dâk-bungalow room and dropped the split-cane curtain back into place.

'Is there need?'

'Great need,' said Niaz, busy with the straps of a dusty valise. 'It was not advisable to speak while there were many to overhear, but now——'

'Here also there are ears,' said Alex with a jerk of his head towards the verandah outside, where the shadow of a loitering servant lay long upon the sun-warmed stone.

Alex and his orderly had left Calcutta by train. The new railway, one of Lord Dalhousie's most admired strides towards the Westernization of his Eastern Empire, now reached as far as Raniganj – a distance of over a hundred and forty miles north of Calcutta. But from this point the remainder of the journey must be accomplished by road, and Alex and Niaz had left the train, hot, dusty and coated with grit and cinders, and having slept the night at Raniganj in company with Colonel Moulson and a varied assortment of troops and travellers moving north, had proceeded for several days' journey towards Benares by dâk-*ghari* – four-wheeled, cab-like vehicles drawn by two horses.

The roads as a result of the monsoon were unspeakably bad, the half-starved ponies made poor time, and Alex's travelling companion, a morose Major on his way to rejoin his Regiment at Benares, did little or nothing towards improving the discomforts of the journey. The space between the seats had been boarded over and bedding spread on top so that the two men could lie down, and the Major spent the larger part of the day lying supine with his eyes closed, arousing himself only for the purpose of uttering some complaint. Niaz rode on the box with the driver, while the Major's servants followed in an *ekka*, a rickety-looking two-wheeled vehicle drawn by a single horse. The horses were changed at every stage, and in addition to frequent stops for repairs to bridles, harness or the *ghari* itself, the passengers had twice been forced to descend and help man-handle the vehicle back onto the road as a result of a wheel leaving the track.

On the fourth day the entire *ghari* overturned down the side of an embankment. Its passengers, including the driver, escaped unhurt, and owing to the fact that the shafts and traces had snapped as though they had been made of so much matchwood and string, the two starveling and evil-tempered horses had not only been unharmed but had bolted across the plain. The dâk-

* Nee-*ahz*.

ghari itself presented a sorry appearance, and one look was sufficient to inform even the meanest intelligence that its long career had come to an inglorious close.

The driver had wasted an unconscionable time in rending his garments and calling down a variety of picturesque curses upon the heads of the absent horses, but eventually, urged forcibly by Niaz, started off in half-hearted pursuit. The Major had high-handedly commandeered the *ekka*, and leaving its lawful occupants to follow on foot, had ordered its driver to proceed to the nearest dâk-bungalow (happily only a matter of two miles ahead) with himself, his bearer and Alex on board. Niaz had elected to remain with the baggage and had arrived at the dâk-bungalow some two and a half hours later, having transferred himself and his master's luggage to a passing bullock cart.

There were several other dâk-*gharis* at the bungalow, where their passengers were partaking of such refreshment as the *khansamah* could provide, and the morose Major lost no time in arranging for one of them to take him up. Fresh horses were brought from the stables, the passengers embarked once more, and after a prolonged and invigorating struggle the reluctant steeds started off at a headlong gallop and the *gharis* disappeared in a cloud of dust. Alex and Niaz were alone in the dâk-bungalow and quiet descended upon the scene.

It would be some little time before a new conveyance could be procured, said Niaz, and since the sun was already low in the sky, they would have to spend the night there. He would prepare a room, and he suggested that it might be possible to procure riding horses locally for very little cost, so that they might dispense with the services of a dâk-*ghari*.

'When there is work to do it is better to travel alone,' said Niaz, his dark face expressionless, 'and I have a friend in the village. A man to whom I was able to do some small service. One does not know when a friend may be of use, so I remained at his house for a night on my way south. I think he will find horses for us.'

Alex nodded and turned to enter the room at the far end of the verandah in which his bedding and valise had been placed. He had had few opportunities for private conversation with Niaz since he had landed, for the hotel in Calcutta had been overcrowded and he had been compelled to share his bedroom with another officer.

Niaz was a Punjabi Mussulman whose home was north of Karnal. Born in the same year as Alex Randall, he came of a family of well-to-do landowners of some consequence whose daughters would seem to have married far from the family acres, since he appeared to possess blood relations in half the provinces of India. He had served in Alex's Regiment and fought at his side at Moodkee and later at Ferozeshah. Alex's horse had been hamstrung at Moodkee by a wounded Sikh in the charge that silenced the guns of the Khalsa, and Niaz had risen in his stirrups and by some miracle of horsemanship had gripped Alex and dragged him clear as the horse fell. A moment later he had slipped to the ground and Alex was in his saddle with Niaz holding the stirrup-leather and fighting beside him in the swaying maddened mêlée, yelling joyfully as he had yelled in the charge: '*Shabash, baiyan! Dauro! Dauro!*' (Well done, brothers! Ride! Ride!)

Four days later, at Ferozeshah, Alex had repaid the debt when Niaz had fallen with a bullet through his chest, and Alex, his own horse killed, bestrode the wounded man and fought above him in the storming of the Sikh entrenchments. Since then Niaz had attached himself to Alex as orderly and body servant, and when Alex had been removed on special duty he had managed, through the judicious use of influence in the right quarters, to gain permission for Niaz to accompany him. Niaz had been granted extended leave during the past year, and Alex had left him certain specific and unofficial instructions that he had no doubt at all would have been carried out.

The shadow of the loitering servant that the evening sun had laid across the dusty verandah did not move, and Alex said reflectively: 'Bring my gun. There will be quail and partridge in the open country beyond, and I am stiff from jolting in that dâk-*ghari*.'

Niaz grinned appreciatively and went out to inform the *khansamah* that the Sahib wished to shoot and would return for an evening meal which had better be of the first quality or he, Niaz, would have something to say on the subject.

Alex strolled down the shallow stone steps of the verandah and walked slowly away through a mango-tope that lay to the left of the bungalow. The low sun thrust shafts of dusty gold between the tree-trunks, and a troop of monkeys chattered and quarrelled among the thick leaves. Facing the bungalow, the jungle through which the road had run swept almost to the compound wall, but behind it and to the left lay comparatively open country; a few fields where crops of maize and sugar-cane had been planted, grazing grounds and a glimmer of water that indicated a distant jheel and the probable presence of waterfowl, and the level plains stretching away to the far horizon.

The ground in the mango-tope was hard and dry and splashed with the droppings of green pigeons, and a warm shaft of sunlight probing the shadows illuminated a slab of stone crudely carved with the lingam, the emblem of fertility, that stood propped against the bole of a tree. The thing was daubed with red paint and there were offerings heaped upon the ground before it. Humble offerings: a handful of parched grain, a bunch of marigold flowers, a string of red jungle beads and the remains of a chuppatti – the flat cake of unleavened bread that is the staple food of half India. Two small striped squirrels were tugging at the chuppatti, and a group of seven-sisters – those drab grey-brown birds who hop and twitter in small gangs like a covey of nervous spinsters – were disposing of the grain.

Alex paused and regarded the crude emblem with some interest. There was nothing at all unusual in the sight, for India is littered with such things. It was the offerings that surprised him. The flowers were unfaded, and the grain and the cake of unleavened bread must have been placed there comparatively recently, for the birds and the squirrels would make short work of them. Yet it was unusual for villagers to bring offerings to a shrine at such an hour – the work of a village restricting such attentions to the late evening or the early morning, when men going out or returning from tilling their fields or tending cattle might pass the spot and leave a small gift at the shrine.

There was a light step behind him and Alex turned to see Niaz who carried a shotgun and a bag of cartridges. Niaz glanced at the red-daubed emblem of Mahadeo and said cheerfully: 'Misbegotten unbelievers!' He spat on the ground and jerked a thumb over his shoulder in the direction of the bungalow: 'The drivers of two of the dâk-*gharis*, and he who drove the *ekka*, brought the offerings. There was, I think, a message also, but it has gone. See, there in the dust——'

The hard dry ground of the mango-tope did not hold the print of footmarks well, but the day was windless, and dust, twigs and fallen leaves betrayed a well-worn track from the bungalow to the shrine, while beyond it the print of unshod feet showed where a single man had approached from the direction of the grazing grounds and the open plain, and returned again.

Niaz moved slowly out of the shadows of the tope, his eyes on the ground, and presently he said: 'Here he turns aside and goes back to the village. It is an old trick to thrust a message into a chuppatti and bake it so that it is well hid. But the driver of that *ekka* was a Mussulman and no Hindu.'

Alex nodded without speaking and turned to look out across the plain, his eyes screwed up against the low sunlight. A black partridge was calling, and he held out his hand for the gun. He was an excellent shot, and Niaz was carrying half a dozen limp feathered forms by the time they reached the edge of the jheel – a shallow stretch of water fringed with straggling rushes, stray clumps of elephant grass and a few scanty palms that stood up against the bright evening sky like worn broomsticks.

Alex sat down on a tussock of dry grass with his back to the open water at the end of a narrow arm of stony ground that reached out into the jheel, and pulling a packet of paper and pouch of tobacco out of his pocket, rolled two cigarettes – a habit he had acquired in the Crimea – and tossed one over to Niaz who squatted beside him.

Niaz struck a sulphur match on the sole of his shoe, and having lit the cigarettes, blew the flame out carefully and flicked the spent match into the placid water. 'There are no ears here,' he remarked approvingly, 'and none can approach by the water. We need watch to landward only.' He drew the tobacco smoke deep into his lungs and expelled it slowly through his nostrils. The evening was warm and very still. So still that they could hear the leap of a little fish a dozen yards away, a quack of water-birds far out on the jheel and the rustle of a small snake that slid through the grass-stems.

Alex had learned patience with much else from the East, and he sat relaxed and silent; watching the shadows lengthen and the smoke from his cigarette rise unwaveringly into the quiet air. He knew that Niaz would speak when he wished to and not before. Meanwhile it was pleasant to sit here and smell the familiar scents of an Indian evening while the sky behind the ragged palm trees blazed with the spectacular glories of a sunset unimaginable to those who live only in Western countries.

At last Niaz said reflectively: 'I did as thou asked. I took my leave and went on horseback, as befits one of the *rissala* (cavalry), to visit those of my relatives in Oudh and Rohilkhand and Jhansi; from whom I heard much. And when that was done I went on foot, no longer as Niaz Mohammed Khan of the Company's *rissala*, but as Rahim, a man of no consequence. From Ludhiana of the Sikhs to the north of my own *ilaqa*, to Benares of the Unbelievers – and even further south to Burdwan went I; listening to much talk in the twilight and hearing many things in the bazaars and by the way...'

He fell silent for a moment or two, drawing deeply at his cigarette while the sunset painted his face with a wash of vivid light so that it seemed to glow like polished bronze, and presently he said: 'Thou wert right, my brother. There is devil's work afoot; and this time it is not a plague that will break out in one spot only and may thereby be kept from others. This runs north and south, and the infection is carried by many and to all men. Even by such as the drivers of these dâk-*gharis*! There are also many tales told of signs and wonders, and the prophecy of the "Hundred Years" is spoken in every village throughout Hind.'

'There is always talk,' said Alex laconically, his eyes on a high-flying wedge of Garganey teal that cut a thin dark pattern against the quiet sky.

'That I know, for when has it ever been otherwise? But this time it is more than talk. Thou dost not remember (it was before thy time) the year in which thy Government ordered the Army to Kabul. The Hindus in that Army became disaffected when they crossed the Indus. They had heard that when Raja Maun Singh crossed that river to wage war against the Afghans he had told all men that the Hindu religion ran no further than the Indus, and had built a temple on the far bank and ordered all Brahmins to leave their sacred threads, the emblems of their caste, in that temple. Then when they reached Afghanistan it was cold – a cold such as they had never known – so that they could no longer bathe before food, as is their custom, and must wear *poshteens*, coats of sheep skin, on account of the cold and the snow: wherefore, since none but the lowest caste will willingly touch the skin of a dead animal, when the Army returned to Ferozepore the Hindus found that their own people would not consort with them because they had lost caste and been defiled. The Mussulmans too were angered, for they said that John

Company had forced them to fight against their co-religionists, which is forbidden in the Koran.'

'This I know,' said Alex quietly. 'It is an old tale. And now?'

'And now, as then, there is a grievance among the sepoys on account of pay: and so the old grievances, that have never slept, are spoken of once more – that the Company desires to destroy all caste. The rail-*ghari* and the telegraph, the jails and hospitals where all are admitted, are looked upon as weapons for the destruction of caste. And the foolish talk of missionary-*log* adds fuel to that fire, since they and many of the Company's officers tell the people of Hind that their customs and practices are evil and must be abolished. Perhaps this is so. I do not know. But their customs are as a tree that is deep-rooted, and if the trunk be cut down there are still the roots.'

Niaz cupped his lean brown hands about the stub of his cigarette and drew on it, letting the smoke trickle slowly through his nostrils, and Alex stayed silent. There was little in what Niaz had said that he did not already know. But he knew better than to hurry him.

'It has long been a custom of Hind,' said Niaz slowly, 'for a man who has no heir to adopt one who shall succeed him; since the son, say the Unbelievers, delivers his father from the hell called *Pat*. If there be no son to perform the funeral rites, they believe that there can be no resurrection to eternal bliss. Therefore their priests and lawgivers have permitted the adoption of sons where the male line has failed. Comes now the order of the Company saying that where there is no male heir of the blood the lands and titles of a prince shall not pass to any adoptive son, but pass instead into the possession of the Company, and that man's line shall die out and cease. Thus many states, by right of lapse, have been swallowed up into the maw of the Company and their ancient names have become as dust . . .'

Niaz's voice had taken on a singsong quality as he spoke, and the pupils of his eyes had widened as though from the effects of a drug: he had forgotten that he, a Mohammedan, spoke of Hindus, and remembered only that he spoke as a native of India:

'Satarah . . . Nagpur . . . Jhansi . . . Sambhalpur . . . Their greatness has departed. The Rajas of Satarah were descended from Shivaji, the founder of the Mahratta Empire. They committed no crime against the Company – save that the last of the Rajas had no son. Yet was their state forfeit. The Peishwa too, the Nana Sahib, smarts under the injustice of the Government who have refused him what is his right under the old laws——'

Alex said softly: 'These be Hindus, O follower of the Prophet.'

'That is so. But now there is Oudh also. In former times the Kings of Oudh rendered assistance to the Company, and because of that help there was a treaty made between them that the state would never be taken by the British – yet now it too has been taken. That it was misgoverned means nothing: that is a word for Councillors and Lat Sahibs, not for the common people. The common people say that Oudh belongs to Wajid Ali and his line, and whether he has governed well or ill as regards his own people he has in no wise broken faith with the Company. If, therefore, the Company dispossess one who has himself – and his forebears also – been faithful to them, who then is safe? Every princeling, every sirdar, every man who has anything to leave or anything to lose, from a small-holding of no more than a quarter acre to a state many *koss** wide, is afraid. And men who are afraid are dangerous. Therefore Hindu and Mussulman, Unbelievers and the Elect of God plot together in fear and hatred; and the word goes up and down the land.'

'And what is that word?'

'That the *feringhis* (foreigners) are few and their councils are divided, and that the men of the North, the Russ-*log*, have made so great a slaughter of their armies that there are none left to come to the aid of those in Hind. That Dost Mohammed Khan, the Amir of Afghanistan, will rise against them and that the Shah of Persia will join with him to drive them into the sea – though that last I know to be fools' talk,' said Niaz, and spat to show his contempt. 'Dost Mohammed would sooner take a live cobra in his hand than ally himself with the Persian! Yet there be many who believe all these things, and the word goes forth, carried into the towns and villages by a hundred different ways. It runs from *pulton* (regiment) to *pulton* – from *rissala* to *rissala*. Men on pilgrimage to the shrines of Kashi and Haramukh; merchants, maulvis, sadhus; Mussulmans, Brahmins, Sikhs and Jains; the woman who draws water at the well and the man who drives a plough – all or any of them may be a carrier of the Word. They spill the powder, and when the train is laid it will need but a spark to ignite it.'

Alex flicked his cigarette-end into the water where it went out with a little hiss, startling a paddy bird which undisturbed by the rise and fall of Niaz's low voice had pricked through the shallows a yard beyond them. The bird flew off with a flapping of wings as a flight of red-necked Brahmini duck swished overhead with a sound like tearing silk to settle down with ruffling importance at the far end of the jheel. The rose and saffron of the sunset had faded, leaving the sky awash with clear green light in which a single star blazed and glittered in lonely splendour.

Alex rolled another cigarette and said: 'Has that spark been found?'

'Not yet. Those who plot seek for one. It wants only that to set the land alight. But it must be something that touches Mussulman and Hindu alike, for if one rise without the other, the Company, few and weak as they have become, may still triumph. Therefore they search diligently, and wait.'

'Yes,' said Alex reflectively, handing over another cigarette, 'but a thing that will make Mussulman, Hindu and Sikh sink their differences and unite against us will not be so easy.'

'Doubtless the Company will of their charity supply it,' said Niaz ironic-

* A *koss* = 2 miles.

ally. 'Are thy people blind or mad, or both, that they cannot see what is toward?'

'Neither,' said Alex. 'It is a national conceit. They – we – can only see ourselves as benefactors whom such as thou' – he grinned maliciously at Niaz – 'must perforce regard only with admiration and gratitude.'

'And do they never learn?' inquired Niaz scornfully.

'No. We *Angrezis* (British) are as God made us. The mould is set. All this that you have told me, word for word and letter for letter, happened once before some two score years and more ago, in the Kingdom that was Haidar Ali's. At that time also there were a few who had eyes and ears and used them, but they were derided and their warnings laughed to scorn. So it is now.'

'I have heard that tale,' grunted Niaz. 'Then too there were injustices pertaining to the payment of allowances, and then as now it needed but a spark to fire the train. That spark thy countrymen supplied by ordering the wearing of leather hats made from the skins of that unclean animal the pig, and of the cow that is sacred to the Hindus. Whereupon the Army rose and massacred their officers, saying that they would rid the land of those who sought to destroy their caste. Those same words are being spoken once again, but this time if the fire be lit it will not be so easy to stamp it out since it will not be in the south only, as it was in that day, but north and west and east also. And many will die in that burning! *I* tell you this. I who have hearkened this past year to the talk in the lines and in the bazaars, in the cities and the *serais* and at the wayside halts.'

Alex shifted restlessly. The swift tropic twilight was almost gone and he could no longer see Niaz's face clearly. He said abruptly: 'All this is talk. Have you proof?'

'*Proof*!' said Niaz and laughed shortly. 'Spoken like a sahib – *Sahib*!' – he gave that title the same scornful emphasis that Kishan Prasad had once done. 'Have I ever lied to thee that thou shouldst demand proof of what I tell thee as though I were some *vakil* (lawyer) of the court?'

'*Gulam* (slave),' said Alex gently, 'were it not that thou art as my brother in all but blood, I would throw thee into the jheel for that word.'

Niaz flung up a hand in mock appeal: '*Marf karo* (have mercy) – Sahib!'

Alex caught the upflung hand about the wrist and bent it backward, and for a moment the two men wrestled silently, hand against hand.

'Is it to be the jheel then?' inquired Alex.

'Nay, it is enough. *Marf karo – bai* (brother).'

'That is better,' said Alex releasing him.

Niaz rubbed his wrist and grinned. 'At least thy sojourn in *Belait* (England) has not softened thee. But what is that gaud thou art wearing? A love token, belike?'

'That . . . ?' Alex looked down at the twisted silver ring with its three small red stones and shook his head. 'No, it was given me by a man whom I would have given much to see dead.'

He told the tale and heard Niaz draw a short hissing breath between his teeth at the mention of that name. 'Kishan Prasad!' said Niaz. 'I have heard of that man. And if all that I have heard is true it had been better that thou hadst cut off thy right hand rather than have given him his life.'

'These things are written,' said Alex philosophically.

'*Beshak*!' (assuredly) said Niaz grimly. 'Nevertheless I think that that bauble will serve its turn. It may yet get thee this proof that thou hast demanded.'

'It is not for myself that I require proof,' said Alex composedly. 'All that thou hast told me I knew without the telling. But those in authority are hard to convince. The Burra-lat-Sahib who has lately gone to his own land has told them that all is well – the land never more peaceful and the people filled with content.'

'More fool he!' grunted Niaz.

'Therefore,' continued Alex, ignoring the interruption, 'those in high places are unwilling to lend an ear to warnings.'

'As they were in the days before the massacre of Vellore,' interjected Niaz scornfully.

'Yes. As in the days before Vellore. There is a saying among our people that those whom the gods would destroy they first make mad.'

'A true saying indeed,' said Niaz. 'But thou shalt have thy proof, though small good will it give thee.'

'Ah!' said Alex, his eyes suddenly bright. 'I thought that there was something more. Tell me swiftly and let us have no more of this talk that runs in circles.'

Niaz laughed. ' "We are as God made us," ' he quoted. ' "The mould is set." It is only the English who rush straight upon the heart of the matter, looking neither to the right nor to the left. Yes, there is indeed something more. I would not have troubled thee on account of bazaar rumours.'

He glanced uneasily over his shoulder as though to make sure that there could be no third person near by, and despite the fact that nothing larger than a jackal could possibly have approached within fifty yards of them without being seen, he lowered his voice until it was barely audible: 'I have learned,' whispered Niaz, 'that there is to be a meeting of certain men in a place near Khanwai that lies to the north of Bithaur within the borders of Oudh. It is dangerous knowledge and known only to a few. Perhaps a hundred in all Hind: no more.'

'And how didst *thou* come by it?' inquired Alex softly.

Niaz threw his hands out palm upwards in a brief, indescribable gesture. 'A woman. How else? Her husband is old and moreover he drinks wine. The Prophet forbade the drinking of wine, and rightly, for by indulgence in this are tongues loosened and many plans brought to ruin. When a woman has discovered a matter that should be hid she will tell it for idleness or mischief or' – Niaz grinned – 'for love's sake.'

'But is it true talk that she has told thee?'

'It is true. That I would swear on my life. I do not know what it is that they who meet will speak of or do, but this I know – that it bodes no good. So I have had the thought that it would be well if we two learned what is afoot. It is set for a night but twelve days hence, when there is a fair at Khanwai. I have been to spy out the land. The place of their meeting is a ruin; no more than a handful of stones and a broken wall which the jungle has swallowed. A foolish spot for such talk, but these men are assuredly bitten with madness. There is but one path to it, for the jungle grows thick behind it, and that path leads through a deep nullah where was once a gateway that has fallen. Only one man at a time can pass through, and each as they pass must say a word. That word I have.'

Once again Niaz paused to peer into the gathering dusk, and in the silence they heard from somewhere far out across the darkening plains a jackal howling at the evening star. Niaz's gaze returned to Alex and even the green dusk could not disguise the glitter of his eyes and the flash of his teeth.

'You old devil!' said Alex in English – the same glitter in his own eyes. 'Niaz, thou wilt surely end thy days in a hangman's noose! Was the overturning of that dâk-*ghari* thy work?'

Niaz waved a deprecatory hand. 'I judged it to be necessary,' he said airily. 'Also the driver was an un-friend of mine. I owed him somewhat in the matter of repayment for certain insolence that he had spoken. He was an eater of opium and he dozed upon the box. A twitch of the reins, and the thing was done.'

'And if my neck had been broken, O son of Eblis?'

'There was no fear of that. A few scratches and a bruise or two at most. No more. It was necessary that we should separate ourselves from those others who travelled by the road. Do we go to Khanwai?'

'Assuredly,' said Alex, and laughed. It was a laugh that men hear sometimes in the heat of battle or as the order is given for a cavalry charge, and that no woman would recognize. Niaz recognized it and his own laugh answered and echoed it.

A rush of wings swept the darkening sky above them and Alex snatched up his gun and fired. There were two splashes within a yard of each other, some twenty feet away, and the placid surface of the jheel broke into ripples that spread out across the water in ever-widening circles to slap against the rushes. Niaz came to his feet in one lithe movement and waded out to retrieve the fallen birds as Alex snapped open the smoking breech and ejected the spent cartridges.

'That is a new toy,' said Niaz returning. 'I have not seen one that is loaded thus before.'

He examined the mechanism of the pin-fire breech-loading gun with interest, peering at it in the dim light, and then snapping it shut he shouldered it and picked up the dead birds. 'Come, it is time we returned.'

They left the jheel and walked companionably back across the darkened plain towards the twinkling lights of the dâk-bungalow while the sky above them blossomed with stars and a jackal-pack howled from beyond the grazing grounds. But as they neared the dense shadows of the mango-tope Niaz fell back, so that they returned to the bungalow with the British officer walking ahead and his silent orderly six paces behind him; to all appearances poles apart.

Alex retired to his bed early that night, but Niaz had work to do. That he did it well was proved by his appearance before the verandah at daybreak accompanied by the headman of the village, several curious onlookers and three horses. These miserable offspring of unmentionable sires and unspeakable dams were, explained Niaz cheerfully, the property of the headman who had agreed to sell them for the exorbitant sum of one hundred and fifty rupees for the three. Here the headman broke into voluble protests, alleging that on the contrary the price was so low that the horses were little less than a gift.

'Send him away before his bellowings deafen me,' said Alex. 'I suppose we can mount these starvelings without them falling dead, but I doubt it.'

'It is better than being slain by the futility of these *ghari* drivers,' said Niaz, paying over the money in silver coin. 'Heaven forfend that any of our own *rissala* see us thus mounted! That third animal is but a pack-pony for the transporting of gear.'

They rode away in the cool of the morning and were swallowed up by the vast, secretive land and the shifting polyglot millions of India as though they had been no more than two grains of dust on the endless plains.

Ten days later an itinerant toy-seller, his pack laden with crudely painted plaster trifles, trudged down the dusty road that led from Cawnpore into Oudh. He had no assistant, but he was of a cheerful and gregarious disposition and always ready to enter into conversation with fellow-travellers upon the road and at the wayside halts. At one of these he had attached himself to a party of jugglers who were proceeding to the fair at Khanwai, a small village on the borders of Oudh not far from Bithaur.

His ready wit and the quick-fire patter with which he accompanied the sale of his gimcrack toys appealed to the leader of the troupe, and after some haggling it was agreed that the man, Jatu by name, should act as barker to the jugglers in the intervals of pursuing his own trade. In return for which the troupe would provide him with food and, if profits allowed, a small percentage of the takings; an arrangement that appeared highly satisfactory to all.

From the opposite direction, that of Fathigarh, a slim, wiry Pathan, sitting astride a bony and bad-tempered down-country mare and trailed by two sorry-looking hacks on a lead rein, was also riding towards the fair at Khanwai. His dress and speech, and the hard, light-coloured eyes in the brown face, proclaimed him as a son of the border tribe of the Usafzai, and he too was of a cheerful disposition, for he sang the songs of the Border – the more questionable ones – as he rode, and was always ready to fall into talk with any he met upon the road.

His cousin Assad Ali, he explained to any who were interested, had brought a string of horses down from the north hoping to sell them for greater profit in the Punjab and Rohilkhand. He had done well with his string, but he had died of the cholera at a village on the outskirts of Delhi, and his horseboys, fearing the disease, had run away taking with them the greater part of the profits, so that now he, Sheredil, with only three unsaleable hacks picked up at Karnal, had taken the road alone, hoping to dispose of them further south. He had heard talk of a fair at Khanwai and intended to try his luck there. He carried a long Pathan knife in his broad waist-belt, and an antiquated but serviceable *jezail* slung over his shoulder, together with a well-stocked cartridge-belt; and he took for preference the centre of the road. Alex had always been a believer in the old saying that it is darkest under the lamp.

The town of Khanwai was little more than a village, and distinguished only by an annual fair which was held in honour of a treaty between two warring clans who centuries ago had endeavoured to exterminate each other for reasons long lost sight of in the mists of time. The fairground was surrounded by the booths of sweetmeat-sellers, toy-makers and hucksters, and there was plenty to entertain the idle: jugglers, acrobats, fire-eaters, a sad and ragged performing bear, snake-charmers and fortune-tellers. And as night fell a troupe of firework-makers brightened the sky with a display of their wares and frightened the timorous with the crash of exploding rockets. But as the fireworks flared, dyeing the awed faces of the spectators red, green and amber by turns, it might have been noted, had any been interested in such a thing, that sundry men were drifting away from the fairground by ones and twos and making their way through the fields beyond the village to the uncultivated land and the dark barrier of the jungle that backed on the grazing grounds.

Sheredil of the Usafzai, following the same path, caught his garments on an unseen branch of a thorn tree and swore softly and fluently in Pushtu as he freed himself, and a shadow that followed noiselessly on his heels lengthened its stride and spoke in a whisper: '*Hai*! thou from the north' – Alex checked and his hand went to the knife in his belt – 'what dost thou here? Thou art a Pathan and no man of Hind.'

'I come that I may carry the word to those who wait beyond the Border,' replied Alex in whispered Hindustani: 'And thou?'

'I likewise; but to Bengal go I: to Berhampore by Murshidabad. Of what *pulton* art thou?'

'Of none. But my cousin's brother-in-law is a daffadar in the Guides,' said Alex mendaciously. 'He too is like-minded with us. And thy Regiment?'

'The 19th Bengal Infantry' – he was a *pūrbeah* sepoy on leave, a lance naik and a man of some influence in his Regiment. He hurried on ahead and was lost in the shadows.

The flare of the fireworks from the fairground lit the path with intermittent flashes of light, and in these brief glimpses Alex could see that there were men ahead and behind him, hastening forward down the narrow track that wound between thickets of thorn, bamboos, *dhâk* trees and elephant grass, but keeping a safe distance from each other. Niaz had studied the ground with the eye of a general, and a map that he had drawn in the dust of the roadside, though crude, had been remarkably accurate, so that even by night and on strange ground Alex could guess the lie of the land and knew what to expect.

The path – it was little more than a goat-track – wandered with apparent aimlessness between tall clumps of grass and finally descended a sandy slope into a dry nullah. To the right the nullah ran straight on into the darkness, but to the left it narrowed and appeared to be blocked by a fall of rock. The sepoy could not have been half a dozen yards ahead, but he had vanished, and Alex, turning unhesitatingly to the left, was once again grateful for the care with which Niaz had reconnoitred the ground. There was a space between two huge slabs of fallen rock that would have been invisible to one who was not aware of it, for the rocks overlapped each other and were overgrown with creepers and the roots of a tree, and only a close inspection by full daylight would have discovered the gap.

It reminded Alex unpleasantly of another nullah more than a hundred miles to the north-west of Oudh, down which he had walked one hot and sunny morning almost seven years ago. That nullah too had apparently ended in a fall of rock, and Alex, idly investigating, had found his way through a narrow gap and come face to face with a full-grown tiger who had been approaching it from the opposite side. He could still remember the stare of the savage yellow eyes in that huge black-barred head . . . the way in which the whiskers had lifted as the lips curled back in a slow soundless snarl and the sight of the muscles under the wonderful painted hide bunching for the spring. There had been no room for either of them to turn, and Alex, who had been out after partridge, carried only a shotgun. He had fired both barrels at point-blank range and the great taloned paw had struck him as the creature died. He carried the mark still, and would always carry it; and now he felt the scar burn as though it were new in his flesh. There would be no jungle beast on the far side of this hidden gap in the rock tonight, but something infinitely more dangerous: man.

The gap was only wide enough to allow one at a time to enter it, and behind it, so Niaz had told him, lay a narrow walled tunnel; for this had once been the outer gateway of a fortress whose walls ran back to left and right, hidden and overgrown by the trees and creeper of the jungle. Alex heard feet slither on the path behind him as another conspirator entered the nullah, and he set his teeth and walked on between the rocks.

He had taken no more than four steps in the blackness when his outstretched hands touched the shaft of a spear that barred his way. It dropped instantly and after a moment's pause he moved forward again and heard it lift once more behind him and heard, too, a man's quick breathing. 'Making sure we go through one at a time,' thought Alex grimly. He could see no glimmer of light and his hands brushed against rough stonework. Niaz had said that the tunnel of the ruined gateway was no more than eight fair paces in length; which meant that there was something or someone blocking the far end of it . . . Then he saw a glimpse of greyness and something touched his chest – an iron-bound *lathi* such as night-watchmen carry – and a voice almost in his ear whispered: 'Give the word.'

'*A white goat for Kali.*'

'Pass, brother.' The *lathi* dropped and Alex moved on into the open air.

The sides of the nullah were steeper and narrower here than on the far side of the concealed entrance, and the jungle arched above it and excluded the moonlight so that the place was almost as dark as the tunnel behind it. Then the darkness thinned and torchlight glowed through the undergrowth ahead, and presently the track ran out into a clearing before the ruins of a long-forgotten fort or palace.

The starlight and a half-moon, the flaming torches and the occasional flare of a rocket illuminated roofless walls and fallen pillars half hidden by weeds and creepers. A giant *peepul* tree split the stones of what might once have been a hall of audience, and in the uncertain light it was difficult to tell which were fallen pillars and which the roots of the great tree. India is full of such ruins; relics of cities and dynasties that have passed away and been forgotten; the haunt of snakes, foxes and monkeys and the lair of the wild boar.

It seemed to Alex an odd spot to choose for a meeting of malcontents, except that there was little doubt that the place had a certain eerie atmosphere about it, and though it lay less than half a mile from Khanwai and the beaten track, its presence would never have been suspected by the casual passer-by. He could see now that the clearing was not a natural one, but the remains of what had once been a large stone-paved courtyard, open to the sky. Thorn bushes and the tough jungle grass had thrust their way between the sandstone blocks, but the jungle had been unable to obliterate them and stood back from it, walling it about with impenetrable vegetation.

The open space was crowded with shadowy figures and sibilant with whispering voices, and Alex stood still, the lance naik of the 19th Bengal Infantry breathing heavily beside him. At the far side of the square, where a broken flight of steps led up to the ruined entrance to a roofless hall, stood two men holding torches – flaring country-made things of dried grass, branches and pitch. They stood as though waiting, and the orange light flickered weirdly on the rolling eyeballs of the shifting, whispering crowd and threw grotesque shadows on the wall of the watching jungle.

Presently there was a stir among the men at Alex's back and the crowd drew aside, Alex with them, as half a dozen men muffled in dark cloaks entered the clearing by way of the nullah. It seemed that they had been expected, for the crowd made a lane for them, parting to left and right, and they passed quickly through and came to a stop before the torch-bearers. They stood for a few moments talking in undertones with a small group of men who had apparently been waiting for them, while the crowd ceased its whispering to listen. But Alex was too far away to hear what was said, and it is doubtful if any but a handful heard, since at that point the fireworks on the distant fairground let off a very fusillade of rockets.

'This is too easy,' thought Alex, waiting for the new arrivals to mount the ruined steps behind them from where he imagined that they would harangue the crowd. 'There must be a catch in it somewhere.' A line from a nursery rhyme jigged through his brain: ' "*Will you walk into my parlour?" said the spider to the fly.*' It had been easy enough to walk in, but would it be as easy to walk out again?

The group of men by the torch-bearers turned, but they did not mount the steps behind them as Alex had half-expected. They walked between the torches and simply disappeared as though the ground had opened and swallowed them up.

From where Alex stood the illusion was so complete that he heard the men about him gasp and shrink back, and saw the sepoy put up a hand to clutch at some hidden amulet he wore concealed under his shirt. Then the crowd began to move forward slowly and he realized that the torch-bearers stood either side of a shaft that descended into the ground, and as he drew nearer he saw that the two men with the torches scrutinized the faces of all who went past them. A hand touched him in the press and he turned to see Jatu, the seller of toys.

'They will never let me pass. Try the ring!' The words were barely a breath against his ear and then the man had melted into the darkness and was gone.

Alex moved forward, a step at a time. He was conscious of a cold tingling sensation between his shoulder-blades and was aware that his mouth was dry. For a fleeting moment he wondered what would happen if the ring meant nothing to the guardians of the shaft. Would they let him stand to one side and wait as others were waiting, or would they—— The light of the torches flared full in his face and his nerves tightened and leapt, but the hand he held out was entirely steady.

The three small stones in Kishan Prasad's ring gleamed redly in the torch-light, and the ring appeared a small and insignificant thing; but the men who held the torches evidently recognized it. One of them, bending forward to stare at it, muttered something that Alex did not catch, and salaamed low, and Alex walked between them and down a narrow flight of steps, aware that the palms of his hands were wet and there were drops of cold sweat on his forehead.

The entrance to the shaft had been concealed by a huge flagstone that had been drawn up with ropes, and it must have taken at least two men, and probably more, to move it. The walls of the shaft were smooth and dry and the worn steps so steep and narrow that only one man at a time could possibly have descended them. They went down further into the ground than Alex would have believed possible, and once again he had the sensation of walking into a trap. A bat flew up past him, its leathery wings brushing his cheek – proof at least that there was some other entrance – and then he had reached the foot of the steps at last and was standing in a vaulted chamber, the roof of which was supported by crude stone pillars.

It was impossible to gauge the full extent of the underground room, for the walls beyond the pillars were lost in darkness and the only illumination was supplied by a single brazier supported on an iron tripod that stood at the far end of the vault, in which an uneasy flame burned flickeringly. The stone floor and the pillars were slimy to the touch, and not dry as were the walls of the stair shaft, and in the faint light of the brazier Alex could see tree-roots that had thrust down between the curved slabs of the vaulted ceiling. That accounted for the bats and the fact that the air was breathable. Perhaps this underground room had once held the hoarded treasures of a king, or been used for some dark priestly purpose. Probably the latter, for there appeared to be carvings on the wall behind the brazier.

There seemed to be between thirty or forty men squatting on the stone floor between the pillars, but it was difficult to tell in that uncertain light whether there were more of them whom Alex could not see. He edged his way towards a pillar and squatted down by it, Indian-fashion, keeping his back to the stone. He could hear hard breathing all about him and smell the rank smell of unwashed human bodies, and as his eyes became accustomed to the dimness he saw that many of those present were sadhus – holy men of all sects and persuasions – wild-eyed and ash-smeared, naked or wearing the ill-cured skins of animals, their long hair matted and hideous. Bairagis, Sannyasis, Bikshus, Paryrajakas; Aghorins whose custom it is to steal and eat the flesh of corpses; devil-worshippers, mendicants and mystics.

Alex shuddered and felt his skin crawl, and was grateful for the feel of the dank stone at his back. But it was not the presence of the Hindu ascetics that made him afraid. It was the unbelievable, impossible fact that there were others in that ill-lit underground vault. Not only Sikhs, but Mussulmans also; followers of the Prophet to whom all Hindus were dogs of unbelievers, crouching side by side with the worshippers of Shiva the Destroyer, of Vishnu and Brahma and Ganesh of the elephant head, of many-armed Mother Kali the drinker of blood, and of a hundred other gods and godlings. It was true, then. Mussulman and Hindu were prepared to combine against the men of 'John Company' – against the white-faced foreign conquerors whose dominion had lasted for a hundred years. Nothing but a common cause and a common hatred could have brought about this weird gathering.

A man stood up at the far end of the chamber, towering above the crouching figures that filled the aisle between the stone pillars. His back was to the fitful flame of the brazier and Alex could not see his face, but the voice and dress told him much.

The man was a Mussulman and probably from Oudh. A tall man with a silver tongue. He spoke quietly and with a curious suggestion of a chant; the voice of a priest or a story-teller; and the tale he told was the story of a conquered people – oppressed, cheated, robbed and exploited by the men from the West, from the land beyond the Black Water. He spoke of kings and princes who had died fighting the Company, or been defrauded of their rights. Of great names and great houses that had become as the blown sands of the deserts of Bikaner. Of cherished laws and customs and religious freedoms that had been curtailed or put aside. Of sheltered zenana women, queens and princesses in their own right, sent to beg their bread in the streets . . .

His voice rose and sank and the men before him swayed and groaned in unison as though they were so many puppets pulled upon a single string. Even Alex, listening – Alex who knew just how much of that tale was truth and how much fable, exaggeration or falsehood – found himself stirred to anger or intolerably moved by that wild, bitter, sorrowful saga. He forgot that he was an Englishman and a servant of the Company, and swayed and groaned with the swaying, groaning mob.

He did not know for how long the man spoke – it might have been for an hour, or two hours, or three. The flame in the brazier flickered and danced and the shadow of the speaker leapt and shrank and leapt again across that motley mob of listening men with an effect as hypnotic as the remarkable voice. The man ended with an impassioned plea for unity: 'They of the Company be few. A handful only, scattered up and down the land. We of Hind have risen against them many times, but the risings have always failed. They have failed because we of this land were divided one against the other. But it is well known that ten men with one heart are equal to a hundred men with different hearts; and it needs only this – that we hold together with one heart – and we are rid of them for ever. Let us put aside our differences and strike as one!'

He flung up his arms with a wild gesture, and the crowd gasped and shrank back as a green fire seemed to run up his arms and leap for a moment from his spread fingers. But the spell had snapped for Alex. He had seen that trick performed by an illusionist at a London theatre, and sanity returned to him: and with it an icy sense of danger. If this man could sway others as he had swayed this bigoted, caste-ridden, creed-divided assembly tonight, he was more dangerous to the Company than anything that had as yet risen against them.

Another man was speaking. A Hindu this time. His theme was the same, but his shrill, impassioned oratory lacked the almost hypnotic appeal of the previous speaker, and Alex allowed his attention to wander and concentrated on trying to memorize as many as possible of the audience and file their features away for future use. It was no easy task in that wavering light, but there were several faces that he thought he would recognize again.

The talk went on and on and Alex shifted restlessly. During his first years in India, when he and Niaz would take leave together and go off shooting, he had taught himself to squat native-fashion on his heels. It had amused him to study and copy the habits and customs and speech of many kinds of men – a game which Niaz, who was a natural mimic, had entered into with enthusiasm – but his grey eyes had made it impossible for him to pass as any but a hillman or a northerner, and so he had selected his present role and worked hard to perfect himself at it. He had used it upon several occasions, in company with Niaz, to gain sorely needed information, but having spent the last year and more in Europe his muscles had grown unused to the treatment they were receiving. They ached abominably and he began to wonder how much longer this performance was going to last, and if he had not already heard sufficient for his purpose? It would be easy to rise and steal up the stair shaft – it was less than six paces behind him and surely no one would dispute his passage if he gave an obvious excuse? But he did not go.

Yet another man was speaking; a sadhu this time. His message was less general and more specific. Spread the word! Carry it into every town and every village. Tell every man to be ready; to procure arms and secrete them; to steal them if necessary! To sharpen his sword, his axe or his knife and to tip his *lathi* with iron. The coming year was the Year of the Prophecy in which the Hundred Years of Subjection would be accomplished. Man, woman and child, the oppressors must be slain, so that not one would remain to carry the tale to the West.

'Carry the word! Carry the word!' The hoarse hysterical voice rang and echoed uncannily under the vaulted stone. 'See! now we prepare a sign as in the old days, so that all men may know!'

A shaven priest arose and threw something on the brazier and the flame flared up with a sudden intolerable brightness that for a brief moment threw the avid faces into harsh relief. It died again and in the near-darkness that followed a second priest began a chant that was taken up by other voices.

The light flickered up again, though dimly, and the two priests moved about it, coming and going. The crowd craned their necks to see, and Alex would have given much to stand upright and look over the heads and backs that obscured his view, but he did not dare to draw attention to himself by doing so. He could catch only glimpses between the silhouetted heads. Something was being poured onto a platter; it appeared to be *ata* – the coarse-ground flour of the villages. A man squatting near the brazier began to beat on a small drum; softly at first, so that it was barely more than a rhythmic accompaniment to the chant, but growing slowly louder and more insistent, until gradually the chant changed its note and became a frenzied incantation, and Alex recognized it as a hymn to Kali:

'*Kali! Kali! Oh, dreadful-toothed Goddess! Devour, cut, destroy all the malignant – cut with an axe! Bind, bind, seize! Drink blood! Secure, secure! Salutation to Kali!*'

The ranks of half-seen men began to jerk and sway and once more one of the two priests flung something on the brazier. But this time the brief flare of the flame was followed by a dense smoke that whirled upward and filled the darkness with a choking smell akin to incense: a heady, stupefying smell that drugged and yet exhilarated. The other priest who had moved back into the shadows returned, dragging something that struggled feebly and gave a small bleating cry. A sacrifice, of course, thought Alex. '*A white goat for Kali.*' They would cut the creature's throat with suitable ritual.

He saw the light glint on the long blade of a knife, and the men nearest the priests and the brazier drew back and caught their breath in a harsh and simultaneous gasp that was clearly audible above the thudding beat of the drum. A shudder swept back through the crowd as a wave sweeps in from the open sea, so that even those who could not see felt the surge of that savage emotion, and Alex was seized with a sudden sick horror, inexplicable and paralyzing. A horror that crisped his hair and dried his mouth and brought cold sweat out on his forehead.

He would have moved then if he could, but his muscles would not obey him, for he was helplessly afraid with a fear that he had never known before. A primitive, primeval fear; not of death, but of Evil . . . He could hear the harsh panting breath of the men about him and it seemed to him as though they breathed as a pack of wolves might breathe; avidly, tongues lolling, circling about a wounded buck.

The smoke from the brazier faded and the flame leapt clear, and as it did so a man near it sprang to his feet with a hoarse cry. It was the tall man who had first spoken, and for a moment his face showed clear in the leaping light; a harsh, hawk-nosed face whose deep-set eyes were white-ringed with horror. He called out something that Alex did not hear, for the drum beat louder and the chant rose to a frenzy. Someone in the crowd pulled the man back, and the knife flashed and fell. There was a bubbling, agonized cry, shrill and high and almost instantly drowned in the concerted groaning howl of the crowd. But it had not been an animal's cry, and Alex stumbled to his feet and stood pressed against the slimy stone of the pillar, and saw what it was that had cried out.

It was not the body of a white goat that lay on the slab of stained and reeking stone below the flickering brazier, but the naked body of a child. A white child. Alex caught a momentary glimpse of yellow hair and a small mouth that gaped from that last shriek of terror above the gaping scarlet gash of the severed throat. It was a boy of no more than three or four years of age, his small body startlingly white against the dark stone and the bright blood.

A blind, killing rage laid hold of Alex, blotting out reason and any thought of caution. His hand fumbled in the breast of the flowing Pathan shirt and closed upon the warm metal of the pistol he carried hidden there. At that range he could not miss the priest who stood above the child's body. He would kill him and his fellow-priest who held the bowl, and three others. And after that there was still his knife . . .

He jerked out the pistol and levelled it, and as he did so the man immediately in front of him rose, momentarily blocking his view, and turned to grope his way into the blackness beyond the line of pillars. But that moment had been enough. Sanity returned to Alex and the red fog of rage cleared from his brain. There were more important things at stake than avenging the slaughter of a child. The lives and safety of other children, and of countless men and women, might hang upon his ability to leave that underground den alive. It would do no good to anyone were he to die too, even though he were to take a dozen of that evil company with him to the grave. The thing was too big. It would go forward and spread, and there would be one less voice to cry a warning. Niaz too would not live to tell that tale, for he too would fight.

Alex slid the pistol back into hiding and wiped the sweat out of his eyes. The horrible ritual of the sacrifice had drawn all eyes and there had been no one watching him. He sank down again onto his heels and found that he was shivering violently. The man who had stolen away into the darkness had left him a clearer field of vision, and once more someone threw a substance on the brazier which hissed and flared and burnt with a bright flame, throwing the faces nearest to it into strong relief. One face in particular caught Alex's attention. A dark gloating face contorted with hate and excitement; the eyes wide and glittering and avid. Red stones – rubies from their colour – adorned his ears and flashed upon his quivering hands. 'I shall know that man again, at least,' thought Alex.

There was some ritual being performed that he could see but not understand, and then he realized that the fresh blood was being mixed with the flour on the platter. He caught the familiar movements of kneading that he had seen a thousand times before in the lines and beside camp-fires and in the bazaars. They were making a chuppatti; the daily bread of India. To the droning accompaniment of strange incantations and the ceaseless, maddening thud of the drum the dough was kneaded, shaped, flattened and baked on a metal platter laid across the glowing brazier. And all the while, to the sound of that chanting, the rows of watching men swayed and bowed and grovelled on the ground in a state of half-hypnotic frenzy.

At last the platter was lifted off the fire and the priests of Kali broke up the bread that smoked upon it, mumbling and grunting invocations to gods and devils – invocations as old and as evil as those chanted in the temples of Moloch. The man with the ruby earrings was handed a square of silk by someone behind him, and laying it across his hands he received the broken pieces of the chuppatti from the priests.

'Let the token be sent forth!' howled the tallest of the priests, tossing his arms above his head. 'Let it go up and down the land. From the North to the South, from the East to the West! And wheresoever it passes, there shall men's hearts be turned to hatred of the oppressors. For this is the pestilence – this is the evil – this is the blood of the British!' His eyeballs rolled in his head and there was froth on his lips. 'Hear me, Kali! Hear me, O drinker of blood! From the North to the South! From the East to the West!'

He fell to the ground and writhed upon the stone floor as the second priest flung oil into the brazier and a crackling flame leapt upward to the roof, blazed furiously for a moment and died. The drum crashed and was still. The chanting ceased on a long wailing note and the vault was plunged into darkness and silence – a darkness in which only the red coals of the brazier gleamed like a single malignant eye.

A voice spoke softly into that silence: 'This that ye have witnessed shall be binding upon all; for were it known, there is not one here whom the *feringhis* would not hang at a rope's end for this night's work. In the eyes of the Company's Government all who have seen it would be held guilty of the blood that has been shed. It were well to remember this, lest any be tempted to speak unwisely.' The voice ceased, and presently man after man rose noiselessly and groped their way to the stair shaft to pass up it and out into the clean night air.

Once there they did not linger, but seemed anxious to avoid each other's company, emerging from the shaft like ants debouching from a hole in the ground, to hurry furtively away into the darkness.

The torch-bearers had gone and the stone-paved square with its surrounding wall of jungle was shadowy under the starlight and the waning moon. Alex made his way down the black length of the nullah, guided by a spark of light that proved to be a single *chirag* – a tiny earthenware saucer filled with oil in which a wisp of cotton did duty as a wick – which had been left on a ledge by the narrow cleft of the gateway. He saw the spark vanish briefly as the man ahead of him passed in front of it and entered the tunnel, and then he himself had reached it.

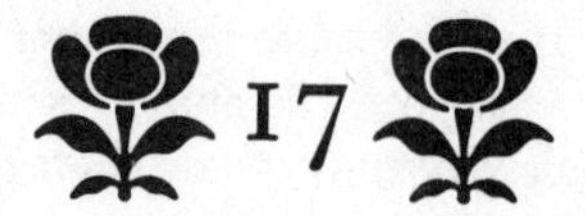

17

Three minutes later Alex was climbing the goat-track on the far side of the nullah and presently he was among the high grass at the end of the plain.

A hand touched his arm as he passed under the black shadow of a thorn tree, and a voice whispered: 'It is I, brother.'

'Back!' said Alex softly. He caught Niaz by the wrist and dragged him swiftly back into the high grass beside the path, crouching down beside him. A moment later another man climbed the slope out of the nullah and passed along the path at a jog-trot. It was a sadhu, his ash-smeared body grey in the moonlight. 'Down,' whispered Alex to Niaz who would have moved. 'Keep down!' They flattened themselves against the dry ground in the shelter of the dusty, sharp-edged grass and lay still as man after man hurried silently along the narrow goat-track towards the distant village, each man keeping his distance from the next and each one glancing furtively from left to right and quickly over his shoulder: sadhus, sepoys, merchants, townsmen and zemindars; followers of the Prophet or wearers of the sacred thread; disciples of Baba Nanak, and worshippers of Kali.

'Divide and rule,' thought Alex watching them as they passed, their feet almost noiseless on the dusty goat-track and their breathing loud in the warm silence of the late September night. As long as these people were divided by their castes and their creeds into antagonistic factions they would always be at the mercy of a conqueror, but if they once combined they could stand against any from sheer weight of numbers. 'But they will never combine,' thought Alex. 'Never. Half of them hate each other more than they hate us. This will not last . . .'

Niaz jerked at his sleeve and whispered: 'Why do we wait? It is not good to linger here. Let us go.'

'Hush,' said Alex softly. 'There is a debt to pay. When these have gone we go back. There are some few who will remain. The priests will leave last, for there is work to do. They cannot leave the dead unburied.'

'Has there been killing, then?'

'Yes. Quiet – here is another——'

Two men this time. One tall and turbaned, his hawk nose clear-cut against the starlight; the other stout and muffled in a shawl that was wound about his shoulders and over his head as though to guard against the night air. The tall man did not walk furtively as the others had done. He strode past, brushing against the grasses, careless of noise, and although he spoke in an undertone his words were clearly audible:

'Dogs and devil-worshippers!' said the tall man furiously. 'Must they stoop to such filth to ensure that none shall betray them for gain? Now are all our heads forfeit for this night's work.'

'Hush – oh hush!' begged the stout man, pausing to peer anxiously over his shoulder. 'Surely thine is forfeit already, Maulvi Sahib, because of the words thou hast spoken against the *Angrezis*.'

'They will not hang me for a word,' said the tall man scornfully, 'for with the purblind vanity of their race they do not fear such talk. But let them hear of this killing and they will hunt us down like mad jackals – each one of us. Dogs and devil-worshippers——' The sound of their voices faded as they disappeared into the darkness.

'That is Ahmed Ullah, a talukdar of Faizabad,' whispered Niaz. 'He is one who goes up and down the land speaking against the Company's Raj. They call him the Maulvi of Faizabad.'

At last the steady procession of shadowy figures ceased and for a full ten minutes no one passed along the narrow path. 'Thirty-seven,' said Niaz. 'I have kept tally. There should be some few more, but not all came this way. Some came along the nullah from the northward. There are two paths that enter it from that end.'

Alex stood up with infinite caution and remained for a further minute or two listening intently. But the night was silent and nothing moved. Niaz said softly: 'It is foolishness to go back into the tiger's lair having once escaped. Forgo thy revenge and come away. There is more in this than one life.'

'It was a child,' said Alex. 'An *Angrezi* child.'

'Ah!' said Niaz. 'Let us go back, then.'

There was no other way of reaching the ruined fort except by the way they had taken before, and they crept down the steep sandy slope that led down into the nullah, their nerves tensing to each rattle of a dislodged pebble or slither of dry earth crumbling beneath their feet. The bed of the nullah was by now in complete darkness, but Niaz possessed eyes like a cat, and though Alex was not his equal in this he could see well enough not to be unduly troubled by it.

The huge stone-paved courtyard lay bathed in starlight in which the clumps of coarse grass, thorn and stunted saplings that had thrust up here and there between the paving-stones took on the appearance of crouching men, but nothing stirred except a breath of night wind in the grasses. The two men stole forward silently, moving from one clump of shadow to the next, until they reached the shelter of the *peepul* tree that straddled the entrance to the roofless hall.

The block of stone that closed the shaft still leant upright against the lowest step of the ruined stair that rose behind it, and from the shaft itself came a faint light and a murmur of voices. Alex left the shelter of the *peepul* tree and creeping forward until he was directly above it, knelt listening. A voice that was faintly familiar was speaking in tones of cold anger:

'. . . so all are endangered!'

'Nay, all are now bound one to another!' replied another voice, a shrill hysterical voice. 'None will dare betray us, since all are guilty of the blood – as thou thyself hast said! They will keep silence now for their lives' sake. And was not this thing thine own scheme? A ruse – an excellent ruse! – for the unsettling of men's minds? The making of this first one with spells and priests and incantations and the calling up of spirits, so that the tale of its beginning might hasten the work? And for such things a sacrifice is necessary – yes, necessary.'

'A goat!' snapped the first voice. 'Had I known that aught else were planned——'

'Yea, a goat,' interrupted the second speaker. '"*A white goat for Kali!*" It was thyself who chose that password! But now' – the voice rose shrilly – 'now is the spell doubly sure! Of what use to Mother Kali is the blood of one starveling *bakri* when we may offer her the blood of a thousand – nay, a hundred thousand *feringhis*? In this sacrifice we have given a sign and a promise of that which is to come. A child of the Abominable Ones – the eaters of cattle, the defilers of caste! – a male child. May it be the first of many! Would that their throats were as one throat, men, women and children together, that I might slit them with a single stroke!' The voice rose until it was a scream of rage.

'That would I too,' said the first speaker. 'But to slaughter a defenceless babe in this fashion is an abomination before Gods and men.'

'Thou would'st spare the young of the serpent? *Pho*! That is indeed folly, since one such, if allowed to live, will one day sire many. They must be destroyed; leaf and branch, root and seed. Not one must be spared. Not one – *not one*!'

Alex heard the man stamp his feet furiously upon the ground so that the vault echoed. There was a brief silence and then the first speaker said shortly: 'Well, it is done now and it cannot be undone. But though this may do well enough for the villages, it will not serve for the sepoys. For them it must be something that strikes deeper and that touches every man. They are already as tinder, but there is as yet no spark. No matter; we will find it.'

Alex felt a touch on his arm and Niaz whispered in his ear: 'Let us let down the stone. I do not think they will lift it from below. They will be trapped like rats and die slowly.'

Alex's eyes gleamed in the starlight and he rose to his feet, and then checked and shook his head. 'No. They could, I think, find a way out. There are bats in that place, and where a bat can enter men might burrow a way out. We will wait. They must come up one by one.'

Niaz nodded and eased his knife from its sheath, and then quite suddenly his head came round with a jerk and he stiffened like a pointer, listening. 'Back!' said Niaz in a harsh whisper. 'There are others here!' They turned from the stair shaft and a moment later were once again among the shadows of the *peepul* tree, crouched down among the twisted roots.

Niaz's ears had not deceived him. There was someone approaching from the dense jungle behind the ruined walls. A branch cracked and grasses rustled, and presently they heard the sound of shod feet on stone. Two men emerged from the blackness beyond a crumbling archway and passing under the shadow of the *peepul* tree stopped by the entrance to the stair shaft. In the clear starlight they were little more than dark silhouettes against the paler expanse of the open courtyard; shadows who carried something in their hands that looked, in the uncertain light, like short-handled axes. A nightjar called from the jungle away to the right and a moment later, from the opposite side, an owl hooted, and one of the shadows spoke:

'The *philao* and the *thiboa* both! The omens are auspicious, though they come late. And the *bhil* is well hidden.'

There was a chink of metal striking against stone as the man rested the thing he carried, and Alex felt Niaz shiver and was aware with a sense of shock that he was frightened. He had never known Niaz show fear before and had thought him a stranger to it. But now he could feel it shudder through the body whose shoulder touched his, and he knew that Niaz was sweating and shivering in the grip of a similar horror to the one he himself had experienced in the vault that lay beneath their feet.

The man who had spoken bent down and called softly down the shaft: '*Ohé, thákur* – it is done.' He was answered from below, and a moment later a head appeared above the hole in the paving. Alex's muscles tensed involuntarily but Niaz's fingers clamped down upon his arm and checked him as four men one after another emerged from the shaft, the light from the vault below glimmering redly on the rubies that one of them wore in his ears. The men conferred together in whispers and he of the earrings said querulously: 'It is late, and I have far to go before morning. The two down there can close the stair. Let us go.' It was the same voice that Alex had heard screaming shrilly of death . . .

One of the men turned and called down the shaft: 'We go now. Close the stone when all is finished.' The faint light from below brightened for a brief moment as though more fuel had been thrown upon the brazier, and for an instant the speaker's face showed clear against the surrounding darkness.

It was Kishan Prasad.

The next moment the group by the stair shaft had turned away and vanished as quietly as they had come, and the night was silent again.

The two who crouched in the shadow of the *peepul* tree did not move for a full five minutes after the last faint rustle had died away, and then at last Niaz released his grip on Alex's arm and put up an unsteady hand to wipe the sweat from his forehead.

'My father's uncle spoke truth,' said Niaz in a shaking whisper. 'They are *not* all dead!'

'Who are not dead?'

'Those two were *lughais* – the diggers of the *bhil*, the buriers of the slain.

Didst thou not see that they carried the *khussee*? They are *Phansigers*. Thugs! The followers of Bhowani. The Stranglers!' Niaz's voice shook and Alex heard his teeth chatter. 'Now do I know that this is an evil thing that must be stamped out, else will the old evils arise again. Two score years ago my father's uncle aided Sleeman Sahib in the hunting down of the Stranglers, and he has told me——' The words broke off in a shiver. 'Let us go from here. Let us go quickly!'

'In a little while,' whispered Alex. 'There are only two below.'

He rose and moved away from the *peepul* tree, and after a moment Niaz followed him. They crouched down on either side of the tilted slab of stone and waited, listening to the faint sounds from below while the shrunken moon sank below the horizon and the sky darkened. A jackal howled mournfully from the plain beyond the jungle and a little breeze awoke and rustled through the surrounding scrub, whispering through the leaves of the *peepul* tree and filling the silent night with a hundred small stealthy sounds.

At last the light below was extinguished and presently feet groped on the stairs and a man's head lifted out of the black well of the stair shaft. Alex waited until his shoulders were clear of the shaft and then reached out and took him round the throat. The man uttered one choking gasp and then he was struggling frantically, his hands clawing the air. His bare feet beat a tattoo against the steep stone steps, and Alex lifted him clear with one savage heave as though he had been of no more weight than a sack of vegetables.

'What is it? Hast thou fallen?' asked a voice from the darkness below, and a second head appeared above the pavement. Niaz's lean fingers closed about the fat throat and he jerked the man up and backward across the rim of the shaft and brought his head down upon the stone with a sharp sound like the cracking of an egg. It was enough.

'This one at least will cut no more throats,' said Niaz. 'Is thine sped?'

'Yes,' said Alex breathlessly, and let the limp thing drop in a huddled heap at his feet. His hands were wet and sticky with the blood that had burst from the man's mouth and nostrils, and he stooped, panting, and wiped them on the priestly robes.

'What now?' asked Niaz.

'Throw them back. If any raise the stone to seek for them, they will find them waiting.'

They tumbled the bodies back into the shaft and lowered the stone above it. They could not see how the thing had been raised or on what principle the two dead priests would have lowered it into place, and they had no time to discover the trick of it. They put their shoulders to it and discovered that it took the last ounce of their combined strength to send it crashing into place. The noise of its fall broke the silence of the night as though it had been the crash of a cannon and awoke a hundred echoes from the ruined walls.

'Quick,' gasped Niaz. 'If there be any within earshot they may return.'

They ran together across the wide, ruined courtyard and plunged into the blackness of the nullah, and ten minutes later they had reached the edge of the grazing grounds and the grove of trees where Alex had tethered the horses.

'Where now?' whispered Niaz, mounting a fidgeting horse with an ease that consorted ill with the character of Jatu the toy-seller. 'We cannot ride together.'

'Lunjore. I go by way of Pari.'

'It were better to take a road south of Gunga,' said Niaz. 'There be few Pathans to be met with in these parts, and it is not safe for thee to ride the roads of Oudh.'

'No roads are safe now,' said Alex grimly.

'True. Let us go swiftly, for in another hour it will be dawn. I would that I had my own mare between my knees in place of this bag of bones!'

By first light they were no more than a dozen miles from Khanwai, for the roads were rough and now that the moon had set the darkness made it necessary for them to keep the horses to a walk. As the dawn broke and the morning mists turned from silver-grey to rose and saffron, and the long low veils of smoke from the cow-dung fires of the villages stretched out across the plain, Niaz fell behind and Alex rode on alone through open country where peacocks screamed from the standing crops and the dew-diamonds on every blade and twig glittered in the first rays of the rising sun.

It was barely more than a hundred miles from Khanwai to Lunjore; less as the crow flies. He should be able to reach there some time during the night, but the horse would need rest. Alex had always been able to sleep in the saddle when necessary, but for the sake of the animal he rode he would be compelled to halt for some part of the day. The thought of any halt oppressed him, since his instinct was to keep going with all possible speed. He could not rid himself of the thought that at any hour the word might go out to look for Sheredil of the Usafzai who had stood in the full glare of the torchlight and shown Kishan Prasad's ring.

Alex looked down at the ring now, and dropping the reins wrenched the thing off in a sudden spasm of loathing, and flung it away into the rank grass by the roadside.

It had been Kishan Prasad whose voice he had heard in the vault protesting against the murder, and it had undoubtedly been the priests and the unknown man with the ruby earrings who had been responsible for that foulness. But Kishan Prasad, whether he had condoned it or not, had convened that unholy coven, and as the instigator of it he could be held to account for all that had happened there, and summarily hanged for his part in the night's work. Alex wondered yet again why he had not let the man die? He had had the chance, and some absurd, inexplicable quixotic streak born of background and upbringing had forced him into saving his life. And yet only a few hours ago he had killed another man, and the dried blood of that killing was still on his hands, spotting his clothing and dark under his fingernails. Yet a hundred such men were less dangerous than one Kishan Prasad. Was rage then, and not justice or reason, the incentive for killing?

Alex scowled down at his stained hands. There must not be a rising! It must be prevented at all costs; for if such a thing were to occur, and the blood-lust that he had witnessed last night were to be let loose, the British, who would do little now for the sake of reason, would do much under the spur of blind rage, and the retribution that would follow an armed rising would be both harsh and horrible, engulfing innocent and guilty alike. His own behaviour was proof enough of that, for he, who had not been able to leave Kishan Prasad to die, had killed a man for rage and revenge – because he had seen that man murder a child. Yet if the fear and hatred that such men as Kishan Prasad were coaxing into flame were to flare out into rebellion, a thousand children would die worse deaths: 'It must not happen,' thought Alex desperately. 'If it does it will leave a legacy of hatred and suspicion that will go on into the future until one day——' The mare shied as a black-buck bounded across the path, and the action brought his thoughts back from the problems of the future to those of the immediate present.

Shortly after mid-day, having watered his horse and tethered it some hundred yards within the borders of the surrounding jungle, he lay down and slept, and an hour later Niaz, jogging along in the hot dust with a party of armed men – the erstwhile retainers of an Oudh noble whose estates now lay under threat of confiscation by the Company's Government, and whose acquaintance he had made on the road – noted that the print of a misshapen horseshoe no longer appeared upon the dusty surface of the road, and nodded to himself, realizing that Alex must have turned aside to rest his horse. That meant night riding, and it was safer to ride by night.

The low sun was shining between the grass stems and the bamboo canes when Alex awoke, and a jungle cock was calling from a cane-brake above the stream. Alex rummaged among the folds of his garment and produced the remains of a chuppatti, which he ate hungrily. The stream would provide water to quench his thirst and he need not stop again for food or rest until he reached Lunjore.

As he ate he thought of the ritual making of the chuppatti that he had witnessed last night, and of stories that he had heard of food prepared in time of plague with special incantations being taken out and left beside the roadside in the belief that any passer-by who picked it up would carry away the infection from the house or village. Was that the meaning of the making of the chuppatti? The symbolic ridding of the community – of Oudh – of the misfortunes that had befallen it?

A flock of parrots fluttered up from the edge of the stream and screeched indignantly away between the trees as Alex emerged from the jungle and bent to scoop the water up in his cupped hands, and a line of egrets flapped overhead, chalk-white against the blue sky, making for the distant river. Alex dried his hands against the full Pathan trousers, and mounting, rode out of the jungle and into the warm evening light.

He made considerably better time over the next twenty miles or so, for the horse appeared to have benefited from its rest. The sun plunged below the horizon and a sharp sweet smell of wood-smoke stole across the plain, and presently a little chill wind arose, a precursor of the cold weather and a promise of cool nights. Alex wrapped a length of cotton cloth about his throat and shoulders, and as the swift dusk swallowed up jungle and plain, and the ghost of the wedge-shaped moon gathered strength in the darkening sky, he settled himself down to ride hard, using all the skill he possessed to coax the best speed from his shoddy mount.

It was late and the road was white in the moonlight as he neared the little town of Pari. He had covered over eighty miles since he had left Khanwai before dawn that day, and only a matter of some six or seven more separated him from the river that formed the border between Oudh and Lunjore. Once across the river, an hour's ride would bring him to the cantonments and Lunjore city that lay barely ten miles from the border.

The road that had run for the past few miles in the shadow of overarching trees ran out into an open plain dotted with tussocks of tall grass and the sparse shadows of thorn trees, on the far side of which a few warm pinpricks of light marked the outskirts of Pari. The plain lay milky in the moonlight, patterned by the misshapen shadows of the grass clumps and an occasional outcrop of rock that loomed tall and sharp-edged against the night sky. Something moved in the black shadow of the rock and Alex reined in hard as Niaz rode out into the open.

Niaz did not speak, but catching the mare's bridle he turned her off the road. He was breathing quickly and the flanks of his own weary beast were white with foam and heaving as though it had been ridden to exhaustion.

'Thou canst not go forward,' said Niaz, speaking in a whisper as though even in that wide plain he feared to be overheard. 'The word has gone out against thee. There were men in Pari asking if any had seen a Pathan horse-dealer – one Sheredil, a man of the Usafzai. Some matter of a stolen horse – or so they said. I rode on through the town and circled back two *koss* through the crops and the grazing grounds, so that none should see me: but this horse is spent. If thine will still carry thee, turn back and ride for the village by the walled tank where the three tombs stand beside the road. There is another path to the southward from there, through the jungle. It is a long way and a rough one, but——'

He stopped suddenly and turned his head, listening. There was a faint rhythmic sound from somewhere far out on the plain. 'Horses!' whispered Niaz. He slipped from the saddle and the next instant Alex was beside him. They ran back to where the road crossed a gully, dragging the unwilling horses with them, and turned up it, stumbling among the stones and the water-worn boulders. The sides steepened as it curved back at a right angle, and they were hidden.

Alex whipped the cloth from about his shoulders and pulled a fold of it about his horse's head, and saw Niaz drag off his turban and use it to bandage the jaws of his own exhausted beast. The sound of its laboured breathing was intolerably loud in the silence, and Niaz wrenched the girths loose and thrust the reins into Alex's hands: 'Keep them still. I would see who comes.'

He turned and crept back down the gully, and for a moment or two Alex heard the stones click and rattle and then there was a silence in which he could hear only the wheezing of the weary horse and, presently, the swift clop of hooves and a muffled jingle of bridles. The mare lifted her head and shivered and her bridle chinked. Alex threw an arm about her neck and held her head against him and she stood quietly. The sound of hoof-beats came nearer and then they were clattering among the dry stones of the gully, breasting the slope on the far side, and were past and fading once more into the silence.

After a moment or two he released the mare's head and unwound the cloth from about it, and she blew heavily through flaring nostrils and stamped uneasily among the water-worn pebbles. A stone clattered and a shadow moved on the wall of the gully, and Niaz was back: 'We are too late,' he said quietly. 'There is no going back.'

Alex had not yet spoken and he did not speak now. He drew out the small pistol he carried slung about his neck, and moving out into the moonlight checked the loading and then tucked it into his wide leather belt where his hand could rest upon the slender butt. Niaz nodded approvingly as he re-wound his turban.

'I do not think there will be more upon the road,' he said. 'They will look for thee to enter the town. We will ride on for half a *koss* and then turn away from the road and make a circle through the fields. It is on the far side that we shall find it difficult, for there is only one place where the river may be crossed – by the bridge of boats into Lunjore – and that will be watched.'

'We will deal with that when we have the town behind us,' said Alex. 'Can that beast bear thee?'

'Needs must,' said Niaz with a laugh. They led the horses back onto the road and mounting again rode on into the moonlight towards the distant town.

Fifteen minutes later they turned off the road and went at a foot-pace, the horses picking their way wearily between rocks and tussocks of grass, and presently they were skirting the cultivated land to the south of Pari. A pariah dog barked at them as they crossed a shallow irrigation ditch where Niaz's horse stumbled and all but threw him, and a second dog and another and another took up the shrill challenge until the night rang to the yapping chorus. Niaz dug his heels savagely into his horse's flanks and urged it forward at a shambling trot down a dusty path that skirted a cactus hedge, and Alex could hear him cursing under his breath.

A watchman, perched in a ramshackle *machan* in a mulberry tree to scare the deer and wild pig from the crops, shouted hoarsely and discharged an ancient fowling piece. The pellets rattled through the leaves and something like a red-hot knife sliced into Alex's arm and he felt the warm blood pour down it and wet the fingers of his left hand. Then water glimmered in the moonlight and they found themselves on a narrow track bordering the marshy margin of a jheel that stretched away and to the left.

The frenzied barking of the pariah dogs died away behind them as the track curved north again under the shadow of a steep bank topped by a towering hedge of cactus, and presently came to what appeared to be a dead end, for the bank and the cactus hedge bent sharply at a right angle, barring their path and continuing on in an unbroken line towards the glimmering stretches of the jheel. Niaz drew rein in the shadows and slid to the ground. 'There is a lane ahead,' he whispered. 'Thou canst not see, for it runs——' He stopped suddenly. 'Art thou hit?'

'It is only a flesh wound,' said Alex, and dismounted awkwardly.

Niaz rolled back the sodden sleeve. A raw-edged fragment of the scrap-iron with which the watchman's gun had been loaded had ploughed through the fleshy part of the arm midway between shoulder and elbow, making an ugly jagged tear that bled freely. Niaz ripped two strips of cloth from Alex's turban and making a pad of the first bound the wound skilfully. 'And the lane?' said Alex.

'It runs back to the right; there, by the turn of the bank. It was not watched when I came by this way, but it may be that there are watchers now. Wait here while I go forward to see.'

He vanished silently into the shadows and Alex waited, listening to the many night noises and calculating the chances of survival. A breath of wind rattled a dead and dried cactus leaf, jackal packs bayed the moon, and from the edges of the jheel frogs croaked in noisy and monotonous chorus while an occasional clucking proclaimed the presence of water-birds feeding further out from the shore.

Niaz returned as noiselessly as he had gone, his shod feet making no sound on the soft carpet of the dust: 'The path is shut' – his voice was barely a breath of sound. 'They have run a cart across the far end and there are two men there. Perhaps three.'

Alex said: 'And the jheel?'

'It would take us until morning to cross it, if we were not drowned among the weeds. Moreover, we could not swim the horses.'

'That may be no loss! There will be a watch kept for a mounted man and the horses may well be recognized. Though it is true that without them——' He was silent for a moment or two, his eyes ranging along the banks and the cactus hedges above them. But the banks were steep and the cactus hedge impenetrable to anything larger than a mongoose. He thrust the reins at Niaz and said: 'Wait while I see.'

He walked soft-footed in the shadow of the bank and found, as Niaz had said, that the bank that apparently took a sharp-angled turn to the left was not the same bank as that which they had followed, but another that cut across it. The two banks turned back towards the town and ran parallel for about thirty yards, forming a narrow steep-sided lane. A country cart had been backed into the mouth of the lane at the far end, and Alex could hear a murmur of voices and see a gleam of firelight. He crept forward to within a dozen feet of the cart and observed with satisfaction that it carried a bale of fodder slung beneath it between the clumsy wheels, and that a blanket hung down between the shafts to provide a rough screen for a small fire of dung-cakes that smouldered on the ground in front of the cart and warmed the feet of the watchers. Two men squatted beside it and were apparently playing cards by its glow, and a third man leant against a wheel and appeared to be asleep. There was just room for a man to pass between the cart and the left-hand bank, but not for a horse. Alex wriggled backwards with infinite caution and presently rejoined Niaz.

'It is easy.'

He outlined a plan in a few terse sentences and Niaz nodded: 'We will try it. If it comes to the worst they are only three to our two, and out of three there is always one who runs away.'

'We cannot allow even one to run away, or the alarm is given. Give me five minutes.' Alex turned and crept back the way he had come.

The lane was inches deep in dust and even the long-thorned fragments of dead cactus with which it was strewn only pressed deeper into it under Alex's feet, while the faint snap of their breaking was drowned by the purr and bubble of the hookah and the slap of the falling cards. A dozen yards short of the cart he flattened himself against the ground once more and began to crawl forward inch by inch, the end of his turban wrapped about his nose and mouth as a protection against the choking dust. Then he had reached the cart and was under it, shielded from view by a bale of fodder and the hanging blanket, with his head barely a foot from the legs of the man who leant against the off-side wheel and less than a yard from the two card-players who muttered, cursed, coughed and drew by turns at the hookah.

The dust and the acrid smoke of the dung-fire penetrated even through the folds of turban cloth and tickled Alex's nostrils unbearably, and the wound in his arm throbbed painfully. A procession of ants crawled across his legs and a host of night-flying insects, attracted by the glow of the fire, fluttered and crept about his face. The slow minutes seemed like hours and he had begun to wonder if some mishap had befallen Niaz when at last he heard the sound he had been waiting for. A voice – a raucous and untuneful voice that sang an obscene ballad enumerating in detail the charms of a certain Delhi courtesan.

The song, interrupted by hiccoughs, came nearer, and the card-players broke off their game and turned to listen, while the dozing sentinel roused himself and unslinging his musket held it at the ready.

'It is only some drunkard from the town,' growled one of the card-players. '*Ohé*! Who comes? Thou canst not pass. The road is closed. Go back, O servant of Bhairon!'

'Go back?' hiccoughed the newcomer. 'Wherefore? And since when has this path been closed to honest men?'

'It is an order of the new Government,' said the man with the musket.

'What *zulum*!' (oppression) First it is a wandering pig of a Pathan whose horse thrusts me into the jheel so that I am besmired with mud, and now the road is closed against me so that I——'

The man with the musket gripped Niaz and dragged him into the light of the fire. 'What is that you say? What Pathan?'

'He is back on the road there. May his horse fall into the jheel and drown. He desired to know where he might obtain a fresh mount, his own being spent. But what do I know of horse-dealing? A song is better. Let us sing together, thus – "O moon of Beauty . . ."'

'It is the very one!' said the man with the musket. 'Hush, fool! Does he come this way?'

'Who?'

'The Pathan, O owl!'

'How should I know? He sits by the path while his horse grazes. Must I indeed go back? What if he should beat me? Pathans be men of evil temper and this one is angry.'

'Let us go,' said one of the card-players, his hand on the handle of a serviceable-looking knife. 'There is a price on his head. Stay by the cart, Dunnoo, and let none pass. And thou, O son of a noseless mother, remain thou here until we return, and if it be that thou hast not spoken truth concerning the Pathan thou shalt suffer a sore beating.'

'Why should I not speak truth?' demanded Niaz, tripping over his feet and sitting down heavily in the dust. 'It is as I have said. He sits by the jheel and curses his gods. If I may go no further I will sleep here. One place is as good as another.'

He staggered to his feet again and yawned largely; a yawn that broke off into a hiccough as two of the men turned and disappeared down the lane. Presently the remaining sentinel turned back to squat by the fire. There was the sound of a dull blow, a coughing grunt and a thud, and Alex crawled out from under the cart and beat the dust off his clothes.

The man who had been addressed as Dunnoo lay face downwards by the smouldering fire and Niaz was composedly replacing a long-hafted knife in its sheath and concealing both in the folds of his clothing.

'I said there was to be no more killing,' said Alex angrily.

'He is not dead,' said Niaz, rolling the man over with his foot. 'I used the hilt only, and these *pūrbeah* pigs have thick heads. It may be that he has a crack in the skull, no more. Do we go now? It will be a long journey on foot.'

'All the more reason to go on horseback,' said Alex. 'Even a spent horse may travel swifter than a man. We will wait. Those two will be back soon, and I think that they will bring us the horses.'

He stooped above the unconscious man and began swiftly to strip off his outer clothing, donning them himself while Niaz bound and gagged the man and rolled him out of sight under the cart.

Ten minutes later the other two returned, leading, as Alex had surmised, the horses that they had found grazing by the jheel. 'We could not find him. But there were two horses and we have brought both away. He cannot get far on foot,' said the man with the musket, edging his way between the wheel and the steep bank of the lane. He crumpled and fell as Alex's fist took him under the jaw, and a choked cry from the rear of the cart showed that Niaz had risen from beneath it and struck down a second victim.

'Pah! It is easy,' said Niaz with scorn, ducking under the wheels and reappearing. 'We must pull this thing clear, else the horses cannot pass.'

They dragged the cart forward, and having led the horses out of the lane, tied up the two groaning men (the first had still not moved) and bundled them into the cart. 'It would be better to kill them,' said Niaz judicially, 'then they can tell no tales.'

'There has been enough killing. They will not be found until morning and we shall be across the river by then.'

'Mayhap,' grunted Niaz pessimistically. 'But there is the bridge to be crossed.'

The brief period of rest appeared to have put new life into the jaded horses and they made good time along the moon-splashed road towards the river, but Alex's arm had begun to stiffen, and from the pain that it gave him he realized that the jagged scrap of metal that had caused the wound must still be embedded in it. He would have to get it out soon or it would fester.

Less than an hour's riding brought them the smell of the river, and they led the horses off the road and tethering them in the jungle went forward on foot to reconnoitre. The unmade road became rougher and more sandy and the air cooled perceptibly and smelt of wet sand and stagnant shallows. There was a square mud toll-house where the road ended, and behind it, screened by plantains and bamboo, lay a meagre huddle of huts that housed the family of the toll-keeper and the bridge guard. Pedestrians were not required to pay a toll, which was only levied on carts and wheeled vehicles whose approach was audible from a considerable distance, and the toll-house was in darkness. Alex and Niaz kept to the shelter of the trees on the far side of the road, and gave it a wide berth.

The near bank was low and fringed with casuarina scrub, and the white sands and wandering shallows stretched far out into the moonlight. But beyond the sands and the shallows the river ran deep and wide, bounded on the far side by a steep bank and a solid wall of jungle. A raised stone causeway ran from the Oudh bank to the edge of the deep water where a bridge of boats spanned the main arm of the river, but there was no sign of life on or near it, and it lay open and innocent in the waning moonlight, creaking to the sluggish pull of the slow-moving current.

'They are on the other side,' muttered Niaz.

Alex nodded, frowning. He knew the far bank of the river well. The jungle that clothed it was so dense as to be almost impenetrable. A horse could not force its way through that tangle of trees and scrub and high grass, and it was no easy task for a man, for there were no paths except those made by wild animals. The only road was the one which wound for almost ten miles from the river to Lunjore, walled in by the jungle. And even if they could swim the horses across there was no point for several miles, either up stream or down, where they could get them ashore, since the current ran strongly on the far side and had worn away the bank until it overhung the river. The only possible landing-place was the cutting where the bridge of boats ended and the road ran up a long, gentle slope to where another brick-built toll-house and half a dozen mud huts huddled on the fringe of the jungle. They would have to leave the horses.

'We must swim,' said Alex slowly.

Niaz did not speak but he pointed silently, and Alex, looking along his raised arm as a man sights along the barrels of a gun, saw a long grey object at the water's edge; something that might have been a log washed down by the river, and which lay at the exact angle that such a log would have grounded. Mugger; the blunt-nosed, man-eating crocodile of the Indian rivers.

'If I die, I will die on land,' said Niaz, 'and not in the belly of such as that. Besides, I am no swimmer, and it will go hard with thee to swim against the current with a wounded arm. No. I will go forward, riding one of the horses. Why should they do me harm? They look for a Pathan. If there be only a few, I may slay them, and then I return for thee.'

'And if there be a dozen of them and they hold thee until first light? The men we bound at Pari will be found at the dawn, and they will follow here and will remember thee.'

'I said we should have killed them,' said Niaz disgustedly. 'It is in my mind to ride back now and slit their throats. But it were better I think to go forward while the night lasts.'

Alex said: 'Try then. It may serve. Take my horse, for it is the least spent. And if there be too many of them, ride for Lunjore and tell Gardener Sahib to send a company with all speed.'

They walked back through the casuarinas and the clogging sand towards the road and the thicket where they had left the horses, but as they reached the road's edge Niaz checked suddenly to listen and Alex, following his example, heard a faint and distant sound that he had heard once before that night. A sound of galloping hoof-beats that came nearer and louder. This time from the direction of Pari.

The two men stood motionless in the shelter of the trees and presently five riders galloped past them in the clear moonlight, raising a choking white cloud of dust. They heard the headlong pace check at the toll-hut and a sound of voices, and then clear in the silence the creak and clop of horsemen crossing the bridge of boats.

Niaz let his breath out in a small sigh. 'One at least of those men is one who watched by the cart. I should have hit harder. The bridge is closed to us. It may be that we can win back to the Khanwai road. They will not look to see us there, and we have the horses. Let us go back.'

'And be hunted through Oudh? No. We must go forward – or die.'

'Then I think we die tonight!' said Niaz grimly.

'If we can reach the bridge it should be possible to swim the river,' said Alex thoughtfully. 'We can hold by the bridge and——'

'We cannot do it,' said Niaz. 'No two men could reach the boats unseen even on their bellies. There is not cover for a tree-rat.'

Alex digested the truth of this statement in silence. The base of the stone causeway was considerably wider than its top and the ramp on either side offered no cover, while from the bank to the bridge lay close on two hundred yards of flat open sand and shallow pools which the river covered in the rainy season. Anything moving on it would be visible while the moon was up, but between moonset and first light there would be at least a short period of darkness, and during that time it might be possible to wriggle unseen to where the bridge began, and there to take to the water. Niaz was no swimmer as he had said, but even he could pull himself over by the boats, for the ropes that tethered them together would provide a handhold. But they had first to reach the bridge . . .

Alex had had barely three hours' sleep in the last two days and his head was aching. His wounded arm was absurdly painful and it throbbed to a steady burning beat of pain that seemed to find an odd rumbling echo in the night. An echo which slowly drowned the throb of his blood, until he realized suddenly what it was. There were carts approaching down the road towards the bridge. A long line of creaking, bullock-drawn carts of the kind that may be met with on any Indian road at any time of the night; their drivers asleep while the patient beasts plod slowly onward hour after hour in the darkness.

Alex touched Niaz on the arm, and jerking his head in the direction of the distant sound, said: 'Turn the horses loose. We shall not need them again. I do not think that we shall die tonight, for these will take us across.'

They left the weary horses to graze in the jungle and ran back along the road towards the carts, keeping to the shadows. There were nine carts rumbling and creaking down the moonlit road, moving as slowly as crawling beetles; the torpid bullocks lumbering through the dust in a ruminative trance, noses almost to the ground and horns swaying, while their drivers crouched upon the cartpoles, miraculously preserving their balance, and slept. A flickering oil-lantern swung from the leading cart and the moonlight showed that four of the carts were piled high with sugar-cane while five carried sacks of *bhoosa*. Alex and Niaz slipped across the road between the carts, and Niaz, walking behind one of them, dragged out several of the light, bulging sacks and flung them away while Alex watched the man on the cart immediately behind for fear that he would wake.

'In!' whispered Niaz, and Alex swung up onto the cart and wriggled into the cave that Niaz had made among the sacks. The plodding bullocks did not slow their crawling pace by a step at the additional weight, and Niaz thrust two sacks on top of Alex and dropped back to burrow his way into the heart of a pile of sugar-cane with the celerity of a grass-snake.

Left alone in the dusty, sweet-smelling darkness, Alex shifted the sack beneath him and worked his way down and further forward into the pile until he lay in the centre of the stifling load. The carts rocked and squeaked and rumbled forward on the rutted dusty road, and presently, as the wheels met the dry sand near the river bank and a sleepy voice called from the toll-hut, they jolted to a stop. The carters, jerked abruptly into wakefulness, entered into surly argument with the yawning toll-keeper, and after some delay the carts started forward once more, and with shoutings, tail twistings and belabourings, jolted down the sandy slope onto the causeway. One by one they rolled out onto the bridge which swayed and groaned beneath the rumbling wheels, and one by one, as the bullocks grunted and strained under a hail of blows and shrill yells of encouragement, they breasted the slope on the far side and were on the road again.

Alex did not catch the shouted orders that checked the carts, for the creaking and rumbling had deafened him and the close-packed sacks muffled all other sounds, but the wheels ground to a halt and there were men all about the carts and hoarse angry voices.

'What is this? Yet another toll?' called one of the carters. 'A Pathan? Nay, we have seen no Pathans . . . Look then and see . . . Horses? Horses? These be no horse-drawn *gharis*! Bullocks only. We carry fodder and such stuff to Lunjore. Are you strangers that you do not know this?'

There was another burst of angry shouting and a man's voice said: 'Any fool would have known that the bridge would be watched once the word had gone out, and this man we seek is no fool. He will have doubled back to the Ganges. Besides, Narain Dass here says that the horses were spent. *Ohé*! thou upon the cart there; didst thou see no horses upon the road?'

'Have I not said that I saw no horses? And no Pathans either! It may be that I slept a little on the way, but if thou thinkest that we carry horses and Pathans in our carts thou art welcome to search for them. Perchance thou wilt find more than horses – elephants belike, and men of Turkistan! Search then – we cannot wait through the night.' A torch flared as men passed along the carts prodding and peering, but the task of unloading and reloading each cart was clearly impossible.

'Thrust with thy spear,' growled a voice.

'And who is to pay me for my sacks?' shrilled the carter furiously.

A voice further down the line said angrily that there was no spear made that could be stabbed down through sugar-cane, adding: 'Do we play at tent-pegging then?' – the speaker's spear had evidently stuck fast in a piece of cane. The wrangling voices passed down the line and presently someone climbed upon the sacks that concealed Alex, crushing them down stiflingly upon him, and something jabbed down, ripping through sacking and *bhoosa*. It missed Alex by a millimetre, but it caught the edge of the bandage that Niaz had tied about his arm and ripped it away. The blood had clotted and dried, but the wrench tore open the wound and he could feel the fresh blood well out once more. But either the spear had been pulled back in the fractional second before the blood flowed, or the *bhoosa* and the sacking had cleaned any traces from the metal, for the man jumped down upon the road again and passed on to the next cart.

Alex pressed his wounded arm against a yielding sack and tried to get his right hand across to cover it, for if blood should drip upon the white dust of the road it would be seen when the carts moved on. He managed to clench his fingers over it, but the warm sticky tide seeped between them. And then, after what seemed an eternity, the carts jerked forward again. It was over – and they were through. The dusty airless darkness closed in upon him, and he was still asleep when Niaz pulled him out from among the blood-stained sacks in the yellow dawn.

Three hours later, bathed, shaved and fed; clothed once more in his own clothes and with his wound probed, cleaned and bound and his arm in a sling, Alex presented himself at the Residency.

The Commissioner was engaged with a visitor and sent out word asking Captain Randall to wait. He would not, he said, be above half an hour.

Alex sat down in a verandah chair, and stretching his legs out before him prepared himself to wait. It was over thirty hours since he had left Khanwai, and an hour's more delay could make little difference one way or another. He could hear a murmur of voices from the large living-room on the far side of the Commissioner's office and supposed that Mr Barton's visitor must have called in a social rather than an official capacity. After a time the gorgeously uniformed *chupprassi* who squatted further down the verandah by one of the outer doors of the living-room, sprang to his feet and held aside the split-cane curtain that hung in front of it, and Alex could hear the Commissioner's voice raised in affable farewell. A man, an Indian, came out past the salaaming *chupprassi* and turned and walked down the length of the verandah. It was Kishan Prasad.

Alex did not move and not a muscle in his face quivered; nor was there any alteration in his lounging pose to betray the shock and the incredulous surprise that the sight of Kishan Prasad had given him. Kishan Prasad, walking softly, came to a stop in front of him and bowed. Alex did not return the greeting. He looked up at Kishan Prasad under his black brows with eyes that were as cold and hard and passionless as grey granite, and smiled.

Kishan Prasad drew back involuntarily and for a fractional moment some of his assurance seemed to drop from him and the lines about his mouth and jaw were suddenly accentuated. Then he recovered himself and his voice was smoothly urbane:

'Ah, Captain Randall. This is an unexpected pleasure. The Commissioner was telling me that he did not expect you back until next week when your replacement, Mr Parbury, is due to leave. I am sorry to see that you have suffered an injury to your arm. Nothing serious, I hope?'

'No, nothing serious,' said Alex from behind that cold smile. 'It was kind of you to come here. It will save me the trouble of sending an escort to bring you in.'

'To bring me where?' inquired Kishan Prasad, affecting polite surprise.

'To the jail – and the gallows.'

'My dear Captain Randall! I must admit that I do not understand you. Is it some English joke?'

'You understand me perfectly,' said Alex softly. 'Murder has always been a capital offence.'

'Murder?'

'What else? "*This thing that ye have seen done shall be binding upon you all, for were it known, there is not one of you whom they would not hang at a rope's end for this night's work,*"' quoted Alex in the vernacular. He saw Kishan Prasad's pupils widen and said: 'Yes, you were right. I am the man whom your cut-throats are hunting through Oudh. You should be more careful whom you admit to your meetings.'

'I do not understand——' repeated Kishan Prasad woodenly.

Alex said: 'But I do. I had heard many tales, but until two nights ago I had no proof. Now I have it. And your life and the life of every man who was there is twice forfeit – for sedition and for murder.'

Kishan Prasad released his breath in an audible sigh and after a moment he said very softly: 'That killing was by no will of mine. I do not war on babes, and had I known what was planned I should have prevented it. I am no ignorant worshipper of devils to dabble in such foulness. As for the rest, I have told you before that I desire to pull down your Company's Raj, and to that end I will use any and every means that lie to my hand. But you cannot hang me, because this proof that you have is no proof. It is only your word, and it will not be believed. No' – he held up a hand to check the words that Alex would have spoken – 'hear me out. I do not know how you knew of that meeting or how you came by the password, but I know that had I not in a foolish moment given you a certain token you would not have seen – what you saw. But having used that token to gain admittance, there was a penalty. It was told to me that a certain Pathan had entered, having shown it. I could not believe – yet it was possible. The word went out against that Pathan; but in case he were not stopped certain other things were done. If you send men now to Khanwai there will be nothing found in proof of your tale. As for me, a hundred witnesses can prove that I was elsewhere, and not at Khanwai, two nights ago.'

Alex said grimly: 'I think you will find, Rao Sahib, that my word will be taken against a hundred thousand of your witnesses.'

'Even when one of those witnesses is the Commissioner of Lunjore?' inquired Kishan Prasad softly.

Alex's face stiffened and there were suddenly two white patches at the corners of his mouth. He came to his feet with a swiftness that made Kishan Prasad flinch as if in expectation of a blow, and said in a harsh whisper: 'That I will not believe!'

'But you will find that it is so. He does not know that he lies,' said Kishan Prasad. 'You see, there was a – a little party that night at the house of a mutual friend, and the Commissioner perhaps indulged too freely in perfumed brandy. He does not remember very much of what occurred and he is convinced that I also was present. He was good enough to admire a trinket that I had brought back from France; an ingenious toy that he was pleased to accept. He has even mentioned it to Colonel Moulson, who is with him now. So you see——?'

Kishan Prasad sketched a deprecatory gesture with one slim brown hand, and Alex saw: saw with a complete and bitter understanding. Kishan Prasad had made full use of both Mr Barton's drunkenness and his vanity. It must have been so easy – so fatally easy. A pre-arranged party at the house of one of the more disreputable noblemen; drink and dancing-girls, champagne laced with brandy and probably opium. A man – any man with a superficial resemblance to Kishan Prasad – and his name repeated until it was impressed upon a fuddled brain. A gift accepted . . .

Alex knew his chief only too well. If the Commissioner had admitted seeing Kishan Prasad at such an affair he would never go back on such a statement, because to do so would be to admit instead that he had been drunk enough to be deceived, and at the house of a prominent Indian.

'They will say that you must have been mistaken,' said Kishan Prasad softly. 'As for this meeting you will tell them of, they will say it was a mere gathering of malcontents. Talk – but no more than talk. Shall I tell you why they will not believe? Because they do not wish to! The colonels who command the sepoy regiments here suspect that their regiments are rank with sedition. Their Indian officers are insolent in many small ways. But for shame's sake they will not admit it and each cries louder than the other that all is well. You see, I speak frankly to you. What need it there for pretence between us, who know what we know?'

He looked at Alex's rigid face and lowered his voice until it was barely a whisper: 'You know that you cannot win this fight. The Company has only a handful of men and its power is an illusion. I have seen the slaughter at Sebastopol and I know that your Queen has no more regiments to send. Do not fight us. Join us! It will not be the first time that men from the West have risen to greatness in the armies of Hind. There have been many – Avitable, George Thomas, Ventura, Potter, Gardiner——'

Alex laughed and the laugh brought a sudden flush into Kishan Prasad's olive cheeks. His hand dropped and he stepped back. Then: 'I am sorry,' he said gravely. 'That was a foolish thing to say.'

'Very,' agreed Alex.

Kishan Prasad smiled. 'I am sorry too that our blood makes us enemies. Perhaps in your next life it may be that you will be born a Hindu.'

'Perhaps,' said Alex. 'When I have hung you in this one.'

'That too may come about,' said Kishan Prasad. 'But the time is not yet.'

He saluted Alex with grave courtesy, and turning, walked down the shallow flight of steps into the bright sunlight of the garden and was driven away in an open carriage, his servants running beside it.

But the hours that followed, and the days that followed those hours, bore out all that he had said. Mr Barton listened with entire incredulity to Alex's story. Alex had made a mistake – a very natural one. All niggers looked as like as two peas when in a crowd. The suggestion that he himself might have been mistaken drove him to blustering and apoplectic indignation. Such an assertion was absurd and insulting! Why, the Rao Sahib had actually shown him a toy that he had bought in Paris – a musical-box ornamented with a naked dancer who contorted her waxen limbs in time to a tinny little tune. There it was, standing on the table to prove his words. Kishan Prasad had begged his acceptance of the trifle and had called only that morning in order to bring the duplicate key – a very sensible idea; these fiddling things were so easily lost . . .

Alex had brought him remorselessly back to the subject under discussion, and Mr Barton had been horrified and disbelieving. It was obvious, he said, that Alex had happened upon some queer religious rite; it never did to pry into such things – leave 'em to wallow was his motto. At such ceremonies the blacks were bound to get above themselves and talk a lot of inflammatory nonsense. It meant nothing. As for Alex's assertion that an English child had been murdered in cold blood, he could only suggest that Alex had been carried away by the – er – the unusual circumstances; the atmosphere, the fumes from the brazier he had spoken of, or the effects of fatigue. He would not like to suggest that Alex had been drinking; although some of these country-brewed spirits were far from mild. Of course it had been a young goat that he had seen killed! A very common form of sacrifice. And if Alex took his advice he would refrain in future from play-acting in native dress and mixing himself up in such affairs. It did not consort well with the dignity of a Company's officer and might lead to a deal of trouble. That wounded arm should be a lesson to him!

And now that that matter was settled, Mr Barton would like to know what news Alex had brought of the Condesa. He hoped that she was well. No beauty, what? – but looks were not everything. A good child, though plain. It was a thousand pities that he had found himself unable to travel to Calcutta, but he had not been well. A bout of fever. It was inconvenient, this journeying to Delhi, but he had thought it better to allow the girl to proceed there in the care of Mrs Abuthnot, as he himself would be going to Delhi shortly on official business. Two birds with one stone——

The past year had done nothing towards improving either Mr Barton's health or his appearance. He had, it is true, intended to take both in hand, and by means of daily exercise and abstaining from over-indulgence in the matter of wine and women, to have effected a considerable improvement. But on consideration he had come to the conclusion that such a course was entirely unnecessary. This was his last year of freedom and he would make the most of it. After this he would have a mewling, puking, scrawny and ill-favoured girl for ever about the house, who would doubtless kick up a fuss at all his amusements and might, if he overstepped the mark, rouse her influential relatives to protest on her behalf. Not that that would make much odds once he had his hands on the girl's money. Still, life would not be the same and so he would enjoy himself for this last year. Having reasoned thus, Mr Barton had abandoned all ideas of abstinence and exercise with a thankful sigh, and the result was the obese, balding, slack-lipped figure who now confronted Alex Randall with a glass clutched in one unsteady hand and his moustache and chin all slopped with brandy.

Alex had dismissed the Condesa in a single brief sentence and returned grimly to the question of Kishan Prasad and the meeting of seditionists at Khanwai. He had argued, expounded and pleaded, but Mr Barton remained obdurate. There was nothing he could do. It was all an unfortunate business and had best be forgotten. No sense in stirring up a hornets' nest.

The same opinion was expressed by Colonels Moulson and Packer, commanding two of the three regiments of Native Infantry stationed at Lunjore, and by Major Beckwith, in temporary command of the third in the absence of Colonel Gardener-Smith.

Colonel Moulson, who had neither forgotten nor forgiven Captain Randall's behaviour at Alexandria, had taken particular pains to be offensive. He had brought all his influence to bear to prevent the Commissioner from taking any official notice of the report, and had done his best to discredit the whole story. Colonel Packer, a bigoted Christian, was content to leave the entire matter in the hands of the Almighty, assisted by prayer, while Major Beckwith, uncertain of himself and convinced of the indestructible loyalty of every sepoy in his Regiment, had listened to Colonel Moulson's scathing and outspoken criticisms of jumped-up over-promoted pets of the Civil Service, and taken refuge in the fact that in Colonel Gardener-Smith's absence he could do nothing. Army officers such as Alex, who were removed from regimental duty and sent to occupy civil posts where both pay and power were greatly in excess of that enjoyed by their fellow-officers, were more often than not regarded with jealous resentment, and Major Beckwith was no exception in this way.

Alex asked for a week's extension of leave on account of his wounded arm, and rode to Agra to see Mr John Colvin, Lieutenant-Governor of the North-West Province. But the mission had proved abortive.

The Lieutenant-Governor was that same Mr Colvin who twenty years ago, as Lord Auckland's Private Secretary, had been one of the primary instigators of the disastrous folly of the Afghan War. He had never been able to forget it or ever again trust entirely to his own judgement. Mr Colvin did not believe that disaffection was rife in the country and still less that the Army was affected. There had been rumours, of course – but then there were always rumours. He could not take it upon himself to order the arrest of men like Kishan Prasad – influential men whom there was no reason to suspect of being anything but loyal – especially when, as Captain Randall had admitted, the Commissioner of Lunjore was prepared to swear that the man had been nowhere near the scene of this – um – gathering at Khanwai. He too thought that Captain Randall must have been mistaken, and that he was surely exaggerating the dangers of the situation. He too suggested that it was hardly suitable for an officer of the Company to take such investigations upon himself. There were paid spies among the native population who were entirely trustworthy, and better qualified for the work on account of their dark skins. He would of course pass on the information Captain Randall had given him to the proper authorities, but in the meantime . . .

Alex had set his teeth and listened with a gathering sense of frustration and bitterness. This was what it must feel like to be a lunatic confined in a cell, beating your head against the padded walls and convinced that it was you, and not your captors, who were sane. Perhaps he had indeed been mad to imagine that anyone would listen to him when men like General John Jacob were written down as alarmists. He had thought that if he could produce proof he must be believed. But it seemed that the evidence of his eyes was not proof and, as Kishan Prasad had truly said, the great majority did not wish to believe: they found it more comfortable to close their eyes and look the other way, in the hope that if they ignored its existence the danger would pass. To take any form of preventive action, they reasoned, would be to advertise a lamentable want of confidence and possibly precipitate thereby the very dangers whose existence they refused to admit.

The most that Alex could gain was permission to take six sowars and three British officers to see if any concrete evidence could be brought back of the murder that he professed to have witnessed. There had been a report of the disappearance of a child a week earlier, admitted Mr Colvin reluctantly. The three-year-old son of a private in a British regiment stationed in Cawnpore; and it was always possible, though hardly credible . . .

Alex had ridden back to Khanwai with six troopers and three sceptical but enthusiastic officers. They had found exactly nothing. The stair shaft leading to the underground chamber was open to the sky and choked with fallen debris that had the appearance of being there for some considerable time. There had been a heavy and recent fall of earth and stonework from the spot where the roots of the *peepul* tree had forced their way downward, and the vault appeared to be in too dangerous a state to encourage a thorough search.

Ten paces within the jungle behind the ruined fort they uncovered a grave, but it contained only the rotting carcass of a white goat.

BOOK THREE

CONWAY

It was over six weeks since the Abuthnots had left Calcutta on the long journey northward to Delhi. A journey on which they had been accompanied, somewhat unexpectedly, by Lord Carlyon and the Gardener-Smiths.

Lord Carlyon, having taken a fancy to visit the old Mogul capital of Delhi, had requested permission to avail himself of the pleasure of their company on what, he said, he must otherwise find to be a singularly tedious journey. Such a pleasantly worded request had been impossible to refuse, and it had been a source of some annoyance to Mrs Abuthnot that the Gardener-Smiths, having made a last-minute change in their plans to allow for a few weeks' visit to Delhi, had also attached themselves to the party.

Delia's mama had announced that the heat and humidity of Calcutta was really not to be borne, but Mrs Abuthnot, without wishing to be uncharitable, could not rid herself of the suspicion that Mrs Gardener-Smith's dislike of the Calcutta climate had only manifested itself when she had heard that Lord Carlyon would be travelling to Delhi with the Abuthnot party. She could also not entirely bring herself to believe that it was the pleasure of their united company that had prompted Lord Carlyon to make his flattering request. He was of course well aware that both Lottie and Winter were affianced and shortly to be married, but could it possibly be that he was attracted by her Sophie? Sophie, though a mere child, was such a sweet little thing! *Could* it be Sophie?

Mrs Abuthnot had indulged in a few maternal daydreams, and her lack of enthusiasm over the addition of the Gardener-Smiths to the party was understandable. Delia, thought Mrs Abuthnot with a sigh, was so *very* striking!

Colonel Gardener-Smith, like Colonel Abuthnot, looked upon the journey as a necessary evil, while his wife and daughter found it uncomfortable, fatiguing, and except for the presence of Lord Carlyon, insufferably tedious. As for Carlyon, he was not impressed with what he saw of India – although he was pleased to approve of the opportunities for rough shooting that it offered to travellers. Winter alone found interest and enchantment in every mile of the road: in each dawn that broke over the plain or the jungle in a wash of saffron yellow, and each evening when the sun would plunge to its rest in a dusty glow of gold and rose and amber, leaving the moon like a silver nutmeg in the sky . . . the silver nutmeg that a 'King of Spain's daughter' had travelled far to see.

The land unrolled itself before her in a pageant of beauty. The tangled jungle, the low hills and the level plains. The wide, wandering curves of the Indian rivers with their silver sandbanks and white flocks of egrets pricking through the shallows. The glimmering jheels from which the wild duck rose in dark skeins against the green evening sky. The palm trees and the yellow, mimosa-like blossoms of the thorny *kikar* trees. The sun-baked silence of the dusty roads and the cheerful tumult of the *paraos.* Little villages with their small bazaars, creaking well-wheels, tanks and temples. The scream of peacocks in the dusk and the cry of wild geese and sarus cranes at dawn . . .

Winter could not understand how anyone travelling through such a land could find it, as Lord Auckland's sister, Emily Eden, had found it, 'a shrivelled cinder of a country', and 'quite hideous'. How was it possible for the self-same thing to hold such enchantment and beauty for one pair of eyes and yet appear only ugly, daunting and repellent to another's?

But there was one aspect of the journey to Delhi which she did not find pleasant. The presence of Lord Carlyon.

Winter had not been favourably impressed by Carlyon on the occasion of their first meeting at Sybella's Summer Ball at Ware, and although his manner towards her since their meeting in Calcutta had been outwardly unexceptionable, she was uneasily aware of hidden undercurrents.

Carlyon's languid gaze had a way of resting on her with a look of insolently comprehensive appraisal, as though she were a slave girl on the block or a blood horse whose purchase he contemplated. His words too, though apparently superficial, frequently contained the same underlying suggestiveness, and he took every opportunity to touch her – gestures that she found hard to avoid without appearing ungracious or childishly rude. The pressure of those lingering hands, as white and well kept as a woman's despite their efficiency with reins or gun, would send a shrinking shiver of dislike and apprehension through her.

Carlyon was aware of that shiver, and he misinterpreted it. He was an egotistical and self-centred man whose languidly disdainful manner and cold eyes disguised a sensual appetite that had never yet had to go unsatisfied. Riches and position, combined with handsome features and excellent physical proportions, had brought him all that he demanded of life. His *amours* had been many, but he had avoided matrimony, or any entanglement of a serious nature, with the same practised skill with which he shot, rode across country or seduced another man's wife. But until now he had never been in the least interested in single young ladies. They were, in his opinion, too raw, too uninstructed and too dangerous, and he had never yet distinguished one of them with his attentions. But Winter de Ballesteros had not been in any way like the general run of demurely blushing debutantes.

Intrigued by her unusual looks he had been sufficiently interested to pay her some attention and considerably taken aback by her reception of the compliment. To be put in his place and given a sharp set-down by one so young and inexperienced had, by its very novelty, both piqued and intrigued him. But he had found the quarry remarkably elusive and presently his good sense had reasserted itself. The pursuit of an unmarried girl of good family could only lead to scandal or the altar, and he did not fancy either.

Now, however, the situation was entirely different, since here there were no influential relatives to interfere. The Abuthnots need not be considered as any impediment, and the girl herself was about to be married to some clod of a Commissioner whom Carlyon dismissed as of no account; it being his considered opinion that any man who elected to serve in such a country as India must of necessity be negligible, both socially and mentally, for were it not so he would remain in England.

Carlyon was the product of an age in which rich members of the aristocracy regarded themselves as being above the laws that governed the behaviour of the lower and middle classes, and he had always considered the *Droit de Seigneur* an admirable institution and regretted that it could no longer be enforced. It could do no harm – and should prove delightful – to give this delicious young innocent an advance course of instruction in the pleasanter aspects of matrimony, and she would enjoy the subsequent embraces of her nonentity of a husband all the more for having been introduced to the delights of passion by an expert. No girl with such a mouth and so sweetly seductive a figure could prove anything but an apt pupil in the art of lovemaking, and a journey of several weeks had seemed to offer endless opportunities for sentimental dalliance by the way.

But however carefully he manoeuvred he found it impossible to speak to the little Ballesteros alone, for she kept close to Lottie or Sophie. She would not be drawn into private talk with him, and Carlyon, who had started the journey in a spirit of pleasurable and entirely confident anticipation, began to lose his temper.

Had he *really* wasted his charm and his conversation on ingratiating himself with this set of middle-class bores, not to mention delaying his departure from India and embarking on a long and uncomfortable journey made the more uncomfortable by the fact that his hitherto faithful valet had flatly refused to accompany him, and all to no purpose? He could not believe it! But as day succeeded day and the travellers drew nearer to Delhi he found himself no nearer to attaining his objective. The other ladies of the party, in particular the lovely Delia, found him charming, while the two Colonels pronounced him an excellent fellow – no side and a first-rate shot. But Winter remained as cool as her name and tantalizingly out of reach.

With his temper Carlyon lost some of his caution, and Mrs Abuthnot began to regard his behaviour towards her charge with anxiety. Naturally he could mean nothing by it and was only paying dear Winter the extra civility that was due to a girl of her position, but all the same . . . She began to keep a closer watch upon Winter; with the result that Lord Carlyon, angry, frustrated and piqued, ended by doing what he had always pronounced to be the very height of folly. He fell in love.

Carlyon had played with that emotion for so long that he did not at first recognize it. Love had been an amusement and the gratifying of a strongly developed sexual appetite, but it had never once touched either his heart or his emotions, so that he had come to believe that he at least was immune from this particular form of madness. The discovery that he – Arthur Veryan St Maur, 10th Baron Carlyon – had actually fallen in love with a chit of seventeen, astounded and angered him. It *could* not be true! It must be the effect of this atrocious climate or the fact that he had kept free of women for the unprecedented space of over eight months.

Nevertheless, he was in love. And being so, he found himself incapable of avoiding any one of the agonies and ecstasies inherent in that condition, or of behaving in a rational manner.

He discovered that he could not sleep, and that the finesse that had led him scatheless through a score of affairs had deserted him. He behaved like a boor and knew it – and could not prevent himself. Mrs Abuthnot took fright and Mrs Gardener-Smith took offence; the older men, with more understanding than their wives would have given them credit for, regarded him with sympathetic concern, while Delia sulked and pouted and Winter remained warily withdrawn.

As Carlyon's desire for her changed its quality, Winter's initial dislike of him changed in turn to something that bordered upon fear, and she longed for the journey to end. Once she was married to Conway she need never be frightened of anyone or anything again. Oh, to be married to Conway! – to be safe and protected from the cold unkindness of the Julias, the kitten-clawed malice of the Sybellas and the crawling gaze of people such as Colonel Moulson and Carlyon! The days that had been a delight ended by becoming a torment of embarrassment and strain, and Carlyon was the only member of the party who was not inexpressibly relieved at the sight of the rose-red walls of Delhi.

The Abuthnots' bungalow was situated in the cantonments on the stony ridge some four miles outside the walled city, and Carlyon had had no difficulty in obtaining an invitation to stay with them, although before the journey was over Mrs Abuthnot would have given much to get out of it.

Lord Carlyon had spoken airily of a 'week or so', but she consoled herself with the reflection that the Commissioner of Lunjore, who had been apprised of the date of their arrival, would certainly be in Delhi to meet his bride, and that the wedding could be counted upon to take place within a few days. A worldly streak in her regretted, for Winter's sake, that it was out of the question for the engagement to be broken off at this late date; Lord Carlyon was such a *very* personable man and a far more dazzling match for the dear child than even a Commissioner. But of course it would not do. It would occasion so much talk. Besides, Winter herself had displayed no partiality towards him – indeed, quite the reverse. One might almost suppose that she held him in aversion. Ridiculous, of course. No young girl could help but be flattered by the marked attentions of such an exceedingly handsome and eligible man, even though she was betrothed to Another.

That Lord Carlyon's affections were deeply engaged was by now painfully obvious, and Mrs Abuthnot wished that she possessed the moral courage to inform him plainly that in the circumstances she did not consider it at all the thing for him to make more than the very briefest stay under her roof. Perhaps George might suggest something of the sort to him? Although why she was worrying she did not know. Except that there was something about Lord Carlyon's manner that alarmed her . . . She had certainly never been aware of it during those few days in Calcutta or on the first half of the journey north, but lately it had seemed to her that under that languid manner and easy charm there lurked a dangerous and egotistical ruthlessness. Or was she imagining things?

What a relief it would be to see Mr Barton! He would be staying until the wedding at Ludlow Castle with Mr Simon Fraser, the Commissioner of Delhi, and would be sure to present himself at their bungalow on the very first evening. She did hope that he would allow dear Winter sufficient time to bathe and change her dress before making his appearance, for the child would wish to look her best for such a momentous meeting. Six years! . . . Mrs Abuthnot sighed sentimentally and remarked encouragingly that another half-hour would see them at the end of their journey.

An imposing array of household servants were lined up on the verandah of the bungalow to receive them, and Kunthi, Mrs Abuthnot's ayah, who had been prevented by illness from travelling to Calcutta to meet her mistress, wept with joy at seeing the two grown young women whom she remembered last as a toddler in socks and sashes and a babe in arms, and enfolded them by turns in a tearful embrace.

There were no less than seven letters for Lottie: fat, sealed packets, each as large, as Sophie remarked teasingly, as one of Mrs Heyman's novels, and all of them from Edward English. But there was neither letter nor message for the Condesa de los Aguilares.

Of course there would be none, thought Winter, comforting herself. There was no longer any need for letters when Conway himself was at Ludlow Castle, only a mile or so from the cantonments. In an hour – perhaps less – she would see him. She must hurry and change into her prettiest dress. Her hair was dull from the dust of the roads and there was dust too on her long lashes and at the corners of her nose and mouth. She must wash and change quickly – quickly!

Teena, a young relative of Kunthi's who had been allotted to the girls as their ayah, was sent running for water, while Winter pulled off her travel-stained dress and Sophie and Kunthi unpacked the dress-box and shook out the folds of the satin striped apple-green *barège*, and a house servant was sent hastily to summon the *dhobi* and his iron.

An hour later Winter took a last anxious look at herself in the looking-glass, wished yet again that she possessed Lottie's blue eyes and yellow curls, and crossing the hall went into the drawing-room to wait for Conway. She could watch the gate from the drawing-room windows and would see him arrive. The servants were already laying dinner and it must be nearly five o'clock . . . surely he would come soon! She heard someone enter the room behind her and close the door, and turned, expecting to see Mrs Abuthnot.

'Who are you waiting for?' asked Carlyon. 'The tardy lover?'

Winter stood quite still. Her dark eyes widened a little and a pulse beat at the base of her throat, for it needed only one look to see that Carlyon had been drinking. He was far from drunk, but his flushed face and over-bright eyes and the slight slurring of his drawling voice were sufficient indication that he was not entirely sober.

She said in a cool, steady voice: 'I am expecting Mr Barton. I will wait in the garden, I think. It is quite pleasantly cool out there now that the sun is so low.' She pressed back the wide flounces of her crinoline and walked quietly towards the door.

Carlyon waited until she was almost level with him and then moved with unexpected swiftness, blocking her way. 'I think not. I haven't had a chance like this before. You've avoided me, haven't you? You've done it very cleverly. Why won't you let me speak to you?'

Winter steadied her voice with an effort, doing her best to keep it light and level: 'But I do. You have often spoken to me.'

'But never alone. Do you know that I have never once been alone with you? – even for a moment? Why do you behave like this? Do you do it to pique me, Winter? No! – don't go. I won't let you.'

She had tried to pass him and he had moved again, keeping between her and the door. Winter said a little breathlessly: 'Lord Carlyon, please let me pass. I – I think I hear Mrs Abuthnot in the hall——'

'No, you don't. And my name is Arthur. Do I have to tell you that? Do I have to tell you that you are the loveliest and most desirable creature that I have ever known? That I——'

'Lord Carlyon, please——'

'Arthur! And I love you. Isn't that absurd?'

'Lord Carlyon, you must not speak to me like this,' said Winter desperately. 'You know that I am to be married shortly and——'

'And to some clod of a Commissioner? What nonsense! What ridiculous, damned nonsense. You know it's nonsense, don't you? Don't you, my beautiful swan – my snow maiden. Shall I melt that snow and teach you to be as warm as summer instead of as cold as your name? Shall I? Shall I——?'

Above his soft, slurred voice Winter could hear horses' hooves on the drive. *Conway*! She tried again to pass Lord Carlyon, and he reached out and caught her wrist. The touch of those hot fingers sent a sudden shock of revulsion through her, but she knew that she must not struggle. It would be fatal to struggle. In a moment the door would open and they would come looking for her: she could hear voices on the verandah. She must not let Conway find her struggling degradingly in the arms of another man. What would he think? He might even think she had encouraged Lord Carlyon. She must keep calm . . .

She said quite steadily: 'If you do not let me go I shall call out.'

Carlyon laughed. 'No, you won't. It would make a vulgar scandal, and this is no moment for a vulgar scandal if this is your chosen clod arriving. So as time is short——'

Before she realized what he meant to do, or had time to cry out, he had jerked her to him and caught her close, pinning her arms to her sides in a grip that was agonizingly painful, and kissing her with a bruising violence that deprived her of breath. She struggled wildly and soundlessly, anger and disgust swamping out thought as the greedy mouth moved to her throat, kissing its cool whiteness with a savage intensity and travelling downwards to the warm hollows of neck and shoulder.

She tried to scream but the only sound she could make was a choking gasp for air. And then the door into the hall opened, and at the sound of it the arms that had held her dropped and she leapt back, one hand to her bruised throat and the other clutching desperately at a chair-back. But it was not Conway who stood there. It was, astonishingly, Captain Randall.

'*Alex*!' She was not in the least aware that she had called him by his Christian name, and the word was barely more than a gasping breath.

Carlyon turned. He was entirely self-possessed and it did not seem possible that this was the same man who only a moment ago had been gripping her in a paroxysm of greedy physical desire. 'Ah,' said Lord Carlyon blandly, 'Mr Barton, I presume?'

Alex's hard grey eyes took in Lord Carlyon from head to foot in one coldly speculative glance, and he raised his brows: 'No, sir. Am I to take it that you were expecting him?' He looked past Carlyon at Winter and bowed slightly: 'Your servant, Condesa.'

A sudden flush burnt in Carlyon's cheeks and his lips tightened. He drew himself up to his full height and said in his coldest drawl: 'You have mistaken the room, sir. You may find Colonel Abuthnot in his office, I think.' He nodded a brief dismissal, but for once that quelling manner which had hitherto invariably succeeded in putting the pretentious in their place entirely failed in its effect.

'Very likely,' said Alex, strolling forward into the room. 'But I did not come to see Colonel Abuthnot. I am charged with a message to the Condesa de los Aguilares.'

'Then pray deliver it, sir, and go,' snapped Lord Carlyon. 'You interrupt us.'

'So I observe,' said Alex, his gaze dwelling lazily on the red blotches that disfigured Winter's white neck and shoulders. 'The message, however, is of a somewhat personal nature, and when I tell you that it is from this lady's future husband I feel sure that you will permit me to deliver it in private. I shall not keep you above a moment.'

The dismissal was entirely plain and Carlyon's languid haughtiness deserted him. He said violently: 'Why, you——!' And then with a rustle of skirts Winter was standing beside Alex, her hand on his sleeve. She did not look at Carlyon but spoke in a small breathless voice: 'Will you take me into the garden please, Captain Randall? You may deliver your message there, and – and it is cooler outside.'

'But very public,' said Alex pleasantly. 'I think you will find it more agreeable in here.'

He walked over to the door, and holding it open smiled at Lord Carlyon. Alex's acquaintances would have recognized that smile. Carlyon did not. The fury died out of his face and contempt took its place. He looked at Winter and said: 'For the moment then, my dear,' and walked past her into the hall. Alex closed the door upon him and Winter sat down very suddenly on the ottoman, feeling ridiculously weak at the knees and seized with an absurd desire to cry.

'Who was that?' inquired Alex without interest.

Winter looked away from him and said in a difficult voice: 'Lord Carlyon. He – accompanied us from Calcutta and is staying here. But you must not think – I would not want you to——'

She broke off and bit her lip. There was, after all, no reason why she should justify herself to Captain Randall, and he could not possibly suppose that she had been a consenting party to the scene that his entrance had interrupted. But how much had he actually witnessed? Carlyon had released her so swiftly, and she had not cried out. Alex must know that if she had cried out he would have heard her. Did he imagine——?

She looked up quickly, the hot colour in her cheeks, and said: 'I know that it must look most singular to you, but——' And then she saw for the first time that Alex carried his left arm in a sling, and forgetting what she had been about to say, said instead: 'You are hurt! What has happened?'

'A shooting accident,' said Alex indifferently.

'An accident?' A sudden recollection of stories of risings and the murder of men in outlying districts drove the blood from her face, and she stood up quickly: 'Conway——! Has there been trouble in Lunjore? Is that what you have come to tell me? Is anything the matter with him? Is he ill?'

'Not as far as I know,' said Alex in a completely expressionless voice.

'Then why are you here?'

'The Commissioner found himself unable to come to Delhi after all. He asked me to explain the matter to you and to arrange if possible for you to travel to Lunjore with the Gardener-Smiths, who will be going there shortly.'

'But...' Winter put out a hand and clutched at a chair-back as though for support, 'but they are not going for nearly three weeks.'

'I know. I am sorry. But there appears to be no one else going there at present, and you cannot travel alone.'

'Why can't I go with you?'

'The Commissioner does not consider it would be suitable,' said Alex drily. 'Besides, I do not go myself for at least two weeks. I have some business here that the Commissioner wishes cleared up.'

Winter sat down slowly, the apple-green flounces that had been intended to please Conway foaming about her. She looked very small and forlorn, and as once before on the deck of the *Glamorgan Castle* at Calcutta, Alex found himself reflecting that strangling was probably too good for Mr Barton. Yet was this slender young thing quite as unsophisticated as she appeared? It would be interesting to know just what was behind that scene that he had interrupted. Young ladies, particularly young ladies who were engaged to be married, did not normally indulge in *tête-à-têtes* with unwelcome admirers, and if she had not wished to be alone with Carlyon she had only to call out. The bungalow appeared to be swarming with servants, not to mention four Abuthnots.

Lord Carlyon, decided Alex dispassionately, appeared to be a strikingly handsome man of a type who might be expected to exercise a considerable appeal to women of all ages; and if he had travelled from Calcutta to Delhi with the Abuthnots, it would not be surprising if he had succeeded in making an impression upon the Commissioner's betrothed. If this was so Alex could not feel sorry for it, since he was of the opinion that almost anyone would be preferable to Mr Barton as a husband for the Condesa.

He wished that he did not feel so responsible for the girl. It was an absurd feeling and it irritated him, for there was no reason for it. What happened to her was no concern of his and she was, when he came to consider the matter, an extremely fortunate young woman and one whom many might envy, being possessed of a title in her own right, a plethora of aristocratic relations, a considerable fortune and unusual personal beauty. Nevertheless he could not rid himself of this nagging feeling of responsibility. It had weighed upon him ever since that night over a year ago when the Commissioner had asked him to take home letters to Ware and escort his bride back to India, and it remained with him still; intensified by his discovery that the girl's august relatives appeared to take little interest in her and were in fact only too anxious to be rid of her.

Alex looked down at the bent head and the small hands that were clasped together so tightly among the absurd apple-green ruffles, and frowned; aware of a disturbing tug at his heart, and thinking again that India was really no place for such women and that if there ever should be a rising on a serious scale they were going to be a devilish responsibility.

Winter, looking up at this point in his reflections, caught that frown and it brought back her courage and a sudden spark of anger. She rose, straight-backed, and said in a cool, composed voice: 'It has been most kind of you to trouble yourself on my behalf. I hope you will not think me ungrateful. Did Mr Barton not send a letter?'

'There was no time. The alteration in plan came at the last moment and I myself left at less than half an hour's notice,' said Alex curtly. He considered it unnecessary to explain that the Commissioner had been in no condition to stand upright, let alone write a legible line, when he had last seen him.

The truth was that Mr Barton, faced with the journey to Delhi, had once more been attacked by his old fears – the same fears that had kept him from sailing to England to claim his bride.

He had refrained from taking the long, hot, uncomfortable journey to Calcutta for no better reason than that the discomfort it entailed did not appeal to him, and that on consideration he had decided that it would serve equally well for him to marry the girl in Delhi. But as the date of his departure for that city drew near, he recollected that Delhi society would be starting a round of cold-weather gaiety, and that he would not cut an impressive figure when contrasted with the gay blades of the Military. Then there were the Abuthnots, who by now must seem like old friends to his betrothed. Supposing – just supposing – that she should not like what she saw of him? Might she not, supported by them, even go so far as to break off her engagement? Better to bring her to Lunjore where she would be in the society of strangers (he did not count Colonel Moulson or the Gardener-Smiths), for once there she would have no chance of changing her mind. He would see to that!

The final touch had been put to these uneasy meditations by Colonel Moulson, who had informed the Commissioner that his betrothed, although not his own idea of a beauty – he preferred 'em blonde and buxom! – was a taking little thing, despite her prunes and prisms air. Mr Barton decided to play safe and cancel any idea of going to Delhi.

He had celebrated this decision by getting exceedingly drunk, and had been barely able, on the morning on which he had originally intended to set out, to do more than mumble a few directions to Captain Randall, the gist of which had been that Alex must see to that Delhi business – he would find the documents relative to it among the office files – and make his excuses to Winter. She would have to come to Lunjore with the Gardener-Smiths. He was damned if he could go chasin' to Delhi to get married. She must come here. Mountain t' Mahomet. Alex must arrange it. He would write when he felt more the thing, and where in the name of damnation that black brute of a contractor had procured the last consignment of brandy from he could not imagine . . .

A description of this scene would, Alex considered, only lead to further misunderstanding, and if the Commissioner's betrothed had indeed found herself growing attached to Lord Carlyon, the problem would probably solve itself without any further interference on his part. He could only hope so, for if the girl did not marry either Carlyon or Barton, he could see himself being landed with the unwelcome task of finding a suitable chaperon to escort her back to Ware.

He said aloud: 'The Commissioner informed me that he would be writing to you. I feel sure you may expect a letter either tomorrow or the next day, although the posts in this country are not always to be relied upon.'

Winter was saved from replying by the arrival of Mrs Abuthnot, who embraced Alex warmly, exclaimed in horrified accents over his wounded arm, and would not hear of him leaving before dinner: 'One of the servants can take a message immediately to Mr Fraser, who I am persuaded will spare you to us for an hour or so,' said Mrs Abuthnot firmly. 'No, of course you must stay, dear boy. Lottie and Sophie will be quite delighted to see you. Colonel Abuthnot has only just this moment told me that you were here, or I should have come in before. I was seeing some of the trunks unpacked. And where is Mr Barton?'

'In Lunjore,' said Alex. 'He was unable to come.'

Mrs Abuthnot turned to Winter with a sympathetic haste that set her crinoline whirling. 'Oh, my love, how *cruelly* disappointing for you! It does not seem right that work should always be considered of more importance than us poor women. But you will have to get used to it, dear. There are times when I barely get a chance to speak two words in the day to Colonel Abuthnot. But it is particularly disappointing for you when it is your wedding that must give way to pressure of work. When will Mr Barton be arriving? I do trust he is not *ill*, Alex?'

'No,' said Alex, and explained the alteration in the Commissioner's plan to the best of his ability. Mrs Abuthnot was desolated to hear that dear Winter would not be able to be married from her house after all, but at least it meant that she would not now miss Lottie's wedding, as the Gardener-Smiths intended to stay on for that and would be leaving the day afterwards . . .

Alex had remained to dinner (it had been hardly possible to avoid doing so) and Carlyon had not been pleased. He was not accustomed to playing second fiddle in any society, and this novel experience, in his present mood, annoyed him considerably. As a result, he drank more than was suitable to the company he was in, and lost a great deal of his languid ease of manner. He considered the Abuthnots to be making an entirely unnecessary fuss over this exceedingly ordinary and, as far as he was concerned, unwelcome guest, and was coolly insolent to Captain Randall. But the fellow appeared to lack the intelligence to know that he was being put in his place, and Carlyon's contempt increased in proportion to his irritation. He had been used to hearing high-ranking officers of the Horse Guards speak slightingly of officers in the Indian Army, and he knew that many British regiments would not accept officers who had seen service there. Presumably because they supported his own view that anyone in the Indian services was bound to be a middle-class mediocrity. He could not understand what Ware was about to permit a member of his family to travel to such an outlandish and impossible country, for the purpose of marrying some petty official of the East India Company.

Carlyon had intended to seat himself next to Winter, but she had slipped past him and taken her place between Colonel Abuthnot and this Captain Randall, while he himself was seated between Mrs Abuthnot and Lottie, both of whom directed far too much of their attention to the newcomer. He took some comfort from the fact that Winter at least appeared to take no interest in the man and did not speak to him at all except on the few occasions on which he addressed her directly. Sophie, on the other hand, who had never been more than shyly polite to Lord Carlyon, appeared unable to take her eyes off Captain Randall and blushed pinkly whenever he spoke to her or so much as glanced in her direction.

Taken altogether, it had proved a tiresome evening, and the only pleasant thing about it, in Carlyon's view, had been the information that the young Condesa's future husband would not now be coming to Delhi, which would necessitate her remaining with the Abuthnots for a further three weeks. Fate appeared to be playing into his hands after all. It had been stupid of him to rush his fences as he had done earlier in the evening. That had been partly due to drink and partly to the overmastering emotion that the girl's unusual beauty had aroused in him. But he would have to be more circumspect if he wished to avoid committing some *bêtise* that would result in Colonel Abuthnot requesting him to remove from the house.

The Colonel was a cheerful and kindly little man who obviously thought and made the best of everyone and everything, but Carlyon imagined that he would be quite capable of acting firmly should the occasion warrant it, and he did not wish to put it to the proof. He was not so sure that he had, after all, overstepped the mark where Winter was concerned. True, she had struggled, which was probably due to maidenly modesty more than anything else, but she had not screamed. Perhaps next time . . . ?

21

Lottie was to be married at St James's Church in Delhi on the twenty-sixth of the month, and preparation for the wedding kept the ladies of the household in a constant ferment over silks and muslins and the mysteries of feminine underwear.

There were also expeditions and picnics, parties and balls, and Carlyon received a flattering amount of attention from the garrison, and was even asked to call upon the ragged old ghost who lived surrounded by a tatterdemalion court in the Palace within the Red Fort of Delhi – Bahadur Shah, descendant of the House of Timur and last of the Moguls. But Winter remained as elusive as ever and Carlyon's exasperation mounted daily.

His temper was not improved by the frequent addition of Captain Randall to the party, since he found that his first and instant dislike of the man increased with every sight of him. The contempt he had at first felt for him had vanished, and try as he would he had been unable to recapture it. There was a look in Captain Randall's coolly observant eyes, and something in his bland manner, that disconcerted and frequently infuriated Lord Carlyon, but it was difficult to pick a quarrel with a wounded man, and in addition to carrying his arm in a sling Captain Randall was not an easy man to quarrel with. He appeared to be entirely uninterested in Lord Carlyon and his proceedings. Nor did he seem particularly interested in the social gaieties of the Delhi season, and Carlyon was frequently puzzled to know why he troubled to accept invitations to affairs that he so obviously found tedious.

Alex was finding this hard to explain to himself. The business that was occupying him in Delhi consisted mainly of the collecting, correlating and checking of evidence in a contested case of accession of territory by lapse, and the bulk of the documentary evidence was being dealt with by the clerks of Mr Fraser and Sir Theophilus Metcalfe. He therefore found himself with a fair amount of time on his hands, and the Abuthnots were pressing with their invitations; but he had previously experienced no difficulty in refusing equally pressing invitations, and he was not entirely sure why he did not refuse these.

Was it only because of that irksome feeling of responsibility that he could not rid himself of? Or because he was aware, without quite knowing why, that Winter was frightened and unhappy? She certainly gave no outward signs of being either, but there was a difference in her that had not escaped him. She had lost that look of expectation, and was once again the withdrawn, wary child of the early spring . . . the girl who had seemed to him to possess something of the stillness and caution of a wild creature who freezes into immobility at the approach of danger, hoping to be overlooked among the protective colouring of its surroundings.

There was nothing that he could do or say to help her back to the happy expectancy of the voyage, but he sensed that in some way – perhaps because she looked upon him as a link between herself and Conway Barton? – his presence reassured her, and in this he was partly right. Winter had understood and forgiven Conway's failure to meet her at Calcutta, for Captain Randall had not been in Lunjore then and possibly there was no one competent to be left in charge of affairs. But if Alex was able to take over the work that was to have brought Conway to Delhi, then surely he could have been left in Lunjore for a matter of a week or ten days in order to allow Conway to come here?

She knew that it was disloyal of her to even think such a thing. Conway must be right, and of course duty must come before personal happiness: he had never failed to impress that upon her in his infrequent letters. Yet she could not help feeling that just this once he might have arranged things so that he could have left his desk for a few days to come for her. If he had been in ill-health she could have understood it better, but Captain Randall had denied that he was ill, and in a letter that arrived a few days later Conway had mentioned only pressure of work. He was, he explained, anxious to clear up the more pressing business of the district so as to enable him to take a really adequate spell of leave for their honeymoon. The letter was a more affectionate one than Conway usually wrote and it had dispelled much of her unhappiness. But despite this she was conscious of a return of that frightening feeling of loneliness and insecurity that had been so familiar a part of her childhood, and which had so nearly vanished with the arrival of the letters that Captain Randall had brought to Ware.

Winter suspected that Captain Randall was inclined to regard her as a somewhat tiresome responsibility, but she could not help feeling grateful for his continued presence in Delhi, if only because it protected her from Lord Carlyon's more than unwelcome attentions. When Alex was there she could forget about Carlyon and relax from the strain of being perpetually upon her guard. She knew that if she were to tell Mrs Abuthnot of the attack he had made upon her on the day of their arrival in Delhi he would instantly be asked to terminate his visit, but since she did not feel capable of facing her kind hostess with such an embarrassing task, she had kept silent and taken pains instead to ensure that there should be no repetition of the incident.

That she was bent upon avoiding him, and was not merely being coy, was gradually borne in upon Carlyon, and he began to realize that vanity and self-assurance had led him into making a grave tactical error. Far from awakening Winter to the delights of dalliance he had only disgusted and frightened her, and if he were not careful he would lose her to the nonentity after all. But he could not make his apologies and set himself right with her in the presence of others, and it seemed as though he were never to see her alone.

His opportunity came at a ball when he stood up with her for a waltz that she had been unable, in the interests of politeness, to refuse him, and he made the most of it. He attributed his unforgivable conduct on the day of their arrival to the brandy and laudanum drops which, he explained, he had taken as a precaution against a suspected bout of fever. He abased himself, and employing all his considerable charm and facility of address, begged for forgiveness. Having received it, he proceeded with confidence to make her a proposal of marriage.

He was fully aware, said Carlyon, of the impropriety of addressing such a proposal to an engaged lady, but he must beg her to make allowances for a man deeply in love. The fact that she had not seen her betrothed since she was a child had given him grounds for hoping that she might bring herself at least to postpone the wedding, in order to allow him time in which to make her change her mind. He had expressed himself with fervour and humility, and had received in return an unqualified refusal that contained nothing which he could conceivably take as encouragement to persist in his suit. The music had ceased, and Winter had not granted him a second dance.

She had been touched by the humility of Carlyon's apology, and disagreeably surprised by his subsequent proposal. But having left him in no doubt as to her feelings she had expected him to leave the Abuthnots' house and Delhi more or less immediately, since if, as he had assured her, she was his sole reason for being there, there could be no further point in his remaining.

Carlyon, however, had not removed. Instead he had written her a carefully worded letter, delivered to her by his bearer, in which he had assured her that he had not intended to distress her, promised never to mention the subject again or enact her any more tragedies, but hoped that he might be honoured at least by her friendship though he must be denied that nearer relationship he had so ardently desired. If he could at any time be of any service to her, his life was at her disposal. He remained——etc.

Winter could not help feeling that she had misjudged Lord Carlyon, and she had smiled at him shyly when they next met. But she was ignorant of the feelings that had prompted the writing of that letter, and had she had any inkling of them she would have been considerably alarmed. For Carlyon was in an exceedingly dangerous mood, and he had written that letter with no other motive than the hope that by doing so he might prevent the little Ballesteros from pressing for his removal from Delhi. He had every intention of removing shortly, but he had made up his mind to take her with him.

Having much to his own amazement decided that he actually wished to marry the girl, it had never occurred to him that she would not be willing to jilt the nonentity to whom she was betrothed once she discovered his intentions to be honourable. He had never proposed marriage to any woman before, and possessed sufficient vanity and bland self-assurance to consider that to do so would be to bestow a very considerable honour. To have his offer incontinently refused was something he had never considered to be remotely possible. He could not believe that she meant it . . . she was leading him on! Yet there was no point in leading him further than a proposal, and she had had that . . .

Carlyon had passed from stunned incredulity to dangerous rage. His languid manner had always disguised a hot and uncertain temper and now suddenly he lost control of himself. He wanted the girl. Wanted her more than he had ever thought it possible to want anything, and by God, he would have her! No clod of an Indian-service official was going to stop him.

His plan was quite a simple one. Make his peace with Winter, and having made a few necessary arrangements, carry her off and compromise her so that she would be glad to marry him. The clod might cause a little trouble at first, but Carlyon could always use his influence to procure him some advancement, and as he had not seen his prospective bride for six years there could be no question of love on either side. The man was obviously only interested in her fortune, and Carlyon was sufficiently rich to apply a generous gold-plaster to any wounds he might receive.

Now that Winter would be staying for Lottie's wedding it had been decided that she as well as Sophie must be a bridesmaid. They were to wear pale blue muslin profusely decorated with satin bows and quilling, and diminutive bonnets of blue straw trimmed with roses. The wedding-dress was pronounced an admirable fit, and Mrs Abuthnot, watching her elder daughter try on her bridal array before the looking-glass, shed motherly tears and announced that she did not know how she should support the loss of her dearest, sweetest Lottie.

'But you will still have me, Mama,' comforted Sophie.

Mrs Abuthnot embraced her and said tearfully that it would not be long before Sophie too would be wearing a wedding-gown.

'I do not think I shall ever marry,' said Sophie with a small unhappy sigh. 'I shall stay single and be a comfort to you and Papa.'

'Nonsense, dear!' said Mrs Abuthnot bracingly. 'Lottie, my love, I really think that we shall have to change your hair-style a little. I am not sure that it would not look better dressed a trifle more forward to suit the wreath.'

'Let me do it,' said Sophie. 'No, don't sit down Lottie, you goose. You will crush the folds.' She mounted precariously on a small stool and placed the wreath with its filmy yards of veil on Lottie's golden head, wondering as she did so if she herself would ever wear a wedding-dress. Would Captain Randall ever look at her as Edward looked at Lottie, or as Lord Carlyon – Sophie was not unobservant – looked at Winter? Sophie doubted it. Captain Randall treated her more as though she were a pleasant child still in the schoolroom, or, worse, as though she were his young sister.

'But I will grow older,' thought Sophie hopefully, 'and perhaps it will be different next year.'

There was a sound of stir and bustle in the hall and Mrs Gardener-Smith's voice was heard to say in plangent tones that she would show herself in. The next moment the door opened and the lady herself swept in, accompanied by Delia, exclaiming that she was sure that dear Mrs Abuthnot would forgive this unceremonious entry, but the butler had told her that the Memsahibs were trying on clothes for the *shadi*, and as she would not dream of dragging any of them away from such an absorbing occupation, she had come to add herself to the admiring audience. She turned her attention to Lottie and uttered a startled shriek:

'My dear! How *can* you! Pray take it off at once!'

'Why, what is the matter?' inquired Lottie, bewildered. 'Do you not like it?'

'Oh, my love, sweetly pretty! But you must not wear your bridal gown and veil before you dress for the church. It is *vilely* unlucky. Surely you know that? Pray remove it immediately. The veil at least. One may safely try on the dress or the veil separately. Indeed one *must* do so, or how is one to know that they will suit? But both together – never!'

Mrs Abuthnot said a little sharply: 'How very absurd. I am sure that I tried on *all* my bridal clothes before I was married.' But Lottie, who had turned quite pale, hurriedly removed the veil and wreath.

Lottie was at that stage of love when it seemed to her that so much happiness could not possibly last; that it was too shining and wonderful to be true, and that she must walk on tiptoe from day to day lest some jealous fate should snatch it from her in envy. She would wake at night terrified for Edward because there were so many things that could happen to people in this cruel country. So many men who had laughed and joked one day and been dead the next. Oh, if only she could marry Edward tomorrow! Every hour that he was out of her sight something terrible might happen to him. If only the days would not go so slowly . . .

Winter saw that her hands were trembling and took the veil from her while Mrs Abuthnot swept the Gardener-Smiths off to the drawing-room, declaring that the remainder of the trousseau dresses were not in a condition to be displayed. A white lie that did not trouble Mrs Gardener-Smith, who was not in the least interested in Lottie's trousseau, but had called in expectation of seeing Lord Carlyon.

There was to be a ball at Metcalfe House, the residence of Sir Theophilus Metcalfe, Chief Magistrate of Delhi, and Mrs Gardener-Smith hoped that Lord Carlyon might, if reminded of her presence, think to engage Delia for a waltz or the cotillion. But Carlyon was not in. He had ridden over to the Artillery Lines to see some carriage horses that an officer wished to sell, and would not be back for at least an hour. Mrs Gardener-Smith signified her willingness to partake of refreshments, and the two ladies fell to discussing the arrangements for the wedding and the various social engagements of the coming week.

A moonlight picnic on the walls of Delhi had been arranged by the livelier spirits among the younger officers, and neither lady was entirely sure that they approved of such a festivity. Naturally no young lady would be attending it unchaperoned, and both Mrs Abuthnot and Mrs Gardener-Smith would be there to keep a maternal eye upon their daughters. But all the same they were not sure that such an entertainment was not a little *fast*.

'Although of course,' said Mrs Abuthnot hopefully, 'when the moon is at the full it really is almost as bright as day, and I hear that it is to be quite a large party. We are to start an hour before sunset so as to be able to observe the moonrise. It should be a very pretty sight.'

'Does Lord Carlyon intend to go?' inquired Mrs Gardener-Smith.

'Yes, indeed. We are all to go. Except Colonel Abuthnot, of course. He says that such things are not at all in his line. But with Carlyon and dear Alex to accompany us we shall not want for male escorts, and shall do very nicely.'

Carlyon returned before the visitors left, and in reply to Mrs Gardener-Smith's questions said that he had purchased a carriage and pair with the object of travelling in his own conveyance instead of by dâk-*ghari* when he left Delhi. He was at present engaged in the purchase of spare horses for the carriage, for although he himself preferred to ride, on a long journey a carriage was sometimes necessary.

Mrs Gardener-Smith was desolated to hear that Lord Carlyon intended to deprive them of his society, and hoped that he would perhaps find the time to visit Lunjore. She was sure that Colonel Gardener-Smith would be able to show him some tiger shooting in the surrounding jungle. She then turned the conversation to the ball at Metcalfe House and tomorrow's moonlight picnic, where it remained until they were interrupted by the return of Colonel Abuthnot, and the two ladies took their leave.

'We shall be seeing you at the picnic then, Lord Carlyon,' said Mrs Gardener-Smith graciously. 'And the dear girls, of course. I can only trust that it does not rain. Not that rain is usual at this season, but there appear to be quite a large number of clouds about. I expect if it does rain it will be only a short storm. Enough to lay the dust. Until tomorrow, then. Come, Delia dear, the Braddocks will be wondering what has become of us.'

The clouds that had attracted Mrs Gardener-Smith's attention produced no rain that day but provided a magnificent sunset, and Winter, riding with Colonel Abuthnot that evening to the Flagstaff Tower on the Ridge, looked out towards the distant city, the gleaming curves of the Jumna river and all the wide plain beyond, and saw them bright gold in the flaring glory of the setting sun.

The minarets and mosques and bastions of Delhi caught the light and glowed as though they were fashioned from molten metal, and in the far distance, rising above the domes of the countless tombs and the ruins of the Seven Cities that stretched away to the eastward, rose the tall tower of the Kutab Minar, a bright, lifted spear against a bank of purple cloud.

Winter drew rein to watch that brief vision of fantastic splendour, and as she watched, the gold turned to rose and the rose faded to lavender, until at last the battlemented walls, the soap-bubble domes, the minarets and the palaces were coldly mauve against the glowing sky, while the river ran blood-red across the darkening plain. And suddenly tears pricked her eyelids, because the evening was no longer full of beauty but of sadness. The sadness of past glory and lost empires. Of change and decay. It seemed to her as though there were something symbolic in that brief flare of beauty that had illuminated the city of the Moguls, and in the swift twilight that was swallowing it up . . .

Somewhere within those walls, a shadow among shadows, the last of the Moguls – an old, frail, withered pantaloon, stripped of all power and King only in name – shuffled through the marble magnificence of the palace built by Shah Jahan, composing Persian couplets to fill his aimless days. And the echo of a long-ago voice seemed to whisper in Winter's ear – the voice of Aziza Begum, telling a small girl stories in the twilight: '. . . *and the sands crept in upon that city and buried it, and it became as if it had never been.*'

Colonel Abuthnot had also been thinking of that same walled city. But his thoughts had evidently taken a different turn from Winter's, for he said unexpectedly and as though he were continuing some argument: 'Yes, I suppose it would be possible. But the Army would soon set it all to rights.'

Winter turned to look at him in some surprise. 'Set what to rights, sir?'

The Colonel awoke from his reverie with a start. 'I'm sorry, my dear. I fear I was talking aloud. Silly habit. Matter of fact, I was thinking of an article that Sir Henry Lawrence wrote – oh, some ten years and more ago. Caused quite a stir at the time; a lot of people were displeased. But I cut it out. It was about Delhi, you know. He pointed out how simple it would be for a hostile party to seize it, and said that if such a thing should ever happen, twenty-four hours would see the rebels joined by thousands of sympathizers, and every ploughshare in Delhi beaten into a sword. Perhaps there is something in it. I have often felt, myself, that it might be a wiser course to have at least one regiment quartered inside the city. We furnish a guard of course, but that would be of little use if the city were to fall into hostile hands.'

'Do you think that is possible?'

'No, no. Of course not. Most unlikely. The country has never been quieter. It is merely a tactical point. In theory, it is possible. But we could take the place again with little trouble. The rabble might turn against us, but they would have no chance against the Army. I would engage to re-take the city with my sepoys alone. No finer troops in the world!'

Colonel Abuthnot's eye lit with the glow of a fanatic and he treated Winter to a lengthy anecdote concerning a minor skirmish of thirty years ago in which a company of native infantry under his command had acquitted themselves with considerable gallantry.

'Should have sent 'em to the Crimea,' concluded Colonel Abuthnot roundly. 'By Gad, they'd have shown some of those Horse Guards fellows what they were made of! Too cold, of course – they couldn't have stood the climate. But give 'em the right officers and there's nothing they can't do. Finest troops in the world! It's an honour to lead 'em, and don't you let anyone tell you different, m'dear. Men like Carlyon don't know what they're talking about – hardly possible of course. No experience. But still——'

Colonel Abuthnot, who fondly and proudly regarded his entire Regiment as a conglomerate favourite son, sounded faintly ruffled, and Winter concluded that Lord Carlyon had been expressing himself tactlessly.

'Odd fellow, Carlyon,' mused Colonel Abuthnot, his cherubic countenance puckered in a thoughtful frown. 'Don't quite know what to make of him. Charming fellow. Excellent shot, and it's a pleasure to see him on a horse. All the same there are times when——'

A bat flittered past the Colonel's head and he awoke from his musings and realized that the swift dusk was closing in upon them and the rock-strewn Ridge was already faintly silver with moonlight. 'Come, my dear. We must be getting back, or Mrs Abuthnot will be thinking that we have met with some accident.'

They turned their horses towards home and cantered sedately back through the dusk to the neat white bungalow in the cantonments where the lights were just beginning to show through the trees.

There were clouds to the north-east of Delhi on the evening of the moonlight picnic: a threatening bar of greyness that lay along the horizon, though elsewhere the sky was clear. Mrs Abuthnot had regarded them with some anxiety, and had been with difficulty restrained from bringing an assortment of capes and umbrellas to the picnic and ordering the closed carriage. But Alex had assured her that their presence merely indicated rain somewhere in the foothills; adding that if it had been raining up north he might well find himself being held up on his way back to Lunjore.

The low sun bathed the walls of the ancient city in warm splendour and dazzled the eyes of the earlier arrivals who strolled upon the broad battlements that lay between the Kashmir Gate and the Water Bastion, overlooking the green tangle of the Kudsia Bagh. Supper would be spread near the guard-house on the bastion near the Main Guard, and meanwhile the guests walked upon the walls to watch the sunset and wait for the moon to rise over the Ridge.

Carlyon, Winter and Alex had ridden to the picnic, while Mrs Abuthnot and her daughters had driven in the carriage. The ride had been a pleasant one, though a trifle dusty, and Carlyon had behaved in an exemplary manner. He could be excellent company when he chose and this evening he had exerted himself to please, so that by the time they arrived at the Kashmir Gate Winter was feeling quite in charity with him. Riding in under the massive arch of the gate they dismounted before the Main Guard, where Alex had stopped to speak to a jemadar of the guard, and had been hailed by a man on horseback who was approaching the gate from the direction of St James's Church.

'Alex, by God!' The man had spurred forward and leaning down from the saddle smitten Captain Randall between the shoulder-blades. 'When did you get back? I haven't had so much as a word from you in half a year, you ingrate.'

Alex had turned swiftly and gripped the proffered hand. 'William! What the devil are you doing here? They told me you were in Dagshai.'

'So I am – officially.'

Alex said: 'Get down off that horse and join us. Condesa, may I introduce Lieutenant Hodson. William, the Condesa de los Aguilares and Lord Carlyon.'

Lieutenant Hodson reached down a hand to Winter and said: 'Will you forgive me if I do not dismount? I have been suffering from a dislocated ankle and can do little more than hobble when on the ground.'

He was a slim wiry man, as slim as Alex, though a little taller, and looked to be a few years older; but where Alex was dark-haired and deeply sunburned, this man was of almost Nordic fairness. The Indian suns, that had apparently had no power to tan his intensely white skin, had bleached his blond hair and long cavalry moustache to a yellow so pale as to be almost white, and only his eyes were dark. They were remarkable eyes, of so deep a blue as to appear black at first sight, and large enough to have graced a girl, but as hard and fierce and glittering as a hawk's.

He shook hands with Winter, favoured Carlyon with a direct look that appeared to sum him up, analyse him and dismiss him in one brief second, said: 'Your servant, sir,' and turned back to Alex with an inquiry as to his injured arm. Winter and Lord Carlyon had continued on their way and joined the remainder of the party on the ramparts, and Alex said: 'William, your manners are as abominable as ever.'

'Nonsense. You cannot expect me to waste time uttering social inanities when I have not seen you for close on two years. Get back onto that spavined animal you have there and ride with me. I can't talk to you here.'

Alex swung himself back into the saddle and the two men rode out through the gate and turned right-handed along the far side of the deep ditch that formed a wide, dry moat between the walls of Delhi and the open country and jungle-like greenery of the Kudsia Bagh.

'Who was the Spanish beauty?' demanded Hodson, 'and what are you doing in such company?'

'Acting as duenna,' said Alex with a grin. 'The Spanish beauty has come out to marry my respected chief, and I have had the thankless task of seeing to her safety during the journey. I escorted her out from England.'

'*What?*' Hodson threw back his head and shouted with laughter. 'Now I have seen everything!'

'It has its humorous side,' admitted Alex with a somewhat wry smile. 'But then I admit I had not visualized, when I joined the Bengal Army, finding myself called upon to act in almost every civil capacity from magistrate to midwife. Being employed to bring out brides for senior officials should be no surprise, and not much worse than being saddled with the care of a stray orphan, which I seem to remember you suffering from on one occasion.'

'My God, yes! Shall I ever forget it? The tasks we are called upon to do in this country would raise the hairs on the head of any Horse Guards officer. Who was the lordling? Don't tell me that you have been press-ganged into bear-leading the globe-trotting nobility in addition to nurse-maiding your unspeakable chief's betrothed?'

'Not yet. Though I daresay I shall come to it – all is grist to the mill in this service. Lord Carlyon is merely visiting in Delhi.'

'Dangerous look in his eye,' commented Hodson. 'I had a horse like that once. Thoroughbred, with the lines of an archangel and as full of vice as Beelzebub. I shot him. Which reminds me, you didn't tell me what you've been doing to your arm. Riding accident? Or did someone put a bullet through you?'

'The latter,' said Alex, drawing rein among the scrub and the grasses that fringed the banks of the Jumna river. 'It's a long story, but I propose to inflict it on you. The sling, however, is merely a façade. It could have been discarded some days ago, but I find it useful.'

He smiled, and Hodson, who unlike Lord Carlyon had reason to know that particular smile, said accusingly: 'What devilry are you up to, Alex?'

Alex laughed. 'No devilry I assure you, Will. But it does not happen to suit me just now to involve myself in a brawl with his noble Lordship, and while I carry one arm in a sling he can hardly be as offensive as he would wish. One cannot insult a man who appears incapable of repaying the insult with a blow.'

The hard blue eyes regarded Alex with a speculative interest not untinged with surprise. 'What's plaguing you, Alex? Afraid of a scandal?'

'Good God, no. It is only that I, like you, distrust the type. He does not care to be crossed and is, I think, egotistical enough to go to almost any lengths to avenge an injury. He has influential friends, and at the present moment I have no particular desire to have complaints laid against me in Calcutta – or anywhere else for that matter – and possibly find some uninstructed Johnny Raw replacing me while I am sent to kick my heels in a useless backwater.'

'As I have been,' said Hodson grimly. 'You heard, did you not, that I had been removed from command of the Guides, and that there had been a court of inquiry on my actions? Yes, of course you did. You wrote.'

'And offered to come up and strangle young Taylor for you,' said Alex. 'It is a pity you didn't accept the offer. How do you do now?'

'Oh, they proved nothing of their case. But the findings exonerating me have been filed in some government pigeon-hole, there to gather dust while I kick my heels in Dagshai. I tell you, Alex, it is damnably hard to begin again as an infantry subaltern after more than eleven years' hard work. I shan't stand it much longer. I shall give 'em another six months, and if by then I have still received no satisfaction, there will be nothing left for it but to decide between suicide, resignation, or desertion to the enemy – or forcing the Governor-General to eat his words and apologize! I rather fancy the latter.'

Alex said: 'Come on down out of that saddle if you can hobble as far as the trees. I have more to say to you than can be comfortably said sitting this fidgeting animal.'

He offered a hand, and having tethered the horses the two men moved off between the tussocks of grass and seated themselves on the river bank, looking out across the Jumna that lay all pearl-pink and glinting in the evening light.

Behind them, a mile or so distant, ran the low line of the Ridge, and to their right the walls of Delhi glowed rose-red in the dusty glamour of the setting sun, while upstream stretched the curves of the river, the wide white sands and the wider plain, with the white roof of Metcalfe House showing above the thick green of trees.

Alex looked over his shoulder at the thicket some ten paces behind them, and Hodson, interpreting the look, said: 'There are peafowl in that cane-brake. I saw them move as we passed. If anyone comes that way they will warn us.'

Alex grinned appreciatively. 'You are a great man, William.'

'Not yet. But I shall be. God willing, I shall be.'

The words were spoken entirely seriously and Alex said abruptly: 'You have not told me yet what you are doing here. Have you taken French leave?'

'More or less.' Hodson put up an impatient hand, and pulling off the peaked pith helmet that he wore, tossed it away into a clump of grass and ran his fingers through his yellow hair. 'I came because I heard that a friend of yours was expected in Delhi. I have a few friends of my own in the city, and I thought it worth while to make some inquiries.'

'A friend of mine?' Alex frowned at the tone of his voice.

'Sparkov.'

'*Gregori*!'

'The same.'

'Then he must have moved damned quickly. I saw him in Malta on my way back here.'

'The devil you did! What was he doing there?'

'Plotting murder and mayhem,' said Alex. And retold the story.

Hodson listened without interruption and when he had finished said:

'Very interesting. But I imagine that means he is not in Delhi – yet. Farid Khan sent me word that he was expected, although he did not say when, nor did he say how he had come by the information. I came down because I thought I might get more out of him, but something or someone has scared him badly and he isn't giving anything away. Still, it's something to know that Kishan Prasad is one of Gregori's contacts: I've met the Rao Sahib. A clever devil and likeable.'

'And damnably dangerous,' said Alex tersely.

'Oh, yes. As a king cobra – or a krait. A bosom friend of your delightful Commissioner Barton's, I gather.'

'That too.' Alex's voice was edged with bitterness and Hodson reached out a hand and gripping his uninjured arm gave it a little shake.

'I know how it is. God – don't I know! Sometimes I've lain awake at night feeling like . . . like Krishna urging Arjuna on to slaying his kin and justifying the deed. If only we could sweep out some of these obese fools what an Empire this would be!'

He threw out a hand in a gesture that seemed to embrace the vast plain and the quiet river, the ancient city of Delhi and all of India, and there was a sudden glow in his eyes. Then his hand dropped again and he said bitterly:

'There are so many men whom one could follow blind; to hell if necessary. Lawrence, Nicholson, Edwards – oh, and a dozen other first-rate fellows. But it takes more than a hundred good men to undo the harm that one Barton can create. Or one hidebound octogenarian, for that matter. I'm not sure which is worse, the frankly venal of whom there are mercifully few, or the aged, osseous ineptitudes which this fatuous seniority system of the Army forces on us by the score. I tell you, Alex, one of the Brigadiers I served under in the affair of '49 could not even see his Regiment. I had to lead his horse by the bridle until the animal's nose was on their bayonets, and even then he had to ask me which way they were facing. A seniority service such as the Company's is very well for poor men, and a godsend to fools, whom it enables to rise equally with men of twenty times their worth. But for the purposes of discipline in peace and effective action in war there never was a worse system, and one day we are going to find that out.'

'Probably sooner than we think,' said Alex grimly.

Hodson looked round at him sharply. 'What do you know?'

Alex told him. And by the time he had finished, their shadows, that the setting sun had thrown long and blue on the white sands of the Jumna at their feet, lay black behind them in the full blaze of the risen moon.

A jackal scuttled out across the silver sands to feed on the rotting remains of a half-burnt corpse that had stranded in shoal water, and a peacock called harshly from the cane-brakes of the Kudsia Bagh. The tethered horses stamped uneasily and Alex's mare whinnied softly. 'That will be Niaz,' said Alex glancing over his shoulder. He stood up, and reaching down his right hand helped Hodson to his feet: 'I shall have to go back and do my social duty. Join us, Will.'

'Not a chance. I must be in Dagshai tomorrow.'

'*Tomorrow*? Are you mad? William, you cannot do it! Not with a bad ankle. Why must you always ride hell-for-leather?'

'Prefer it. And it may come in useful one day. Besides, you know I can sleep in the saddle, and as for the ankle I've got it strapped into splints for the occasion. That's why I'm so lame. Damnably painful but entirely serviceable.'

He limped over to his horse and called out: '*Ohé*, Niaz Mohammed Khan. Is it thou?'

Niaz rode forward into the moonlight, and slipping from his horse gave the salute that is given only to elders of high rank.

'*Salaam Aleikum.* Is it well with thee, Hodson Bahadur?'

'Nay, ill. My star is sinking.'

'That I have heard,' said Niaz gravely. 'No matter. It will rise again.'

He held the stirrup for Hodson to mount and Alex said: 'Have they sent thee to look for me?'

'Nay; I followed, for there was a sadhu who also came this way. A Shakta of the Left Hand. He came very quietly, keeping among the trees, and I came after to see what he would do. But hearing my horse move among the dried grass he turned back and went away to the northward. I waited to see that he did not return.'

'Some more of your friends, Alex?' inquired Hodson over his shoulder as his horse picked its way across the rough ground to the narrow footpath at the edge of the counterscarp.

Alex shrugged his shoulders. 'India is full of sadhus. Do you really ride for Dagshai tonight, William?'

'I am afraid so.'

'Then I shall not be seeing you for some time. I'm for Lunjore on Monday. The business here is cleared up a good three or four days earlier than was expected, but Fraser has asked me to remain on over the week-end. I should get back, but I have accepted because he is having a guest whom I shall be interested to meet. Dundu Pant. The Peishwa's heir. Met him?'

'Once. Another krait. What is he doing here?'

'Oh, purely a private visit I gather. Unofficial. He stays in Delhi for only two days. I admit I have always had a certain amount of sympathy for the man. There is no getting away from it, the Hindu law has allowed the right of adoption for centuries, and we cannot sweep it out of court merely because it is not a custom of the West. Sir John Malcolm had pledged the Government to bestow that pension, and had this man been the true son of the old Peishwa he would have fallen heir to it. I cannot help feeling that it was a niggardly gesture to refuse it to him on the ground that he was adopted, when in the eyes of every Hindu in India he is the legal heir.'

'Trouble with you, Alex,' Hodson threw over his shoulder, 'is that you always will see the other fellow's side of a question as well as your own. It makes life too complicated.'

Alex made a wry grimace. 'I am aware of it. I wish I had your singleness of purpose. What is your star, William?'

'Leadership,' said Hodson promptly. 'I would like to be able to make men follow me blind – as I would follow a man like John Nicholson. To damnation, if necessary.'

'They will,' said Alex with a smile. 'Niaz does not hold my stirrup, nor call me Bahadur.'

Hodson laughed. 'Do you know, I believe they will. That is, if I can prevent myself being hamstrung by a lot of incompetent old women in trousers. But I'll get my chance one day, and then, by God, I'll show 'em!' He reined in his horse as they reached the Main Guard and held out his hand. 'God bless you, Alex.'

Their hands met in a brief hard grip and then he touched his spur to his horse's flank and galloped back under the dark arch of the Kashmir Gate while Niaz, who had dismounted, stood stiffly to the salute. Alex heard his horse's hooves drum hollowly on the bridge over the moat and then he had gone.

'What does Hodson Bahadur do here?' inquired Niaz in an undertone, holding the horse for Alex to dismount.

'He sees a friend in the city.'

'Does he so!' said Niaz thoughtfully. 'Dost thou remember how in the year following the taking of the Punjab an astrologer in Amritsar city cast his horoscope and foretold that in seven years his star would arise and burn bright among much blood? Those years be all but sped, and it may be that he smells that blood.'

He took the reins and led the horses away into the shadows, while Alex walked up the ramp to the battlements and into a babel of voices and laughter and the clink of glasses and silver.

The picnickers were grouped about a long white cloth that had been spread over a carpet on the warm stone, the older ladies seated in wicker chairs and the younger ones on cushions on the carpet, with their wide skirts spreading about them like full-blown roses. The men sat cross-legged beside them or leaned against the embrasures of the battlements, while white-clad servants handed around an impressive selection of cold foods and drink. Candles had been placed upon the cloth, but the flames had attracted so many winged and crawling insects that they had been quickly extinguished, so that now only the white blaze of the moonlight lit the scene. That Indian moon whose light is as clear and as bright as many a spring evening in the West.

'My dear Alex, we had quite given you up. Where have you been?' Mrs Abuthnot edged her chair back a little and pulled aside her ample skirts, and Alex came over and subsided onto the carpet at her feet.

'I'm sorry. I met a friend whom I had not seen for over two years and who leaves Delhi tonight.'

He accepted a plate of cold food and ate it abstractedly, his mind still on his conversation with William, but presently he became aware that someone had addressed him by name, and rousing himself he turned to find that it was Winter who sat on his left.

Winter had kept close to Mrs Abuthnot since her arrival, for although Carlyon had of late conducted himself with so much propriety, charm and consideration that she had lost a great part of her antipathy towards him, this evening she was aware of an odd feeling of disquiet. An uneasiness that had become sharply increased by Captain Randall's failure to put in an appearance on the battlements, for were he to remain below in conversation with the lean blond man with the remarkable eyes she would either have to ride home alone with Lord Carlyon, or plead fatigue and beg a place in the carriage. Alex had no *right* to leave her like this! Conway expected him to protect her from annoyance and alarm, and he ought not to ride off with strangers and abandon her to the care of men like Arthur Carlyon.

In fact, his Lordship, having left her with Mrs Abuthnot, had made himself agreeable to Mrs Gardener-Smith, and when the sunset had duly been admired and the moonrise exclaimed over, had taken his place between Delia and a Miss Clifford who was making a stay in Delhi with her friend Miss Jennings, daughter of the Chaplain.

The party was a gay one, and the noise of talk and laughter disturbed the roosting birds in the trees behind the Main Guard and brought inquisitive sightseers from the purlieus of the city to crane their necks and peer up at the strange doings of the *feringhis*. But try as she would, Winter could not bring herself to share in the universal high spirits. She had done her best to appear interested and entertained, but the pain that had struck at her heart when she learned that Conway would not be coming to Delhi had returned to torment her among the prevailing merriment. A shy young Lieutenant of Bengal Artillery, George Willoughby, had been seated on her left, and Mrs Abuthnot's voluminous skirts had effectively protected her right until Alex materialized out of the moonlight and sat down at her chaperon's feet.

With his arrival some of her fear and tension and doubt faded. There was something about Alex that was instantly reassuring, and Winter fought down a sudden and childish desire to clutch at his sleeve and hold it tightly. She doubted if he would have noticed had she done so, for he appeared to be singularly *distrait* and as if his own thoughts were of sufficient interest to make him oblivious of the babble of talk around him. She answered Lieutenant Willoughby's shy attempts at conversation so much at random that he could only feel relieved when at length she turned to Alex and said: 'Who was that man you introduced to me, Captain Randall? Is he stationed in Delhi?'

Alex turned towards her with something like a frown and then his face cleared and he said: 'Oh, it's you. I'm sorry. I was not attending. What did you say?'

Winter repeated the question and Alex said: 'William Hodson. No, he was only here for a day. His Regiment is at present in the Simla hills. I rather think he has taken French leave.'

'You mean, left without permission? Are officers allowed to do that?'

'No. But William is a law unto himself – which has caused him a great deal of trouble in the past and will probably cause him more in the future. But if ever we get into another war in this country, I would rather have William at my back than a whole army corps. Not that he'd be at one's back. He'd be twenty paces ahead!'

Winter said: 'You are fond of him, aren't you?'

'Yes,' said Alex briefly.

'Tell me about him.'

Somewhat to his surprise Alex found himself complying with the request and telling her something of William – that dynamic, unpredictable person whose physical endurance matched his enthusiasm and impatience. How he had worked under the object of their mutual admiration, Sir Henry Lawrence, and had at Sir Henry's behest taken in hand the building and superintending of the Lawrence Asylum for the Children of European Soldiers, on a spur of the Kussowli hills. How he had acted as secretary, overseer and a hundred other roles, helped to raise the Corps of Guides, fought with them through the Sikh war and risen to command them. How the promotion of a young officer to so coveted a position, and Hodson's unorthodox methods, had aroused the enmity and spite of lesser men whose jealousy had led to his removal from command, while official indolence had pigeon-holed and suppressed the findings of the court of inquiry that had exonerated him . . .

'The trouble with William,' concluded Alex, 'is that he says what he thinks, and people don't like that. And what he does is usually proved right, which they like even less. He has been sent to kick his heels doing a subaltern's job in Dagshai – and this at a time when we need his kind of man more than we have ever needed them before! My only consolation is that if there ever is any serious trouble no one will be able to hold him.'

Alex had forgotten that he was talking to the promised wife of Mr Commissioner Barton who had caused him a great deal of inconvenience and irritation. He had been speaking, as he had done once before in the Malta moonlight, to someone with whom he was entirely at ease, and he looked down at her now and smiled a little wryly, realizing suddenly that he had been talking uninterruptedly through three courses, and as though the two of them had been alone: which indeed they might have been, for Mrs Abuthnot and a Mrs Forster had kept up an animated discussion above their heads and Lieutenant Willoughby had been engaged in conversation by Miss Jennings, daughter of the Chaplain of Delhi.

Alex looked away again and caught a smouldering glance that momentarily held his own. So Carlyon, at least, had noticed that he had been monopolizing the little Ballesteros for the last twenty minutes or so! Observing that look Alex was reminded vividly of Hodson's comment of an hour ago. 'Dangerous look in his eye,' William had said, and he had been right. Alex looked thoughtfully back at Winter and then reached out and removed the empty plate that she held in her hands.

He said: 'I seem to have been talking a deal too much. What a subject for a moonlight picnic. William should feel honoured. Have I bored you?'

'No.'

A swift and appreciative smile lit Alex's eyes. He found the brief monosyllable, shorn of the polite protestations with which a more socially experienced young lady would have adorned it, curiously touching. Alex, himself a man who did not trouble to say 'Yes' or 'No' unless he meant it, appreciated not only its obvious sincerity but the fact that the speaker was as yet sufficiently unversed in social small-talk to say exactly what she meant and no more.

He bent to remove a large moth that appeared to be in danger of drowning in a bowl of fruit salad, and said: 'Why were you interested in him?'

But this time the answer took him completely by surprise, for Winter said simply: 'Because he was a friend of yours.'

Alex looked up, startled. 'You see,' said Winter slowly, and as though she were explaining something to herself as much as to Alex, 'I do not really know very much about you, but one gets to know a little more about people when you know something of their friends.'

'And do you know more about me now?' inquired Alex with an odd note in his voice.

'I think so.' She looked away from him and traced a small aimless pattern with one finger on the close pile of the Persian rug before her. 'Alex——' Once again she was unaware of having used his Christian name.

'Yes?'

'Why could not Conway come to Delhi? Was there any – any other reason?'

Alex did not answer and Winter said: 'Other than his work, I mean?'

Damnation! thought Alex, taken off guard and completely at a loss. How did one answer a question like that and at a time like this? And what was the good of answering it? He had told her once and been slashed across the face for his pains. Was that because he had been a stranger? Now that she knew him better would she take it from him and believe it? or . . . 'I cannot throw it in her face in the middle of this bloody picnic party,' thought Alex, 'I *cannot*. It will have to wait——'

'Was there?' persisted Winter.

'No,' said Alex shortly. 'That is – no. I——'

He was interrupted by Mrs Abuthnot who leant forward and tapped him upon the shoulder with her fan. 'Alex, dear boy, you are sitting on my flounce and I wish to move. Thank you——' She rose and shook out her skirts as Alex came swiftly to his feet. 'The servants are to clear away and then we are to have some singing, I believe. I see that Lieutenant Larrabie has brought a guitar and Miss Clifford has her mandolin. Winter, my love, Mrs Forster tells me that we are to remove for a while so that the gentlemen may finish their wine. Come, dear. Come, Lottie.'

There was a ruffle and a rustle of silks and muslins as the crinolines ceased to be flattened circles and their owners drifted away in the moonlight like a flight of enormous bubbles blown along by a light breeze.

By the time they returned the debris of the picnic had been cleared away. Only the carpets and cushions remained, and an officer possessed of impressive whiskers and a luxuriant moustache was playing a sentimental ballad on a guitar. The majority of the guests did not immediately re-seat themselves in a compact group, but scattered along the ramparts talking, laughing and admiring the moonlight and the view, and Winter was relieved to see Carlyon attach himself to Delia and lead her away to look at the river – a proceeding that drew only a complacent smile from Mrs Gardener-Smith.

She could see no sign of Alex and wondered uneasily if he had gone home, but Lottie informed her that he had walked along the wall towards the Water

Bastion: 'Sophie wished to go too,' confided Lottie, 'but she did not have the courage to ask him to escort her, and he did not offer. He looked a little put out and as though he did not wish for company. Oh Winter, is it not a lovely night? I wonder if Edward is looking at that moon too? How I wish he were here!'

'Perhaps Conway is looking at it,' thought Winter. Why had Alex looked so disconcerted when she had asked him about Conway? He had looked . . . guilty.

'Winter, my love,' said Mrs Abuthnot, bearing down upon her accompanied by an unknown gentleman, 'here is someone whom I am sure you must be pleased to meet. Only fancy, Mr Carroll here passed through Lunjore less than a week ago and stayed the night with Colonel Moulson – you remember Colonel Moulson, do you not, dear? They dined with Mr Barton, so he can give you the latest news of him. Mr Carroll, this is the lady who is shortly to marry Mr Barton. The Condesa de los Aguilares.'

Mr Carroll, a large man with a red face that even the white moonlight could not pale, stared at Winter and muttered that he was honoured to meet her. He took her hand doubtfully and bowed over it, and in reply to her eager questions said that he had indeed seen the Commissioner at the previous week-end. He was often in Lunjore and had had the pleasure of his acquaintance for some years. Mr Barton had in fact been kind enough to urge him to stay on and keep him company, there being little to occupy him at present. But though the Commissioner of Lunjore might find time hanging heavily on his hands, he himself had too many calls upon his time to allow him to——

Mr Carroll became aware of the amazement and shock reflected on the faces of the Abuthnot ladies and the young Condesa, and stopped, disconcerted and alarmed.

'But that is absurd!' said Mrs Abuthnot sharply. 'Perhaps you did not know that we expected Mr Barton in Delhi, but pressure of work did not permit him to leave Lunjore. You must be mistaken.'

'Oh – er – yes,' said Mr Carroll unhappily. 'I must have misunderstood. Yes, of course. I——'

Winter broke in upon his flounderings. 'Mr Carroll, please tell me. Why could not my – the Commissioner – come to Delhi? Is he – is he not well?'

Mr Carroll, embarrassed and distressed, caught at the excuse with the fervour of a drowning man snatching at a passing straw, and over-played his hand:

'Yes. Yes, I am afraid that is it. He – er – did not wish to distress you. Naturally wished to spare you anxiety. Most awkward, being taken ill at a time like this – felt it very keenly.'

'But – but why did he not tell me?' asked Winter, her hands gripped tightly together.

Mr Carroll gulped, groped wildly for a suitable answer, and was visited by inspiration: 'Would not mention it, of course, for fear that you would consider it your duty to proceed immediately to his side. Sickroom no place for a delicately nurtured lady. Fever you know – er——' Mr Carroll had a momentary vision of the corpulent, bloated face of the Commissioner of Lunjore, and improvised glibly: 'A swelling fever. No, no, nothing serious I assure you. Merely – er – disfiguring. Not catching. But no man of sensibility would wish to meet his betrothed looking so.'

'Oh, the poor, dear man!' exclaimed Mrs Abuthnot, touched. 'How well I understand! How could he wish to allow you to see him in such a sad state? And of *course* he would not permit you to endure the discomforts of a sickroom. Perhaps that is also why he could not come to Calcutta? I expect he hoped to be well enough to proceed to Delhi instead, and suffered a relapse.'

Winter said in an eager, breathless voice: 'Is that so, Mr Carroll? How long has he been ill?'

Mr Carroll looked unhappily at the pale, tense face. He had roistered with Mr Barton on more than one occasion and considered him a bad man with a bottle or with women; but he could not tell this white-faced young woman the truth. A lie was better, and he'd drop a line to Con in the morning, giving him the tip.

'Er – not above six weeks,' said Mr Carroll. 'Or it may be a little more. Slow business. He hopes to be recovered shortly. On the mend now. You will not let him know that I have told upon him? He – he did not wish you to suffer any anxiety on his account.'

'No,' said Winter unsteadily. 'No, I will not tell him. But I am so *very* glad to know – to know that he is better. Thank you, Mr Carroll. I am *truly* grateful to you.'

She gave him her hand and Mr Carroll bowed over it and removed himself hurriedly, mopping his brow with a large bandana handkerchief and breathing hard.

'The poor, dear man!' said Mrs Abuthnot, presumably referring again to the absent Mr Barton. 'How truly noble of him to wish to spare you anxiety. And how very *human* to wish not to be seen by you except when looking his best. Gentlemen would like us to think that it is only we who are vain of our looks, but *we* know better. Ah, I see that we are to have some music. Let us join the others. I believe Miss Clifford to be an exceptional performer on the mandolin . . . such a treat. Come, Sophie dear. Why, Winter – where are you going, my love?'

Winter did not answer her and it is doubtful if she even heard the question. She caught up the short train of her riding-habit, and turning from them went quickly away down the long stretch of the moonlit ramparts towards the Water Bastion.

There were few people strolling now upon the broad ramparts. Most of them had returned to join the party and seat themselves on the carpets and cushions preparatory to being entertained by the talented Miss Clifford and the romantic Lieutenant Larrabie, and the few who passed Winter were returning from the far end of the wall. There was still, however, a lone gentleman who remained seated in an embrasure of the battlements overlooking the river, the end of his cigar making a small warm pin-point of light in the blue and black and silver of the night.

Alex had no wish for company. He was feeling angry and irritable and irrationally guilty. He had hoped that he need do no more in the way of warning off Mr Barton's betrothed, for once she reached Lunjore and saw the man, the whole affair – apart from arranging for her return to England – would be over. And, what was more to the point, the breaking of the engagement would have nothing whatever to do with him, Alex Randall, and therefore it would not lead to the Commissioner having him removed from Lunjore and sent to eat his heart out – as William was doing – in some useless and junior appointment. But Winter had asked him a direct question and it must be answered. He had answered it with a lie because she had taken him off-guard and it had been impossible to answer it truthfully in those surroundings. She had asked it because she was frightened and unsure. He knew that. But had she also asked it because now that she had come to know him better, and to regard him with less hostility, she had remembered what he had told her in the avenue at Ware, and begun to wonder if, after all, it could be true?

He would have to tell her, and this time she would believe him and go back to Calcutta and to England instead of to Lunjore. And that meant that the Commissioner would ask questions and—— 'Oh, damn all women!' thought Alex savagely. What had come over him? Surely this was no time to allow one young, white, frightened face to come between him and the work there was to do? And yet——

Various couples passed him, chattering and laughing, but he kept his shoulder turned to them and no one broke in upon his thoughts, and presently they drifted back towards the Main Guard again and he was alone with the moonlight, the glittering river that wound between the wide, ghostly sandbanks below the walls, and a white egret that had alighted softly on the battlements some half a dozen yards to his right.

Someone at the far end of the wall was singing 'Where are the flowers we gathered at morning?' to the accompaniment of a mandolin: a plaintive ballad that he had last heard in England. He heard a sound of quick light footsteps and the rustle of a woman's dress, and the egret rose with a flap of silver wings and flew off into the night as the footsteps came to a stop beside him. Alex tossed the end of his cigar over the battlements, turned, and rose to his feet.

Winter's face appeared drained of all colour in the white moonlight and she breathed unevenly as though she had been running. The close-fitting pearl-grey habit she wore in place of a crinoline moulded the lovely lines of her figure and lent her an illusion of maturity and height, but she could not control the childish trembling of her lips or keep the hurt and anger from her eyes, and Alex, looking at her in the full moonlight with his own face in shadow, felt an odd pain at his heart, and a hurt and anger that matched her own.

She said in a quick breathless voice that she tried to keep steady: 'You knew what was the matter with Conway, didn't you? You knew all the time. You could have told me, even if he did not want me to know. I had a right to know! And all these weeks I've thought – I've thought——'

Her voice broke and Alex said curtly: 'I did try and tell you once, but you would not listen.'

'You never told me! I asked you, on the day that you came to tell me that he could not come, if there was anything the matter with him, and you said there was not. And I asked you again tonight——'

'I'm sorry,' repeated Alex, relief and pity submerging that inexplicable anger. It did not not occur to him to wonder how she could have come by the knowledge. It was enough that she knew the truth at last without any further attempt on his part to force her to it. Yet, unaccountably, the fact that she had trusted him to tell her the truth hurt him unbearably.

Winter said: 'You knew the reason why he did not come to meet me in Calcutta. You had a letter from him too. He must have told you in that.'

Alex's brows twitched together in a sudden frown. 'Told me what?'

'Oh, I know that he did not want me to know. Mr Carroll told me so. He thought it would distress me, and – and he wished to spare me anxiety. And I know he cannot have wished me to see him looking——' Her voice stopped on a sudden gasp of horror and her eyes widened: 'Why – why, he may even have thought that I might turn from him if his illness had affected his appearance. He should have known I would not! But he has not seen me for so long. *You* knew though! You must have known that I was not like that. If you had told me——'

Alex cut harshly across the sentence: 'We seem to be at cross-purposes. I find I have not the remotest idea what you are talking about. What is it that Mr Carroll has told you?'

'He told me the truth. That Conway has been ill.'

'*Ill*?'

Winter's chin came up with a jerk. 'I hope you do not mean to deny having had any knowledge of it?'

'I most certainly do,' said Alex, 'although I suppose it is just possible to describe his condition in such a term. But it is not one I would have used myself. Perhaps you will be good enough to tell me just exactly what Mr Carroll had to say?'

Winter told him; her voice quick with indignation and reproach. 'I – I suppose you meant it for the best,' she finished, 'but you should have known that I would prefer to be told the truth. I did not think it of you. I thought that you——'

She stopped and bit her lip and Alex said curtly: 'You are right. I should have told you the truth. Will you hear it now?'

'I know it now.'

'Oh no, you do not. No——' His hand shot out and grasped her wrist as she made a move to leave him. 'This time you are not going until I have said what I have to say.'

Winter tugged furiously at her imprisoned wrist but Alex's lean fingers were hard and unyielding, and realizing that she could not free herself without an undignified struggle she let her arm go slack and stood still:

'Very well. I will listen.'

He released her and she snatched her hand away and stood rubbing it, her breath coming unevenly. There was doubt, and something else in her face – a dawning apprehension.

Alex said: 'Mr Barton is not ill. Not in the accepted sense of the word.'

'What – what do you mean?' The words were barely a whisper.

'I mean,' said Alex with brutal clarity, 'that Mr Barton suffers from over-indulgence in drink, drugs and women.'

Winter caught her breath in a harsh gasp and turned swiftly, but again Alex was too quick for her. He caught her by the arm and jerked her round to face him.

'I'm sorry, but you are going to hear me out. I told you once before that Barton was not a fit person for you to have anything to do with, let alone marry. I meant it. A libertine and a drunkard is hardly a suitable husband for such a woman as yourself – or for any woman, for that matter. He would not come to England to marry you because he must have been well aware that should he do so, one look at what he had become would have been enough to ensure that the engagement was broken. I do not know why he did not meet you in Calcutta. Probably for the same reason. I do know, however, that the after-effects of a debauch, if nothing else, prevented him from leaving for Delhi. He was incapable of standing upright when I left him.'

He let her go, but Winter did not move. She stood quite still, her eyes wide and frightened, and once again Alex was conscious of that bewildering pain in his heart. He said harshly: 'Well, now that you know the truth, I can only suggest that you return to Calcutta and sail for England as soon as there is a passage available.'

She did not answer him, and the moment seemed to stretch out interminably. A mongoose ran along the parapet, keeping to the shadows, and checked by the sight of the two motionless humans, fluffed out its tail and whisked away with a little chattering cry of rage. But neither of them moved or spoke, and in the moonlit silence the words of a tender, plaintive melody that drifted down the long length of the ramparts, sung by a dozen voices and blurred and sweetened by distance, filled the night with a strange, nostalgic magic——

> '*Believe me, if all those endearing young charms,*
> *Which I gaze on so fondly today,*
> *Were to fade by tomorrow, and fleet in my arms . . .*'

Winter saw Alex's set mouth soften and twitch, and she spoke in a whisper: 'No! Oh no . . . I don't believe it. Alex——'

She stretched out a groping hand in a gesture that begged for reassurance, and as it touched him something as vivid and as elemental as a flicker of lightning seemed to shiver between them. The next instant his arm was about her and he was holding her hard and close. For a brief moment she resisted him violently, her body taut with shock. Then his mouth came down on hers, and all at once the rigidity and resistance left her and the ground was no longer solid under her feet . . .

'Thou wouldst still be adored as this moment thou art . . .'

Her skin smelt faintly of lavender and her body was soft and sweet and fragrant in his embrace; as soft and sweet and fragrant as her lips and her closed eyelids and her shining hair. Alex's mouth was not hot and greedy as Carlyon's had been. His lips were cool and firm and his slow-moving kisses were a warm, drugging wonder that deprived her of all power of thought or movement and narrowed the night and the moonlight, the wide world and the wider sky, down to nothing more than the close circle of his arm.

She felt him free his left arm from the sling, and then his fingers were on the nape of her neck, pressing upwards slowly and caressingly through the thick soft waves of hair; fondling the curve of her head and holding it as closely and possessively as his right arm held her body. His mouth moved from hers at last, and his cheek was cool and harsh against her smooth warm one:

'*Darling . . . darling . . .*' His voice was no more than a breathed caress, but at the sound of it the passionate spell broke and dissolved before the cold inrush of reality. Winter tore herself free and backed away from him, shaking with rage and shame and the shock of a sudden revelation:

'So *that's* why you hate him . . .!'

Her voice was low and breathless and edged with scorn: 'You're jealous of Conway, and so you made it all up! You haven't even enough honour and – and decency to prevent you making love to his future wife. *You!* – you and Carlyon! Mr Carroll *did* tell me the truth. Why should he lie to me? Conway is ill – and because you are jealous of him you do your best to blacken him to me so that you can make love to me behind his back. I hope – I hope I never have to see you again!'

Her voice broke on a sob, and then she had whirled about and had run from him, and he heard the sound of her flying feet die out along the wall and lose itself in the sound of the distant singing.

Alex made no attempt to follow her. He stood where she had left him, staring into nothingness. Presently he lifted an uncertain hand and rubbed it dazedly across his forehead, and sitting down slowly in the embrasure, felt mechanically in his pockets for tobacco and matches. He rolled a cigarette with careful concentration and struck a match against the worn stonework. It lit with a hiss and crackle of sulphur, and the vivid flare of the small yellow flame momentarily dimmed the brightness of the moonlight.

> *'. . . the heart that has truly lov'd never forgets,*
> *But as truly loves on to the close;*
> *As the sun-flower turns on her god when he sets*
> *The same look which she turn'd when he rose.'*

The singing ceased and the night was silent once more. Alex appeared to have forgotten about the match, for it burnt out between his fingers. He dropped it with a quick grimace of pain, and removing the cigarette from his mouth, flicked it away into the shadows.

'*Hell*!' said Alex aloud and softly, addressing the moonlight, the ancient city of Delhi, and all India.

Lord Carlyon's plans were at last reaching some sort of shape, and in pursuance of the policy of lulling Winter's fears he had studiously avoided her and had devoted himself instead to entertaining Delia Gardener-Smith.

He had seated himself as far away from Winter as possible, but this had not prevented him from observing that Randall had held her in conversation for the greater part of the meal, or that they appeared to be on remarkably easy terms with one another. He had tried not to watch them, but he could not keep himself from doing so, and the unusual animation on Randall's face and the interest on Winter's had infuriated and alarmed him. Thank heaven Randall would shortly be leaving Delhi, and that he himself would before long be shaking the dust of this deadly place off his shoes! Only a few more days – he could not stand it much longer.

Carlyon looked across the laden cloth at Winter, trying to observe her dispassionately and decide what it was about her that had become such a fever in his blood. He had known many beautiful women: women far lovelier than this slender young creature whose wide-set eyes were full of a sweet unsureness that gave the lie to the full-lipped, passionate mouth.

Perhaps it was that – the youth and unsureness and the unawakened passion – that attracted him? To a palate jaded by experience, inexperience alone had a charm that was strangely and sharply new. He had been a fool. He, with all his knowledge of women, had handled this unsophisticated girl as though she had been some opera dancer to be seduced for the price of a trinket. Did she know that she was disturbing and desirable? . . . What had Randall been saying to her?

He had met Alex's reflective gaze and for a long moment he had stared at him, his throat tight with rage. And later that evening, when the singing had begun, he had not failed to mark that neither Winter nor Randall was present, and judging from the direction of Sophie's anxious gaze he had little doubt as to where they were.

He had endured it as long as he could, but as the minutes slipped by and they did not return, his jealous rage had increased until it had suddenly become past bearing, and he had risen and walked quickly away in the direction of the Water Bastion. Half-way down the stretch of wall the shadow of a huge *neem* tree lay across his path, and as he reached it he heard a sound of running footsteps and someone ran into him and would have fallen but for his arms.

'Oh, it's you——' Winter's voice was breathless and sobbing and she had forgotten that she disliked this man. She had forgotten everything but the fact that Alex had betrayed her – lied to her – shamed her. 'Take me home. Please take me home. I cannot stay here.'

Carlyon drew her out of the shadows and into the bright moonlight, and looking down at her distorted face saw that it was wet with tears. He said furiously: 'What has he done to you? My dear – don't! I'll go back and break his damned neck for you!'

'No – no, please don't.' Winter's fingers clung to his arm. 'I want to go back to the bungalow. Please take me back.'

'Of course.' He took her hand and drew it through his arm and turned back towards the group near the Kashmir Gate, but they had not taken more than a dozen steps when he stopped: 'We shall have to pass through all those people. There is no other way down. You will not like them to see you like this. May I——?'

He proffered a clean handkerchief and Winter accepted it gratefully. Presently she said in a more rational voice: 'You are very kind.'

'No, I am not.' There was an unexpected bitterness and sincerity in his voice and Winter looked up, startled. Carlyon recovered himself swiftly: 'I told you, did I not, that if I could serve you in any way it would give me great happiness to do so? I meant it, you know.'

'I – I know.'

Did she know? Had she been wrong about Lord Carlyon? She had been wrong about Alex. If she could be wrong about Alex——

Quite suddenly she found herself telling him everything. Conway's illness. Captain Randall's perfidy, her own fears and doubts when Conway had failed to come to Delhi: 'I could not understand it. I thought that he could surely have left the work to Alex – Captain Randall – just for a few days. Just to fetch me. But now that I know, I must go to him at once; I cannot wait another week in Delhi! I could help nurse him – I would not mind a sick-room. He might have another relapse and I not there. If he is ill he needs me. Will you – would you help me to go to him?'

Carlyon looked down into the wide, appealing eyes and saw that she was shivering violently. He knew nothing of this man that the young Condesa was to marry, but what he had seen of Captain Randall led him to suppose that the Captain's revelations concerning his chief were probably correct. Randall did not give him the impression of a man given to that particular form of lying. On the other hand Randall appeared to have made – or attempted to make – advances to his superior officer's future wife, and Carlyon found himself torn between an entirely primitive rage that he should have dared to touch her, and satisfaction in that by doing so he had played his, Carlyon's, game for him by presenting him with an opportunity that appeared to be little less than a gift from the gods.

'I will take you to Lunjore myself,' said Carlyon. 'You cannot go unescorted.'

Winter drew a quick breath, her hands clasping and unclasping against her grey habit. 'Would you? Would you really?'

'Of course. It is a piece of the greatest good luck that I purchased that carriage. You and your serving-woman can travel in it and I will ride. There is only one thing——' He paused, frowning, and Winter said anxiously: 'What is it?'

'Well, I do not know,' Carlyon spoke doubtfully, 'but I think perhaps it would be as well if you did not mention this matter to the Abuthnots.' He saw that he had startled her and said quickly: 'I am sure that they would sympathize with your intentions, but they would be obliged to prevent you from going until you could do so under the charge of Mrs Gardener-Smith. They would not consider it at all suitable for you to travel either alone or in my care, and I do not imagine that Mrs Gardener-Smith could be prevailed upon to put forward the date of her departure.'

'No,' said Winter slowly. 'No, she would not. And you are right about the Abuthnots. But I will not wait. I will not! I – I am my own mistress. No one can stop me.'

'They will try,' said Carlyon drily.

'Yes, I suppose so.' Her eyes were suddenly dry and bright and she straightened her slim shoulders and lifted her chin, stilling the trembling of her body with a visible effort of will. 'When can we leave? Tomorrow?'

'I could arrange it.'

'You are very kind. I will speak to Mrs Abuthnot tonight and tell her that I wish to leave immediately for Lunjore. I must do that. If she will assist me I will not have to trouble you. But if she will not, then – then I think it will be better if we leave as early as possible.'

Carlyon said gravely: 'You are quite right, of course. Let us hope she may assist you.'

He had no qualms on that score, since he was quite certain that the Abuthnots would do no such thing. He offered his arm to Winter and said: 'Shall we go now? Do you ride home, or shall you go in the carriage? I can tell Mrs Abuthnot that you have a headache. I do not think, you know, that you should leave without her. It would be remarked.'

Winter had returned in the carriage, and Mrs Abuthnot, who had been alarmed by the girl's pallor, had hurried her into bed and prescribed hot milk and chlorodyne drops. Her solicitude provided the opportunity Winter had needed to beg her permission and approval for an immediate departure to Lunjore, but Mrs Abuthnot, although deeply sympathetic, would not hear of it. Such a plan was out of the question.

'After waiting for so long, dear, you can surely wait another eight days. Only think of poor Mr Barton's chagrin if you were to see him after all these years when he is not in looks.' To Winter's passionate assertion that Conway's looks could not make a particle of difference to her feeling for him, Mrs Abuthnot had replied that it was not dear Winter's feelings that were in question, but poor Mr Barton's. Winter had argued and pleaded and Mrs Abuthnot had wept sympathetic tears, kissed her fondly but remained adamant.

'You will see that Colonel Abuthnot will agree with me. And Alex too.' She had turned out the light and left the room, and Winter had lain awake in the darkness and made her own decision. She would not wait another eight days – or even one day. She would leave at once. Alex would be leaving Delhi on Monday and if she left tomorrow she would be in Lunjore by then: married to Conway and safe from him. She did not know why she had to be safe from Alex, or stop to realize that a part of the driving impulse to get to Lunjore and to Conway arose from a panic desire to escape from him.

Conway would have to get rid of Alex. He must arrange for him to be sent to some other appointment, and until that happened she at least need not see him again. As for Carlyon, she had forgotten both her dislike and distrust of the man and thought of him as no more than a means to an end. He was no longer a person with a character and passions of his own, but something of no more, or not so much, importance as the carriage and horses that would take her to Conway.

Winter groped for matches, and having found and lit a candle, slipped out of bed and wrote a brief note to Carlyon. The ayah should deliver it first thing in the morning. She wrote a second and longer one to Mrs Abuthnot, sealed it with a wafer, addressed it and put it away. Her trunks would have to be sent after her. To be packing trunks would not do at all. She lit a second candle, and making a selection of garments and other necessities, packed a small valise and a capacious carpet-bag. Carlyon would have to devise some means of smuggling them into the carriage. As for the ayahs, she would not be able to take either of them with her, but that could not be helped. And Conway would surely forgive the unconventionality of her proceedings once she was safely with him and had explained the circumstances. Struck by another thought she scribbled a hurried and loving note to Lottie – Lottie at least would understand!

That done she blew out the candles, and fell at last into an uneasy sleep.

Mrs Abuthnot had evidently given the question of Winter's proceeding immediately to Lunjore no further thought, for she did not refer to it on the following morning, and having inquired affectionately as to whether Winter had quite recovered from her headache, was full of plans for pre-wedding festivities in the forthcoming week. A seemingly endless list of engagements tripped off her tongue, from which she was only interrupted by Carlyon inquiring of Winter if she would care to drive out with him that morning to try the new carriage?

Mrs Abuthnot was not at all sure that it was quite the thing for dear Winter to be seen driving *à deux* with Lord Carlyon, but consoled herself with the reflection that she was, after all, engaged to be married. Besides the child really did look remarkably pale, and a drive, even in the heat of the morning, would doubtless be of benefit to her. As they drove away she saw that Carlyon did not intend to sit in the carriage with his guest, but to ride beside it. The hood of the carriage had been raised against the morning sun and Mrs Abuthnot did not leave the shade of the verandah. Winter kissed her with unusual affection and Mrs Abuthnot, unsuspicious by nature, was touched.

The carriage rolled out of the drive under the shadows of the pepper trees, and ten minutes later, happening to look out of her bedroom window, Mrs Abuthnot saw Carlyon's down-country bearer and two of his syces riding out of the side gate that led from the stables, taking with them the two spare carriage horses. She supposed that they must have had their orders, but it seemed to her an odd time of day to exercise horses, and she could only imagine that it was Carlyon's ignorance of the country that had led him to order them out in the hottest part of the day. For a moment an odd twinge of uneasiness disturbed her, but Lottie demanding advice on the set of a ruched sleeve turned her thoughts into more congenial channels.

Twelve o'clock brought no sign of the carriage, and by one o'clock Mrs Abuthnot was seriously disturbed. Neither Winter nor Carlyon, she was persuaded, would be so thoughtlessly inconsiderate as to hold up luncheon to this extent. There could be only one explanation. The carriage must have broken down, or – horrifying thought – the horses had bolted with it.

Mrs Abuthnot was immediately seized with the conviction that Winter was at that moment lying in some nullah with a broken neck. 'Oh no, Mama!' cried Lottie turning alarmingly pale. 'You cannot think . . . You cannot really believe . . . But Lord Carlyon would have sent back word had there been an accident. One of the syces would have ridden back.'

Investigation, however, proved that the procession that Mrs Abuthnot had witnessed leaving the stables that morning had also not returned. 'Mama,' said Sophie thoughtfully, 'you do not suppose that they can have eloped?'

Mrs Abuthnot uttered a small shriek. 'Sophie! How can you suggest such a thing!'

'I am sorry, Mama, but you must own it is a little strange that all Lord Carlyon's servants and his horses have left, and not one of them returned. And anyone could see that he admires Winter.'

'Dear Winter would never——' began Mrs Abuthnot, and stopped. She had suddenly recalled the kiss that Winter had given her before setting out that morning. The kiss that had seemed so unusually demonstrative for that undemonstrative child. She had imagined at the time that it was intended in part as an apology for her outbreak on the previous night when she had pleaded to be allowed to leave immediately for Lunjore.

Lunjore——! Mrs Abuthnot fell back in her chair with a groan that brought Lottie and Sophie running to her side. 'Oh no!' gasped Mrs Abuthnot pressing her plump hands to her ample bosom. 'Oh no! She *could* not do such a thing! She would at *least* have left a letter!'

Lottie flew for the hartshorn while Sophie, more practical, departed in the direction of Winter's bedroom, to return a few minutes later with two letters that she had found propped up on the chimney-piece where they could not fail to catch the eye of the first comer.

Colonel Abuthnot, summoned from the lines by an entirely unintelligible missive from his wife, gave it as his opinion that Carlyon had behaved shockingly, and that come to think of it he had never quite trusted the fellow. Something a sight too smooth and cynical about him. But he had not thought it of the little Condesa. Probably foreign ways; he had heard that they were surprisingly lax on the Continent.

To his wife's plea that he would set off immediately in pursuit of the runaways he had replied with an unqualified refusal. He was far too busy a man to go tearing about the country in pursuit of a young chit who was old enough to know better:

'It's no good, Milly, my dear. I will not do it. The girl is going to her future husband. Very understandable. I cannot conceive what possessed Carlyon to agree to such a mad scheme, but if she was set upon going he may have considered that her protection on the journey was of paramount importance. Though he must also have realized that his presence was enough to ruin her reputation. I can only hope that the Commissioner of Lunjore will take a lenient view of it. As for suggesting that I should go in pursuit of them, the idea is preposterous. If anyone is to go in pursuit it had better be Captain Randall. The girl is betrothed to *his* superior officer, not mine. And he is a deal younger than I am; he might even overtake 'em. I should not.'

'*Alex*!' exclaimed Mrs Abuthnot frantically. '*Why* did I not think of that!'

She hurried away to dash off a brief note requesting Alex's immediate presence, and having underlined 'immediate' with three black lines that tore the paper, added a postscript, also underlined, stressing the urgency of the matter. This missive had been dispatched post-haste to Ludlow Castle, the residence of Alex's host, Mr Fraser, with instructions to the bearer of it that it must be delivered into the Captain Sahib's own hand. But Alex had been out, and the bearer of the letter, whose instructions had not included scouring Delhi for the Captain Sahib, had settled down to sleep away the afternoon in a convenient patch of shade in the compound, until such time as the Sahib should return.

Alex had arrived back barely half an hour before sunset in no very good humour, and had not been pleased to receive Mrs Abuthnot's agitated summons. He dismissed the servant with a verbal message to the effect that he would present himself within the hour, and went off to take a bath and change out of the dusty, sweat-soaked clothes he had worn all through the hot day. Having done this, he picked up the crumpled piece of letter-paper again and read it through, scowled at it, and tearing it into several pieces dropped them on the floor and told Niaz to have Latif saddle Shalini and bring her round to the verandah in ten minutes' time.

He rode over to the cantonments in the warm, pearl-coloured aftermath of the sunset, when all the tints of earth and sky and river gather themselves together and merge into a brief opalescent twilight, and the first stars swim in a cool green sky like silver fish in clear water.

There were a good many carriages and riders on the roads; residents from Delhi and the cantonments driving out to enjoy the cool evening air. Alex passed several people whom he knew, but since his expression was anything but encouraging none of them had attempted to engage him in conversation. He had no idea what Mrs Abuthnot's note portended, but imagined that Winter had poured out to her something of the scene last night, and that she wished to hear from himself if he had really made such accusations against the Commissioner, and were they true.

Alex supposed that he would now have to convince the Abuthnots that he had, if anything, understated the case, and perhaps they would be able to prevent the girl from proceeding to Lunjore at the end of the month. The possibility that she might leave at once, and with Carlyon, had never occurred to him, and he was entirely unprepared for the announcement with which the tearful Mrs Abuthnot greeted him.

She saw the colour leave his face and a white line show about his mouth. He said: 'What time did they leave?'

'Quite early,' sobbed Mrs Abuthnot, dabbing her eyes with a handkerchief. 'Nine o'clock, I think.'

'Good God, ma'am,' said Alex violently, 'could you not have sent for me before?'

'But we did not realize what had occurred until Sophie found this letter——'

She held it out to Alex, who having read it with eyes that were almost black with anger, crushed it into a ball and thrust it into his pocket. 'And then you were out,' explained Mrs Abuthnot, 'and the stupid man never thought to inquire after you. And George – Colonel Abuthnot – positively declines to go after them.'

'Quite out of the question,' confirmed Colonel Abuthnot, who had caught the end of the sentence. He entered the room by the verandah door, and having nodded gloomily at Alex said: 'What do you propose to do about it, my boy?'

'Bring her back,' said Alex tersely.

'Too late for that now. She'll have been out all night with that fellow before you can catch up with her. Besides, I can't see that it will do any good for you to go along as well. Two men ain't any better than one when it comes to playing propriety. Worse, if you ask me. Not sure I'd trust Carlyon very far. He had an eye to that girl. Wanted her himself, any fool could see that. Probably ruined her by now.'

He caught Alex's eye and took an involuntary step backwards, saying hastily: 'No, no, I don't expect he'd do such a thing. But as far as her reputation is concerned——'

Alex cut him short. 'May I take it that you would be willing to allow her to remain here when I bring her back, Mrs Abuthnot?'

'Of course I should. I know only too well that the dear child means no harm. It was only that she was upset by the news of Mr Barton's illness and wished to go to his side without loss of time. One can understand that so well. The *best* of motives! But she may not wish to come back.'

'Her wishes,' said Alex through shut teeth, 'have nothing whatever to do with the matter. I shall hope to be back at a tolerably early hour tomorrow, and if this matter has not been mentioned outside the house I see no reason why it should become known.'

'You need have no fears on that score, my boy,' said Colonel Abuthnot firmly. 'We ain't likely to blab about such an affair. Though if it were not for that fellow Carlyon fancying himself in love with the girl, I'd advise you to let well alone and let her press on for Lunjore. I daresay Barton may be persuaded to take a lenient view of the matter once he has her safe, and if you don't try fetching her back it's he who'll have the handling of her.'

Alex, who had turned to leave the room, stopped with his hand on the doorknob and looked back. 'It is precisely on that account,' he said savagely, 'that I intend to bring her back. Lord Carlyon can go to the devil!'

The door slammed behind him, and Colonel Abuthnot, who had been giving the matter thought, said reflectively: 'Damme if I don't believe he's fallen in love with the girl himself. Now look what you've done, Milly.'

'Done? What have I done? I've sent him after her. Someone had to go. And of course he is not in love with her!'

'You're a fool, Milly,' said Colonel Abuthnot affectionately. 'Always were. Why else should he be in such a taking? He ain't the type to lose his temper for nothing. Now there'll be the devil to pay.'

'What *can* you mean, George?'

'Mean? I mean that if I'm right about him, and he overtakes those two before they reach Lunjore, he'll murder that fellow Carlyon. And if he doesn't, he'll probably murder Barton!'

Mrs Abuthnot, who had borne enough, took refuge in a strong attack of the vapours.

Alex's mood was so nearly murderous that Colonel Abuthnot's prediction might have come unpleasantly near the mark had it not been for one factor that he had not taken into his calculations. The ford at Jathghat.

He had stopped at Ludlow Castle barely long enough to inform his host that he would be unavoidably absent, and to collect Niaz, a third horse and his revolver. He had proffered no explanation for his actions and had left, riding at a breakneck speed that had taken them far on the road by the time the moon was high. He knew that the carriage could not travel at any great speed owing to the poorness of the roads, and he imagined that it would halt at some dâk-bungalow for the night, so he calculated, with luck, on being able to come up with it well before midnight.

He had no very clear idea of what he intended to do when he did overtake it. Carlyon was bound to be difficult and he apparently had at least half a dozen servants with him. Niaz, however, could be trusted to deal with the latter, and as for Carlyon, it would give Alex the greatest pleasure to deal with his languid Lordship himself. He had not given much thought to Carlyon – beyond considering him a more suitable husband for Winter de Ballesteros than the Commissioner of Lunjore – and the murderous rage that had taken possession of him at the news of their flight had been almost entirely on account of Mr Barton.

If Winter had gone to Lunjore in the care of the Gardener-Smiths they could not have refused to shelter her and assist her to return to Delhi or Calcutta when she discovered, as she must almost immediately do, the impossibility of marrying the Commissioner. But if she were to arrive in Lunjore alone, with no one to turn to, there was no knowing what might happen. In all probability Mr Barton would see to it that any return was made impossible, and Alex had turned sick at the thought.

Even Colonel Abuthnot's reference to Carlyon's wanting the girl himself had done little more at the time than add to his fury; but now he remembered it again, and a cold fear took the place of that fury as he remembered also the scene he had interrupted on the evening of Winter's arrival in Delhi, and the look he had seen in Carlyon's eyes only last night. 'If he has harmed her——' thought Alex savagely. 'If he has harmed her——' He set his teeth and bent far forward in the saddle, riding as though he rode in a race, and with a recklessness that startled Niaz.

But he had forgotten the ford at Jathghat and the unseasonable clouds that Mrs Abuthnot had commented upon on the previous evening.

There had been rain in the foothills and on the plains beyond Moradabad and Rampur, and now, twenty-four hours and more later, the river had risen and was still rising. It had been dangerously high, though still fordable, when Winter and Carlyon had reached it some four hours earlier. But what had then been a ford of no more than fifty yards in length was now a brown, turgid torrent measuring a quarter of a mile from bank to bank, swirling sullenly past in the moonlight with an ominous chuckling gurgle that spoke of whirlpools and hidden currents.

Alex had been riding at a hand-gallop and paying little attention to the road, and he reined in hard at Niaz's shout of warning and dismounted to stare at the ugly stretch of water in blank dismay. He knew that road only too well, and knew too that when the river ran high there was nothing to do but wait for it to fall again, since the nearest alternative route meant a detour of fifty miles, and over such country as to make it, on a normal occasion, a matter of less delay to wait for the flood-water to pass. But this was no normal occasion, for an interview with a sleepy villager aroused by Niaz had elicited the information that a memsahib in a carriage, accompanied by a sahib and several servants on horseback, had crossed the ford less than half an hour before it became impassable.

Alex swung himself back into the saddle, his face harsh and haggard in the bright moonlight, and turned north on the long detour to the nearest bridge.

Half an hour later a python slithered across the narrow and little-used track almost under the hooves of his tired horse. Shalini shied wildly and the low branch of a *kikar* tree slammed against Alex's wounded arm. He hit the ground with the point of his shoulder, and in the fractional second before his head struck against the rocks by the roadside, heard his collar-bone snap as he went down into darkness.

Winter lay back in a corner of the carriage and closed her eyes. The setting sun shone in under the heavy leather hood above her with a golden glare, and the surface of the road was unbelievably bad. The carriage wheels jolted into ruts and out again, and every jolt threw her body sideways or jerked it back against the squabs until her head began to ache dully.

She told herself again that she was going to Conway and that in four days' time – less if the roads improved – she would be with him at last. No more waiting: no more doubts or fears or loneliness. But the spell had begun to lose some of its first potent charm.

Perhaps it had first failed a little at the ford. The horses had jibbed at the swirling brown water and the coachman had looked frightened and had protested that it would be better to turn back or to wait until the water fell. For one inexplicable moment Winter had experienced a feeling of overwhelming relief. They would have to go back! The next second shame at such cowardice had stiffened her resolution and she had feverishly seconded Carlyon's decision to cross.

The sight of the rising river had given Carlyon an exceedingly unpleasant shock, for the prospect of having to return to Delhi was not one that he cared to contemplate. Such an absurd anticlimax did not bear thinking of. The frightened faces of the coachman and the servants had infuriated him, but threats and bribery having prevailed, they had made the crossing.

Resting awhile on the far bank, they had watched the river rise steadily, inch by inch. 'No more will pass that way for some days,' remarked a villager who had crossed with them, and Winter had looked back at the swirling water and thought, 'Now there is no going back. Now, whatever happens, we must go on.' The thought had been oddly frightening. She did not want to go back. Of course she did not want to go back! Yet now, even if she had wanted to do so, the road was barred behind her and the flooded river lay between her and Alex. *Alex* – her mind shrank violently away from the thought of him as though it had touched something that could not be faced. She would not even think of Alex.

The road on the far side of the river had been almost worse than the one they had travelled on since leaving Delhi, but Carlyon had handed the reins of his horse to one of the syces and joined Winter in the carriage. She had had little speech with him since they had started out, for it had been impossible to carry on a conversation with anyone riding beside the carriage. Carlyon had seen to it that the horses kept up a creditable speed, and his behaviour during the brief halts had been courteous and considerate. But now that the river had been crossed and lay impassable behind them, his manner had undergone a noticeable change. Or was it only weariness that made her imagine that it had?

Ever since the scene in the Abuthnots' bungalow that Alex Randall's arrival had interrupted, Carlyon had appeared to avoid looking directly at her, and she had not again encountered that slow appraising gaze that had so often disturbed her on the journey from Calcutta. Now, however, as though the need for restraint were gone, she found that she could not look up without finding his eyes upon her.

He did not talk much and Winter, finding the silence obscurely alarming, did her best to keep up some show of conversation. As the sun sank behind the trees and the carriage began to fill with shadow she asked that the hood might be lowered so that they could get the benefit of the cooler air, for with the open sky above her and the accompanying servants in full view, she fancied that the uncomfortable tension would be largely relieved. But Carlyon, although he had stopped the carriage and complied with her request, had laughed and said: 'Why? Are you afraid of what I might do?'

There had been no possible answer to that, and Winter had forced herself to meet his gaze calmly and with a faint touch of disdain that had aroused his admiration. Despite her youth and inexperience this was no vapourish miss who would fall into a swoon and capitulate to a show of masculine force. She would be a wife worth having. His gaze rested upon her with possessive appreciation, and it crossed his mind that he must remember to see that none of the horses were left unattended and within her reach. There was apparently a dâk-bungalow some few miles further on which they should reach before darkness fell, and though Winter had wished to travel by night, he had been able to make her see the impracticability of such a course; explaining that the horses would not be able to proceed without rest, but refraining from mentioning that he had no intention of travelling further than this particular dâk-bungalow.

The providential flood that had closed the ford behind them had solved one problem: he had felt tolerably certain that Randall at least would not take the news of their departure with equanimity, but now there was no longer any need to look over his shoulder or listen for the sound of hoof-beats on the road behind them. And though the dâk-bungalow would in all probability be no better, and possibly worse, than any they had met with on the long journey from Calcutta, it would serve. They would spend a brief, premature honeymoon under its roof. A wedding night that would only anticipate the wedding by a few days.

They might even, if the surroundings were not too sordid and the ford remained impassable, remain there for several days. Days that would be made idyllic by the possession of a loved and desired object that he had come to covet beyond the reach of reason. Then when the river fell they would return to Delhi and be married quietly and without fuss, and leave immediately for Bombay, from where they would take ship for England.

Winter would be frightened at first. Possibly even frantic, since she appeared to cherish a romantic and childish attachment for this man Barton which she mistook for love. But she would give way to the inevitable. Carlyon had a shrewd suspicion that the young Condesa possessed little knowledge, if any, of the physical aspects of marriage. So much the better, since she would be the more easily brought to realize, in the shock of the discovery, that marriage with any other man was now quite impossible. And he had no fear whatsoever that he could not eventually make her love him.

He was surprised to discover that he wanted her love almost as much as he desired her body. Perhaps the first would take a little longer to obtain, because he could not obtain it by force. But it would come to him in the end. Too many women had loved him for him to have any doubts on that score.

His annoyance on finding that the dâk-bungalow, when they reached it just before moonrise, was already sheltering what looked to be a large party, was considerable. It had not occurred to him that they might have company, and for a moment fury at such a disruption of his plans made him consider giving a reckless order to drive on. But both horses and riders were tired, and the next dâk-bungalow was twelve miles ahead. As he hesitated, his Calcutta bearer, who spoke sufficient English to make himself understood by his master, returned with the information that it was only an Indian lady and her servants who had broken her journey at the dâk-bungalow. There were rooms in plenty for his master and the Miss-sahib. Carlyon, who regarded all Indians with less interest than he would the furniture of a room, drew a sigh of relief and helped Winter to alight.

The dâk-bungalow was little different from a score of others he had seen. It stood back from the road in a compound containing a large and solitary *neem* tree and bounded by a low stone wall. A verandah ran round it on three sides, and the high, whitewashed rooms were almost bare of furniture. There was dusty matting on the floor and white ants had built long, thin, wandering tunnels of dried mud upon the walls and eaten their way through what little furniture the rest of the house had boasted. The string beds were of Indian make; wide, low cots without head- or foot-boards, that looked to be uncomfortable but were capable of providing an excellent night's rest when not, as too frequently, infested by bugs.

Winter had not been able to bring any bedding, but Carlyon assured her that he had brought sufficient for both, and sent his bearer, to whom he had given certain instructions, to prepare her room. They ate a tolerable meal in the main room of the bungalow while the moon rose over the plain and someone – the *khansamah* said it was the Mohammedan lady in the room at the far end of the verandah – played a tinkling tune on a stringed instrument.

It was a haunting thread of sound, oddly familiar, and Winter found herself listening to it with a feeling that she had heard that particular plaintive tune before. She was tired, and anxious to get to her own room where she would be free of Carlyon's disturbing gaze and the necessity to appear calm and composed, and the meal seemed interminable. She had excused herself as soon as it was over, and stepping out onto the verandah, had seen a *ruth*, a closed, double-domed cart, to which a pair of trotting bullocks were being harnessed.

'It is the Begum Sahiba,' said one of the bungalow servants in reply to Winter's question. 'She stopped only on account of a broken wheel, which has now been repaired. She stays the night at a village further on the road. She is from Oudh and returns to her home.'

Winter turned away and walked slowly to the door of her room, her wide skirts rustling on the dusty stone of the verandah. 'I am from Oudh,' she thought, 'and I too am returning home.' The thought gave her fresh courage and she turned and gave her hand to Carlyon, who had followed her, thanking him once more for his help and escort and bidding him good night.

Carlyon took her hand but he did not release it. He held it in a hard grasp with fingers that were feverishly hot and unsteady, and lifting it suddenly to his lips, he kissed it.

It was not a light gesture of gallantry, but a kiss as greedily passionate as the kisses he had forced on her once before, and that the shock of Mr Carroll's revelations, Alex's perfidy and her frantic desire to escape to Conway had allowed her to thrust into the background of her mind. She tried to drag her hand away but he held it hard, kissing it again and again, moving his hot, hungry mouth against its cool softness. And when he lifted his head at last and looked at her, his cold eyes were cold no longer, but as hot and avid as his mouth had been.

He stared at her for a long moment, breathing hard and unevenly, a dark flush on his cheeks and his eyes bright with a feverish excitement that was as inexplicable to Winter as it was terrifying, and her body shrank and turned cold with a primitive fear and a misty comprehension that the passion she had aroused in him was beyond her control – and his.

She had been disgusted and shocked and furiously angry when he had kissed her that day in the Abuthnots' drawing-room. But she had not been frightened. It had not occurred to her to be frightened, for it had happened in broad daylight and there had been a dozen people within call, and her only fear had been that Conway might find her thus embraced. But she was frightened now. So frightened that for an appalling moment she thought that she was going to be physically sick from the fear that cramped her stomach and dried her mouth. Then Carlyon had released her hand at last and she had turned and stumbled through the open doorway of her room.

She closed the door behind her and threw her weight against it, terrified that he might follow her. Her heart was racing and her teeth chattered as though with cold, and when at last she fumbled for the bolt her shaking hands could not find it. There seemed to be nothing there but an empty useless socket.

The absence of a bolt sent another sickening wave of terror through her, and she turned and ran across the room, stumbling and tripping on the coarse matting, and fetched the oil-lamp that stood on a rickety table beside the bed. Her hands shook and her hooped crinoline sent huge, swaying shadows up the walls as she bent to examine the place where the bolt should have been. The wavering light showed clearly where the clamps that had held it had been removed; and also that it had been recently done . . .

She stared at it for a long moment and found herself wondering illogically how much Carlyon had paid that oily Calcutta bearer to remove the bolt, and what the man had thought on receiving such an order? But the discovery of this evidence of his intentions had an unexpectedly steadying effect upon her. This was no longer some nebulous evil that she had to deal with, but a concrete thing. There was only one way out of this tangle of her own devising, and that was instant flight. There were the horses . . . She could go through the bathroom and out through the back door to the stables, and once there she could saddle a horse and escape. But she would have to be quick, for at any moment the door might open and she was no match for Carlyon in the matter of physical strength.

Winter pulled up her foaming skirts – those spreading yards of chintz-flowered balzarine that had looked suitable for going out for a short drive in a carriage – and unfastened her crinoline. The hooped underskirt fell to the ground with a rustle and a click, and she stepped out of it and ran to fetch the carpet-bag . . . the valise would have to be abandoned. There was no time to change, but without her hoops she could ride.

But the outer door of the bathroom was locked and the key removed, and the latch of the inner door had been wrenched off.

Panic rose in her once more but she fought it down. She would have to leave by the verandah door. There was no other way, and she did not believe that Carlyon would be waiting out there. He would wait in his own room until the Indian lady and her retinue had left and the bungalow servants had retired to bed. It would not occur to him that she would run away, for where was she to run to?

The thought checked her abruptly. There *was* no place to run to. The road back to Delhi was blocked by the swollen ford, and if she continued on her way she would not outdistance him for long. He would soon find that she had gone, and overtake her. A choking hopelessness caught her by the throat and she leaned against the bedroom door, suddenly weak and shivering once more.

A sound of wrangling voices and an occasional laugh came from the compound outside, and her ear caught the jingle of bells as one of the bullocks tossed its horns. The other travellers, who were to leave tonight. Of course!

She would beg help of the lady from Oudh. Surely another woman would not refuse to help her?

Winter eased open the door onto the verandah with infinite caution. The hinges squeaked protestingly, but there was no one on the verandah. A flare of torches and oil-lamps and a talkative group of retainers surrounded the tinselled *ruth*, and a square of light from the window of the end room showed that the Indian lady had not yet left. Winter gathered up her trailing skirts in one hand and the carpet-bag in the other and ran lightly down the moonlit verandah.

The door was not locked and she could hear a woman talking on the other side of it. She pushed it open and went in.

There were three women in the room. A young and strikingly beautiful woman wearing the silk tunic and full trousers of a Mohammedan lady of family, and two older ones who were obviously servants, the younger of whom uttered a small scream of alarm at the sudden appearance of a stranger.

Winter put a finger to her lips in a gesture that implored silence and spoke in a soft, breathless whisper, explaining what little she could of her predicament and begging that they would take her with them. The Indian girl – she could not have been very many years older than Winter – listened in wide-eyed astonishment, and when she had finished, clapped her hands like a child and said: 'But it is wonderful!' She turned to the elderly serving-maid: 'Is it not wonderful to hear a *feringhi* speak as one of us? Who art thou? What is thy name?'

'Winter. Winter de Ballesteros. If the Begum Sahiba would be so kind as——'

'*What*? What is that you say?' said the girl sharply. She snatched up the oil-lamp that stood on the floor and held it so that the light fell full on Winter's face.

Winter blinked at the sudden blaze and the girl stared in silence, moving the lamp so that it lit first one side of Winter's face and then the other, lifting it so that the light poured down upon the black waves of hair.

'It is!' said the girl. '*Allah Kerimast*! It is so. Little sister, do you not know me?'

'I – I do not think——' began Winter breathlessly.

'Ameera! – dost thou not remember Ameera? Hast thou indeed forgotten the Gulab Mahal and my mother Juanita Begum, and the tales that *nani* told us on the roof-top?'

The older serving-woman threw up her arms with a little wailing cry: '*Aié*! *Aié*! It is the *Chota Moti*! It is Zobeida's baba whom I nursed as a babe!'

Winter's eyes widened until they were dark pools in her white face, and she looked from the elderly woman to the girl who had called herself Ameera.

'*Anne Marie*!' All at once there were tears in Winter's eyes and her voice was a shaken whisper: 'It is Anne Marie!'

And then quite suddenly they were in each other's arms, laughing and crying and pulling away to look at each other and clinging together again.

The soft silk, the smell of sandalwood and attar of roses; the liquid Eastern vowels. The touch and the scent and the sound of home . . .

A sudden tumult from the compound outside brought Winter back from the past to the recollection of her present position, and she pulled away, listening, her face once more strained with alarm.

'Quick, Anne Marie – quick! Take me with you. If he should find that I am gone——'

'Hush, hush,' said Ameera, who was Juanita's daughter. 'We go now. Those are my servants out there, and they shall protect thee.'

'No!' said Winter urgently. 'There must not be fighting. He has guns. Let us go quickly before he finds that I am not in my room.'

'As thou wilt,' said Ameera. 'And on the road thou shalt tell me who this *feringhi* is who has frightened thee so. Is it thy husband from whom thou wouldst escape?'

'No. It is someone who—— Anne Marie, I cannot go out there. There are lights, and his servants will see me go. Cannot the *ruth* be brought nearer?'

Ameera laughed. 'No one shall see thee, Little Pearl – dost thou remember thy pet name in the zenana? – see, we will put Hamida's *bourka* upon thee, thus.' She snatched up a voluminous white cotton garment that lay on the floor and dropped it over Winter's head. It was a long, full, tent-like cloak that shrouded her from head to foot leaving only an inset of coarse net over the upper part of the face, through which the wearer could see but not be seen. 'There,' said Ameera triumphantly, 'It is done. Hamida must cover her face with her *chuddah* if she fears that men will attack her for the sake of her beauty!'

The older waiting-woman, who had been the infant Winter's wet nurse, mopped the tears from her face and chuckled like a parrot. 'I will go out by the back way lest any of the *nauker-log* should see four women go out where but three came in.'

'That is well thought of,' said Ameera, donning her own *bourka*. 'Come now. We are ready.'

'No – wait,' said Winter suddenly. 'I must leave a message. If I do not, he will think me lost and rouse the country looking for me, or go to the police. He could not just leave me and go back. Hast thou paper and ink?'

'Paper and ink? No. But Atiya here shall fetch some from the *khansamah*. Quick, Atiya – run!'

Ameera gave the girl a push, and she scuttled away, looking like a Hallowe'en ghost, to return a few minutes later, breathing hard and bearing a soft sheet of native paper, a bowl of black and gritty ink and a quill-pen. Winter threw back the folds of the *bourka* and wrote swiftly, Ameera holding the lamp. She thanked Lord Carlyon for his kind assistance, but she had met with a relative, a cousin, and so need put him to no further trouble on her behalf. He need be in no anxiety about her as she would be quite safe, and was continuing her journey immediately.

She held the paper above the lamp to dry the ink, her hands shaking with nervous haste, and folding it, begged Atiya to take it to her room and leave it there, but to make no sound that might attract attention. The woman had slipped out again, and Winter had waited in a fever of impatience and dread until she had returned, giggling reassuringly and carrying the small valise: 'No need to leave thy gear,' said Atiya. 'We will cover it with a *chuddah*, so, and it will pass unnoticed.'

They hurried down the verandah steps and out into the night, and a moment later they were in the dark, close-curtained *ruth*. There was a startled ejaculation from one of the entourage, and a fierce request to be silent from Hamida, as a fourth figure crept into the *ruth*. 'That son of an owl will ruin all,' muttered Hamida angrily. The man who had exclaimed at the sight of four women where he had expected three inquired anxiously if all were well. 'All is well, Fateh Ali,' called Ameera. 'Drive on. It is late.'

The driver of the *ruth* shouted, the bullocks grunted and the *ruth* jolted forward and precipitated Winter into Ameera's lap, where the pent-up strains and anxieties and emotions of the last twenty-four hours found relief in a gale of laughter. She clung to Ameera and laughed, and Ameera and the two serving-women laughed with her, so that the driver and the four elderly mounted retainers who accompanied the *ruth* stared at each other in bewilderment and ended by chuckling in sympathy with that joyous sound.

'And now,' said Ameera, drawing breath and dabbing her eyes with the edge of her veil, 'tell me all. How dost thou come to be here? Art thou not yet wed? And who is this *feringhi* from whom we escape?'

But she received no answer. Winter's head was still against her shoulder, but she had fallen asleep.

Carlyon had waited until the sound of quarrelling voices and the wheels of the Indian women's equipage had been swallowed up by the night. He had heard the *khansamah* and others of the dâk-bungalow servants pass along the verandah, and had waited until the voices from the stables and the servants' quarters at the back of the house sank to a murmur and there was silence at last. He was in no hurry. He could afford to wait.

He adjusted his long silk dressing-gown to his satisfaction, ran a hand over his hair, and smiling a little, went out onto the deserted verandah. The light still burned in Winter's room and he pushed the door open and went in, and finding the room empty supposed that she must be in the bathroom; she had evidently prepared for bed, for her discarded crinoline was lying on the floor. He closed the door softly behind him, and crossing the room sat down on the bed to wait.

It was not until several minutes later when, disturbed by the silence, his eye fell upon a paper that bore his name, and less than a minute later he was on the verandah shouting for horses, servants and lights.

He dressed with desperate raging haste, but he had allowed too much time to elapse, and he did not know of the narrow side lane that led off the road to the house where Ameera was to pass the night. A lane down which the *ruth* and its escort had turned less than five minutes before he galloped past it.

An hour later he was forced to realize that Winter had escaped him, and he turned back, rage contending with fear for her safety. Whom had she gone with? How could she have left without his knowledge? A *relative*? How could she have met a relative? Had she planned it all, and known that there would be someone here to meet her? The Indian woman in the end room did not so much as cross his mind, for Carlyon had never heard of Juanita de Ballesteros, who had married Wali Dad of Oudh.

The frightened servants could give him no information, and he cursed his inability to understand this barbarous language and the incapacity of his Calcutta bearer as an interpreter. He had headed for the ford on the chance that Winter's letter had been a blind and that she had, after all, turned back to Delhi. But a raging torrent ran where the ford had been and Carlyon had returned to the dâk-bungalow, white with fury and convinced at last that Winter had tricked him. He had spent two appalling days of enforced idleness at the bungalow, alternating between the extremes of rage and boredom, and on the morning of the third day, having heard that the river had fallen, he had returned to Delhi.

Winter awoke to find sunlight lying across her in a fretted pattern thrown by a carved wooden shutter. She was still wearing the crushed and crumpled morning-dress of balzarine that she had put on in her bedroom at the Abuthnots' bungalow in Delhi Cantonment . . . how long ago? It seemed an age; another existence.

She pushed away the thin cotton *chuddah* that covered her and stretched her arms above her head. She was lying on a *charpoy*, a low string bed with carved and painted legs, in a small bare room whose walls were coloured a gay pink while the floor was covered with rush-matting. Except for the *charpoy* and the matting the room was devoid of furniture, and once again Winter had a sudden mental vision of her room at Ware with its clutter of cumbersome furniture, gloomy wallpaper, dark heavily-framed engravings and thick fringed and tasselled draperies. The contrast made her laugh aloud, and there was a rustle of silk and a scent of sandalwood, and Ameera was there, smiling down at her.

'We did not like to wake thee,' said Ameera, 'but the sun is high and if we do not wish to lose a day's journey we must be on our way.'

Winter sprang up and immediately tripped on the voluminous folds of her crumpled dress and would have fallen if Ameera had not caught her.

'*Tenga cuidado*!' exclaimed Ameera, unexpectedly relapsing into Spanish. 'Why do you wear a garment in which it is impossible to walk?'

'My hoops,' exclaimed Winter looking ruefully at her trailing skirts, 'I took them off, and I suppose they are still on the floor of that dâk-bungalow.' Forgetting more pressing matters she described to the fascinated Ameera the workings of a crinoline: 'They hold the skirts out – so.'

'Like a tent!' exclaimed Ameera, delighted. 'But it is ridiculous, is it not so? How does one sit down? Or walk through a door?'

Winter demonstrated and Ameera went off into peals of laughter.

'But have you never seen one?' asked Winter curiously. 'Are there no European women in Oudh?'

Ameera's laughing face sobered. 'Yes,' she said slowly, 'there are European women, but I do not meet them.'

'But your mother?'

'My mother is dead,' said Ameera. 'Did you not know?'

'No. I am sorry. She used to write, and then she wrote no more, and – and that is all I ever knew.'

'She died in the year of the cholera, when more than five hundred died in one day in Lucknow,' said Ameera. '*Ai de me*! you will find few who remember you at the Gulab Mahal.'

'Yet you still speak Spanish,' said Winter.

'As you see. But badly now. We kept it as a child's language amongst us. I do not often speak it in these days, for my husband – my husband does not care for *feringhis* and their ways.'

'Your husband! You are married, then?'

'But of course,' said Ameera in surprise. 'I have been married these five years. Have *you* no husband as yet?'

Winter laughed. 'You are taking me to my wedding!'

Ameera clapped her hands in a child-like gesture of delight. 'Is it really so? Then there is all the more need for haste. You shall tell me the whole; but first you must eat, and then we will find you some clothes. You cannot travel in comfort in such garments as you wear now.'

She ran to the door and called a variety of orders down the steep little stair, and presently Winter was being bathed and fed, and dressed in a replica of Ameera's own graceful costume by a horde of chattering, inquisitive, laughing women.

'Zobeida has cared for this well,' said Hamida approvingly, combing out the heavy silken waves of hair that reached almost to Winter's knee. 'It is softer and finer and even longer than Ameera Begum's. Is Zobeida no longer alive that she is not with thee now?'

Winter shook her head and Hamida sighed. '*Hai mai*! We all grow old. Stand still, child, while I braid it. We shall need no black sheeps' wool to lengthen this.'

Her gnarled brown fingers braided the rippling silken cloak into two long thick plaits, and fastened them with coloured thread. 'There! It is finished. Now thou art no longer of *Belait* but of Hind.'

'And is not that dress more comfortable than thy tent of wires and fish-bones?' demanded Ameera. 'Thus do I remember thee when we played together in the women's quarters of the Gulab Mahal.'

Dressed alike in full trousers, loose tunics and veils of fine *shabnam* from Dacca, with their blue-black hair braided to the knee, the relationship between the two women was suddenly apparent. Winter, daughter of Marcos, but with the small bones of her mother Sabrina, was not so tall as Ameera. But their eyes were the same; de Ballesteros' eyes, dark brown, not black. Enormous, liquid and lovely. The eyes of some gentle Moorish maiden, centuries dead, who had married a knight of Castile. Their black hair swept back from their foreheads in the same line, springing from a deep widow's peak and glinting blue and not bronze where the light struck it, and their small, high-bridged, delicate noses and slim, swallow-wing brows were the same. But there the resemblance ended.

The face of Juanita's daughter was not broad at the brow and pointed at the chin like Winter's, nor did it possess Winter's gravity, or the faintly hollowed planes that were an indication of the beauty of bone beneath it. Ameera's face was a smooth, laughing oval, and though her lips were as red as Winter's they resembled a pomegranate bud rather than a full-blown rose, while her wheat-gold skin made Winter's warm-tinted ivory appear velvet-white by contrast.

She was the elder by less than two years, but early marriage and her Eastern blood had ripened her to an opulent maturity that would have made her seem the younger girl's senior by as much as ten, had it not been for the laughter that danced perpetually in her dark eyes and lurked in the dimples at the corners of her small curving mouth.

Winter, whom life at Ware had starved of laughter, looked into Ameera's merry eyes and experienced a sudden relief of tension. An uprush of gaiety and high spirits and an irrational desire to run out into the sunlight and shout and play foolish games. To laugh for the sheer joy of laughing – and to make up for all the laughter that had been lost during the lonely years at Ware.

'A *bourka* for the bride!' called Ameera. 'My little cousin goes to her wedding, and we cannot let other men's eyes peer at her by the way.'

And at that they had all laughed together with a noise like a flock of starlings, and swept out to the door of the women's quarters to see the guests off on their journey.

That journey was perhaps the happiest time that Winter de Ballesteros, going to her wedding, had known since the long-ago days of the Gulab Mahal. Here was a friend and a companion of her own age, and here once more was all the warmth and wonder of the old happy memories coming alive again. The very scent and sound of the days that she had kept alive with Zobeida's help and a desperate and tenacious effort of will, because it had so often seemed to be all that she had to cling to. She told Ameera all that had happened to her, and heard in return all the news of the Gulab Mahal.

There were, as Ameera had said, few left in the Rose Palace who would remember the Little Pearl, for the cholera had taken a heavy toll. Dasim, son of old Ali Shah's brother, the young and handsome man who had looked too often at the white and gold Sabrina for Aziza Begum's peace of mind, was now an elderly gentleman whose wife, a soured and shrewish woman from Faizabad – Ameera pulled her laughing face into an expression of mock malice – was the senior lady of the household, though Dasim had acquired two junior wives and now possessed the three permitted by the Prophet.

Ameera's sister, a baby who had been born in the fateful January that had seen the retreat from Kabul and the disastrous end of the first Afghan War, had died too of the cholera, but the son who had been born in the same year as Winter was now a young man nearing his eighteenth birthday:

'A wild youth,' said Ameera, shaking her head sadly. 'But he is young. He will learn. At the moment it is all drink and devilry with him, and he is easily led by bad companions. It will pass.'

Ameera had married her second cousin, Walayat Shah; a petty nobleman who had occupied one of the numerous hereditary and lucrative sinecures at the dissolute court of the King of Oudh. The annexation had dispossessed him of employment and livelihood and he and his family lived now at the Gulab Mahal. The loss of power, privilege and revenue had enraged Walayat Shah against the *feringhis*, so that it would be better, explained Ameera regretfully, if Winter did not visit the Gulab Mahal just yet. Men were apt to get hot and angry. They had less patience than women, and although she herself considered that the action of the Company had been high-handed and unnecessary – for were there not others of the royal line to replace Wajid Ali if he had offended? – she was happy to be back in the Gulab Mahal and had no wish to kill and burn. She had heard no good of Wajid Ali while he had reigned, and now that he had been deposed she could see little point in plunging the state into bloodshed in order to reinstate him. She had her children's safety to think of, and for their sake would be content to live quietly in the Gulab Mahal under any government that could be trusted to keep order.

'Your children?' exclaimed Winter, instantly diverted from politics to the personal. 'Have you children? How lovely. How many?'

'I have two sons,' said Ameera proudly. One was four years old and the other three, and they had been left in the care of her husband's mother while she had been away on a visit to attend the wedding of a near relative: she would have taken them with her, but that her husband's mother had forbidden it for fear that they might fall ill or meet with some accident on the journey, and now she could not wait to get back to them.

'Three weeks! I have not seen them for three weeks – and it has been like three years. If it were not that I cannot spare even another hour from them, I would remain for thy *shadi*, Little Pearl. When thou art wed and have sons of thine own thou wilt know how it is with me.'

Ameera's road lay through Lunjore and across the bridge of boats, but when some five days later they neared the outskirts of the city she would not come to the Residency, but stopped the *ruth* and sent one of her servants to fetch a hired carriage: 'I have thought,' said Ameera lovingly, 'that it were better if thou didst not arrive at thy bridegroom's house with a cousin who is not of thy own race. I have heard that there are those among the sahib-*log* who do not look kindly on such things. But we will meet again. Surely, surely we will meet again! And now, as thou hast no woman of thine own to attend thee, Hamida here will go with thee. Nay, nay, we arranged it all last night whilst thou wert asleep. It is not seemly for thee to go to thy husband with no woman to attend thee. If he has procured another for thee, then she can return.'

The two young women embraced, and Hamida collected her own and Winter's belongings and followed her out into the road. A moment later the gaily decorated *ruth* with its mounted escort had rumbled away down the long, tree-shaded road. A slim hand waved briefly from between the embroidered curtains and Ameera was gone.

Winter, no longer in native dress but wearing a light-coloured riding-habit, stood by the side of the road looking after the dust cloud that hid the *ruth* and blinking back tears from her eyes, until Hamida, scandalized by the staring crowd of country folk who had paused to gape at the sight of a strange memsahib, hurried her into the hired carriage.

They were driven away through the hot sunlight towards the cantonments, and presently they reached a long white road bordered by trees and a high wall, and came at last to a huge castellated gateway of whitewashed stone, wide enough to admit a carriage and high enough to allow for the passage of a howdahed elephant. A gateway splashed with flamboyant colour from the bougainvillea that climbed its sides and hung in vivid masses from the parapet, and under whose deep, shadowed archway Sabrina Grantham, Condesa de los Aguilares, had ridden eighteen long years ago, to stay with her Uncle Ebenezer as a guest at the Residency where his nephew Conway was now Commissioner.

25

Sabrina's daughter did not look up at the gateway but forward at the long drive that curled through the chequered shadows towards the high, single-storied house that was to be her home. She was here at last. Conway was in that house, and very soon now she would be married to him.

The carriage drew up under a stone porch festooned with flowering creeper, and a startled *chupprassi* gaped at the girl in the close-fitting riding-habit who descended from it. The Residency servants had been aware for many months of their master's approaching marriage, but they had not expected the bride for another two weeks, and several of them gathered to stare and exchange agitated whispers.

Yes, agreed Durga Charan the head *chupprassi* cautiously, straightening his turban with an agitated hand, the Commissioner Sahib was at home, but he could see no one. He was indisposed – far too sick to receive visitors.

'I know,' said Winter. 'That is why I have come. I will see the Sahib at once. Show me to his room.'

The head *chupprassi*, already bewildered by this young Miss-sahib who showed such an unexpected command of his own language, made an ineffectual attempt to stop her, but Winter swept past him and into the wide hall.

Conway's bedroom was darkened by curtains drawn across the windows. It smelt unpleasant, and there was a woman in it. A plump native woman dressed in brightly coloured spangled muslin, who crouched on the floor beside the bed and waved a palm-leaf fan. The woman looked up, startled by Winter's entrance, and rose with a clash of anklets and jewellery. She was fat and past her first youth, but in a bold, florid manner, not unbeautiful. She had been chewing *pan*, and the smell of it, allied to the musk with which she was scented, almost overpowered the stench of sickness and brandy. She seemed an unsuitable sickroom attendant, and she stared at Winter in indignation and hostility, her *kohl*-blackened eyes enormous in her plump dark face.

'The Sahib is not well,' said the woman in a shrill, angry voice. 'He can see no one. No one!'

'He will see me,' said Winter, and walked past her to the bed.

The heap on the bed moaned, grunted and stirred, and said in a thick voice: 'Wha's that? Wha's that? Shurrup, can't you! Filthy din——'

It turned over on its back and groaned aloud, and Winter looked down at a bloated, unrecognizable face. Was this – *could* this be Conway? She had expected to find a worn, haggard, perhaps even grey-haired skeleton of a man, wasted by fever, and this fat bloated face, yellow in the dim light of the curtained room, was entirely and unexpectedly shocking. A reek of stale spirits and foul breath made her draw back sharply. They had been dosing him with brandy! Surely that could not be a good thing for fever?

And then suddenly she remembered what Mr Carroll had said. 'A swelling fever.' Of course! That was why Conway looked so bulky and bloated. No wonder he had not wished her to see him like this. No wonder, not knowing her well enough to trust in her devotion to him, he had feared the effect it might have upon her. Pity and love choked her and her eyes filled with compassionate tears. She bent over him and laid a cool hand on his forehead.

Conway grunted and opened his eyes with an effort. He stared up at her for a long time, trying to focus her and completely at a loss. Must have been drunker than he had thought last night – or was it the opium? God, what a head he had! Tongue like a roll of dusty matting. He'd seen things before, but they had been strange spotted things that had crawled or hopped. Not women. Not young and beautiful women. Couldn't be the brandy. Must be the opium. The creature was speaking. He wished that she would stop speaking and go away. He liked women, but not after a thick night. At the moment noise – any noise – hurt his head abominably . . .

' . . . Winter. Conway, it's Winter. Conway dear, don't you know me? Why did you not tell me you were ill? I have come to look after you. You will be well soon, dearest. Conway, it's I – Winter. Dearest, I am here——'

At long last, through the thick, sick, agonizing torment that filled his head and stomach, the sense of the words penetrated . . . *Winter*! It wasn't the opium or the brandy. This was the fortune that he was going to marry. The ugly, skinny, dark-eyed creature from Ware. She was here. How she had got here he did not know . . . Surely he could not have collapsed from the effects of a debauch and been unconscious for weeks? Hardly. What did it matter anyway? The girl was here. Must get rid of her. He was going to be sick again any minute, and that would finish it. Must get rid of her——

He was sick. Exceedingly sick. But in the more lucid interval that followed he discovered with amazement that she was holding his head and bathing his forehead with cold water; whispering endearments and telling him that he would soon be well. Yasmin, standing by in stunned fury, began to protest, and Conway turned his head slowly – he could not turn his eyes – and spoke a single virulent word of dismissal.

The small, cool hands pressed his head back upon the pillow and he lay still with closed eyes, trying to think; dimly aware of disaster and the need for action. Presently he opened his eyes a little, peering at her under puffy, half-closed lids, and said thickly: 'Didn't expect you. Good of you t'come. Call Ismail, there's a good girl. M'bearer.'

The portly bearer, who had been hovering outside the door with a whispering and curious crowd of servants, hurried to his master's side, and after a brief and muttered colloquy turned to Winter and salaamed deeply. If the

Miss-sahib would follow him he would show her to her room, and refreshments would be brought. The Huzoor wished Ismail to attend upon him.

'Go with him,' said Conway, forcing the words with an effort. 'Y' can come back later.'

When the door had closed upon her he crawled out of bed and dragged himself to the bathroom. The water in the earthenware *gurra* was cold from the cool night, and he took a tin dipper and sloshed it over his head and shoulders, shuddering at the shock of the chilly cataract on his hot, sweating body and coldly sweating head. Ismail, returning, applied a variety of well-tried remedies, and the Commissioner groaned and staggered back to his bedroom to subside heavily into a chair, and demanded brandy.

'Hot milk is better for the opium,' advised Ismail, leering.

'Well, mix 'em together then. Quickly! And tell that bitch Yasmin to keep to her own quarters.'

He drank the brew of hot milk and brandy and felt sufficiently recovered to demand an explanation of his future wife's arrival. Ismail had heard it all from those who had witnessed the Miss-sahib's arrival, and also from the ayah whom the Miss-sahib had brought with her.

Conway listened, dazed, half-stupid and racked with recurrent waves of nausea and futile rage. Damn the girl! What had possessed her to come gallivanting off on her own? It was unheard of! It would ruin all. He would not have had this happen for the world. He had intended to arrange for the wedding to take place within an hour or two of her arrival, so as to allow her no time to change her mind. And now she had arrived unexpectedly, and alone, and had found him suffering from the after-effects of a debauch in a house stinking of spirits and the sandalwood and essences of the five *nautch*-girls from the city who, with Yasmin, had entertained his guests at a bachelor party he had given on the previous night. What had possessed the girl to descend upon him like this? Or had she heard rumours, and wished to catch him out unawares?

'The Miss-sahib, hearing that the Huzoor was suffering from illness, hurried from Delhi in her haste to care for him,' said Ismail, laying out clean linen.

Illness. She had said something to that effect, so she had. Why, of course! An innocent creature like that could have had no experience of drunkenness. She had imagined him to be suffering from some illness!

The way opened before him with such surprising simplicity that he would have laughed aloud if such a physical effort had not been too painful. She was here alone and unattended. There was no one she knew in Lunjore and she could not stay the night in his house unless she were married to him. It was all going to be quite easy after all. He would send for the padre and explain why, in order to protect the young bride's reputation, the wedding must be performed immediately, and until the knot was tied he must keep up the fiction that he had been suffering from fever. It could not be better!

Revived and invigorated by the prospect he stumbled back to bed and ordered Ismail to send a message instantly to the padre-sahib requesting his immediate presence, and another to Colonel Moulson to say that he wished to see him. 'And send in the barber to me, and get this room cleaned up, and open all the windows and clear the air a bit – no, don't draw the curtains, you black bastard! Oh, and keep the Miss-sahib out of here, d'you hear? Tell her I'm asleep – in me bath – anything. But keep her out. Now *hut jao* – and *jeldi*!'

The padre, a thin young man suffering from weak eyes and incipient malaria, listened with an attempt at concentration to the explanation of the young Condesa's unexpected arrival and unprotected state, and agreed, shivering with ague, that immediate marriage seemed the best solution to the difficulty, and that as the bridegroom was unfortunately in poor health the ceremony should be performed in the house. He would make the necessary arrangements, but the Commissioner must procure two witnesses.

Three hours later, in the cool, dim drawing-room, Sabrina's daughter stood before a makeshift altar between burning candles and was married to the nephew of Emily and Ebenezer.

She had brought her wedding-dress with her, but she did not wear it, for she had no hoops to support its spreading folds, and no desire to explain at this juncture why she should be without a crinoline. She wore instead the pale grey riding-habit in which she had arrived, and carried a bunch of the white jasmine that grew by the porch. Hamida had tucked jasmine blossoms into her black hair, and dropping the filmy bridal veil over her head had frowned, saying that white veils were more suited to widows than to brides.

Hamida was uneasy. She had no knowledge of the ways of 'sahib-*log*', but the Commissioner's servants appeared to hold him in scant respect behind his back, and half an hour in the Residency had left her under no delusions as to what type of woman it was who occupied the *bibi-gurh* – the small detached house that lay behind the main building and was screened from it by a discreet hedge of poinsettia and a cluster of pepper trees.

It had been no unusual thing in the past for the sahibs to install Indian women in their compounds, and there had been a time when such a practice was encouraged. Not only because the lack of white women drove men to consort with prostitutes, and therefore to take a morganatic wife or a mistress from among the women of the country was considered preferable, but because close association with such women taught them more of the country, and gave them a better understanding of the men under their command. Many had married Indian women, and Lady Wheeler, wife of the British General commanding at Cawnpore, was known to be an Indian lady of good family. But with the arrival of more and more white women in the country these relationships became fewer, and Hamida considered that out of respect to his bride the Commissioner-Sahib should have pensioned off the occupants of the *bibi-gurh* before her arrival. Hamida viewed the situation with suspicion and took an instant dislike to the Commissioner's servants, whom she considered lax and insolent.

But if Hamida had qualms, Winter had none. Her only anxiety was on the score of Conway's health, and she was alarmed at hearing of his intention to leave his bed for the ceremony. Surely a man who had been ill for so long should not be allowed to rise and be kept standing even for a short time? Supposing he should suffer a relapse? Conway had, however, assured her that her arrival had already worked such wonders on his spirits that he felt himself to be a new man, and as he was already on the mend such a small exertion on so happy an occasion could do him no harm.

That had been in the course of a brief interview in the darkened bedroom where the curtains had remained drawn against the strong sunlight. The Reverend Eustace Chillingham, who had also been present, had been surprised to learn that the Commissioner had been so ill, since he had previously heard nothing of such a thing; but he was feeling too ill himself to pay much attention to the matter.

Winter had not seen Conway again until Colonel Moulson had appeared to lead her to the drawing-room. The sight of Colonel Moulson, whom she had never liked, and whom later, following the incident on the night that the *Sirius* had anchored off Alexandria, she had actually disliked, was a shock to her. She had forgotten that he would be in Lunjore, and although she knew him to be acquainted with Conway, she had not expected him to be on such intimate terms with her betrothed as to warrant his being asked to give away the bride. She would rather have had anyone but Colonel Moulson to give her away, when but for Alex——

She had a momentary and disturbing vision of Alex's face, as real and as sharply defined as though for a fractional moment he were standing between her and Colonel Moulson – Alex who had lied to her and tried to prevent her from marrying Conway. Well, he had not prevented her and he did not matter any more. As for Colonel Moulson, Conway must know that she had met him, and it was out of delicacy and consideration for her that he had asked Colonel Moulson to give her away rather than some stranger. He could not be expected to know that she would have preferred a stranger.

Winter looked at Colonel Moulson, her pale cheeks pink, her eyes very bright and young and a little frightened; not seeing him at all, but seeing instead the old, familiar picture of Conway, golden-haired, blue-eyed, wearing bright armour and standing between her and Cousin Julia and unhappiness.

That picture did not fade when she looked through the mist of her veil at the gross elderly man with the pale protuberant eyes, greying hair and slack, twitching mouth who stood or knelt beside her, and whose damp fleshy fingers were so unsteady that it was only with difficulty that he managed to put the ring upon her finger.

There was nothing about this bulky stranger that was familiar; but he was

Conway, and he had been ill. So ill, and so disfigured by illness, that he had not wanted her to see him. That was proof enough of his affection for her, and of his kindness. The change that she saw in him was only physical, and now that she was here to nurse him and take care of him, to help him and to love him, he would recover soon enough and become strong and well again. She looked down at the ring that was too loose for her finger, as the first ring that he had given her had been, and her eyes were suddenly full of happy tears.

Through the mist of those tears and the gossamer whiteness of her veil, she turned to look up at her bridegroom and saw, beyond his shoulder, that there was, after all, another woman at her wedding – a young woman, slight and fair, with enormous shadowy eyes and wearing an unusual style of dress. But it had only been a trick of the light that filtered through the heavy split-cane *chiks* that hung before the line of french windows, for when she blinked the tears away there was no one there except Colonel Moulson and a Major Mottisham, the Reverend Eustace Chillingham whose weak eyes were already bright with fever, and Conway Barton – who was now her husband.

But half an hour later there had been a good many more people, and a considerable quantity of champagne.

The Reverend Chillingham had left immediately after the ceremony, but to Winter's distress Conway had refused to return to his bed.

'Bed? Nonsense! Nonsense! Never felt better in m' life. Told you I was on the mend. Don't get married every day of the week. I've sent out to tell some of m' friends, and they'll soon be over. They'll want to see the bride. You're the Commissioner's Lady now, m'dear. You'll have to learn to do the honours. Have some champagne. Capital stuff for putting life into you. You'll find we keep a good cellar. Hey there, Rassul, bring another bottle!'

He toasted Winter and looked her over with considerable approval. Between pain and nausea, and fear that her unexpected arrival might result in his losing the fortune that she represented, he had been able to spare little attention for her personal appearance. Now, however, secure and in triumph, he took stock of his bride and decided that fate had indeed been kind to him.

Who could have believed that the plain, skinny, owl-eyed child whom he had last seen six years ago would have turned out so well? She was not precisely in his style – there were enough dark-haired women in India, and when it came to European ones he preferred 'em blonde and buxom – but she was well enough. Those eyes were magnificent, and if he knew anything of women, that mouth promised a very pleasant wedding night. As for her figure, if her riding-habit did not lie he would find little to complain of.

'Fred told me you had turned out quite a beauty,' said the Commissioner, 'and by Gad, he was right! A fortune and a beauty too – I'm a lucky man.' He put an arm about Winter's slim waist and squeezed it, and the champagne slopped over and splashed down his waistcoat.

Winter said anxiously: 'Conway, please sit down. I'm sure that you cannot be strong enough to stand. Colonel Moulson, please persuade him to return to his bed.'

'Persuade him to go to bed?' exclaimed Colonel Moulson, who had been lacing his champagne with brandy and had already downed three glasses in rapid succession. 'You shouldn't have any difficulty about gettin' him there! If I were in his place, the difficulty would be in holdin' me back from it – the lucky dog!'

Winter had not fully understood the allusion, but the coarseness of the laugh which accompanied it had made her colour hotly and draw back from the Colonel in shocked distaste, her slim body stiffening with disgust. But Conway had only laughed and said: 'Time and to spare for that, Fred – time and to spare!' And then carriages and men on horseback had begun to arrive and the room had filled with noisy strangers.

There had not been many of them – perhaps a dozen in all – and only two of them had been women; but to Winter there had appeared to be twice or three times that number. The noise, the loud laughter and congratulations, the curious, appraising stares and the bold approval of the men bewildered and disconcerted her, and the women were neither of them of the kind whom she would ever have felt drawn towards. They made her feel young and stiff and gauche, and they appeared to know Conway very well, for they addressed him – and every other man in the room – by his Christian name, so that Winter had some difficulty in deciding which were their husbands.

Mrs Wilkinson was small, plump and pretty, and made no secret of the fact that she used rouge. She jangled a great many bracelets, smelt strongly of violet essence and had rolling blue eyes and a high-pitched laugh.

Mrs Cottar, on the other hand, was tall and thin, red-haired, green-eyed and ugly. She was dressed with extreme smartness, though in a somewhat *outré* style, and she appeared to be a general favourite with the men. Her remarks were invariably greeted with a burst of laughter and applause, but as they were mostly delivered *sotto voce* Winter heard few of them, and since those she did hear conveyed nothing to her, she could not understand why they should so amuse the gentlemen who hung on Mrs Cottar's words, applauding her and addressing her as 'Lou'.

Winter herself stood silent, a small rigid smile fixed on her face and her anxious eyes on Conway. Once, when a particularly uproarious burst of laughter had greeted one of Mrs Cottar's more audible sallies, he noticed that his bride had failed to join in the general mirth, and urged her in rousing tones not to be such a little innocent.

'She ain't likely to remain one long; not in your company, Con,' observed Colonel Moulson with a hiccough.

'Damn you, Fred,' protested the bridegroom; adding jovially: 'Not that I wouldn't say you were right.'

'Not like you to take to milk and water after years of champagne and country-brewed brandy, eh, what?' said Colonel Moulson. 'Shouldn't have said it would suit you at all.'

'But then I do not suppose that he will be disposing of his cellar,' said Mrs Cottar softly.

There was another burst of laughter in which the Commissioner joined uproariously, and Mrs Cottar looked from the bridegroom's face to the bride's, and frowned.

Lucy Cottar possessed a caustic and malicious wit, and little kindness towards her own sex; an attitude which the majority of them reciprocated with active dislike, since despite her lack of beauty many men found her attractive as well as entertaining, and Mrs Cottar enjoyed playing with fire and had no conscience in the matter of other women's husbands. But something in Winter's bewildered eyes gave her a momentary twinge of compunction.

'Con,' said Mrs Cottar in an undertone, 'you shouldn't have done it. It isn't decent.'

'What ain't decent?' demanded Mr Barton.

'You aren't. What possessed that child's family to send her out to you? Why, it's no better than rape. Didn't they know you?'

'I took dam' good care that they didn't!' said Mr Barton, and shouted with laughter. He was feeling light-headed with triumph. All over – all the waiting. All the work. He'd married a fortune. He was a rich man. A rich man and a dam' clever one! He'd planned it all, and it had all come about just as he had planned it. Not a hitch. Clever!

Mrs Cottar, still under the influence of that unexpected feeling of compunction, left him and addressed herself to his wife:

'You must find it a little bewildering at first – meeting so many people whom you do not know and who all know your husband so well. But you will soon get to know us just as well as he does. Though you must not expect much gaiety in Lunjore. We do our best, but if you have been led to expect a gay life from what you will have seen of Calcutta and Delhi, I am afraid you may be sadly disappointed in Lunjore.'

'Oh, but I never expected it to be gay,' Winter hastened to assure her, 'and I know that Conway – Mr Barton – will be far too hard-worked, once he is well again, to have much time for entertainments.'

'Has he been ill?' inquired Mrs Cottar in some surprise. 'I did not know. But then I have not seen him for above a week. You must know that that is most unusual, for we all meet a great deal. Your husband has been used to give a small party as a regular thing each Tuesday night for his special cronies, and you do not know how welcome they have been during the hot weather. To sit at home all day in the heat is bad enough, but to be compelled to sit there every night as well would be insupportable! And this is such a cool house. But I had a migraine last week and could not attend, although Josh went – the selfish creature.'

She saw that Winter was looking at her with a stunned bewilderment and said in explanation: 'Josh – Joshua – is my husband. The large dark one by the door——' She pointed with her fan.

Winter said slowly and as if she found it difficult to articulate: 'But – but Conway – Mr Barton, has been ill you know. Since – since late August.'

'Ill? Feathers! Did he tell you that? He was joking. Perhaps he meant you to believe that he was sick for love.'

'But Mr Carroll told me——'

'Carroll? Do you mean Jack Carroll? So you know him? Oh, that would be just his way of saying that Con gave one of his bachelor parties when Jack was last here, and they were all in a melancholy way the next morning. I know Josh was! I told him that the next time he came home from one of Con's bachelor dinners he could sleep it off on the verandah. I am afraid that the men will sadly miss those parties now that Con is married, but I hope that you do not mean to discontinue our Tuesday sociables? We gamble, you know. Not very heavy stakes, but enough to make it exciting. Do you play cards?'

'No,' said Winter. 'No, I – I have never . . .'

'We must teach you. And you need not be afraid that Con will be too overworked to enter into our few entertainments. Why, he is the idlest of creatures – and so we all tell him. He lets Alex Randall do all the work while he takes all the credit. Quite shocking – is it not, Con?'

'No idea what you're talking about, Lou, my witch. But I am ready to be shocked,' said Mr Barton coming to anchor beside them. 'What is it? A new scandal?'

'On the contrary. An old one. It is you I was referring to. I was telling your wife that you allow Alex Randall to do all the work while you take all the credit.'

'What's shockin' about that?' demanded Mr Barton. 'Randall likes work. Meat and drink to the man. Peculiar taste. Shockin' fool I'd be if I wore myself out doing what someone else will do for me. *I've* better use f' my time, m' dear. But Alex is a cold fish.'

'Oh, no, he is not,' said Mrs Cottar with a twisted smile. 'You're out there, Con.'

'Ha! I am, am I? Trust you to know! Speakin' from personal experience, Lou?'

'No, alas.'

'Which means that you tried your lures on him, eh?'

'But of course. Any woman of spirit would have done the same. But he does not mix business with pleasure, and Lunjore is business. Such a pity.'

'Not for me,' said the Commissioner, holding out his glass to be refilled by an obsequious *khidmatgar*. 'He deals with the business while I take care of the pleasure. Very satisfactory arrangement, Lou, my love.' He drank deeply and looked down at his wife's white, rigid face. 'Mustn't forget I'm a married man now. Have to watch m'self. Not so much straying from the straight and narrow, eh, Lou? Eh, m'dear?' He pinched his wife's chin and slopped a quantity of brandy down her dress in the process.

The rest of the evening was a nightmare to Winter. A dreadful, feverish dream of babel and noise and the clink of glasses, in which she did not hear one word of what was said. She sat on a sofa with her back straight and her head high and a small social smile frozen on her face. She answered when she was spoken to, but her voice did not seem to belong to her any more.

The sun sank and the room filled with shadows. Lamps and candles were lit and the *chiks* rolled up to let in the cool night air, but still the noise went on and still no one left. Hours later – or so it seemed – a meal was served in the big dining-room, and Winter sat beside her bridegroom at the head of the table, white-faced and dry-eyed, smiling with stiff lips and trying to force herself to eat the food that was placed before her. Toasts were drunk and speeches were made, and still she sat there as if she were held in a strange trance in which her body had turned into some inanimate jointed thing and her mind had ceased to function. She was aroused from it at last by someone plucking at her arm, and turned stiffly to see Mrs Cottar.

'Do forgive me, dear Mrs Barton, but I do not expect you are used to playing hostess as yet, and we are waiting for you to leave the table,' explained Mrs Cottar. 'If we do not leave the men to their port soon, we shall none of us get to bed this night.'

It was midnight before the guests departed, and they would not have gone then but for Major Mottisham, the second witness at the marriage ceremony, who, suddenly recollecting that this was a wedding party and not a carouse, had made a short and garbled speech full of distressingly broad allusions, and herded the wedding guests into the hall.

Winter stood on the porch steps beside her husband with her hands hanging at her sides and her face still wearing that frozen smile, while carriage wheels rolled away and horses' hooves scattered the gravel. They had gone at last, and the house was quiet.

The garden was full of moonlight, and in the drawing-room the servants were stacking glasses and removing cigar-stubs, turning out lamps and blowing out candles. 'Well, we may not have had a full-dress weddin',' said Conway, 'but we cer'nly had a capital celebration. Don't get married every day of yer life, s'just as well to enjoy it. Eat, drink and ge' married! That's it, ain't it, m'dear?'

He appeared to expect some reply and Winter said in a stiff, expressionless voice: 'I am very tired. I think, if you do not mind, that I will go to bed.'

'Tha's right. You go to bed. I won't keep y' waiting!' He laughed uproariously and Winter turned away and walked slowly and unsteadily to her room, as though it were she and not Conway who was drunk.

Hamida was waiting for her, and the sight of the girl's white face and dazed eyes filled her with clucking alarm. But Winter paid no attention to her words and did not even hear them. She allowed herself to be undressed and bathed and put to bed as though she were not even a child but a large doll. Her world – the dream world that she had built up for years and planned for and longed and lived for – was in ruins about her, but she could not even think.

At least it was quiet at last. The noise and the babel, the meaningless talk, the incomprehensible jests, the shouts of laughter and the clink of glasses had stopped, and she was alone; for now even Hamida was gone. Now perhaps she could think again – could cry, to ease the terrible pain in her heart. And then the door opened and Conway was there.

Winter sat up swiftly, pulling the sheets up about her, wondering dully why he was here and what he wished to say to her so late at night. She had not taken in the sense of his last remark to her, and in the dazed nightmare of that terrible wedding party she had forgotten that people who were married shared the same bed. She watched stupidly while he came towards her, weaving a little in his walk, and put his candle down upon the bedside table and began to remove his dressing-gown. And then, quite suddenly, the numbness left her and gave place to sheer panic and horror.

This man – this gross, repulsive, drunken stranger – was going to get into the same bed with her. To lie down beside her – perhaps touch her – kiss her! She dragged the sheets up to her chin and her eyes widened until they were enormous in her white face.

'Go away! Please go away at once!' Her voice was hoarse with fear and loathing. 'You cannot sleep here tonight – not tonight. Go away!'

Conway gave a drunken chuckle of approval. 'Coy are you, my shy little virgin? Tha's as it should be. But yer a wife now.' He looked down at her and his red-rimmed eyes lit with a look that she had seen before. A look that had been in Carlyon's eyes.

'By gad, yer a beauty after all!' The thick voice held a note of awe. 'It would a' been worth marryin' any ugly wench with that fortune, but to get a beauty into the bargain——!'

He reached out an unsteady hand and lifted a long tress of the black unbound hair, and Winter struck at his hand in fury and terror.

'Don't touch me! Don't dare to touch me!'

Conway lunged towards her across the bed and she flung aside the sheets and leapt out, in the grip of the same frantic, shuddering panic that she had experienced when Carlyon had looked at her by the door of her room at the dâk-bungalow beyond the ford. But her husband's clutching hands were on her hair and they gripped it and jerked it brutally, so that she fell back and was caught. And this time there was no escape.

26

Alex was both strong and healthy, and Niaz had sufficient knowledge of such matters as concussion and broken collar-bones to deal more than adequately with the situation. Having assured himself that the injury was not serious he had eased off Alex's coat and set the collar-bone, binding it securely with his *puggari*, and having retrieved Shalini had ridden back to a small village they had recently passed, where he had procured a ramshackle palanquin and bearers to carry it. An hour later Alex had been installed in the hut of the village headman and under the care of a wrinkled crone well versed in the use of healing herbs.

He had not recovered consciousness until well after dawn, and all through that day, while Niaz held him down so that he should do no further injury to his arm and shoulder, he had talked; sometimes in English, sometimes in Hindustani or Pushtu, muttering and raving. Exhorting a gang of labourers who built a road through wild and trackless territory; shouting in a cavalry charge; whispering to a havildar eight years dead as they crawled forward under cover of darkness to attack a fort; discussing philosophy with a mullah in the foothills beyond Hoti Mardan, or arguing with the Commissioner of Lunjore – expounding policies, pressing for action, explaining patiently the need for reforms.

Once he spoke in a strange tongue. An odd sentence, twice repeated: '*Kogo zakhochet Bog pogubit, togo sperva lishit razuma.*' Niaz did not know that he spoke in Russian, or that the words were those that he heard Gregori Sparkov speak in a moonlit garden in Malta: 'Whom the Gods would destroy, they first make mad.'

Alex tossed and turned and muttered of Khanwai and white goats, of sharks and sacrifices and the stupidity of fools who would neither see nor hear, look nor listen. But towards sunset he became quieter and lay still at last, talking to Winter, his hoarse, exhausted voice barely a whisper.

Niaz slept, stretched on the ground beside the low *charpoy* on which Alex lay, his shoulder touching it so that he should wake to any urgent movement, while the aged crone crouched at the far side of the bed coaxing occasional strange herbal draughts between Alex's dry lips and down his parched throat, listening to the endless, incomprehensible murmuring, and aware, through some feminine instinct, that the Sahib spoke of a woman . . .

Twenty-four hours later the invalid woke to drugged sanity and a splitting headache. He could remember nothing of the past few weeks; his last coherent recollection being of a dâk-*ghari* overturning on the journey up from Calcutta. He supposed that he must have suffered some injury in the accident and wondered what had happened to his fellow-passenger, the morose Major?

Niaz, discovering this gap in his memory, made no move to repair it, for instinct told him that once Alex remembered what it was that he had set out for, he would start off again long before it was safe for him to do so. But since there had been no driving urgency to reach Lunjore from Calcutta within a given time, as long as Alex imagined himself to be on that journey he might be persuaded to remain where he was and lie quiet. The beldame's drugs helped in this. Alex was drowsy and stupid and in pain, and he drank them obediently and slept; woke to a smell of dung-fires and sun-baked earth, the aromatic scents of masala and cardamons and all the familiar sounds and smells of an Indian village, grinned at Niaz and swallowed the infusion of herbs and hot milk that he was offered, and slept again.

It was not until the morning of the sixth day when, awaking to the first brilliant rays of the sun and the squeaking of a well-wheel, he remembered Delhi and all that had happened there. It had taken him some time to realize how many days had elapsed since he had ridden in pursuit of Winter and Carlyon, and when he had done so he had propped himself on his unwounded arm and cursed Niaz with a savage, concentrated fury for having let him lie there; for having given him drugs and for not having put him on his horse and taken him on to Lunjore or back to Delhi.

'Had I done so, it had gone ill with thee,' said Niaz, unmoved.

'Saddle the horses. We go now.'

'To Delhi?'

'To Lunjore.'

Niaz shook his head. 'If we go today thou wilt be able to ride two *koss*. Perchance three, but no more. Wait here yet another day and I will ride to Delhi for Latif and our gear. I sent word to Fraser Sahib in Delhi, and also to Barton Sahib, that thou hadst met with an accident and would be delayed. There is no need for thee to ride to Delhi and back. I will go; and tomorrow, if I return in time, we will go on to Lunjore.'

'We will go today, and within the hour,' said Alex.

Niaz observed him with a thoughtful eye and said in a non-committal voice: 'I sent a man to get news at the ford. The river fell three days back, and the Lord-Sahib returned with the carriage and horses and his *nauker-log*. They go to Delhi.'

Alex looked at him for a long moment. Then he said: 'Was the Lady-Sahib with him?'

'No. But the man spoke with one of the syces, and it was said that she had met with friends upon the road and had gone forward with them to Lunjore.'

Alex lay back slowly on the string bed and stared up at the smoke-blackened ceiling above his head. He was silent for so long that at last Niaz cleared his throat and said carefully: 'Do we ride today?'

'No.' Alex closed his eyes and spoke without looking at him. 'I will wait here. Fetch the gear from Delhi.' He turned over on his right side with his face to the wall and did not speak again.

Niaz did not return for two days, and those days had given Alex plenty of time for thought. His shoulder still pained him and his head still ached, but the dizzy stupidity had gone. He would drink no more of the old woman's drugs and his brain was clear. There had been a moment when he had been tempted to return to Delhi and demand an account of his behaviour from Lord Carlyon, but five minutes' reflection had convinced him of the uselessness of such a proceeding. He had no shadow of right to take Carlyon to task, and Colonel Abuthnot could be counted upon to say all that was necessary upon that head. As for Winter, if she had indeed met with friends upon the road she would have reached Lunjore days ago, and there was nothing more that he could do about that either. She would have learned by now what sort of a man Conway Barton was, and would probably be staying with these friends until she could arrange to return to England.

Whether he wished her to return there was another matter, and one which he was not in the least desirous of facing. He had kept free of entanglements with women of his own class and kind, largely because of a conviction that work and women in such a country and climate, and under the conditions that prevailed in India, did not mix. One or the other of them were bound to suffer. Those wives who endured the heats and hazards of hot weather in the plains in order to be with their husbands grew old before their time, yet to go to the hills meant months of separation. And children were less a blessing than a continual and terrible anxiety. Hodson had lost his only and beloved child the previous year, and India was strewn with the graves of children.

One day, when conditions improved and such things as railways and good roads had linked up the provinces and states, it might be different. But in the present state of the country, Alex considered that marriage was something to be avoided, while if there should ever be a rising on the scale that he suspected was being plotted, then all women would not only be an anxiety but a deadly handicap. Remembering the capacity for cruelty, the indifference towards suffering, the fanatical hatreds and blood-feuds that obtained in the East, Alex imagined that there might well come a time when a man might wish with all his heart that there had never been such a thing as a woman; or that he himself had never known or loved one.

Winter . . . If he should see her again, would he try and stop her from returning to England, or would he let her go? He did not know. Barely more than a week ago he would have been thankful to see her go. But that had been before he had kissed her. He had kissed other women, lightly or passionately, and had forgotten them. But he could still feel that warm, rounded slenderness in his arms and the way in which, for a long moment, she had seemed to melt against him and become so much a part of him that her every nerve and pulse and breath and heartbeat had been as though it were his own.

Her mind could deceive her with the pretty pictures that it had made up and hugged for comfort during the past six years, and her tongue could talk of her love for Conway: but her body had betrayed her. If she had known anything of love – if her love for Conway Barton had gone deeper than a lonely child's romantic attachment and hero-worship – Alex's arms and his kisses would have been unendurable to her. But they had not been. For a long, long moment they had not been . . .

Behind his closed eyelids Alex saw the young heart-shaped face, and the dark eyes that were so unsure; one moment so brimful of hope and happiness, and the next so still and so wary – and sometimes so frightened. She had learned to school her face. To wear a dignity and calm and composure beyond her years. To hold her chin high and her slim figure erect, and to hide loneliness and hope and hurt. Perhaps in time she would learn to force her eyes to do these things too, unless happiness and security saved her from that sad necessity. But he, Alex, was the last person who could offer her either.

She had better go home, and soon. He would not see her again, and for all he knew she might already have left Lunjore. He should have refused point-blank to have anything to do with bringing her out to this country. Yet if he had quarrelled with the Commissioner . . . Once again he found himself back in the old, infuriating impasse.

To come into direct conflict with the Commissioner would have meant, without a shadow of doubt, that he would end up being sent to some non-essential post where he could do neither harm nor good, and to Alex, pupil and disciple of Sir Henry Lawrence, the necessity of doing to the best of his ability the work that lay to his hand, no matter how many obstacles officialdom placed in his way, took precedence over every other consideration.

Officialdom, in the person of Lord Dalhousie, had disagreed with Sir Henry's moderation and humanity, and removed him from the Punjab, leaving it to be settled by the harsher hand of his brother John who preferred force to persuasion. And Alex knew that the Commissioner of Lunjore, left to himself or assisted by someone possessing less understanding and sympathy with the problems of the district than he, Alex, did, would be capable of alienating the local talukdars and small-holders beyond any hope of counting upon their co-operation except under the threat of force.

His mind turned from the problem of Winter to the problems inherent in controlling and administering the one small piece of India whose welfare was his own responsibility: 'Why in hell's name,' thought Alex with impatience, 'haven't the Governor's Council the sense to send Lawrence to Oudh? If anyone could settle it without bitterness and injustice, he could. If he had it in charge for a year he could hold it quiet even if the rest of India rose all round it. Oudh is the plague-spot now, and Lunjore is right on its borders . . .'

In the evenings, when the cooking-fires were lit, the headman and some of the village elders, finding that he was sufficiently recovered to sit up and eat the first solid meal he had eaten in days, came to squat by the door, smoke their hookahs and converse.

Their talk was a talk that Alex understood and had listened to on many occasions – the all-important problems of village life. Crops and harvesting, the drying up of a well, the damage done by deer and wild pig, the failure of certain crops owing to a poor monsoon, a dispute over a marriage dowry – the half of which had not been paid – and a vexed question of grazing rights. This was the India that he knew and loved, and which, as far as any European may understand the mind of India, he understood.

India, to Alex, was the land. The cultivator and the herdsman and the hundreds of thousands of small, humble village communities whose way of life had not changed in the slow centuries since Alexander of Macedonia and his warriors had poured through the passes to conquer the unknown land that had been old when Greece was young. He had little love for the cities, for to him they seemed to contain all that was worst in the East, and he could never ride through them without experiencing horror and pity and despair.

The sight of filth and disease and the callous indifference towards the suffering of man and beast was something that he could not accept or ignore, as the majority of his fellow-countrymen appeared able to do. The naked, starveling children of the poor with their spindle legs, bloated bellies and eye-sores on which the flies clustered, the diseased deformities who begged their bread in the gutters, and the noseless, eyeless lepers who wandered at large through the narrow streets, seemed to him an offence before God, and, in some way, a thing for which he himself bore a personal responsibility. Scarcely less terrible in his eyes was the sight of dumb animals, starving, diseased or mutilated, who were left to die slowly and in agony because none would take upon themselves the sin of destroying life.

The cities spawned as much evil as filth. Murder and prostitution, theft and trickery, intolerance, hatred and talk: a froth of talk that went in circles and was seldom concerned with essentials . . . windy poison with which to disturb the hearts and minds of the credulous, and which stirred up bloody riots between sects and the followers of different gods upon holy days. Talk that was never of building up but always of pulling down, and which could whip up hysteria with the speed of a whirlwind. But there were few such talkers in the villages, for the work of the land pressed hard upon the heels of those who took their livelihood from her.

Ploughing, sowing, reaping and irrigation would not wait while men sat in circles and listened to windy and grandiloquent phrase-makers who promised overnight Utopias provided that this or that class or sect, creed or colour were first destroyed or routed. The villages had their own failings. Their methods of cultivation did not change. They never learned better and they did not wish to. What was good enough for their forefathers was good enough for them, and so they lived always with the spectre of starvation grinning at their shoulder. But they toiled hard and they were kindly people, and Alex listened to them now and felt more relaxed and at peace than he had for many days.

They requested his opinions and deferred courteously to them, and he found himself arbitrating, as by right, in a vexed dispute (it concerned the ownership of a cow) that had been dividing the village into opposing camps for some weeks past. His decision was accepted with applause, and the headman hastened to lay before him another and more personal problem. It was not one that would normally have been raised in Western society, but Alex had heard many such and he listened gravely and gave the headman the benefit of his advice. The talk drifted to theology; a long, wandering discussion such as Asiatics love, until the elderly headman, observing that Alex appeared tired, dismissed the assembly, and expressing the hope that his guest would enjoy a good night's sleep and find himself greatly refreshed the next morning, withdrew into the darkness.

The meeting convened again on the following evening, but this time Alex sat under the night sky and the stars on the baked ground beneath a huge *neem* tree where the villagers met as men might meet at a club to discuss the day's doings. His collar-bone, thanks to Niaz's prompt attention, had set well, and apart from a faint headache the after-effects of concussion were vanishing rapidly. He was impatient to be gone, for there was a land dispute coming up in Lunjore which he particularly wished to settle with the minimum interference from the Commissioner, and Niaz, watching him without appearing to do so, withdrew him tactfully from the assembly at an early hour, saying that they would need a good night's rest as there was a long ride before them on the morrow.

They left in the cool brightness of the early morning after a plentiful meal prepared by the headman's wife; the headman and some others escorting them a mile upon their way. 'If it is necessary that the land be governed by *feringhis*,' remarked the headman, watching the horsemen ride away between the tall grass and the *kikar* trees, 'that is the sort they should send us, and not fools such as that fat sahib who passed this way last year and brought with him an evil rogue from Delhi to speak for him because he had insufficient understanding of our tongue and less still of our ways.'

Alex accomplished the remainder of the journey by easier stages than he would normally have done, for he found the long hours in the saddle more tiring than he would admit; and Winter had been married almost a week by the time he rode down the long dusty road that led past the Residency to his own house.

His lamp-lit bungalow was pleasantly cool after the heat of the dusty roads, and Alam Din, who combined the offices of butler and bearer, had prepared a meal, for Niaz had sent forward word of their arrival. Alex had ridden less than thirty miles that day, but he was intolerably tired and impatient with himself for being so. He had intended to go straight to bed and merely send word of his arrival to the Commissioner, reporting to him on the following morning; but Mr Barton had sent over to say that he wished to see him that same evening.

Alam Din, handing dishes, had mentioned the Commissioner's marriage – it being a matter of considerable interest in Lunjore – and had expressed approval that there should at last be a Memsahib at the Residency, but Alex had answered at random and had not taken in a word of what had been said. Alam Din was inclined to be talkative and Alex's mind was on other things.

He walked over to the Residency in the starlight and stopped under the dark arch of the gateway to speak to Akbar Khan, the gatekeeper, who rose up at his approach, the orange glow of a small oil-lamp illuminating his white robes and flowing beard so that he looked like some prophet of the Old Testament. He had been speaking with someone, for Alex's quick ear had caught the almost inaudible murmur of voices as he approached; but there was no one else visible now. The little stone cell in the thickness of the gateway, where Akbar Khan spent much of his time when on duty, was dark, and he had moved so as to block the doorway.

Akbar Khan salaamed, expressing regret that the Huzoor should have met with an accident and hoping that he was by now entirely recovered. But his eyes in the lamplight avoided Alex's and he seemed anxious for him to pass on. Aware of this, Alex lingered, talking trivialities and wondering who it was who lurked in the blackness behind Akbar Khan's back? There was no reason why the gatekeeper should not have a friend there should he wish. Perhaps it was some woman of his household. And yet . . .

There was a faint, familiar odour under the airless archway. A smell that was quite distinct and separate from the mingled scents of dust and watered earth, stonework, bougainvillea, the hot lamp and the cheap tobacco in the hookah that Akbar Khan smoked. It was a rank, almost animal odour, that suggested an unwashed human body and reminded Alex of the smell of the naked ash-smeared Bairagis in the underground chamber at Khanwai. His eyes narrowed and he said softly: 'Who is it who sits within there and stays so still? Bid him come out.'

Akbar Khan's face did not alter and now his eyes were no longer uneasy. They met Alex's grey gaze blandly and his voice was gently deprecatory: 'It is my wife, Huzoor. She brought more oil for the lamp, and hearing the Huzoor approach she hid within, for it being dark she had come here without a head covering.'

Alex looked at him thoughtfully. Instinct – instinct and that faint nauseous odour – told him that the man was lying. But if he were mistaken and it was indeed Akbar Khan's wife who lurked in the darkness, to force her out into the lamplight, unveiled, would lead to considerable unpleasantness.

'Tell thy . . . *wife*,' said Alex grimly, 'that to go abroad thus, even by night, is unwise, since there be others besides myself who might chance to see. And to speak of it.'

The inference and the threat were not lost upon Akbar Khan, for his eyes flickered sideways for a fractional second, and then he salaamed low as though in agreement, and Alex passed on, thinking of Khanwai and, as so often of late, of the night a year and more ago when he had witnessed that curious gathering under the banyan tree. Mussulmans (and Akbar Khan was a bigoted Mussulman) did not consort with Hindu holy men . . . Yet the hawk-faced man who had addressed the gathering at Khanwai had been both a Mussulman and a Maulvi. Alex stopped on the dark drive and half turned as though he would have gone back, but thinking better of it he went on, and he was still frowning and lost in thought when he walked up the porch steps and was ushered into the Commissioner's drawing-room.

The big room was brightly lit and empty, and there was something unusual about it. It was no longer the untidy and somewhat raffish apartment with which he was familiar. The furniture had been rearranged and the place was clean, and there were no less than three vases of flowers. Alex was frowning abstractedly at an arrangement of orange lilies and yellow jasmine, his mind still on the subject of Akbar Khan, when a door at the far end of the room opened and he looked up and saw Winter.

He should have been prepared for it, but he was not. He had been so sure that, young as she was, she possessed too much character and courage to allow herself to be forced by circumstances into this marriage once she had seen the man to whom she was betrothed, and had realized, as she must immediately do, what he had become. It had indeed occurred to him that she might still be in Lunjore, but he considered it more likely that the friends she had met with on the road – possibly friends she had met at Ware or at Sir Ebenezer's? – had already helped her to return to the Abuthnots or to Calcutta, and he could only be grateful for it. That she could have married that sodden debauchee was – must be – impossible. He was neither prepared for the sight of her nor for what it did to him.

Winter had not known of Alex's return. Conway had not thought to mention it, and she had not imagined that she need ever see him again. Knowing her husband to be sitting over the wine with two of his friends, she had slipped into the drawing-room by the side door to fetch a pair of embroidery scissors that she had left there earlier in the evening. She had opened the door and seen Alex . . .

They stood quite still and looked at each other; their faces white and drawn with shock, and their eyes wide and fixed and unbelieving. There was a clock in the room; a massive affair of marble and gilt. The pendulum swung to and fro counting the ticking seconds into the silence, and the sound of them seemed to grow louder and louder in the stillness. Alex put out a hand with the groping gesture of a blind man and caught the back of a chair and held it, and Winter saw his knuckles shine white, and saw too that there were bright beads of sweat on his forehead.

Her own fingers tightened about the door-knob, gripping it desperately as she fought with a tide of shame and despair that equalled the shame and desperation of her wedding night. Alex had told her the truth about Conway and she had not believed him. He had done what he could to prevent her from being trapped by this horrible quicksand into which her own foolishness had led her, and it was unbearable that she should have to face him now.

Alex said harshly: 'Did you marry him?'

'Yes.' The word was barely a breath.

'Why?'

Winter did not answer him, but she moved her head in a slight, helpless gesture that was less a refusal to answer than hopelessness.

Something in that small despairing movement hurt Alex with savage pain that was as entirely physical as the touch of a hot iron. 'Was it because you had no one else to go to? You could have——' He stopped abruptly, aware of the futility of questions or answers. What did the whys and wherefores matter now? The thing was done. His hand tightened for another instant on the chair-back and then fell to his side. His head was aching abominably and it was suddenly an effort to stand erect. He said in a curiously formal voice that somehow gave the impression that he was a little drunk:

'I suppose I must offer my congratulations. Will you make my excuses to your husband? He sent for me, but I have had a somewhat tiring day and I feel sure he will forgive me if I postpone the interview until the morning. Good night.'

He turned on his heel, and Winter heard him stumble as he went down the porch steps, and then the sound of his footsteps died away into the silence until there was only the clock ticking again, louder and louder, and presently a muffled bellow of laughter from the direction of the dining-room where Conway and his friends were finishing the port.

Alex had gone. She had let him go, though she could have stopped him. Even now, if she ran after him, he might help her. He could not dissolve her marriage. That was irrevocable. But he would not refuse to help her. He would do something – she did not know what – but something. Yet how could she possibly appeal to him after what had occurred in Delhi? – after the insults she had hurled at him? She could only hope that she need not see him again. And there was no one else she could appeal to.

She would have run to Ameera, but that Ameera had told her that she could not ask her to the Gulab Mahal at that time; and she could not return to Delhi because Carlyon might be there – or upon the road. And because she had no money and no means of getting any, for Conway had taken charge of her jewel box and any valuables she possessed, saying that such things were better under lock and key. Even Hamida had gone . . .

The morning after her wedding Winter had awakened from the deep sleep of utter mental and physical exhaustion to the full and despairing realization of what she had done. There had been a heavy outflung arm lying across her, its inert weight hurting her breasts, and beside her, his mouth open, her bridegroom snored in sodden slumber. He had groaned and rolled his head on the pillow when she had moved, but he had not awakened, and Winter had crept shuddering from under that arm and from the bed, dizzy, bruised, sick with loathing and despair, and huddling a shawl about her had stumbled into the dressing-room and bolted the door behind her.

Hamida had been there waiting for her, and Winter had clung to her; shivering, dry-eyed and desperate. Hamida had crooned over her and petted her, but it was obvious that she considered that these things were but a normal part of life. She herself, said Hamida, had been many years younger than Winter when she had been wed, and her husband had been a lusty man – a bear! – so that Hamida too had screamed in terror on her wedding night and had wept and shivered for many days afterwards. But in time she had come to love her husband and to welcome his embraces, and she had borne him five sons of whom four still lived, so that her grandsons were many. Husbands, said Hamida, were often rough and brutal in the marriage bed, but wives must bear such things and learn to please their lords, lest their lords turned to light women.

Winter's hysterical assertion that she intended to leave Lunjore immediately was received with scandalized horror. Such a thing was impossible – unthinkable! Wives did not behave thus. They had their duties and their responsibilities, and to run away because they found a bridegroom not entirely to their taste was unheard of. She was married now, and that could not be undone. She had not even been forced into the marriage. It had been of her own choosing, and she could not now run away from it.

Hamida read Winter a lecture on the duties of wives. A wife must submit herself to her husband and try by meekness, diligence and obedience to win his regard. Let his defects be what they may, a wife should always look upon her husband as a god, lavishing upon him her attention and care and paying no heed to his displeasure. If her husband should threaten her, abuse her, even beat her unjustly, she must answer meekly and beg his forgiveness, instead of uttering loud outcries and running from his house.

Winter had listened numbly to Hamida's voice, but only one thing that Hamida had said made sense to her – she was married now, and that could not be undone. Hamida was right. But within a week Hamida had gone.

It was the plump painted woman whom Winter had found sitting beside Conway's bed on the morning of her arrival who was responsible: Yasmin, the woman who lived in the *bibi-gurh* behind the scarlet poinsettias and the feathery screen of pepper trees, with her sister and her own serving-women. Yasmin had recognized an enemy in Hamida and had taken steps to remove her. Conway had told his wife that she must dismiss the woman she had brought with her, as he had already made arrangements for an ayah, and an outsider would only cause trouble among the other servants.

Winter had refused flatly to part with Hamida, and Conway, to his wrath, had found that he could do nothing to alter her decision. He had lost his temper and had said things that had stripped the last rags of her illusions from her. She had not given way, but the next day Hamida had been taken ill, and had whispered to Winter that her food had been poisoned. 'Do not fear, child. I ate only a little, and tomorrow I shall be well again. But after this I must buy all my own food and cook it apart, letting no one near, so that they cannot try again.'

But Winter would not hear of it. She would not risk Hamida's life and she sent her away, sending gifts and messages by her to Ameera. And with Hamida went her only link with the outside world until the Gardener-Smiths should arrive in Lunjore. Perhaps they would be able to help her; lend her money so that she could return to England and to Ware. To Ware! She had never believed that she could ever desire to return there, but anything – *anything* – was better than life in this horrible house with this coarse, gross, brutal stranger who was her husband, and who had told her furiously to her face that he had married her only for her money.

Alex Randall had still not returned and Winter could only be thankful that she was spared the humiliation of facing him. Conway had mentioned casually that he had met with some accident that would delay his return and that it was curst careless of him. But Winter had not believed it. She had been sure that after the incident on Delhi wall Alex would prefer not to return to Lunjore, and was probably arranging to get himself transferred to some other post. She had no knowledge of officialdom and it seemed to her an obvious course of action. Alex had no illusions about his chief. He had spoken of him in unmeasured terms, and he had kissed his chief's betrothed and had been accused by her of jealousy and lying. No, he would not wish to return to Lunjore and she would not be seeing him again.

There remained Mrs Gardener-Smith, who had called upon her from mixed motives on the afternoon of their arrival. The motives appeared to be curiosity, a desire to impart all the news of Lottie Abuthnot's wedding and to lose no time in making the acquaintance of so senior an official as the Commissioner, coupled with a wish to express disapproval of Winter's unmaidenly conduct.

Mrs Gardener-Smith was most affable to Mr Barton, and Mr Barton, much taken by the looks of her daughter Delia, who was in every way exactly his idea of a handsome young woman, had set himself out to be pleasant. Mrs Gardener-Smith was favourably impressed by his manner and surprised to see that his bride was not in looks. The girl appeared to have aged ten years. The drawn pallor of her face was noticeable even in the shaded drawing-room where the blinds were drawn against the sun, and there were dark shadows beneath her eyes that made them look too large for her face. She was, however, perfectly composed and much interested to hear of Lottie's wedding. She had asked permission to call upon Mrs Gardener-Smith on the following day, and had arrived at eleven o'clock. But the interview that had followed had been painful to both.

Mrs Gardener-Smith's views on young wives and their duties towards husbands – especially husbands as senior and affable as the Commissioner of Lunjore – appeared to be much the same as Hamida's. She had not only been unsympathetic, she had been scandalized. Of course all men drank! and on occasions drank too much and behaved accordingly. But ladies did not mention such things. They looked the other way. As for the suggestion that she should assist Winter to leave her husband, she would have nothing whatever to do with such a preposterous proposal. Such a course could only involve her in unpleasantness with the Commissioner, and on those grounds alone she would not think of it. But even if Winter *should* be mad enough to run away, she would not get far, since the law would be on Mr Barton's side and could force her to return. Mrs Gardener-Smith had pronounced herself shocked that dear Winter should be so lacking in restraint, and so lost to all sense of responsibility towards her husband and to society, as to even think of such a thing! She must remember that she was no longer a heedless girl but a married woman, and marriage entailed responsibilities . . .

Winter had driven away down the dusty, shadow-barred roads of the cantonment with her last hope gone. Mrs Gardener-Smith had been right, as Hamida had been right. She had married Conway and she could not run away; because there was nowhere to run to, and because however far she ran it would not be far enough, for the law would send her back to her lawful husband. She had indeed made her bed and now she must lie on it.

Returning wearily to the big white house that was now her home she had not thought it possible to experience more humiliation or more despair. Until on the evening of that same day she had opened the door into the drawing-room and had seen Alex Randall, and known that she was wrong.

In the slow days and weeks that followed Winter had seen Alex only rarely and never to speak to. He had not left Lunjore, and she who had once – how long ago it seemed! – meant to influence Conway to send him away, had grown to be almost glad of it. The fact that he was here, even if she did not speak to him or see him, was curiously comforting; the one strong link in a rotted and rusty chain. If ever life and living became more than she could endure, there was Alex. He at least would not refuse to help her. He knew Conway.

Alex spent a large part of his time in the outlying areas of the district, and when he was not on tour he avoided entering the living-rooms of the Residency. But he was often in the Commissioner's office and Winter would hear the murmur of his level voice that always seemed to her, when he was addressing her husband, to hold something of the restraint of an adult explaining a problem patiently and tactfully to a spoilt, backward and fractious child. She was obscurely aware that Alex rode his temper on a tight rein, and often wondered why he should trouble to do so, for the truth of Mrs Cottar's flippant remark that Captain Randall did the work while Mr Commissioner Barton took the credit was soon patently obvious.

Conway did little work and was content to leave the greater part of his duties in Alex's hands. He signed papers that Alex laid before him, and agreed to decisions that Alex had made, imagining, from the way in which they were presented to him, that the decisions were his own. He had not, after all, sent in his resignation, for rumour had it that the Governor-General was contemplating an extensive tour, which would include Lunjore, in the following year, and the Commissioner scented a possible knighthood. The prospect of being able to retire not only as a rich man but as 'Sir Conway' appealed strongly to his vanity, and he decided to postpone his resignation for a year; and also to make that year as pleasant as possible. He ceased to take even a casual interest in the affairs of Lunjore, and Alex's work was greatly simplified thereby, though it meant that he spent more time in Lunjore itself and less out in the district.

Secure now in the possession of large wealth, the Commissioner entertained lavishly and the Residency was always full of guests. He ordered new furniture and furnishings from Calcutta so that his house should be fit to entertain the Governor-General and his Staff in, and talked of building a new wing. He was proud of his wife's looks and poise, and it pleased him that her dresses and jewels and her youthful dignity made an impression on his guests. But he had early tired of her as a woman. She had never again screamed and wept and fought him, but the passive, rigid disgust with which she had endured his subsequent embraces had soon robbed them of any pleasure, and he had returned to the coarser and more co-operative Yasmin for his entertainment.

There had been a brief period, while his interest in his wife had lasted, when Winter too had eaten food that made her unaccountably ill, although the Commissioner appeared to suffer no ill-effects. And she had remembered Hamida and been frightened. But who in the house would want to get rid of her? Hamida had been different, for she had been a rival servant and her presence would have deprived the woman whom Conway had employed to look after his wife of profitable employment. No, it could not have been poison! She was allowing her imagination to run away with her.

Her illness had kept Conway out of her room for several days, and when she had recovered she had been careful to eat only from those dishes that Conway must also eat from. She had despised herself for doing so, but at least she had not been taken ill again – and Conway had returned to her bed.

Two days later she had had a narrow escape from a more unpleasant death. She had been about to take a bath in the small bathroom that led out of her dressing-room. It was in the oldest part of the house, a room with walls three feet thick and a vaulted stone ceiling which made the smallest sound echo eerily. The bath, a tin affair that was filled from buckets, stood in a shallow depression with a raised brick rim from which a sluice ran out through the thickness of the wall. At night the room was lit by a single oil-lamp that stood on a wooden bracket by the door, and on this occasion the lamp had been burning unevenly, blackening the glass. Winter had picked it up to adjust the wick, and the action had saved her, for she would never have seen the cobra whose raised head swung two feet above its coils until it was too late. But the movement of the lamp threw its menacing shadow, enormously exaggerated, on the wall behind the bath.

The slow sway of that shadow caught her eye, and she stared at it for a moment in bewilderment before she saw the thing that threw it – the slim, gleaming terror with its flickering tongue and spread, speckled hood that reared up beside the bath. She had not screamed, but her hand had moved involuntarily and the wick that she had been turning down had flared and gone out, leaving her in the black darkness with the hissing, angry snake. She had backed away, groping for the door, and after what had seemed an eternity she had found it, and turning the handle, stumbled into the dressing-room.

The cobra had been killed, but there had been no satisfactory explanation as to how it had got into the bathroom. It must have come through the sluice that took off the bath water, said Conway. But that was hardly possible, since the high verandah that surrounded the house raised the floor level of the rooms over three feet above the ground in the front and nearer five at the back, where the ground fell away in a slight gradient. In addition to which the verandah did not extend further than one wall of the bathroom. The other two walls, together with one wall of the dressing-room, were blank and windowless and backed onto a shallow gutter and open ground where a fig tree flourished luxuriantly, nourished by the bath water. The exit of the sluice jutted out in a stone lip from which the water fell clear of the wall into the gutter, and no snake could have come that way unless it had received assistance. It might, of course, have come up the steps of the bathroom verandah on the opposite side and entered by the doorway; though that seemed even more unlikely.

Winter was more shaken than she would have admitted. But there had been no more such incidents, and it did not occur to her that the fact that Conway had lost interest in her and had taken to sleeping in his own room again could have had anything to do with this.

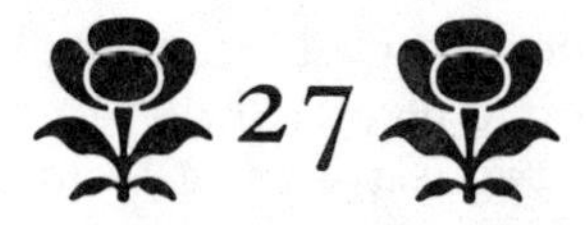

Mr Barton did not allow the fact that he was now married to alter his way of life to any great extent, and his more raffish friends were frequent visitors at the Residency. Mrs Cottar, acidly witty, and Mrs Wilkinson, plump, pouting and feline, were often to be seen there, with or without their husbands, and the Tuesday parties of which Mrs Cottar had spoken were not discontinued. Winter played hostess at any of the Commissioner's parties that might be considered official entertaining, but she had refused to preside at the long sessions of gambling and drinking that constituted these particular entertainments, and on Tuesdays she would retire early to bed with the plea of a headache.

Conway had attempted to take her to task on this score and to insist on her remaining, on the grounds that her early retirement was an insult to his guests. But here he had found, as he had found over the question of Hamida, that his young wife was not to be browbeaten. She would perform the duties of the Commissioner's wife to the best of her ability, but these duties did not include lending her countenance to such questionable and noisy entertainments as the Tuesday parties.

She made no friends among the British community in Lunjore, and she did not like the Residency servants; in particular her ayah, Johara, the sister of the woman in the *bibi-gurh* who, so Conway had informed her – his eyes sliding away from hers – was the wife of his butler, Iman Bux, whom he had permitted to occupy the quarter. But she was given no opportunity to dismiss them. The capacity for gaiety and warmth and happiness that had shown itself, although shyly, on the long voyage from England, and the laughter that Ameera had released, had been cut off like flowers in a black frost, and Lunjore society found young Mrs Barton a cold little thing.

Mrs Gardener-Smith did indeed claim that her daughter Delia was Mrs Barton's greatest friend, and Delia was often to be met with at the Residency. But if the truth were known she came there more on Colonel Moulson's account than Winter's. Winter had been surprised and disconcerted to find that Delia was becoming one of the 'Tuesday Crowd' at the Residency, for she had not thought that Mrs Gardener-Smith would permit it, and she was sure that Colonel Gardener-Smith – a silent, elderly, earnest man, wrapped up in his beloved Regiment – would not wish his daughter to attend such affairs.

Winter liked Colonel Gardener-Smith. He reminded her a little of her Great-Uncle Ashby, whose bookish tastes had insulated him from real life. Colonel Gardener-Smith's narrow absorption in his Regiment and its welfare gave him much the same immunity from outside interests.

The Colonel had lately succeeded in putting into practice a long-cherished scheme for improving the lot of his sepoys' families: the opening of a school for their children, run on European lines, and a medical centre for both parents and children. He had hoped that his wife and daughter would interest themselves in these admirable ventures, but Mrs Gardener-Smith and Delia had displayed nothing but dismay at such an idea, and the scheme itself was proving a disappointment. Colonel Gardener-Smith had lately discovered that his philanthropic venture was regarded by his sepoys as a subtle method of destroying their caste, and he had no hesitation in laying the blame for this attitude at the door of Colonel Packer, the commanding officer of the 105th Bengal Infantry Regiment stationed at Lunjore.

Colonel Packer, a bigoted Christian, placed his duty towards his God above that of his duty as an army officer. An admirable attitude with which no one could quarrel, save on the score that as his interpretation of these duties conflicted, it would have been wiser for him to resign his command.

Colonel Packer's duty towards God impelled him to make every effort to spread the Gospel to the heathen, and he was at present engaged in an earnest attempt to convert his entire Regiment to Christianity: a project that Colonel Gardener-Smith, together with almost every other thinking British officer and every sepoy in Lunjore, regarded with hostility and dismay, and that had caused Captain Randall, in the name of the Commissioner of Lunjore, to send a strongly worded protest to the Commander-in-Chief, General Anson, suggesting that Colonel Packer should either be restrained from 'spreading the Word' or instantly removed from his command.

Colonel Gardener-Smith refused to see that the suspicion with which his own schemes towards bettering the lot of his sepoys was regarded was anything more than a reflection of the alarm and dismay that Colonel Packer's assaults upon the religion of his men had produced among the native regiments stationed in Lunjore, and he did not abandon hope of popularizing both school and medical centre.

In these circumstances he had too much on his mind to pay overmuch attention to the social activities of his wife and daughter, and though he could not like Colonel Moulson, the man was, as far as he knew, a tolerably efficient commanding officer, a gentleman by birth and apparently possessed of adequate private means above his army pay. He could, therefore, see why Eugenia considered him eligible, but he had no fears that his daughter Delia would ever seriously consider marrying the fellow. She was far more likely, if he knew anything of young women, to fall in love with some penniless sprig of an ensign rather than with a man of Moulson's age!

In point of fact Colonel Gardener-Smith knew nothing of young women, least of all his daughter. Delia was not in the least in love with Colonel Moulson, but she was intrigued and flattered by his attentions and had every intention of marrying him. He had as yet made no declaration, but she was sure that given time and the opportunity he would do so. She intended to give him both, and as he was most often to be found in the Commissioner's company, she developed a fondness for young Mrs Barton's society, and was often to be seen driving over to the Residency.

Winter had endeavoured to warn Delia's mama of the style of the Tuesday parties, but Mrs Gardener-Smith had been either genuinely or intentionally obtuse. She was persuaded, she said, that dear Delia could come to no harm at any party where Winter was her hostess. And after all, the dear child was young, and young people could not be expected to attend only formal parties with senior officials.

'Colonel Moulson is not young,' said Winter. 'And neither are Mr Cottar or Major Mottisham. You do not understand. You see I – I do not attend these parties myself, and I would prefer them not to be held in my house. But they were established before – before I married Mr Barton, and he wished to continue them.'

Mrs Gardener-Smith had smiled tolerantly, for an explanation for Winter's embarrassed disclosure had just occurred to her. The little bride was jealous of the attentions that Delia was receiving from the Commissioner and his friends! Quite understandable, since Delia, in Mrs Gardener-Smith's eyes, was by *far* the more beautiful of the two. The cards of invitation continued to go out from the Residency and Mrs Gardener-Smith continued to permit her daughter to attend the Tuesday-night parties. And Winter made no further attempt to interfere.

She had made one friend within the walls of the Residency. Zeb-un-Nissa, the nine-year-old grand-daughter of Akbar Khan, the gatekeeper. Nissa was a frail little creature whose enormous dark eyes had a curiously blind look as though they looked through people and not at them. She was reported to be subject to fits and to have second sight, and the servants were afraid of her.

She was a solitary child who spent much of her time among the roots of the big banyan tree near the Residency gate, watching the birds and squirrels, who appeared to have no fear of her and would feed from her hand and take grain from between her lips. Winter had noticed a flock of green parrots fluttering about the roots of the tree early one morning, and had gone out to see what had attracted them. She had stayed to talk to Nissa, and the two had become fast friends.

Winter had asked permission for the child to help in the house, with the idea of training her to be her personal servant in place of Johara, but the suggestion had not been well received, and she suspected that the main opposition came from Johara's sister, Yasmin. Nissa's mother, a frightened-looking, slatternly woman, had seemed only too pleased, and Akbar Khan had salaamed deeply and thanked the gracious Lady-sahib for her kind interest in his all too unworthy grand-daughter, but expressed regret that the child was not strong enough for the work. Nissa did not enter the house, but Winter spoke with her often in the garden, and they would wave to each other when Winter passed the banyan tree on her daily rides.

She became less actively unhappy as the weeks passed, and a dull resignation took the place of the raw wound in her heart. There was still India, and that alone, in the ruin of her dreams, had not betrayed her. She would ride out every evening and in the early morning before the sun rose, galloping across the plain and along the banks of the distant river, or riding through the dew-wet crops where the peafowl screamed at the dawn and skeins of wild geese honked overhead on their way to the jheels of Hazrat Bagh and Pari.

The glory of the sunrise over the limitless plains and the wide, winding river; the quiet beauty of the evenings when the sun sank with incredible swiftness, dyeing the river and the long silver sandbanks, the city and the plain and every tree and cane-brake to a warm, glowing apricot; the swift, opal twilight, and night unfolding like a peacock's tail, green and blue and violet, flecked with the last gold of day and spangled with stars – these were things that comforted Winter and held for her a never-failing enchantment, daily renewed.

The wide land, the wide river and the enormous sky were beautiful to her. The vastness soothed her. The sense of space – of the plains stretching away and away to the deserts of Bikaner, the blue waters of Cape Comorin and the jungles and valleys of Nepal; wrinkling up into the foothills, to rise in range after range to the white barrier of the Himalayas where the remote passes led into the unknown land of Tibet, into Persia and the Pamirs and the great plains and lakes and ranges of Central Asia – the Kara-Koram, the Hindu Kush, Tien Shan and Turkestan; Balkash and Baskal; the white wastes of Siberia and the yellow leagues of China. Here there was none of the sense of being shut in and enclosed behind high walls that she had sometimes experienced at Ware. The mile-wide rivers and the enormous mountain ranges seemed less of a barrier than the neat English hedges and the trout stream that had separated the paddocks from the park.

There was a fatalism too about the East that appealed to her, and the filth and squalor and cruelty that everywhere underlay the beauty did not in any way lessen her love for the land. The city was ugly and foetid and full of sights that were unbelievably horrible to Western eyes, and Winter's eyes did not miss them. But she loved the city too. The heaped colours of fruits and vegetables and grain in the bazaar. The rich smell of mustard oil and masala, of musk and spices and *ghee*. The shops of the potter and the silver-smith. The stalls that sold glass bangles as fine and light as silk and as fragile as a dried leaf, in glittering, sparkling, burning colours – red and blue and gold and grass-green. The silk shops with their gay bales piled high in the shadows. The drifting, jostling crowds and the great, lazy Brahmini bulls, sacred to Shiva, who shouldered through the narrow streets taking toll of the baskets of the vegetable-sellers.

White women were seldom to be seen in the city, and on the rare occasions on which they went there they went in carriages and escorted by white men. But Winter would go with only Yusaf, the syce, and at first the crowds would collect to giggle and stare and follow her, peering and whispering. But she went so often that they became used to her and to the fact that she spoke their language with an idiomatic fluency that they had rarely met with in others of the sahib-*log*. She came to have many friends and acquaintances in the city. Unexpected friends and strange acquaintances who would have horrified and disgusted her husband had he known of it. But then Conway took little interest in his wife's doings, and did not know or care where she went.

Alex knew, and though it had at first disturbed him that Winter should go so freely and so far afield about the countryside and the city, he had come to the conclusion that her greatest safety might one day lie in such friendships, and he had withdrawn the unobtrusive watch he had set on her.

He too, when he was not out in camp, rode every morning before sunrise, and Winter had sometimes caught a distant glimpse of him, though she was unaware that he often rode where he could keep her within sight and see that she came to no harm. He had heard the story of the cobra in the bathroom and had drawn his own conclusions. The woman in the *bibi-gurh*, the ex-dancing-girl who had once flaunted Kishan Prasad's great emerald, feared a rival, and she or her relations had attempted to remove that rival.

His complete helplessness in the matter filled Alex with a sick fury, but he had taken what steps he could. He had spoken to Iman Bux, whom he knew to be an ally of the woman's, and had informed him that should any more such accidents befall the Memsahib, or if he heard again that she had fallen ill from something she had eaten, exceedingly unpleasant consequences would descend upon the heads of several members of the household, and not all the Commissioner's influence would avert them:

'And I think it is known that I am a man of my word,' said Alex softly. Iman Bux, looking into those merciless long-lashed eyes, had quailed visibly, and instead of pouring out a flood of injured and bewildered protest had found himself mumbling instead: 'It is known.'

But the fact that there might be nothing more attempted against the Commissioner's bride in the house did not preclude the possibility of some accident being engineered while she was out of it, and Alex was uneasy at the way in which her husband permitted her to ride abroad daily with no other escort than a syce. He had eventually succeeded in getting a nominee of his own into that post. With Yusaf to ride behind her he knew that she would come to no harm, and after that Winter seldom saw him when she rode before sunrise or at sunset.

She was happier when she was away from the house. The house held Conway, who had once been a child's dream of all goodness and romance and was now a horrible parody of that knight in armour. Or there would be strangers there – people whose faces were by now only too familiar to her, but who remained strangers. Men and women with overloud voices and overloud laughter, who still made her feel stiff and young and gauche and cold with distaste. Josh Cottar, that coarse, rich vulgarian who had made a fortune out of beer and army contracts, Major Wilkinson, red-faced, glassy-eyed and maudlin, and others of their ilk. There would be Johara too, Yasmin's sister, with her sly eyes and veiled insolence. And sometimes, in the twilight, there would be a slim fair girl who wore an oddly outdated dress.

Winter did not see this girl often, and then only when she was particularly overstrained or weary. But there were many occasions when she knew that she heard someone who was not there. This house was different from other houses. While there were lights in the rooms, and her husband or the servants or any guests moved about them, they were just rooms. A background for the people who occupied them. But on the rare occasions when she was alone it was different. Then the empty rooms held someone else. Winter would walk through an open doorway into a silent room and there would be someone else there. Someone whom her entrance had alarmed. It was not she who was frightened, but that other one, who could – she was sure of it – feel her unhappiness and desperation and strain, and was disturbed by it. Sometimes she would even hear voices. Not whispering, but as though they came from a long way away and yet were no farther than a few paces from her. Once she had thought she heard a few words, clearly spoken: '*There is someone here who is unhappy. As if – as if it were* me!' An odd thing to imagine.

But one night there had been other whispers.

It had been early in the new year and Winter had awakened feeling cold. She slept alone in the wide bed, for Conway had taken to sleeping in his old room once more and seldom visited her. Rain had fallen during the day, but towards sunset the sky had cleared and now the moon rode high and shone into the windows of her room. Winter sat up and reached for the quilt that normally lay folded at the foot of her bed, but it was not there and she remembered that she had taken it into the dressing-room earlier that evening.

She slipped out of bed, shivering, and pulling a light Cashmere shawl about her shoulders, crossed the room and pushed open the door of the dressing-room. She had left the quilt on the couch by the bathroom door and her hand was upon it when she became aware of the whispers, and stood still, listening: thinking for a moment that it was once again those ghostly, half-heard voices that she had imagined so often before.

The sibilant sound held something of the faint, hollow clarity of an echo and seemed to come from the bathroom, the door into which had been left open. Winter stood clutching the quilt, shivering and a little frightened, until quite suddenly she realized that the voices were speaking in Hindustani and that the ghostly echoing quality was accounted for by the wide stone sluice pipe that carried off the bath water. Someone was squatting on the far side of the bathroom wall, safely out of sight and hearing of anyone within the house, but unaware of the fact that the exit of the sluice was acting as a speaking tube so that it seemed as though a soft, echoing voice whispered under the curved roof of the bathroom.

Winter heard the bubbling sound of a hookah, and supposed that it must be Dunde Khan, the night-watchman, whiling away the long hours with a wakeful friend from the servants' quarters. She had a sudden childish impulse – the first young or gay impulse she had experienced in three months – to creep into the bathroom and wail down the sluice pipe. The windowless wall would be in black shadow, and such a sound, coming out of nothingness, would startle old Dunde Khan considerably. She dismissed it reluctantly, visualizing the household aroused by a piercing yell of panic, and was turning away when the soft, disembodied voice whispered again in the silence:

'He will be riding Chytuc or Shalini, for the Eagle has cast a shoe. And either one will show up far against the crops——'

Winter stood still, her attention suddenly arrested. Those were Captain Randall's horses. Was it Alex Randall whom the men in the darkness by the blind wall were speaking of? She waited, listening intently, and then a second voice spoke, less distinct this time but still audible:

'But what of Niaz Mohammed Khan? It is seldom that Randall Sahib rides without him.'

'That has been arranged. By now I think he will be suffering from a little sickness. Only a little – it would be unwise to arouse suspicions – but enough to keep him to his bed tomorrow. And the syce has a poisoned hand. I think the Sahib will ride alone.'

Yet another voice spoke, but this time the speaker must have been further away, for Winter could not catch the whispered words. She found that she was shivering again, but not with cold, and she crept forward into the darkness, feeling for each step and with a hand outstretched before her. The window shutters were closed and there was no gleam of light in the dead blackness of the bathroom. The matting whispered under her bare feet, and then her foot touched the raised rim that surrounded the space where the bath stood and from where the sluice led out. She crouched down so that her head was nearer the level of the pipe, and started as a voice appeared to speak almost in her ear:

'And what if he does not ride by way of Chunwar?'

'He will. There is a report that the canal bank has been breached by Mohammed Afzal for his fields, and sitting by the office door I heard him tell the Commissioner Sahib that he would go on the morrow, when he rides at dawn, to see if the report be true. And as all know, to ride to Chunwar he must cross the nullah near the *dhâk* trees. There is no other way for a horseman. It will be thought an accident.'

'But – but if I should fail——' The voice had a shiver in it, either from cold or fear.

'Thou wilt not fail. A child could not. Remember, there will be Mehan Lal also. And afterwards there will be witnesses to tell that the Sahib's horse took fright, which all will believe, for did not he fall from his horse not three months agone and lie sick with a cracked head? When a man has been dragged by a foot that is caught in the stirrup of a bolting horse it is difficult to tell which injury caused his death. I have seen one such in my time.'

Another voice growled: 'Why not a gun or a knife, and be done? There are two score times a day when a man might bring him down with either.'

'And be caught! No. Besides, we want no open killing. If he be killed openly it might be that word would go out that Lunjore is a place of trouble, and then, who knows, an *Angrezi* regiment might be sent here, and that we do not want. He must not be killed unless it be made to look an accident. That is the order that has been given.'

There was a pause in which the hookah bubbled again, and a faint scent of tobacco smoke drifted into the cold blackness of the bathroom. Winter heard a man clear his throat and spit, and then the voice with the shiver in it said: 'Why is this necessary? It is but one sahib, and there are many.'

'There be many fools to one wise man,' grunted the first speaker. 'Up by Peshawar way they say that there are many sahibs – but only one Nikal Seyn (Nicholson). It is the same everywhere and with all men. If those who see where others are blind be removed from the path, the matter is thereby made easier.'

'But – but this is a good man——' Another voice, further away and almost inaudible. 'He knows our ways, and though at times he is hot and very angry, he is just. He righted the matter of the crop tax, and Baloo Ram has said——'

'*Fool!*' – the epithet echoed hollowly in the cold room – 'it is not those who spit upon us and treat us as dogs and slaves who are of danger to us, for they do but light a fire for their own burning. It is men such as Randall Sahib, who speak our tongues as one of us, and who have many friends amongst us and are seen to do justice to all men, who are a stumbling block in the path; because many of our people will listen to their words and many more follow them to the death, taking up arms even against those of their own blood. It is these who must first be slain.'

There was a murmur of agreement and again the purr and bubble of the hookah. Winter's teeth began to chatter with cold but she clenched them tightly and continued to crouch in the darkness, straining her ears to listen. But something had evidently startled the group outside, for she heard sounds of hurried movements and an unintelligible mutter, and after that for a long time there was silence and she did not know whether the men had gone or were still crouching against the wall. Then there was a sound of footsteps, an asthmatic cough and the rattling of a chain from beyond the shuttered window at her back, and she realized that it was old Dunde Khan, the night-watchman, making his rounds, whom the men by the wall must have heard approaching.

She waited for perhaps a quarter of an hour longer, huddled in her shawl and numb with cold, but she heard no more voices, though the night was so silent that she could hear the sound of her own breathing and the rustle of a mouse that scuttled across the matting in the darkness. At last she stood up stiffly and crept back to bed, closing the dressing-room door softly behind her. She had forgotten about the quilt and she did not go to sleep, but dragged the blankets up about her and sat with her chin on her knees, shivering and thinking and waiting for the dawn.

Chunwar . . . That was a village to the south of the city. She had ridden out that way before, though she did not often ride in that direction, for the first mile or so was crop-land threaded by water-courses, and to walk a fresh and restless horse along the narrow paths between the crops or along the crumbling edge of irrigation channels was tedious. Beyond that there lay several miles of open dusty plain dotted with *kikar* and *dhâk* trees; rough, stony ground, full of unexpected potholes and dry nullahs.

The nullah that the man had spoken of cut diagonally across the plain a mile or so short of the village which lay behind a thick belt of trees. It was more a wide, steep-sided ravine, and riding to Chunwar from the direction of the cantonments there was only one practicable place where it might be crossed; where the narrow, rutted cart-track ran. The ravine was full of trees and scrub and high grass, and someone – perhaps several men – would be waiting there for Captain Randall to pass. It would be easy enough to unhorse a man in such a place, for they would see him coming from a long way off across the plain. A rope or a wire laid across the steep path and suddenly jerked taut. A man dropping from an overhanging bough onto the shoulders of a horseman passing beneath. There would be a dozen ways. And when they had dragged him off and stunned him, his foot would be jammed into a stirrup and his horse lashed forward to drag him at a gallop across the sharp stony plain.

Winter had a sudden vision of Alex Randall's brown, clean-cut face torn and battered into a shapeless mass of blood and dirt, and she shuddered as she stared into the darkness. The hours crawled past and the moonlight left the window and then the verandah beyond, and the room was dark and very cold. The cold began to make her drowsy, but she dared not sleep for fear that she should awake too late and not be in time to stop Alex from riding to his death.

At long last a hint of grey crept into the blackness, and a cock crowed from somewhere behind the servants' quarters at the far side of the compound. Winter lit a candle and began to dress herself hurriedly; her fingers clumsy from cold and weariness and a sudden fear that perhaps after all she might be too late. The thought terrified her and she ran through the quiet house and shook awake the sheeted, corpse-like figure of one of the house servants who slept in the hall at night, and told him to tell her syce that she wished her horse brought round immediately.

The household were by now too accustomed to her early rising for the man to feel any surprise, and he stumbled off, yawning and adjusting his *puggari*, to deliver the message. Yusaf must have been up already, although it was almost an hour before her usual time for riding; and barely fifteen minutes later she was cantering down the long drive in the grey, aqueous light of the early morning. She had never been to Captain Randall's bungalow, though she had passed it almost daily. There was a light burning in one of the rooms and a groom was walking a restive horse up and down in front of the verandah. So he had not yet left! Winter restrained her mount with difficulty, for Furiante was feeling fresh and above himself and did not relish being kept to a gentle canter; but Winter had no intention of going too far ahead. She reined him in and made him walk sedately down a narrow lane under a feathery canopy of tamarisk boughs while she listened for the sound of Chytuc's hooves behind her.

She did not know the identity of the men who had whispered against the wall last night, and she had heard only one name – an unfamiliar one. But the men would not have been there if some at least had not been connected with the Residency. One, or all of them, must be in the Commissioner's employ. Winter could not believe that her syce Yusaf had been one of them, but she had been too frightened by what she had heard to take any chances, and she would have left him behind except that she had never ridden out without him before, and to do so now might cause comment.

If it were the servants in Conway's house – she did not think of it as hers – who plotted to murder Captain Randall, it would be just as well if it did not appear that she had warned him, for were it known that she had done so, it must follow that she had overheard them or that one of their number had betrayed them to her. She had no idea how to deal with that problem. Alex would know, but in the meantime she must avoid any appearance of deliberately turning him back from Chunwar, and must make it look as though she had met him by chance.

The lane came out upon an open stretch of ground beyond which lay a mango-tope and a deep belt of crop-lands. To the right lay the city and the river while half a mile to the left lay the *maidan* (parade-ground) and the rifle-range. Winter drew rein a little beyond the mouth of the lane as though undecided which way to turn. She heard Shiraz, the horse Yusaf rode, fidgeting behind her, and then the sound that she had been waiting for, and turned; swinging Furiante so that Alex had no choice but to stop. He pulled up, and Winter saw that he was alone. So they had been right in that at least.

She said on a note of surprise, and for the benefit of Yusaf: 'Captain Randall! How fortunate that I should have met you. I have been wishing to see you. May I ride with you?'

It was the first time that she had met or spoken to him since the night of his arrival in Lunjore almost three months previously, but if Alex was in any way surprised at being thus accosted he gave no sign of it. He bowed slightly and said in his most expressionless voice: 'Certainly, Mrs Barton, if you wish. But I am riding to Chunwar this morning and I am afraid that you would not find it very amusing. The going is rather rough.'

'Then perhaps you will ride with me to the *maidan* instead,' said Winter, turning her horse's head. 'You can ride to Chunwar some other morning.'

'I am sorry to sound disobliging,' began Alex, 'but——'

Winter looked over her shoulder at him with raised brows, letting the reins lie loose, and under cover of her long habit used her spur on Furiante. Furiante needed no second invitation. He had been sidling and snorting and seething with impatience for the past quarter of an hour, and he responded to the spur with all the outraged velocity of an exploding rocket.

Winter screamed once for Captain Randall's benefit, and thereafter concentrated on remaining in the saddle without making the smallest attempt to arrest Furiante's headlong flight. She was not, if the truth be known, in the least sure that she could do so if she wished, for Furiante had the bit between his teeth and was galloping as though he were pursued by seven devils.

Mercifully the ground was level, and once they were through the trees the vast stretch of the *maidan* lay ahead. The path through the trees was a narrow one and branches whipped at Winter's skirt; her hat fell off and her hair streamed out behind her like a black silk flag, and then they were racing across the open *maidan*. She could hear Chytuc's hooves behind her and Alex's voice shouting 'Left! – pull left!' and only then remembered the wide ditch that bounded the far side of the ground. She pulled on the near-side rein with all her strength, but she could not turn the maddened horse. And then Alex was gaining on her and she saw Chytuc's black head and laid-back ears draw level with her, and Alex had caught her bridle and turned Furiante – still galloping at full stretch but tiring at last – away from the ditch and towards the open country. Two minutes later he had brought them to a stop.

Winter bowed over Furiante's neck in sudden weakness and felt Alex's hard fingers grip her shoulder and heard him say: 'Are you all right?'

She lifted her head and looked at him – and saw the sudden comprehension in his face as he met that look. His hand dropped and he said incredulously: 'Did you do that on purpose?'

Winter straightened up and drew a deep breath to steady herself. 'I – I had to. I'm sorry. But I had to talk to you. *I had to*! Tell Yusaf to keep behind.'

Alex looked at her for a long moment. His eyes were black with anger and his mouth had closed in a hard, unpleasant line. He threw a curt word of command over his shoulder and touched Chytuc with his heel, and the two horses moved forward at a sober pace, Yusaf falling back out of earshot and following at a discreet distance.

Alex said curtly: 'You had better do something about your hair. Give me the reins.'

He leant across and took them from her, and watched her as she attempted to gather up and re-roll the shining mass into some sort of order. The anger went out of his face and he smiled a little crookedly:

'You might almost be one of the Spartans "combing their long hair for death" in the pass of Thermopylae. Don't look so tragic. What is it?'

Winter said: 'I – I'm sorry about – about that, but I had to stop you from going to Chunwar.' Her voice was all at once small and unsteady and she glanced at him and saw that his brows had drawn together and his eyes held a look that was hard to read. She said abruptly: 'Why did you ride alone today? Doesn't your orderly usually ride with you?'

'He is ill,' said Alex briefly. 'Why do you ask?'

Winter drew a little gasping breath. 'Because – because that means it is true. I didn't imagine it all.'

Alex looked at her, frowning. 'What is true? What is all this?'

'They were going to kill you,' said Winter. 'In the ravine on the road to Chunwar. I heard them talking last night, and I had to stop you. But – but I did not want them to know that I knew, so when you would not come with me I had to do something to make you. That is why I made Furiante bolt, and pretended that I was being run away with, so that you——'

Alex said: 'Wait a minute. Do you mind saying that all over again, and slowly? I must be singularly slow-witted this morning.'

Quite suddenly there was a hint of a laugh in his voice, and Winter stiffened and the colour rushed up into her face. 'You don't believe me. You think that I am—— But it's true! They said that Niaz Mohammed would be given something to make him ill, and that your syce had a poisoned hand and so you would be riding alone, and——' She checked and said: 'I – I am sorry. I do not seem to be telling it very well.'

'Begin at the beginning,' advised Alex. 'Who are "they"?'

'I don't know. I only heard voices——' She told him the story of those voices that had whispered in the shadow of the blank wall where the bathroom sluice ran out, and of how it was that she had come to hear them, and Alex listened without interruption. When she had finished he was silent for a moment or two and then he asked if she had recognized any of the voices. Winter shook her head. 'No. They were speaking very quietly, and the echo made it sound strange.'

'No names?'

'Only one. A man named Mehan Lal would be in the ravine to – to help. There is no one of that name among the servants.'

'But there is among my acquaintances,' said Alex grimly.

He snapped his fingers at the level of his shoulder without turning his head. It was a brief and almost inaudible gesture, but Yusaf, twenty yards behind, saw it and spurred forward. 'Huzoor?'

'Hast thou a gun?'

Yusaf thrust a hand into the bosom of his coat and produced a small five-chambered Colt pistol; a surprising item of equipment for a syce. Alex held out his hand for it and slid it into his own pocket, and said: 'I may have need of two. Take the Memsahib home by way of the cantonments, and keep a still tongue in thy head.'

He noticed Winter's startled face and smiled: a smile that did not quite reach his eyes. 'It's all right. Yusaf is one of my own men. I did not think that you should ride so far afield without a trustworthy escort. The times are not as settled as some people suppose.'

He made as though to turn Chytuc and Winter snatched at his rein.

'No! Alex, no!' Her voice was sharp with panic.

Alex looked down at her white frightened face and the harsh lines of his own face softened. He dropped his hand over hers for a brief moment and gripped it hard and reassuringly.

'I shall be all right. I promise you. Forewarned is forearmed, you know.'

But Winter's fingers still clung to the bridle. 'What are you going to do?' she demanded breathlessly.

Alex grinned unexpectedly. 'To tell the truth, I am not sure. But I do not like being gunned for, and I intend to discourage it. There is a deal of difference between falling into an ambush and walking into one with your eyes open.'

Winter said: 'I'm coming with you – and Yusaf can come too, and——'

Alex shook his head. 'Oh, no, you're not. That would spoil everything. They are expecting me to come alone, and if they see anyone with me they will abandon the idea and wait for another opportunity. And I might not be warned next time.'

'Alex——'

Alex wrenched her hand from the bridle and said suddenly and savagely: 'For God's sake don't look at me like that!' He saw her flinch as though he had struck her, and said with harsh impatience: 'I'm sorry. I am very grateful to you for warning me. Now get on – go on back to the house.'

He wheeled Chytuc, and was gone, galloping back across the open ground towards the distant belt of trees, and Winter turned her horse's head and sat watching him grow smaller and smaller across the colourless plain until at last the trees swallowed him up.

The sky that had been pearl-grey when she had ridden out under the arch of the Residency gate was growing bright now with the sunrise, and only the morning star still shimmered faintly in the wash of saffron light that flooded upwards from the east – the morning star and a pale segment of moon, drowning in the rising tide of the dawn. It was less than an hour since she had left the Residency, but it seemed as though hours had passed – or years. As though she were not even the same person who had ridden out under that gate.

Why had she not known before that she loved Alex Randall? Why was it only now, when he was riding away from her, perhaps to his death, that she could realize how much he meant to her? She had loved him for so long and been too obsessed with her childish, foolish, pasteboard-and-tinsel image of Conway to recognize it. Once, in Malta, she had wanted him to kiss her, and been horrified at herself – because of Conway. And when he had kissed her at Delhi she had been shamed and startled by her own instinctive response, because it had seemed a betrayal of Conway and she had hated herself for it. And hated Alex who had trapped her into it.

She had been blind and stupid and stubborn. She must always have known that she could trust Alex, but the shock of Mr Carroll's desperate fictions and Alex's cruel repudiation of them, followed by the sudden tumult of feeling that had taken control of her when he had held her and kissed her, had swept her out of her depth and into a helpless maelstrom of emotions that she had been unable to understand or control, and in which Conway – the rock to which she had clung for so many years – had seemed the only safe and solid refuge in a treacherous world. It was only now, facing the possibility of Alex's death, that all the mixed and unmanageable emotions had suddenly sorted themselves out and left only the one fact – that she loved him. But whether he lived or died, it was too late, because she had married Conway Barton.

Yusaf cleared his throat in a gently deprecatory hint that his orders had been to see that she returned to the Residency, and Winter straightened her slim shoulders and lifted her chin in the familiar gesture of her childhood when she had braced herself to meet reproof or hurt or humiliation and to endure it in silence, and turning Furiante she rode back through the brightening dawn to her husband's house.

But she did not enter it. Instead, she dismounted within the gate, and dismissing Yusaf and the horses, went across to the great banyan tree to sit silent among the roots and watch Akbar Khan's little grand-daughter share her morning meal with the birds. The sight of the small, still figure with its slow unhurried movements, surrounded by a host of friendly birds and squirrels, was always a soothing one to Winter, and the creatures had become sufficiently used to her frequent presence to pay little attention to her. But today they appeared wilder than usual, and would barely come to Zeb-un-Nissa's soft, wordless call.

'It is because they know that thou art afraid,' said Zeb-un-Nissa. She turned her enormous unfocused eyes on Winter and smiled her sweet vague smile. 'There is no need. He will come to no harm.'

The words were spoken with entire conviction, and though she could only have been referring to a bird or a squirrel, Winter was suddenly and strangely reassured. The terror and the tension ebbed away from her, and a bold blue jay, its plumage glinting like a handful of jewels in the morning sunlight, swooped down to take a fragment of bread from Nissa's small palm.

BOOK FOUR

MOONRISE

The sun was still below the horizon when Alex left the green crop-lands behind him, and gave Chytuc his head across the wide stretch of the open plain where his hooves clicked against the bleached bones of cattle and his black body as yet cast no shadow.

The line of the ravine was still invisible, but the tall group of *dhâk* trees made a small dark landmark against the dun-coloured level of the plain. The morning air was sharp and cold and exhilarating. Partridges called from among the tussocks of grass and thorn-scrub, and in the far distance a slow-moving line of dark dots betrayed a herd of blackbuck.

A rough cart-track idled across the plain towards the ravine and Chunwar, but the heavy dew and the rain of the previous day had laid the dust, and the prints of Chytuc's hooves lay clear on a surface that showed that no cart and only two men on foot had passed within the last few hours. Alex noted the fact, but without optimism. There was no reason to suppose that reinforcements had not entered the ravine from the opposite side, and he could only hope that there were not more than three or at the most four men lying in wait for him. The conversation that Winter had repeated to him made it seem likely that there would be only two, but it was not safe to count on that.

Mehan Lal . . . Yes, he remembered Mehan Lal, and he had a fairly clear idea as to why the man had been selected to carry out this particular form of assassination. Mehan Lal possessed an unusual accomplishment, and Alex had once seen him use it to bring down a galloping leopard that had broken cover during a partridge shoot. The creature had bounded across an open stretch of ground, and Mehan Lal had swung and released a weighted silken rope with unbelievable swiftness and accuracy. The rope, swung by its weights, had whipped about the leopard's fore-paws and brought it to a rolling, snarling stop. It was said of Mehan Lal that he could bring down anything from a galloping horse to a long-legged heron with his weighted rope, and Alex did not doubt it.

He slowed Chytuc to a canter as the clump of *dhâk* trees loomed larger and the tops of the scrub and trees and cane that choked the ravine showed as a dark line above its rim. As he neared it he reined in to a walk: there was no necessity to risk Chytuc breaking a leg, though he doubted if anything would be tried in the way of tripping the horse. That Chytuc should be capable of dragging his dead body for a reasonable distance appeared to be an essential part of the scheme.

Alex had ridden through the ravine comparatively frequently, and he tried now to visualize it and put himself in the place of two men who wished to ambush a third and kill him, preferably by a blow on the head. There was a tree that grew on the bed of the ravine and spread its branches above the track. A man lying along one of those branches might strike down at the head of a horseman riding beneath. But would the leaves be thick enough to hide such a man? He could not remember, but of one thing he was sure; on the downward slope it would be easier to see into the branches, for they would for a moment be on a level with the eye. Therefore there would be nobody in that tree. It would be as he breasted the slope on the opposite side.

Alex drew out the slim skinning knife that he carried under the saddle flap. It was an item of equipment that was useful on long rides in rough country, and had in its day been put to a multitude of uses. Niaz kept the blade sharpened to a razor-like edge and Alex ran his thumb lightly along it and grinned appreciatively to see the blood start at its touch. He held the knife with the blade uppermost against his sleeve and touched Chytuc with his heel, and they passed by the *dhâk* trees and down over the rim of the ravine.

Chytuc's hooves slipped a little on the slope and Alex spoke softly. He was riding loosely, sitting relaxed in the saddle, and there was nothing about him to betray the fact that every nerve and faculty was tense and alert. He heard the faint rustle to one side of the track, and the whistle of the weighted rope; and because he had been waiting for it he pulled back on the rein and brought up his left hand in the same movement.

The rope whipped about him like a live thing with a life of its own, but instead of pinning his arms to his sides, his arm was raised to meet it. The knife blade shored upwards severing the rope, and Chytuc, reined in savagely, had backed instead of plunging forward.

Almost simultaneously a man rose from the high grass by the track and clawed at Alex's boot, but Alex had dropped the reins after that one savage jerk and there was a pistol in his right hand. The explosion and the howl of pain sent Chytuc rearing wildly on the narrow track, and the slashing blow of an iron-tipped *lathi* from the opposite side missed its mark and caught the horse's flank, raising a vicious weal. Alex dropped the knife and fired again, as with a squeal of rage Chytuc reared up with flaying hooves. The next moment horse and rider had burst out of the ravine and onto the level plain with the speed and violence of a thunderbolt.

Alex made no attempt to check the infuriated horse but let him have his head until his pain and panic had subsided. They rode into Chunwar by way of the canal bank, and Alex noted that the report that it had been illegally breached was correct, but that it was another cultivator, and not Mohammed Afzal, whose fields had reaped the benefit. He called upon the Kotwal – the village headman – and having dealt with the matter of the breached canal, rode back to the ravine accompanied by the Kotwal and some of the more responsible villagers.

A man who gave his name as Sobha Chand was discovered hiding in the thickets a quarter of a mile above the track. It had not been difficult to trace him for he had a bullet through the shoulder and was suffering from severe loss of blood. He appeared to imagine that he was either dead or dying. Mehan Lal had not gone so far. A smashed knee is a painful thing, and he crouched in the tall grass by the path and groaned. There had been a third man, but he had fled.

Alex had seen the two wounded men loaded into a bullock-cart, their wounds roughly bandaged, and had ridden slowly back to the cantonments in the wake of the cart, where having handed the groaning pair of would-be assassins over to the care of the police, he had returned to his bungalow for breakfast. He hoped that the morning's work might act as a deterrent to others interested in his removal, since the average native of the country, though for the most part careless of death, possessed a disproportionate fear of being painfully wounded.

Having breakfasted he walked over to the Commissioner's office and paid particular attention, without appearing to do so, to the demeanour of every servant whom he met. No face expressed any surprise at his appearance, but he noted with interest that although Durga Charan, the head *chupprassi,* could control both his face and his bland, unwinking eyes, he could not prevent his hands from quivering. Alex dropped his gaze to those unsteady hands and allowed it to linger on them thoughtfully.

'Durga Charan,' said Alex softly, 'I think that I have heard some talk of *taklief* (trouble) in thy village. It may be that thou shouldst take leave and see that all is well with thy house . . . while thy health permits.' The man had said nothing, but an hour later he had asked the Commissioner for leave to go to his home.

Winter had heard Alex's footsteps and his quiet voice, and she had gone to her bedroom and locked the door behind her and wept for the first time since her wedding night: weeping for relief and thankfulness as she never wept for the loss of her illusions.

It had been a Tuesday, and that evening the 'Tuesday Crowd' were to dine as usual at the Residency. Winter had been too tired and too worn out by the anxieties of the previous night and the varied emotions of the day to be able to stand up to a scene with Conway, and she had agreed to dine with them on the understanding that she could retire immediately afterwards. Provided she sat at his table, said Conway, he had not the smallest objection to her feigning a headache and retiring at the conclusion of the meal. In fact he would appreciate it, by God he would! She cast a damned damper on such parties, and they would do very well without her.

He looked at her with scowling irritation, wondering how he could ever have imagined, even for so short a time, that she had grown into a beauty? He had not paid much attention to her of late, and it suddenly struck him that she had lost a lot of weight and was looking remarkably sallow. A pity.

He disliked skinny women. And her eyes were too big. He had thought them amazingly fine when she had first arrived in Lunjore. The most speaking eyes he had ever seen in a woman's head. Lashes like – like black butterflies! dammit, mused the Commissioner, surprised at himself for such an unusually poetical flight of fancy. But now there was a blankness about them and they seemed to look round him or through him, but never at him, and there were blue shadows beneath them like bruises.

He said a little uneasily: 'You are not looking at all the thing, my dear. Are you not feeling well? Lunjore is not held to be a good station for women. The climate is not all it should be. Perhaps it might be a good thing if you were to go away on a short visit, to set you up before the hot weather. The Abuthnots would I feel sure be pleased to see you. Or we might consider a visit to Lucknow. You will like to see your father's house – our house. What do you say to that?'

He saw the bright, transient colour flood up into his wife's pale face and her eyes lose their blankness and become brilliant again, and thought with baffled amazement: 'Why dammit, she *is* a beauty——'

Winter said with a tremor in her voice: 'Could I really go to Lucknow? I have wanted to so much. Could I really?'

The Commissioner was gratified by her response to his careless suggestion, though he considered that she should have shown a more proper reluctance to leave him. But she was, on the whole, an amenable little thing, and except for stubborn moments, such as her refusal to enter into the spirit of his gayer evenings, she gave no trouble. And she was – or wasn't she? – good looking. It was odd that he could never make up his mind on that point. He patted her shoulder with condescending affection, and said well, well, they would see about it. It might not be a bad idea at all. The Casa de Ballesteros – he believed that it had once been called something fanciful to do with peacocks – was really a very fine house. He had stayed there once or twice when inspecting the property on behalf of her guardian.

Pleased with that momentary flicker of beauty and his own magnanimity, he had put an arm about her waist, and pulling her against him had planted a wetly alcoholic kiss upon her cheek. It had been intended for her lips, but Winter had turned her head away, though she had done nothing else to avoid his embrace but had stood quite still, enduring it with closed eyes; wishing with a sudden passionate intensity that it was Alex who held her. She heard footsteps in the hall and Iman Bux's murmured 'Huzoor', and realizing that in the next moment a visitor would be ushered into the drawing-room, attempted to free herself: 'Conway – please. Someone is coming in——'

'Let 'em!' mumbled Conway thickly. He had started his drinking early so as to be in good spirits for the arrival of his guests, and had found, as always, that the feel of a woman's body in his arms – even that of so slim and unyielding a one as his wife's – was remarkably pleasant.

Winter's arms had been hanging stiffly at her sides, but now she put up her hands and caught at his coat sleeves in an endeavour to thrust him away, so that for a moment it appeared as though she were returning her husband's embrace. She heard the door open and found herself looking into Alex Randall's expressionless face.

It was a sudden and nightmare repetition of the day at Delhi when he had walked in and found her in Carlyon's arms. A nightmare with a cruel twist to it, because then she had been so afraid that it would be Conway who would find her in that degrading position; but it had been Alex. And now it was Conway who held her, and again it was Alex. But it was Alex whom she loved.

Conway released her and turned. 'Hullo, Alex m'boy. Walked right in on the turtle doves, dammit! Have a drink. Make yerself at home. Nothin' urgent, is it? because I ain't got the time to look to it now. Here's Mrs Barton already dressed, and I still have to have a bath and change.'

He shouted for drinks to be brought, took one himself and moved to the door. 'Don't go. M' wife 'll look after you. Why don't you stay t' dinner? Good party on tonight. Capital crowd. We shall all be as jolly as grigs. Time you got yourself out of a rut. Shall expect you.'

'I am afraid, sir——' began Alex, and stopped. He looked at Winter's drawn rigid face, and after a perceptible pause said quite deliberately and as though he had intended to finish the sentence that way '– that I have been neglecting my social duties of late. I should be glad to.'

'Good, good,' approved the Commissioner heartily. 'Look after him, m' dear.'

He removed himself, and Winter said stiffly: 'I am sorry that Mr Barton should be unable to give you his attention, but we are expecting guests within the hour. I hope that your business with him will keep?'

Alex strolled across the room and came to a stop before her. He was feeling angrier than he had ever felt in his life. An entirely illogical anger, for surely he should be glad that she was not, after all, as unhappy in her marriage as he had supposed. Because of that anger his slight suggestion of a drawl was suddenly more marked.

He put his glass down on the chimney-piece and said: 'I did not come here to see Mr Barton. I came to pay my debts.'

'Your debts?'

'Let us say, my thanks. I am afraid that I cannot have appeared particularly grateful to you this morning. But I am. I think I owe you my life, and the least I can do is to thank you properly for the gift.' He looked down at her and smiled, not entirely pleasantly, and added: 'I believe that I had intended to say something to the effect that it is now of course wholly at your disposal, but such statements are apt to sound better in a theatre, do you not think? So I will confine myself to saying "thank you". I am indeed grateful.'

He reached out, and before she had realized what he meant to do he had taken her hand and bent above it formally, lifting it so that it barely touched his tight mouth.

Winter snatched it away and took a quick step backwards: afraid of his proximity and what it did to her, and bewildered by the derisive note in his voice. She said a little breathlessly: 'You have nothing to thank me for, Captain Randall. I did nothing that anyone else would not have done in the same circumstances.'

Making a determined effort to steady her voice and appear calm and composed, she moved to a chair and sat down, her wide skirts spreading crisply about her, and said: 'You have not told me what occurred this morning. Was there no one in the ravine, then?'

'No, they were there,' said Alex. He did not accept her invitation to be seated, but leaned his shoulders against the chimney-piece and looked down at her, his hands – which like Durga Charan's were not quite steady – driven deep in his pockets.

He gave her an edited and colourless version of the happenings in the ravine, and passed on to other topics, mentioning that he had recently received a letter from Mrs Abuthnot, and inquiring if Winter had had any news of Lottie.

Winter had, in fact, received a long and rapturous letter from Lottie by the last dâk, but as it had been largely concerned with the many perfections of Edward and the sweetly pretty furnishings that Lottie had contrived for her drawing-room, there was little in it that could be expected to interest Captain Randall, while its only really important item of news – that Lottie had begun to cherish hopes of a child who would be born in midsummer – could not be imparted, since such things were unmentionable before gentlemen.

Captain Randall, however, did not stay long. He finished his drink and excused himself, saying that if he were to dine at the Residency that night he would have to change into more formal wear.

Winter rose with a rustle of yellow *gros de chine*. She had not looked directly at him during the past ten minutes or so, but she looked at him now. 'Why did you change your mind about dining here tonight, when you had meant to refuse?' she demanded abruptly. 'I know that you do not like parties, and if you only wished for an opportunity to thank me, you have done that, and need not dine here if you do not wish to. I will make your excuses to Mr Barton.'

'What makes you think I do not wish to?'

'Well . . . you have never accepted any previous invitation to dine.'

Alex lifted one faintly ironic eyebrow. 'Have I not? You must put it down to pressure of work. I daresay I offered some such excuse. But you are quite wrong. I like parties. It is only their after-effects that I have sometimes found tiresome. And I seem to have attended several this season.'

'But none in this house.'

'That was churlish of me,' said Alex gravely. 'But it will be remedied tonight.' He bowed and went away, leaving her question unanswered.

He had returned some thirty minutes later, and Winter had had the doubtful felicity of observing that he appeared entirely at his ease among the inner circle of the Commissioner's friends. Mrs Cottar addressed him familiarly by his Christian name and devoted a large part of her attention to him, and her conversation seemed to afford him considerable amusement. He had also made himself unusually pleasant to Delia Gardener-Smith, while at the same time blandly refusing to be drawn into any argument with Colonel Moulson, who continued to regard him with a hostile eye.

At the conclusion of the meal the guests had repaired to the drawing-room, where the furniture had been moved to allow space for a long table covered with a baize cloth on which cards and dice were laid out. There were usually several Indian guests on these occasions: rich landowners and noblemen, or their sons, who gambled heavily, and were on that account on easy terms with the Commissioner and his more raffish friends. Those who were Hindu, and whose caste raised difficulties in the matter of eating, would arrive after dinner, and tonight they were joined by Kishan Prasad, whom Winter had not seen since the day of her arrival at Calcutta.

She had been about to excuse herself on the plea of a headache, but two things had made her change her mind. The arrival of Kishan Prasad and something that had been in Alex's face when he had seen him.

Alex had been standing at the far end of the room among a noisy group which had gathered about Mrs Cottar, and Winter had been covertly watching him. She had seen his gaze rest briefly upon Kishan Prasad, and had been suddenly aware that he had known that the Rao Sahib would be present that evening, and it was for this reason that he had accepted her husband's invitation to dine. Perhaps he had even arrived at that particular moment in the hope of obtaining such an invitation, and for reasons of his own had made it appear as though he had at first intended to refuse? His expression had not altered noticeably at the sight of Kishan Prasad, but it seemed to Winter as though there was a glint of satisfaction in his eyes, as though he had bet on the turn of a card and won. Then he had turned his back and engaged Mrs Cottar in conversation as Winter moved forward to greet the Rao Sahib.

Kishan Prasad bowed formally in the Indian fashion and expressed his pleasure at meeting her again. She had never been able to rid herself of a slight feeling of repulsion towards him ever since the day that she had surprised that look of gloating hate on his face as he watched a sinking, water-logged wreck in the wild dusk four days out of Aden. But he was of a very different kidney to those few of his fellow-countrymen who frequented the Commissioner's less reputable parties, and she could not imagine him tipsy, obsequious or insolent, or permitting himself to be cheated at cards – treatment that she uneasily suspected was not unknown when the Tuesday parties had lasted well into Wednesday morning.

Card-play had not yet begun, and Kishan Prasad, having greeted Colonel Moulson and one or two other acquaintances, had drawn up a chair beside the sofa on which Winter had seated herself, and addressed her in his own tongue. Since she was well aware of his proficiency in English, she appreciated the compliment; together with the fact that he did not talk the trivialities of the Station. Kishan Prasad's conversation was drily entertaining and rich with the imagery of the East, and Winter found herself conversing with him with more ease and interest than she had as yet enjoyed since her arrival in Lunjore, and could only be sorry when they were joined all too soon by Colonel Moulson and Delia Gardener-Smith and he reverted to English.

He inquired politely where Mrs Barton intended to spend the summer months, and on hearing that she would not be removing to the hills, advised her most earnestly to do so. She would, he assured her, find Lunjore unpleasantly hot from mid-April until the monsoon broke, and it had an unenviable reputation in the matter of high temperatures during May and June. He himself had visited Simla on more than one occasion, and he dilated upon its charms. She must persuade the Commissioner to permit her to sample the delights of the cool airs and the pines.

Delia had been pleased to be arch. She had informed Kishan Prasad that no loving wife would ever voluntarily allow herself to be separated from her husband, and that were *she* married she knew that for her part she could never endure to leave her husband's side even for a week. No mountain airs could compensate for such deprivation! She had allowed her gaze to rest innocently upon Colonel Moulson, who had twirled his moustache and expressed approval of such womanly sentiments.

Kishan Prasad remarked drily that Miss Gardener-Smith had yet to experience a hot weather in the plains, and turned the conversation to the forthcoming duck shoot at Hazrat Bagh, a jheel that lay some fifteen miles to the west of the cantonments. Hazrat Bagh – the 'Grove of a Thousand Trees' – had once been the site of a hunting park of some forgotten king, but nothing remained of it now except the lonely stretches of water and the intersecting bunds on which the 'thousand trees' – *kikar* and an occasional *peepul* tree – stood among high grass and reeds and provided excellent cover for sportsmen. And since there were no villages near the jheel, the waterfowl came there in their thousands.

The shoot was being arranged by some of the local talukdars, and food and beaters on an elaborate scale were being provided for the guests, who included most of the British officers stationed in Lunjore. Those ladies who had been invited to attend as spectators would watch the *battue* from the tree-lined bunds or from an artificial 'hide' to one side of the jheel, and several hundred sepoys were to be lent for the occasion to keep the birds from settling on outlying jheels and inaccessible stretches of water. A road was in process of construction so that the ladies would be able to drive there in their carriages, since the jheel lay far from any made road and was at present difficult to reach even on horseback, owing to the roughness of the going.

'I hope that we are to have the pleasure of seeing you there, Mrs Barton?' said Kishan Prasad. 'I am to be one of the hosts, you know.'

'No, I did not know,' confessed Winter. 'But I shall certainly be there. I have never been out on a big shoot before.'

'You must let me arrange a tiger shoot later on,' said Kishan Prasad. 'One may shoot duck in Europe, but a tiger shoot is something that you will see only in the East.'

'For my part, I could not endure to attend such a thing,' declared Delia with a shudder. 'I am sure I cannot conceive how *any* lady could do so.'

'Why?' inquired Kishan Prasad. 'Would it distress you to see so beautiful a creature shot? But tigers are vermin, you know. They prey upon the herds of the villagers, and in their old age they often take to killing men, while the duck you will see shot do no harm.'

'Oh, but I did not mean *that*,' said Delia, opening her eyes at him. 'I meant the danger, of course. There can be no danger in a duck shoot, but a tiger shoot cannot help but be dangerous.'

'That is why it is exciting,' said Kishan Prasad with a smile. 'No sport is worthy of the name that does not include an element of risk.'

'Is that a creed, or merely an opinion?' inquired a pleasant voice behind them. 'Good evening, Rao Sahib. When did you arrive in Lunjore?'

They had none of them observed Alex approach, and Winter saw Kishan Prasad's slight involuntary start at the sound of that voice; but he turned a bland countenance and his voice was as pleasant as Alex's own:

'A creed, of course, Captain Randall. I seldom advance opinions. I arrived at mid-day.'

'In good time for the obsequies, in fact,' said Alex with a grin. 'I am sorry to have had to disappoint you.'

'Yes?' Kishan Prasad's slim brows rose and he looked puzzled though polite, as though he imagined Alex to have attempted some Western joke, the point of which had escaped him.

Winter looked sharply from one face to the other, for Alex's apparently pointless remark was entirely clear to her, though she could not conceive why he had made it. To suggest that Kishan Prasad could have had any hand in an attempt upon his life was absurd, since the man owed his own life to him and was not likely to forget it. Yet she did not think that Alex was in the habit of making pointless remarks.

Had Kishan Prasad known that there was to have been an attempt to kill Alex? No, of course that was impossible! . . . Or was it? She could not be sure, and because she was not, she was all at once afraid.

Alex laughed, but did not explain himself. He said instead: 'I hope you mean to invite me to your tiger shoot. When is it to be?'

'I have not thought,' said Kishan Prasad gravely. 'It was not a plan, merely a suggestion.' He met Alex's gaze blandly, holding it for a long moment, and then said gently: 'Some time in the hot weather, shall we say? They are always easier to deal with in the hot months, for instead of ranging at large they are forced to keep near water, and are less active.'

'That is not a thing that I should care to count on,' said Alex, regarding him under drooping eyelids.

Kishan Prasad shrugged his shoulders: 'But of course not. Did I not say that there is always an element of risk? It is for that reason that one should take particular precautions when ladies are of the party. But there can be few ladies who would care to go on such a shoot during the hot weather, and I do not imagine that Mrs Barton will be with us then. I feel sure that she will have removed to some hill station to escape the worst of the heat. I have just been warning the ladies that Lunjore can be a veritable furnace in the months before the monsoon breaks, but coming from Europe they have as yet little idea of how fierce our Indian hot weathers can be.'

'I shall do my best to impress it upon them,' said Alex.

'I am sure you will, Captain Randall,' said Kishan Prasad with a smile. 'Though I fear your warnings are doomed to be disregarded. You will find that those ladies who have not yet experienced a hot weather will be sure that you are grossly exaggerating the discomforts, while those who have will have forgotten just how bad they can be. So you see I am really quite safe in playing traitor to the climate of my native land.'

Delia said brightly: 'Maudie Chilton, who has spent four seasons in Lunjore, says that it is best not to think of such things while it is cool, as once it becomes hot there is nothing to be done about it, and when it is over one can forget all about it until the next time.'

Winter could see nothing amusing in the remark, but both Alex and Kishan Prasad laughed, and their laughs contained a disturbing and identical note of grimness. It was almost, thought Winter uneasily, as though their casual conversation had possessed two separate and distinct meanings, and that each knew exactly what the other had implied. She looked at the two men, and for a fleeting moment it seemed to her that there was a strange likeness between them. A likeness that had nothing to do with colouring or feature, but that went deeper than externals.

Kishan Prasad rose at the approach of Mrs Cottar and presently walked away with Alex, amicably discussing the forthcoming duck shoot, and Winter decided that she was letting her imagination run away with her. Yet she had not, after all, left the party early that night. She had stayed for the first time; watching Alex and Kishan Prasad, and telling herself that there was nothing there – nothing. That Kishan Prasad had not blandly presented Alex with some obscure piece of information or warning, or Alex recognized it as such.

The Commissioner had as usual drunk too much, and had eventually abandoned cards in favour of lolling upon a sofa at the far end of the room with his arm about Mrs Wilkinson's waist – Major Wilkinson being at present in no state to resent such behaviour, having succumbed early to the effects of the Commissioner's port.

Winter looked at her husband's coarse, flushed face with its pale, protuberant eyes and drooping brandy-sodden moustache, and watched him fondle Chrissie Wilkinson's plump bare shoulder while he whispered something in her ear that sent her off into peals of laughter. She knew that she should not remain and lend her countenance to such proceedings, and that she need not even trouble to make any excuses for her removal, since few if any of her guests would notice that she had gone. Yet she did not go. She sat stiffly upright, the yellow silk flounces of her wide skirt spreading out from below her slim waist like the petals of an overblown rose, and the same small frozen smile on her face that she had worn during the nightmare hours that had followed her wedding.

She could not leave, because Alex was there, and all at once it had become enough to be in the same room with him: to be able to watch his face and to hear his voice and his laugh. To realize, having visualized him dead, that he was alive and safe and real; and to feel the ache of loving him tug at her heart. Tomorrow, or the next day or the next, he might meet with another carefully planned accident, or die of cholera or typhus or black-water fever, or any one of the deadly diseases that ravaged India. Life was cheap in such a country, and a face seen laughing across a luncheon-table one day might well lie slack-mouthed in death less than twenty-four hours later, and be hidden under six feet of earth before another sun had set.

Death was an all too familiar visitant, and as Maudie Chilton had said of the hot weather, it was better not to think of such things. But there were also other and less disastrous things that could remove Alex from her orbit just as effectually. He might be transferred to some other district, or be returned to regimental duty. He might fall in love and marry some pretty creature like Sophie Abuthnot who, with infinitely more sense than Winter, had wasted no time over falling in love with him. Or someone like Delia—— No, surely not Delia! He had never been more than polite to Delia. But he was being more than polite to her now . . .

Winter watched him unobtrusively across the width of the room and suspected him of being a little drunk. His eyes were very bright and his thick dark hair was ruffled, and he appeared to be in excellent spirits and to have no objection to entertaining Miss Gardener-Smith – or, for that matter, Mrs Josh Cottar. Josh Cottar, who had the reputation of being able to drink any man in Lunjore under the table and still remain sober, was discussing a business deal in a far corner of the room with one of the Commissioner's Indian guests, but Colonel Moulson, who was seated at Delia's left, was showing every sign of losing his temper.

Kishan Prasad had left at midnight, but his departure had not been the signal for any of the other guests to leave, since the Tuesday parties seldom ended before three and sometimes four o'clock in the morning. But shortly before one o'clock the Commissioner, who had passed successively through the convivial, the amorous, the quarrelsome and the maudlin stages of intoxication, finally arrived at the unconscious; and as though he had been waiting for that, Alex put down his unfinished drink, flung his cards face upwards on the table, and rose.

'Where are you going, Alex?' demanded Mrs Cottar.

'Bed,' said Alex briefly. 'And so are the rest of you.'

Unbelievably, he had managed to get rid of them. Winter did not know how he had done it, but within a quarter of an hour the last carriage had rolled away down the drive and only Alex remained. He had looked thoughtfully at the Commissioner's snoring bulk and then at Winter and said: 'Do you need any help?'

Winter had not been entirely certain as to what he had meant by that question, but she had chosen to put the obvious interpretation upon it and had said a little stiffly: 'You need not trouble. Ismail will help him to bed.'

Alex shrugged his shoulders very slightly and had been turning to go when she had stopped him.

'Captain Randall——'

Alex turned back. 'Mrs Barton?'

Winter said: 'Did you know that the Rao Sahib would be coming to the house tonight?'

'I had heard that he might be.'

'Is that why you were here tonight?'

Alex regarded her with raised brows. 'My dear Mrs Barton, I was here tonight because your husband invited me.'

'But you would have refused if you had not thought that the Rao Sahib might be coming.'

Alex shrugged again, 'Perhaps. Why do you ask?'

'Why did you want to see him?'

Alex's lazy glance dwelt reflectively on her for a moment or two and then he said: 'Because I happen to be interested in him. There is a reason for everything that Kishan Prasad does, and it is always the same reason. He is a man with only one idea.'

'What idea?'

'My dear girl,' said Alex with sudden impatience, 'you know as well as I do. You once saw his face in the raw when we passed the wreck of that transport. He has only one aim in life. To throw off the rule of the Company. And to achieve it he would, if it were necessary, be prepared to cut the throat of every white man in this country with his own hands – with one possible exception.'

'You mean – yourself? But you thought that he had told those men to kill you. You told him so! That is what you meant, didn't you?'

Alex shook his head. 'No. He will not deliberately take my life, or plot to take it, because I once made the grave mistake of saving his. But if someone else should do it, that would be quite a different matter.'

Winter sat down again a little abruptly. She said, looking up at him: 'What were you talking about? It sounded just like ordinary talk, but it wasn't, was it?'

Alex subsided onto the sofa opposite her and drove his hands into his pockets. He said slowly: 'Not exactly. I think that he intended to do you a service – or me – and that he is sufficiently sure of himself to be able to afford to do so. Perhaps he is right.'

Winter said: 'I don't understand,' and Alex looked at her under lowered lashes.

'That may be just as well. Are you going to the hills this summer?'

'No. I do not think that I shall mind the heat so much. Why are you changing the subject?'

'I'm not. I think you should go, and I shall do all that I can to see that you do. Are you so particularly anxious to stay?' His gaze wandered to the sofa on the far side of the room where her husband lay and snored.

'Yes,' said Winter, watching the turn of his head against the lamplight. Had that been what Kishan Prasad meant? Had he been hinting that there might be trouble in Lunjore in the coming months? But if that were so, how could she go to the hills, knowing that Alex would still be in Lunjore?

She said almost inaudibly: 'There are times when – when one would so much rather not be sent away.'

Alex misinterpreted the hesitant words. He turned sharply, his mouth suddenly white. 'Are you going to have a child?' he inquired bluntly.

Winter did not move, but he saw her face set in a dreadful silent stare and felt the shudder that went through her body as clearly as though she had been touching him instead of separated from him by a full two paces.

It would be absurd to say that Winter had never contemplated such an eventuality, for she had often imagined herself as the mother of Conway's children. But that had been before her marriage. It had, incredibly enough, never once occurred to her since; perhaps because, subconsciously, she could not believe that anything could be conceived as a result of happenings that inspired only fear and repulsion. Alex's abrupt question had faced her with something that filled her with sick horror; as though she had been a sleep-walker waking to find herself balanced on the lip of a yawning gulf. The colour drained out of her face, leaving it pinched and sallow. That could not happen to her – it could not! Children should be born of love——

Alex said: 'Are you?' The harshness of his own voice surprised him.

Winter steadied her white lips with an effort, too shaken to resent the question. 'No.'

Alex stood up abruptly, and crossing to the table that was still littered with cards and dice, picked up his unfinished drink. The brandy burned his throat and he drank it as though he were parched with thirst, and refilling the glass at a side-table by the door, came back with it in his hand and stood looking down at her:

'I'm sorry. Perhaps I should not have asked you that.'

Winter did not raise her eyes further than the glass in his hand, and noting the direction of her gaze he smiled a little wryly: 'No, I am afraid I don't get drunk. It does not happen to be one of my failings, so I cannot excuse myself on that score. I thought that was what you meant, and it seemed to make it even more necessary that you should remove from Lunjore for the hot weather.'

Winter did not look at him. She said: 'I only meant that I will not run away.'

'From what?'

'From – from anything.'

'No,' said Alex thoughtfully, 'I don't believe you will.'

He sat down again, and stretching his legs out before him, leant his head against the back of the sofa, and the silence lengthened and drew out and filled slowly with small sounds; the Commissioner's stertorous breathing, the ticking of the clock, the chirrup of a gekko lizard and the monotonous fluttering of a large moth that had found its way in from the night and was battering its wings against the glass of the large oil-lamp, throwing whirling, wavering shadows across the walls and the high white ceiling.

Winter sat motionless, her body still rigid from shock. She did not look at Alex's face where it lay thrown back against the gold-coloured brocade of the high-backed sofa. She looked at the hand that held his glass: brown, thin, long-fingered and nervous; a hand possessed of unexpected strength and equally unexpected gentleness; and she seemed to see beside it the damp, fleshy, unsteady fingers of the man she had married. She knew then that she could not bear children to Conway. To do so would be the ultimate indecency. She would go to Lucknow as he had suggested. Not to the house that had been her father's, but to the one that had been her only home. To the Gulab Mahal. To Ameera, who might understand, and even if she did not, would be loving. If she could only get back to the Gulab Mahal she might be able to see things clearer; to stand back and get them into some sort of perspective. She could not do that while Alex was here and her need for him was so great. While Conway was here and her shuddering aversion for him filled her with such sick despair. She would go home . . .

She saw Alex's body relax, slackening perceptibly until the glass that he held tilted a little as his fingers loosened about it, holding it only lightly. He was still silent, but his silence was as devoid of tension as his body, and the familiar sense of safety and reassurance that his presence could bring her gradually smoothed out the turmoil in Winter's mind. The taut rigidity left her and she leant back tiredly against the furry plush upholstery of the tall chair-back, feeling the strain and tension of the last twenty-four hours seep slowly away from her.

The drawing-room smelt stalely of cigar-smoke and spirits, of fading roses and the heavy violet scent affected by Mrs Wilkinson, and the furniture still stood pushed out of the way of the card-table and against the walls. The room looked as cluttered and untidy and forlorn as any room when a party is over and the guests are gone, but despite its unattractive aspect it was all at once curiously peaceful. Alex had always been able to give her this feeling of security, and looking at his abstracted face Winter thought how strange it was that this should still be so. Surely, now that she had discovered that she loved him, she should feel embarrassed or shy or ashamed in his presence? She was a married woman, and it was shockingly improper of her to allow herself to fall in love with another man. She should by rights be overcome with shame. But then she had not allowed herself to fall in love with Alex. She had only discovered the fact when it was far too late to do anything about it. She had not even had sense enough to realize it when he had kissed her. She wondered, now, why he had done so? Had it only been a sudden impulse, born of the romantic beauty of the warm moonlight and the strains of a sentimental song? Or had he after all loved her a little? She knew that he had felt responsible for her and that the feeling of responsibility had irked him. She knew too that it had not died with her marriage. Sitting relaxed and silent she watched his quiet face and wondered what he was thinking of.

Alex was not thinking of Winter. He seldom had time to think of her, or allowed himself to do so. There were too many other things to think about. Too much that needed to be done, and always too little time in which to do it . . .

So Kishan Prasad was to be one of the hosts at the duck shoot – Kishan Prasad who never did anything without a reason. What then was behind this shoot at Hazrat Bagh? Could there be an ulterior motive behind such an arrangement? or was its aim merely to lull the senior officers and officials into a deeper sense of security and belief in the good-will of the local talukdars than they already possessed? It would, of course, mean that for the best part of a day the station would be practically denuded of British officers, as the majority of them were attending the shoot. Had anything been planned to take place in their absence? The armoury – the magazine——?

No, that was absurd. Kishan Prasad had said the hot weather. He would not have troubled to say that if it had not been true, and the real hot weather did not officially start until the end of April or the first week of May. Or had he been playing a double game? That would be like him. And yet—— No, he had meant it. He could afford to hand Alex that piece of information, carelessly secure in the knowledge that no one else would believe it.

Sepoys . . . They had asked for sepoys to help put up the birds. Why, when there were so many villagers and coolies that they could call upon? Was there anything in that? '*. . . this may do well enough for the villages, but it will not serve for the sepoys. For them it must be something that strikes deeper and touches every man. They are already as tinder, but there is as yet no spark. No matter; we will find it.*' Had Kishan Prasad found the spark he had spoken of? What had made him sure enough of himself to give that warning? – for it *had* been a warning . . .

'I must see Packer and Gardener-Smith and Moulson in the morning,' thought Alex, 'though they will none of them believe a word of it. However, they may be prepared to believe that the other man's regiment is rotten, and that may help. Surely they must know that their sepoys are being got at? What the devil is behind this damned duck shoot? There is something. I've felt it in my bones long before I even knew that Kishan Prasad was mixed up in it. Maynard says the police are firm. I wonder. Oh God, why won't they send out more British officers – call off the civil from mucking about with the Army, and throw out some of these decrepit senior officers! . . . William was quite right when he said that at the age at which officers become colonels and majors not one in fifty is able to stand the wear and tear of Indian service. Look at the way the magazines and arsenals have been left unguarded. If there is a rising in Lunjore, who is going to hold the magazine if they are all involved in it? Thank God, we've only got a small one! But there's the arsenal at Suthragunj: guns, arms, powder enough to blow up half of India, and only one Queen's regiment against three of Native Infantry and one of Native Cavalry if it ever came to —— Oh, what's the good of thinking of it! It's not my pigeon . . .' His thoughts left the wider issues and drifted into the familiar pattern of planning for the welfare of his own district.

The clock on the chimney-piece struck two and Alex removed his abstracted gaze from the ceiling and turned his head to look at Winter. He said slowly: 'I didn't mean to keep you up so late. I'm sorry . . . Riding this morning?'

'Yes.'

'Where?'

'Anywhere. To Parry's mound?'

'All right. Six o'clock, then.'

They smiled at each other, their faces dim and peaceful, and Alex finished his drink and stood up. Winter rose with a rustle of silk and walked beside him into the hall where a sleepy servant squatted nodding by the dining-room door.

Alex said curtly: 'Send the Sahib's bearer to him,' and the man scrambled to his feet and scurried away into the darkness as Alex turned to Winter and held out his hand:

'Good night. Or Good morning. And I suppose I should also say, "Thank you for a very pleasant evening." '

'Was it pleasant?'

Alex considered the question, still holding the hand she had put into his. He had a habit of considering a question before he answered it, rather than returning a conventionally empty reply. He said thoughtfully: 'Instructive, at all events. And I suppose tolerably amusing.'

He seemed about to say something else, but he changed his mind and was silent for a moment or two, looking down at Winter and not quite smiling, the line of his mouth unexpectedly tender. Then he lifted the hand he held, and turning it palm upwards, kissed it lightly and deliberately, and folding her fingers upon the kiss, released it.

There had been nothing in the least passionate in the gesture: it might have been either a wordless apology or a comforting caress given to a child. Then he had turned and gone out into the night, and Winter had heard him speak to a servant in the porch, and had waited, standing in the silent hall, until the sound of his footsteps died away in the darkness.

Less than four hours later Alex had been waiting for her on the Residency road, and they had ridden out through the quiet cantonments and across the rifle-range to the open country beyond, Niaz and Yusaf riding behind them.

The rifle-range was hard and level and the horses were fresh, so they did not talk much. But beyond the range the ground became broken, and they slowed to a walk, threading their way between rough tussocks of grass, *kikar* trees and thorn bushes, feathery clumps of pampas and outcrops of rock, to draw rein on the crest of a lonely knoll that was crowned by a banyan tree and the weather-worn slab of an ancient grave whose inscription was still faintly legible: *Here lyes the body of Ezra Parry of the Honourable Company of Merchants of London trading to the East Indies, the son of Thos: Parry and Susanna, who departed this lyfe the eleventh of October 1666.*

The sun rose as they reached it, and they sat looking out across the country beyond, while every blade and spear of grass flashed and glittered with dew-drops and the morning mists lifted in veil after veil so that the land seemed to unroll itself, stretching back and back into limitless distance.

Doves cooed among the branches of the banyan tree and a flight of wild duck whistled overhead, making for the jheel that lay ten miles and more to the northward. Winter turned to watch them as they dwindled into specks against the pale blue of the morning, and saw that there were other lines in the sky, long and wavering or forming neat dark arrow-heads; duck and teal and geese flying in from a night spent on the river or among the ploughed lands.

Alex turned his horse, and following the direction of her gaze said: 'They will be leaving soon. This shoot will mark the end of the season.'

'Where do they go?'

Alex jerked his chin to the north-west. 'Central Asia – Outer Mongolia – Siberia. To breed. They will come back this way when the next cold weather sets in.'

'That is Hazrat Bagh out there, isn't it? What lies on the other side of it?'

'Nothing nearer than Suthragunj. But there are no roads.'

'They are making a road,' said Winter, and pointed with her riding-crop to a thin brown line that wandered away across the plain.

'Yes. That's a temporary track so that the ladies of the garrison can all drive out in comfort to watch the duck shoot. No expense is being spared to impress upon your husband and the garrison how friendly and co-operative our local landowners are, and I should dearly like to know——'

He did not finished the sentence, and Winter said curiously: 'What do you wonder?'

Alex did not answer. Winter had discovered that he seldom answered a question unless he wished to do so; he merely ignored it. He turned now, screwing up his eyes against the dazzle of the newly risen sun, and said, 'Listen to those partridges calling. I must bring a gun out here one evening.'

Winter was silent for a moment or two, listening to the clangour of the partridges and thinking of other things, and presently she said: 'You had one yesterday, didn't you? A pistol, I mean. Do you always carry one?'

'No. Only recently.'

'Have you got one now?' inquired Winter.

Alex nodded, his eyes on a covey of partridges that whirred up from among the low thorn-scrub and skimmed away across the tops of the sun-gilt grass where Niaz sat his fidgeting horse at the foot of the knoll.

Winter said abruptly: 'Will you give it to me?'

Alex turned sharply. 'What?'

'Will you give me a pistol?'

'What for?'

'I should feel – safer,' said Winter lightly, affecting an interest in a pair of weaver-birds who were fluttering anxiously about their dangling nest in a thorn tree below.

Alex surveyed her with narrowed eyes and said drily: 'Thinking of shooting anyone?'

'No,' said Winter soberly. 'Not even myself.'

The Eagle snorted and backed as though he had felt a sudden jerk on the bridle, and there was a momentary silence while Alex brought him under control. When he had done so he inquired shortly if she had ever used firearms before.

Winter shook her head. 'No. But I do not suppose it is very difficult, is it?'

'Try.' Alex dismounted, and pulling the Eagle's reins over his head, whistled to Niaz and turned to help Winter from the saddle. The sunlight glinted on the barrel of the small Tranter revolver as he explained its mechanism.

'Is it loaded?' inquired Winter.

'My dear girl,' said Alex impatiently, 'do you really imagine that I should carry one that wasn't? Here – take it. No, don't aim as low as that. Fire it in the air.'

The report sent Furiante dancing and snorting indignantly, and startled a peacock and his five demure brown wives who had been roosting unseen on the far side of a clump of pampas grass, sending them squawking away.

'Well done,' said Alex approvingly. 'You didn't jump; but you must allow for the recoil.'

'Show me how.'

She handed it back to him and Alex said sharply: 'Don't ever hand anyone a loaded weapon in that way again!'

There was a bright blue jay's feather caught among the thorns of a *kikar* tree less than a dozen yards away, and he jerked up his hand and fired. The feather vanished and Niaz, behind them, gave a grunt of approval.

Winter said: 'Is that really the way to do it? Not taking aim?'

'No,' admitted Alex with a grin. 'That was just showing off. I apologize. I'll do it for you slowly this time. Stand behind my shoulder and look along the barrel.'

He levelled the revolver and fired. 'Think you can do better now?'

'Yes, I think so.'

Winter took the weapon less gingerly, selected a mark and pulled the trigger. Her slim wrist jerked to the kick of the discharge and the bullet went high of the mark. Alex made her fire the remaining rounds and then remarked: 'Not bad. You can keep it.'

'Thank you,' said Winter gravely. She held it out to him and said: 'Will you reload it for me, please.'

Alex shook his head. 'No. Not until I've taught you how to use it. For the present it is safer unloaded. And probably just as effective as a deterrent.'

He saw the hot colour rise in a wave from her throat to the roots of her hair, and had a sudden startled suspicion as to why she had wanted a pistol. Winter thrust the weapon into the pocket of her riding-habit and turned away to where Yusaf held the indignant Furiante, and Alex, following her, helped her to the saddle and stood holding her stirrup-leather and looking up at her under frowning brows. Winter did not return his look. The bright colour was fading from her face and her expression gave nothing away, and after a moment he dropped his hand without speaking.

They cantered back in single file between the high tufts of grass, the rocks and the flat-topped thorn trees, and when they reached the rifle-range broke into a gallop and did not draw rein until they came to the outskirts of the cantonments. Alex had stopped before the gate of the Residency, for his own bungalow lay barely a hundred yards beyond it, and said briefly: 'Bring that pistol with you tomorrow and I'll teach you how to use it. It may come in useful.' He watched her turn in under the shadow of the gateway, and rode back to his own bungalow with an expression on his face that was anything but pleasant.

Winter had proved an apt pupil. She had an excellent eye and no tendency to gasp or flinch at loud noises, and within a week she could be trusted to hit a reasonable mark at ten paces and a larger one at twenty.

Alex had asked no further questions as to why she had wanted a pistol, and he did not know that three days after he had given it to her she had used it, unloaded but with, as he had predicted, a satisfactorily deterrent effect, against his superior officer.

Conway rarely visited his wife's room, but he had done so on the night following the Tuesday party and had found it locked against him. He had created a scene, which availed him nothing. The next night, finding it still locked, he had decided to teach his wife a lesson, and on the following evening he had walked in upon her as she was dressing for dinner. He had been tolerably sober and therefore more dangerous, and had bellowed to Johara, who was sulkily assisting with his wife's toilet, to get out and stay out.

'Now, my dear wife,' said Conway unpleasantly, his pale eyes red-rimmed with rage and brandy, 'you will find that there are other times of day when I can demand your obedience. You can take that dress off again. You won't need it.'

Winter had remained unruffled. She had opened a drawer of her dressing-table and turned towards him with the Tranter revolver in her hand. She had been perfectly polite and quite definite. He had not married her for love, but for money, and he had got what he wanted and must be content with that. She would fulfil her duties as his wife in every way except this, but if he ever attempted to force his attentions upon her again she would shoot him.

'Not to kill you, Conway. I shall stop short of murder. But just to hurt you painfully enough to ensure that such a thing does not occur again. I hope you realize that I mean it?'

If she had screamed or raged Conway might not have believed it. Because she did neither, but faced him with white-lipped calm, he had blustered and shouted and called her unprintable names, but had backed out of her room and had not attempted to enter it again. Later he had made an effort to find the revolver and remove it, but he had been unable to do so, and neither Yasmin or Johara had given him any help in the matter. After that, as he had little enough desire for her, he had left his wife severely alone. The revolver had served its purpose, but Winter continued to take instruction in how to fire it. Partly because it amused her, but largely because it gave her an excuse to see Alex.

Alex had taught her with a grim, unsmiling efficiency, making her load and fire, reload and fire again until her wrist ached. 'You never know when it may come in useful,' was all he would say.

One day he had brought a rifle with him on the morning ride, and had told her to fire it. It was, he said, one of the new issue; the Enfield rifle that was to replace the old-fashioned infantry musket – the famous 'Brown Bess' that had long outlived its usefulness.

He had made her lie down to fire it, holding the heavy weapon as though she had been on the range, and had lain beside her on the dew-wet ground explaining the method and mechanism and exhorting her not to hold it as though it were made of glass. The recoil had bruised her cheek and shoulder badly, and the bullet had gone far wide of the towering ant-hill, over two hundred yards distant, at which she had been aiming. Alex had refused to let her fire it again. He had fired it himself, and Niaz, seeing the distant explosion of dust, sucked in his breath and said '*Wah!*' in an awed voice.

Both Niaz and Yusaf had regarded the rifle with considerable interest. 'Is it true that this thing will fire a ball many times the distance of the old ones?' inquired Niaz. 'How is it done?'

'It has grooved bores,' said Alex.

'They will be difficult to load; especially when they are fouled,' commented Niaz, squinting down the barrel.

Alex shook his head. 'Not so, for the cartridge papers are greased.' He took one out of the pocket of his riding-coat, and biting off the end, rammed it down the barrel to demonstrate, and fired again.

'May I try?' inquired Niaz.

Alex handed over the gun and another cartridge and Niaz bit off the end and spat it out upon the ground. '*Pah*!' he said with a grimace. 'With what is that greased?' He lay down, cuddling the butt against his cheek, sighted carefully and fired. A fluff of dust showed that the bullet had chipped the ant-hill, and Niaz laughed.

'*Hai*! This is indeed a good weapon. Now all that we require is a war so that we may try it on an enemy!'

'May a man buy such a gun for his own use?' inquired Yusaf, his eyes sparkling. 'Beyond the Border such a thing would be worth many times its weight in silver.' Yusaf was by birth a Pathan, and blood-feuds added much to the excitements and hazards of life in his own territory.

Alex did not answer. He was staring down at the small scrap of greased paper that Niaz had spat out upon the ground, and there was an odd, still look on his face. He drew another cartridge from his pocket and stood looking at it, turning it over in his hand and rubbing the ball of his thumb slowly across the greased paper wrapping, until at last Winter said: 'What is it?'

'Hmm?' He turned towards her, but his eyes were blank and unfocused and they looked past her as though she was not there.

Yusaf said: 'Huzoor, may I too try the gun?'

Alex's eyes narrowed suddenly. The abstraction left them and his hand clenched hard over the cartridge that he held. 'Assuredly.' He turned slowly and held out the cartridge, and Winter, watching him as she always watched him when he was not looking at her, was all at once aware that behind that casual gesture his nerves were tense and alert as if he were waiting for something to happen; for some expected – or unexpected? – reaction. She was so sure of it that she turned quickly to look at Yusaf, half-expecting to see him recoil from Alex's outstretched hand; but he took the cartridge without hesitation, and biting off the end of it as Alex and Niaz had done, rammed it home.

Yusaf did not lie down to fire in the manner of a sepoy. He handled the musket as a tribesman, and the ball struck the top of the ant-hill and disintegrated it. '*Shabash*!' applauded Niaz.

Alex handed him a second cartridge without ever taking that quiet, intent gaze from him, and a curious spark leapt to life in his eyes as Yusaf, having bitten off the top of the second cartridge, rubbed his mouth swiftly with the back of his hand.

Yusaf fired again, and missed. 'That is bad shooting,' said Niaz. 'Thou shouldst come and fire on the range. The second shot should be better than the first.'

'In my country,' said Yusaf, 'it is the first shot that counts. If a man fail with his first, he may not live to fire a second. Come over the Border on thy next leave, Niaz Mohammed, and we will show thee!' He handed the rifle to Niaz and once more drew the back of his hand across his mouth.

Alex saw the gesture, and he turned away and stood looking out across the plain with his hands in his pockets, and after a moment or two Winter heard him say something under his breath that sounded like '. . . and furnish the pretence'.

'What is it?' she asked, as she had asked five minutes earlier, troubled by something in his manner that she could not understand.

Alex looked round at her with a faint frown as though he had forgotten that she was there. 'What is what?'

'You said something about furnishing a pretence.'

'Did I? I must have been thinking aloud.'

'What about?' inquired Winter, unaccountably disturbed.

Alex gave a short laugh. 'I was thinking of some lines of Dryden's. "*When churls rebel against their native prince, I arm their hands and furnish the pretence, and housing in the lion's hateful sign, bought senates and deserting troops are mine.*" It seemed remarkably appropriate.'

He turned on his heel, and although it was still early they rode no further that day, but turned back to the cantonments – Alex riding with a speed and recklessness that he had never shown before when he had been out with Winter, and as though he had once again forgotten that she was there.

An hour later he had been ushered into Colonel Gardener-Smith's office where he had been forced to wait for some considerable time.

'Good morning, Captain Randall,' said the Colonel making a belated appearance and eyeing Alex with some uneasiness. 'Sorry to have kept you waiting. Awkward time of the day for me——'

He wondered what Randall had come about this time, and hoped that it was no more alarmist nonsense about an armed rising planned for the coming hot weather. Efficient young man, very. Colonel Gardener-Smith had a profound respect for Captain Randall's knowledge and ability. But all these outstanding young men who were pets of the political – 'Lawrence's Young Men' – had bees in their bonnets. Randall's was the fear of mutiny; not a localized affair, but something on a far larger scale that would involve the whole of the Bengal Army and not merely one, or at the most two, regiments.

Such an idea was of course complete nonsense. Not that Colonel Gardener-Smith imagined that India had seen the last of mutinies and rebellions. That was perhaps too much to hope for. Now and again one was likely to hear of some dissatisfied and mismanaged regiment causing trouble, but as for the entire Army, nonsense! It would need something more than local grievances to do that – a common denominator that would set off a panic among all sepoys everywhere. But misuses and abuses of authority were always localized affairs, and could not disturb the Army as a whole. His own Regiment, for instance, was loyal to the core, and he had recently written a letter to the *Calcutta Times* expressing his indignation on the subject of those men who had so little respect for the known character and fidelity of the British-led sepoy as to attempt to blacken him in the public prints by suggesting that he was ready to turn against his masters. No such thing! The Colonel was almost tempted to agree with Colonel Moulson (a man whom he could not bring himself to like) that men who expressed such views must be considered to be losing their nerve and should resign from the service of the Company.

Not that Randall appeared to be deficient in either physical or moral courage, but that last interview, at which both Colonel Packer of the 105th N.I. and Colonel Moulson of the 2nd Regiment of Lunjore Irregulars had been present, had been distinctly trying. One could not help thinking that Captain Randall was, at the very least, guilty of exaggeration. And at the worst must be suffering from overstrain or sunstroke. He had put his case with a convincing lack of heat, and had kept his temper remarkably well in the face of what the Colonel could not help thinking was unnecessarily insulting behaviour on the part of Moulson; but all the same . . .

Colonel Gardener-Smith frowned and said with more hostility than he had intended: 'Well, what is it now?'

Alex had been standing by the window when he entered, looking out over the sun-baked parade-ground and turning something over and over in his hand. He had replied briefly to the Colonel's greeting and now he walked over to the table and tossed the object down upon it and said without preamble: 'That is one of the cartridges for the new Enfield, sir. Can you tell me what they are greased with?'

The Colonel stared, considerably taken aback both by the question and the tone in which it was uttered. He picked the thing up, examined it and dropped it, and marked his displeasure by seating himself behind his desk and keeping Alex standing. Randall might occupy a reasonably senior civilian post in Lunjore, but in the presence of a commanding officer he was a mere brevet captain and must remember to conduct himself as such.

He said coldly: 'I have no idea. And I hardly think that the composition of cartridge-grease lies within your province.'

Alex said: 'Perhaps not, sir, but it must be within yours. Those cartridge-papers have to be bitten, and if there is any doubt as to the composition of the grease, it is a thing that will affect the caste of every sepoy in the Army. A grievance that will unite men of every regiment – a common denominator.'

The mention of a term that had so recently passed through his own mind checked the Colonel's rising anger, and he cast a startled glance at the innocent-seeming object that Alex had thrown down on his desk. He looked at it for a minute or two in silence and then looked up again at Alex's expressionless face and thought fleetingly that Randall appeared to have aged a lot recently. He said slowly: 'You mean, if it were animal fat——?'

'If it should contain any lard or animal fat,' said Alex harshly, 'no sepoy should be asked to touch it, let alone bite it. The pig is an unclean animal to a Mussulman and the cow a sacred animal to the Hindu, while the fat of any dead creature is an abomination to both. But no one knows that better than you, sir.'

Colonel Gardener-Smith's worried gaze returned to the cartridge and he frowned at it, pulling at his lip. He said uneasily, but without conviction: 'That is a point that cannot have escaped the attention of the responsible authorities.'

'Why not? The method and manufacture of these things was worked out in England, not India, and the men responsible for it are not likely to possess any special knowledge of the caste system that prevails here.'

'I do not believe . . .' began the Colonel unhappily; and then once more a sense of irritation and frustration came over him. Of *course* there was always the danger of trouble breaking out in a conquered country! And despite the fact that he, like most other regimental soldiers of the old school, took little interest in affairs outside his immediate command, he too had lately been aware of a changing atmosphere and a lack of that sympathy and close co-operation between officers and men that had obtained in earlier and more troublous days. He could feel it in the air and sense it in the very faces and voices of his men, and he did not like it. But it was the New Order, that was all. New methods. New men. A new outlook. The lack of large-scale wars and operations to keep the troops occupied, and an inevitable slackening of discipline. Not what it had been in his young days. But the Bengal Army was still the finest fighting machine in the world. He was sure of that. This new feeling of restlessness in the ranks meant nothing; it would pass, and if only men like Randall would stop croaking of disaster life would be a much pleasanter affair. *His* men were all right. They were his own men and he could handle them; they would follow him anywhere – hadn't he proved that? He wished Randall would leave well alone and stop this continual harrying . . . Bees in the bonnet. *Buzz-buzz-buzz* . . .

He banged the table suddenly with his clenched fist and said violently: 'What do you expect me to do about it, anyway? It's none of my business – or yours! I'm not Master General of the Ordnance! These things will shortly be issued to every regiment in India.'

'I know,' said Alex tiredly. He reached out a hand and picked up the cartridge, and his face was suddenly blank: 'But at least it can do no harm to ask for the official analysis of this stuff, and in the meantime it might be possible to manufacture our own wrapping papers here in Lunjore, so that the men can see for themselves what is used.'

'That would be impossible,' said Colonel Gardener-Smith shortly.

'Nothing is impossible now,' said Alex slowly. 'Not even a mutiny of the Bengal Army.'

Colonel Gardener-Smith stood up abruptly and pushed his chair back with unnecessary violence. 'That is a point upon which we are unlikely to agree. If that is all you wished to see me about, I must ask you to excuse me, as I have a great many calls upon my time. I will bear in mind what you have said, and write at once to inquire into the composition of the lubrication which is being used. But you may be quite confident – as I am – that your fears will be proved groundless.'

'Thank you, sir,' said Alex in a colourless voice, and went out into the bright blaze of the mid-morning sunlight.

He rode less with Winter after that and he did not again take out the Enfield rifle.

Winter missed those early morning rides in his company, and did not know that the reason for their curtailment was the fact that it is difficult to arrive home in the early hours of the morning and still wake in time to ride before sunrise.

Alex spent a great many of his nights in unexpected places; listening, watching, and occasionally – very occasionally – asking questions. It was an easier matter by night to pass unnoticed in the crowded bazaars and alleyways of the city, and he had sources of information there whose usefulness would have been severely curtailed had they been observed coming to his house. It was better that he should meet them outside the cantonments and in some other guise, and he had managed in this way to acquire a considerable quantity of curious information.

Niaz too spent much of his time similarly occupied, but he did not frequent the city. Niaz had friends among the sepoys and was often to be found visiting the lines. Much of his information tallied with Alex's, and none of it was in any way reassuring.

'It is said,' reported Niaz, chewing a grass-stem while Alex, lying full length in a small patch of dusty casuarina scrub, sighted carefully along the barrel of a heavy Westley Richards rifle, 'that it is the purpose of the Government to convert all men, by force or fraud, to be Christians. This a jemadar of Colonel Gardener-Smith Sahib's *Pulton* himself told me. But they say that as the *feringhis* are few, to force their faith upon all in Hind would be difficult; therefore they will accomplish it by fraud.'

'With what purpose?' asked Alex, screwing up his eyes against the low sunlight that glowed on the river.

'So that they may use the sepoys to conquer all the world for them. When the sepoys go on ships, and to far countries, they become sick and do not fight so well; but it is not so with the sahib-*log*, and this, it is said, is because of the food that the sahibs eat. Therefore, if the Army were all of one caste – Christians – they too would eat the same food and be as strong, and as slaves of the sahib-*log* would fight their battles in a hundred countries. There is even now a tale that to this end the Company have ground up the bones of pigs and cattle and mixed that dust with the flour and with the grain, so that all who eat of it will thereby lose their caste. And being casteless will have to become Christians, and – hast thou heard this then?'

Alex nodded. 'I have heard. Do they in the lines believe it?'

'Many believe, for they say that as the *feringhis* won many cities and provinces – and Oudh also – by fraud, why should they not do this? It is also well known that children purchased during years of famine have been placed in Christian schools. What do they say in the city?'

'They have refused the last consignment of Government flour,' said Alex. 'It lies still unloaded in the carts. I have sent for grain from Deesa, so that they may grind it for themselves. Are there no elder men among the *pultons* who can see that these are lies made to frighten the foolish into ruin?'

'They are like sheep,' said Niaz scornfully. 'The leading one tumbles down, and all the rest fall over him. And surely the days of the Company are numbered when those who command the *pultons* no longer know the minds of their men.'

Alex said: 'There was a man who wrote from Kabul in the war of '38, saying, "God may help us, for we are not allowed to help ourselves."'

'And if I remember aright,' growled Niaz, 'in that war thy God withheld his help. Ah!' – his voice dropped from an undertone to a whisper – 'that *manji* (boatman) spoke truth. He said that it came daily at this hour——'

A ripple broke the gleaming surface of the river and glittered in a dazzling shiver of light, and presently, inch by inch, an iron-grey shape drifted in towards the flat white sandbank and grounded as gently as a floating log.

'It is a long shot,' murmured Niaz, 'and into the eye of the sun. We should have gone lower.'

Alex said nothing. He waited patiently, as he had waited for the best part of the last two hours, until the creature drew its sixteen feet of ugly armour-plating out of the water and turned slowly and clumsily, lying full-length at an angle to the stream.

The crashing detonation of the shot echoed along the quiet river and sent a score of basking mud-turtles flipping back into the water and a flock of paddy-birds flapping off the far shallows. The big mugger jerked once and was still. Alex fired a second time and rose to his feet, beating the sand off his clothes as Niaz ran forward.

The bullets had ploughed into the beast's neck, severing the spinal cord, and it had moved no more than a foot.

'Do we keep the skin?' inquired Niaz, pacing the length from jaws to tail on the wet sand.

'No. That creature has taken the lives of over twenty men to my knowledge, and I have no wish to be reminded of it. Leave it to the kites. They will make short work of it.' Alex turned on his heel and walked back across the hot white sand with the evening sun stretching his shadow long and blue before him.

The mugger had taken a heavy toll of the city and the village five miles above it for many years, and only the day before it had taken Mothi, the eight-year-old son of Alex's grass-cutter. Mothi had been a friend of Alex's, and Alex had taken an afternoon off to lie up for the killer. But as he walked back across the sand he wondered why he had done so. To kill a dumb beast for revenge was surely a pointless action, since the creature had killed by instinct and for food, and its death would not bring back the child or any of the countless other humans whom it had fattened upon. The mugger too had a right to live, and who was to say that its victims had not been born and appointed to their end?

'We interfere too much,' thought Alex tiredly. 'Am I God that I should arbitrate?' He looked out across the flat lands and the quiet river, dusty gold in the low sunlight, and thought wryly: 'I am thinking like a Hindu.'

A slow-moving shadow sailed across the white sands as a raw-necked vulture flapped clumsily to rest a yard or two beyond the red and grey shape at the water's edge, and waddled cautiously towards it.

'That too was appointed,' said Niaz quietly, 'for none may die before their allotted time.'

Alex turned his head and looked at Niaz reflectively, wondering how it was that this man should be able to follow his thoughts when there were so few of his own kind who could do so. His own kind, as represented by the garrison and officials of Lunjore, were as far out of touch with him at the present time as though they had been occupying separate worlds and speaking different languages. He had been unable to do more than scratch the surface of their determined blindness and complacency, and they were inclined to take anything he said as a reflection upon their own efficiency.

There had been that matter of the Government issue of flour. He had brought up at a general conference earlier that day the question of the refusal of the bazaars to accept or handle it, but the Commissioner had merely observed that if they didn't like it they could go without, and the majority view appeared to be that the whole thing was a storm in a teacup which would blow over if ignored. Colonel Packer was of the opinion that it was merely a trick on the part of the local farmers to force up the price of their own grain, Colonel Gardener-Smith, for his part, was sure that a few words of calm explanation would soon put his own Regiment to rights on the matter, and Colonel Moulson had remarked unpleasantly that he did not know what the garrison was coming to when members of it allowed themselves to be panicked by every petty rumour in the bazaars.

Alex had glanced down at his hands in the shadow of the table and had been surprised to see that they were comparatively steady when he felt physically sick with rage and exasperation. The windy, unconstructive debate had dawdled to an indecisive close, and he had flung out into the sunlight without consulting the Commissioner or anyone else.

Two hours later, still possessed by that fury, he had gone out after the mugger. The long crawl across the hot open sands to the dusty and inadequate shelter of a thin outcrop of grass and casuarina that provided the only possible cover within rifle-shot, and the enforced stillness of the lengthy wait that followed, had done a great deal towards calming him. And looking down at the dead creature he had tasted a brief satisfaction in the knowledge that he had avenged the death of a friendly brown imp of whom he had been fond. But the satisfaction had been only momentary, and Niaz, watching him, had by some alchemy of friendship followed his thought and replied to it.

Yet the thought recurred as they walked back in the evening light along the river bank and across the dun-coloured plain towards the green-belt of trees that hid the cantonments. 'I have taken the life of that creature for the sake of Mothi, who will not care, and to work off my rage, which will return; and yet I could not kill Kishan Prasad, or even leave him to drown, although that might have saved the lives of many more men, women and children than the mugger would have taken in all his life. Why? Because I believe that Kishan Prasad has a soul, and the beast has not? But if that were so, I have taken all that the mugger had, while Kishan Prasad would still have a soul. But then so had that priest at Khanwai, whose life I took. And so has that girl who would have burned herself with her husband on his funeral pyre if I had not heard in time and prevented it. But is she any happier for being forced to keep her life? If she had committed *suttee* she would have gone with her man, and her name would have been honoured in the villages: her very ashes would have been sacred. Now she can never re-marry, but will live out her life as a childless drudge, despised and neglected. We interfere too much. We take too much upon ourselves. By what right? – by what right?'

'And why in the name of the four hundred and ninety-nine thousand angels,' thought Alex impatiently, as he had thought so often before, 'can I not rid myself of this habit of seeing both sides of a thing instead of only my own? Which one *is* my own . . .?'

He had been dining out that evening, the occasion being a Guest Night of the 105th N.I., and had been half-inclined to send his excuses until it had occurred to him that his absence would undoubtedly be regarded as a fit of the sulks, and as it behoved him to try and keep on terms with the senior officers he had donned the tight, high-collared mess-dress of his Regiment, with its elaborate frogging and jingling spurs, and driven over to the barracks which lay two miles distant on the far side of the cantonments.

The Guest Night had been late and noisy, and it was long after midnight before he had been able to leave. The sleepy syce deposited him in the porch and drove the trap round to the stable, and Alex walked stiffly up the verandah steps, tugging at the fastening of the braided collar and throwing it open with a sense of relief.

There was a light burning in his room, and the *chowkidar*, his blanket drawn over his head, lay sleeping soundly on a string cot in the porch and did not stir as Alex passed him. But as the spurs jingled in the silence, two shadows rose to their feet from the far side of the soft square of orange light that the oil-lamp in his bedroom threw across the matting of the verandah. One of them moved forward and lifted the *chik* that hung over the doorway to allow him to pass in.

'Who have you there?' asked Alex in an undertone.

'It is the Kotwal of Jalodri,' said Niaz. 'He would have gone away, saying that he would come again in the morning, but I constrained him to stay, for he has news that concerns thee somewhat.'

'Send him in,' said Alex.

The man slipped in under the lifted *chik* and stood blinking nervously in the yellow lamplight. Alex greeted him gravely and offered an apology for his having been kept so late. 'What is the trouble with thee, Chuman Lal?'

'I do not know,' whispered the Kotwal, his eyes rolling and starting like those of a frightened horse. 'It is a thing I do not understand, and therefore I brought one to thee, and by night. But they told me thou hadst gone out to eat with the *Pulton*, and I would have gone back to my house, but thy servant constrained me to wait. He – he said that this was a matter of which thou hadst knowledge. If that be true, and there be some evil charm in this, it may be that thou canst draw it out.'

The man looked back quickly over his shoulder, but there was only Niaz behind him, and thrusting a trembling hand into the folds of his garments he drew out a chuppatti.

Alex's expression did not alter, but it was a moment or two before he spoke:

'What evil is there in that?'

'I do not know,' whispered the Kotwal, shuddering. 'It was brought to me last night by a runner from Chumri, which is four *koss* to the north. He brought with him five of these things, together with a fragment of goat's flesh, and told me that I must prepare five more, breaking one of these which he had brought and mixing a little of it with the new five. These I must dispatch by a runner to the next village, sending also a portion of goat's flesh, to be given into the hand of the headman of that village, saying to him that he must do likewise and send in turn to the next village. And with it must also be said certain words that the runner from Chumri had spoken to me: "From the North to the South, and from the East to the West." Then did I know that it was a charm.'

Alex stretched out his hand and took the thin flat cake of coarse-ground flour, and stood looking down at it with the smile that he had taught himself to wear when his face was being watched by tense or frightened men for a clue to his thoughts. Niaz, who knew that faint, abstracted smile, grinned in recognition of it, and the Kotwal, looking anxiously from one to the other, visibly relaxed.

'Here it comes,' thought Alex. 'The fiery cross. This is what he spoke of in Malta; "... *as before the Mahratta rising.*" It was cakes and millet that were distributed through the villages then. This is the fruit of that devildom at Khanwai. "... *this may well do enough for the villages, but it will not serve for the sepoys* ..."'

He handed the chuppatti back to the Kotwal and said: 'And what hast thou done?'

'I did as it was told me,' said the Kotwal. 'Five I prepared and had sent by runner. Those that I received, saving only this one, I have wrapped in a cloth and buried deep. Huzoor, what is the meaning of this thing? I am a poor man and ignorant, and I fear that it may bring misfortune upon my house and my fields.'

'There is nothing to fear,' said Alex quietly. 'It is only, as thou knowest, that last year the rains failed and many of the crops failed also. That thing in thy hand is the food of all, and if it be a charm it is one that is sent for good; in propitiation, so that this year the rains will not fail and the crops of every village through which the chuppattis pass may be good.'

'Ah!' said the Kotwal gratefully. 'That is good talk. I will tell the village, for they feared greatly, wondering what evil this might portend. I will strew these things about the fields, and then surely my crops will prosper. And the goat's flesh? What is the meaning of that? Tara Chand, whose fields lie by mine, said that it foretold the fall of the Company's Government, for is it not said that——' The Kotwal stopped abruptly and coughed a small dry cough of embarrassment.

'—— that he who kills an Englishman sacrifices a goat to Kali,' finished Alex grimly. 'So I also have heard. But the goat's flesh that was sent thee is but a sign that the flocks and herds shall increase, for in a good year there is grass and water for many. Tell them this in the villages, that they may know that it is a sign for good.'

The Kotwal salaamed deeply, and stowing the crumbling chuppatti with reverent care among the folds of the blanket he wore wound about him, he backed out of the room, and they heard his feet patter away on the matting of the verandah.

'So it comes at last,' said Niaz softly, echoing Alex's own thought. 'That was quick thinking. Will he believe?'

'Let us hope so. It is the Government who will not!'

'All Governments,' said Niaz cheerfully, 'are as blind as the monkey of Mataram who did not wish to see.' And he squatted down to help Alex remove his boots and to regale him with the gossip of the lines.

Alex wrote a report on the mysterious distribution of the chuppattis the following morning and sent it across in triplicate to the Commissioner, who was pleased to be facetious on the subject that evening.

'Damned if I ain't beginning to think Fred Moulson is right about you, Alex. Bees in the bonnet. Though its more like bats in the belfry, if y' ask me! Yes, yes, yes – I know y' had a wild tale last year about some hocus-pocus at Khanwai. But as I told y' then, it's a mistake to go pokin' about in that side of native life. Probably no connection with this at all. Far more likely that this is only some local big-wig propitiating the gods by a distribution of cakes; it ain't unusual – you should know that! And if you think I'm going to forward such a farrago of nonsense to the Governor, y' *must* be mad! Fiery cross indeed! No such thing! . . . Mahratta rising? What's that got to do with it? . . . Oh, nonsense! I don't believe a word of it – coincidence. That other business happened half a century ago.'

Alex said slowly: 'The people round here say that the numerical values of this year form an anagram: "*Angrez tubbah shood ba hur soorat.*" ' (The British shall be annihilated.)

'Bah!' said the Commissioner. 'A triviality.'

'Or a straw in the wind?' suggested Alex.

'Nonsense! Rubbish! Tell you what, you should relax. You're gettin' a sight too vapourish. Get a woman instead – do you all the good in the world! Comin' on this shoot tomorrow? Good, good. Day in the open will blow some of these cobwebs away.'

Alex, who spent the larger part of his day in the open dealing less with paper-work than with people, and who had recently spent half his nights there as well, forbore to comment. He refused the offer of a drink, and walked back to his bungalow wondering if he had ever really imagined for a moment that the Commissioner would take any other attitude. He supposed not, and he felt slightly ashamed of that report in triplicate, realizing that he had only put it in writing so that he could justify himself later from the files. But of what use to him, or to anyone else, would such justification be? 'I told you so' was a cheap form of satisfaction at the best of times, and he despised himself for having given way to it. He would have to go more often to the villages and talk with the headmen and the elders, and see what he could do towards allaying any panic that the distribution of the chuppattis might have caused.

Did the things also carry any specific message? or were they merely a means of creating an atmosphere of suspicion and alarm, and thus providing a fruitful breeding ground for deeper and more savage hates and fears? Five . . . . Did that mean anything? Alex knew the Indian custom of sending a message by means of a handful of oddments – flowers, leaves, fruits, bangles; things that each carried their own meaning in the language of signs, and were in common use as messages between lovers. In that language any object appearing in duplicate stood for a number indicating time, unless it were accompanied by a pinch of saffron or incense, in which case it stood for place. Five chuppattis . . . The fifth month? That would be May, and Kishan Prasad had said 'in the hot weather'.

An open carriage passed him bearing a Captain and Mrs Hossack, their four children and an ayah. Mrs Hossack was a pleasant woman with a somewhat anxious manner, and the four children, the youngest of whom, wrapped in innumerable shawls, lay in the arms of the ayah, were pale-cheeked, leggy little creatures whose pallid fragility was a cause of endless anxiety to their mama. The two older children, recognizing Alex, waved enthusiastically as they passed, and Mrs Hossack smiled and bowed.

'Thank God I'm not married!' thought Alex with sudden vehemence. 'At least I have not that fear to face.' And thought instantly: 'I must get him to send her to the hills. She will have to go if he orders her. After all, he *is* her husband.'

But he was not thinking of Mrs Hossack.

The duck shoot at Hazrat Bagh was timed to begin soon after eight o'clock in the morning, to allow the guns and the guests to assemble and breakfast to be eaten on a prepared ground half a mile from the jheel.

Previously it had always taken several hours of riding over difficult country to reach the jheel, and no carriage or cart could have attempted the trip. But the temporary road that the hosts had caused to be constructed for the convenience of their guests proved remarkably good, and the carriages that had started from Lunjore as the dawn was breaking reached the rendezvous in ample time for breakfast.

To Winter's surprise many of the guests proved to be strangers to her, and she found on inquiry that they were officers and officials from Suthragunj, a large cantonment town beyond the borders of Lunjore.

As the crow flies Suthragunj lay less than thirty miles from the Lunjore Cantonments, but the main road ran far to the southward for more than double that distance before a branch road to Suthragunj added yet another fifteen miles to the score. There were various small footpaths and side tracks that wandered between the villages, but since none was capable of taking a carriage, the British residents of Suthragunj and Lunjore seldom met. Now, however, two of the hosts having acquaintances among the Suthragunj garrison, the *kutcha* (makeshift) road had been extended beyond the jheel so that they too might attend, and at least a dozen members of the garrison were present.

Also present were three exceedingly vivacious ladies and four seedy-looking gentlemen of assorted European extraction: the members of a so-called 'Italian Opera Company', touring the East, whose successes in Calcutta and Bombay had emboldened them to try their luck in other towns. Having found few that were provided with facilities for the presentation of opera, they had abandoned that in favour of playing farce and singing at private parties, and after recently appearing in Lucknow were now on their way to Delhi. One, at least, came from Goa, and a second from the French settlement of Pondicherry, and none of them was Italian. But the leading lady (lately the soprano), a languishing auburn-haired charmer who rejoiced in the improbable name of Aurora Resina, was noticeably handsome, and the two older ladies, though highly coloured, were by no means unattractive.

They had arrived at the shoot unsuitably attired in the gayest of garments: their crinolines the widest for day wear yet seen in Lunjore, their inadequate hats decorated with innumerable ribbons, frizzes and bobs, and their complexions shielded from the sun by frilled parasols guaranteed to scare any wild bird into the neighbouring province.

The Commissioner, who had made their acquaintance at a small supper-party given by Colonel Moulson on the previous evening, had been particularly taken with the opulent charms of the leading lady, but even his partiality was not proof against the conviction that she would be better kept well out of sight of the duck and discouraged from taking her stand near the jheel. The opera company had been an eleventh-hour addition to the shoot at the request of Colonel Moulson, and though two of the gentlemen had stayed in the tents with the ladies, the other two had borrowed guns and expressed their intention of 'trying a shot'.

'For God's sake,' begged Captain Garrowby of the 93rd, eyeing with lively apprehension the way in which one of these gentlemen held his gun, 'put 'em somewhere where they can do no harm. That feller will fire down the bund, or I'm a Dutchman!'

The other gentleman – a Mr Juan Devant on the playbills, who claimed to be of Franco-Hungarian descent and hailed from Pondicherry – handled his gun with more authority and in a manner that made Alex regard him with sudden interest. 'Cossack-trained,' thought Alex, and murmured inaudibly to Niaz, who could presently have been seen in idle conversation with one of the villagers who had come out the night before to act as beaters and retrieve the fallen duck.

'Mullu will watch him,' reported Niaz rejoining Alex as they took up their allotted stations on the grass-grown, tree-shaded bunds that wandered around and across the jheel.

The jheel was not in the least as Winter had pictured it. She had imagined a mile-long lake fringed with reeds, but the narrow bunds divided the shallow water into numerous squares and triangles, few of which were more than a hundred yards across. *Kikar* trees and high grass grew thickly along the bunds, which were fringed with reeds and red waterweed, and the guns with their loaders and beaters took up their positions at intervals of fifty to a hundred yards apart.

Winter had seated herself on the hard ground with her back to a tree-trunk a few yards from where her husband had taken up his stand, and removed her wide-brimmed hat to let the breeze ruffle her hair. There was a continuous coming and going among the thousands of water-fowl who blackened the open water, and the noise of quacking and quarrelling birds and the ruffle of wings made a soothing and monotonous music. Doves cooed among the *kikar* trees, and the soft, warm breeze whispered through the reeds and the thorny branches, rustling the dry grasses and bringing with it a sweet scent of pollen and water-weeds. The bright morning sunlight chequered the banks with patterns of light and shade, and the sky no longer appeared to weigh down upon the wide earth as it often seemed to do in the heat of the day, but to curve high and cool and cloudless; as full of peace and serenity as the placid water that reflected it.

A little striped-backed Indian squirrel crept within a yard of Winter's foot and stood up, small paws dangling and the pale soft fur of its tiny stomach making a white splotch against the tree shadows. It regarded her with bright curious eyes, and as she did not move and her grey riding-habit was a pleasant and unobtrusive colour against the dusty ground and the rough grey bark of the tree, it dropped down on all fours again and continued to search for seeds. A hoopoe alighted nearby and paraded upon the bund, its crest rising and falling, and a ruffle of wings swept along the reeds as a flight of teal moved further down the jheel.

'I should like to build a house here,' thought Winter, her thoughts moving as slowly as the slow shadows. 'Not a house . . . a hut of dry reeds. And live here all by myself, and sit by the door and watch and listen; like Nissa does . . .' A green-bronze feather drifted down through the warm air and came to rest in her lap, and she thought of all the places to which the birds would soon go, and all the wild, strange forests and lakes and tundras that they would see. Alex had said they would go to Central Asia and Outer Mongolia and Siberia. But next cold weather they would come back again to Hazrat Bagh – flight upon flight of mallard and teal, widgeon, pintail and pink-feet, white-fronted geese and the long-legged storks that built their nests in the isolated *kikar* trees that grew out in the open water of the jheel, and reared their foolish, flapping babies. And in the summer there would still be the doves and the hoopoes, the black and white kingfishers, the green pigeons and the blue jays, and a hundred other birds and beasts who lived their placid lives beside the jheel . . .

The striped squirrel whisked away with an indignant chirr and Winter, turning to see what had alarmed it, saw the loader hand her husband a gun, and was suddenly seized with an absurd desire to cry out to him, begging him not to fire.

The first shot broke the drowsy, murmurous peace of the morning with a shattering impact, and instantly the day was no longer peaceful, but full of noise and violence, for it was followed by a crashing fusillade and a sound that Winter had never heard before – the slow, rushing roar of a hundred thousand birds rising off the water.

The quiet air was ripped by wings and deafening explosions that crashed and echoed and crashed again as the panic-stricken birds whirled towards the bunds, banked and rose, wheeled and broke, to sweep up over the tree-tops and rise higher and higher in dark, lacy patterns against the high blue sky.

An elephant who had been walked out into the widest stretch of water, to keep the birds from coming down out of range, squealed and trumpeted, splashing and backing while its mahout yelled encouragement. And then the birds began to fall; plummeting into the water to float inertly or flutter wounded into the temporary shelter of the reeds.

Winter leapt to her feet and backed against the rough bark of the tree, pressing her hands over her ears to keep out the noise of the shots and the shouting, and staring in shuddering horror at the falling birds and their helpless, dying flurries as they strove to dive and could not do so, or thrashed upon the water with broken wings, striving to evade the men who waded in to retrieve them, but whose caste forbade them to put a dying creature out of its misery.

She shut her eyes, trying to shut out the sight; but she could not shut out the sounds. And then something crashed through the thin branches and struck against her, and she opened her eyes to see a huge goose struggling on the ground at her feet. It dragged itself away, one wing trailing and its beak wide as though it gasped from fear or for air.

'Good shot, that,' commented Conway lumbering up. 'Better wring its neck, or it'll get away. Surprising how tough these birds are——'

He stooped, but Winter was before him. She caught the great bird in her arms, her face white with all the accumulated pain and horror and panic of the last months, and backed away from him, her mouth open in a soundless scream.

'Here, give it to me,' said Conway. 'Can't kill it yourself. You'll find it takes a deal of doing.'

'Don't touch it!' The words were almost a scream. 'It's only hurt. It isn't going to die. You shan't kill it!'

Conway stared, his pale eyes bulging with anger. 'Don't be a fool! Put it down at once, d'you hear me?'

He lurched towards her and Winter evaded him with a frantic leap, and turning, fled down the bund clutching the wounded bird to her breast, its warm neck across her shoulder and one huge helpless wing almost brushing the ground as she ran.

The bund bent at a right angle less than fifty yards from where her husband had taken up his position, and high grass closed in about it, reaching up to the lower branches of the thorn trees. Winter ran blindly, in the grip of a breathless, reasonless, gasping panic, and she did not see Alex until she had run into him.

Captain Randall had been given a less exposed position, just beyond the turn of the bund, but he had not been shooting well that morning. He had been thinking of other things. Seeing at last and very clearly the reason for this elaborate shooting party, and wondering why it had not occurred to him before, when it was so simple and so entirely obvious. Was it this climate? Did the hot suns that sapped one's strength also slow down one's thinking? Well, it was too late now. He should have stopped it before. How? . . . Barton would never have let him. But perhaps – who knew? – it would cut both ways. So simple, and yet he had not seen it!

'*Mark*!' yelled an unseen man – Captain Garrowby of the 93rd – from fifty yards further down the tree-shaded bund. A lone goose swished overhead and Alex fired and saw the bird fall wounded somewhere along the further arm of the bund. Niaz gave a grunt of disapproval and Alex threw the gun across to him and said: 'Damn the birds!' He turned away and walked towards the turn of the bund, feeling in his pockets for a cigarette, and Winter brushed through the grass and stumbled against him.

Alex caught her by the shoulders and held them in a hard grasp, staring down into the wide, panic-stricken eyes. For a moment she had tried to wrench herself free, and then she had seen who it was who held her.

'*Alex*! – Alex, don't let him kill it! Don't let him——' She thrust the warm heavy body at him, and as she did so the soft, feathered neck slid down from her shoulder and hung limp.

'It's dead, dear,' said Alex quietly, and took it from her.

'No! No, it can't be dead. It was only wounded.' Her dress was splotched and spattered with bright scarlet drops, and a wide patch of blood stained the breast of the grey habit as though it were she who had been shot and not the bird; and at the sight of it a savage wave of fear lashed at Alex as though something had struck him over the heart.

He let the bird slip to the grass, and Winter caught at his arm as though she would have snatched it from him. And then quite suddenly she dropped her head against him and wept.

Alex stood very still, holding her: feeling the shuddering of the slim warm body under his hands. Her hair smelt faintly of lavender as it had on the walls of Delhi, and he held her quite gently because he wanted so much to hold her hard against him . . . because he wanted so much to thrust her away from him! The sound of her helpless, broken sobbing tore at his heart, and his face above her bent head was twisted with pain and scored with harsh lines that had not been there before. 'Oh God,' thought Alex, 'not this! Not now. I can't stand it.' The sun was hot on his shoulders and the warm silence was drowsy with the hum of bees among the *kikar* blossoms and sweet with the scent of lavender, and the crackle of shots seemed to come from very far off as though he were hearing them from the other end of a long tunnel. At last the choking, shuddering sobs quietened and ceased, and he put her gently away from him.

She made no attempt to turn away, but stood facing him, her long lashes sticking wetly together and her face streaked with tears, searching in the pocket of her habit for a handkerchief. It was a flimsy enough affair, and stained too with the blood that had run down the great wing. Alex produced his own and handed it over. His nostrils were pinched and there was a white shade about his mouth, but he spoke quite pleasantly: 'Try this one,' he advised. 'It's larger and a good deal cleaner.'

He watched her with a wrenching tenderness as she dried her eyes and blew her small nose with a complete lack of self-consciousness, and wondered how many women would have been sufficiently oblivious of their own looks as to face his direct gaze instead of turning away to repair the ravages of tear-stains and dishevelled hair.

Winter folded his handkerchief into a careful square and drew a deep breath. 'I'm sorry,' she apologized, her voice under control once more. 'I don't know why I should have behaved so stupidly.'

She considered the matter gravely, looking down at the dead bird that lay beside them on the grass, its strong wings and soft breast dabbled with bright blood, and said slowly: 'I think it was because it was such a lovely day, and when the shooting began that seemed to make it worse . . . because it had been so beautiful before, and so peaceful. I couldn't bear it being spoilt. And then the goose came down on top of me, and it was hurt. Conway wounded it – he wanted to kill it, and——'

'I wounded it,' said Alex.

'You?' she looked up at him, startled, frowning a little.

'Yes, I saw it fall and I was coming to get it.'

'Oh.' She was silent for a moment or two, and Alex watching her, said gently: 'Does that make a difference?'

Her gaze came back to him and she said thoughtfully: 'Yes. But I don't know why it should.'

'Better? – or worse?'

She did not answer him and Alex lifted a hand that was not quite steady and brushed his fingers lightly across her forehead: 'Don't frown, dear. It can't matter as much as all that. Give me that handkerchief.'

She held it out to him and he took it and pushed through the grass and reeds to the water's edge, and returning with it wet and dripping, washed the worst of the stains from her habit, remarking that it would dry very quickly in the sun: 'And now come and try a shot at a duck yourself. You've never tried to fire a sporting-gun.'

Winter shuddered and jerked back, her face blank with hurt, and Alex met the look squarely. 'You think that's callous and brutal of me, don't you? – after what has just happened. But it's sense, you know. Like getting back into the saddle after you have been badly thrown, when you're learning to ride. Didn't they ever make you do that? Besides, you'll find that hitting a moving target isn't as easy as you think. It takes a lot of skill, and that makes a difference too.'

Winter said, shuddering: 'I don't want to kill anything – *anything*! And if I hit a bird I might only wound it, and not kill it outright. Like – like that goose.'

Alex said with deliberate harshness: 'What do you suppose happens to any wild creature when it gets old? Nine times out of ten it dies a slow and very painful death. And it's the same with most of the animals in this country. I passed a buffalo yesterday that had fallen into a nullah and broken two of its legs. The crows had already picked out its eyes and the pariah dogs were tearing at it. It was near the village track and twenty people an hour passed it, but though it was still alive not one of them would have dreamt of killing it.'

Winter swallowed convulsively. 'Did you kill it?'

'I did. And got lectured by the local Brahmin for doing so. He's a friend of mine, but bigoted. Shooting duck isn't really slaughter, whatever you may think. For one thing, it's food, and none of it will be wasted. And it takes skill. You may not like the idea of trying it yourself, but it will take the bad taste out of your mouth to see it in a different light. An antidote to sentimentality.'

His voice was suddenly mocking and devoid of pity or sympathy, and its hardness had a tonic effect upon Winter. She had needed that hardness. She came reluctantly but she came. Alex handed her a shotgun and gave a few brief directions.

'You won't find it the same as firing at a stationary object. Swing with your mark and allow for its speed. Those are pintail coming in from your left. Now——!' Winter fired, and the three birds that had been flying towards her jinked and rose and were gone. 'Not far enough ahead. Try again.'

He made her fire again and again, and after the first three or four attempts the panic and sick distaste that had begun to rise again to her throat died down, and she thought only of the science and theory of the shot, concentrating tensely on the flashing marks, so that when, fifteen minutes later, Alex took the gun from her and demonstrated, bringing down two birds within a yard of each other, interest had replaced horror.

'Well?' inquired Alex looking down at her where she sat among the freckled shadows. 'Feeling better about it now?'

Winter nodded. 'Yes. But I still don't want to shoot anything myself.'

'There's no reason why you should. But a sense of proportion is a useful thing to cultivate.' He laid the shotgun away and sat down on the warm grass beside her. 'I've suffered from the same kind of mental indigestion myself. I killed something the other day – not for food nor even for the sport of trying out my skill on a difficult target, but for revenge and because I was in a damnably bad temper. I wasn't sorry for it, but it seemed pointless, and for some reason or other I lost a lot of sleep over it – at least ten minutes!'

'A man?' asked Winter with a catch in her voice.

Alex gave a short laugh. 'No. That is where the inconsistency comes in. I killed a man not so long ago for precisely the same reasons; but it did not seem in the least pointless, and neither did I lose any sleep over it. Don't let yourself get hurt over something like this' – he jerked his chin in the general direction of the jheel. 'Put it in its proper place. I dislike these large scale *battues* myself. I prefer to do my shooting on my own or with one or two people at most, instead of indulging in this type of mass slaughter.'

'Then why did you come? – if you knew what it would be like?'

'Curiosity. I wanted to see if I could find out why Kishan Prasad and his friends had arranged this elaborate shoot.'

'And have you found out?'

'Yes.'

Alex did not add anything to the affirmative, but looked out across the stretch of sunlit water that lay beyond a narrow belt of grass and reeds that fringed the bund, his eyes narrowed against the sun-glare. There were fewer birds moving now, for many had risen far out of range and were making for the quieter reaches of the river or the jheels within the borders of Oudh, and those that remained were too wild to offer a reasonable mark. The firing had died down to no more than an occasional shot, and a warm, sleepy silence returned to the morning, broken only by the soft monotonous cooing of the imperturbable doves.

Winter pulled a grass-stem and bit it thoughtfully, watching Alex's brown profile against the sharp criss-cross lines of sunlight that fell between the branches of the *kikar* trees and the tall spears of dry grass. His silence contained no quality of withdrawal, and presently she said: 'Why do you think that they gave this duck shoot?'

'Hmm?' said Alex absently. Winter repeated the question.

'It isn't a duck shoot,' said Alex, his eyes still on the glittering expanse of water. 'That was merely a means to an end – and also, possibly, a rehearsal.'

'A rehearsal? I don't understand. What are they rehearsing for?'

'They aren't. We are very kindly doing it for them.'

He stretched out at full length and turned, lying on the warm ground and facing her. 'It was quite simple really. Lunjore lies across one of the main roadways into Oudh, and that road crosses an iron bridge ten miles to the south. If there should be a rising in the Punjab, or Delhi way, we could hold that bridge; or if the worst came to the worst, blow it up and not only isolate ourselves from rebel troops, but prevent them from using this route into Oudh, which is at the moment a hot-bed of disaffection. There is an arsenal at Suthragunj. A very large one which is, in my opinion, inadequately protected against the possibility of a large-scale rising. Some of our local talukdars have not missed that point, and under cover of a lavish and well-organized entertainment for the garrisons and officials of both districts they have constructed a very adequate road that avoids the bridge and brings Suthragunj within roughly twenty miles of us. We in Lunjore have very kindly tested it for them, both from the point of surface and timing, by driving a variety of carriages along it, while the officers from Suthragunj have done the same from the opposite direction. And where a carriage can go, guns and ammunition-wagons can follow.'

Alex rolled over on his back with his hands linked beneath his head and watched an industrious procession of red ants hurrying along the underside of a branch above him, until presently Winter said a little uncertainly: 'Are you – do you really think that there is going to be trouble?'

She had half-expected that he would not reply, because Alex, when he chose to answer a question, did not lie, and she knew that the majority of men, when faced with such a query from a woman, would resort to denial or some soothing generality; but Alex said bluntly: 'Not trouble. A rising. Yes, I do. I've thought so for about five years. We've been asking for it. Napier warned us that there would be one sooner or later if certain reforms were not instituted, but no one paid any attention to him. We cherish a theory that to listen to warnings, or act upon them, is a sign of panic and shows loss of confidence, and we would rather lose our lives any day than be accused of either. It is an exasperating trait. The kind that curls in on itself and ends by eating its own tail, because precautions that are not taken in time of peace cannot be taken when a crisis is imminent, for the simple reason that to take them then creates panic and loss of confidence at a time when one can afford to do neither.'

'What will happen?' asked Winter.

Alex was silent for a moment or two, and when he spoke his voice held a savage bitterness that startled her:

'We shall see the ruin, in one day or in twenty days, of what might have been the finest army in the world. And though we shall build it up again, it will never be quite the same. We shall turn half that army against its fellows, and play off Sikh against Mussulman and Mussulman against Hindu, and Gurkhas against both. There will be atrocities on both sides – all sides. The East drops straight into barbarism when it is frightened or enraged, and we shall follow its example and call it revenge – as I myself have done! There will be murders and massacres, because these people have no conception of the ultimate strength that we can bring out of Europe against them, and they will imagine that they can stamp us out——' Once again Alex was talking more to himself than to Winter – talking angrily and despairingly:

'Even men like Kishan Prasad have no idea what they are challenging. Kishan Prasad watched the shambles at Sebastopol when the Russians threw us back and we failed to take the Redan. He saw the mess and the muddle and the raging incompetence, and missed the fact that, despite it, sheer physical courage and guts and endurance triumphed over it. He and men like him do not realize that even if they murder every white man, woman and child in the whole of India, England, and not 'John Company', will go on sending out troops until she has smashed all opposition. And the reprisals that will follow will leave a legacy of hatred that will be handed down to future generations, from father to son and from mother to daughter. We shall forget – but they will not!'

A breath of breeze whispered across the jheel, ruffling the water and rustling through the reeds and the harsh grasses, and bringing with it a sharp reek of black powder to mingle with the faint scent of the yellow, mimosa-like blossoms of the *kikar* trees and the dusty incense of the dried grass. There was another burst of firing from away to the left and the voice of Captain Garrowby arose once more upon the quiet air: '*Mark*!'

A dozen teal, bunched together, swished overhead almost brushing the tree-tops with their wings, and Alex came reluctantly to his feet. 'Energetic beggar——' He appeared to refer to Captain Garrowby. 'Perhaps I had better do something towards upholding the honour of the visiting team.' He glanced down at Winter and said: 'Your habit seems to have dried. Hadn't you better be getting back?'

Winter ignored the remark. 'Is that why you wanted me to go to the hills? – and taught me to shoot?' she inquired, leaping womanlike from the general to the personal.

'Yes,' said Alex briefly and without qualifying the statement.

Winter stood up and shook out the grey folds of her skirt. She said quite lightly, 'I will think about it,' and was turning away when she remembered the goose. She hesitated for a moment and then said a little diffidently: 'The – that goose. Conway thought that he had shot it. Can I take it back? Then perhaps he will not be so——'

She stopped, flushing painfully, and bit her lip; suddenly ashamed of her desire to placate her husband in this unworthy manner. But Conway would be angry enough as it was, and she could not bear another scene just now.

Alex was watching a flight of mallard who were approaching from the open water too high to allow them to pass within range. He said: 'Of course,' without turning his head.

He did not look round as she went away, but he heard the tall grass rustle behind her, and he stood quite still, listening, until he could hear it no longer; his face drawn and bleak in the harsh sunlight.

'Why,' demanded Alex, asking the despairing question that has been asked so often of heaven, 'does this have to happen to me?'

An hour and a half later a horn blew, conjuring odd echoes from the water and the wandering, intersecting lines of the bunds. Beaters and *shikaris* collected the dead birds, and the guns walked back to the tents where refreshments awaited them. During the afternoon they had walked up partridge and sand grouse over the open country to the west of the jheel, leaving the duck to settle again, and only moved back to the bunds for the evening flighting.

Alex had had speech with both Kishan Prasad and the Brigadier in command at Suthragunj that afternoon. He had walked alone with Kishan Prasad to the top of a low, stony ridge that overlooked the distant jheel, and spoken bluntly and to the point, telling Kishan Prasad what he had told Winter earlier that day – that British regiments would be sent out to take over the country if the Company fell.

'If the Company fall, it is enough,' said Kishan Prasad. 'If I can but live to see that, I will die content.'

'But we shall still hold India,' said Alex. 'If it takes a year – five years, ten, twenty! – we shall go on fighting you, if only for the sake of one thing – the women. If there is a rising there will be women of ours, and children too – many of them – who will be murdered by your friends without mercy. Who should know that better than you, who were at Khanwai? You will not be able to prevent it, and it is the one thing that my countrymen will not forgive. All else perhaps, but not that. Their deaths will arouse a hatred and a rage that will seek only revenge and not rest until it is obtained. And that revenge will fall on the heads of the innocent as well as the guilty, because men are blinded by such rage. I have seen troops run amuck, and it is not pleasant. In the last it will be your own people who will suffer most, and all to no purpose; for you will not be rid of us.'

He read the look on Kishan Prasad's face and said more quietly: 'You do not believe that, because of what you saw in the Crimea. But it is true. We shall send out more and more British regiments.'

'You will find it too costly,' said Kishan Prasad. 'Your Queen and your Queen's Ministers will say, "Let be. It is not worth it."'

'Never. You do not understand. We are a rising power, and with every day we become richer and more powerful, and over-proud to stomach such an affront. When we have had our day the time may come when we will think as you have said, and turn from a fight. But not now. Not yet.'

'Then I will wait for that day,' said Kishan Prasad softly. 'And if I am dead, then my son will be ready – or if it be not him, then his son's son – or the son of that son! Would you yourself not do likewise?'

Alex did not answer and Kishan Prasad repeated the question in Hindustani, using the familiar title: 'Tell me, Sahib, wouldst thou not do likewise wert thou of my blood and this thine own land?'

Alex stared at him, his eyes hot with a helpless anger that was as much against himself as Kishan Prasad, and he said violently and as though the words were wrenched from him: '*Yes* – God damn you!' and turned on his heel and walked away without once looking back to where Kishan Prasad followed more slowly behind him.

The Brigadier had been no more amenable. He was seventy-four, white-haired and exceedingly deaf, and having served in India for more than half a century, was convinced that no one had a better knowledge of the country and its inhabitants than himself.

He had listened, with one hand cupped about his ear, to Alex's views on the subject of the newly made *kutcha* road between Lunjore and Suthragunj, and had remarked that in his opinion it was a demned useful thing. If the garrison in Lunjore ever had any trouble with their men (he was aware that some of the new lot of colonels were shockin'ly incompetent and did not know how to handle natives – very different in his day; he, b'gad, had known every one of his men by name!) then the regiments in Suthragunj, loyal to a man, could now be sent over at a moment's notice to restore order. Not that there was the slightest danger of any disturbance. He himself had an ear to the ground and he would be the first to get wind of any trouble brewing. Captain Randall need have no anxiety.

Alex turned on his heel and left him without wasting further words.

31

The carriages and the ladies had left Hazrat Bagh early so as to get home before dark, but the guns had remained to shoot once more on the jheel, and had ridden back three hours later by the light of a half-moon to attend a large party given by the Commissioner to round off the day's festivities.

The gathering at the Residency had consisted of the larger part of those who had been at Hazrat Bagh, and had included the members of the self-styled Italian Opera Company, who had sung excerpts from a number of light operas and followed them by a selection of popular songs.

Alex had attended the party for reasons not unconnected with the gentleman who called himself Mr Juan Devant. He had arrived in a singularly unpleasant frame of mind, and for perhaps the first time in his life had deliberately set himself to drink too much.

Wine and spirits always circulated freely at the Commissioner's parties, even in mixed company, and although the heavy drinking of the Regency days had become a thing of the past, it remained a hard-drinking age in which a man who could not account for a bottle and more of port at a sitting was considered to be a poor specimen. But though the Commissioner's port, wine and brandy were of the best obtainable, they had little effect upon Alex beyond increasing his ill-temper, which the sight of Mr Barton openly making amorous advances to the auburn-haired ornament of the Opera Company, in complete disregard of his wife's presence, did nothing to mitigate.

It was verging on midnight when Mr Juan Devant's not unpleasing baritone embarked upon a familiar ballad:

'Believe me if all those endearing young charms,
Which I gaze on so fondly today,
Were to change by tomorrow and fleet in my arms . . .'

The music and a memory hit at Alex with an unexpected, wrenching pain, and some control in him seemed to snap, as though a wire drawn taut had parted. He put down his glass, walked across the room and calmly removed Signorina Aurora Resina from the Commissioner's orbit. He had some experience of such women, and he had drunk enough to make him reckless for once of arousing the Commissioner's hostility. It suddenly did not seem to matter any longer if he did so or not. And besides, there was Winter, who should not be made to endure the insult of her husband's behaviour towards this ogling actress. But he did not want to think of Winter . . .

Alex could be charming enough when he chose, and he chose now. He had blandly ignored the glowering indignation of his chief, the hostility of Colonel Moulson and the momentary shock he had seen on Winter's face, and had taken the lady away – ostensibly to view the garden by moonlight. They had not returned, though the majority of the guests, despite a long and tiring day spent in the open, had stayed until well after two o'clock.

The Commissioner had been crudely outspoken on the subject of Captain Randall's behaviour when the guests had departed, and had ended by observing that Lou Cottar had been right about the man, by God! – he was a dark horse, and they were always the worst with women: trust a woman like Lou to know! Lou had always said that Randall was no cold fish, and he'd certainly taken home a hot enough piece to keep him warm tonight. It was only he, Conway Barton, who had a cursed cold fish on his hands.

The Commissioner had returned to the deserted drawing-room to drink more brandy, and Winter had gone to her room and had sat for a long time on the edge of her bed, staring before her and thinking of Alex. Alex with his hard, nervous fingers caressing another woman's hair; Alex's slow kisses on another woman's mouth, and his dark head lying pillowed on that opulent powdered breast or buried in the suspicious brightness of those auburn curls.

She had cried only that morning for a dead bird. No, surely not for a dead bird? – for the wanton destruction of something beautiful. Was it for the beautiful day, or the strong, beautiful bird? or for her illusions and all that had happened to them? She did not know. But she could not cry now because Alex could be like Carlyon and Colonel Moulson, and Edmund Rathley who had kissed her so long ago at Ware, and – and Conway.

'I must go away,' thought Winter, as she had thought on that day when she had first discovered that she loved Alex. 'I will go home to the Gulab Mahal. If only I can get back there I shall be safe again – safe from everything!' And she thought, as she had thought so often, of the rose-pink walls and the brilliant flowers, and the brightly coloured birds who had been so tame that they had allowed her to touch them, and of old Aziza Begum's comfortable, sandalwood-scented lap where she had sat in the warm, star-twinkled dusk to listen to tales of Gods and Heroes.

'I will go back,' thought Winter, staring dry-eyed into the shadows of her room. 'If I can get back to the beginning again – the beginning of all that I remember – I can start again. If only I can get back I can start again . . .'

She had fallen asleep at last, fully clothed, and she had not ridden that day, either in the morning or the evening, because she had been afraid of seeing Alex.

She had not seen him again for some considerable time. Alex had taken care of that. The night he had spent in the arms of the Signorina had resolved nothing and solved no problems. It had not even made him forget, as he held her, the feel of Winter's slim body in his arms. In the cold grey light of the early morning the auburn-haired Aurora had looked blowsy and coarse – the lip rouge with which she had deepened the red of her pouting mouth smeared and ugly, and the black from her lashes smudging her cheeks. She smelt faintly of perspiration and rice powder and overpoweringly of patchouli, and Alex had looked at her with impatience and pity and a twinge of disgust, and thought of Winter sobbing jerkily against his shoulder for the death of a wild bird. And had found that his anger had not evaporated with the morning but was still a hard, hot stone in his breast.

The complexity of his emotions exasperated him, and he had woken the woman and driven her back in the dawn light to the dâk-bungalow where the troupe were lodging, from where she and they had left later that morning for Delhi: Alex having sent word ahead of them to Mr Simon Fraser, and arranged for an unobtrusive individual to be attached to their seedy retinue of servants in a minor capacity – the previous holder of the office having been unaccountably taken ill and being unable to proceed further.

'Am I seeing danger in every shadow?' thought Alex. 'That man *can* sing. But so can a good many Russians. Theatrical companies do not usually get further than Calcutta or Madras, and these people have been to Lucknow. Oh well – at least we shall know now who he meets on the road and who he talks to, and Fraser can deal with it in Delhi.'

Alex attended no more parties at the Residency, and he had not ridden again with Winter. His bungalow had not seen him for days at a time, for he spent more and more of his time in the outlying villages of the district, picking up what information he could between and in the course of his official duties, and doing what lay in his power to allay the uneasiness that he could see and sense in and behind every cautiously worded greeting or inquiry.

The villagers would bring him rumours – tales such as the story of the bone-dust that was reported to have been mixed with the Government flour – and he would deny them, explaining and exhorting, and his listeners would agree. Yes, yes, he was right. The Huzoor was right. It was only a tale, and untrue. A tale spread by evil men to alarm the simple . . . But he knew that they did not eat the flour, and that it lay rotting in the Government-stamped sacks in warehouses and carts.

He could not reach them. Their processes of thought were not of the West. They accepted an order if it were backed by force, but that did not mean that it was of itself acceptable. They respected Alex, and many of them liked him; but he was a *feringhi* – a foreigner. Impassable gulfs gaped between them, across which they looked at each other helplessly; seeing the same things by entirely different lights and weighing them by different standards so that they appeared as dissimilar as rocks and rivers. 'Is there a meeting-point?' thought Alex. 'Is there any real neutral ground?' But there was Niaz, who was as much his friend as William. How did one explain his strong kinship for this man of his own age who could turn from his own race to serve one of alien blood?

He had asked Niaz that question one evening when they were lying up in a patch of high grass waiting for a slow-moving herd of blackbuck to pass within range (Alex was in camp and they were shooting for the pot), and Niaz had replied lightly: 'I have eaten the Company's salt.'

'That is no answer. Many have done so, but the bread that is eaten is soon forgotten.'

Niaz shrugged. 'We are brothers, thou and I. Who can say why? Were I a dog of a Hindu I would say that perchance in some other life we were indeed kin, for I have met none other among thy race whose mind I knew – or cared to know. Yet I know thine.'

'And if it come to bloodshed, as it may come, wouldst thou stay with me against thine own kin?'

'*Beshak*!' The answer was prompt and leisurely. 'I owe thee my life – and thine is forfeit to me. That alone were a rope that is hard to cut. Quiet now! They move this way . . .'

It was Niaz who had brought him a copy of a pamphlet that was being circulated in the city calling on all Mohammedans to prepare for a *Jehad* – a Holy War. 'This thing is in the hands of all Mussulmans,' said Niaz, 'and in the mosques also they preach a *Jehad*. I have heard too that it has been promised that Ghazi-ud-din Bahadur Shah, the King of Delhi, shall be restored to his own, so that once more the Mogul will rule in Hind.'

'And what say the Hindus who hear such talk?' asked Alex.

'They do not speak against it. And that is a strange thing, for they would not wish to see us rule them as once we did. Yet they say that they will accept the Mogul because he is of Hind, and no foreigner. Sikunder Dulkhan (Alexander the Great)' – Niaz looked at Alex with a half-smile – 'I will fight at thy side and take thy orders when the bloodshed begins – and *I* do not say "if it begin" – but I too would like to see a Mussulman rule once more in Delhi; Sunni though he be, while we of my family be Shiahs.'

Alex said: 'Art thou so sure then that it will come to an uprising?'

'As sure as thou art! And were it not for thee I myself might well cry *Deen*! *Deen*! for the Faith.'

Alex shivered involuntarily. He had heard that fanatical war-cry in his time and had seen the green flags wave and the hot-eyed hordes of the Faithful sweep yelling up to and onto and over the guns, and he had not forgotten. He said now: 'Who is behind this thing that comes? Is it the Hindus or the Mussulmans? Or is it the work of foreigners – Russians and Persians?'

Niaz laughed and made a gesture of negation with his hand. 'There are many Russian spies; and Persian too. They, the Russ-*log*, plot with both, as is their custom – but always against thy people! And in despite of the police and the spies of the Company they still go about the land, even to the walls of Delhi, bringing money and arms and many promises, and their sayings and promises are printed openly in the Hindu press. But their words are of little account: they help to boil the pot, that is all. Nay; this that will come is the Rising of the Moon,' said Niaz with oriental imagery. 'We who were once great in the land have lost almost all that we had of power, and revolt may serve us where peace will not. This will be a *Jehad*. And I think it comes close. Dost thou remember the night of the earthquake at Hoti Mardan?'

Alex nodded. He knew only too well what Niaz meant, for the same thought had occurred to him more than once of late. Over seven years had passed since the night that Niaz had referred to, but he had never forgotten the weird, waiting hush that had preceded that violent convulsion of the earth, or the way in which the dogs and the horses had known what was coming and had striven with uneasy whining, shivering, sweating apprehension to give a warning that had not been heeded. Alex was aware again of that same uncanny, ominous feeling of expectant stillness. But it was a stillness that was not to last long, and the first warning mutter came from faraway Bengal.

The thing that Alex had visualized in the moment following Niaz's casual comment on the greased cartridge paper – the fire that unthinking officialdom had put into the hands of Kishan Prasad and his like – had caught the fuel that had been prepared. And the fuel was dry and ready.

On that same January morning that had seen the garrison of Lunjore ride gaily out to shoot duck at Hazrat Bagh, a man of low caste, a lascar who worked in the ammunition factory at Dum Dum near Calcutta, had stopped a high-caste sepoy during the heat of the day and begged a drink from his *lotah* – the brass water-pot carried by every caste Hindu and religiously preserved from defilement. The sepoy had stared less in anger than astonishment at the outrageous request. 'How can that be, fool? I am a Brahmin, and my caste forbids it.'

'Caste? What is caste?' grinned the lascar. 'The cartridges that we prepare here are defiled with the fat of hogs and cattle, and soon ye will be as one – casteless together – when the new guns are given out to the *pultons* and ye bite the cartridges daily.'

'What is that?' said the sepoy thickly. 'Tell again!'

The lascar had done so, with embellishments, and the sepoy had not waited to hear to the end, but had run to his comrades in the lines. Here was proof at last of the duplicity of the *feringhis*! The hated policies of Annexation and Lapse, the suppression of *suttee*, the seizure of land, the deposing of kings and the curtailment of pay and power and privilege were as nothing to this; for this struck at the deepest beliefs of men, in that it destroyed their souls.

Hindu and Mohammedan together recoiled in horror from sacrilege and defilement. Panic spread through the lines, and from there, with the incredible swiftness that fear lends to evil tidings, it swept out across India, its progress sped and fanned by those who had been ready and waiting for such an opportunity, and who made the best use of this brand that had been given into their hands.

A hundred men – a hundred thousand – picked up the fearful whisper and passed it on: 'It is an order from *Belait*! from the Queen and her Council, that by means of the cartridges all sepoys, both Mussulman and Hindu, be defiled – as all men in the towns and cities are defiled by the eating of bone-dust in their flour – so that being made casteless they shall do the will of the sahib-*log* as slaves for ever! We are betrayed by the *feringhis* who have stolen our country and now wish to steal our souls!'

It was then that the nocturnal fires started. Suddenly, in the night, the thatch of an officer's bungalow would catch fire, set alight, more often than not, by a blazing arrow shot by some unseen hand. The telegraph station of the big cantonment of Barrackpore burned to the ground, and night after night, despite guards and sentries, flames would glow bright in the darkness, spreading up northward from Calcutta and Barrackpore . . .

There were midnight meetings of men with muffled faces who kept to the shadows of walls and where no guards challenged them. There were letters (for the sepoy had learned to use the post in the days before the privilege of free postage to the Army had been abolished). Letters that went out by every dâk, calling upon the soldiery to resist the attempts to defile them. The news that the 19th Regiment of Native Infantry at Berhampur, a hundred miles to the north of Calcutta, had broken out into mutiny spread upwards through India and fanned the panic.

But that mutiny which had flared up so suddenly died out, and without violence. An inquiry into the question of the greased cartridges was instituted and proceeded upon its ponderous way, and officers who had begun to eye the men under their command with an anxiety they would not own to, relaxed again.

The rumours died down, and the Commissioner of Lunjore, who had consistently pooh-poohed the possibility of any serious trouble arising, remarked complacently that he had always known it was a mere tempest in a teapot, and there was too much panic about among fellows who ought to know better. Why, he had even heard some preposterous story of a manifesto being circulated to all Mohammedans, calling for a *Jehad*! All nonsense of course. There hadn't been any such thing circulated in *his* district.

'About eight hundred of them, I think, sir,' said Alex expressionlessly.

'*What's that?*' The Commissioner's voice cracked with angry amazement. 'You're telling me we've had 'em in Lunjore? Then why the devil wasn't I told!'

'You were, sir. I sent in a full report – in triplicate. It will be somewhere in the files.'

'Oh,' said the Commissioner, disconcerted. He glowered angrily for a moment or two and then observed sulkily that he hadn't had the time to read every damned, panicky paper that came into the office.

Relieved by the passing of the temporary uneasiness caused by the cartridge scare and the abortive mutiny of the 19th N.I., he had at long last turned his attention to the question of leave and a visit to the Casa de Ballesteros in Lucknow.

The January rains had been plentiful that year and the river ran high, so that the bridge of boats creaked and pulled to the current.

There were carts crossing it from the Oudh side, and Winter, who had preferred to ride rather than accompany her husband in the carriage, waited for them to pass, and while Conway fretted angrily at the delay, fell into conversation with a gaunt, white-haired Mussulman who was also waiting to cross.

Looking across at the dense line of the jungle that walled in the sandbanks and the wide, seemingly slow-flowing river with its placid surface and treacherous currents, they had seen a half-burned corpse bob slowly past, turning and twisting as though it were alive as the fish and the turtles tugged at it. It came to rest against the side of the bridge and Winter shuddered, wondering how long it would stay there before someone felt it necessary to push it off with a pole. But the hideous, bloated thing vanished suddenly, pulled under as though by a hand that had reached up from the deep water and drawn it down, and the old gentleman, observing her start, said: 'That will be the mugger of the bridge. He keeps it free of all such things. Doubtless the All-Wise appointed him to the work. Where does the Memsahib go?'

'I go to my home,' said Winter, her face lighting to a smile – the first it had worn for more days than she could remember.

'Thy home? Is thy husband then one of the sahibs newly come to Oudh?'

Winter shook her head. 'Nay. I was born in Lucknow city. In the house of Aziza Begum, wife of Mirza Ali Shah, that is called the Gulab Mahal. But my father's house lies to the west of the city. It is named the "House of the Peacocks". Know you Lucknow?'

'Who better?' said the old man. 'Yea, yea, I know the house and I have heard the tale. But this is a sad time for home-going, my daughter. In Lucknow the courtyards are empty and the *kutcharis* (law courts) are full, and many who were pensioners of the King starve while the new Government decide what is to be paid to them, and by whom. When one is old and has lived by means of such a grant from the King – a few rupees only each month – and the grant ceases while the new Government talk of whether it is fit that it be paid, then there is nothing left but to die . . . if the talk lasts longer than an old man and an ageing woman can live without bread.'

His voice was devoid of either animosity or bitterness. He was simply stating a fact, dispassionately and without heat. It had been promised that pensions, wherever possible, would still be paid. But claims to pensions had to be proved, and the wheels ground slowly, for in the turmoil and disorganization caused by the change of Governments, the processes of justice were necessarily slow.

Ameera and Alex and many of Winter's friends and acquaintances in Lunjore city had spoken of Lucknow and the troublous times that had befallen it, and Winter had listened because it was of her own secret city that they spoke. But it was not until now, when an old man who waited patiently beside her to cross the bridge spoke of those troubles without heat or indignation, that a sudden fear came upon her.

Ameera's husband had also lost employment and livelihood through the annexation of Oudh. Were they, too, in want? Winter thought again, and uneasily, of Ameera's letter . . .

She had written to Ameera, telling her of the proposed visit to Lucknow, and Ameera had replied with expressions of delight and had promised to call upon her at the earliest possible moment. But she had suggested – it had been barely more than a hint – that she still could not ask her to the Gulab Mahal. They would be able, she wrote, to talk over such matters when they met. The letter had ended with the bald information that her brother, the young Khalig Dad, was dead.

Winter had sent condolences, and had not given over-much thought to the hint that she might still not be welcome at the Gulab Mahal. But she remembered it now. It could not be true that Ameera did not want her at the Gulab Mahal! . . . or was it the wife of a British official who was unwelcome?

There was nothing in Winter's first sight of the beautiful, barbaric city of Lucknow that awoke even an echo of memory.

They had reached it on the evening of the following day, when the wide sweep of the river, the massed, scented greenery of the gardens, the fantastic silhouettes of golden-domed palaces and soaring minarets, fretted balconies and pointed temple-tops, were bathed in the full glow of the sunset.

There were many British on the wide, shady roads enjoying the evening air: officers and civilians on horseback, ladies in light-coloured dresses driving out in buggies, victorias and high dog-carts, and children bowling hoops under the indulgent and watchful eyes of ayahs or orderlies. Many of them had turned their heads to watch the girl in the grey habit ride past, their attention caught by the bright look of eager expectancy on the young face under the ugly, wide-brimmed pith hat.

Alex would have recognized that expression. But even he had not seen it for many months, and no one else in Lunjore had ever seen it at all.

A long high wall enclosed the grounds of the Casa de Ballesteros, and the gateway of Moorish design was splashed over by the vivid brilliance of bougainvillea. The gateman salaamed low as Winter rode in under the arch, and his bright old eyes followed her approvingly. 'That is indeed Marcos

Sahib's daughter,' he said, addressing a peering group who had gathered by the gate. 'I who have been many years in the service of the house, remember. The very look of her father! What a pity she were not a son. It is many years since my young Sahib, his wife being dead of the birth of this daughter, rode away to fight for the *Sikar* (Government) in Afghanistan, and would not take me with him because I lay sick of a fever. *Hai mai*! The house has been empty overlong. It is not good for a house to lie empty ... or a heart.'

Her father's house was as unfamiliar to Winter as the city had been. But the golden ghost of Sabrina would have found little changed, for the years had been kind to the House of the Peacocks, and it seemed that here time had stood still. The groves of lemon trees and pomegranates still scented the twilight, roses and jasmine and climbing begonia still filled the great stone jars along the river terrace with cascades of colour, and the fountains still made a splashing, tinkling music in the patios.

Mr Saumarez and his wife, the caretakers whom Marcos had installed so many years ago, had done their work well, and an army of servants, many of whom had served Winter's grandparents, had stayed on under the terms of the young Conde's will and had faithfully swept and polished and dusted the huge empty rooms, taking care always to replace everything in the exact position in which it had been found.

The raging heat and the drenching rains, the dust-storms and the brief cold weathers of close on eighteen years, had taken toll of the house; but on that first evening it was difficult to see to what extent they had done so, for the kindly light of candles hid many blemishes. It was only in the full daylight that the ravages of the years became apparent, and Winter could see where the brocades had faded and frayed until a touch would tear them, where the woodwork had warped and cracked, and the dark, beautiful Spanish portraits on the walls had become stained and blotched with damp.

The servants who remembered her parents had pressed about her with smiles and tears and garlands, and she had been touched; though a little saddened because she could not remember even one face among all those faces. But it had been pleasant to talk to people who had known her parents and spoke of them as though they had only lately lived in that house. People who could remember her mother's wedding-day, and how a dress for the bridal had been found among her grandmother's boxes because the bride had only a riding-habit and had brought nothing with her.

It had been a white dress, they told her, and that had been a bad omen, since white, as all knew, was for widows and for the dead. Red was for bridals! – red and gold, the colours of rejoicing. Though it might be that she had worn white in mourning for the father and mother of her husband, who had died but a short while before ... And Winter heard again, from the lips of the old night-watchman who had helped open the heavy door of the tomb, how her grandfather, Don Ramon, had kept vigil by his wife's coffin and had died of it. The stories that Zobeida had told her, told again and in the house that had seen them happen – the great Spanish Casa that Don Ramon had built in his romantic youth on the banks of the Goomti, and named the 'House of the Peacocks'.

The peacocks still cried in the dusk and at dawn, and sometimes Winter would find a glittering, gold-powdered tail-feather lying on the grass or on the stone flags of the river terrace. The servants would collect them, tying them together and using the gorgeous things as feather dusters to brush the pictures and portraits that Don Ramon had brought from Spain.

Conway strongly disapproved of what he termed her habit of 'gossiping with the *nauker-log*'. It was, he said, undignified and ridiculous and merely tended to encourage familiarity, insolence and idleness. There was also, in his opinion, something definitely objectionable about her proficiency in their language. Dammit, what with her black hair and those eyes, not to mention her yellow skin (all this goin' out riding was making her devilish sunburnt) people might even get the idea that he had married a half-caste! To possess a smattering of Hindustani was useful – but to talk it like a native was not at all the thing, and he trusted that she would not display that talent in Lucknow society.

They had not been left long alone, for the news that the Commissioner of Lunjore and his Anglo-Spanish bride were in residence at the Casa de Ballesteros had brought a host of callers to the house, and Conway accepted and issued numerous invitations. This was not what Winter had wished to come to Lucknow for. This was Lunjore again – the endless luncheons, dinners, assemblies, card-parties and races. But she did not know how they could be avoided except on a plea of ill-health, and she could not plead ill-health and then ride in the park and about the city, and she would not hide indoors. There was only one person she had wanted to see in Lucknow, and that was Ameera. And only one place – the Gulab Mahal.

Hamida had brought a message and a gift of flowers and fruit from Ameera on that first evening, but the message had only been to say that Ameera would come and see her as soon as it could be arranged.

'Then am I not to go to the Gulab Mahal?' asked Winter bluntly of Hamida.

'Presently, my bird, presently,' said Hamida. 'But wait until thou hast first seen the Begum Sahiba. She will come soon.'

Ameera had arrived at dusk one evening in a palanquin with tinselled curtains borne by bearers in shabby finery; and by good fortune Conway had been out. She had embraced Winter with tears in her eyes, and they had walked together on the river terrace in the cool twilight while Hamida and two of the grizzled retainers from the Gulab Mahal kept watch to warn away any intrusive males.

They had talked of many things, but the news that Ameera brought had been a bitter blow, for it meant no more than this – Winter must not come to the Rose Palace. Not now. Not yet. Some day, promised Ameera, but not at this time.

Khalig Dad, son of Wali Dad and Juanita, who had been born less than three months before Winter – Khalig Dad who was to have been 'a great king and have seven sons' – had been killed in a street brawl. He had died from a blow on the head received when a drunken and truculent crowd of young dandies, of whom he had been the ringleader, had been mistaken for rioters by some fuddled British officers who were returning late at night from a party in one of the recently commandeered palaces. The true story had never come out and no action had been taken by the authorities, for there had been many unpleasant incidents in Lucknow since the annexation of Oudh, and one more was only one among many. But the incident had been exaggerated to stir up trouble and ill-feeling, and the body of Juanita's son had been paraded through the streets by a howling mob who had had to be dispersed by force.

'He was my brother,' said Ameera, 'and I should not speak against him, for he was only a youth, and foolish, and might have grown out of his wild ways. But I have heard from one who was there that he had drunk overmuch wine, and that seeing the *Angrezi* officers he thought to make sport of them, and he and those who were with him threw firecrackers beneath the feet of their horses and danced about them, shouting. I have heard also that though the sahibs became hot and angry and laid about them with their riding-crops, there were no shots fired. Only the *partarkars* (crackers). But Dasim's wife, Mumtaz, will not have it. She is like my husband and hates all foreigners.'

Ameera sighed, thinking of her husband Walayat Shah, and the hatred that had soured him since the Company's Government had deposed the King of Oudh. She had attempted to explain something of his attitude to Winter, though it had been difficult, since he no longer spoke his mind to his wife . . .

Walayat Shah had at no time felt any friendship towards the British, but he had admired force – when it was successful – and as long as the British won battles and crowned their mercenary armies with glory, he had been prepared to view them with toleration and a certain degree of respect. Now, however, they had deprived him at one stroke of all rights and privileges and put an end to his means of livelihood, so that almost overnight, from holding a position of some power and authority, he had become little more than a pauper; forced even to prove his claim before a British official to land that his family had held for generations, and which was now his only source of income. And the proving of such claims, in a land where the sword had always carried more weight than the pen, was no easy matter when written evidence of possession was virtually non-existent.

Walayat Shah's toleration of the *feringhis* changed to a corroding and vindictive hatred. And with that hatred had arisen, like a phoenix from the fire, the memory of the past glories of his race. He had rarely thought of the history of his people while the Muslim kingdom of Oudh still stood, but now that Oudh – almost the last Mohammedan state in India – had fallen, he and many like him turned to look at the glorious past when the horned moon of Islam had blazed above India from Peshawar to the Deccan, and the Great Moguls had ruled all Hind. The fire of that great Empire had sunk now to a feeble flicker, as though it had been no more than the light of a thousand *chirags* – the small oil-lamps lit for the festival of Dewali – that together blaze like a golden bonfire, but which die out one by one as the oil burns low or the night winds blow. Only a few of the lamps that had once made that bright glare remained, for the hot winds of the warlike Mahrattas, of the Rajputs, of Guru Narnak, founder of the Sikhs, had extinguished them one by one. And then a greater wind had arisen: the cold wind of 'John Company', blowing in from beyond the Black Water and breathing upon the last dying flicker of the Empire of the Moguls.

The British had conquered the conquerors: Mahratta, Rajput and Sikh; and now, if the British themselves were to fall, chaos would follow. Out of that chaos might not the moon of Islam rise once more, and the followers of the Prophet rule the land as they had ruled it in the great days of Akbar – of Jehangir – of Shahjehan – of Aurungzebe, 'Holder of the World'?

Walayat Shah, brooding on present calamity and past glory, listened to the words of those who preached a *Jehad*, and dreamed the Mohammedan dream. For now a *Jehad* meant far more than the spreading of the Faith and the slaying of unbelievers. It meant revenge; and perhaps, once more, an Empire.

'He is changed even towards me, his wife, because my mother was a *feringhi*,' said Ameera sadly, 'and therefore I cannot ask thee to enter the Gulab Mahal. Some day, surely. But for the present it were better to keep away.'

And so that door was closed to Winter.

She had come back at last to Lucknow. But not to that charmed and peaceful starting-point whence she had hoped to recoup her strength, and find a purpose in the pattern of her life so that she might start out again with surer feet; no longer a child at the mercy of incomprehensible adult orders, but as herself, Winter de Ballesteros, released from her foolish dependence on the pasteboard figure of a non-existent knight, free of fear and loneliness and the agonizing, strangling, dragging ties of love, and able to stand alone.

The reiterated promise that one day she would return to the Gulab Mahal and then all would be well with her had grown too deeply into her consciousness to be eradicated, so that the Gulab Mahal had become far more than a mere memory of happiness. It was a spell . . . a charm . . . a philosopher's stone that could transmute base metal into gold. The moon out of reach. She had seemed within reach of it at last, but she could not stretch out her hand and touch it, because the gate was shut against her.

Not wishing to distress Ameera, Winter did not even ask the way to the Rose Palace or in what part of the city it lay, and therefore did not even know if she passed it when she drove through Lucknow. She did not think so, since the houses in which the Europeans lived lay on the outskirts of the city or in the cantonments.

The city itself was a rabbit-warren of houses, shops, mosques, temples and palaces, narrow streets, narrower alleyways and crowded bazaars. Few Europeans chose to go there, for it seethed with discontent and bitterness, rage and rumours: 'The sahibs will not rest until they have all Hind,' ran the whispers. 'Did they not have a treaty with the King, and have they not broken it? It is said that the last *Lat* Sahib gained honours from the Queen for stealing so much land, and now the new one means to steal more so that his honours may be the greater. Soon there will be no kingdoms in Hind, but only one land – and all of it the Company's!'

The scores of men who besieged the courts daily, asking who would now pay their pensions, were told to wait. To wait . . . to wait. And while they waited, they starved.

'Couldn't be helped,' said Mr Samuel Coombs, discussing the matter with the Commissioner of Lunjore over the port. 'You can't take over a chaotic mess like Oudh and turn it into a smooth-running concern in a few weeks. It's not possible. Augean Stables wasn't in it, and Coverley Jackson ain't a Hercules! He did his best of course, but his best wasn't good enough . . . not much sympathy or understanding for the plight of all the poor devils who lost their livelihood and saw their way of life being swept into Limbo when we took over. And it was no secret that he spent half his time quarrelling with his assistants – all Oudh knew it, and that sort of thing don't inspire confidence. Good thing he's gone.'

Mr Coombs, like Mr Josh Cottar, was in business, and dealt in army contracts which were in the process of amassing him a large fortune. His business methods left much to be desired, but he was a shrewd man with a considerable knowledge of Oudh, and his independent status and large financial stake in the country gave him a clearer vision of the dangers inherent in the situation than those officials whose horizons were necessarily bounded by paper reports and red tape.

Mr Barton, who had no sympathy and little understanding for any problem regarding a subjugated race, contented himself with remarking that in his opinion far too much fuss was made over the natives these days. 'Napoleon was right, b' Gad,' said Mr Barton. 'A whiff of grapeshot is the only medicine that a rabble understands. But now that Lawrence has taken over, I suppose we shall see the population being pampered and petted beyond all bearing.'

Mr Coombs shook his head. 'Not Lawrence. Justice ain't pampering. By God, he's a marvel!' – Mr Coombs's hoarse voice held an unexpected note of awe. 'He hasn't been in the place ten days, yet already one can feel the difference. Pity he wasn't sent here at the start, I say.'

'Very nearly was,' interjected another guest, a burly, grizzled man with a bloodshot eye. 'Fact! I'm told he offered for the post but his letter arrived too late, Canning had just appointed Jackson. Great pity. Jackson's an able feller, but too hot-tempered. Lawrence has a temper too, but he seldom loses it. Patience of the East – and that's a virtue in this country! Jackson should have been superseded months ago.'

'The trouble is that Canning's too kindly a man,' said Mr Coombs. 'Wouldn't like to ask for Jackson's resignation after having appointed the fellow himself, and hoped things would improve, I suppose. But I understand that the stream of complaints about the mismanagement here grew too much even for his butter-hearted Lordship, and drove him to take the plunge and throw out his nominee in favour of Sir Henry.'

'Well, I say it was a mistake,' said Mr Barton thickly. 'S' Henry's a sick man. Anyone c'n see it with half an eye. And a sick nigger-lover ain't what I'd have prescribed for this province. No, by God it ain't! I hear he was due to leave f' England when the Governor-General's letter came. He should 'a gone!'

Mr Coombs surveyed his host with palpable distaste. 'It's plain you don't know Sir Henry,' he remarked. 'He'd have come if he was dying. *He* knew! He knows how it is. He'll do his best, and his best is a sight better than any other man's in India. If anyone can check the rot, he will – though it's my opinion the rot's gone too far to check without bloodletting.'

'Qui' right,' agreed the Commissioner. 'What did I tell you? Whiff o' grapeshot, that's the answer! Barnwell, the port's with you——'

Sir Henry Lawrence, perhaps the best-loved man in India, had arrived in Lucknow late in March to take over the administration of Oudh from Mr Coverley Jackson. He was aged by grief and disappointment, and as Mr Barton had observed, in failing health. But at Canning's request he had once again abandoned the hope of sorely needed home leave and had hurried to the help of Oudh. '*... man can die but once,*' wrote Lawrence to his friend and pupil, Herbert Edwards, '*and if I die in Oudh – after saving some poor fellow's health or skin or* izzat (honour) – *I shall have no reason for discontent ... But the price I pay is high for I had set my heart on going Home ...*'

No one knew better than the man who had settled the conquered Punjab and won the respect and affection of the defeated Sikhs what unavoidable tragedies resulted from such a change in Government, or how best to soften and mitigate the hardships and heartaches and hopelessness that inevitably followed in its wake. The news of his appointment sent a sigh of relief through half India. If anyone could tame the sulky, suspicious, wild-eyed stallion that was Oudh, it was Henry Lawrence.

The Conway Bartons had been invited to dine at the Residency, and Winter had had her first sight of the man whom Alex had spoken of as men speak of a god or a hero.

He was a tall man, thin to emaciation, and his grey hair and scanty straggling beard were already turning white. His haggard, hollow-cheeked face was scored with the lines of weariness and anxiety and the unending strain of sorrow for his wife Honoria, who had died three years before. But the grey, deep-set eyes were quiet and far-seeing, and they could still glow with the same fire and fervour and enthusiasm with which he had faced his task as a young man newly come to India, and which had inspired and led such men as John Nicholson and Herbert Edwards, Hodson and Alex and many others, to look upon him with affection and admiration as the best and wisest of all administrators.

The Residency was always full of guests these days, for the newly appointed Chief Commissioner kept open house for the nobles, landowners and gentry of the district, as one method of inspiring confidence and getting in touch with the opinions prevailing in Oudh. His jurisdiction did not extend beyond the borders of his own province, but as Lunjore touched upon those borders he had been anxious to meet its Commissioner, of whom he had heard little good. Mr Barton had not impressed him favourably:

'As you are at the moment on leave, Mr Barton, you will possibly not have heard that there has been a serious incident in Barrackpore,' said Sir Henry. 'It will soon be common property, but I thought that you might like to know of it as soon as possible, in case you think it advisable, in the circumstances, to return to your district.'

'*Return?*' said Mr Barton, his pale eyes bulging. 'Did you say Barrackpore? But that can hardly affect us. It is a far cry from Calcutta and Barrackpore to Lunjore.'

' "*Delhi dur ust,*" ' said Sir Henry with a wry smile.

'I beg your pardon?'

'It is an old saying in this country,' said Sir Henry. ' "*It is a far cry to Delhi.*" ' But I do not think that distance will serve to protect any of us, because what has happened in Barrackpore is likely to affect us all. The cartridge question was at the back of it again. It seems that a sepoy of the 38th Native Infantry fired on and then cut down the Adjutant and a sergeant-major who ran to his assistance, while a jemadar and twenty men who were watching refused to help. General Hearsey appears to have ridden at the man, who then shot himself. That happened the day before the 19th N.I., who mutinied at Berhampur, were disbanded, and I fear it may have unpleasant repercussions in every cantonment in India. There has already been a certain amount of trouble in Ambala, and the cartridge scare is spreading.'

'It will blow over,' said Mr Barton comfortably.

'I wonder. I confess I do not like this business of the cartridges. It is the worse in that it contains a substratum of truth, as there is no doubt at all that proper care was not exercised, and denials may save us less than a frank acknowledgement of error and every effort to put it right. But in that I can have no say. I do not know how you have found it in your district, but in my opinion it is the Army and not the nobles and talukdars that we have to worry about; although I cannot in all honesty deny that the nobles have, in many instances, just cause for complaint. I have always thought that we are too apt to under-value Indian forms of Government and measure too much by British rules: and in defiance of common sense we still appear to expect that the erstwhile rulers of this country should welcome our taking to ourselves all authority and all emoluments! If we cannot treat them, particularly the soldiers, as having the same ambitions as ourselves, we shall never be safe. There has been bad feeling for many years among the Bengal Army, but now that they are beginning to realize how few we are they are discovering a dangerous consciousness of power. A havildar to whom I was speaking only the other day warned me that if we did not speedily redress their wrongs they would redress them themselves.'

'I trust the brute was hanged as an example?' said Mr Barton, his face crimsoning with affront.

The grey eyes under the beetling brows regarded him with dislike. 'I do not punish men for telling me the truth,' said Sir Henry coldly. 'It has always been a wise policy – I am sure you will have found it so yourself – to allow men to speak their minds, since to prevent them from doing so is only to remain in ignorance oneself. Your district lies at so little distance from my own that disaffection here is bound to affect you in Lunjore, and I will not disguise from you that I am not without forebodings and apprehension as to the future. You have no Queen's troops in Lunjore, I believe?'

'No. There are three Regiments of Native Infantry. The 93rd and the 105th, a Regiment of Lunjore Irregulars and a contingent of Military Police. But I can assure you, Sir Henry, that we have had no reason for alarm or anxiety. Neither do I anticipate any. My district has never been quieter, and the Regiments are loyal to a man. I have every confidence in them.'

'I envy you,' said Sir Henry quietly. 'I wish I could say the same. You have of course a very able assistant. How is Randall? I had hoped to be able to see him. He has the makings of a very promising administrator.'

Mr Barton shrugged. 'Tolerable. Very tolerable. I won't deny that he is a hard worker, but he takes too much upon himself. Does a thing and asks afterwards.'

Sir Henry smiled. 'I fear that is a trait that I am responsible for. All my most promising pupils have suffered for it in consequence. But you know, Barton, it is, within limits, no bad thing. We suffer too much from the dead hand of officialdom in this country. Too many people are not prepared to take a risk or to do what they feel to be right, without first obtaining sanction in writing from a superior. And that wastes everyone's time. I used to tell 'em to act on their own judgement and do what they thought was right. There are only three golden rules for an administrator. Settle the country. Make the people happy. Take care there are no rows!'

'If Randall had his way,' said Mr Barton sourly, 'we'd have plenty of rows. He's losing his usefulness and that's a fact. Beginning to see a burglar under every bed, just like some pesky old maid!'

'Indeed? That does not sound like Alex Randall. What particular burglars has he been envisaging?'

Mr Barton appeared slightly discomforted, for it had just occurred to him that there was a certain similarity between Captain Randall's views and the ones expressed by his host. He said uncomfortably: 'Oh, nothing much. Nothing much. Some nonsense about a plot for an organized rebellion. He got hold of some tale of chuppattis being circulated locally among the villages in my district, and would have it that this was a signal – a "fiery cross" he called it.'

Sir Henry surveyed him thoughtfully. 'Not locally, Mr Barton,' he said gently, 'those chuppattis have been distributed through a large part of India, and I too am inclined to take them as something in the nature of . . . I cannot better Randall's phrase, "a fiery cross".'

Mr Barton's countenance became dangerously empurpled, but he swallowed his annoyance and managed a shrug of the shoulders. 'I had not heard that they had been observed in other districts,' he admitted. 'But I can assure you that as far as Lunjore is concerned, Captain Randall's fears are entirely groundless. I cannot of course speak for the rest of India, but I am happy to say that *my* district is completely free from any taint of disaffection. And I know that in saying so I can speak for the regiments stationed there, for their commanding officers have severally and together assured me of their entire confidence in their men.'

'Nevertheless,' said Sir Henry, rising, 'I hope you may not think me impertinent if I suggest that the closest possible watch should be kept on the activities of the sepoys, and that an examination of the letters they receive or write might be rewarding. The times are troublous, Mr Barton, and it behoves us all to be on our guard, while at the same time giving of our best. Let us join the ladies.'

'What did I tell you?' demanded Mr Barton, relating this conversation with strong indignation to his wife as they drove homeward in the warm darkness to the Casa de Ballesteros. 'He's a sick man, and no fit person for the post. Listening to every bazaar rumour and allowing it to prey on his nerves! The iron hand, that's all these natives understand. They respect force and despise weakness. "*I do not punish men for telling me the truth*" – Bah! *I'd* have known how to treat any damned nigger who had the impertinence to talk to me like that! To listen to that sort of inflammatory stuff is just to encourage them.'

Mr Barton would have found himself in agreement with Honoria Lawrence, though not in the same spirit, when she had written of her husband almost five years previously: '*If the new doctrine holds that sympathy with a people unfits a man to rule them, then indeed Sir Henry shows himself unfit for his position.'* In Mr Barton's opinion, Sir Henry was entirely unfit, but as he had no desire to offend so notable a person, he had kept a guard upon his tongue excepting before his wife.

They had both attended several other functions at the Residency, and though Mr Barton had had no further private conversation with the Chief Commissioner of Oudh, Winter had struck up a friendship with a Mrs Daly who had been acting as hostess and housekeeper for Sir Henry.

Mrs Daly, her little son, and her husband Captain Harry Daly, who had just been appointed to command of the Corps of Guides, were staying as guests at the Residency, and Mrs Daly had temporarily taken on the management of the vast, scantily furnished house. She had taken a great fancy to young Mrs Barton, and a few days before her departure with her husband and child to Hoti Mardan on the North-West Frontier, where the Guides were stationed, she had asked if she might invite Winter to spend a few nights at the Residency.

Conway had offered no objection, since it had occurred to him that his wife's absence would provide an excellent opportunity to arrange a few entertainments of his own at the Casa de Ballesteros. He had therefore given the scheme his cordial approval, and having seen Winter off to the Residency, had settled down with a large glass of brandy to plan a week of pleasurable and unrestricted amusement.

33

The Lucknow Residency was a large, three-storeyed building whose deep verandahs and pillared porticos looked out over the beautiful city and the winding river. It stood on high ground, among green lawns and gardens full of roses and flowering trees that held at bay an area of crowding, crowded buildings that surrounded and pressed about it, and which housed a numberless horde of unemployed musicians, entertainers and other humble hangers-on of the vanished court of Wajid Ali Shah, last King of Oudh.

'Sir Henry does what he can for them,' Mrs Daly told Winter, walking with her guest in the gardens in the cool of the evening, 'though I do not think it can be easy. He cannot give them *all* employment. But he is always so ready to listen to anyone who asks for help, and to give any aid he can. I think a good deal of it comes from his own pocket, and I do not believe that there can be a kinder or more truly charitable man to be met with anywhere. Harry – my husband – says that already he has done more than anyone thought possible towards tranquillizing the province, for he is seeing that the promised pensions are paid, and has done much towards pacifying the bad feeling among the shopkeepers and tradesmen in Lucknow. But I believe it to be the ex-King's army that is providing the main source of anxiety. Harry says that Sir Henry had hoped to enlist them in the Military Police or the local corps, but they say that they have eaten the King's salt and will eat no other's. But he does not despair. He has been holding a great many Durbars, you know, where the nobles and landowners may state their complaints freely so that he may do what he can to remedy them. I do not believe he ever sleeps!'

Winter had been happier during these past few days than she had been for months past. The relief of being free of Conway's society was itself immeasurable, and she had been charmed by the atmosphere that prevailed at the Residency, and the casualness and complete lack of ceremony shown by its host.

'Harry and I had to procure a great deal of furniture and fittings for the house,' confided Mrs Daly, 'for Sir Henry declared that he had no more than a single knife and fork to his name. He cannot be bothered with such minor details and leaves them to anyone who will attend to them for him. And I never know how many guests to expect. He will ask me to send out cards for a party of fifteen, and an hour before dinner George Lawrence will come in and tell me that his uncle has invited another twenty, and clean forgotten to mention it! And then there are always the unexpected visitors.'

One of these unexpected visitors walked in on a breakfast-party on the last day but one of Winter's stay.

Breakfast at the Residency was a long-drawn-out and pleasant meal, lasting from ten o'clock until twelve, and attended on this occasion (in addition to Sir Henry and his nephew George, the Dalys and Winter) by a Colonel Edwards, a Mr Christian, Commissioner of Sitapur, and a Dr Ogilvie. They had been animatedly discussing the rival merits of Buddha and Confucius as religious teachers, when a caller had been announced, and Captain Daly had looked up and jumped to his feet:

'Alex – by all that's wonderful!'

Winter had been peeling an orange and her hands were suddenly still. As still as her heart. Alex's voice spoke behind her:

'Hello, Harry; I hadn't heard you were here. I hope you may forgive me for walking in on you like this, Sir Henry? I arrived an hour or so ago, but Mr Barton cannot see me until later, so I thought——'

'You know that you need no apology for walking in on me at any hour, Alex,' said Sir Henry, and smiled.

Winter laid the orange down very carefully on her plate and turned slowly, but Alex was not looking at her. He was not even aware that she was present. He was looking at his old chief, and Winter was seized by a helpless, foolish pang of pure jealousy. A resentment, as keen as it was ridiculous, because neither she nor any woman would ever be able to bring that look to Alex's face – or to any man's face.

Sir Henry pushed away his plate and stood up to grip Alex's hand, and Captain Daly beckoned to a *khidmatgar* to bring another chair.

'Had any breakfast?' inquired Sir Henry.

'At about five o'clock this morning, sir.'

'Then you can do with another one now. *Hazri lao Sahib kirwasti*, Ahmed Ali. What are you doing in Lucknow, Alex?'

'The Commissioner sent for me, sir.'

Alex's voice was entirely expressionless, but Sir Henry regarded him with a twinkling eye in which there was a good deal of comprehension: 'Called up to explain yourself, eh? What high-handed action have you been taking this time without consulting the higher authorities?'

Alex laughed. 'Something like that. You are too acute, sir.'

'And entirely mannerless, for I have not yet made you known to my guests. But then I think you know all of them except Dr Ogilvie. Mrs Barton is staying with us for a few days to keep Mrs Daly company.'

Alex looked round with a sudden startled frown in his eyes. 'I'm sorry, Mrs Barton; I did not see you were here. Hullo, Mrs Daly. It's good to see you again. How do you do, sir – no, I do not think we have met.'

'How long will you be staying?' inquired Sir Henry.

'Not above a day, I imagine, sir. It depends on the Commissioner, but I hope to start back before dawn tomorrow. This is no time to be——'

He bit back the sentence, and his mouth shut hard as though he were annoyed with himself for being betrayed into an unguarded statement. But the thought was entirely clear. This was no time to be dragged away from Lunjore to explain some official peccadillo in person to its absent Commissioner.

Sir Henry said: 'Only one night? That is not long. You'll stay here, of course.'

'I would like to, sir, if you are sure——'

'Oh, Mrs Daly will arrange it. You need not worry. She is in charge just now. I cannot think what I am to do when she leaves me, but her husband is selfishly removing her on the thirteenth. Daly is off to take over command of the Guides.'

Alex turned quickly: 'Is that true? Congratulations, Harry, I had not heard. You always were a lucky devil. Pleased?'

'Who wouldn't be! But I could wish it had come at any other time. It is hard to have to leave Lucknow just as Sir Henry arrives.'

Sir Henry smiled. 'My dear Harry, don't think that I do not appreciate the compliment, but as I told you before, you could not dream of refusing the finest appointment open to a soldier.'

Alex said: 'You couldn't try pulling a few strings, sir, so that he can stay on here and I can go instead?'

Sir Henry looked at him reflectively. 'I might try, though it would not have a particle of effect. But would you really go if it did?'

Alex returned the look, and his mouth twisted in a wry smile. 'No, sir.' There was an odd note of bitterness in his voice and Sir Henry nodded understandingly: 'I did not think so. Not at this time.' He pushed back his chair and stood up. 'Well, if you will all excuse me, I must go. I'll see you later, Alex. When you have had your wigging!'

The conversation had become general after his departure, but although Alex had borne a part in it he had appeared *distrait*, and Winter found that he did not even glance in her direction. Looking at him across the wide table she was filled with despair. Nothing had changed. She might just as well have never come to Lucknow – have never left Lunjore. She had found no solution to her problems or her unhappiness or her love for Alex. Perhaps there was no solution. And no answer except fortitude.

Alex had left at the conclusion of the meal, and she did not see him again until he entered the crowded drawing-room just before dinner that night. She thought that he looked tired and cross, and she would have given much to have been able to go to him and run her fingers over his forehead to smooth away the frown lines as he had once done to her at Hazrat Bagh. She wondered what he had done that had annoyed Conway sufficiently to send for him to Lucknow at a time like this, and what the interview had been like? The fact that her husband had been unable to see him at eleven o'clock in the morning had not been lost upon her: Conway must either have given or attended a late party last night. She hoped the latter, for the picture of a motley crowd composed of the least reputable members of the British community carousing in the cool stately rooms of the Casa de los Pavos Reales was a singularly unpleasant one.

Winter had not seen her husband since her arrival at the Residency. He had announced his intention of driving over, but he had not done so, and she could only be thankful for it. This was the first time since the day of her wedding that she had not been under the same roof as Conway, and she found the relief it occasioned her more than a little frightening. Was it really going to be possible to spend the rest of her life in the company of a man whose absence brought her such infinite and blessed relief? Could marriage really be regarded as a sacred and binding sacrament under such conditions?

'Perhaps it is my fault,' thought Winter. 'Perhaps if I tried very hard I could make him care for me, which might turn him from the sort of life he likes to lead. If I tried——' But then to Conway, love meant only lust. It would be easy enough to make him lust after her, but when he had satisfied that lust he would care no more for her than he had in the past. Mr Barton regarded women with a single mind. They were either physically attractive, or not. It was as simple as that. Eastern opinion held that women have no souls and are put into the world solely for the use of men; to pleasure them, serve them, bear their children, and (on behalf of the devil) to tempt them from the paths of duty and righteousness. Conway Barton would have been found to be in complete agreement with these views, and he loved only one person: himself.

Winter had come to see this quite clearly, but nevertheless she had thought again and again during those few peaceful days at the Lucknow Residency that perhaps if she tried hard – if she forced herself to swallow her disgust of him and fought against the shrinking of her flesh at the very thought of his touch – she might gradually wean him from the vices that were rotting his mind and body. Yet now, looking at Alex Randall across the candle-lit table at the Residency, she knew with a helpless and despairing certainty that she could not do it. Not while she could not even look at Alex without a contraction of the heart.

There had been a large dinner-party that night, and from his seat at the head of the long table Sir Henry's bright, tired gaze had wandered from one to another of his guests: noting the lack of interest or means of communication between many of his British guests and their Indian neighbours, and the animated three-sided conversation between young Mrs Barton and two Oudh nobles, one of whom sat on either side of her. She at least would not lack friends if the need arose. But of how many others could this be said? As for her husband, Sir Henry could only be thankful that there were few officials of his stamp in India, but it embittered him to think that the harm one such man could do easily outweighed all the good performed by twenty able ones.

His gaze moved on to Alex Randall and rested there with affection and approval. These were the proper men to govern the country. Men who would keep the peace by mixing freely with the people and doing prompt justice in their shirt-sleeves, and who did not consider *jaghirdars* and pensioners as nuisances and enemies, but felt themselves doubly bound to treat ex-foes with kindness because they were down . . . and because they still retained influence among their own people. Once, nearly nine years ago, Alex had said hotly in the course of an argument: 'No, I don't believe in a divine right to govern! But I do believe that now we've got this country it is up to us to govern it to the best of our ability.' He was probably still of the same mind, mused Sir Henry, and he possessed the right kind of ability. He must find an opportunity to talk with Alex after the guests had gone.

But it was not until the last carriage had driven away shortly after eleven o'clock, and the house-party had dispersed to their own rooms, that he found himself alone with Captain Randall in the cool darkness of the high verandah whose tall, supporting pillars stood black against the moon-flooded garden.

'Well, Alex?' inquired Sir Henry after an appreciable interval of silence.

Alex turned from his contemplation of the white lawns and the tree shadows. 'Far from it, sir. Will you forgive me if I omit the reasons for my visit here? I do not feel capable at present of discussing them in a rational manner.'

'In fact,' said Sir Henry softly, 'if anyone were now to offer you command of the Guides you would return a different answer to the one you gave me this morning.'

Alex gave a short laugh. 'If anyone were to offer me any post whatsoever that would enable me to return to regimental duty, I should accept it!'

'Oh, no, you would not,' said Sir Henry placidly. 'If you think that, you know less about yourself than I do. I have been wanting to see you for some weeks past. I would have written, except that there has been so much to do. Colvin gave me news of you when I stayed with him in Agra on my way here. It seems you saw him in October.'

'I did,' said Alex grimly. 'I had a story to tell him which he was not prepared to believe.'

'So I gathered,' said Sir Henry, settling himself comfortably in a long verandah chair. 'Perhaps you will find me less hard to convince. Sit down and tell me about it.'

'Thank you, sir, but I think I'll stand. I have had a long spell in the saddle, and there is another ahead of me in the morning.'

'Can you not stay over tomorrow? We have the Nana of Bithaur in Lucknow on a visit, and I shall be seeing him tomorrow. I have my suspicions of the Nana Sahib, and I should be interested to hear what you make of him. Have you ever met him?'

'No, sir. I missed meeting him once in Delhi, owing to – to unexpected circumstances. And I am afraid that I shall have to miss him again. I cannot delay.'

'I am sorry for it. Tell me this story that you told Colvin. I imagine that your version differs somewhat from his.'

Alex propped his shoulders against the nearest pillar and told again the story he had told in the previous autumn to Mr Colvin, Lieutenant-Governor of the North-West Provinces. He told it all, beginning with a moonlight night in Malta and ending with his second visit to the ruins near Khanwai with an escort of cavalry and three sceptical British officers, and Sir Henry listened calmly and without interruption and when he had finished asked only one question.

'Who,' said Sir Henry, 'was the man with the ruby earrings? Did you ever find out?'

'No. I should recognize him again if I saw him, but that's the most I can say.'

'A pity. It is a help to know for certain who one's enemies are. He sounds as though he were a man of some standing, and at this time it is more than useful to know whom we can trust and whom we cannot. Kishan Prasad I know. And the Maulvi too. The latter has been preaching here in the city and he has a very large following. A rabble-rouser and a born leader of men. They say too that he is a miracle worker. I presume he works the same sort of tricks with greek-fire that you saw him use, for the benefit of the credulous. The man's a charlatan, but he's a patriot and a fanatic and he uses his head. The same may be said of Kishan Prasad; though with less truth, since he might have been a stout ally if we had not done our imbecile best to alienate him, whereas the Maulvi would never have bent the knee. But they are in general birds of a very different feather, and it is disturbing to find them in the same nest. Have you come up against any signs of serious disaffection in your district?'

'One. The building, under cover of providing a shoot for the garrison, of a *kutcha* road between Lunjore and Suthragunj——' Alex gave details, and Sir Henry listened and nodded.

'Kishan Prasad again. Any trouble in the villages?'

'Not as yet, sir. The chuppattis have been in circulation and there has been a bit of *taklief* (trouble) over the flour being suspected of containing bone dust; but the villages have been quiet enough. They are uneasy of course, what with the chuppattis and the bone-dust rumour, and a deal of talk about omens and portents – you know the sort of thing, sir. Signs in the sky, monstrous births, two-headed calves and the like. Not to mention the old centenary of Plassey prophecy that is being circulated so freely. But the regiments are a different matter. I rely on Niaz Mohammed for my information in that line. He has friends among the sepoys.'

'He is still with you then?'

'He is; and he hears things in the lines that I would not. Not much, as he is suspect. But enough. What do you think is going to happen, sir?'

'*Khuda ke malum*!' (God knows) said Sir Henry. 'Let us have your views. I am on the bench tonight, and I should like to hear what you think.'

Alex frowned abstractedly at the contents of his glass, swirling the liquid slowly so that the moonlight that was beginning to encroach on the darkness of the verandah caught in it and sent pale, circling lights across the matting on the floor.

'Well?' inquired Sir Henry after an interval of silence.

Alex looked at the face that was dim in the moon-thinned shadows and the eyes that burnt so brightly in the hollow sockets, and spoke with deliberation:

'I think it is the Army that we have to fear, sir.'

'A mutiny.' The word was a confirmation rather than a query.

'Yes, sir. Not a spontaneous outbreak, but a planned one. Set to take place simultaneously in every cantonment in India on a given date. A few months ago I would not have believed such a thing possible, because to achieve it there would have to have been some exceedingly strong grievance that was common to both Mussulmans and Hindus – strong enough to unite them against us. We have, however, very thoughtfully provided that common bond in the greased cartridges. That was all that was needed. Having armed their hands, we have furnished the pretence.'

Sir Henry was silent for a moment or two, stroking his beard, and presently he said gently: 'Any evidence, Alex?'

Alex flung the contents of his glass with a violent gesture over the roses below the verandah rail, and said bitterly: 'None that is acceptable to the Commissioner or those purblind, pig-headed—— I *beg* your pardon, sir!'

Sir Henry laughed and getting up from his chair put out a thin hand, gripping the younger man's shoulder in a hard grasp.

'Hipped, Alex?'

'Damnably,' admitted Alex, meeting his look.

'I know. It's like banging one's head against a stone wall. What's the evidence?'

Alex told him; repeating the words that Kishan Prasad had spoken in the drawing-room of the Residency at Lunjore.

'In the hot weather . . .' said Sir Henry thoughtfully. He had returned to his chair while Alex talked, and now he leant back in it, fingering his lip. 'Why are you so sure that he was presenting you with the truth in this oblique manner?'

'I saved his life once,' said Alex shortly. 'It was possibly the greatest mistake I ever made, but he feels some sense of obligation towards me. And I also think he has a liking for Winter – Mrs Barton. Or else——'

Alex checked; wondering, as he had done once before, if it might not be that Kishan Prasad suspected Alex of liking Mrs Barton, and for that reason had warned him to send her to safety? He did not complete the sentence but said instead: 'There is another thing that seems to suggest he was speaking the truth. That road, if I am right about it, will have to be used before the monsoon breaks, because it will be useless afterwards. And that limits it to this side of mid-June. Something will happen before then.'

Sir Henry nodded and leaned forward in his chair, his clasped hands on his knees and his head silvered by the moonlight. He said slowly: 'I am in agreement with you. Although I still cling to the hope that we may yet avoid the deluge that our blindness has earned.'

'Then you do not think that I am "harbouring bees in my bonnet", as my chief is pleased to term it?'

Sir Henry laughed. 'Hardly! Unless I harbour the same bees. In fact I am so much in accord with your views that I will tell you something that few people are aware of. I have already begun to prepare the Residency to stand a siege.'

'Then you think——?'

'I hope!' interrupted Sir Henry. 'And I will go on hoping until the last possible moment. But I am also doing what I can to prepare, in case that hope fails me. Perhaps it will not. I have a deal of faith in the Punjab. Nicholson and Edwards are there, and my brother John. They will hold the Punjab quiet. I believe that Nicholson could do it single-handed, and if there were three of him instead of only one I should have no fears for India. But I cannot feel any optimism on the score of the North-Western Provinces, and should Oudh revolt it will go hard with us all. Given time, I believe I may be able to hold Oudh quiet even if the rest of India rises; but it is *time* we need – time most of all: and that is a thing which God and the Government may not grant me. The sands are running out, Alex.'

Alex said slowly and after a brief pause: 'How the devil do they get their information, sir? The telegraph doesn't account for it, for we aren't on the line at Lunjore and have to get our news by runner. We didn't get word of that Barrackpore business for a full week, but the city knew it all within two days.'

'It's the same everywhere,' said Sir Henry. 'I don't pretend to account for it, but if I were a superstitious man I'd say that in times like these the very wind carries bad news. I believe that it is done with drums in Africa, but here one would almost say that they are able to transfer their thoughts from one agitator to another.'

'Talking of agitators,' said Alex, 'Gregori Sparkov was expected in Delhi. Hodson told me that – he appears to have sources of information in Delhi. And there was a travelling theatrical company who came through Lunjore a month or so ago. They had spent several weeks in Lucknow, and before that they were in Cawnpore and Agra. I had reason to believe that one of them might be a friend of Sparkov's – or an agent. They were proceeding to Delhi, and I sent word to Mr Fraser. I heard lately that the man disappeared the day after the troupe arrived there. They think that he is in the Palace, but as it cannot be searched he is safe enough. Intriguing with the King, I suppose.'

'More likely to be the Queen,' said Sir Henry. 'The old Padishah is too enfeebled and futile a personage to be of much danger except as a lay figure to prop up on a throne. But Zeenut Mahal is a very different matter. She has brains and drive and fury, and she is burnt up with hate and ambition. I imagine it is she who is the focus of this Russian–Persian intrigue.'

'Do you suppose there is much in it, sir?'

'A certain amount. Russia has always wanted India. She has always wanted the whole world! But particularly the East. She can't get it while we are here, and she knows it. But if she can help to get us out she can crawl in through a hundred cracks and crannies and rot it from top to bottom until it falls into her hand like an over-ripe pear. Naturally she's doing all she can to fan the flames. That was only to be expected.'

Alex turned instinctively to look towards the north, and he jerked his shoulders in an oddly uneasy gesture and said: 'Is it true that the native press in Delhi has been printing a good deal of Russian propaganda?'

'It is,' said Sir Henry serenely. 'I believe there was something to the effect that the Tsar had placed an army of half a million at the disposal of the Shah of Persia for the purpose of ridding India of the British. On the other hand, there was also an article that said the Russians were the cause of our war with Persia, and were merely using the Persians to cloak their own intention of conquering Hindustan.'

'From what I know of them, I should think that is more than probable,' said Alex grimly.

Sir Henry shrugged. 'Possibly. But then India has believed for many years that the "Russ-*log*" would one day fight us for the mastery of India, and when we made the mistake of withdrawing troops from this country to fight in the Crimea it was immediately taken as proof that the Russians had so decimated our armies that we had no fighting men left save those out here. But Russia is not the villain of this present drama. We have relieved her of the responsibility by casting ourselves in that role.'

He looked up at Alex and smiled his tired, charming smile. 'I am taking a dreary view of the future tonight, am I not? But though I can feel the wind and hear the thunder, I do not yet despair of avoiding the storm. And if it comes – it comes! and I shall look to you to hold the western road for me, so that if you should be right, and the regiments at Suthragunj mutiny and seize the arsenal, they will not reach Oudh by Kishan Prasad's road.'

'I will do my best, sir. You know that.'

'Even if you were offered command of the Guides tomorrow?'

Alex threw up his hand in the gesture of a swordsman acknowledging a hit, and laughed, but this time without bitterness. 'You could offer me no greater inducement, sir, but I will content myself with trying to hold the western road for you.'

'Let us hope it will not come to that,' said Sir Henry. 'You mentioned Hodson just now. Have you seen anything of him of late?'

They talked of other things for a space, until at last Sir Henry rose and held out his hand. 'If you are making an early start, I shall not be seeing you again before you go. Good luck to you, Alex. God bless you, and——' He hesitated for a moment and then said thoughtfully, and as though the word were not a light one, 'Good-bye.'

His thin hand gripped Alex's for a brief moment and then he turned and walked away, and Alex had a last glimpse of his tall figure outlined against the lighted square of the open doorway as he passed through it and was gone.

'I shall not see him again,' thought Alex with sudden conviction; and was startled by the unbidden thought. Why should he think such a thing? Was it only because he was tired and overworked that he had imagined something indefinably final in that last word of farewell? He found that he was staring at the lighted doorway as though he could drag back that spare tall figure by an effort of will, and that there was an uncomfortable constriction in his throat.

The last months had been full of anxiety and strain and infuriating frustration for Alex, and his recent interview with Mr Barton had driven him dangerously near to breaking point. To be dragged from his district, at a time like this, to explain a wholly justified action taken against a wealthy and dissolute nobleman who had only escaped his just deserts in the past on account of bribes paid to the Commissioner, was beyond bearing. Yet he had set his teeth and borne it, and as a result had arrived at the Residency that evening in no very amiable frame of mind. He had, for the moment, quite genuinely meant what he said when he told Sir Henry Lawrence that he would accept any post that would allow him to return to regimental duty, and he had been seriously considering sending Mr Barton his resignation. But ten minutes of Lawrence's society had been enough to restore a sense of proportion and sanity. Perhaps that was why men as remarkable and as different as Nicholson and Hodson could regard Sir Henry with so much respect and affection, and why, when he had left the Punjab, thousands had come to bid him farewell and to follow him for many miles as though loath to see the last of him.

'Of course I shall see him again!' thought Alex. 'He is not an old man. He is barely fifty . . .' But in spite of the windless warmth of the night he shivered as though he were cold, and could not rid himself of a sense of foreboding.

It was late, and in a few hours' time he would have to start for Lunjore again. He knew that he should get what sleep he could, but he had seldom felt less like sleeping. The house was hot and it was too warm even in the shadows of the verandah, but the garden looked cool and inviting. Alex walked the length of the verandah and went down a shallow flight of steps and out into the quiet moonlight.

Although it was almost mid-April the night was fresh and cool, for the hot weather was unusually late that year and it might well have been early March, so green and pleasant were the grass and the flowering trees. The roses were colourless in the milky light, but the late-blooming orange blossom and foaming masses of jasmine were star-white, and the night air was sweet with the scent of flowers and lately watered earth.

Alex strolled across the wide lawns, his footsteps inaudible on the grass that the gardeners had watered at sunset, and came by chance to a group of flame trees whose shadows lay velvet-black in the moonlight.

There was someone standing at the far edge of that belt of soft darkness, her wide, pale skirts luminous in the shadows, and despite the fact that her outline was barely distinguishable and that she had her back to him, he knew that it was Winter. He stopped, and would have turned back except that something in the pose of the dimly seen figure arrested his attention. She was watching something, and there was a suggestion of alertness in the tilt of her head that even the deep shadows could not disguise. Curiosity overcame discretion and he went forward and came to stand beside her.

She heard the quiet footsteps and turned her head, but she made no movement of surprise or alarm and seemed as instantly aware of his identity as he had been of hers. She might almost have been waiting for him, though for once she had not even been thinking of him. But it seemed entirely natural to her that he should be there. The warm stillness of the garden was another world which had nothing in common with the turmoil and tensions and restlessness that were a part of the daylight hours. She accepted his presence as a matter of course, and turned back to her contemplation of the stretch of gardens beyond the trees, as though her interest in what lay there had absorbed her attention to the exclusion of all else.

Standing beside her Alex could see the pale outline of her profile against the massed darkness of the leaves, and smell the clean, cool scent of lavender that he had come to associate with her. As his eyes became accustomed to the shadows he could make out the curving line of the long lashes, the faint, puzzled crease between her brows and a stray tendril of black hair that curled childishly above her ear.

Winter did not appear to be aware of his gaze and presently she inquired in a whisper: 'What are they doing?'

Alex looked away from her, and for the first time became aware of what it was that had caught her interest. There were things moving across the open ground between the sharp-edged shadows of buildings that lay within the precincts of the Residency: things that moved in complete silence, keeping for the most part to the shadows and flitting noiselessly across the moonlit spaces like a frieze of trolls; bowed, hunchbacked and grotesque, silhouetted briefly against the silver-washed grass or the wall of a house; lost again in shadow and emerging only to be swallowed up by the ground.

It took him a moment or two to realize that they were men carrying heavy loads, shouldering sacks or bent under weighted boxes, and stowing them away in the underground cellars that lay beneath some of the Residency buildings. He said lightly enough: 'They are only men laying in supplies for the summer. Grain and——'

'And ammunition,' finished Winter. 'Why? And why are they doing it by night? George Lawrence was there a little while ago. I saw him. He said he was going to bed, but he came out here to see that there was no one about. They were doing it last night too. And the night before. They cannot need so many supplies unless . . . unless they think this place will be besieged. Is it that?'

Alex did not answer the question. He said instead: 'Why have you come out here to watch them every night?'

'I haven't. I mean, I did not come out to watch them. I only came out to walk in the garden.'

'At this time of night? It's very late.'

'I could not sleep, and this gave me something else to think about,' said Winter simply. 'Is there really going to be a rising? Ameera says——'

She stopped and after a moment Alex said: 'What does Ameera say? And who is Ameera?'

Winter turned to look at him in surprise. It seemed incredible to her that Alex should not know about Ameera. Until she remembered that she had barely seen him, and then only at a distance, for almost three months after her marriage, and that he did not even know the story of how she had come to Lunjore. She told him something of it now, and of Juanita and Aziza Begum and the Gulab Mahal; standing among the scented shadows of a garden that overlooked the teeming city of Lucknow and the house in which she had been born.

It had been April when Marcos de Ballesteros, riding out through the gateway of the Gulab Mahal, had turned in the saddle to see Sabrina standing among the hard-fretted shadows of the gold-mohur trees, and had not known that he was seeing her for the last time. Eighteen years ago. And now it was April again, and Sabrina's daughter told that tale as it had been told to her by Zobeida . . .

'We never knew what had become of them – Aziza Begum and my Aunt Juanita and the others,' said Winter in conclusion. 'The letters stopped. That was all. I did not even know if Ameera was alive; or anyone I had known.'

She was silent for a time and then she said slowly: 'I think Ameera is afraid. Her husband does not like the British, and I think – I think he does not trust her because of her Western blood. She will not let me go to the Gulab Mahal, and I have only seen her twice. She says it is not easy for her to see me, and I do not think her husband knows that she has done so. Perhaps he would punish her if he did. You don't think he would, do you? Jehan Khan told me that Nila Ram cut off his wife's hands because she disobeyed him——' Her voice had a sudden tremor of fear in it and she put out a hand and caught at Alex's sleeve: 'Alex, you don't think he would do anything like that, do you?'

Alex looked down at the small hand on his arm and found himself unable to resist the impulse to cover it with his own. His touch appeared to startle her, for he felt the slim fingers stiffen and become quite still under the light clasp of his own. They withdrew gently and without haste, but her unconscious acceptance of his presence was gone and the ease between them was broken.

Alex said in a matter-of-fact voice: 'No, I don't. I expect you would find that Nila Ram's wife was conducting a clandestine affair. To visit a first cousin, even if that cousin is a European, is hardly a major offence. Does she seem to think there is any danger of an armed rising?'

Winter shook her head. 'She said that the city was full of strange rumours, but she would not say what they were. Only – only she said that I must go to the hills, and not stay in Lunjore.'

Alex said drily: 'I seem to remember saying that myself.'

'I know you did. But there are twenty or more other women in Lunjore, and——' She broke off abruptly, wishing that she had not spoken. The inference was so obvious, and what did she expect Alex to say? That she was the only one whose safety he cared about? She drew back from him involuntarily, feeling the hot colour flood up and burn in her cheeks, and grateful for the darkness that would conceal it. But Alex's voice was clipped and cool:

'I am aware of it. And if I had the authority to do so, I would have every one of you sent to the nearest hill station where there are British troops while there is still time. Not for your safety, but for ours.'

'For yours?' said Winter uncertainly. 'I don't understand——'

'Don't you? I should have thought it was obvious,' said Alex brutally. 'Because men are sentimental over women they will throw away military advantages, and hesitate and weigh the chances of failure when attack is their best or only hope, and lose their opportunity because they "have to think of the women and children". Men who would not otherwise dream of surrendering will make terms with an enemy in return for the safety of a handful of women. If a man is killed, it is an accident of war; but if a woman or a child is killed it is a barbarous murder and a hundred lives – or a thousand – are sacrificed to avenge it. It is only a man like John Nicholson who has the courage to write, and mean it, that the safety of "women and children in some crises is such a very minor consideration that it ceases to be a consideration at all". If only more men thought like that you could all stay in Lunjore and be damned to you!'

There was exasperation and bitterness in his voice, as though some prophetic vision of the future had risen before him in all its tragic futility. And then a dry leaf crunched behind them and he turned quickly to see George Lawrence standing beyond the rim of the tree shadows.

'Who is it?' George Lawrence spoke softly but sharply, and as Alex moved out of the shadows he said with undisguised relief: 'Oh, it's you, Alex. I thought——' He checked at the sight of Winter. 'Mrs Barton!'

His eyebrows twitched together in a sudden frown and Winter said: 'I'm sorry, Mr Lawrence. Did we startle you? I came down to walk in the garden because I couldn't sleep, and Captain Randall found me here.'

The Chief Commissioner's nephew cleared his throat in nervous embarrassment and shot a quick look at Alex that needed no interpretation.

Alex grinned a little maliciously and said: 'No such luck,' as though in answer to a spoken question.

The moonlight did not disguise the dark colour that showed briefly in George Lawrence's face. He said sharply: 'I did not for a moment suppose——' and checked again, and then said abruptly and as though Winter were not there: 'How much has she seen?'

'Quite enough,' said Alex laconically. 'But she won't talk.'

George Lawrence turned to look at Winter and she answered an unspoken question as Alex had done: 'I promise. I didn't mean to spy on you, and I won't speak of it to anyone. Word of honour.' She smiled at him and his set face relaxed in an answering smile.

'Thank you. It is not a thing that my uncle would wish to become generally known. It is only a precautionary measure, you understand, but if it were to be talked about it might give rise to panic at a time when it is essential to give the appearance of calm.'

He turned to Alex and said a little stiffly: 'I thought that you were intending to make a five o'clock start, Alex? It is near one o'clock already. Had you not better be getting some sleep? I will see Mrs Barton to her room.'

Alex regarded him with a good deal of sardonic comprehension in his gaze. So George considered that he had been gravely imperilling young Mrs Barton's reputation by being found talking to her in the garden at one o'clock in the morning, did he? He wondered what impression would be gained by anyone who might happen to see Mr Lawrence escorting Mrs Barton to her bedroom at that hour. George would not have thought of that! He said gravely: 'I am sure I could leave her in no better hands. Good night, Mrs Barton. Good-bye, George. I hear you return to Sikora soon? Good luck to you.'

'Thank you,' said George Lawrence soberly. 'I may need it.'

Alex lifted his hand in a brief gesture of farewell, and turning on his heel walked away across the moonlit lawn and was swallowed up by the foreshortened shadow of the Residency tower.

The Dalys had left shortly after twelve o'clock on the following day, and an hour after their departure Winter drove back in Sir Henry's barouche to the Casa de Ballesteros.

Her husband, she was informed, was still abed. There had been a party last night; not a large one, half a dozen sahibs in all. But they had stayed until the small hours.

Despite the lateness of the season, every door and window in the big drawing-room stood wide, but the hot air of mid-day and the scent of fresh-cut flowers could not disguise the stale reek of cigar-smoke, spilled brandy and another smell that reminded Winter of Hazrat Bagh. There was also something in the room that had not been there before: a large square of faded velvet that she recognized as a bedspread from one of the upstairs rooms had been hung neatly over Velasquez's portrait of Don Cristobal de Ballesteros.

Winter looked at it, puzzled and frowning, and sent for old Muddeh Khan, the head bearer. Muddeh Khan had looked unhappy and had avoided her eye. The Huzoors, he explained apologetically, had been in a merry mood and had damaged the portrait somewhat in sport. He would have removed it, save that the wall also——

Winter dismissed him, and when he had gone she crossed to the portrait and pulled away the square of olive-green velvet, and knew why the smell in the room had reminded her of Hazrat Bagh. Conway and his guests had used the vast painting as a target, and the dark beauty of the magnificent canvas was spattered with bullet holes which had smashed through it and broken and pitted the wall at its back. The haughty, hollow-cheeked Spanish face with its faint suggestion of scornful amusement was a mess of ruined canvas, and there was nothing left of the portrait that was worth repairing.

Looking at it, Winter was dragged down without warning into helpless rage. That he could do this to her father's house! to Pavos Reales! That he should bring his coarse, drunken friends and his cheap, loud women to this beautiful, silent house and vulgarize it as he had done last night!

She turned and walked out of the house and down to the river terrace; hatless in the hot sunlight and shivering with shock and anger and disgust as she had shivered on the morning that had followed the nightmare of her wedding.

'I can't bear it!' thought Winter, staring out across the wide reaches of the river with eyes that only saw the senseless ruin of that magnificent canvas. 'I can't bear it . . .!' Yet what was she to do? Neither Church nor Law would release her, and she remembered again what Mrs Gardener-Smith had told her. That the law would be on Conway's side.

'I will go to the hills,' thought Winter. 'At once – today! That should at least please Alex. Or . . . or will it? No, not please him. He does not want me to go because I am I, but because I am merely one of all the women he would like to be rid of so that we cannot get in the way of military decisions if there is a crisis. Alex thinks that there is going to be a crisis. And so does Sir Henry, or he would not be taking all those precautions. Ameera does too – or is it only that she is frightened of her husband? or *for* him?' What was it Alex had said? or Nicholson had said? . . . '*women . . . in some crises are such a very minor consideration that they cease to be a consideration at all*'.

Quite suddenly her anger and despair fell away from her, for if a crisis was indeed brewing in India her own difficulties were trivial, and she could not, at this juncture, add to the problems and anxieties that the times were laying upon the shoulders of all men by creating a public scandal in Lunjore and Lucknow. Conway intended to return to Lunjore at the end of the month, and she would go with him and arrange to leave for Simla or Naini Tal towards the middle of May. That at least could create no scandal, and Conway could not very well refuse to let her go. She must do nothing until then; except the hardest thing of all. To wait . . .

It was mid-afternoon and the quietest time of the day. Few went abroad while the sun sucked the moisture from the earth and the marrow from men's bones, and all who could do so lay still in the shade and waited for the cool of the evening. The river and the stone-flagged terrace lay empty in the sun-glare, and the far bank was deserted. A mile or so upstream the city shimmered in the heat-haze, and there was no cloud in the sky and nothing moved except the soundless river and a solitary boat that drifted down with the stream.

It was a flat-bottomed country boat with a matting roof curved above it to keep out the sun, poled by an ancient rheumy-eyed man in the scanty garb of a fisherman, and it drifted closer and closer into the bank until it bumped gently against the stone wall of the river terrace and its prow grated on the water-steps. It was a small enough sound but astonishingly loud in the hot, silent stillness of the afternoon, and Winter moved to the balustrade and looked down.

A woman's partially veiled face peered out from beneath the matting screen and looked cautiously up and down the empty reaches of the river, eyes narrowed against the sun-glare, and then glancing upwards, saw Winter. The eyes widened suddenly and a dark claw-like hand beckoned. There was something so furtive and yet so urgent in that gesture that Winter turned involuntarily to look behind her. But the terrace and the park beyond it were deserted, and not even a butterfly moved in the blinding sunlight.

She went quickly to the water-steps, holding her wide skirts clear of the hot flagstones, but at the top of them she hesitated for a moment. There was no one within sight or call, and she did not know who was in the boat. The hand beckoned again imperiously and Winter descended the steps slowly and stooped to peer under the shadows of the curved matting. The face that looked up at her dropped its *chuddah* for a brief moment. It was Hamida.

Winter gathered up her skirts and holding them about her scrambled into the darkness of the tent-like enclosure. There was a clink of silver bracelets and a scent of attar-of-roses, and a soft, slender hand that was not Hamida's stretched out of the gloom and caught her bare arm.

'Ameera! Is it thou?'

'It is I, *querida*——' Ameera spoke in halting Spanish. 'Luck is indeed with me, for I did not think to find you here. Hamida was to fetch you from the house. I came at this time because I knew that there would be few abroad at such an hour, and I cannot stay long.'

She spoke with a soft, breathless haste that made Winter say sharply: 'What is it? What has happened?'

'Nothing. Nothing as yet. But I cannot come to see you again. It is not safe, either for you or for me. And if it were known that I have come now——'

The sentence broke off into a shiver and all at once the hot dimness of the little matting shelter, the bright stillness of the land and the wide, slow-flowing river were full of fear, and even the sly chuckle of the water under the wooden boat seemed a sound full of menace.

Winter took Ameera's hand between her own small cool palms and held it tightly. 'Tell me what has happened.'

Ameera sank her voice to a whisper: 'I must not come again, but I could not – I did not dare send word for fear that it would not reach you, or that you would not believe. You must go, *querida*. Quickly! Very quickly. There is danger here for all of your blood. No, not in Lucknow only, or in Oudh, but in all India. I have heard .... things. Things I dare not tell you. But it is true what I say. Only yesterday there was found a proclamation posted by the gate of the Jumma Masjid in Delhi, saying that the Shah-in-Roos (the Tsar) would send an army that would sweep all the British into the sea and——'

'*Yesterday*?' said Winter. 'How can you know that? It is two hundred miles and more to Delhi.'

'There are ways,' whispered Ameera. 'Ill news travels swiftly, and there is much ill news; therefore I come to tell you that you must not go to the hills but to the sea, and take ship and return at once to your own country.'

'This is my country.'

'It is not – it is *not*!' said Ameera passionately. 'I am of this land, but you are not! But for love of you, because we two played together as children and because your father was brother to my mother, I betray my countrymen by warning you to go.'

Winter said slowly: 'Dear, you must tell me more. I cannot go just for this. I – I am married. There is my husband – can you not tell me——'

'I can tell you nothing – *nothing*! Already I have said too much. I also love my husband, though his heart is turned away from me because of my mother's blood that runs in my veins – do you think I would not rid myself of it if I could, for his sake? He will turn to me again, of that I am sure. How could I live if it were not so? But men are not as we are. For us, they are all of life. But for them love is but a small part of living, forgotten when the kissing is done. My husband thinks first of his own people and his own Padishah and of his own wrongs. If he knew that I had told you aught, he would kill me – even me, who am the mother of his sons, and whom he loves.'

Winter's eyes, accustomed now to the gloom after the sun-glare of the terrace, could see that Ameera's face was drawn and haggard with fear and anxiety, and that the same fear was on Hamida's face too. But she had to know more. She had to know *when*, but there was little trace of the West in Ameera who had once been 'Anne Marie'; her love and her loyalty lay with her husband's people, and she would not tell more than she must . . .

Winter said carefully, trying to keep the urgency from her voice: 'I will try to go, but it will not be easy to leave soon. We do not return to Lunjore until the end of this month, and I had planned to go to the hills by mid-May.'

Ameera said: '*No*! not to the hills! To England. Even the hills may not be safe.'

'It will take three weeks to reach Calcutta,' said Winter slowly.

'That I know. Did I not say that you must leave at once? Before the first week of May is out.'

Winter's fingers released the slim hand she held, and she said as though frightened: 'But is it safe to travel? If there is danger, would it not be safer to stay where there are regiments?'

'No harm will come to you before the last day of May. But after that there will be no safety anywhere – least of all where there are regiments! You will go? Promise me you will go.'

Winter drew a long breath and found that the palms of her hands were wet: a wetness that had nothing to do with the airless heat of the small boat. She had got what she wanted. She leant forward and kissed Ameera swiftly: 'I will try, *querida*. But if my – my husband will not go, then I cannot.'

'Then go to the hills. It may serve . . . I do not know. And now I must go. Already I have stayed overlong. Good-bye, *querida*——' She lapsed into Hindustani: 'Farewell, Little Pearl. Do not forget me. I will make prayer to my God and to Bibi Miriam (the Virgin Mary) also, who was a woman and may hear me, for thy sake and thy safety.' The tears were running down her cheeks and she clung to Winter for a moment and then tore herself free and thrust her away. 'Go now – go quickly! It is late. Hamida, tell the *manji* to make haste!'

Winter stood on the water-steps in the hard sunlight and saw the old man thrust off with his pole, backing the narrow boat into the stream. She raised her hand in farewell, and then the boat had swung and the old *manji* was poling it away upstream towards the city.

The little ripples lapped and hissed softly against the hot stone steps, and Winter watched the small boat through a mist of tears until the sun-dazzle on the water blotted it out. Something moved on the terrace above her and she whirled about, her heart in her throat. But it was only a peacock rustling his splendid tail along the flagstones.

Her sudden movement and the swish of her hooped skirts startled the bird, and lifting his tail clear of the ground he scuttled for the shelter of the bamboos with undignified haste. But the momentary panic he had caused her served to remind Winter – if she had needed reminding – that Ameera had risked her life to bring that warning. It was a horrible thought, and it sent a small, icy prickle of fear down Winter's spine. She shivered in the afternoon heat and turned back again to the river, peering under the palm of her hand. But the boat had gone and the river ran quiet and undisturbed from bank to bank and nothing moved upon it save a corpse that drifted down on the stream turning lazily with the current, and a slow-moving mud-turtle who crawled up out of the water to bask with his basking fellows on the edge of a sand bar.

Had anyone seen Ameera's boat stop at the water-steps? There were so many eyes in India. But Ameera had been right: now that the hot weather had set in this was the safest time of day. Safer than the night, when every tree and shrub and shadow could hide a pair of eyes. No, there was no one on the river terrace, and no one in the gardens or the park. Only herself and the peacock. It was absurd to feel afraid. And yet she was afraid.

Winter stood on the deserted terrace and looked out across the wide river and the wide land beyond, as her mother Sabrina had stood on an evening almost eighteen years ago: and was seized as Sabrina had been by a sudden horror of India. Of the savage, alien land that lay all about her, stretching away for hundreds of miles and yet hemming her in; of the dark, secretive, sideways-looking eyes and the tortuous, unreadable minds behind the bland, expressionless faces. Of Nila Ram, who had cut off his young wife's hands . . .

'I must be careful,' thought Winter. 'I must be very careful. Not for my sake, but for Ameera's.'

If only Alex were still here. She wondered if she could write to him, and then knew that she could not take the risk because she had no means of ensuring that her letter would not be read, and if she appeared to be in possession of dangerous information, Ameera would be suspected of having given it to her. She was not frightened for herself. Perhaps because she was too young to be able to visualize death in connection with herself, or perhaps because her life at present did not seem to contain much that made it worth living, But Ameera had so much to live for, and she was afraid for Ameera as she could never be afraid for herself.

'I must be careful,' repeated Winter, speaking aloud to the empty sun-soaked spaces of the river terrace: '. . . *careful*' whispered the echo from the curved stone wall that bounded its far end.

She did nothing for three long days. Forcing herself to inactivity and her face to smiles, for fear that her actions or her expression should be watched by someone who might have had knowledge of Ameera's visit. She wrote no letters and paid no visits. She received and entertained her husband's guests, and gave no outward sign that might be interpreted as alarm or disquiet: feeling like a traitor to her own race because she did not run at once to Sir Henry with that vital information.

On the fourth day her chance came when she and her husband attended an evening party at the Residency. It was a very large party, and *shamianahs* had been erected on the lawns, and the trees hung with coloured lanterns. The band of one of the regiments stationed in the cantonments provided music while the guests, who numbered several hundred and included almost all the British residents and a large proportion of the nobility and gentry of Lucknow and its environs, moved about the gardens chattering, laughing, admiring the illuminations, partaking of a large variety of refreshments, and watching the performance of a troupe of jugglers.

Perhaps the most spectacular guest, and certainly the one who aroused most interest, was Dundu Pant, the Nana of Bithaur, who attended the party accompanied by an impressively large retinue.

The Nana was a man who cherished a grievance against the British, the Government having refused to recognize him as the legal heir or to allow him the pension granted to the Peishwa, Baje Rao, who having no son had adopted him under Hindu law. But he did not appear to have allowed his grievances to sour him. He was most friendly and affable towards the British guests, with several of whom he seemed to be on excellent terms, and Winter saw him in animated converse with Sir Henry Lawrence. He was a fat man, strangely dark-skinned for a Mahratta, and very splendidly dressed; and he wore a pair of large diamond earrings which flashed and glittered in the light of the coloured paper lanterns. Alex, had he been present, would not have recognized the earrings – the ones he had seen had been rubies – but he would have had no difficulty at all in recognizing the wearer.

The Chief Commissioner had been surrounded by a ring of guests wherever he moved, and it was clearly impossible to have any private conversation with him. But Winter had managed to speak with George Lawrence. She had asked him to show her the rose garden and had put her hand on his arm and walked away with him, talking with unusual animation. There were strollers in the rose garden too, but far fewer of them, so it was possible to speak here without being overheard.

'I have something to tell you,' said Winter, her hand urgent on his arm. 'It is Sir Henry I wished to speak to, but the people follow him about so, and as I do not wish to go apart with him, you must tell him.' She looked up into her companion's face and said: 'Please will you smile as though I were telling you something of no matter?' – and laughed herself as she spoke.

George Lawrence smiled an obedient and somewhat puzzled smile, and managed to retain it, though with some difficulty, through the next few minutes. He listened attentively while Winter walked beside him, smiling as she talked, and breaking off to admire the roses and the lanterns or comment on the music or the illumination, whenever any other guests passed within earshot. He found the resulting information a little confusing, but realized at least that young Mrs Barton was in deadly earnest, although he was inclined to treat her story with some reserve. There had been so many rumours of late, and this was just one more – and apparently one that had been brought by an over-excited Indian woman who by some curious twist of fate was first cousin to this girl who walked beside him. He was not inclined to take the information as much more than another straw that showed the way in which the wind was blowing, but he promised, nevertheless, to relay it to Sir Henry.

'You must not tell it to him where you can be overheard,' begged Winter earnestly. 'And he must tell no one who it came from. It is true – tell him that I am *sure* that it is true! Ameera risked her life to tell me, and I am risking hers by telling you. Tell him that.'

She looked up into his face and smiled as she spoke, but her eyes were wide and bright and full of a desperate urgency.

'I will tell him,' promised George Lawrence. 'But you must not allow yourself to become over-anxious, Mrs Barton. We hear many of these rumours. There has been a deal of dissatisfaction in Oudh, for the annexation was pressed through without sufficient thought, and the original policy was needlessly harsh. But Sir Henry is changing all that, and I feel sure that this cloud will blow away as others have done. You have not been out in India very long, I think; but when you have experienced some of our hot weather, you will notice that there are days when the clouds gather until the whole sky is covered with them, and it seems that it must rain. Yet they disperse without a drop falling. It will be the same with this you will find. It will pass.'

It will pass . . . It has passed . . .

In cantonments and offices, in Residencies and British bungalows, in Government Houses and Council chambers and in the home of the Governor-General himself, wherever the British met to talk, those soothing words were spoken again and again. The brief flare-up at Berhampur in February and the uglier and more recent outbreak in Barrackpore had died down without leading to any further demonstrations, and men who had been smelling the wind uneasily relaxed again, and concurred with the popular conviction that the peak of the general unrest had passed, and that any serious danger (if there had ever been any, which the majority were inclined to discount) was now over.

Winter received no further news of Ameera, but Lottie wrote from Delhi. Edward had been transferred there from Meerut on special duty, but they were not living in the cantonments, as they had been lent a delightful house inside the city, not far from the Kashmir Gate:

'*I fear Mama is a little disappointed that we would not reside with Papa and her*,' wrote Lottie, '*but I see so little of Edward that I like to have him to myself when he is off duty. Sophie is away on a visit to friends in Cawnpore, and will be returning on the fifteenth of the next month. It is really not so very hot as yet, and I begin to think that reports as to the heat of the plains have been greatly exaggerated, although I am told that this is quite an exceptionally cool year, and many old hands say they have known nothing like it before. If it gets no worse I do not believe I shall be greatly incommoded. I wish you will come and stay with me. It would be so delightful to see you again. You must come next cold weather, and only think! I shall have a little Edward to show you then! I cannot bring myself to believe it. Mama sends you her love . . .*'

Winter read the letter and thought again of Ameera . . . and of George Lawrence. Which of them was right?

Lottie's news disturbed her, because she had thought that Lottie at least was safe. There were well over a thousand British soldiers in Meerut, forming the strongest European garrison in the North-Western Provinces, and surely any woman would be safe there? But Delhi——

She wrote to Lottie, urging her for the sake of the coming child to go to the hills and to take Sophie with her:

'*You do not know how hot it can get in the plains, and it will be so bad for you at this time. You should think of the child. I expect to be going to the hills about the middle of May, and shall be so lonely there that if you will come and stay with me as my guests, and keep me company, you will be doing me a great kindness.*'

She wrote also to Edward English and to Mrs Abuthnot, urging it upon them, and begging Mrs Abuthnot to accompany her daughters – they would all spend the hot months together in a bungalow among the pines and be cool and have pleasant times. But Lottie would not leave her Edward or Mrs Abuthnot her George. It was too kind of dear Winter, but they were sure that she would understand. Perhaps Sophie might pay her a visit later on?

Winter wrote again, and more urgently, but they were not to be persuaded. 'Even if I told them all that Ameera had said, they would still not come,' thought Winter, 'because they would not believe it. Or they would hope that it was not true, and soon they would make themselves believe that it could not be. There is nothing I can do.'

On the last day of her stay in Lucknow she went again to the river terrace in mid-afternoon. It was hotter now than it had been on the day when she had last seen Ameera, and even the wide pith hat she wore could not prevent the sun from scorching her slim shoulders. The afternoon was as still and as breathless as that other afternoon had been. And as silent. Even the peacock had gone. There was only Winter, with her shadow black and foreshortened on the hot flagstones, and a little snake, sunning himself by the water-steps, who slid away with a dry rustle as she passed.

Conway had given a farewell party that last night. It had been a riotous affair that had lasted well into the small hours of the morning, and he had to be carried to the carriage in which they were to make the journey to Lunjore. He had expressly forbidden Winter to ride, saying that he had no desire to have her down with heat-stroke on the journey – nothing could be more inconvenient. But the sight of her husband's brandy-sodden and inanimate bulk being disposed in the carriage proved too much for her, and she had ordered Furiante to be saddled.

She looked back over her shoulder at the Casa de los Pavos Reales as she rode away. At the orange trees and the lemon groves, the pomegranates and the tree-shaded levels of the park that had changed so little with the long years. And thought, as Sabrina had thought: 'Perhaps I shall never see it again.' But she did not think it with love and longing as Sabrina had done. The gracious, peaceful house did not mean to her what it had meant to Sabrina: it held no happiness and no memories. It was the Gulab Mahal that held those, but the Gulab Mahal was closed to her. It was still a *fata morgana* – a glimmering mirage. The moon out of reach.

The journey to Lunjore had been hot and tedious, and though the distance was not great they had taken four days to cover it, because the heat tired the horses. Conway had grumbled and cursed and complained, and solaced himself freely with brandy. The snows were melting in the ranges to the north and the river was higher than when they had crossed it coming to Lucknow. The bridge of boats rang hollowly to the clop of the horses' hooves, and jerked and creaked and swayed to the wheels of the carriage: and then they were over, and Oudh was behind them.

It was evening, and the last day of April, when the Commissioner and his wife drove once more through the massive gateway of the Lunjore Residency, and barely two hours later they were dining with the same raffish company that had celebrated the Commissioner's wedding.

They were all there, with the exception of Mr Josh Cottar who had departed to Calcutta on a business trip: Lou Cottar, Chrissie and Edgar Wilkinson, Colonel Moulson, Major Mottisham and half a dozen others. 'Wrote ahead and invited 'em,' said Conway. 'Didn't think that we'd take that extra day, but what's the odds? Nothin' like havin' a celebration to welcome us home, eh?'

'I assure you the place has been like a morgue or a Quakers' Meeting while you have been away,' said Lou Cottar. 'I have had such a fit of the bore that I have yawned two more lines into my face, and heaven knows that it has enough already. I get asked to so few amusing parties when you are away, Con, for the majority of your female parishioners do not consider me quite respectable. Odd, is it not? Or else they do not trust their husbands! Though I cannot think why they should not, when their husbands are almost without exception dull enough to send one into a decline!'

'Who are the exceptions, Lou?' inquired the Commissioner with a chuckle. 'Am I one?'

Mrs Cottar raised her brows at him. 'Not any longer. But you do at least provide the only tolerably amusing parties in Lunjore.'

'It wasn't only my parties you found amusing once,' said the Commissioner, reaching out to pat her arm. 'Eh, Lou?'

'Ah, but that was at least five years ago. Or was it more? You were a heavy, handsome brute in those days, and I believe I actually lost almost two nights' sleep over you once.'

'Shall I see if I can make you lose two more?'

'You couldn't do it. You're gross, Con. You're fat and bald and you drink a deal too much, and if it wasn't for your parties I'd be tempted to drop you. But you're a habit with me and I'm too idle to break it.'

The Commissioner glowered at her. 'You've got the most poisonous tongue of any woman I know, Lou. By God, I don't know why I put up with you!'

'Because I'm a habit with you, and you've never been able to break yourself of bad habits,' said Mrs Cottar. She laughed her low, throaty laugh and crossing to the piano, threw up the lid and began to sing a music-hall song to her own accompaniment for the amusement of the company:

'Hamlet loved a maid,
Calumny had passed her.
She never had played tricks,
'Cause nobody had ask'd her!'

'Nothing has changed,' thought Winter. 'It is just the same. It's as though I had never been away to Lucknow . . .'

But that was not true. She herself had changed. The noisy, raffish party and the sight of her husband with his arm about Chrissie Wilkinson's waist no longer had any power to hurt or disgust her. A night in the garden of the Lucknow Residency and an afternoon on the river terrace of the House of the Peacocks had changed all that, for now she too could feel the wind and hear the thunder.

If Ameera was right, all these people here might die within a few months – perhaps in less. The last day of May, Ameera had said – 'and after that there will be no safety anywhere'. It was the first of May tomorrow. In English villages they would be going to bed early so as to be up with the dawn to pick flowers with which May Queens would be crowned and garlanded on countless village greens. The hedges and the orchards would be bright with blossom, and there would be cowslips and primroses in the woods and fields, and beribboned maypoles on the greens. May Day. Thirty days more. *Was* Ameera right? – or was George Lawrence? *It will pass . . . it will pass . . . It has passed.* Had it?

Winter did not ride the following morning. The horses needed rest, and she slept late, but when she had breakfasted she wrote to Alex.

It was a short letter and the first she had ever written to him. She gave it to a servant to deliver, but the man said that Randall Sahib was in camp among the outlying villages. 'Then someone must take it to him,' said Winter. 'Send Yusaf to me.' The man looked slantingly at her under lowered lids and went away to summon the syce. But the look had frightened Winter.

Quite suddenly, in that brief moment, the full meaning of what a major insurrection in this country would entail came home to her. She had never really visualized it in its entirety before. She had, indeed, imagined Ameera being killed or maimed as a punishment for having warned her, and she had visualized Lottie and kind Mrs Abuthnot and hero-worshipping Sophie being cut down by a howling mob. But these had been isolated pictures, and behind them had been a whispering voice that said: *'We hear many of these rumours . . . it will pass.'* But now, standing in the big, cool drawing-room of her husband's house, she thought for the first time of exactly what such a rising would mean. Of the handful of white people who held this vast country, and the dark, teeming millions who surrounded them and who lived cheek by jowl with them, watching their every movement and listening to their every word – and waiting. There was little privacy to be had in a land where a dozen servants were always within call, and where a punkah-coolie, a *chupprassi*, or a *dazi* sitting cross-legged before a pile of sewing, were as natural a part of every verandah as the matting on the floor.

She had trusted the servants in her father's house at Lucknow, but she had still been careful for fear that they might be questioned by others. And if she had been careful there, she must be doubly careful here. She tore up the letter that she had written to Alex and burnt the pieces, and wrote another. It was not that she did not trust Yusaf, who was Alex's own servant, but she preferred to take no chances. She handed the letter to him, telling him in a tone that was sufficiently clear to carry to the punkah-coolie and a loitering gardener who was cutting off the dead heads of the canna lilies in a flower-bed below the verandah, that a friend of the Captain Sahib's whom she had met in Lucknow wished to come over for some *shikar* (shooting), and as the Sahib was in camp he must be informed in case he wished to return.

Yusaf had ridden with the letter, and Alex had read it late that evening by the light of a flaring oil-lamp. There had been only two lines, but he had read them and re-read them and then folded the paper carefully and put it into the inner pocket of his coat. He whistled softly and Niaz materialized out of the darkness. 'We return tomorrow,' said Alex.

Niaz raised his eyebrows, but made no other comment on the unexpected order beyond inquiring when they were to start.

'*Panch baji* (five o'clock). That should do. No it won't——' Alex was speaking in English for the first time in over two weeks and was unconscious of it. 'There is that business of Puran Chand's. I can't leave that in the air. The rest can slide . . .'

When he was on tour in the district Alex seldom had occasion to speak his own tongue, and was apt to find himself thinking and even dreaming in Hindustani. He reverted to it now: 'Tell the Kotwal that I will see him at sunrise. There is still some work here that cannot wait. We will leave as soon as it is finished. Where is Yusaf?'

'Huzoor?' A second shadow moved out of the darkness and saluted.

'Tell the Memsahib that I return tomorrow or the next day.'

Yusaf saluted again and slipped back into the darkness, and Alex returned to his tent and blew out the light that was attracting too many creeping and flying things to their doom.

Niaz had put up the camp-bed in the open, and lying on it later that night Alex stared up through the mosquito net at the blaze of stars, and saw a comet cross the heavens from east to west, not with the rush of a falling star, but slowly, dragging a long train of glowing light that appeared red rather than white or golden, and taking a full ten minutes to traverse the spangled ceiling of the sky. From a dozen yards to his left he heard Niaz move, and looking in his direction saw the silhouette of his lifted head and knew that he had seen it too.

'They will say that too is a sign – or an omen,' thought Alex, 'and I am not sure that one can blame them for it.'

A red star, smearing a trail of blood from the east to the west. Were there such things as signs and wonders in the sky? A star had once brought Wise Men out of the East to search for that Sword that had come into the world so many centuries ago and had not yet been sheathed. That the heavens foretold the future was perhaps the oldest superstition in the world, and men had watched the skies for three thousand years and more, believing that their fate could be read there. In the hot weather many men slept out in the open, in roadways and on roof-tops and at the doors of their huts. How many of them would have seen the red comet, and how many – or how few? – would not regard it as a sign from heaven? An evil sign: not because of its colour, for red is worn in the East for rejoicing, but because the times and men's thoughts were evil.

A hundred yards away a pariah dog thrust its gaunt nose at the sky and howled long and very mournfully, and the howl was taken up and repeated again and again in a barking, wailing chorus by all the dogs of the near-by village, as though they bayed the moon. Beyond the tank and the mango-tope where Alex's camp was pitched, a light pricked the darkness; and another and another; and presently a conch brayed in the temple and a tom-tom beat. 'They have seen it,' thought Alex. 'This is how legends are born.'

He heard Niaz mutter something in an undertone. It appeared to be uncomplimentary to the villagers. The red-tailed comet sank behind the mango trees, its reflection lingering for a moment longer in the dark waters of the tank, and as the glow faded from the sky the dogs stopped howling as though at an order. But the conch brayed and the tom-toms beat for hour after hour, and Alex heard them in his sleep, mingling with his uneasy dreams.

He did not start for Lunjore until early next afternoon when, leaving the servants to break camp and follow, he and Niaz rode hard through the heat of the day and into the dusty sunset and the brief green dusk. As the sun sank below the horizon they had stopped in order to eat and drink, for the Mohammedan fast of Ramadan had begun with the new moon, and while it lasted Niaz and all other followers of the Prophet might not eat or drink between sunrise and sunset. Alex too kept the fast when he was away from the cantonments and out among the villages, for he had found it to be good training, and there were times when he needed to keep it.

They had drawn rein at the edge of a tank, and as they dismounted a lone pigeon with a hawk on its tail flew low above their heads, twisting and turning in its flight, and flumped heavily into a large *peepul* tree on the far side of the tank. A flock of crows rose up from the *peepul*, cawing hoarsely, and the hawk flew off. Presently the pigeon, undisturbed by the narrowness of its escape, fluttered down onto a half-submerged slab of stone at the edge of the green scum-covered water to drink. But almost instantly it rose again with a noisy, startled flap of wings, as though something had frightened it, and they saw it circle upwards and then turn and make for the west where the glow of the setting sun was turning the dust veils to gold.

Alex looked across the tank with narrowed eyes, trying to see what it was that had startled the bird, and became aware that there was a man seated among the roots of the *peepul* tree. A naked ash-smeared sadhu who sat so still that he might almost have been part of the tree. The squirrels played about him, running casually to and fro, and a dozen birds who were making preparations to roost quarrelled and twittered within reach of his hand, as completely undisturbed by his presence as the crows and the parrots who perched in the boughs over his head. He had made no movement: Alex was sure of that, because had he done so he would have alarmed the other wild creatures about him. Yet the pigeon had been frightened. It was a trivial incident, but it occupied Alex's mind to the exclusion of much else for the remainder of the ride.

It was dark by the time they reached the bungalow, and having taken a hot bath to remove the dust and sweat of the long ride, he changed into the white mess-jacket that was almost a uniform of the hot weather, and walked across in the starlight to the Residency.

The big house was ablaze with lights and there was a trap and a high dog-cart standing on the wide drive. 'Moulson again,' thought Alex, 'and Gidney and Mottisham, I suppose.' He nodded to the *chowkidar* and went up the verandah steps. A servant lifted the *chik* before the hall door and murmured that the Huzoors were playing cards in the small *ghol-kumra* (drawing-room) and the Memsahib was in the big drawing-room.

Winter was sitting on a sofa in the centre of the room with the slow-moving punkah stirring the air above her. She had a book in her hands, but it was obvious that she had heard his voice in the hall. There was a suggestion of rigidity about her slight figure, and she was smiling. It was a pleasant smile; the smile an actress might have employed to indicate pleasurable surprise. But she was not as a rule, reflected Alex, walking leisurely towards her, much given to smiling, and it occurred to him to wonder if that smile was for his benefit or for Rassul, who had shown him in. Some instinct for danger made him return it, and as he took the hand that she held out to him he knew that he had been right, for her fingers were cold and not quite steady and they tightened warningly upon his for a moment before they were withdrawn.

She said gaily and on the same note of pleased surprise that was in her smile: 'How kind of you to come so promptly! I hope it was not inconvenient? I was entrusted with a message from a friend of yours whom I met in Lucknow.' Her gaze went past him and she spoke to the servant who lingered by the door: 'Bring drinks for the Sahib, Rassul.'

'*Hukkum*,' murmured Rassul and the door closed softly behind him.

Winter said: 'Do sit down, Captain Randall. Have you ridden far today? I am afraid my husband is busy just now. A card-party, you know. How much English do these people understand? I did not expect to see you until tomorrow.' She laughed as though she had made some joke.

Alex's eyes narrowed suddenly but he replied without the least hesitation: 'There was nothing much to keep me, and camping is hot work in this weather. A good deal more than most people would think.'

He saw Winter's quick breath of relief, and smiled. Had she really been afraid that he would misunderstand her and demand explanations? She threw an anxious glance at the two doors that opened onto the verandah. *Chiks* hung before both to keep the room from filling with bats and night-flying insects, but there were, he knew, at least three servants on the verandah. He shook his head very slightly, and the door behind him swung open silently and Rassul was back with a laden tray.

Winter said: 'Yes, I thought it might be so. Mr – Brown wished to know if there was any good shooting to be had in Lunjore at this time of the year. He has a few weeks' leave soon and was considering coming here. I told him that I could not possibly say, but that you would write.'

Rassul poured out a drink and withdrew and Alex talked trivialities for a quarter of an hour by the drawing-room clock. Whatever it was that Winter wished to tell him, he had no intention of hearing it now. She had established her point, and no one listening to her voice and her light laugh could suspect her of having anything in the least disturbing on her mind. He finished his drink and rose: 'I must say a few words to the Commissioner if you will excuse me. Do you ride tomorrow?'

'Yes. A little before five. It is too hot now once the sun is up.'

Alex said: 'You should ride by the river. It is cooler there. I expect I may see you. Good night, Mrs Barton.' He went into the small drawing-room that led off the larger one and was greeted ungraciously by the Commissioner, stayed to watch a hand of whist, and left.

There were no signs in the skies that night and the pariah dogs were silent; but the city was not. The city was awake and restless. Tom-toms throbbed and conches blared as they had in the little village beyond the tank and the mango-tope, and there were an unusual number of pedestrians upon the road that led past the Residency gateway from the cantonments to the city.

'It is Ramadan,' said Niaz; but he said it uneasily, looking over his shoulder.

'It is *dewanee* – the madness,' retorted Alex; and added as Niaz prepared to leave, 'We ride before sunrise. Bring a gun.'

'Which? Do we shoot partridge or *kala hirren* (blackbuck)?'

'Pigeon,' said Alex briefly.

'*Ah!*'

Alex turned swiftly at the tone. 'Didst thou see, then?'

'Nay. It was too far. But that *bairagi* (holy man) did not wish us to see the bird, and therefore he told it to go. Wherefore, I wondered——'

'I too,' said Alex. He had seen such things done before, and it did not strike him as in the least impossible that the man could order a bird's departure without speech or movement. He had heard it said that even little silent Zeb-un-Nissa, Akbar Khan's grand-daughter, could do the same.

It was cool in the early light of the May morning, cooler than Alex ever remembered it to have been at this time of the year. May and June were normally burning months in the plains, but this May was not like others, and he could only regret it, since an early hot weather and soaring temperatures would have sent many women hurrying to the hills with their children, while this unusual mildness was causing them to linger and put off the day of separation.

The land and the river and the sky were all one colour in the dawn light: a clear, opalescent grey in which only the morning star still shivered as a challenging point of brightness. There was a faint swathe of mist smoking off the river, and a pair of sarus cranes cried harshly from among the crops as Alex and Niaz rode along the narrow, embanked roadway that curved across the plain.

Winter had ridden out by the wooden bridge that spanned the nullah behind the house, instead of by the main gateway. She saw the two horsemen far out on the plain ahead of her as she emerged from the thick belt of scrub and jungle that covered the far bank of the nullah and was an arm of the denser jungle that stretched away eastward, closing in upon the river bank three miles further down where the river joined the main stream that formed the boundary between Lunjore and Oudh. The distant horsemen were as small as marionettes, and though they appeared to be moving slowly, a long white cloud of dust behind them showed that their horses were at full gallop, and Winter threaded Furiante between the rough tussocks of grass where the narrow jungle track ran out onto the plain, and giving him his head, rode to cut them off before they reached the river bank. The exhilaration of speed and the rush of the morning air brought a glow of colour to her cheeks and she was laughing as she reined in beside a clump of three tall palm trees where Alex had pulled up to wait for her.

'Good morning, Captain Randall. Have you brought that shotgun for more target practice?'

'Perhaps,' said Alex, unsmiling. He wheeled his horse beside her and they moved off together parallel to the river bank, Niaz and Yusaf falling back out of earshot: 'What is it that you wished to tell me?' Winter's face sobered and she threw a quick look over her shoulder. 'It's all right. They can't hear, and it wouldn't matter if they did. What is it?'

'It's something that Ameera said,' replied Winter, and she told him of that hot, still afternoon on the river terrace of Pavos Reales: of the little covered boat that had drifted in to the water-steps, and the thing that Ameera had told her in halting Spanish so that even Hamida should not know what it was that she had said.

Alex did not say any of the soothing and reassuring things that George Lawrence had said. He said nothing at all for a long time, riding beside her in silence and looking out over the brightening river through narrowed eyes.

So he had been right. A day and a date. He was sure that it must be so, for men like Kishan Prasad and the Maulvi of Faizabad would not content themselves with stirring up general discontent. That was an easy thing to do – too easy. And though sporadic outbreaks of mutiny and violence would embarrass the authorities, they could be dealt with and stamped out provided they were localized. It was a general mutiny of the Bengal Army, coupled with a popular rising, that was to be feared. And such a thing called for a day and a date . . .

The last day of May . . . and it was already the third. Three days gone. Twenty-seven left. Twenty-seven days in which to turn aside the wind that was rising steadily and blowing hot and fitfully through every cantonment in India. How did one stop a wind that had been whistled up by the blindness and obstinacy and egotism of men who imagined that it was a simple matter, and one worthy of all praise, to pry the East loose from its centuries-old laws and customs and force it into a Western mould?

'I can do nothing about the regiments,' thought Alex, 'but some of the talukdars will stand behind me – or at least stay quiet. And so I think will the villages. The city is the trouble. There are always *budmarshes* (scoundrels) by the score in the kennels of any city, and the scum of the bazaars and the back alleys will rise at a word simply for the chance of murder and loot . . . Will the police stand if the Army breaks? I must see Maynard again . . . Can I get Barton to demand plenary military powers in Lunjore that would give him the right to order the sepoys to be disarmed if their Colonels refuse to take action? I could always get him drunk enough to sign anything, and do the job myself. How does one prove to a set of courageous, pig-headed, devoted die-hards that their beloved men are listening nightly to treason? To suggest as much to a man like Gardener-Smith is almost on a par with telling him his wife is unfaithful to him. Worse if anything, as it deprives him of the satisfaction of knocking me down! "*. . . there will be no safety anywhere; least of all where there are regiments.*"'

Alex said abruptly: 'Have you told anyone else?'

'I told George Lawrence, but I don't think he believed me. No, I don't mean that – I mean he believed that Ameera had said it, but he thought that she was only repeating another bazaar rumour. Do *you* think that?'

'I wish I did. But it fits in too well with my own view of the situation.' He relapsed into silence again, riding with a slack rein.

The land and the sky and the still river were no longer grey, but filled with a soft, luminous brilliance, and an almost visible shiver ran over the vast plain as the light lifted in the east. 'The Wings of the Morning,' thought Winter, 'it is like wings – invisible wings – or like someone running, with wings on their feet.'

A white egret flew slowly along the shallows, its reflection mirrored in the quiet water, and a line of dust showed where goats and cattle were being driven out to the grazing grounds. A flock of pigeons, dark against the brightening sky, swept up out of the distant city and circled upwards until their wings paled and shone to the sun that was still below the dusty horizon.

Alex reined in and dismounted swiftly, and Niaz cantered forward without a word and handed over the shotgun he carried as though he had received an order. A partridge called from a clump of dry grass: *Fakiri! Fakiri! Fakiri!* But neither Alex nor Niaz moved in its direction. They were watching the pigeons, and Winter, observing them with a puzzled frown, was startled by the look of grim concentration on the two faces. She turned to follow the direction of their intent gaze, and saw a single pigeon separate itself from the wheeling flock and fly towards them, but at an angle that took it across the river.

'It is out of range,' muttered Niaz.

Alex nodded. He had not raised the gun and now he handed it back and Niaz received it, neither of them taking their eyes off the solitary bird as it dwindled into a speck against the immensity of the sky.

Winter would have asked a question, but Alex's face did not invite questions and she remained silent. He swung himself back into the saddle and they rode back down the river bank and across the plain at a gallop, and reached the outskirts of the cantonments as the first dazzling rim of the sun lipped the horizon.

There was plenty of traffic upon the cantonment roads, for the early mornings were by far the most pleasant (and would soon be the only possible times) in which to walk or ride. Today being Sunday the bells were ringing for the six o'clock service and there were a quantity of early church-goers to be seen driving along the shaded roads, and Alex abandoned his taciturnity and conversed with the utmost cordiality as though he had nothing in the least disturbing on his mind. He accompanied Winter to the Residency gates, acknowledged Akbar Khan's dignified salutation, and returned to his own bungalow for breakfast. He did not keep the Ramadan fast when within reach of his own kind.

Niaz, who had eaten before dawn, was sitting cross-legged on the verandah rolling a supply of cigarettes when he came out. He stood up, slapping the fallen tobacco from his clothes, and said as though continuing a conversation: 'I will tell Amir Nath. I do not think he will talk. But it must be done on the far bank. That was too close.'

Alex nodded, he seldom wasted words on the obvious. 'Tell him, tomorrow at five,' he said.

It was barely light when he rode out on the following morning, and he was not pleased to find Winter at the far side of the wooden bridge that spanned the river a mile above the city. Reining in with unnecessary violence, he demanded to know what she thought she was doing there.

Winter arched her brows at him. 'Riding,' she said lightly. 'Why do you ask?' Alex favoured her with a penetrating look and she laughed and said: 'Very well – I'll confess. I wanted to watch.'

'Watch what?' Alex's voice and face were not encouraging.

'Perhaps you do not know,' said Winter pleasantly, 'that Amir Nath is a friend of mine. He has let me fly his *shahin*.' She saw Alex's mouth tighten ominously and said quickly: 'He didn't tell me. I promise you. I saw him going this way yesterday evening and I stopped to talk to him. He only said that he thought of taking them out into the open country on the far bank to try them against the partridge there, so I thought I would ride this way and watch. It was only when I saw you that I remembered the pigeon. It is that, isn't it?'

'Yes,' said Alex briefly.

'Can I come? I won't if you'd——'

'You may as well,' said Alex ungraciously. He called down a greeting to the old fisherman who lived in a reed hut below the bridge, and touched Chytuc with his heel.

A mile and a half down the far bank of the river and out of sight of the city they turned inland through grass and low scrub and drifts of sand, and presently a small white-bearded man, thin as an arrow, rose up apparently out of the ground, and Alex stopped and dismounted.

'The Huzoor is in good time,' said Amir Nath. 'Will he fly the *jurra* himself?' He lifted the hooded goshawk that held to his wrist, and the bird turned its head with a faint jingle of bells and flexed and unflexed its taloned feet, stretching a little and ruffling its feathers.

Alex shook his head. 'No. I have not handled one for too long, and I would not have him miss.' He held out his hand in a heavy leather riding-glove and took the goshawk from the old falconer, stroking it and talking to it while Winter dismounted and talked to Amir Nath. 'Is Nunni here?' she asked presently. 'Assuredly,' said the old man, and gave a shrill call.

A small boy rose up from the tall grass and grinned shyly at Winter. He carried a peregrine falcon on his wrist, and was Amir Nath's great-grandson. Winter sat down on a tussock of grass and they carried on an animated three-cornered conversation while the sky paled above them and the partridges awoke, and a flight of parrots swished overhead, making for the river. The goshawk on Alex's hand stretched its neck, turning its head eagerly from left to right and tugging at its jesses, and Alex returned it to Amir Nath.

Five hundred yards above them Yusaf, sitting his horse at the bend of the river, stood up in his stirrups and raised his arm, and Niaz, three hundred yards below him, whistled. Alex said: 'It will come over high.'

'High and to the left,' agreed Amir Nath composedly. 'But he is a king of birds.'

Alex had brought a gun again, but the pigeon was well out of range. It came flying steadily, as had the one they had seen on the previous morning, making for the borders of Oudh.

'It is too high,' thought Alex. 'The hawk will never see it——' Amir Nath had removed the hood and now, with a shrill cry, he hurled the bird up and into the air. There was a rush and a whirr of wings and the goshawk mounted with the speed of a feathered arrow, circling upward. It hung for a moment, motionless, sixty feet above them, and then it had sighted the pigeon and was away.

'*Shabash*' shrilled little Nunni, dancing among the tussocks of grass.

'Said I not he was a king of birds?' said Amir Nath. 'Watch him bound to his prey. *Maro*! *Maro*!'

Niaz, who had ridden up, stooped from the saddle, and Nunni, thrusting the tercel at his great-grandfather, clutched at his hand and scrambled up before him with the agility of a squirrel, and then they were away in pursuit.

The pigeon flapped and jinked, turning and twisting, making for the shelter of the dense miles of jungle that blanketed the borders of Lunjore and Oudh. But she did not reach it. The goshawk towered above her, seized her and clung to her and dropped to the ground.

Three hours later Alex was confronting the Commissioner with a small strip of native-made paper on which were written a few lines in *shikust*. 'And that, I think, sir,' he concluded, 'is how bad news seems to get about this country so quickly. There's probably a chain system of 'em.'

'What the devil does it say?' demanded the Commissioner peevishly.

'"*It is too soon. Be patient and await the auspicious day.*"'

'Well – well? What of it? Can't see any harm in that? Too soon for what? Doesn't make sense!'

'I take it to refer to some premature outbreak in Oudh,' said Alex with exemplary patience. 'If we hear within the next day or so that any such incident has occurred, I think we can take it as conclusive. I know that it does not prove much by itself, but added to all the rest it seems to me to have points of interest. Not the least of them being that we now know that we have leading agents and agitators in the city. It also bears out the theory that what is planned is a simultaneous rising on a given date – "the auspicious day".'

'Nonsense!' said the Commissioner. 'Probably refers to a wedding.'

'As you like, sir,' said Alex in his most expressionless voice.

'Why do I do it?' he thought, walking back to his bungalow. 'Why in hell's name do I do it? It's a waste of time and it only puts his back up. Yet I cannot keep him in the dark. I can't have him saying when the mine goes off, "Why did you never tell me?" Justifying myself in advance again! – as if it mattered. Oh, well, I suppose I may as well do the thing thoroughly and be damned to it——'

He spent another exhausting and abortive morning on his feet (he was not offered a chair) placing his views yet again before the three commanding officers of the regiments stationed in Lunjore. But with no better results than before. Colonel Gardener-Smith still steadfastly refused to believe anything against his men, though Alex suspected him of feeling less confident than usual, and was sorry for the old gentleman.

'You don't understand, Randall,' the Colonel had burst out, striking his hands together passionately. 'You are young and you have never commanded a regiment – you have barely served with one! Can you not see that it is you, and men like you, who are responsible for any feeling of – of unrest that there may be in the Bengal Army? Where there is complete confidence there can be no suspicion and distrust, and it is distrust – this distrust that you are doing your best to arouse – that breeds disaffection! I *cannot* distrust my men. To do so would destroy them – and myself!'

Colonel Moulson had been offensive, and Colonel Packer had announced that he trusted in the Lord and therefore feared no evil. Alex went down to the police lines and discussed the possibility of disaffection among the police with Major Maynard who commanded them.

Major Maynard alone confessed to uneasiness, but not on account of his police, whom he believed to be staunch.

'It's old Packer,' he said. 'Unless something can be done to stop him preaching the Word to his men we shall find ourselves in the basket. Can nothing be done to gag the old fool?'

'I've tried,' said Alex tiredly. 'I got him an official wigging, which he holds against me. I gather I am one of those "by whom the offence cometh"! But that was the best I could do.'

'It doesn't appear to have damped his proselytizing ardour,' commented Major Maynard. 'Perhaps he yearns for a martyr's crown?'

'I daresay he does – and at this rate he'll get it! But I have no desire to qualify for one myself. Doesn't he know he's playing with gunpowder? He told me that he was "rendering unto Caesar the things that are Caesar's and to God the things that are God's", and that as, in temporal matters, he obeyed the orders of his superior officers in the Army, so in spiritual matters, as a Soldier of Christ, he obeyed the orders of the Lord, which instructed him to save the heathen from damnation. He has a great deal of support in Lunjore.'

'Among the sepoys?'

'Good God, no! Among the ladies. They look upon him as a saintly man and a shining example to the less devout – such as Moulson!'

'Moulson's too much of a martinet,' said Major Maynard gloomily. 'Seems to be no happy medium! There's old Gardener pottering around with his watering-can, cherishin' his fellows as though they were tender plants, and Packer looking upon his as erring sheep to be gathered into the fold, while Moulson goes to the other extreme and slings his sepoys into irons if they so much as blink on parade. He'll go too far one day, but there's no denying that his lot are the best disciplined of the bunch. I'd say there was a lot less chance of them cracking than of Packer's strayed lambs.'

'Or your own?' inquired Alex.

'Oh, they're all right,' said Major Maynard easily. 'But I'll bear in mind what you say and keep a sharp eye on 'em. Personally, I'm inclined to think that the worst is past. I hear they hanged that Jack who touched off the Barrackpore business – Mangal Pandy? And the jemadar as well. That ought to stop the rot.'

'I envy you your optimism,' said Alex drily, and rode back slowly to his bungalow through the blinding sunlight and the hot shadows of the wide cantonment road.

The telegraph did not as yet operate in Lunjore, and so it was not until two days later that the news trickled over the border from Oudh that on Sunday, May 3rd, the 7th Regiment of Oudh Irregulars had refused to accept their cartridges, and had mutinied. Sir Henry Lawrence had apparently acted with great promptness and succeeded in disarming the Regiment – a good many of whom had absconded – and fifty of the ringleaders had been seized.

'"*It is too soon,*"' said Alex, rereading that laconic dispatch. '"*Be patient and await the auspicious day.*"' He crumpled up the tiny scrap of paper and flung it from him in sudden rage, and rode out in the heat of the day to visit one of the influential landowners in his district.

It was that night that Niaz woke him at one o'clock in the morning.

Alex slept out in the open in the hot weather, and had, in other years, slept in the garden. But this year his bed had been carried up nightly to the flat roof of his bungalow, and Alam Din slept across the stair that led up to it. Alex was a light sleeper at the best of times, and the whispers woke him. There was a quality of urgency about them that sent him out of bed and across the roof within less than ten seconds of his waking.

'*Kaun hai?*' (Who is it?)

'Come down, Huzoor,' whispered Alam Din. 'It is Niaz, and I think he is sorely hurt.'

Alex ran down the stairs and his bare foot slid on something wet. He knew the feel of that sticky wetness of old, and caught the dark figure that sagged against the bottom of the stair, and said sharply to Alam Din: 'Take his feet.'

'No,' gasped Niaz with an attempt at a laugh. 'I can walk. Give me thy shoulder, brother.'

Alex thrust Alam Din ahead of him: 'Light a lamp in my room – quickly! Where art thou hurt?'

'In the back, to the left. But it has missed its mark. Do not fear.'

Alex pulled Niaz's right arm about his shoulder and half-carried him to the bedroom, where he could see the flicker of a light as Alam Din lit the oil-lamp and drew the curtains. He could feel the warm wetness that soaked Niaz's clothing, and in spite of the heat of the May night he found that his hands were cold with rage. The wound was an unpleasant one, but as Niaz had said, it had missed its mark, for it had been deflected by the shoulder-blade and Niaz was suffering more from loss of blood than from anything else. He had walked a mile or more after he had been knifed.

'It was in the lines,' said Niaz. 'I had——'

'Quiet,' said Alex curtly. 'Tell me later. We will bind thee first.' He cut away the blood-soaked clothing, and with Alam Din's assistance washed and bound up the wound and sent him off to brew strong tea.

'I can go no more to the lines,' said Niaz ruefully. 'It is finished. For long they have not trusted me, and I too have carried a knife for fear of this thing. And then to be caught off guard like a fledgling! *Pah!*' He grimaced with pain and drank the hot, sweet liquid thirstily.

'Who was it?'

'I do not know. I went to talk with those whom I thought to be friends of mine in the lines of the 93rd, and to listen. But tonight they would not talk, and they looked at me out of their eyes, sideways, and there was a constraint upon them. There was a *bairagi* in the lines – a sadhu. I saw him standing in the shadows of a hut. He stayed silent and did not move as I passed, and I made as though I had not seen him. When I came away I looked to see if he was still there, but he had gone, and I put my hand upon my knife and walked as a cat walks in an alley full of dogs.'

Niaz grinned to hide another spasm of pain and drank again, his teeth chattering on the rim of the mug. 'There is a lamp by the *peepul* tree at the turn of the lines, by the *bunnia*'s shop,' he said between mouthfuls, 'and there was a gun lying in the dust . . . A revolver such as the sahibs carry. A child's trick that should not have deceived a babe, yet I stooped for it. I heard the step but I could not avoid the blow. Had I not heard it, that knife would have struck true.'

Alex said: 'Was there nothing to tell who it was?'

'I did not see. I fell, and turned as I fell, but he had gone like a shadow, and I did not wait. But I think it was the sadhu.'

'Why?'

Niaz wrinkled his nose expressively and Alex nodded. He too knew the characteristic smell of the ash-smeared, unwashed ascetics of India.

Niaz had a touch of fever the next day, but the ugly wound had bled itself clean, and he suffered remarkably few ill-effects from it. The weather continued unusually mild, and all over India women who had intended to leave for the hills delayed and put off the day of departure while the nights remained cool, and the Commissioner of Lunjore informed his wife that he could not arrange for her to leave for the hills before the twenty-second of the month. It seemed that Mrs Gardener-Smith and Delia, Mrs Hossack and her four children, and a Captain and Mrs Batterslea and their young family were all leaving on that date, and therefore it would be more convenient if she were to travel with them, since Captain Batterslea's presence would save him from having to arrange for an escort for her.

Winter acquiesced without interest. She would have gone willingly enough if Lottie or Sophie and Mrs Abuthnot had gone with her, because she would then at least have been more assured as to their safety, but she could not feel disturbed as to her own. She still rode every morning before sunrise and again in the cool of the evening, but she saw nothing of Alex for several days and heard nothing of him until Colonel Moulson remarked in her hearing one evening that he understood that Captain Randall had taken shooting-leave.

'So much for all this hot air he has been talking,' said Colonel Moulson with scorn. 'Shows how much he believes in it if he can chuck his responsibilities and go off after jungle-cock. Tried to set us all by the ears, and when he found he couldn't panic us, goes off and sulks in the *terai*. I wonder you let him go, Con. I'm damned if I'd have done so! What that cub needs is five years of regimental soldiering under a C.O. who'd knock the conceit out of him. Wish I had him under my command!'

'You *have* got your knife into him, haven't you, Fred?' said Mrs Cottar pleasantly. 'Now I wonder why? Did he snap some lovely creature from under your nose? Con used to feel quite kindly towards him until the Aurora Borealis preferred him to his Excellency the Commissioner – didn't you, Con? But ever since then he's gone sour on him too – just like you. How vain you men are!'

The Commissioner cast her a glance of dislike and said sourly: 'I don't know why I put up with you, Lou. As for you, Fred, to hear you talk anyone 'ud think I'd given the man a month's leave instead of three days.'

'You can give him three years for all I care,' said Colonel Moulson. 'Place is a sight better off without him. Your deal——'

Alex resented the lost days considerably more than Colonel Moulson, but there were certain preparations that he thought it necessary to make, and they could not be made in a night. Niaz, he considered, could hardly have selected a worse moment to be laid up with a knife wound, but time was too short to wait until he had recovered. Niaz himself had angrily asserted that he had taken no harm, and had begged to go with him, but Alex had been adamant. He would take Alam Din and, for the look of the thing, his *shikari*, Kashmera; those two could do all that was necessary, and he would need Niaz later on.

A thin-shanked, grizzled little man, wearing a vast dust-coloured *puggari* and a tattered coat ornamented with the tarnished buttons of a long-forgotten regiment of Indian Cavalry, arrived at Alex's bungalow in the dark hour before dawn, and Alam Din coughed discreetly outside the bedroom door and murmured: 'Huzoor, the *shikari* has come and the trap is at the door.' Kashmera knew more about game, both furred and feathered, and more about the dense miles of jungle, than any other man in the district, and he had often accompanied Alex and Niaz on shooting camps. He and Alam Din loaded the trap by the light of an oil-lamp with a variety of packages and several guns.

'Let be!' said Alex sharply to Niaz, who had heard the sound of the wheels as the trap was brought round from the stables and had come out to lend a hand. He took a small square box quickly from Niaz's hands: 'Thy time will come. There is the road to be thought of, and thou art of no use to me maimed. Keep to thy bed while I am gone.'

Niaz jerked his head at the *shikari* and said in an undertone: 'Does he know?'

'Not yet. But he will see that we do not bring back what we take out, and so I must tell him something . . . though not all. We will go upriver and make camp beyond Bardari as though we would shoot *kala hirren*, and Alam Din and I will come down by boat and at night, which will be easy. It is the getting back that will be hard, because the stream will be against us. See that no *bairagis* visit thee while I am gone!'

Three days later they returned after dark, with the horns of a blackbuck and a dozen partridges on the floorboards of the trap. Kashmera had been driving, for both Alex and Alam Din were sound asleep: they had had little sleep, and then only in the day-time, during the last three days.

'How is the wound?' inquired Alex on the following morning.

'It is healed,' said Niaz impatiently. 'It was but a flesh wound. How much longer do I stay here?'

'For another week, I think,' said Alex. He smiled a little grimly at Niaz's face of disgust and said softly: 'It is in my mind that thou wert so sorely wounded that I must ride abroad with a syce for some days yet, so that all will know that thou art still a sick man and unable to go about.'

'Aah!' said Niaz, and smiled. 'What now?'

Alex explained. '. . . and if thou and one other go, on foot and by night, and while it is known that thou art sick, I think that the thing may be done.'

'So do I also,' said Niaz. 'Give out that I am like to die. That should please those dogs in the lines! Who goes with me? Yusaf?'

Alex considered the matter, frowning, and after a moment or two said curtly: 'It will have to be.'

He found Winter sitting under the punkah of the small drawing-room on the following morning, writing a letter to Lottie. It was Sunday, and she had just returned from church. Her formal dress of grey, white-spotted *mousseline de chine* looked fresh and cool, and her discarded bonnet lay on the sofa. She looked up in surprise when he entered and he saw her cheeks flush with sudden colour. She seemed to be aware of this herself, for she stood up rather quickly and turned so that her back was to the light.

'I came to ask if I might borrow Yusaf for a few days,' said Alex, dispensing with formalities. 'Niaz is sick and there is a certain amount of work I need done that I think Yusaf could do for me. It will only be for a few days. Can you spare him?'

'Yes, of course. But——'

'Thank you. It will mean that you will have to take one of the Commissioner's syces with you when you ride. Don't go too far afield, and stay away from the city. I'll send him back as soon as I can.'

He turned to leave and Winter said: 'I heard that you had taken shooting-leave. When did you get back?'

'Last night,' said Alex uncommunicatively, and left.

The door closed behind him and Winter regarded it with a smouldering eye. 'There are times,' she said aloud and deliberately, 'when I am almost glad that I once hit you!'

She returned to her desk and the sheet of letter-paper that so far bore only the address, and picking up her pen, dipped it in the standish. But she did not write. She sat nibbling the end of it thoughtfully while the minutes ticked by and the ink dried on the nib.

The punkah creaked and flapped gently and monotonously overhead and a pair of gecko lizards on the wall behind the desk chirruped a small, shrill accompaniment. In the garden outside, a *köil*, 'the brain-fever bird', was singing its maddening hot-weather song on a long, rising scale: *brain fever* . . . *brain fever* . . . *brain fever* ! sang the *köil*, finishing at the top of the scale and starting all over again at the bottom, as tirelessly monotonous as the creaking of the punkah. It was hot today. Hotter than it had been for many days, and in every room the doors and windows had been closed before sunrise to keep in the cooler air of the night and exclude the burning heat of May. 'There will be no more cool nights now until the *bursat* (the rains),' Iman Bux had said that morning.

'I was a fool not to have sent in m' papers before,' grumbled the Commissioner, mopping at the sweat that trickled down his thick neck. 'I don't believe that dam' man Canning is coming on tour this year after all. Pretty fool I shall look if he don't – stewing through another hot weather for nothing! Should have gone a month ago. No – take that damned coffee away and give me a cold drink. Hair of the dog!'

He mixed champagne and brandy and started the day with a 'Raja's peg'.

Alex sat at his desk in the room that he used as an office, and listened with only half his attention to the droning voice of the head clerk who was reading out a lengthy and involved petition. 'We have only one chance,' thought Alex, 'and that is that the ringleaders will not be able to hold 'em until the day they have set. They're too worked up. Some ass will put his foot in it somewhere, and there will be a premature explosion which will sound the alarm. But if it does go off on time, and all over India, they can write our obituaries now . . .'

In far-away Calcutta a senior Member of the Supreme Council finished reading Sir Henry Lawrence's telegraphed report on the mutinous behaviour of the Oudh Irregulars, and picked up his pen. '*The sooner this epidemic of mutiny is put a stop to, the better*,' wrote the Member of the Supreme Council. '*Mild measures won't do. A severe example is needed . . . I am convinced that timely severity will be leniency in the long run . . .*'

In a large bungalow in the Cantonment of Meerut, forty miles to the north-east of Delhi, Colonel Carmichael Smyth, the commanding officer of the 3rd Light Cavalry, sat at breakfast. 'The sentence was entirely just!' said

Colonel Smyth. The Colonel was a man whose views were identical with those expressed by the senior Member of Council, and hurrying back from leave to set an example, he had ordered that fifteen picked men from each troop were to parade on the following morning to learn to use the new cartridges. 'I'm not standing any dam' silly nonsense from *my* men!' said Colonel Smyth.

The ninety men were duly paraded – and eighty-five of them had refused to handle the caste-breaking cartridges. They were immediately tried by court-martial and sentenced to ten years' imprisonment, and a parade of all troops had been ordered by the aged divisional commander, Major-General Hewitt, to watch the sentence put into execution. For hour after hour, in the broiling sun on the Meerut parade-ground, the regiments stood in stony-faced silence to watch eighty-five picked men of a picked regiment stripped of their uniforms and fettered one by one with the iron fetters that they would drag with them through ten dreary years of captivity; and when at long last the ordeal was over, the terrible, clanking file of manacled men were marched away in the bright merciless sunlight, calling and crying to their comrades: 'Is this justice? Because we will not lose our caste so that none of our own will speak with us or eat with us, must we suffer this fate? Is there no justice? Help us, brothers! Help us!'

'Entirely just!' snapped Colonel Smyth, helping himself to scrambled eggs. 'Harsh? Nonsense! These mutinous fools need a sharp lesson. This will serve to stop the rot.'

'Wait, brothers! Wait . . . wait. Have patience. Remember the auspicious day! It is too soon!' urged the agents of Ahmed Ullah the Maulvi of Faizabad; of Dundu Pant the Nana of Bithaur; of Kishan Prasad . . .

'Art thou of the *rissala*?' shrilled a harpy in the Street-of-the-Harlots in Meerut city to a group of prospective clients as night fell. 'The 3rd *Rissala*, sayest thou? Then thou canst not enter here. Out – out! We do not lie with cowards! Where are thy comrades who eat dirt and walk in chains? *They* were men! But thou——! Chicken-hearts – children – cowards all! *Pah*!' She spat in derision, and a chorus of jeering painted faces applauded her from a dozen latticed windows and balconies, screaming like peacocks: 'Out! Out! – we lie with no cowards! If ye indeed be men and not the boneless babes we take you for, release your brothers from bondage!'

Their taunts and jeers pursued the men of the 3rd Cavalry through the hot, crowded, snarling bazaars of Meerut city, driving them from rage to a murderous frenzy.

Winter dipped her pen once more into the standish and added a date below the address that she had already written at the top of the blank sheet of letter-paper: '*Sunday, May 10th 1857. Dear Lottie . . .*'

The night was hot and very still. So still that every small sound of all the small sounds that go to make up silence separated itself from its fellows, and emphasized that stillness. The cheep of a musk-rat; the dry scrape of a scorpion crawling up the wall; the flitter of a bat's wings in the dark verandah; the drone of the mosquitoes and, from very far away, the echo of a jackal-pack which howled on the plains beyond the river.

Winter lay and listened to those sounds, and could not sleep. Once she thought that she heard whispering voices, and remembering the night that she had listened in the bathroom, she slipped noiselessly out of bed and tip-toed to the bathroom door. But there were no voices. Only the dry whisper of dead and dying *neem* leaves that drifted down through the hot, windless air and came to rest on the parched stone of the roof or the dry, brittle grass.

'There are no tom-toms in the city tonight,' thought Winter, listening by her open window. 'And no conches. This is the first night for almost ten nights that I have not heard them. Perhaps it is the heat. It has not been really hot until now——'

Somewhere in the dark recesses of the house a clock struck one. Three more hours before she could dress and go out to ride by the river. Would it be cooler by the river? It was so hot here, and so airless. Because the noise of the flapping punkah had irritated her she had sent the punkah-coolie away, saying that she could sleep better without it. But when he had gone she wished that she could call him back, for the sweltering, breathless stillness that had closed down upon the room with the cessation of the slow sway of the punkah had been worse than the nerve-racking monotony of that creak and flap.

'I will go up to the roof,' she thought, turning restlessly away from the window. 'It will be cooler up there.' She groped for her slippers in the darkness, shook them mechanically for fear they harboured centipedes or scorpions, donned them, and slipped her arms into the wide sleeves of the muslin wrap that lay at the foot of her bed. There was a dim light burning in the hall, and a slow regular snuffle and snore came from a corpse-like figure who lay rolled in a thin cotton *chuddah* near the front door. Winter walked softly past it, and lifting the *chik* went down the verandah and up the steep flight of stone steps to the first level of the flat-topped roof.

It was certainly cooler here, but the brickwork and the stone were still warm to the touch, and the wall supporting the second and higher-level roof gave off waves of stored heat. She made a half-circuit of the lower level and came to where six stone steps led up to the larger area that covered the high main rooms of the Residency.

A shadow moved on the stonework and she looked up, startled, to see a small white figure standing above her by the narrow parapet that surrounded the upper roof. It was Zeb-un-Nissa.

Winter called up to her in a whisper, but the child did not answer or make any movement to show that she had heard. She was staring out across the garden and the distant bulk of the Residency gateway towards the south-west, and her face and body looked curiously rigid, as though she were straining to catch some far-away and almost inaudible sound.

'I believe she's sleep-walking,' thought Winter, suddenly anxious. She waited for a moment or two, looking up at the child's tense face, and then went up the steps very softly so as not to frighten her, for she had heard that it was harmful to waken a sleep-walker too suddenly. Zeb-un-Nissa did not move. Her eyes were wide and fixed, and standing beside her Winter could see that her small face was drawn with fear. She laid a gentle hand on the child's thin arm and spoke softly: 'Nissa——'

Zeb-un-Nissa did not start or turn, but she moved her head a little and looked at Winter as though she were perfectly aware of her; her eyes full of horror. 'Hark!' she said in a hoarse whisper. 'Dost thou not hear them?' She began to shiver, and Winter put an arm about the frail little shoulders and drew the child against her: 'What is it, *piara*? (darling) What is there to hear?'

The child pulled herself free and turned again to the parapet, clutching at the stone with small claw-like hands and listening to some sound that Winter could not hear.

'It is the mem-*log* – the memsahibs. They are screaming. Canst thou not hear them scream? Surely thou canst hear them – there be children also . . . Listen! – *Listen*! They are killing the mem-*log*. Thou canst hear the sword cuts . . . and the flames. There! that was a child! – hark to its mother shriek! *Ai*! *Ai*!——' She wailed aloud and put her hands over her ears, cowering down below the parapet and weeping. 'I cannot bear to hear them scream! . . . They are killing the mem-*log* . . . they are killing the mem-*log*!'

Winter dropped to her knees and gathered the small wailing figure into her arms. 'Nissa – Nissa! There is no one screaming. It is all quiet. Listen – there is no sound. It is only a dream, *piara*. Only a bad dream. There is no killing——'

She had heard no sound behind her, but a shadow fell across them, black in the moonlight, and she turned swiftly, her heart in her mouth, to see Akbar Khan, the gatekeeper, salaaming deferentially behind her. His face was dark against the moon and the night sky, but Winter could see the gleam of his teeth and the glitter of his eyes, and though her first momentary panic had died at sight of him, an odd flicker of fear went through her, making her pull the child closer.

'Her mother missed the unworthy one from her bed,' said Akbar Khan softly. 'She has been sick with a fever these few days past and she must have left her bed while her mother slept. I am sorry that the child should have troubled the Lady-sahib.'

'She has not troubled me,' said Winter. 'Let her be. She can sleep in my room for what is left of the night.'

'Nay, nay!' said Akbar Khan, shocked. 'The Lady-sahib is the fount of all goodness, but it would not be seemly. And her mother is anxious, and sent me in search of her.'

Winter felt the frail body in her arms stiffen and writhe and become rigid, and then quite slowly it relaxed. Nissa sighed as her head nestled down against the shoulder that supported it, and looking down at the small face and feeling the shallow, even breathing, Winter realized that she had fallen asleep.

Akbar Khan reached down and took the child from her. 'It was a fit,' he said placidly. 'She has always been a sickly child, and I fear that the time of her release is near. Her mother will grieve; but what is written is written.' He cradled the thin body of his grandchild comfortably in his arms and said: 'Her mother will be very honoured that the gracious Lady-sahib troubled herself with the child. Shall I call a servant to light the Lady-sahib back to her room?'

'No,' said Winter curtly. 'I will remain here. Tell Zeb-un-Nissa's mother that I will come tomorrow to see how the child fares.'

'The Lady-sahib is my father and my mother,' murmured Akbar Khan politely, and went away, his bare feet making no sound on the warm stone.

Winter watched him go and she shivered in the hot night air; a shiver that was not caused by cold but by uneasiness and foreboding. Akbar Khan had always been courteous and placid, and his greeting to her whenever she passed through the gateway contained no trace of the veiled insolence that she had sometimes detected in the manner of Conway's other servants. But tonight there had been something in his manner that frightened her. No – not in his manner; there had been nothing wrong in that. In what then? In the fact that he himself had for some reason been afraid? In the glitter of the eyes in that shadowed, bearded face as they had stared down at the wailing, muttering figure of his little grand-daughter? No, she was being foolishly imaginative. But he had told a lie when he had said that Nissa had been sick for some days. That at least was not true, for she had seen Nissa daily at dawn.

What did the child think that she had heard? It was a dream, of course. She had been dreaming. And yet she had not behaved as Winter imagined that a sleep-walker would do. She had appeared to be aware of Winter, and awake; caught up in horror, but awake.

The servants said that Akbar Khan's little grand-daughter had second sight, and they were afraid of her. And there had been that day when she had said – or seemed to say – that Alex would come to no harm; and he had come to no harm. But then she could not have known that he was in any danger. It had been a coincidence. 'They are killing the mem-*log*, surely thou canst hear them scream?' Surely, in this waiting stillness, the sound of a scream would carry from the cantonments beyond the trees? But there was no scream – no sound. Only silence.

Almost against her will Winter went to lean on the parapet as Nissa had done, and strained her ears to listen. But she could hear no sound in the silence; not even a jackal's wail or the fall of a dead leaf. 'She was dreaming!' said Winter aloud and firmly. But she shivered again, and drawing her thin beruffled wrap tighter about her, she left the roof and returned to the hot, dark, silent rooms and her hot, tumbled bed.

Alex heard her running along the verandah of his bungalow at eleven o'clock on the following morning, and knew who it was even before the startled *chupprassi* lifted the *chik* and she was standing before him, tense and white-faced, her hands clutching at the edge of his desk.

There were five other men in the office, but she appeared to be oblivious of them. Alex stood up swiftly and dismissed them with a brief word, and they melted out into the sunlight. Winter did not see them go. She said in a hard, breathless voice that she fought to control: 'Alex, do something! They've killed her! I know they've killed her! Conway won't do anything. He says it's all nonsense. It's her grandfather – it's Akbar Khan. He did it. I know he did it! Alex, you can't let him do that and – and——'

Alex came round the desk and caught her by the shoulders and propelled her forcibly out of the office and into the living-room. He pushed her down into a chair, splashed a generous quantity of brandy into a glass and held it to her mouth while she drank it. Winter gasped and choked, but it took some of the shivering rigidity from her.

'Now tell me.'

'It's Nissa,' said Winter, tears standing in her eyes. 'She – she had a nightmare last night. At least I think it was a nightmare. Akbar Khan said it was a fit——' She described the happening on the roof: 'Then he took her away, and I went to see her this morning and – and they said she was dead. They didn't want me to see her, but I made them. Her mother was crying, and she tried to tell me something, but they pulled her away and said she was hysterical. I – I have never seen anyone dead before. Only Great-Grandfather, and he—— But I don't believe – I think they smothered her——' Her voice broke suddenly on a shudder of horror.

Alex said quietly: 'You can't know that.'

'No. They said she had had another fit, and—— I don't believe it! He heard what she said – Akbar Khan – and he was afraid. I know he was afraid. I knew it last night.'

Alex said: 'I'll see what I can do.'

He walked back with her in the full glare of the blazing morning and saw her go into the house, and an hour later he sent over a brief message asking if she would ride with him that evening.

Winter heard the wailing in the servants' quarters for half that hot afternoon, and later a small wooden box was carried out by a side door in the wall to the Mohammedan burial ground outside the city; but she did not see it go.

'There is nothing we can do,' said Alex. 'The child appears to have been subject to epileptic fits, and Dr O'Dwyer, whom I asked to look at the body, says that it is quite possible that she died as a result of one – with general debility and the heat as contributory causes. He was not prepared to take any further action on it. He said – and rightly – that there was enough tension in the place already without giving rise to any more alarm and excitement. I'm sorry, but that is all there is to it.'

Winter said in a small, hard voice: 'And what do you think yourself?'

'What I think has nothing whatever to do with it,' said Alex at his curtest.

'Then you won't do anything?'

'There is nothing I can do beyond what I have already done. The child was buried at four o'clock. *Ab khutam hogai.*' (Now it is finished.) He turned his head and looked at the set white face beside him and said after a moment: 'I'm sorry, Winter.'

She did not look at him and her own hurt made her desire to hurt him also. 'No, you're not. You didn't know her. To you and Conway she was only another Indian child. A "native"; what does she matter? You would both of you have made more fuss over a dog, and a great deal more over a horse. Do you mind if we do not discuss it any more?'

Alex gave a slight shrug of his shoulders and said nothing further. He did not wish to discuss it himself. He knew something of Zeb-un-Nissa and her reputation. Epileptics were often regarded in India as being possessed of devils or favoured by God, and he had seen himself the power that the child had over wild creatures, though he had attributed it to the simple fact, unusual in a child, that she possessed infinite patience, never made any movement that was not slow and unhurried, and could sit motionless for hours at a time. But Winter's account of what the child had said last night disturbed him.

It was not that he believed Zeb-un-Nissa to have had second sight, but it seemed to him quite likely that she was repeating something, or dreaming of something, that she had heard discussed. If so, that would account for Winter's conviction that Akbar Khan had been afraid. If Akbar Khan had imagined the child to be talking of something she had overheard, she might well have been assisted to die. However, as O'Dwyer had not been prepared to interfere, there was nothing further that could be done about it. But the words that the child had said repeated themselves again and again in his brain as they had repeated themselves in Winter's last night – 'They are killing the mem-*log*! – they are killing the mem-*log*! . . .'

Perhaps it was just as well that Zeb-un-Nissa was dead, and that there had been no one to call out during that long, burning day that they could hear the mem-*log* screaming.

Delhi was far away, hidden behind the dust and the dancing heat-haze and the parched, blazing plains, and Mrs Abuthnot had not screamed as she died in the hot sunlight within the Kashmir Gate where so short a time before the officers from the cantonments by the Ridge had held that gay moonlight picnic. But little Miss Jennings, the Chaplain's daughter, and young Miss Clifford, who had sung 'Where are the flowers?' to the accompaniment of her mandolin and Captain Larrabie's guitar, had screamed and shrieked as the clawing, blood-stained hands snatched at them and the reddened sabres cut and slashed. And all through that long hot day the shrieks of women and the terrified screaming of children, the crackle of flames and the howl of the mob, had risen from Duryagunj – that once quiet quarter of Delhi where the European and Eurasian clerks and pensioners and Indian Christians had lived and were now dying in terror and agony in the blinding, merciless sunlight.

All through that long hot day frantic officers in Meerut – where the terror had broken out and from where the mutineers, after a night of murder, had ridden for Delhi – ground their teeth and waited, or pleaded for permission to ride after them. There were more British troops in Meerut than in almost any other garrison in India, and not all the native regiments had revolted; only let them follow up the mutineers and save Delhi before it was too late – or at least send warning! But General Hewitt was old and fat and infirm. The magnitude of the crisis had left him too bewildered to take any decisive action, and Brigadier Wilson, left to take the initiative, hesitated and was lost: 'We cannot spare any men: we have to think of the women and children,' said Brigadier Wilson uneasily. 'We cannot risk a repetition of last night's massacres. We must protect the remaining women and children.' He would not sanction any pursuit . . .

All through that long hot day the Delhi garrison waited and hoped, watching the Meerut road for the help that they could not believe would fail them. And every moment that the help delayed, the mutineers of the 3rd Cavalry and those who had joined them grew bolder, and more and more of the city rabble gathered before the Palace where the tatterdemalion court of the aged King of Delhi grew hourly more confident.

'It is true – it is true!' urged Zeenut Mahal, the scheming favourite of old Bahadur Shah. 'They say that they have killed every *feringhi* in Meerut; men, women, and children also. It must be true, for see – there is no dust cloud on the Meerut road. If any remained alive, think you they would not ride with all speed for Delhi to take vengeance? They are dead. They must all be dead. Let us kill all the *feringhis* in Delhi also, and then thou wilt be King indeed!'

'It is true – it must be true,' said the scum of the city, sharpening swords and knives for the slaughter. 'They have killed every *feringhi* in Meerut! Let us do the like here.'

'It is true!' yelled the men of the 3rd Cavalry, who had fled to Delhi in dread of pursuit and the vengeance that they had imagined to be on their heels and who now saw, with incredulity, that none pursued. 'Did we not tell you that we have slain them all? The King! The King of Delhi! Help us, O King! *Deen! Deen! Maro! Maro!*'

Lottie had seen her father cut down by his own men, an expression of utter disbelief upon his rubicund, cherubic face, as though he could not and would not believe, even in the moment of his death, that this thing was possible. She had made no sound, because she herself did not believe what she had seen. Standing with her mother and a dozen other women and their children who had taken refuge at the Main Guard within the Kashmir Gate, she had seen him ride up to the gate with his men; placid and confident, but hurrying them forward so that this preposterous situation, the details of which he could not believe to have been correctly reported, should be put to an end at once. She had heard his fussy, fatherly voice – this pleasant, kindly little man of whom she knew so little – raised in expostulation when his men had checked before the gate. And a minute later she had seen him dragged from his horse and three bayonets plunged into his body.

His Subadar-Major and his Indian orderly had fired on the murderers and been themselves cut down, and Lottie, looking down dazedly from the rose-red walls where she had picnicked and walked in the peaceful autumn days of the vanished year, had thought how red and bright the blood looked on the hot white dust.

'It cannot be happening,' thought Lottie. 'It cannot be true . . .'

'I don't see 'as 'ow we can 'old out much longer, sir,' said Conductor Buckley to Lieutenant Willoughby who commanded the Delhi Magazine. 'Them perishers 'av brought scalin' ladders——' His words were barely audible above the howling of the mob and the incessant rattle and crash of gunfire.

They had been holding the Magazine since morning, and now the sun was moving down the sky again. Was it only four o'clock? Nine of them, against a howling, yelling mob of thousands. Nine of them to man ten guns——

'Scully says the train's laid, sir!' yelled Conductor Buckley. 'Any sign from the Meerut road yet, sir?'

Young Lieutenant Willoughby ran to the river bastion and strained his eyes for a last look down the hot, empty road where the heat-haze danced and shimmered under the brazen sky. 'No. They are not coming. Perhaps they are all dead. We cannot wait any longer.'

He looked up at the blue of the sky, his eyes calm and youthful in the sweating, dust-grimed, powder-blackened mask that was his face, and then glanced at the swarming thousands who clambered in, monkey-wise, over the walls, hemming the defenders into the last narrow square of ground.

'We shall take a good many of them with us,' said Lieutenant Willoughby. 'All right, Buckley. Give him the signal to fire it.'

The ground and the buildings and the very sky seemed to rock and reel and sway to the appalling crash of sound that silenced the savage roar of the maddened city, and a vast cloud, rose-red and beautiful in the level sunlight, lifted up above the domes and minarets; above the groves and gardens of the city of the Moguls; reaching up higher and higher into the still air and spreading out like a blossoming flower on a tall white stem.

It hung there for hours, an ephemeral memorial to gallantry. But as though the sound of the explosion had been a signal, the sullen, hesitating sepoys within the Main Guard turned upon those who had taken refuge there, and Lottie, who had run down from the wall at the sight of Edward, saw her mother fall without a sound, a hole through her temple, and saw a sabre slash down through her husband's head, laying it open almost to the shoulder.

She had screamed then, and fought to go to him, but someone had caught her arms and dragged her struggling and shrieking to the battlements, and then hands were gripping her wrists and she was being lowered down from the wall, swaying and turning against the hot stone, and screaming for Edward. The makeshift life-line of hastily knotted belts broke, and she fell and struck the hard ground and rolled into the ditch, the breath knocked out of her body, to be caught again and dragged on and up the steep escarpment, running and stumbling over the rough ground to plunge headlong into the tangled thickets of the Kudsia Bagh . . .

The crash of the explosion shivered through the hot stillness and rocked the Flagstaff Tower on the Ridge, where the terrified families from the cantonments had been crowded together in helpless confusion all that long day, waiting for news and straining their eyes through the heat-haze towards the city and the empty Meerut road. The women gasped and flinched to the hammerblow of the sound, while their servants wailed aloud and the children shrieked excitedly as a white column of smoke shot up from the distant city to spread into a slow rose-red corona that hung above the mangled bodies of the thousand dead who had died in the explosion of the Magazine.

'We can't wait here any longer,' said a haggard-faced officer pacing the Ridge. 'What in hell's name are they doing in Meerut? They *cannot* all be dead! For God's sake, why don't we do something to help those poor devils in the city? There's still the river arsenal to draw on. We could have made some sort of a show, instead of just leaving them to be slaughtered!'

'Don't be a fool, Mellish! We've got to think of the women and children. As it was, we had to weaken the city garrison in order to keep sufficient men here for their protection. We can't try any "forlorn hopes" while we have their safety to consider.'

'Then why didn't we send them off to Karnal as soon as we got the first news? Why the devil don't we send them now? Every moment that we hesitate increases the danger for them and for us, and most of all for those who are trapped in the city. No one seems to have done a dam' thing in Meerut, and no one is doing anything here – except young Willoughby who has evidently had the guts to blow up the Magazine. Surely anything is better than standing by like this and watching the few men who might remain loyal losing all confidence in us? *Look*——! What's that – there's a cart coming up the road! Is it news at last?'

A bullock-cart creaked and jolted slowly up the road in a cloud of dust, to halt by the Flagstaff Tower where the sinking sun illuminated its contents with brutal clarity: the slashed, stiffening, blood-stained bodies of half a dozen British officers, thrown in as carelessly as though they had been so many bales of straw. A challenge flung at the Ridge by the triumphant city. A challenge that would not be taken up for many days.

The moon gathered light as the last of the daylight faded, and those who had stood all day on the Ridge of Delhi, hoping and fearing and waiting for the help from Meerut that never came, prepared to leave at last. 'It will be dark in half an hour,' said the Brigadier, his eyes still straining towards the empty Meerut road. 'The women had better go, and they will need protection. You had all better go while the road to Karnal is still open.'

The glare of burning bungalows in the cantonments made a second sunset in the sky as carriages and dog-carts and men on foot and on horseback streamed away into the gathering darkness, to begin that long torment of flight through a hostile land during which so many were to die. The Brigadier waited until they had gone, and then with the last remaining officer on his staff he faced the sullen remnants of his command. 'Sound the Assembly,' said the Brigadier, and heard the familiar bugle-call ring out in the silence.

A single figure, a sepoy of the 74th Bengal Native Infantry, answered the summons; standing stiffly to attention, lonely and obedient in the gathering dusk. The only one to remain faithful to his salt out of all those serried ranks of men who twenty-four hours ago would have obeyed that call.

The Brigadier's shoulders sagged tiredly, and he turned at last and rode away from the Ridge, leaving the deserted cantonments to the night and the looters, while behind him, high above the darkening city, the last of the daylight and the first rays of the moon lit a fading cloud that still hung above the shattered Magazine and marked the only decisive stand that had been made in all that terrible day.

Winter had not spoken again during that evening ride and Alex was too occupied with his own thoughts to notice the fact. He was sorry for her, but it occurred to him that there were going to be a great many other things to be sorry for soon. He could not send Niaz to the lines any more, and his various sources of information in the city and the surrounding towns and villages were becoming less and less easy to get in touch with. They were afraid of being seen near his bungalow, and what news they brought was inconclusive and disturbing.

He looked up at the pale segment of moon floating high above the veil of dust that blurred the horizon. A flight of cormorants making for Hazrat Bagh jheel drew a thin dark arrowhead against the opal sky, and a flock of purple pigeons circled above the jostling roof-tops of the city. He wondered how Niaz and Yusaf were faring? It would be far hotter out on the plain than in the cantonments, and they would have had nothing to eat or drink since before dawn. Ramadan, when it fell in the hot weather, was no mean test of endurance, and the knife-wound in Niaz's back was not yet fully healed. 'I shall have to go myself tonight,' thought Alex. Night work was all very well for Niaz and Yusaf, who could spare the time to sleep by day, but it came hard on Alex, who could not.

He drew rein before the Residency gate and spoke for the first time in almost an hour. 'When do you leave for the hills?'

'On the twenty-second,' said Winter listlessly. Her anger had left her and she felt curiously apathetic.

'Which gives you a week in which to get there,' said Alex. 'Eight days to be precise. That should be enough. I expect I shall see you before then. Good night.'

He turned his horse and cantered away in the direction of his bungalow and Winter went on under the arch of the gateway past the stately, salaaming figure of Akbar Khan. An hour ago she would not have acknowledged that salutation. An hour ago she had thought him a murderer and had hated both Alex and her husband because they would not hang him for murder. But now, in the grip of the apathy that had taken hold of her, she was not sure. Perhaps Nissa had died a natural death after all.

The high, white-walled rooms of the Residency were unexpectedly cool after the sultry heat of the plain where even the air of the late evening held a breathless suggestion of an open furnace. The lamps had been lit, the doors and windows thrown open and the paths about the house watered to lay the dust. The scent of wet earth was as strong as incense, but though it permeated the lamp-lit rooms and filled the house with a clean fragrance, it could not disguise another scent: the cloying smell of musk and betel nut that belonged to the fat woman who lived in the *bibi-gurh*. So Yasmin had been in the house during her absence. That was unusual. Winter was well aware that the woman visited Conway's rooms by night, but she had never known her to come into the main part of the house before. But tonight she had obviously been there; in the drawing-room and the morning-room. Even in Winter's bedroom.

Conway was in the drawing-room, sprawled on the sofa with a glass of brandy in one hand. He was wearing a thin native-style shirt over white cotton trousers, and both were dark with sweat. It was not late, but he was already unmistakably drunk. There was a silver-mounted hookah on the floor, and the cushions of the sofa were indented as though someone had recently been sitting beside him. Winter had not seen him dressed in such a fashion before, and she did not know if it constituted his usual garb in the hot weather, or if he were slipping back into a way of life that his marriage had temporarily interrupted. She had told him once that if the woman Yasmin entered the house – she excepted his private rooms – she herself would leave it, and she wondered now what had made Yasmin bold enough to return. Should she make a stand now and carry out her threat?

She surveyed her husband's flushed, vacant face and sodden, sweat-soaked body, and realized that it was useless to talk to him when he was in this condition, since he would not understand a word she said. The apathy that had descended upon her an hour ago pressed down on her with an almost tangible weight. She had not slept at all during the previous night and now she was very tired. Too tired to care about Conway and his fat, musk-scented mistress. It did not matter any more. Nothing mattered any more. Perhaps it was true that their lives were plotted out for them and none could avoid their fate. 'What is written, is written . . .'

Someone moved in the shadows behind the lamp that stood on the table at Conway's elbow. It was the pale girl with the yellow hair whom Winter had seen before in this room. Her grey eyes were wide and frightened as though it were she, and not Winter, who was looking at a ghost. Had she died in this house? Was that why something still held her there? *'They are killing the mem-log . . .'*

Conway said thickly: 'Well, what ish it? Wan' anything?' . . . and there was no one behind the lamp. Only a white curtain and a vase full of yellow canna lilies, and the shadows . . .

Winter slept soundly that night despite the heat and the creaking of the punkah. As soundly as Zeb-un-Nissa who lay in the Mohammedan cemetery and did not hear the yelling of the jackal-packs who slunk among the graves. As exhaustedly as Lottie who lay asleep, her thin slippers and frilly skirts torn and ripped by thorns and stained with dust and blood, in a curtained *ekka* whose kindly owner had found her and her two companions crouching in a ditch by the roadside, and had befriended them.

'I go to Lunjore, and with all speed,' said the driver of the *ekka*. 'Delhi will be no place for a man of peace for many moons, and I have a brother in Lunjore with whom I will abide until this madness is past.'

Alex and Yusaf returned to the bungalow in the dark hour before dawn and by different routes, but Niaz remained invisible. He was reported to be still suffering from fever and unable to leave his bed.

Alex had hoped to sleep late but he was awakened at sunrise by Alam Din. 'Huzoor,' said Alam Din softly, 'there is a red kite caught in the thorn tree by the city road.'

'Damn!' said Alex wearily. 'Damn and blast! Oh, all right. *Acha*, Alam Din, *main jaunga*.'

He shook himself awake, and twenty minutes later he was riding through the crop-lands in the direction of Chunwar. The mile-long road that led across the open plain to the city boasted a solitary thorn tree that grew near its edge some two hundred yards from the cantonment end, and this morning there was a cheap paper kite such as children fly caught up in its scanty spiked foliage. A vivid scarlet thing, visible from some considerable distance.

Gaily coloured kites flew all day and at all seasons in the sky above the city, and a strayed one that had broken its string was frequently to be found tangled among the branches of trees on the plain. Alex did not pass the thorn tree and barely glanced at it. He took a narrow side-path that skirted a field of mustard, and checking the Eagle by a culvert where the elephant grass grew high and a wild fig tree threw a patch of shadow, he dismounted as though to tighten a girth.

There was a rustle in the grasses and a voice whose owner remained invisible spoke in a whisper that was barely audible above the creaking of a distant well-wheel and the indignant chittering of a striped squirrel:

'There is word in the bazaar that the *pultons* have risen in Meerut, and have slain all the *Angrezi-log* and ridden on Delhi, which has fallen also. It is said that they have proclaimed Bahadur Shah as Mogul and put all *feringhis* to the sword.'

'When?' asked Alex, wrestling with a strap.

'Yesterday only. The news was told at dawn by a fakir at the steps of the Pearl Masjid.'

'It is not possible,' said Alex. 'Delhi is far.'

'Do not the very birds of the air speak to the *bairagis*?' whispered the voice.

Alex said: 'Is there aught else said?'

'Nay. What need of more? The city hums like a hive.'

'Will they rise?'

'Who knows? There be many *budmarshes* in the bazaars, but the Maulvi's men call upon them to hold back and to wait for the Word. It were better that none of thy people were seen in the city today. Keep them close. If even a stone were thrown there is no knowing what might follow. Thou knowest the temper of crowds. If they see blood, they run mad like jackals.'

Alex said softly: 'Go back and bring me word tonight. I will ride by the tomb of Amin-u-din at sunset.'

'I will try. But I am afraid – afraid. If it were known, they would tear me in pieces!' Alex could hear the man's teeth chatter, and he laid a handful of silver coins in the dust by the rim of the culvert and said: 'There will be fifty more tonight,' and mounting again rode on in the general direction of Chunwar.

He made a circuit of the crop-lands and returned to the cantonments by way of the rifle-range, riding for the most part at a leisurely walk that necessitated a considerable effort of will, and it was well past eight o'clock by the time he reached the Residency.

He found the Commissioner still abed and naked save for a width of thin cotton cloth wrapped about his waist in the manner of a Burmese *lungi*. The room reeked of musk and stale spirits, and the green-tinted *chiks* over the closed windows toned the light to a twilight dimness. Alex's foot struck against a cluster of little silver bells such as often adorn an Indian woman's anklet, and he found it an effort to restrain a grimace of disgust.

'Well?' demanded Mr Barton sourly. 'What is it now? More bees?'

'I hope it may turn out to be no more than that,' said Alex curtly. 'There is a tale being circulated in the city of a rising in Meerut and in Delhi. It may be entirely untrue, or there may have been some trouble there that has been grossly exaggerated by rumour. But the story is that the regiments in both places have mutinied and killed all the Europeans, and that Bahadur Shah has been acclaimed as King.'

'What rubbish!' said the Commissioner angrily. He sat upright and the movement appeared to be painful, for he groaned and put a hand to his head. He glowered at Captain Randall and said: 'Why, Meerut's crammed with British troops. Crammed with 'em! – at least two thousand. Strongest garrison in India. Poppycock! It's only another bazaar rumour.'

'Perhaps, sir,' said Alex shortly. 'The point is not so much whether it is true, as that the city believes it to be true. Such a rumour is bound to give rise to a good deal of excitement, and I should like, with your permission, to put the city out of bounds to all Europeans until the excitement has had time to die down.'

'Why?'

God give me patience! prayed Alex, setting his teeth. He said calmly and pleasantly, as though reasoning with a backward and fractious child: 'It takes very little to start a riot among people who have been systematically worked up into a state of excitement and tension as these have been. With this sort of rumour flying round the bazaars, a white face in the city might lead to stone-throwing. And as you know, sir, with a mob that is only a short step from murder. We cannot afford any unpleasant incidents at the moment. In a day or two at most we should hear if there is anything at all behind the rumours, and if there is not, the excitement will die down. May I take it that you agree to putting the city out of bounds?'

'Oh yes, I suppose so,' said the Commissioner ungraciously. 'Don't believe a word of it, but—— Well, go on, go on! – do what you like about it and leave me in peace.'

Alex did not linger. He did not return to his own office but went instead to the Commissioner's where he wrote briefly, swiftly and to the point, using the Commissioner's official paper, and then returned to the darkened bedroom with pen and inkwell to demand the Commissioner's signature. Having seen the *chupprassi* leave with the sealed documents, he asked if he might see Mrs Barton, but Winter had gone out.

'The Memsahib left but half an hour ago,' Iman Bux informed him. 'She has gone to the city.'

Alex whipped round on the speaker with a suddenness that startled him considerably. '*Where?*'

'To the city,' faltered Iman Bux. 'To the shop of Ditta Mull the silk merchant, near the Sudder Bazaar.'

'Who is with her?'

'Huzoor, the Memsahib went on horseback. I do not know which syce – I will make inquiry, if the Huzoor——'

But Alex had gone.

It was after nine and the tree shadows were shortening on the white dust, while already the heat danced on the open plain so that the mile-distant city appeared to shimmer and waver in the blinding sunlight as though it were made of molten glass. There was a white foam of lather streaking the Eagle's neck and flanks, and Alex's coat was wet with sweat, but his hands and his stomach were cold with fear and rage – a rage that was entirely directed at himself.

'If I get myself involved in a riot, I may have to shoot,' thought Alex, 'and if I do that—— They won't harm her! They know her too well. They know me too, but I represent Authority, and that may set them off . . . I ought to let her take her chance. If they kill me that fool Barton will lose his head, and I have not given the order about the bridge, and – I *can't* risk everything just because of one woman! . . . Nicholson was right – the safeguarding of women and children in some crises is such a very minor consideration that it ceases to be a consideration at all – I must not go . . .' But he went.

He reined to a canter as he neared the city gate, and fought down his fear, for a mob was a purely animal thing and like an animal could sense fear. He rode in under the gate at a walk, sitting loosely in the saddle, and called a greeting to the police havildar who saluted him as he passed.

He could feel the pulse and panic of the city swirling about him from the very dust and beating down upon him in the blinding heat. There was an ominous silence as he passed and a menacing mutter that rose at his back, and the faces that watched him were avid or insolent or uneasy. Those men he knew and spoke to as the Eagle shouldered his way through the crowded bazaar avoided his gaze and shifted unhappily, observing their neighbours with furtive anxiety. Normally, when he rode through the city, they cleared a path for him, but today he found that he must force the Eagle between men who made no attempt to move out of his way, and who jostled and obstructed him with deliberate insolence. His progress became slower and slower; and then a stone hurtled out of the crowd. It missed him and struck a woman, who screamed shrilly.

An indescribable sound rose from the crowd; a sound like the soft, growling snarl of a gigantic cat; and Alex rose in his stirrups, and facing the quarter from whence the stone had been thrown, raised his voice and called a jest across the heads of the crowd. It was a coarse and untranslatable jest relative to the proper treatment of prostitutes, and the crowd, taken by surprise, laughed. The tension snapped and a man called out: 'Has the Sahib heard the news from Delhi?'

'*Beshak!* I hear many lies with every morn, Karter Singh. But I wait for the evening, and when the heat of the day is past the truth becomes known.'

'Is it then the truth?' cried another voice.

'The heat has surely turned thy brain, Sohan Lal,' said Alex with a laugh. 'Abide a little, and let it cool!'

The laugh had its effect upon the crowd. Hostility waned and doubt took its place. Perhaps the rumours that had spread like wildfire through the bazaars since dawn were false? for the Sahib, it was plain, had also heard news – yet he laughed. Would he laugh if the news were bad? The crowd drew back and let him pass, their faces sullen and unsure, and twenty yards ahead Alex caught sight of the Maulvi of one of the city mosques making his way along the street. He urged the Eagle to a quicker pace, and drawing level with the man, leaned out and touched him on the shoulder. The Maulvi turned sharply.

'*As Salaam aleikum*, Maulvi Sahib,' said Alex pleasantly. 'Canst thou spare the time to lead me to the shop of Ditta Mull in the street of the silk merchants? I cannot call to mind the way.'

He saw the anger flash in the man's eyes, and the cunning replace it as the Maulvi looked up at him and then back at the watching crowd; and knew that he had guessed aright. This was one of Ahmed Ullah of Faizabad's men, and Gopal Nath, hidden in the culvert by the fig tree, had whispered that the Maulvi of Faizabad's men were preaching patience. It was no part of their plan to touch off premature riots, and if there was any truth at all in the rumours concerning Delhi and Meerut they must be feeling alarmed for the success of their carefully laid plans. The man who stood at Alex's stirrup knew quite well that he was familiar with every street and alley and shop in the city and was demanding protection, and he would have given much to refuse it. But it was as much in his interests as in Alex's own to prevent a premature outbreak in Lunjore, so he smiled sourly and murmured the conventional reply to the greeting:

'*Wa aleikum Salaam.* If the Sahib will come with me I will show him.'

Furiante's impatiently tossing head, and the frightened face of the syce who was endeavouring to control both horses, were visible above the heads of a noisy jostling crowd who packed the narrow street before Ditta Mull's shop and swayed dangerously to and fro. The panic on the face of the syce did nothing to reassure Alex, and once again he felt fear clutch at his throat, and forced it back. The Maulvi, walking beside him, took the Eagle's bridle and thrust his way through the crowd, who fell back and cleared a passage to the bottom of the five rickety wooden steps that led up to the shop front.

Winter was not visible, for Ditta Mull had hurriedly dropped the heavy split-cane *chiks* before the open entrance at his shop. He peered out anxiously on hearing Alex's voice and grasped feverishly at his sleeve: 'Take her away, Huzoor!' begged Ditta Mull. 'By the back way. I do not know what madness has taken hold on the city this morning. There is a tale that—— But no matter. I fear that some may do her harm because she is the wife of the Commissioner Sahib. Already there have been stones flung at my shop. It is not our own people. They know her well. But there are others – *budmarshes* from Suthragunj and Shahjehanpur and Bareilly who have been stirring up trouble in the city with wild tales. The Memsahib is with my wife and children. She wished to leave, fearing the people might harm my shop on her account, but I would not let her. It is well that thou hast come! I will tell the Memsahib.'

He hurried away through a dark doorway in the back of the shop, wringing his small fat hands and making little moaning noises, and returned a minute or two later with Winter. She was perfectly calm, and quite uninterested, thought Alex furiously – irrationally swinging from the extremes of fear to the limits of exasperation – in the dangers of the situation. She frowned a little at the sight of him, but refused to leave without a large quantity of rose-coloured sari silk that she had previously selected. She watched Ditta Mull wrap it up in a length of muslin, his hands shaking like leaves in a wind, and having accepted and paid for it, said with a touch of impatience: 'Do not show them that face, *Lala-ji*. If they see that thou art afraid, then they too may behave foolishly. But not otherwise.'

She handed the package to Alex who received it in grim silence, and went out under the lifted *chik* into the fierce glare of the sunlight. The crowd had ceased to shout and sway and had become silent, gazing curiously at the split-cane *chik* that concealed the interior of the shop, and at the impassive Maulvi who stood at the foot of the steps outside it. As Winter stepped out into the sunlight a mutter rose from them and swelled ominously, but she appeared unconscious of it and Alex saw her look up to smile at someone in a second-storey window at the far side of the narrow street, and sketch the Hindu gesture of salutation with one hand.

The crowd, instantly diverted, turned as one to see who it was whom the Memsahib had greeted, and saw a small plump child hanging out over the edge of a fretted window ledge and beckoning. Winter shook her head at it and called out: 'Have a care, Bappa, or thou wilt surely fall. I cannot come today, but I will come soon.'

'Tomorrow?' shrilled the child.

'Not tomorrow. Perhaps next week.'

The brief conversation changed the mood of the crowd as Alex's jest had changed the mood of the mob in the Sudder Bazaar, but he could feel the dangerous pendulum-swing of their emotions with every nerve in his body, and knew how little it would take to sway them towards senseless savagery. Was Winter unaware of it? She seemed to be. He heard her murmur a polite and conventional greeting to the Maulvi, and then she was in the saddle and moving off down the packed street, controlling the nervous impatience of Furiante with apparent ease.

The next fifteen minutes seemed endless to Alex, riding behind her and frequently separated from her by the shifting, jostling crowds. He heard her speak to a dozen people as they edged their way through the streets, her voice light and gay. He noted as they passed that more than half the shops were closed and shuttered – sure sign of panic. That despite the intense heat, the narrow stifling streets and alleyways were as full of people as though it had been a fair day or a festival, and that the people talked in whispers and muttered in undertones.

The Maulvi left them abruptly at the turn into the wide stretch of the Sudder Bazaar that ended at the Rohilkhand Gate, and vanished down a side street. Three hundred yards to go . . . Two hundred . . . One hundred . . . Fifty. Slowly; keep to a walk . . . A man was holding forth excitedly to a dense knot of people as thick as a swarm of bees, and scraps of sentences separated themselves from the sullen murmur of the crowd. '. . . with two heads! My cousin's wife's brother saw it . . . it is a sign! What else but a sign? Their days are accomplished . . .!' Muttered curses and a man spitting loudly and contemptuously as they passed. A low-caste woman shouting at the frightened, furious syce: '*Hai*, *ghora wallah*, do they feed thee on bone-dust now that thou hast taken service with the sahib-*log*?'

And then they were through the gate and out on the open empty glaring road that led across the plain to the cantonments, and Furiante had broken into a canter and then into a gallop. Winter had attempted to slow him after the first hundred yards or so, but Alex had brought his whip down on the horse's quarters and they had flashed at full gallop under the shadows of the trees that lined the cantonment roads. He reined in at last before the gate of his own bungalow and waited for the syce to come up with them. He had not spoken once since he entered Ditta Mull's shop, and he did not speak now. He put up a hand and wiped the sweat out of his eyes, and knew that his hand was shaking.

Winter said uncertainly: 'You're very angry, aren't you? But I did not know that there was trouble in the city. I know you told me to keep away from it. I'm sorry. But you should not have come for me. I do not think that they would have done me any harm. They were more likely to harm you.'

This was precisely what Alex himself had thought, and his anger against himself for not having had the moral courage to leave her to take her chance kept him silent.

Winter looked at him doubtfully and added: 'It was – kind of you to come. Thank you.'

'You have nothing to thank me for,' Alex said brusquely. 'I probably endangered your life, and that of everyone else in the cantonment, by going there.'

The syce cantered up, dusty and sullen but still clutching the package of rose-coloured silk, and Alex observed him tight-lipped, and then turned back to Winter. He said: 'The city is out of bounds until further notice, and I should be obliged if you would curtail your rides in future, and keep only to the cantonments and the *maidan*.'

'But——'

'That is an order,' said Alex, and turned into his own gateway.

He had ridden out at sundown that evening to the ruined tomb of Amin-u-din on the far bank of the river, but Gopal Nath had not been there. There had been no one there but the bats and the lizards and a flock of green parrots, for Gopal Nath was lying face downwards among the high grass at the edge of the grazing grounds with his throat cut from ear to ear, and the work that the jackals and the hyenas began that night was completed the next day by the kites and the vultures and the remorseless heat, so that twenty-four hours later no one could be sure who those reddened, scattered bones had once belonged to.

Alex had ridden home in the last of the brief twilight knowing that it was no use to wait any longer, and later that night he had gone out over the back wall of the bungalow compound where the loquat trees made a belt of shadow, and near some tamarisk scrub at the edge of the cantonments had been met by Yusaf and two skinny village ponies.

There had been a party at the Residency that night. The last of the Tuesday parties, although no one there knew that it would be the last. It had been a late one, and Alex, returning at four o'clock in the morning with the sky already greying to the dawn, heard the voices and laughter of the guests as they drove away from the Residency, before he fell into an exhausted sleep.

Lottie was almost thirty miles nearer to Lunjore that night. At Meerut General Hewitt and Brigadier Wilson, with a strong force of British troops at their command, still remained in a state of helpless inaction, and on the Ridge at Delhi only the putrefying bodies of six officers, still piled one upon the other in the abandoned cart that had dragged them from the shambles of the Kashmir Gate, were the only British who remained to tell of all those who, two short days ago, had lived and laughed in the now gutted and empty cantonment.

A dispatch rider from Suthragunj on a lathered horse arrived in Lunjore at noon on Wednesday. He had waited only long enough to deliver the sealed letter he carried to the Commissioner's head *chupprassi*, and to water his horse, before setting out on the return journey. Alex had not been told of his arrival, and the Commissioner, handed the letter on a salver by Iman Bux during luncheon, had stuffed it into his pocket, unread, and forgotten about it until the following morning. It had been nearly midday when he read it at last, and then he could not at first take in the baldly worded statement it contained.

His first reaction had been incredulity. The thing was a hoax – a ridiculous practical joke! It must be, because it could not possibly be true. Yet it was written on official paper, and he knew that scrawled signature. The blood seemed to leave his heart and drain out of his body. His pale eyes bulged with shock and the paper dropped from his nerveless hand and slid to the floor, where the draught from the punkah sent it fluttering lazily across the drawing-room carpet like a bird with a broken wing.

It had been Winter who had picked it up and Winter who had sent for Alex. He had arrived to find the Commissioner gulping down his third glass of brandy, and under its influence returning to his first view of the situation. 'Hoax,' said Mr Barton thickly. 'Can't be anything else.'

'I'm afraid not, sir,' said Alex, running his eye down the single sheet of paper. He looked at the quivering bulk that slumped upon the sofa, glass in hand, and said curtly: 'Where is the man who brought this? When did it arrive?'

The Commissioner swallowed the remainder of the brandy in his glass and poured himself out a fourth peg, slopping the liquid onto the carpet. 'Can't be expected to deal with everything!' he said loudly and defensively. 'How was I to know it was important? Might have been an invitation to a shoot f'r all one knew. Put it in m' pocket. Forgot it. Very natural.'

'It arrived during luncheon yesterday,' Winter said quietly. 'I think that the man left almost immediately.'

Alex said nothing. He looked at his chief with a contempt and exasperation which he made no attempt to disguise, and turned and went out of the room.

'Damned impertinence!' said Mr Barton querulously, and finished his fourth brandy.

Less than an hour later a hurriedly convened conference of a dozen appalled men met around the Commissioner's dining-room table to discuss the emergency arising out of the incredible – the impossible news – and to decide what measures, if any, might belatedly be taken to safeguard Lunjore from the mutiny and massacre that had overtaken Meerut and Delhi. Alex had urged the supreme measure of disarming the regiments, but the suggestion had been treated as an outrage.

'If I should ever be ordered by the General to insult my men in such a manner,' declared Colonel Gardener-Smith roundly, 'he would first have to disarm me, and after me, every one of my officers!'

'Your suggestion, Captain Randall,' said Colonel Moulson, 'is not only beneath contempt, but one which it is not your place to advance.'

Alex gave a faint shrug of his shoulders. 'I am sorry, sir. Then may I suggest that we send the women and children to Naini Tal immediately? Today if possible. There may still be time.'

There was an immediate outbreak of protest. If disaffection was rife, travelling would be dangerous and difficult. The women were safer where they were. An adequate escort could not be spared. To send them to the hills now was to run too great a risk.

'To leave it until it is too late will be a greater one,' said Alex. 'The mutinies at Meerut and Delhi were premature. I am sure of that. As I have already told you, I have reason to believe that a date for a general outbreak has been set for the end of this month; and that belief is not only supported by information, but confirmed by the behaviour of the city. There is still time to send the women and children to safety.'

'We cannot do it,' said Colonel Gardener-Smith heavily. 'It is too late.'

'It is *not* too late!' said Alex passionately. 'At least there is a chance.'

'Perhaps. But it is a chance that we cannot take. At this stage it is surely a matter of vital importance not to show any sign of panic. You must see that.'

'I doubt it,' said Colonel Moulson with a sneer. 'It is a thing that Captain Randall has never been able to see. And I agree with you, Colonel. It is of course out of the question for any of the women to leave. Their departure at this juncture would be taken as a clear sign that we had lost our nerve, and I am sure that I speak for the majority when I say that this is far from being the case.'

'I agree. I entirely agree,' said Colonel Packer. 'To show panic may precipitate the very crisis we seek to avoid. We must place our trust in the Lord. His rod and His staff shall not fail us.'

'Possibly not, sir,' said Alex drily. 'But will the sepoys? Are we to take it that the sight of our women and children being sent to safety will unsettle the regiments to the extent of driving them to mutiny? I had understood that you believed them to be loyal?'

'The loyalty of my Regiment,' said Colonel Gardener-Smith quietly, 'has never yet been called in question, and to send my wife and daughter away would amount to a public declaration that I had lost confidence in their loyalty. That I will not do. At this time it is doubly necessary not only to show confidence, but to avoid any action that can be construed as alarm.'

'Which means,' said Alex with shut teeth, 'that no precautionary measures whatever can be taken, for fear that any change in the present routine may be translated as panic.'

'You exaggerate, Captain Randall,' said Colonel Gardener-Smith coldly. 'Reasonable precautions will of course be taken.'

'Will you name one, sir?' demanded Alex harshly.

There was a sudden silence about the table. It was broken by Colonel Packer, who remarked pontifically that those who put their trust in the Lord needed no other armour.

'Nonsense!' snapped Colonel Gardener-Smith. 'The Lord helps those who help themselves, Packer. But at the present juncture I maintain that all that is necessary is to remain calm. There must be no appearance of alarm or any alteration of our normal practices that might be likely to call forth comment and arouse uneasiness. For which reason I myself am against sending the women and children away. What do you say, Barton?'

'Qui' ri',' said Mr Barton. 'Mush keep calm. 'Ssential to keep calm. Where's the brandy?'

Alex came to his feet and leaned on the table, his hands gripping the edge. 'May I *beg* you to reconsider, sir? I am well aware that it will give rise to panic if we send them away. Good God, I am not entirely——' He controlled himself with an effort and continued more quietly: 'But I feel that it should be possible to explain to the regiments, through the medium of their Indian officers, that the families are only being sent away because the services of every officer and every sepoy may be needed for action, and not for being kept hamstrung in cantonments protecting a parcel of women.'

'I reshent that,' said the Commissioner with dignity. 'Wha' d'yer mean, "parcel o' women"? Sweet creatures! . . . Privilege to protect 'em!'

Alex ignored the interruption: 'I beg of you to send them away while there is still time. It is the lesser of the two evils, and our paramount duty at this time is surely not their protection, but the saving of the country. The maximum efficiency cannot be obtained while the garrison is hampered by a horde of women whose personal safety will be placed above military expediency . . .'

The memory of his own fatuous action of the previous day, when he had followed his chief's wife into the city against all reason and judgement, caught in his throat and seemed to choke him, and he struck the table with the flat of his hand: 'Can you not see that if they remain here they will hamper and handicap us into virtual uselessness? How can any man make a cool-headed decision which he knows may involve grave risk, while he is thinking that to take that risk may mean the murder and mutilation of his wife and child? There are a hundred chances that we would all cheerfully take without them, yet would hesitate to take while we have their safety to consider.'

He looked about the table at the circle of grim, drawn faces and saw hesitation and doubt; and, for a moment only, he was hopeful. Then Colonel Moulson spoke:

'My dear Captain Randall,' he drawled. 'You allow your fears to run away with you. It is my opinion that the news from Delhi will be found to be greatly exaggerated. And in any case the Meerut Brigade will have moved by now, and Delhi has almost certainly been recaptured. But even if that were not so, I would like to point out that we have three Infantry Regiments here as well as half a Regiment of Military Police, and if we had only one – my own – I would still engage to keep the city in order and protect double the number of women and children without the smallest difficulty. The rabble are notoriously chicken-hearted, and a dose of grape will be quite enough to cool their tempers should they show any signs of violence. I advocated such a course only yesterday, but I understand that it was you who preferred the more cautious method of putting the city out of bounds? A pity. Now, I should have marched my men through the streets and shot down every black bastard who raised his voice. That would have ended any nonsense quickly enough!'

'Hear! Hear!' interjected Major Mottisham.

'So you must really not expect us,' concluded Colonel Moulson, 'to make a public exhibition of ourselves by ordering a panic-stricken exodus of all the women and children, just because you yourself feel nervous.'

Alex said softly: 'I can only say, sir, that in the event of my timorous fears proving justified, I hope that you will obtain some comfort from the realization that you will have sacrificed the lives of these women, and jeopardized the safety of the Company's possessions, in order to demonstrate a confidence in the fidelity of your sepoys which you do not wholly possess.'

Colonel Moulson's face was suddenly scarlet with rage and he half rose from his chair. 'You are impertinent, Captain Randall! Must I again remind you that you are a junior officer – and can be disciplined?'

'Because I speak the truth, sir?' Alex's precarious hold on his temper had departed and his voice was raw-edged with a rage that matched Colonel Moulson's. 'You all have your doubts! Every one of you! But not one of you will admit it. You will not even institute a few inquiries because to do so would be tantamount to an admission that disloyalty among your men might be possible, and so you prefer to shut your eyes rather than cast what you consider to be a slur on the good name of your regiments. All very laudable. But in the present crisis, you will give me leave to say that it is hardly practical.'

'In the present crisis,' said Colonel Moulson furiously, 'it is the panic-mongers that we have to fear! If we could rid ourselves of them we should be a deal better off! There is no lack of confidence here, I assure you. But as you yourself feel so insecure, I can only suggest that you should apply for sick-leave and set off immediately for Naini Tal!'

Alex's right hand that lay flat upon the table clenched slowly into a fist – and as slowly relaxed again. It was no use. They were courageous enough, but they did not even now realize the magnitude of this thing that was overtaking them. They had refused to take any precautions while the emergency was far away, and now that it was upon them they would take none – for fear of showing fear. They had done nothing while they could, and dared do nothing when they would.

'Qui' ri',' repeated the Commissioner with a hiccough, ''tirely agree. Mush keep calm!'

Alex sat down without further words and did not speak again while the conference dragged to its inconclusive close. But when it was over he dispatched a telegram to the Governor-General, in the name of the Commissioner of Lunjore, requesting plenary military powers. The nearest telegraph post had until recently been seventy-five miles away in Suthragunj, but it was not twenty by the Hazrat Bagh route, and Alex reflected grimly that Kishan Prasad's road was proving its usefulness in a way that had not been foreseen by those who made it.

That night the first of the fires started in Lunjore, and the surgeon of the 105th N.I., Colonel Packer's Regiment, had his bungalow burnt to the ground. It had been a thatched bungalow and an arrow wrapped in blazing, oil-soaked rags had been fired into the roof shortly before midnight.

Less than fifty miles to the south-west, Lottie and her companions, though suffering tortures from the heat in the closely curtained *ekka*, were still safe in the charge of its kindly driver and drawing hourly nearer to Lunjore. But behind them, scattered over the sun-scorched countryside that surrounded the captured city of the Moguls, the majority of the fugitives from Delhi hid and starved and died.

Men, women and children crouched all day in ditches and cane-brakes, gasping in the relentless heat: stripping themselves of uniforms and crinolines, wading rivers, crawling through dying grass, skulking in the jungle. Scratching shallow graves with their bare hands in the hot, iron-hard earth to cover the corpse of a child, and leaving the bodies of the adult dead to the vultures and the jackal-packs. Robbed, stripped, insulted; hunted through the crop-lands and murdered for sport. Lured by promises of protection into villages whose inhabitants gathered to watch them die and laughed as the naked, blood-stained bodies were flung on the village dung-heaps.

A few – a very few – fell into the hands of kindly people who gave them food and shelter and risked their own lives, and the lives of all their families, in order to save a hunted, helpless fellow-creature. And within the walls of Delhi, in a stifling, windowless dungeon below the Palace of the aged, timorous Bahadur Shah, newly proclaimed King of all Hindustan, fifty prisoners – the last of the British and the Christians left in Delhi – had still two days to live.

Niaz had reappeared in public and was once again to be seen riding with Captain Randall through the villages.

They were in the saddle for the greater part of every day, for Alex returned each night to Lunjore. He heard cases and gave judgements, sitting on horseback in the shade of a tree throughout the long, blazing days: seeing in the faces of the villagers the ominous signs of the sickness that was sweeping through India; the open insolence and hostility that must be stared down or disregarded; the quick-leaping panic that must be allayed.

The quiet countryside was alive with rumours. 'The Shah of Persia has sent an army to the help of Bahadur Shah, who is now King of all Hind, and that army is already in Delhi!' . . . 'There are but a handful of *feringhis* left in the land, and the defeated remnants of the *Angrezi* regiments have been forced back and back until they drowned in the sea!' . . .

There were stories and more stories, but no proof. Until one day three men arrived in a village not ten miles from Lunjore city and brought the proof with them, in the form of two flounced muslin dresses, a sword, and a long tress of silky blonde hair. The soft muslin of the flounces and the soft gold of the hair were stiffened and patched with the ugly brown stains of dried blood, and there was blood too on the blade of the sword that had once belonged to a British officer.

'We found them hiding in a ditch by the roadside,' boasted one of the men. 'Two memsahibs and a sahib, five *koss* from Delhi. There was a child also, whose crying betrayed them. The sahib was sore wounded, but when Abdullah here ran his *tulwar* through the child he struck at him with this sword. But his arm had no strength and I took it from him and slew him with it, and the young woman also. *Arré* – how she shrieked! Like a peacock. I caught her by the hair – see, here is the lock. All the Hell-born are dead, and——'

'Not all,' said a hard clear voice behind him, and the gaping villagers drew back hastily.

Alex rode forward, Niaz at his elbow, and looked long and steadily at the three men, and no one spoke. Then he crooked his finger without turning his head and said softly: 'Kotwal-*ji*, bind me those men.'

The headman flinched and hesitated, and suddenly there was a revolver in Alex's hand and another in Niaz's.

'Be swift, my father,' said Niaz pleasantly. 'Do not keep the Huzoor waiting – or Hell either, which languishes to receive these three.'

There was a stir and a babble among the crowd and Alex raised his voice. '*Chup*! Be still! The first who moves without an order will go quickly to his account. And if it be a woman who moves, then her man will pay in her stead. Use thy *puggari*, O Kotwal; it will serve if thou canst not find a rope. That is better! Mohammed Latif, and thou, Duar Chand, bind me these other two.'

The three men looked wildly about them, jaws dropped and eyes starting in disbelief; but the village had known Alex for several years, and the habit of obedience, backed by the threat of firearms, was strong. If he had looked away or hesitated they would have broken and run, and guns and knives and *lathis* would have appeared as though by magic, and stones would have been thrown. But he did not look away and his eyes were cold and unpleasant. As unpleasant as Niaz's narrow-lipped grin.

One of the three men turned suddenly and ran, and Niaz fired. The man tripped and fell face downwards in the dust, twitched once and was still. 'That was too good a death for such carrion,' said Niaz cheerfully, controlling his horse more by the pressure of his knees than by the reins in his left hand.

The Eagle flung up his head and backed a pace, but he had been trained to stand the sound of a shot and he gave no trouble. When the two remaining murderers dangled at a rope's end, Alex gestured at the third body on the ground: 'Hang him beside his friends, so that all may see.'

They strung up the corpse without a word and Niaz took up the sword, the stained clothing and the lock of yellow hair, and tying them swiftly into a bundle, fastened it to his saddle. Alex surveyed the shivering Kotwal and the silent villagers and said: 'If any others come saying that all the sahibs be slain, show them these three. And tell any who ask, that though every sahib now in Hind were slain, a hundred thousand more – and ten times a hundred thousand – would come from *Belait* to exact vengeance for the slaying of their women and their babes. For the blood of such helpless ones is as seed which, falling to the ground, springs up in the likeness of armed men.'

He rode on out of the village without a backward look. '*Ho*!' said Niaz, putting up a hand to wipe the sweat from his forehead, 'I did not think to leave that place alive. It needed but one among them to show his teeth and they would have been at our throats like wolves. Wast thou not afraid?'

Alex gave a short laugh and held out one hand, palm downwards, by way of answer. It was shaking uncontrollably.

'Mine also!' said Niaz. 'I counted each breath as though it were my last. Is it true then that thy people are hunted through Hind?'

'It is true. But the end is not yet. In the end there will be a vengeance which will be as harsh, or harsher, than the offence. That is the evil that springs from such killing.'

Alex's voice was suddenly rough with anger and despair, and Niaz said quietly: 'It is none of thy doing, brother. What is written is written.'

'That is taught by thy Prophet, not mine,' said Alex bitterly. 'Mine would have me be my brother's keeper. Here – take the gun.'

He sent in a brief report of the incident to the Commissioner and was sent for to explain himself. 'You had no authority to do such a thing!' fumed the Commissioner. 'Disgraceful! Supposing it should come to the ears of the Authorities that men had been hung in my district without trial? Why, I might be—— Upon my word, Randall, you take too much upon yourself! The men should have been brought back here to stand their trial by the processes of the law and——'

'And been turned into heroes and martyrs,' interrupted Alex bluntly. 'This is war, sir! What do these people know of Western laws, which are not even their own? Those men were boasting to the villagers of murdering women and children and a wounded man. They had the evidence in their hands – you've seen it yourself. Do you suppose that if I had brought them back here it would have had a fraction of the effect on the village that seeing immediate justice done to them will have had? They understand justice – not law! And if I had taken those men into custody they might have been rescued ten times over on the way here, while if they had stood trial, half the city and possibly half the troops would have acclaimed them as heroes who had struck a blow against the British. We can afford no trials of that description, sir.'

'It will create a bad impression in the district,' said the Commissioner, with less certainty.

'On the contrary, it will create a very good one,' said Alex shortly. He forced his voice to a more conciliatory tone and said: 'If you will allow me unfettered action, sir, I can maintain order in the district as long as the regiments in Lunjore remain quiet. At the moment the sepoys are quiet, but if they should revolt it would be a different matter, and I would again urge you most strongly to impress upon their commanding officers the advisability of disarming them while there is still time.'

'I shall do no such thing!' snapped the Commissioner, his pallid face becoming dangerously suffused. 'What would happen if they did? Why – we'd be left with no defenders and no defence at all! Disarm the sepoys, and we'd be at the mercy of the scum of the city and every villager who could carry a rifle or a *lathi*!'

'It is not they whom we have to fear,' said Alex, and went out into the furnace glare of the noonday sun. That same sun that was even now blazing down on an open courtyard in the purlieus of the palace of the King of Delhi, where there stood a little cistern shaded by a *peepul* tree . . .

There were some fifty dazed and terrified people herded together like sheep in that hot courtyard, of whom all but six were women or children. The last of the Europeans and Christians left alive in Delhi, dragged up from the heat and stench and darkness of the dungeon in which they had spent five days, to be butchered in the harsh sunlight by men whom the sight and scent of blood had turned into beasts: men who cut and slashed and howled in frenzy until the last scream and the last moan was silenced, and who drew back then, shuddering, from the shambles and the stench of fresh-spilled blood and brains and entrails that steamed up from the pile of the newly dead.

Now at last there were no more *feringhis* in Delhi! Now at last the reluctant, trembling old King and every man, woman and child in the city was committed irretrievably to the path that had been chosen. There could be no drawing back now, for the massacre of the women and children whose mutilated bodies strewed the courtyard and whose blood soaked into the silent stones and curled and dried in the searing heat, had sealed them to their path. This was irrevocable. The die had been cast.

All that day while the shadows of the *peepul* tree and the cistern crawled across the paving-stones and the quiet dead, a shifting, peering crowd pressed ten deep about the courtyard, gaping and whispering. And towards evening half a dozen *mehtars*, men of low caste who act as sweepers and disposers of filth, heaped the stiffened, mangled bodies onto carts which dragged them to the bank of the placid Jumna, and flung them one by one into the river. Food for the crocodiles and the mud-turtles, the jackals and the scavenger birds: and a sign and a warning to a hundred villages as the bodies drifted down with the slow stream to be stranded on sand bars and burning-ghats and fish traps, or caught in the eddies that washed the walls of fortified towns.

Alex walked back to his bungalow in the sweltering heat and thought about the city and the district. There was no point in thinking about the sepoys; he could do nothing there, but as long as they remained quiet there were still things he could do among the uneasy, frightened, rumour-ridden population. Things that would have to be done on his own responsibility. 'I shall have to have his authority, or they will stop me,' thought Alex; and returned to his bungalow to make plans.

'Niaz, are there any among the *pultons* who will stand by their salt?'

'None that I would gamble a single *pice* of my pay on with any certainty of return,' said Niaz flippantly. 'But the Sikhs be the least unstable. They have no love for us Mussulmans and little liking for the Hindus. They strike always for themselves.'

'And the Mussulmans?'

'We strike for the Faith,' said Niaz with a grin, ' – save for such renegades as myself!'

'Give me the names of a dozen Sikhs from the *pultons*. Those who be the least disloyal,' said Alex, and returned to the Residency.

He found no difficulty in assisting the Commissioner to reach that state of intoxication where he would sign a paper without reading it – he signed many such. And on the following day, backed by the authority of a dozen mounted men (there was no cavalry in Lunjore but the cantonment was plentifully supplied with horses) he had ridden thirty miles to arrest an influential talukdar whose treasonable activities had been interesting him for some time past. Habib Ullah Khan had been taken by surprise, and a search of his house and his person had produced a remarkable quantity of ammunition and documentary information. His armed retainers had numbered some forty in all, and Alex had given them five minutes in which to lay down their arms. They had been three to one – nearer ten to one, if one counted the swarm of relatives, servants and villagers – but the sight of Alex sitting his horse in grim silence, watch in hand and counting the minutes, proved too much for them, and sullenly they threw down their arms.

There were too many weapons to allow for them to be taken away, and Alex watched while the growing heap of swords, muskets and *jezails* mounted to sizable proportions, with the addition of the very considerable quantity of arms taken from the house itself or discovered in the course of a ruthless search of the village. When the tally was complete he had ordered wood and dry grass heaped upon them and oil poured upon the pyre. It burned merrily, and the exploding cartridges provided a pyrotechnic display that enthralled the villagers.

Alex waited until he was sure that nothing but melted and twisted metal could be salvaged, and then rode back to the cantonments at a speed that left the majority of his escort toiling far behind him. The documentary evidence found in Habib Ullah Khan's house and on his person, together with certain unguarded statements made by Habib Ullah Khan himself – now lodged in the jail – carried conviction even to the brandy-sodden intelligence of the Commissioner of Lunjore.

'The head of the whole trouble in the city is Maulvi Amanullah of the Moti Masjid, and Abdul Majid, the Talukdar's nephew. If we can get those two, the city will be left with only petty agitators, but no real leaders,' said Alex. 'But if we try to take them openly we shall have a first-class riot on our hands, and I do not think that the——' He checked abruptly and then put what he had been about to say into different words: 'I think it would be putting too much strain on the loyalty of the sepoys to ask them to fight a street action at this point. But if you will hold a Durbar, I think we can manage it. Call a conference of all the influential men in the city. The larger shopkeepers included. It's the only hope.'

It had taken an hour and the best part of a bottle of brandy to persuade the Commissioner, and it had proved harder still to persuade the Military that the risk was worth taking, but the battle had been won by Colonel Moulson's dislike of Alex, and Alex's deliberate suggestion that Colonel Moulson did not trust his Regiment.

A stately conference had been held under the sweltering shade of a vast *shamianah* erected in the coolest part of the Residency grounds, and there were speeches and expressions of loyalty: genuine enough at the moment of their making, thought Alex wryly, remembering that ten minutes' conversation with an agitator could swing the pendulum as far East as it was now West. Views were canvassed and listened to with respect, and the guests withdrew as the sun began to set. All except two of them. Maulvi Amanullah and Abdul Majid Khan, wealthy nephew of the Talukdar, were delayed in conversation, and when they would have left, were detained.

There was considerable uneasiness in the city that night. The patrolling Magistrate, who had been covertly assisting the work of spreading disaffection, found himself arrested, and the following morning a proclamation was issued calling upon all inhabitants of the city to give up their arms within twenty-four hours; followed by another, imposing a curfew. It was backed by the appearance of four heavy guns that were plainly to be seen in position commanding the Rohilkhand Gate and the main road to the city.

Deprived of its leaders the city capitulated, and the arms were collected – but not destroyed. 'For God's sake,' begged Alex, 'burn 'em. Blow 'em up! There's enough stuff there to fit out an army. Now that we've got it, don't let's take any chances of it falling into their hands again.'

'It could be in no safer place than in the care of the Military Police,' snapped Colonel Moulson.

Alex bit back the retort he had almost made, and was silent. For the moment at least the danger was averted. The villages and the city would stay quiet – for just as long as the sepoys stayed quiet. 'The thirty-first of May' . . . Ten more days. If they would only disarm them *now*!

There had been no reply to the message he had dispatched to Suthragunj to be telegraphed to the Governor-General in Calcutta, and he did not know that it had never reached Lord Canning, but was gathering dust in a pigeon-hole while the junior official who had received it occupied himself with panic-stricken plans for evacuating his wife and family on the first ship to sail for Europe.

Calcutta was filled with panic in these days, as telegram after telegram, message after message, brought news of disaster. Delhi snatched from the hands of the British in an hour! Meerut, with one of the strongest British garrisons in India, bewildered and helpless and apparently unable to do more than protect itself from a peril that had passed from it to spread out like a forest fire over half India. A hundred pleas a day poured in upon Canning begging for troops – for British troops. 'We cannot hold out without troops. Send us help.' 'The sepoys have mutinied. Send us troops.'

He did what he could, but it was little. Help would be slow in coming. They must fend for themselves yet awhile.

Lottie had arrived in Lunjore at last. Lottie and Mr Dacosta and Mrs Holly – that same Mrs Holly who had embarked on the steamship *Sirius* and had nursed Mrs Abuthnot and her daughters through a bout of seasickness.

Stout, cheerful, sensible Mrs Holly was considerably less stout and no longer cheerful. Her clothes hung in folds and her round pleasant face sagged in deep harsh lines; for she had seen her husband's head struck from his body with a single swing of a sharpened *tulwar* in the blazing charnel house of Duryagunj, and only the sudden collapse of a burning roof-beam had saved her from a similar fate. Somehow – she could not remember how – she and Mr Dacosta had escaped from the carnage and reached the Main Guard at the Kashmir Gate, where they had witnessed the final tragedy and escaped over the battlements. But although her stoutness and her cheerfulness had gone, her placid good sense remained. She had taken Lottie and Mr Dacosta under her wing and it was she who had cajoled the driver of the *ekka* into taking them up, and so brought them at last to Lunjore.

Mr Dacosta was an olive-skinned, middle-aged Eurasian, a clerk in a Government department. He had been wounded by a sword-cut and badly burned, but he had struggled on valiantly and had not complained. Mrs Holly had bound up his wounds and taken charge of him as she had of Lottie: 'You know, ma'am,' she explained to Winter, 'it was just as well, them being sick. It give me something to do, and something else to think about than – than the things I seen that day. It was Miss Lottie 'oo said you was 'ere when that *ekka-wallah* says as 'e was goin' to Lunjore. She would 'ave it that we must come 'ere, an' I don't know but what she wasn't right. We 'ad no place special to go to, you see. She said – she said as you'd invited 'er for a visit, pore young thing.'

'Mrs Holly,' said Winter unhappily, 'do you – do you think she will remember?'

'Some day,' said Mrs Holly. 'It'll be a pity when she does, for she's better off this way, and that's the truth.'

For Lottie had been delighted to see Winter, and she had forgotten Delhi. She wondered sometimes, a little hazily, why it was that she should suddenly have decided to come to Lunjore. Something had happened, surely? But then she had always meant to visit Winter one day, and Edward—— Why had she allowed Edward to send her on a visit just now? She had told him that she would not think of leaving him. Edward must have insisted. It was odd that she could not remember. Perhaps it was something to do with having a baby that made thinking an effort? It was easier not to think – so much easier. Thinking made her head ache, and with that ache fear would well up inside her like ice-cold water bubbling up out of an unseen spring, and her heart would begin to hammer and her breath come short. Yet there was nothing to be afraid of. Nothing. Winter was here. She was only paying a visit to Winter, and soon she would go back to her pretty bungalow in Meerut and be with Edward again. She must not think. It made her feel ill, and that was bad for the child. 'You must not think of yourself, Lottie; think of the child' . . . 'You must rest more, Lottie; think of the child' . . . 'You do not eat enough, Lottie; think of the child.' Edward and Mama and Mama's friends had said such things so often, and they were right. She must think of the child. Edward's child——

'Edward wants a girl, you know,' she confided to Winter, 'but I want the first one to be a boy and just like Edward. He is to be christened Edward – I have quite made up my mind. But he will have to be Teddy, because we cannot have two Edwards. I am sure that Teddy will be exactly like his papa. Edward says that red hair is very catching!'

'Alex,' said Winter desperately, 'do you think she will ever remember?'

'One day,' said Alex, and added as Mrs Holly had done: 'She's better off as she is at the moment. When is that baby due?' He had frowned at the sight of the sudden colour that burned in Winter's cheeks and had said impatiently: 'You don't really suppose that hitching a hoop higher and carrying round a shawl disguises a thing like that, do you?'

Winter had been taught that babies, until they were born, were an unmentionable subject in the presence of gentlemen, but the impatience in Alex's voice made her ashamed of the blush. She said with as much composure as she could muster: 'I think she expects it in about two months' time. But Mrs Holly says one can never be sure with a first child, and that it may not be born until——'

She stopped abruptly and put her hands up to her hot cheeks. It was one thing to answer a direct question, but one did not – one *could* not – discuss such things with a man!

A corner of Alex's mouth curved in the shadow of a grin and he said: 'Don't be missish, Mrs Barton. It's a perfectly natural function. How soon can you leave?'

'*Leave*? I can't leave now! Lottie can't go any further. Not after what she has been through. Dr O'Dwyer says that she must not be moved, but have complete quiet. He says that she could not support any further journeyings in this heat, and that he cannot understand why she has not had – a – a——'

'A miscarriage,' finished Alex with curt impatience. 'Yes, I've heard of those too. Then you will not be leaving either?'

'How could I?'

'No,' said Alex bleakly, 'you could not. And I think in any case it is too late.'

For Alex had talked to Mr Dacosta – Mrs Holly avoided questions – and had heard the first true account of that last day of the British rule in Delhi. The ease with which Delhi had been captured had horrified him; as had the news that although young Willoughby had blown up the Magazine in the city rather than allow it to fall into the hands of the rabble, the far larger Magazine near the river above Metcalf House had apparently not been similarly destroyed, which meant that an ample supply of ammunition of every description would by now be at the disposal of the mutineers.

'We looked all day for thee troops from Meerut,' whispered Mr Dacosta, hoarse with weakness and fever, 'but they did not come. If only twenty British troops had appeared before thee gates that morning, those men would have run away. They were veree fearful. Oah yess, they feared pursuit. But it is all lost – all lost. My whole family – Mama-*ji* and Clara and the *butchas*. Twelve we had, though five died when they were onlee small. My Clara, she cried for them. She would not have cried if she had known how she and thee others would die. It is not right that I should see that and still live. I was in thee office, Mister Randall, and when I heard that there was some *juggra* in thee city, I did not believe that it would be veree bad. I laughed at young Pereira and said, "Nonsense, man! It is nothing," and I stayed at my desk. That is right, is it not, Mister Randall? One must stay by thee work and set an example when others are fearful. We cannot run away and leave thee work. But if I had run then, I might have saved them! No, no – that is not true. But I would have died with them. My poor Clara! She was veree jolly always. Always laughing and joking. Later – later I ran back through the streets and searched my house and saw – and saw . . . Mister Randall, they were all dead! Even Chiri, thee little one. She was onlee two, you know. Her they had . . . No, it is not good to have seen what I have seen and still live. It is not right!'

Two days later he had died, and Mrs Holly, who had been unable to weep for her Alfred, had wept for frail, middle-aged, sallow-skinned Mr Dacosta, who had conceived it his duty to stay at his work and set an example of courage.

Almost every night now there were mysterious fires in the cantonments, and though extra guards patrolled the area, they never made any arrests. The Police Lines burned down one night and then the Post Office, and the following night the bungalow of Lieutenant Dewar, whose wife and young family were only saved with difficulty, for they had been sleeping on the roof on account of the heat, and the fire, which broke out in the living-room, had taken firm hold before they were aroused.

It was difficult to allay panic among the families of the officers who lived in bungalows surrounded by large gardens where trees and shrubs provided cover for lurking incendiarists, and few women slept at night, while parents of children lay awake, starting in terror at every night noise.

Only the children showed no signs of strain. They grew pallid from the heat and the enforced inactivity in shuttered rooms during the day-time, but the children had always been favourites with the servants in the bungalows and the sepoys in the lines. They loved them, trusted them, spoke their language with far more fluency than their mother-tongue, bullied them and ordered them about, and ran to them with their woes. The Indians – any Indians – were their friends and allies and playmates, and they would no more have conceived of receiving harm at their hands than at the hands of their own parents. Less! for parents could be stern at times and administer punishment and rebuke, but Mali-*ji* and Ayah-*ji*, and Makhan Khan and Piari Lal and Sobra Singh, Havildar Jewrakun Tewary and Sepoy Dhoolee Sookul, the *dhobi*, the *dazi*, the sweetmeat-seller and old Khundoo the *chowkidar* – never! From all these and a hundred more the children had never received anything but kindness and petting. But their mothers grew thin-faced with fear and their fathers walked with neck and shoulder muscles taut with strained alertness.

The three commanding officers still refused even to consider disarming their men, although now, when it was too late, they would have sent the women away – and dared not do so, because each day new reports of disaffection and murder came in. Lunjore was still quiet, with the tensed, twitching quietness of a cat at a mousehole, but it was not so with the districts that surrounded it. 'They are safer here,' said Colonel Gardener-Smith, whom the past ten days appeared to have aged by as many years. And even those who had previously made arrangements to send their families to the hills, cancelled them.

The Commissioner did not appear to notice that his wife had put off her departure. He noticed little in these days, and that little through an alcoholic haze. The whole situation was beyond him. He was afraid, and his fear drove him to his familiar refuge, the bottle. Even Yasmin had forsaken him. She had packed her clothes and her jewels and everything else she could manage to lay her hands on, and had slipped away one night with her three fat, half-caste children, her relations and her servants and Nilam, the blue macaw, and had not come back. Her defection had frightened the Commissioner far more than the nightly fires, the news from Delhi, the inaction of the Meerut Brigade or the endless tales of murder and massacre that trickled in daily from the outside world.

'Rats leavin' the sinkin' ship!' whispered the Commissioner hoarsely, staring into space with eyes that did not see the sly, inscrutable face of Iman Bux who had broken the news. 'That's what it is. They know. The rats know! We're sinking. She knew it, and she's gone – the lying, cheating black bitch!'

He had flung his glass furiously at the impassive butler and that afternoon he had advocated immediate flight. They must all of them go, and by night, in boats down the river. The Company's Raj was finished. Unless they were all to die, those who were not already dead must fly the country – reach the coast, using the rivers and avoiding the roads, and abandon India. They could not hold it. If they stayed they would all be murdered.

'Better that than to turn tail,' snorted Colonel Moulson, observing him with disapproval. 'I hope you don't speak in this fashion before your servants, Con. If we can keep our heads we shall weather the storm. Calcutta can't be idle, and strong reinforcements are certain to be on their way.'

'How do we know that there are any Europeans left alive in Calcutta?' whispered the Commissioner. 'If the native regiments at Barrackpore have mutinied they could wipe out the Europeans in Calcutta in a night. How do we know it hasn't happened already? – how do we know?'

'Y' know, Con,' said Colonel Moulson judicially, 'you're better when you're drunk. Nothing to get worked up about – troops as quiet as lambs. If it's these fires that are gettin' on your nerves, forget 'em! Work of bazaar *budmarshes*. The sepoys have worked like trojans puttin' 'em out.'

The Commissioner had retreated to the brandy bottle, and had taken no interest in the information relayed to him three hours later that the sepoys of Colonel Packer's Regiment had refused to accept their consignment of Commissariat flour, saying that it was known to be adulterated with bone-dust for the purpose of destroying their caste. Colonel Packer and his officers had expostulated, lectured and finally pleaded, but the men had remained obdurate. They would not touch the flour, and moreover they insisted that it must be thrown into the river to ensure that it was not returned to them again or handed to any of their comrades in the other regiments. The flour had been duly taken away and thrown into the distant river.

'Thank God it wasn't Moulson's lot,' said Alex to Major Maynard. 'He'd have ordered 'em to eat it or else – and it would have been "or else"!'

The sepoys, having won their point, had become noticeably insolent and out of hand, and many of them, from all three regiments, had that same evening openly looted the ripe fruit from the gardens of the cantonment bungalows. Their officers had soon succeeded in putting a stop to it, but it was plain that discipline was deteriorating rapidly.

'They are a little out of hand,' admitted Colonel Gardener-Smith reluctantly, 'but that is understandable in the exceptional circumstances. We are all only human. It is nothing serious – though Packer's Regiment is not behaving at all well. I begin to fear we may have a little trouble with them. Nothing of course that my own men will not be able to set to rights.'

'Old Gardener's sepoys are all to pieces,' said Colonel Packer. 'I don't like the look of it. Thank God my men have never given me any serious cause for anxiety. I have assured them that for the present we will discontinue the supplies of Government flour and obtain it locally, and they are quite content.'

'Wouldn't trust Packer's fellows a yard!' said Colonel Moulson. 'Or old Nannie Gardener's either, for that matter! No discipline; that's their trouble. Now *my* lot . . .'

That night Major Wilkinson, who had dined at the Residency and returned drunk to his bungalow, fired at and wounded one of a patrol who challenged him. There was an inquiry held on the following day and Major Wilkinson was acquitted of any intent to wound – on a plea of being unconscious from intoxication at the time.

'Bloody fools!' said Alex, exasperated. 'They should have cashiered him – sent him off to be court-martialled at Suthragunj. Anything but this. To acquit him of wounding a sepoy at a time like this, and on a plea of drunkenness – are they mad? If it had been the other way round, they'd have given the sepoy ten years' penal servitude or hanged him! If this doesn't start something, I'm a bigger fool than Packer!'

There was a ball to celebrate the Queen's birthday on the first day of the new week. Victoria's birthday had fallen on a Sunday that year, so the ball had been held on the day following it. It had been the end, too, of the fast of

Ramadan, and there was a new slim sickle moon in the sky. It hung in the green of the evening, a curved thread of silver; like the crescent of Islam embroidered on the green banners of the Faithful – like an omen in the sky.

'*La Ill-ah ha! il Ill-ah ho!*' cried the muezzins from the minarets of the mosques in the city. 'There is no God but God!'

The band of the 1st Regiment of Lunjore Irregulars stood smartly to attention, their dark faces creased with concentration, and watched the Conductor's baton fall. '*God Save our Gracious Queen, Long live our Noble Queen——*' The familiar tune, the National Anthem of an alien race, blared out through the open windows across the dark parade-ground and the sepoy lines.

She was thirty-eight – that dumpy, imperious, self-confident housewife who had ascended the throne as a slim self-confident girl in the year that Sabrina Grantham had met Marcos de Ballesteros; the year that Anne Marie the second, who was Ameera, wife of Walayat Shah, had been born to Juanita in the little pink stucco palace in Lucknow city.

'*Send her victorious, happy and glorious . . .*'

Sabrina's daughter danced at the Queen's Birthday Ball in a wide-skirted ball-gown of water-green tarlatan looped up with garlands of camellias. She smiled as she danced – the same smile that was on the face of every woman who danced in that flag-and-flower decorated room, or sat against the walls listening to the sepoy band playing the 'Imogene Waltz', the 'Sultan's Polka', the Laurel; 'Angelina', 'Belle of the Village' and 'Lily of the Valley'. A smile that did not reach the eyes and hurt the heart. The smile of women who watch their men and strain their ears to listen, and will not show that they are afraid.

Alex too had attended that ball and there was nothing in his face to show that he had spent the greater part of the afternoon arguing, urging, pleading fruitlessly and for the last time with three courageous, obdurate men for the disarming of the sepoys.

'It can be done,' urged Alex. 'There are enough of us to do it, and this ball will provide the opportunity. No one will expect anything on the night of a ball.' He had outlined a plan; rash, but possible; and the verdict had been unanimously against it.

'Until we have actual evidence of mutinous intentions,' said Colonel Gardener-Smith, 'no sepoy of mine shall be so insulted or——'

'I have yet to learn,' said Alex shortly, abandoning diplomacy and brusquely interrupting that familiar speech, 'that cure is preferable to prevention. And this Wilkinson affair may well prove to be in the nature of a last straw. I understand that the verdict was not well received in the lines?'

But they were not to be persuaded. They did, however, decide on taking one precautionary measure, for the sake of the ladies, whose nerves were beginning to suffer from the strain of constantly being on the alert. It was the custom among the European families in Lunjore to drive out in the early mornings to get what little fresh air they could before the sun rose and the heat forced them into the dimness of shuttered rooms. Word was conveyed to the families that on the morning following the ball the women and children were to drive instead to the Residency, taking with them such clothing and necessities as they would need for a stay of a few days. The Residency was sufficiently large to shelter them all without too much discomfort, and a party of Military Police was to be posted in the grounds as extra protection, while four guns under the charge of native gunners of Colonel Moulson's Regiment were to be placed in between the Residency and the lines, and another two between the Residency and the city.

'The Residency is admirably situated for defence,' said Colonel Gardener-Smith. 'With that nullah and the jungle behind it, and a wall round the rest of it, nothing could be better.'

'I agree,' said Alex, 'providing one was defending it against a rabble from the city. But if the sepoys should mutiny it will turn into a trap.'

'My sepoys will not mutiny,' said Colonel Gardener-Smith obstinately. 'I will stake my life on that.'

Alex said nothing more. He was tired of vain repetitions. He had gone across to the Residency and spoken to Winter. 'I'm taking Yusaf again. I need him. What have you done with that revolver I gave you?'

'I have it.'

'Good. Keep it loaded and keep it within reach. I've brought you some more ammunition for it. And see that there is always a horse kept saddled, and——' He did not complete the sentence but looked past Winter's shoulder at the blank wall for a long minute, his brows drawn together in a frown, and then shrugged and went away without further words. What was the good of saying anything else? He had done what he could. Had that woman – Ameera? – spoken the truth? Had there been a day set, and had the Meerut rising been premature? It had been remarkably successful, and its success had touched off a series of localized risings. Were those too a mistake? '*Await the auspicious day*' . . .

'Two more days to go,' thought Alex that night, leaning against the wall and watching a quadrille danced at the Queen's Birthday Ball.

But there were no more days. Only hours.

BOOK FIVE

THE HIRREN MINAR

40

It was Major Beckwith, second-in-command to Colonel Gardener-Smith, who informed his commanding officer half an hour before sunrise on the morning after the ball that the Regiment had not dispersed after parade, and could no longer be trusted. He had wept as he had said it, for Major Beckwith, like his Colonel, had believed with a whole-hearted belief in the fidelity of his men.

'I will go back and speak to them,' said Colonel Gardener-Smith.

'It's no good, sir. They will listen to no one.'

'They will listen to me,' said Colonel Gardener-Smith stubbornly.

But they had not listened.

'We will not harm thee, or permit thee to be harmed,' said their spokesman, 'for thou art a good man. But we take no more orders from *feringhis* who have plotted to destroy our caste and enslave us. Go quickly while there is yet time, for we know what we know, and the men of the 105th are not as us, and if they can, may slay thee.'

They had thrust him from the lines, shouting down his words, and had rushed to the bells of arms and seizing their rifles had announced their intention of marching immediately for Delhi to offer their services to the Mogul. They had opened fire on their officers, two of whom had been badly wounded, and there had been nothing for it but to leave before worse befell, and the Colonel had left.

His bungalow was empty, for his wife and daughter were already at the Residency, and it seemed intolerably dark and quiet. As quiet as the tomb. As quiet as old age. 'I am an old man,' thought Colonel Gardener-Smith. 'An old man and a fool. I have given my life to a lie. They will disband the 93rd and remove its name from the Army list. *My* 93rd!'

His mind went back to the days when he had first joined the Regiment as a young ensign, and he remembered men long dead; sepoys and subadars, men who had fought with him and followed him. The names of old fights and old battles spoke their names in his brain like a roll of drums. He forgot his wife and Delia. Their faces and their names meant nothing to him, and awoke no echo in his mind to drown or disturb the memory of the men among whom and beside whom and for whom he had spent his life.

'They will disband the 93rd as they did the 19th. It will go down in the records – *Disbanded for Mutiny*. My 93rd . . .'

He left the bungalow and went to the deserted Mess, walking bareheaded in the blaze of the newly risen sun, and took down the colours and burned them in the grate, pouring lamp-oil on them and watching until there was nothing left but a heap of evil-smelling black ash. And then he shot himself.

'The bloody idiot!' said Alex furiously, hearing of it half an hour later – he had ridden out to speak to the Kotwal of a village beyond the city and had returned late – 'Just when we need every man who can fire a gun. When one man is worth his weight in – God damn these sentimentalists! Art thou ready, Yusaf? It may be that thou wilt have to wait two days. Three even. But I do not think so, for Fazal Hussain has brought word that a horseman took that road at first light. No matter, there is food and water enough for a long wait. If they come, wait until the first of them are abreast of the rocks by the two palm trees. Go now and go swiftly. *B'ism Illah*——'

Colonel Moulson had been breakfasting at the Residency, together with several officers who were engaged in assuring the ladies assembled there that there was no cause for alarm and that their presence in the Residency was merely a precautionary measure which would only be necessary for a day or two.

The Residency was noisy with women's voices and the laughter or yells of children, the rustle of poplin, muslin and *barège* dresses and ruffled pantalettes. Almost every woman there had danced until a late hour at the ball, and many had had no sleep before starting out for the Residency. But all were gay and in good heart, for the presence of the Police Guard, the sight of the guns with their attendant crews of native gunners, the high white wall of the Residency and, above all, the company of their fellows, had worked wonders on their failing spirits. They felt safer together and in such surroundings than they had separately in their scattered bungalows, and there was a light-hearted and picnic-like atmosphere in the crowded rooms that even the non-appearance of their host, and the news that he was indisposed, did nothing to dispel.

The information that it had been considered advisable to urge all the women and children to take refuge in the Residency, to place guns at the approaches and mount a strong guard of Military Police had been too much for the Commissioner, and it had been a matter of the greatest difficulty to get him into a fit state to make an appearance at the Birthday Ball. Once there, however, surrounded by women in ball-gowns, officers in Mess-dress, flags and flowers and no lack of liquid refreshment, he had recovered his courage. The music and the lights, the laughter and the wine had combined to persuade him that all was well, and that any danger that threatened had been averted.

But this happy frame of mind had not lasted. Awakening with the headache and dry mouth that was the usual aftermath of celebration, the presence of a crowd of women and children whose chattering could be heard all over the house had brought all his fears flooding back. These women were here because they were in danger, and the danger must indeed be great to warrant such measures, yet Fred Moulson had assured him—— Where was the brandy? Brandy and yet more brandy was the only refuge from a world that was disintegrating around him. Brandy warmed him and comforted him and cushioned him against fear.

Delia, unlike the majority of the women present, had elected to wear her widest crinoline and a dress that was more suitable for an afternoon party than an early breakfast. Four airy flounces of pale blue muslin edged with narrow velvet ribbon composed the full skirt, and the tight little bodice boasted small puffed sleeves and a wide matching sash of watered silk. Her beautiful hair was not confined in a net, but tied back with a demure bow of ribbon that allowed it to cascade down her back in glossy chestnut ringlets. Colonel Moulson found her enchanting, and was in process of telling her so when the sound of galloping hooves interrupted him . . .

'I might have known it!' fumed Colonel Moulson. 'Always said that fool Gardener was too soft with his men. I'll show 'em! Marching to Delhi with the treasure, are they? Where the hell's my horse? If we double three companies across the *maidan* we'll cut 'em off and cut 'em to bits!'

He galloped off into the glare of the morning, his Adjutant and a senior captain riding behind him, and his Regiment received him in silence. They listened to his bellowed commands, and no man moved – their shadows lying motionless on the hot ground. Then a man laughed, loud and scornfully, and another took aim and fired.

Ten minutes later the Adjutant, his arm pouring a bright scarlet flood, slid from his wounded horse onto Alex's sunny verandah and gasped out the news.

'They shot him down . . . and Mottisham too . . . and Halliwell and Reeves and Charlie and little Jenks. They're all dead. Packer's fellows have broken too. They've killed him – saw his body. Cut to bits. And old Gardener has——'

'I know,' said Alex, knotting a strip torn from a curtain with furious haste about the man's shattered arm and shoulder. He turned his head and called out to Niaz who had ridden full-tilt round the corner of the bungalow from the direction of the stables:

'The Lunjore *Pulton* also! Ride for the river. Get the charges from the Hirren Minar. I will meet thee there. Go quickly!'

Niaz lifted a hand in salute and turned his rearing, frantic horse as Alex helped the Adjutant back into his saddle. 'If Moulson's men have broken that means the gunners will go,' said Alex. 'Get over to the Residency and tell 'em to get the women and children away over the nullah and into the jungle at once – *at once*, do you hear! Think you can do it? Good. Alam Din, run with the Sahib – be swift!'

He leapt down the verandah steps and caught at the bridle of his horse. 'Where – are you going?' gasped the Adjutant, wheeling his own wounded animal.

'Magazine.'

Niaz, already half-way to the gate, caught the word and reined in hard.

'What is it?' called Alex, spurring down the drive.

'I go with thee,' said Niaz between his teeth, and rode out level with him.

'Do as I tell you!' said Alex savagely and in English. He cut at Niaz's horse with his whip and drew ahead, the Eagle easily outdistancing the heavier horse, and yelled back over his shoulder in the vernacular: 'It is an order! This is in thy hands. Do not fail me, brother!'

The Magazine was a small, square, unpretentious building of whitewashed stone that stood near the centre of the cantonment area and was surrounded by a high wall and several shade trees. There was a yelling crowd of sepoys milling round it, and Alex heard the crackle of musketry and reined back in the shadow of a clump of bamboos. Someone was holding the Magazine, then. He caught a brief glimpse of a pink boyish face, hatless, the red hair bright against the whitewashed stone about the inner parapet, and recognized young Eyton, one of the new-joined 'griffins', barely a month out from England. The other lay face downwards thirty yards from the gate and on the edge of the yelling crowd, his brains splashed in an oddly symmetrical star-shaped pattern on the hot dust.

Another face appeared beside young Eyton – a dark, bearded face that showed a gleam of white teeth; a rifle cracked and another man in the crowd fell. Alex could hear words from among the howling din: 'Join us! Do not fight for those who have betrayed us! We be thy brothers! Kill the *feringhis* and join us!' The answer was another shot fired into the thick of the mob. There were some then who had remained true to their salt. But the fight was an unequal one, for already fifty men or more had swarmed over the outer wall, and the gate was creaking under a heavy log of wood wielded by a dozen men as a battering ram.

Alex knew that he should go. There was nothing he could do. But he did not move. He saw the boy appear briefly again on the parapet and peer down at the yelling besiegers, duck to avoid the shots, and hold up his hand as though he gave a signal – and even as he watched Alex knew what that signal meant, and he turned his horse and set him at a low wall fifty yards away, cleared it and was racing across a stretch of open ground. As he reached the far side of it he heard the roar of the explosion and felt the shock of the blast like a blow between his shoulders. '*Well done*!' cried Alex, unaware that he was shouting aloud, 'Oh, well done!' He spurred across another piece of open ground, leapt a compound wall and found himself among the flowers of Captain Batterslea's garden.

Mrs Batterslea had been one of the five women who had considered the move to the Residency quite unnecessary and had elected to remain in her own bungalow: 'The children are far better off here. Why, my servants adore them! I am quite sure they would die for them.'

Mrs Batterslea's extravagant statement had proved to be no more than the truth. Her ayah lay huddled among the plumbago bushes below the verandah, in death as in life striving to protect the small silent figure in its white frock and blue sash that her stiffening body and outstretched arms still covered, while in the servants' quarters behind the bungalow portly Farid, the butler, the thin-legged *pūrbeah* grass-cutter, Captain Batterslea's Brahmin orderly and Bulaki, the low-caste sweeper, had died side by side, fighting to protect the three small boys who had been reached at last only over the bodies of four men of an alien race and divergent faiths who had fought their own kind in defence of a foreigner's children.

The bungalow was burning and the heat of the flames joined the furnace heat of the sun to shrivel the few plants that still brightened the flower-beds. The flower-beds had been Mrs Batterslea's special pride, and in them she had striven, not always with success, to grow the flowers that reminded her of home – larkspur and mignonette, pansies, gillyflowers and roses. Of these only the roses now remained, wilting in the relentless heat. The rose-bushes and Mrs Batterslea herself, who lay wide-eyed and open-mouthed among the withered flowers, staring up at the brassy sky. The frilly pink-and-white wrap she had worn had been torn away, and where her breasts had been there was now only blood. And she had been raped before she died. 'That means the bazaar scum and the city have broken out already,' thought Alex automatically, knowing that no sepoy would have done such a thing, for to do so would have defiled him.

It did not need more than one look to see that she was dead, but the sight of her mutilated body checked Alex and turned him back from the road he had meant to take.

From the moment that he had heard the first news of the outbreak he had thought of only one thing and seen only one thing: the thin, tired, dauntless face of Henry Lawrence who had said: 'If it comes, I shall look to you to hold the western road for me.' And when he had learned that the 93rd had expressed their intention of marching for Delhi he had been conscious only of relief. Let them go to Delhi – let them go anywhere as long as it was not eastward into Oudh. '*Given time, I believe I may be able to hold Oudh quiet even if the rest of India rises; but it is time we need! – time most of all: and that is a thing which God and the Government may not grant me. The sands are running out, Alex . . .*'

'If I can help to give him even one more day,' had been the driving thought in Alex's brain ever since the morning that Gopal Nath had whispered the first news of the Meerut mutiny and the fall of Delhi, and it had filled his mind to the exclusion of all else during the past half-hour. But now, looking down at Mrs Batterslea's dead, staring face and breastless, outraged body, he saw another face. Winter's. Saw it as clearly and as distinctly as though it were she and not Alice Batterslea who was lying at his feet among the trampled rose-bushes. And turning back, he rode for the Residency, hating himself; cursing aloud in a breathless, blasphemous whisper, but driven by an emotion and a fear that he could not control.

The heavy, iron-studded doors of the Residency gate had been closed that morning and the police guard ordered to keep them barred, but the door of the narrow wicket in the main gate, through which only one at a time could enter, stood ajar. There was a crowd before the gate; a swaying, yelling, crowd who were being harangued by a wild-eyed figure in a green turban – Akbar Khan, the gatekeeper.

'Kill them!' screamed Akbar Khan. 'Slay all, and let not one escape! For the Faith! For the Faith! *Maro*! *Maro*!'

They heard the sound of the furious galloping hoof-beats and scattered like a whirl of dead leaves as Alex rode into them. He fired only once and saw Akbar Khan topple forward with an expression of ludicrous surprise on his face, and then he had flung himself from the saddle, the Eagle's rearing body protecting him momentarily from the crowd, and in that fractional moment he was through the narrow wicket. A bullet fired by someone within the gate smacked into the woodwork within an inch of him and he stumbled over the body of a man who lay across the threshold, and turning, threw himself against the narrow door and dropped the heavy bar into place.

He turned from it, revolver in hand, and saw the faces of the police guard, sullen and unsure as they fidgeted uneasily with their muskets, and knew that there was no security there.

'Sorry, Randall,' said a gasping voice from the shadows of the gate. 'Nearly got you. Thought it was another of those swine.'

Major Maynard, commanding the Military Police, was sitting on the ground with his back to the wall and one hand pressed to his side in a vain attempt to stem the red tide that welled out between his fingers. He held a smoking revolver in the other, a bullet from which had narrowly missed Alex, and his men watched him and did not move.

'Y'r just in time,' said Major Maynard. 'Tell 'em up at the house – run for it.' He saw the movement of the revolver in Alex's hand and said: 'No. It wasn't them. They ain't as far gone as that. It was that gatekeeper of yours.'

Alex faced the watching men and said harshly: 'Take up the Sahib and carry him to the house. Quickly!'

'*No*!' gasped Major Maynard. 'No . . . wouldn't be any use. I know that . . . so do you. I've got . . . fifteen minutes perhaps . . . and as long as . . . I'm here . . . they'll do nothing. When I'm gone . . . they'll open the gate, and run fer it. Get up to the house . . . tell 'em t' get out. I'll hold these for . . . a few minutes . . .'

Alex did not wait. He had told Wardle twenty minutes ago to get the women away, and they must have gone already. But he had to be sure. He turned and ran for the distant house, across the iron-hard lawn and over the flower-beds, and reaching the verandah leapt up the steps with the noise of the mob beyond the Residency gate rising into a roar behind him.

But no one had gone. They were all there still. Perhaps a dozen men and more than twice as many women and children. A flower garden of women in preposterous, pale-coloured, wide-hooped skirts, tight-fitted bodices and thin, inadequate, flat-heeled slippers. Women whose faces, sallow from the heat and inactivity of the hot weather, were now greenish-white with fear.

'Good God!' said Alex furiously, 'what the hell d'you think you're doing? Go on – get these women away! Wardle, I thought I told you——'

'Safer here,' gasped Captain Wardle. 'The gunners are loyal and the police'll hold . . .'

'The gunners have broken and the police will run within five minutes – and half the riff-raff of the city is out there,' snapped Alex. 'Go on – out by the back and over the bridge. Get into the jungle! It's your only chance. *Run*!'

He saw Winter's face across the width of the room. She had one arm about Lottie and her eyes were wide and enormous but quite steady. There was a sudden and louder burst of yelling and a crash that told its own tale, and Alex ran to the window, took one look and was across the room and had flung open the door that led out of the drawing-room and to the back of the house: '*Run*!'

They ran; picking up screaming children, clasping babies, sobbing and panting, tripping over their wide skirts. Winter said: 'Take Lottie, Mrs Holly,' and pushed them out through the door, 'you know the way.' She stood back, urging the women to speed, and then Alex had caught her wrist and was running with her, dragging her. He pulled her down the steps of the back verandah and thrusting her ahead of him said breathlessly: 'Over the bridge – quick as you can!' and then he had left her.

After the dimness of the shuttered house the sunlight was unbelievably hot and bright. The heat and the glare met her like the blaze from a blast furnace and added to the complete unreality of the moment. Far across the gardens, through the intervening trees and shadows, she could see a crowd of little figures pouring through the gate. For Major Maynard had been right. He had lived considerably less than the fifteen minutes that he had hoped for, and when they saw that he was dead his men had thrown away their muskets and unbarred the gates, letting in the maddened mob of sepoys who had now been reinforced by a rabble from the city.

'Run, damn you!' shouted Alex from the turn of the house. She saw him jerk up his arm and fire, and picking up her wide skirts she ran as he had told her to – ran after Lottie and Mrs Holly and a dozen others who had made for the bridge over the nullah.

But they had not all run for the bridge. Many of them had checked and turned back, daunted by the glare and the empty spaces and the yelling of the mob, and deeming the shuttered house a safer refuge had run to hide instead in closets and cupboards and under the frilled valances of beds, locking themselves into darkened rooms and cowering behind the furniture. Others, confused by terror and the blinding sunlight, had lost their sense of direction and were running helplessly to and fro like panic-stricken animals, dodging behind trees and shrubs.

Winter saw Lottie and Mrs Holly reach the bridge and cross it and run on towards the tangled thickets thirty yards beyond it. Her wide skirts swayed and swooped and the ground under her thin flat-heeled slippers felt unbelievably hot. She had almost reached the bridge when she saw someone on horseback galloping towards her from the far side of the nullah. A fair-haired girl on a chestnut horse. The shadowy horse – surely she could see the trees through it? – saw her and shied violently, and instinctively Winter flung herself to one side, and a bullet that would have struck her between the shoulders passed harmlessly by.

She did not see what happened to the horse and rider, for a shriek behind her made her check and turn, and it was Delia, running towards her from the direction of the house.

Delia's muslin ruffles flared about her like the petals of a huge peony in the wind, and the ribbon had fallen from her hair so that her long chestnut curls streamed out behind her. Her face was a mask of terror and her mouth a screaming square. Men were running behind her, covering the ground with great bounds – two men wearing dirty turbans and scanty garments that were spattered with blood, one of whom had armed himself with a grass-cutter's sickle. His teeth looked astonishingly white in his dark face and he was gaining on Delia easily.

This is not happening, said something in Winter's brain. Her hand went to the deep pocket in her skirt and she pulled out the revolver and levelled it, but she could not fire because Delia was directly between her and the pursuing man; and even as she hesitated, he caught her. A dark, sinewy hand clutched at Delia's curls, caught them and dragged her back. The sickle swept, and Delia's severed head, its mouth still open and its blue eyes wide in terror, remained in the man's hand dangling by its curls, while her body fell sideways in a foam of gay muslin flounces.

Winter fired and the man tripped and fell, and Delia's head, released from his outflung hand, struck the bridge, rolled and came to a stop almost at Winter's feet. The second man had stumbled over the body of the first and fallen also, but he pulled himself to his knees. He carried a butcher's knife in his hand and there were fresh blood-stains upon it. Winter recognized him as a butcher from the cantonment bazaar, and as he scrambled to his feet she fired again and missed, and then the revolver jammed. The man ran forward, howling threats and obscenities, and Winter flung the useless weapon in his face. She heard a shot and saw him stagger and fall, and then from somewhere Alex had appeared, running towards her. He leapt the sprawled body of the man on the bridge, stooped swiftly to snatch up the fallen revolver, and said breathlessly: 'Run——'

'No!' gasped Winter, catching at the rail, 'we can't! Look——'

There were screaming women and children in the Residency garden, running across the lawns, blind with terror; dodging like hunted hares while muskets cracked and dark-faced, blood-stained, blood-crazed men pursued them, yelling and laughing.

Alex thrust the revolver into his belt, and gripping her arms tore her free and dragged her by main force across the bridge and down the path that stretched for thirty yards or so over open ground before entering the narrow arm of jungle that lay between the back of the Residency and the plain. He did not keep to the path but plunged off it right-handed, dragging her with him and thrusting his way between the high grass and thin scrub, the bamboo-brakes and the *dhâk* trees; and when he stopped it was only because Winter's crinoline was hopelessly impeding their progress. From behind them they could still hear clearly a bedlam of shots and shouts and screams, but they did not appear to have been pursued. There were too many victims in the grounds of the Residency, and a too-alluring prospect of loot, for anyone to bother with chasing the few fugitives who had vanished into the jungle.

Winter was sobbing and struggling. 'Let me go! You can't leave them! You can't! There are children there – listen to them – *listen*! You coward – you *coward*!' She struck at him wildly, trying to break his hold.

Alex slapped her across the face with the flat of his palm. It was a hard blow and it jerked her back against a tree-trunk and effectually checked the torrent of words and her rising hysteria. 'I may yet be more use alive than dead,' said Alex brutally. 'Get those hoops off – hurry!' He released her wrist and stood waiting, breathing quickly and listening, his revolver in his hand.

The pain of the blow had made her head ring and Alex's curt voice did not permit of argument. She pulled up the voluminous poplin skirts and the frilled petticoat and unfastened the hooped crinoline with feverish haste, wincing and gasping at the sound of those distant appalling screams that seemed to tear thin scarlet gashes through the hot sunlit morning. She saw Alex's face flinch and stiffen but he made no move to return. He reloaded her revolver with steady hands and gave it back to her. 'Come on!'

It was easier to move without the hooped skirt, though her dress had to be lifted up to prevent it trailing on the ground. But her shoes were not made for rough walking and she knew that they would not stand up to it for long. Something rustled in the shadows, and two women who had been crouching among a tangle of grass and creepers stood up, white-faced and breathing in short gasps. Lottie and Lou Cottar. And behind them, in a panting huddle on the ground, sat Mrs Holly.

'*Winter*!' cried Lottie in a sob. She ran to Winter and clutched her, her eyes wide and glittering: 'I thought – I thought—— What happened? Why did they make me run? Why? *Why*?' Her voice rose to a scream and Winter, remembering the murderous rabble so short a distance behind them, spoke frantically: 'Hush, Lottie! You must be quiet. Hush, dear!'

'Why?' sobbed Lottie. '*Why*!'

Alex reached out and caught her, pressing her head against his breast and holding it there with one hand. His eyes were anxious and alert but his voice was neither. He spoke to Lottie in an entirely matter-of-fact tone that somehow carried complete conviction: 'We have to go to Meerut, Lottie. You want to see Edward, don't you? The carriage has broken down, you know, so I am afraid we must walk. We were only running to get out of the sun. You would not want to get sunstroke just as you are going to Meerut, would you? This is a short cut. And you must not make too much noise because – because I have a bad headache.'

Over Lottie's small head his eyes met the blaze of anger in Winter's. 'How could you! How *could* you!' Her lips formed the words soundlessly. He looked away again and down at Lottie. The hysterical tension ebbed from Lottie's body and she lifted her head and smiled her sweet, dazed smile. 'I didn't know. I'm sorry. Why, of course I want to see Edward! Mrs Holly did not tell me that we were going to Meerut, and I thought—— Let us hurry!'

Alex shut his eyes for a brief moment, then he released her and said quietly: 'Are there any more of you?'

Mrs Cottar shook her head and answered him in a whisper: 'Only the three of us. I think there are others hiding in the nullah, and some of them ran on down the path.' Her face was chalk-white except where a thorn had scratched it deeply, and her hair had tumbled down her back. Her smart morning-dress – she too had discarded her hooped underskirt – was ripped and torn, and she was trembling violently. But her eyes and her voice were steady.

'They'll have to take their chance,' said Alex curtly. 'We can't wait.' He glanced at Lottie and said: 'She'll have to take those hoops off. And you'd better do something about your shoes, or we shan't get far. Tie 'em with strips off your skirts – we can spare a few minutes. I don't think they'll look for us yet, they have too much to——' He did not finish the sentence but knelt swiftly to help Mrs Cottar, who was already ripping the frills from her petticoat with quick unsteady fingers. 'You've got a pistol, I see. Can you use it?'

'Yes,' said Mrs Cottar briefly, and sat down to tie the strips of cloth round her shoes, binding them strongly about the ankle. Alex performed a similar office for Lottie while Winter, having tied her own slippers with a ruffle torn from her petticoat, coaxed Lottie out of her crinoline and turned to Mrs Holly who had not moved.

'Hurry, Mrs Holly – you must take off your hoops. Let me help you——'

'It's no use, dearie,' said Mrs Holly hoarsely. 'I can't go no further.'

'Of course you can!' began Winter, but Lou Cottar, who had heard the words, whipped round. She said in a harsh whisper: 'So he got you? I – I thought——'

'Yes, dearie,' said Mrs Holly.

Winter dropped to her knees beside the huddled figure among the thick grass. 'What is it? – what is it? I don't understand. Get up, Mrs Holly – please! We have to go.'

Lou Cottar said: 'It was a man in the servants' quarters. He had a musket and he fired at us as we went past. I shot him. I thought he'd missed——'

Alex pushed Winter to one side and knelt to put an arm about Mrs Holly, lifting her a little. His hand touched a warm wetness that there was no mistaking and he saw the grey look on the plump, homely face, and recognized it.

There was a sudden renewed clamour of shots and shouting from the direction of the Residency and the screaming of someone in intolerable pain, muffled by the distance but still horribly audible in the stillness of the morning. Lottie flinched and began to breathe quickly again, and Mrs Holly said urgently: 'Go on, sir. Make 'em go on. It ain't safe to wait. Get the ladies away. You can't do nothing for me. I know that. Go on quick.'

Alex laid her back very gently and stood up, and at the sight of his face Winter drew in her breath in a harsh gasp and caught at his sleeve. 'No, Alex! No. You can't leave her – you can't. They'll look for us, and they'll find her. And if they didn't she would—— Mrs Holly, please get up – *please*! We can carry you – we——'

'It's no good, dearie,' said Mrs Holly. 'I'm too 'eavy – an' too bad 'urt. An' there's Miss Lottie to think of. I don't know as 'ow I could look 'er ma in the face, or 'er Mr Edward neither, if I was to let 'em get 'er. You go on, dearie . . . I shall be all right soon.'

Winter flung her arms about Mrs Holly, holding her tightly; feeling, as Alex had felt, the warm tide that soaked out upon the grass. She looked up at Alex and said jerkily: 'You and Lou can take care of Lottie. I'm going to stay here.'

'That you're not!' said Mrs Holly with sudden energy, the instincts of one who had been a children's nurse in her day rising to the surface. 'You'll do what you're told, Miss Winter!' She looked up into the young, drawn face above her and her voice softened: 'I won't 'ave it, dearie. I shall be all right. I 'aven't been 'appy since Alfred went. It'll be a pleasure to know . . .' The words were coming with more difficulty and she fought for breath.

Alex glanced back uneasily in the direction of the Residency. He put out a hand as though he would have pulled Winter away, and then clenched it and let it fall; knowing that she would not come for him. Mrs Holly said urgently: 'An' there's Miss Lottie. She knows you. She'd be that scared without you. 'Er ma was good to you. You owe 'er something. Get along now, dearie – hurry now.'

Winter looked back at Lottie who was staring at them with bewilderment and a renewal of panic in her face. She looked up at Alex with wide, imploring eyes and he shook his head in answer to the question they asked. Her cheeks were suddenly wet with tears and she bent and kissed Mrs Holly, released her and stood up.

'That's a good girl,' approved Mrs Holly. 'Don't you fret.' She looked at Alex and her lips moved. He bent swiftly. 'Take me shoes,' whispered Mrs

Holly. 'She'll need 'em. Stout they are. Not like those flimsy . . . I can't reach . . . Alex turned without a word and removed the stout, sensible shoes and thrust them into his pocket. He jerked the revolver from its holster, looked at it for a fractional moment and then laid it beside her on the grass.

'No, sir,' whispered Mrs Holly. 'You'll maybe need it, and I won't.'

'You may,' said Alex in a hard voice.

'I'd rather not, sir. I might use it if they come, an' . . . an' I don't 'old with it. The Commandments is plain. The Lord didn't say kill 'em if they kills you. 'E jus' said . . . *don't*! I know it's different for you, sir . . . an' if I could 'a killed to save Alfred, I know as I would 'av done. An' . . . an' then you see . . . I might be tempted ter use it on meself, sir, an' that wouldn't be right neither. Take it——'

Alex picked it up again. He lifted one of the rough, work-worn hands, kissed it swiftly and rose to his feet. He knew that she had no chance; he knew that she might take hours to die; but he had other things to think of and he had to reach the river. He would have shot her himself and taken her death on his conscience, but he did not dare, because there was no knowing who might hear that shot and follow it up.

He swung round on the three white-lipped women who watched him and said savagely: 'Don't stand there! For God's sake get on – quickly.' He thrust them ahead of him into the hot, rustling grass and the shadows of the *runi* trees, and did not look back.

Two and a half hours later they had covered less than four miles. The intolerable heat, the absence of trodden paths and the necessity of forcing their way through high grass and scrub, raging thirst and the unsuitable shoes and garments of the women had combined to slow them down to a mere matter of keeping moving.

Lottie had struggled on manfully, supported at first by Winter or Lou Cottar, while Alex went ahead, but it had soon become obvious that she could not keep up with them, and eventually Alex had carried her. Lottie, even seven months pregnant, weighed astonishingly little, but the lightest weight becomes intolerable after a time, and Alex's muscles ached and the blood drummed in his ears and he had been forced to stop and lay her down at shorter and shorter intervals.

It was Winter who said suddenly, watching his grim, exhausted face as he rested for a moment, sitting with closed eyes and his back to a tree-trunk, 'Where are we going? What is it you want to do?'

Alex opened his eyes and looked at her and his face was suddenly bleak. But for her and Lottie and Lou Cottar he could have turned back and tried to get a horse from the stables and make a detour by the plain, and he might still have reached the bridge in time. But for them he could still reach it in an hour. The bridge was ten miles by road, but barely half that through the jungle, and he had gone this way on foot often enough before, though the jungle was thick and there were no paths. But for Winter – Winter and Alice Batterslea – he would not be here at all . . . *'the safety of women and children in some crises is such a very minor consideration that it ceases to be a consideration at all . . .'*

He said in a parched whisper: 'I know this jungle . . . it runs to the river . . . there's a ruin . . . use it for *shikar* . . . mile above the bridge. Put the stuff there . . . weeks ago.' He closed his eyes again.

'What stuff? What stuff, Alex?' Winter knelt beside him, shaking him.

'Gunpowder,' said Alex without opening his eyes.

'*Gunpowder*? What for?'

'Blow up the bridge,' said Alex briefly.

Across his body Winter's eyes met Lou Cottar's. She had never liked Lou Cottar, but now something in the older woman that matched something in herself made a sudden bond between them. They looked at each other for a long moment and it was as if each of them had asked the other a question, and answered it.

Winter looked back at Alex. 'How much further is it?'

'Hmm? Oh – mile. Get there soon.' He moved his shoulders uneasily and dragged himself to his feet.

Winter said with a break in her voice: 'Alex, you fool! You should have left us!'

Alex said: 'You don't know these jungles. You'd have gone round and round in circles until——' He shrugged his shoulders uneasily and winced with the pain of the movement.

'Well, we are all right now. We'll bring Lottie. Go on as quick as you can, but – but mark the way so we won't miss it. If it's only a mile we'll be able to manage that.'

Alex did not argue. He looked at Lottie who lay asleep with her head in Lou Cottar's lap, and then at Lou Cottar and Winter. They were exhausted from heat and thirst and the slow miles they had walked. Their faces and hands were scratched by thorn-scrub and sharp-edged grasses; their feet were blistered – Lou was already wearing Mrs Holly's shoes – and their clothing was torn and soaked with sweat. But their eyes were calm and they looked back at him steadily. Two pairs of eyes, so very different; so entirely alike.

He said: 'Don't rest too long or you'll find you can't move. Keep moving, even if it's slowly. I'll mark the way. Hide if you hear anyone, and don't fire unless as a last resort. The sound of a shot carries.' He turned away, and the high grass and the thorn-scrub, the choking bamboo, the *runi* trees and lantana and the chequered shadows closed behind him, and he was gone.

They listened to the sounds of movement fade and die, and all at once the jungle was intolerably still. Nothing seemed to stir in that hot, breathless stillness; no twig or leaf or dry spear of grass. There seemed to be nothing alive in it except themselves.

A soft, monotonous ticking crept into the silence and Winter looked down and saw that it was Alex's watch which must have fallen from his pocket. She reached out and picked it up and the broken chain clinked as she lifted it . . . Alex must have forgotten to wind it, for the hands pointed at ten minutes to eleven.

The watch ticked gently. Ten minutes to eleven. Only ten minutes to eleven! It had been just on seven o'clock when the first news of the mutiny of the 93rd had taken Colonel Moulson from the Residency. Less than half past seven when Captain Wardle had ridden in on a wounded horse with his shattered arm and shoulder roughly bound with one of Alex's bungalow curtains and Alam Din running at his stirrup, bringing Alex's message warning them to leave the house and take refuge in the jungle. The warning had been disregarded, as had all Alex's warnings, for the native gunners were still at their posts and the police were loyal, but – so argued Captain Wardle and those men who had been detailed to remain in the Residency – if they should see the women and children leaving it might unsettle them and create an atmosphere of distrust and panic which must be avoided at all costs. So they had stayed; and less than quarter of an hour later they had heard the roar of the explosion as young Eyton and the five men of the guard from the 93rd who had remained loyal had blown up the Magazine, and themselves with it.

It had not been eight o'clock when Alex had burst into the crowded Residency and told them to run – and to keep running. Surely that had been a year ago . . . a lifetime . . . an aeon ago? How many people had died in the hour that preceded that? In the quarter of an hour that had followed it? How many people were dying now? How many were hiding in the jungle like themselves, and how long would they – and those others – be able to stay alive? Ten minutes to eleven . . .

Lou Cottar spoke in a whisper. A whisper that was not on account of the sleeping Lottie, but enforced upon her by the deathly stillness of the jungle: 'He was right. We'd better keep moving. We can follow him fairly easily if we go now, but the grass stands up again so quickly.'

Lottie rolled her head in Mrs Cottar's lap and muttered: 'Water – please. So thirsty.'

The two women looked at each other and looked away quickly; their own throats parched.

'We shouldn't have thrown our hoops away,' said Lou Cottar getting stiffly to her feet. 'We could have made a hammock out of them. Oh well – too late now. It will have to be my dress. It may hold.' She slipped out of it as she spoke, and they folded it and tied it with strips torn from Winter's petticoat and made a rough-and-ready hammock in which they laid Lottie. It was a precarious enough conveyance and put an intolerable strain on them, but they managed it somehow, with the aid of a makeshift harness that took the weight on their shoulders.

It was an agonizingly slow performance, but they kept moving. The sun scorched them and blistered Lou's arms and face – Winter's, more inured to the sun of late, suffered less. Once something moved ahead of them that was not a shadow, and Winter, who was leading, stopped with a gasp of fear as a tiger moved into the trodden track and stood still, staring at them. 'What is it?' whispered Lou, who could not see. Winter did not reply, not daring to move or speak; barely daring to breathe. The tiger too did not stir, until suddenly Lottie moaned and said: 'Water!' and at the sound a growl rumbled in the great cat's throat, and Winter heard Lou draw a hissing breath of comprehension. The creature's tail began to twitch in the dry grass as they stared at each other for what seemed like an hour, though it could not have been more than a minute or two at most. She could feel the sweat trickling down her face and running in little cold rivulets down her neck; and then the tiger backed away and the grass closed over the place where it had stood.

They heard no further sound for several minutes, not even a rustle in the grass; and presently Winter put up a shaking hand and wiped the sweat out of her eyes, and the two women lowered their burden to the ground and sat down abruptly.

'Has it gone?' whispered Lou Cottar through dry lips.

'Yes.'

'It may be waiting; why didn't you fire?'

Winter turned and looked at her. She said: 'You didn't see what happened to – to some of the others this morning, but I did. We are safer with animals. A shot might be heard.'

Mrs Cottar licked her dry lips and shivered in the stifling heat. 'Yes. You are right. We must get on. Help me up, my muscles have gone stiff.'

They heard no more movements in the jungle, and almost an hour later they saw something loom up out of the tangle of scrub and *sal* trees and bamboo that was not a shadow but a solid wall of creeper-covered stone, and knew that they had reached the end of that day's journey.

The ruin that Alex and Niaz had stumbled across three years ago while tracking a wounded leopard through the dense jungle had perhaps once been the hunting lodge of some forgotten king, or all that remained of a long-vanished city. Niaz had named it the Hirren Minar – the Deer Tower – because they had found the antlers of a buck in the grass by the threshold, and they had kept its discovery to themselves. Only Alam Din was aware of its existence, for despite the fact that it lay barely a mile from the bridge of boats, the jungle here was not only dense but scored with deep nullahs, choked with scrub and high grass, and known to be the haunt of tigers. They had frequently used it as a base when on shooting leave, and over the last three years there had lurked at the back of Alex's mind the germ of the thought that some day a hiding place such as this might prove more than useful.

All that remained was part of a two-storeyed building topped by a low, ruined dome. Thickets of bamboo grew closely about it, and lantana and the rank jungle grass smothered the fallen blocks of stone and pressed up between the paving. It was hot and very dark inside, and smelt strongly of the wild boar and his family who had recently been inhabiting it. There was also a distinct smell of leopard. The stairway that led up to the top storey had fallen centuries ago, and only a gaping hole remained in one corner of the black, bat-haunted ceiling of the single cell-like lower room.

The trodden grass showed where Alex and at least one other had passed in, but the ruin was as silent as the silent jungle, the hot sunlight and the chequered shadows.

'There is no one here,' whispered Lou Cottar, and the dark stone walls about her whispered back, '. . . *no one here*.'

'But there is a ladder,' said Winter. 'Look!'

Hanging from the jagged hole in the roof was a serviceable rope ladder, and they tugged at it tentatively. It appeared to be quite fast. Winter set her foot on it, but Lou Cottar caught her arm: 'Be careful! there could be someone up there.'

They stood still and listened, holding their breath, but they could hear no sound. 'Water——' moaned Lottie, '. . . *Water*,' whispered the echo. Winter gave a little jerk of her shoulders and started upward, and a minute later she had vanished through the broken aperture. Presently her head reappeared. 'It's all right. Can you get Lottie up? There's water here. There's – there's everything!' Her voice broke.

Two rough and ready beds, a roll of matting, some tin boxes, an oil-lamp and an earthenware *chatti* containing water would not have been considered 'everything' – or even 'anything' – a few hours ago. But the world had dissolved under their feet during those hours, and the sight of these few and homely objects helped in some way to solidify it again.

The water in the *chatti* was warm and stale and there was not a great deal of it. There was a tin mug, recently used, standing beside it and they watched while Lottie drank, and then drank thirstily but sparingly themselves, and wetted their handkerchiefs in it to cool Lottie's hot body.

'There, there, darling,' said Winter, forcing her voice to placid reassurance. 'You'll be all right now. You must rest. We're safe now . . . we're safe.'

But for how long?

41

'How much longer?' muttered Yusaf, crouched between two rocks on the burning plain five miles beyond the cantonments and overlooking the *kutcha* road that stretched across the rough open country towards Hazrat Bagh. 'Pray Allah they do not wait until nightfall!'

He took a drink from his water bottle and was grateful that the month of Ramadan at least was over. To have kept that vigil fasting and without being permitted to quench his thirst would have been hard indeed.

It was noon, for the sun stood directly overhead; but there was still no cloud of dust on the plain. Yusaf settled himself more comfortably and waited.

'How much longer – dear God, how much longer!' whimpered Chrissie Wilkinson, lying where she had fallen when they had battered down the door of Winter's bedroom and dragged her out screaming from under the bed. The blood from her wounds was caked and drying, and it seemed impossible that anyone could be so mutilated and in such agony and still live.

She had lain there for hours, hearing the screams and the shouting and the horrible confusion of noise. Hearing at last only her own hoarse, laboured breathing – each breath an unbelievable torture. There was someone lying beside her whose head rested upon her, and whose outflung arm lay across her, its weight adding to her agony. Someone who surely was also alive? Her glazing eyes lit with a last flicker of recognition: 'Con,' she whimpered. 'Con——' But he did not move. Nothing moved in all that silent house except the scarlet waves of pain that washed over her but would not drown her.

'They are all dead,' thought Chrissie Wilkinson. 'All dead – how much longer——'

She tried to move her head, and died.

But they were not all dead. Twenty-seven of those who had taken refuge in the Residency that morning were dead, but others had escaped into the jungle and one had escaped in a different manner.

The mutineers and the mob who had rushed the Residency had burst into the empty hall to be met by the Commissioner of Lunjore, clad only in a pair of thin cotton pantaloons and a gaily coloured dressing-gown, and swaying dangerously on his feet.

'C'mon in!' urged the Commissioner expansively. 'Plen'y of drink. Welcome!'

He advanced unsteadily towards them and the men drew back. 'He is mad!' muttered one. 'He is surely mad.'

The East is tolerant of madness, believing those who suffer from it to be afflicted by God and therefore under divine protection. They did not touch the Commissioner, but one of them, pushing past the others, slashed with a *tulwar* at a large oil painting that hung on the wall and ripped the canvas from top to bottom.

'Thash the idea!' yelled the Commissioner with enthusiasm. The destructive instinct that brandy was apt to unloose in him caught fire, and lunging at a large pottery jar full of canna lilies that stood on the hall table, he sent it toppling. It crashed to the floor, sending water, flowers and chips of pottery flying, and the Commissioner bellowed with laughter, and stumbling to the door into the drawing-room, flung it open and waved in the mob. 'C'mon! Lesh break it up – thash th' shpirit!'

He had raged through the house, shouting and yelling with the shouting, yelling, frenzied horde, assisting them with howls of drunken laughter to smash and destroy; oblivious, in the tumult, of the shrieks of women and children dragged out of hiding and butchered among the wreckage; blind to the blood and the agony, and seeing only a noisy drunken mob of fellow-revellers rioting through the rooms in jolly carouse.

'He is mad——'; 'He is afflicted of Allah——' They had not harmed him and at last they had gone; rushing out of the blood-stained shambles they had made, their arms laden with loot, to seek other victims and wreck other bungalows.

The Commissioner of Lunjore, left alone in the silent house, had reeled towards his room shouting for his bearer and for Iman Bux. But no one had answered him.

Where the devil had they all got to? It was Winter's fault . . . where was she? It was a wife's duty to see that a house was properly run – servants on duty. Disgraceful! – he would tell her so at once.

He stumbled over the threshold of his wife's room and stopped. Why, there was Chrissie! Dear Chrissie. Always been fond of Chrissie – good for anything. Worth six of his wife . . .

He wavered towards her, tripped, collapsed onto the floor beside her and plunged into oblivion.

Niaz had meant to ride to within half a mile of the bridge and then, striking off at a tangent into the thick jungle, make for the Hirren Minar by a route which he and Alex had often used before. He should by rights have reached it several hours before Alex, but he did not do so.

By the irony of fate it was a bullet fired by one of the five British women who had preferred to remain in their own bungalows rather than take refuge at the Residency, that had brought down his horse. Laura Campion, standing over the body of her dying husband on the verandah of her bungalow, had fired his musket at a mob of sepoys who had pursued the wounded man from the lines. The bullet went wide, and Niaz's horse, neck stretched at a gallop, had crossed the line of fire.

Niaz struck the dry grass verge of the roadway, rolled into a ditch and lay still.

He recovered consciousness within a few minutes, and not long afterwards, shaken and badly bruised but otherwise unhurt, he was crawling down the ditch towards a culvert where the drive leading into Captain Garrowby's bungalow branched off the road. As he did so he had heard the explosion of the Magazine, and had not known if it also signalled Alex's death. But he did not turn back.

There was a tangle of oleanders growing by the gate of Captain Garrowby's bungalow, and Niaz, waiting his opportunity, left the culvert and took refuge among them. Since the night that he had been knifed leaving the lines he had had few illusions on the score of his safety if the sepoys should mutiny, and he preferred to keep out of the public eye. But he must have a horse, and there would be horses in the stables behind the bungalow.

There was a smell of smoke in the hot air and a crackling sound, and emerging from the shelter of the oleanders he saw that the bungalow was on fire. He ran across the garden, keeping to the shelter of the shrubs and trees, and saw a mob of sepoys between the back of the bungalow and the stables, cutting off his approach. Niaz did not linger. He scrambled over the compound wall and fifteen minutes later he was a quarter of a mile away, wriggling along a drain behind Mr Joshua Cottar's stables. But Josh Cottar had taken four of his horses with him when he had left for Calcutta, and Mrs Cottar had driven to the Residency in a carriage and pair, accompanied by a syce riding the remaining horse. The stable doors stood open and the stables were empty.

It had not proved in the least easy to steal a horse that morning, for the mutinous sepoys and the bazaar rabble had scattered through the cantonments, shouting and firing off their muskets, hunting down the British and attacking, looting and burning the bungalows. But Alex might be dead, and if so it was doubly necessary that he, Niaz, should reach the Hirren Minar and the bridge. He would have to do so even if it meant walking.

Crouched behind a prickly cactus hedge he heard a mob of men stream past, coming from the direction of the city – a mob who shouted the battle-cry of his creed: *Deen! Deen! Fatteh Mohammed!* An odd shiver tingled through him at the sound and he set his teeth and tried to shut his ears to the fierce cry that had been a clarion call to all men of his faith for over a thousand years.

A dried finger of the cactus overhead, withered by the sun, threw a shadow on the hot, hard ground before him. A curved shadow in the shape of the sickle moon – the emblem of that faith. Niaz stared at it, seeing it, in a sudden wave of superstition, as a sign. The sign of the once great Empire of the Moguls, shrunk now to no more than a shadow on the ground. Men of his race and creed were fighting now to raise that Empire from the dust into which it had fallen, and if they succeeded, a Mogul of the House of Timur would once again rule over the greater part of India. Once again there would be Mohammedan Viceroys and Generals and Governors.

'*Ya Allah! Ya Allah! Allah ho Akhbar! Fatteh Mohammed*' . . . The sounds died away, but the echoes still rang in his ears as he ran on, keeping to the cover of trees and walls, taking short cuts across the compounds of burning bungalows, and making for the road that led out of Lunjore towards Oudh.

He had eventually stolen a *dhobi*'s donkey, and mounted on this had made good time, his dangling feet barely clearing the ground as the thin little beast ambled briskly along through the choking dust. And he might well have covered several miles in this manner had it not been for a sadhu. But he had turned a bend in the road and come upon a sadhu who stood upon a little brick platform before a shrine under a *peepul* tree by the roadside, exhorting an excited mob of villagers.

The sadhu had apparently recognized Niaz, for he had flung out a skinny arm and a pointing finger, and screamed a string of imprecations, and the villagers, armed with sticks and stones and other primitive but painful weapons had moved to the attack, but paused at the sight of the revolver in Niaz's hand. 'Kill!' howled the sadhu. 'Kill the follower of the *feringhis* – the traitor – the betrayer!'

Niaz fired and the man fell forward, coughing blood. 'That for thy knife in my back!' called Niaz, and abandoning the donkey took to his heels and the shelter of the high grass and scrub at the edge of a cane-field. A second shot discouraged the villagers from pursuit, and he made his escape across an irrigation ditch and into an orange orchard.

An hour later he had dragged a portly *bunnia* from the back of a starved-looking pony, and was riding as hard as he could persuade the animal to gallop in the direction of the bridge of boats.

There was seldom much traffic on the roads in the heat of the day during the hot weather, and he passed an occasional lumbering bullock cart, but nothing else. He had abandoned the pony by the roadside when he took to the jungle, finding it easier to make his way on foot, and had arrived at the ruined hide-out barely fifteen minutes before Alex.

Something grunted and crashed away through the undergrowth as he approached it, and Niaz had entered the jungle-choked ruin with caution and groped in the gloom for the length of stout bamboo that he knew he would find against one wall. A moment or two later he had operated the primitive mechanism that released the rope ladder, and was in the upper room collecting sundry packages with feverish haste.

He had been descending with his load when Alex arrived and both of them had been too exhausted for speech. They had looked at each other for a long moment and then Alex had climbed the ladder. He dipped a tin mug into the water that stood in the covered earthenware *chatti* and drank it thirstily. The water was warm and stale and there was not overmuch of it for a good deal had evaporated since he had filled the *chatti* almost three weeks ago. There was brandy there too, and he drank some of that, and fetching the Westley Richards rifle from its hiding-place in the ruined dome above, loaded it. Niaz returned from below and fetched a shotgun from the same place, and Alex looked up and shook his head: 'Nay, leave it. I have this' – he touched the revolver. 'How much time have we?'

Niaz shrugged his shoulders. 'An hour – two hours – a day. Who knows?'

He saw Alex draw a quick breath of relief and said: 'I was delayed, and therefore I came slowly' – he gave a brief account of that delay. 'But there are none on the road as yet, and there being no *rissala* they must come on foot. I do not think they will come too soon. They are mad from killing and they are breaking into the bungalows to rob and burn.'

'When there are no more left to kill they will be afraid and come away quickly,' said Alex, filling his pockets with spare ammunition and reaching for powder-flask and shot.

'Assuredly,' said Niaz, following his example. 'But there is little shade on that road, and they must march. How didst thou come?'

'By the jungle,' said Alex briefly.

'On foot then?'

Alex nodded. 'All but a few of those who were in the Residency *Koti* were slain. I came away across the nullah with three memsahibs whom I left half a *koss* from here. They follow, but slowly. I have marked the way. Let us go.'

They descended the swaying ladder and shouldering their burdens went out into the hot shadows of the forest. The river ran past less than two hundred yards from the Hirren Minar, but the banks were steep and overhung by the dense jungle so that none passed that way, and the road and the bridge of boats lay away to the right, a scant mile from the hidden ruin. No paths led there, but Alex and Niaz knew this part of the jungle well, and they had their own tracks through the apparently trackless thickets and the man-high grass, the trees and the cane-brakes.

They moved with more and more caution as they neared the road, and presently the jungle thinned out a little and they heard the gurgle of the river running between the boats, and the creak and strain of the bridge.

'Wait here,' whispered Niaz. 'I will go forward and see if the road be clear.' He laid down the load he carried and wriggled away like a lizard through the thick scrub.

Alex sat down with his back to a tree-trunk and tried not to think of a dozen things that he had seen that morning. Things that made his stomach heave and cramp with rage, and a red haze swim in his brain so that some primitive, unreasoning, tribal instinct had made him, for one dreadful instant, want to get his hands round Niaz's throat at the Hirren Minar – because of the things that men of Niaz's race had done that day. He had seen, too, for a fractional moment, a like antagonism in Niaz's face, and known that the drag of race and blood had pulled at him also. It had been there for less than a breath, but he had recognized it for what it was.

'But we are not only our people – we are ourselves,' thought Alex, '*ourselves*! No we are not – we are chained together by environment and customs and blood . . . "*I arm their hands and furnish the pretence . . .*"' He found that he was unable to think clearly and wished that he need never think again.

The undergrowth rustled and gave up Niaz who said cheerfully and without troubling to lower his voice: 'I have locked the toll-keeper and the police guard in the toll-house and have taken away their muskets. Remains now those on the far side.'

Alex said: 'Had they heard aught?'

'Nay; for two slept, and that they would not have done had the news been told.' He lifted his discarded burden and said: 'Why do we not cut the boats loose? That would suffice.'

'For a time only, for the boats would strand and they would use them again. And I would close this road.'

They came out cautiously into the thinner belt of jungle by the bridgehead where the grass was trampled down and the ashes of old fires showed where travellers had stopped for the night. The road lay long and empty under the dancing waves of heat, and the small stone-built toll-house was silent. There was no sound to be heard except the gurgling of water between the close-lashed boats.

Alex glanced at the toll-house under frowning brows and Niaz said sweetly: 'They will not cry out. I have bound them.'

'And the others in the huts behind?'

'They sleep. And all the muskets were in the toll-house. They will not move for some hours yet. Why should they? There was no outcry.'

They walked down the slope of the road onto the bridge, into the full blaze of the blinding noonday and the sun-dazzled water, the creaking planks hot under their feet. The heat shimmered off the wood in quivering waves that smelt of tar, and the glittering river that slid beneath them did not cool it. The banks narrowed and the river ran deep from a hundred yards above the bridge to a mile below, for the bridge spanned it at its narrowest point. But upstream the sand bars and the shallows widened until they were lost in the heat haze. There were row upon row of mud-turtles basking in the glare at the edge of the sand bars on the far side of the river, but except for the turtles there seemed to be nothing else alive within a dozen miles, and the hollow sound of their footsteps on the planks of the bridge was loud in the hot silence.

A drowsy toll-keeper heard it and came reluctantly to the door of the mud hut that served as a toll-house on the Oudh bank of the river. Seeing a sahib he salaamed and hurriedly straightened his turban. Alex returned the salute and inquired as to the prospects of *shikar* in the jungles by the bridge. He had, he said, glancing down at the stain that Mrs Holly's blood had left on the sleeve of his coat, shot a leopard that morning not a mile up the road. While he talked Niaz moved between them and the hut.

Five minutes later the horrified toll-keeper and the two men in the hut who constituted the bridge guard were sitting gagged and bound in the inner room, and Niaz was making fast the door. He carried the two antiquated muskets out and flung them into the water as he and Alex ran back along the causeway and onto the bridge.

They worked swiftly and methodically in the boiling sun, laying the charges, tamping and connecting fuses, never certain that the intense heat of the hot wood and the burning metal would not detonate the explosive of itself. The sweat poured off them and the dazzling glare off the river scorched their faces and hurt their eyeballs.

'Listen!' said Niaz suddenly. 'There are horses on the road.'

Alex leapt to his feet and stood for a moment listening intently; and heard the faint faraway sound that Niaz had heard. He snatched up the rifle and thrust it at Niaz. 'Four more and we have done. Hold them off for a little——'

Niaz turned and raced for the bridge-head and Alex bent to the charges again, working with feverish speed. The sound of horses' hooves was clearer now and presently he heard the crack of a rifle-shot, but he did not lift his head or look round. He must have more time – only a little more time. The noise of the river was astonishingly loud under his feet, and the heat of the iron bands that reinforced the planking burnt his hands as though it were red-hot. Once again he seemed to hear Sir Henry's voice speaking from the shadows of the verandah in the Lucknow Residency – '. . . *it is time we need – time most of all*——'

'Only five minutes!' prayed Alex, 'it isn't much to ask – only five minutes ——!'

He heard a fusillade of shots and a bullet sang past his head like a hornet, but still he did not look round.

Niaz reached the toll-house, and leaping the step of the shallow verandah, unbarred the door and ran to the small window that looked down the long Lunjore road, ignoring the groans of the three bound and gagged men who watched him from the floor with starting eyes.

There were perhaps twelve or fifteen riders, sepoys from Lunjore, advancing at a leisurely trot for the bridge; either men bringing the news of the rising to Oudh, or an advance party sent to secure the bridge for the main body of the mutineers who would cross later that day to swell the ranks of the malcontents in the newly annexed province.

Niaz waited until they were within range, and fired; aiming deliberately for the leading horse in order to create the maximum confusion. He saw the horse rear and fall, and the dust rose in a choking cloud as the men drew rein and came to a sudden stop. He re-loaded swiftly and fired into the dusty smother; heard a yell and the scream of a wounded horse and saw the riders scatter to either side of the road.

Knowing that they were unlikely to come any further for several minutes, he fetched the muskets belonging to the police guard that he had piled against the wall out of their reach. With several muskets and Alex's rifle, he should be able to save time on loading. He looked at the priming of one and noted with irritation that its owner had permitted the weapon to reach an unsoldierly state of dirt. '*Police*!' said Niaz, and spat scornfully to show his disgust.

He re-loaded the rifle again and watched with interest, reserving his fire, while the skirmishers at the road's edge conferred together. Presently one of them cupped his hands about his mouth and, evidently under the impression that it was the bridge guard and the toll-keeper who were firing upon them, bellowed that they were friends and urged the guard to join them – the *feringhis* being dead and all Lunjore in the hands of its rightful owners.

The man moved incautiously out into the road and Niaz shot him and watched his riderless horse bolt down the road and gallop wildly past the toll-house. There was a crash and a splash as the frenzied animal went wide of the bridge and plunged headlong into the deep water, and Niaz heard shrill feminine screams from the three small huts twenty yards behind the toll-house where the toll-keeper's family lived. A fusillade of shots spattered up the dust and chipped flakes of stone from the walls, and he saw the remaining horsemen hurriedly dismount and disappear into the jungle.

'Now they will come up under cover on either side of the road,' thought Niaz, and remembered with dread that Alex, working alone on the empty bridge, would provide an admirable target. He fired again at random into the jungle just ahead of where the men had entered it, discharging each of the muskets in turn and re-loading with feverish haste.

A woman ran out across the sun-scorched ground opposite the window, and a musket-ball fired from the jungle on the far side of the road whipped past her and smacked against the corner of the toll-house, sending a shower of chips flying. She shrieked and ran back again and Niaz grinned and fired in the direction from which the shot had come. Three more riderless horses galloped past with trailing reins and he heard their hooves thunder on the bridge and hoped that they had not ridden Alex into the water.

There was a back door to the toll-house and a woman beat upon it and screeched to her husband to come out and take refuge in the jungle for they were being attacked by *dacoits*, but the remainder of the police guard had presumably either run away or joined the sepoys. There were men now in the jungle opposite, and a bullet entered the open door and ricochetted round the small room.

Niaz turned from the narrow, iron-barred window in the end wall, and running to the door fired into the thick scrub on the opposite side of the road. As he did so something struck his chest and he fell sideways, the rifle jerking from his hand to slide along the floor and come to rest against the far wall.

After a moment he came dizzily to his knees and crawled towards the rifle, but he could not reach it. He groped instead for his revolver and dragging it painfully from its holster, raised himself a little and fired at a face that peered through the high grass at the road's edge, and saw a man lurch forward and fall on his face in the dust. And then he heard the sound of running feet, a crash of shots, and Alex had leapt the stone step of the verandah, stumbled over him and turning, had fired his revolver at a man on horseback who rode shouting for the bridge.

The shouting voice stopped as though cut off with a knife and there was the sound of a fall, a clatter of hooves and a brief moment of silence. And then the crashing blast of an explosion; and another and another, joining together in a single shuddering roar of sound, and the glaring day was dark with flying splinters of wood and choked with the scent of cordite and the reek of black powder. Then silence slammed down like an iron shutter and the river gurgled no longer, but ran quiet and unimpeded from bank to bank.

Alex spoke breathlessly into that silence: 'Quickly, before they recover – out by the back!' He had barred the door behind him and was across the room, pulling at the heavy bolts that closed the back door. He drew it open a crack and said: 'There is no one there – quick!'

'I cannot,' said Niaz.

Alex whipped round, seeing for the first time that Niaz had not been merely kneeling to fire, but was wounded, and he crossed the floor in a single bound. He knelt swiftly and thrust an arm under him, lifting him: 'Hold about my neck and I can carry thee.'

'No,' said Niaz urgently. 'This is the end for me. Go – and go swiftly while there is yet time – *mera kham hōgya* (my work is finished).'

Alex looked down at the greying face against his arm and the bright, swiftly spreading stain that soaked the dusty tunic, and pulling back the reddened cloth he saw that there was nothing that he or anyone could do, and a desperation and a wrenching rage beyond anything he had felt that day tore at him with the savagery of a taloned paw. He heard dimly and as though through a roaring fog, the crack of rifle-fire, but he did not move.

Niaz said: 'Thou hast seen how it is with me . . . go now. I can still . . . fire a gun . . . it will hold them . . . for a little. Get to the jungle . . . there be the memsahibs to be . . . thought of——'

Winter – Lottie – Lou Cottar . . . If it had not been for them he, Alex, would have reached the river an hour or more ago. This would never have happened. How long would they live if he died? He had left Mrs Holly to die alone and slowly. He had had to – because of those three women. And because of the bridge. But the bridge had gone. He had stopped at least one road into Oudh, and perhaps by doing so had bought, at the price of his friend's life, a little more time. Only a very little more, for there were so many other roads. Winter had courage, and so had Lou Cottar. And there was ammunition and a certain amount of food at the Hirren Minar.

Once again, and for a brief moment, he saw Winter's face quite clearly, against the rough stone walls of the shadowed room; as clearly as he had seen it in Alice Batterslea's garden. But it did not mean anything to him any more. She would have to take her chance. He would not leave Niaz to die alone as he had left Mrs Holly.

Alex drew his arm away very gently, laying Niaz back, and getting to his feet he closed and bolted the back door and dropped the shutters across the two windows, fitting the iron bars that held them into the sockets. He took up the guns one by one and loaded them methodically. There was an earthenware jar of water in the room and he fetched a brass *lotah*, stepping over the bodies of the three bound men who lay in a terrified huddle on the floor at the far end of the room, and filling it, brought it to Niaz.

He lifted him carefully against his shoulder and Niaz's eyes narrowed in the gloom as he strove to focus him. He drank a mouthful of the water and said again and urgently: 'Go!'

'We will go together,' said Alex. 'Has it not been said that "death in the company of friends is a feast"?'

A bullet struck the heavy wood of the door and another cracked against the stone. He looked down at Niaz and smiled, and Niaz grinned back at him – the old carefree grin with which he had greeted every chance and mischance of life through the twelve eventful years that they had known each other – and he said in a clear strong voice: 'It is better this way. It is not good to have a divided heart, and there is that in me which, were it not for thee, would have me follow such men as the Maulvi of Faizabad. We have had a good life, Sikunder Dulkhan – a good life – and though thou art an unbeliever, and therefore Hell-doomed, thou hast been as my brother. Lift me up, brother – it will be a good fight——'

His voice failed, and presently he began to mutter names and odd scraps of sentences, and Alex realized that in imagination he was back at Moodkee, watching the opening of the Khalsa cannonade and fretting for the order to charge. Then suddenly he laughed and raised himself in Alex's arms; pressing up as though he rose in his stirrups, and shouted aloud as he had shouted on the day of that charge – '*Shabash baiyan! Dauro! – Dauro! – Da*——' A rush of blood choked him, pouring from his mouth and dyeing Alex's coat and hands, and he fell back and was still.

A musket-ball struck a leaf of the wooden shutter over the window and filled the room with flying splinters. There were shouting voices and another fusillade of shots from outside the toll-house, and the bound men on the floor writhed and groaned in terror as a second bullet smashed through the shutter and struck the wall above their heads; but Alex did not move. He stayed quite still, holding Niaz's body in his arms; his mind entirely blank.

The noise outside the toll-house seemed to come from very far away and to have nothing whatever to do with him, and he was only aroused at last by a bullet fired at much closer range that smashed through the panel of the door and passed within an inch of his shoulder.

He laid Niaz down very carefully and stood up. His gaze fell on the water jar and he picked it up and drank thirstily, and poured what remained of it over his head and neck. He did not know how many men there were outside. A dozen? Twenty? They would get him in the end, but he should be able to account for some of them before the ammunition in the toll-house ran out. He took stock of it, and discovered that unless the police guard kept their ammunition elsewhere they had only been issued with a few rounds each. But there was still the supply he had brought for the rifle.

He picked up Niaz's revolver and loaded the single chamber that had been fired. A rifle, five muskets, two revolvers. A pocketful of ammunition. He might hold them off for an hour – perhaps a little longer——

There were two string *charpoys* in the stifling room and he stooped, and lifting Niaz laid him on one of them. He took up the rifle and loaded it, and crossing to the window lifted the bar of the shutter and pulled it aside. There were three sepoys not a dozen yards away, and putting down the rifle he jerked the revolver from its holster and fired, killing one and wounding a second.

It was nearing five o'clock when Alex fired the last round and dropped the useless weapon to the floor.

The heat of the closed stone building was appalling and his head and every muscle of his body ached abominably. The sun was sinking down towards the tree-tops and the walls of the room were hot to the touch. The three bound men who lay against the wall had ceased to move or whimper, and he wondered incuriously if they were dead from fear or thirst or one of the ricochetting bullets? He closed the shutter again, and sitting down on the *charpoy* beside Niaz, leaned his head against the wall and waited, watching the patch of sunlight from the broken shutter creep slowly across the floor and up the wall, and thinking odd disjointed thoughts. For the moment there was silence outside, but he knew that it would not be long before it dawned upon those outside that he must have come to the end of his ammunition. He had met every move with a shot so far and made it too dangerous to approach across the open, but after a time they would find that they could move without one, and draw their own conclusions.

He heard horses' hooves galloping down the Lunjore road towards the river, and heard them check some way above the toll-house. Reinforcements? He wondered how soon the mutinous regiments would arrive. They should be here by now. Unless, which seemed unlikely, someone had ridden back to tell them that the bridge had been destroyed and that there was no further point in their coming that way.

He wondered how Yusaf had fared, and if the destruction of the Hazrat Bagh road had been as successful as the blowing up of the bridge. It should have been – they had worked it out with considerable care. He hoped that Yusaf would not be too impatient, but would wait until all the guns and the wagons were well on the mined stretch of road. That should not only effectively block the road, but dispose of a considerable quantity of ammunition at the same time. Would they come that day, or would they wait until the thirty-first? A harlot's taunt had sprung the mine of the mutiny before its time, but now that it had been sprung that premature explosion, like the charges he had laid on the bridge, was setting off a succession of other explosions, and not all the pleas of the leaders could prevent the inflammable material they had prepared from catching fire from the flying sparks.

The hot room stank of sweat and urine, black powder, betel-nut and blood, and the gloom was noisy with the buzz of flies. Alex pulled down the end of Niaz's *puggari* so that it covered his face, and folded the quiet hands across his chest. They were beginning to stiffen already. It must be getting late. He rose and turned the *charpoy* so that the dead man's head was towards Mecca. There was no more water, so he could not wash as the ritual prescribed, but he rubbed his hands partially clean on his soiled handkerchief, and spoke the words of the *Du'a* over the quiet body – there being no one else who would ever speak them for Niaz:

'*May the Lord God, abundant in mercy, keep thee with the true speech: may he lead thee to the perfect path; may he grant thee knowledge of him and his prophets. May the mercy of God be fixed upon thee for ever. Ameen . . . O great and glorious God, we beseech thee with humility, make the earth comfortable to this thy servant's side, and raise his soul to thee, and with thee may he find mercy and forgiveness.*'

The murmured words awoke a soft echo in the shuttered stone-walled room, and when they ceased there was only the buzz of the swarms of flies once more. Alex sat down again, and presently, from very far away, borne on the hot stillness and scarcely more than a vibration of sound, he heard the faint boom of an explosion. It was followed a second or two later by another and then a third—— 'Yusaf!' thought Alex contentedly. The Hazrat Bagh road had gone, and with it a large proportion of the contents of the Suthragunj arsenal, for the charges that he and Niaz and Yusaf had laid had not been sufficient to account for that sound at so long a range. That had been ammunition wagons blowing up. He leaned back against the wall and closed his eyes.

A voice from outside the toll-house shouted for those within to come out and give themselves up. Alex made no reply, and emboldened by the silence, footsteps clattered at last on the shallow stone verandah and rifle butts battered on the door and the window shutters. These were followed after an interval by other sounds; dragging sounds and footsteps and voices all about the small building, and quite suddenly Alex realized what it was that they were doing. They were piling wood and dry grass against the doors and windows and about the house. They were going to make a pyre of it. Well, he might as well go that way as any other. A funeral pyre for Niaz and himself. He settled himself more comfortably against the wall, and as he did so one of the men on the floor stirred and moaned.

The sound seemed to clear some numbness from his brain, and he remembered that he and Niaz were not the only occupants of the toll-house. There were three other men there, and he could not let them be burnt alive. 'Wait a minute——' said Alex, speaking aloud. 'Wait a minute——'

He dragged himself to his feet and walked unsteadily to the door, and as he did so he heard a man outside say triumphantly: 'Did I not say so? It *is* a sahib! There are sahib-*log* in there!' and realized that he had spoken in English and that they did not know who was within.

A voice immediately outside the door said loudly: 'Who is it? Who is within there?' and Alex's hand dropped from the bolt, for he knew that voice. He leant against the door because it was an effort to stand, and said: 'It is I, Rao Sahib. Call off your butchers, for there are three in here who are bound hand and foot and who had no part in this. You cannot burn them alive. I will come out.'

He heard Kishan Prasad catch his breath. 'Who else is with thee?'

'None but Niaz Mohammed Khan, who is dead.'

There was a shouting and a rush of feet and he heard Kishan Prasad say furiously: 'Stand back! – stand back, I say!' and a moment later the sound of a grumbling and reluctant retreat.

'Open then,' said Kishan Prasad.

Alex picked up the empty revolver from the floor and thrust it into the holster with a gesture that was purely mechanical, and straightening his shoulders with an effort, he drew back the bolts and opened the door.

Kishan Prasad stared at him for a long moment and then stepped over the threshold and threw a quick look about the small room. He looked at Alex again and then turned away and stood blocking the narrow door, facing men whom Alex could not see.

'There is but one sahib here,' he said. 'The other man is dead and the three men they have bound are alive. This sahib I know, and because he once gave me my life at risk of his own, I say that he shall go free. Stand away!'

There was an ugly growl and a babble of voices: 'And what of Heera Lal who lies dead? and Dhoolee Gookul – and Suddhoo and Jagraj and the others? – and Mohan whose leg is broken? It is a *feringhi* – kill him! Kill him!'

There was a rush of shouting men, but Kishan Prasad did not move from the narrow doorway and his voice rose clearly above the tumult: 'Stand back!' cried Kishan Prasad. 'I am a Brahmin; and if you would kill this man, you will have first to kill me.'

The babble died abruptly and the men drew back, for they were Hindus, and to kill a Brahmin would be sacrilege unspeakable, dooming them to the nethermost of hells, and to become outcasts among their fellow-men.

'Go,' said Kishan Prasad, speaking over his shoulder to Alex. 'Move out behind me and run for the jungle. I can do no more. The debt is paid.'

Alex said tiredly and without emotion: 'Rao Sahib, if I had one bullet left in this gun, I would shoot you now for the things that have been done this day because of men like you.'

'That may yet come,' said Kishan Prasad. 'Go now——'

He moved out of the doorway, keeping between Alex and the group of snarling men at the far end of the verandah, and Alex backed away behind him, one hand against the wall, and reaching the end of the verandah, stepped down and to one side behind the shelter of the house, and turning, ran for the jungle behind the toll-house and the huts.

He heard the uproar break out behind him, and a lone shot whistled past his head. And then he was into the high grass and had turned parallel to the road and was running and stumbling through the thickets, keeping as close to the road as he dared in the belief that the pursuit would imagine him to be making straight for the thicker jungle instead of turning back up the Lunjore road. They would watch to see that he did not cross the road, and would not search the far side of it, so he must cross as soon as he could do so without being seen.

He wriggled into a thick patch of thorn-bamboo and lay still, listening for sounds of pursuit. There were no more shots, and though he could still hear shouting it seemed to go further and further away, and prove that his guess had been correct, and that they had expected him to run in a straight line, and were beating the jungle behind the toll-house. The sounds did not come his way, and after a time he heard horses' hooves on the road that lay barely a dozen yards from his hiding-place. Two of the men at least were riding back to Lunjore, and the voice of one of them, high-pitched and angry, came clearly to his ears:

'What matter? He cannot cross the river and he has no food or arms. He will die slowly in the jungle. I am for Delhi; that is the place for such as . . .' The voices faded.

When he thought that they had gone far enough Alex crawled with infinite caution to within sight of the road and lay there for a long time, wondering if he dared cross it. He had reached a point roughly five hundred yards above the toll-house, but the road here ran straight as a spear for a mile or more, and there would be men watching it from the toll-house. He must not draw them to the far side of it. At present it lay empty on either side of him, but he could see men moving before the toll-house.

The sun touched the rim of the jungle and slid slowly below it, and a peacock called from the thickets behind him. Another horseman galloped towards him from the direction of the river, raising a long cloud of dust. And suddenly it was simple.

The rider drew level with him and passed him, and Alex leapt to his feet and ran for the opposite side of the road, screened by the choking cloud of dust.

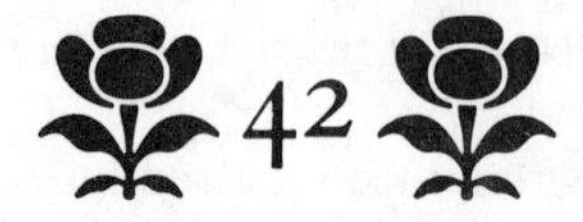

In Lunjore city the conches brayed and horns blared in the temples. Tom-toms beat and rockets flared while men rioted through the streets shouting that all Hind was freed forever from the 'Company Sahib's' rule – that all the *feringhis* were dead, and the great days had returned. They wore stolen finery and displayed stolen goods, and boasted of the deeds they had done and the sahib-*log* they had slaughtered; they made wild and grandiose plans for the future, and fell to quarrelling over who should be governors, generals or captains of their provinces and armies.

A mile outside the city the cantonments lay silent and deserted. Here and there a bungalow still burned and creeping figures still slunk between the silent houses, searching for any loot that might have been overlooked during the day-long orgy of murder and robbery. But as the evening shadows lengthened, the dead who lay about the cantonments filled even the scum of the city with uneasiness and superstitious fear, and they fired a few more bungalows, leaving the night breeze to carry the sparks and fan the flames, and ran away shuddering.

The sepoys whom it had been intended to march into Oudh for the re-taking of that province had turned westwards towards Delhi when the news had been brought that the bridge had gone, and the lines were deserted. In the silent Residency where the dead lay scattered through the quiet gardens and the darkening rooms, the Commissioner of Lunjore lay fathoms deep in drunken slumber, and a quarter of a mile away, in the jungle beyond the nullah, Mrs Holly died at last.

The jackals and the hyenas, the crows and the kites and the naked-necked vultures, would feast to the full for many days to come, for there were other dead on the plain that stretched towards Hazrat Bagh. The garrison of Suthragunj had risen at the news of the mutiny at Lunjore, and had killed their officers and seized the treasury and the arsenal, and left, as Kishan Prasad and his friends had planned, by the *kutcha* road to join with their fellow-mutineers and march in strength upon Oudh.

They had taken the guns and wagon-loads of powder and ammunition, and Yusaf had waited until those guns and wagons lay between given marks. He had fired then, at a target that Alex had set for him. And, as he had once told Niaz, he did not miss with a first shot, though he might be careless with a second. The charges set each other off for a quarter of a mile, and the wagon-loads of ammunition exploded with a crash and a detonation that was heard ten miles and more away. And when the smoke and the flame cleared there was no road, and what remained to be seen was not pleasant to look upon.

Yusaf waited until the shadows lengthened and the partridges began to call from among the grass and the thorn-scrub; until the last of the men from Suthragunj who were able to do so had disappeared in the direction from which they had come, and until there was no more movement from the shattered road. Then he drank deeply from his water-bottle, ate his fill of cold food, and wriggled out backwards from between the rocks.

He did not return to Lunjore, but moved off westwards, making like a homing pigeon for the North-West Frontier. From what he knew of Nikal Seyn and Jan Larr'in and Daly Sahib, the Guides at least would be fully employed, and he had many friends among the Guides. Who knew – they might already be marching to attack Delhi? And if so, he would join them on that march.

Yusaf slung his rifle Frontier-fashion across his shoulder and set off towards the red ball of the setting sun.

Winter and Lou Cottar had heard the faint, faraway crack of rifle-fire at the bridge-head, and the distant roar of the explosion. All that afternoon the firing had continued, and they had guessed what it meant and watched and listened – and waited.

Once Winter had picked up the shotgun that Niaz had left on the floor of the upper room, and had said desperately: 'I'm going! – it can't be far away – he said it wasn't more than a mile. Listen! – it can't be as far as that. I – I might help.'

Lou Cottar had taken the gun from her. 'He wouldn't thank you for it,' she said, and Winter had known that to be true.

For want of anything else to do they had set about turning the stone chamber into some semblance of a room. It had at least kept them occupied. Alex and Niaz had once spent two weeks in the Hirren Minar, shooting in the surrounding jungles, and they had made themselves tolerably comfortable. The room was large and square, and windowless on three sides. The fourth side consisted of three pillared arches, two of which still retained broken fragments of stone tracery. These led out onto a flat roof surrounded by a low, ruined parapet.

There were several *chiks* in one corner of the room, and though the white ants had damaged one or two of them they were in reasonably good repair, and Lou Cottar had hung them between the pillars, remarking that they would keep out the worst of the flies and mosquitoes. They had also curtained off a section of the room with sacking for Alex's use, convinced as they did so that he would not return, but denying the fear by that action.

Bamboo and dried grass had made primitive but efficient brooms, and they had swept and dusted, cleaned and tidied, in a desperate attempt to keep their hands occupied and their minds from thinking of the many things that did not bear thinking of. Of Mrs Holly, left to die alone in the jungle. Of Delia

Gardener-Smith's pretty head, with its wide eyes and open mouth, rolling along the planks of the bridge above the nullah. And of what must have happened to so many others whom they had known and left behind in the shambles of Lunjore. How many were dead? How many – or how few – were hiding and hunted like themselves, but with no refuge such as this?

It was no use thinking of these things. To think of them was to sink into clutching quicksands of panic and horror. It was better to occupy themselves with make-believe domesticity, and they were grateful to Lottie because she needed attention and care, and because to keep from frightening her they themselves must not show fear.

Lou Cottar, standing at the edge of the open roof by the crumbling parapet, had reported that she could see a glimpse of river and would fetch water. She had taken the *chatti* – Winter had lowered it after her on a rope – and set out to find her way through the dense jungle to the river bank that lay so near and yet took so long to reach. She had not returned for over an hour and Winter had received her with breathless relief. 'I'm sorry,' said Mrs Cottar apologetically, 'but it's so thick out there that I lost my way coming back, even though it is so near. We must mark the way when we go again. We'll have to pull the water up. I can't carry it up that ladder.'

Winter drank thirstily while Lou Cottar filled a small rusted tin with water and arranged a spray of wild gourd and jungle berries in it for Lottie. 'I bathed,' said Lou Cottar, knotting up her wet hair. 'It was wonderful. The bank is very steep and there are no shallows on this side, but there is a place where the river has cut in behind a tree and made a little beach, and I held onto the roots. You had better go too, before it gets dark. It gets dark so soon once the sun is down and——' She stopped as though she had forgotten what it was that she had meant to say.

The sun was almost at the level of the tree-tops, and they had heard no shots for some time. They looked at each other and looked away again; and said nothing because they were both thinking the same thing – that Alex must be dead.

'We are on our own now,' thought Lou Cottar. 'We shall have to get out of this by ourselves – if there is a way out. I expect we can do it. It's a pity about Lottie English – it's going to be difficult with her on our hands. I wonder if Josh will hear what happened? I wonder if—— No. I won't think about it. I won't think of it!'

'He is dead,' thought Winter. 'If he were not, he would have come back by now. The bridge went hours ago – hours. And I called him a coward because I thought he should have stayed and been killed at the Residency instead of doing something sensible and dying at the bridge instead. I wish I hadn't said that. I wish I had told him that I didn't mean it. I wish I were dead too; it would be so much easier to be dead. But there is Lottie – and Mrs Cottar. And – and perhaps there are others somewhere. Or are they all dead?'

Conway must be dead . . . He at least had been in no condition to make his escape. It was odd to think that he had been her husband and now he was dead – and that she could feel nothing at all. The only emotion she could feel was a dull regret that she had made no apology to Alex. In the circumstances, a trivial emotion. But everything else was blunted and numb. Alex had told her once that you felt nothing but the blow when a bullet hit you, and that the pain only came when air reached the wound. The air had not breathed upon her brain or her heart yet, for she could feel no pain. Only numbness.

The faint, faraway crack of a lone shot broke the brooding stillness, and the two women turned their heads as one to listen. But there were no more shots. It was, somehow, a very final sound. Like a period at the end of a chapter.

'I'll take some of Lottie's clothes and wash them in the river,' said Winter abruptly, 'and my own. They'll dry in an hour.'

She removed her own torn, dusty, sweat-soaked clothes and wrapped herself in a length of faded blue cotton cloth that they had found rolled up in a bundle and stuffed in among a collection of odds and ends in one of the tin boxes. It made a skimpy though adequate sari, and she wound it about her in the fashion of the Indian women.

'You know,' said Lou Cottar thoughtfully, 'you could almost pass as an Indian if you'd get a little more sunburnt. It's your hair and eyes. It may be a help yet.'

'I should have to learn to walk without shoes,' said Winter.

'We may both have to,' said Lou Cottar grimly, and turned away to collect a few of Lottie's underclothes for Winter to rinse in the river.

They made a bundle of the clothes and Winter took the loaded revolver and went down the rope ladder. The jungle that had been so silent all day was waking to life as the shadows lengthened, and there were rustlings among the dry, golden grass, and birds sang and twittered and called from the thickets. A peacock fluttered up to a low bough of a tree, his gorgeous tail glinting in the low rays of the sun, and a chinkara fawn looked at Winter with soft, startled eyes over a tussock of grass before bounding away in the direction of the river.

Making her way through the tangle of dry grass and leaves and creepers her ears were filled with the sound of her own progress, but she could hear the bird-song above it, and with a vivid remembrance of the tiger they had seen that morning, she kept the revolver in her hand, though she had little fear that she would need to use it. The shots and the blowing-up of the bridge would have scared any large animal for miles, and after the heat and sweat of that terrible day the lure of cool water was not to be resisted.

The river ran gold in the evening light by the time she reached it, and the far bank was already in shadow. The water slid past like silk, so smooth and still that it seemed impossible that there could be strong and treacherous currents beneath that placid surface. It chuckled softly between the exposed roots of a great tree that the wash of the stream had undermined, and lapped against a small shelving beach below the steep bank.

Something slid into the water with a splash, and Winter started back, remembering with sudden horror the corpse that she had seen pulled under the water near the bridge two months ago, and the words of the elderly gentleman who had said: 'It is the mugger of the bridge.' But it was only a piece of the overhanging bank that had fallen, for she saw the soil and the grasses sweep past her with surprising swiftness. The bridge was a mile downstream, and the little beach looked safe enough. She clambered cautiously down the steep bank, and removing her makeshift sari, tucked it and the bundle of soiled clothing in a crutch among the tree roots, and let herself down into the water.

It was cool and delicious beyond belief, and she lay along the shelf of the bank and let the river run over her, drawing the heat and the ache from her tired body. Her hair spread out and rippled like water-weed in the pull of the stream, and the voice of the current slipping through the tree-roots made a soothing monotonous murmur in the silence.

She did not know how long she lay there, mindless and still, with closed eyes, but presently the slow thought drifted through her brain that it would be easy – easy and pleasant – to slide into the main stream and let the current carry her out and down into the cool darkness of the deep water. There was nothing to live for and she was very tired . . .

But even as she thought it, the voice of the water whispering against her ears seemed to change into another voice: a laboured, whispering voice that had spoken to her that morning – '*. . . 'er ma was good to you. You owe 'er something. Get along now, dearie . . .*'

Dear Mrs Holly! Was she dead? or was she still alive and alone and frightened? 'She was braver than I am,' thought Winter. 'Braver than all of us. I couldn't have done that. I must stay alive as long as I can because of Lottie – and Mrs Holly. Because Lottie is going to need help. There is nothing else to stay alive for——'

She turned her head in the shallows and opened her eyes. The sky and the river were no longer gold but rose-pink, and the leaves and flowers of the tree that leaned over her made a stiff, formal pattern against that wash of colour. Something moved in the pattern, a green parrot with a scarlet beak and long green and blue tail feathers . . . And all at once the Gulab Mahal was there before her. The enchanted garden of her childhood. The formal patterns of leaves and flowers and brightly coloured birds that moved against a sunset sky, and that had remained fixed in her memory as a bright promise through all the grey, intervening years.

The whisper of the water was no longer Mrs Holly's voice, but old Aziza Begum's, telling her stories in the twilight: Zobeida's, making the old promise – 'one day we will return to the Gulab Mahal, and all will be well . . .' There was something else to stay alive for after all. Somehow, some day, she would reach the Rose Palace. She had promised herself that for too long to relinquish it now.

A new energy seemed to flow through her with the thought, and she came to her feet and wrung out her wet hair, and reaching for the bundle of clothing among the roots, washed out the torn, soiled garments in the river. They made a damp, heavy bundle when she had finished but they would dry quickly. She climbed the bank again and wrapped the makeshift sari about her once more, leaving her wet hair hanging loose.

A peacock cried in the jungle, and the call echoed across the wide river and was answered by another on the far bank. Pea-or . . . *Pea-or* . . . *Pea-or!* The cry seemed to underline the loneliness of the silent river and the dense miles of jungle, and to wail for all those who lay dead and who had been alive when that sun rose that was setting now. A savage and unbearable pain stabbed through the numbness about Winter's heart. 'The air is getting to it,' she thought, and she picked up the wet bundle and the revolver and turned from the river to make her way back to the Hirren Minar, stumbling through the tangled grass and the thickets as though she had been blind and must feel her way.

She had stayed far longer by the river than she had meant to do, and now the sun had gone and the swift twilight was closing in. She had marked her way carefully, but in the fading light the marks were no longer visible and she was unsure of her direction. Fear replaced the pain in her breast, and she stood still, trying to remember the landmarks that she had taken note of when she had left the ruined building. Presently she began to move again, though with more care, but she had gone less than a dozen yards when she stopped again at the edge of a small clearing.

Something was moving in the jungle ahead of her, as though some large animal was walking slowly towards her through the dry, rustling undergrowth; and remembering the tiger she froze into stillness, her hand gripping the revolver. The sound came nearer and nearer, and now she could see the grass and the bushes on the far side of the clearing sway to the movement of something or someone who was moving directly towards her. *Someone* – was the hunt so close?

Winter crouched down where she stood, seeing again in an ugly flash of memory the dark, contorted face of the man who had pursued and murdered the screaming Delia. Her finger tightened upon the trigger of the revolver as the high grass rustled and parted, and Alex walked out into the clearing.

For a moment she did not believe it. She had given him up for dead, and the sight of him – filthy, blood-stained, dazed but alive – was a greater shock by far than the sight of his dead body would have been. The revolver slipped from her hand and she stood up with a choking cry and took a swift step forward, the bundle of clothing falling unheeded to the ground.

Alex checked, swaying, and his hand moved automatically to the butt of his useless revolver. Through the haze before his eyes he saw a slim Indian girl confronting him in the dusk, the blue of her thin cotton sari and the blue-black of her long, unbound hair melting into the shadows of the darkening jungle behind her. Then the haze cleared – and it was Winter.

They stood staring at each other for a minute that seemed like an hour, and then Alex stumbled forward, and as she ran to him he dropped on his knees and she caught him, holding him to her, and felt his arms go about her in a desperate grip.

She held his head against her, rocking him as though he had been a child. His hair smelt of dust and sweat and the reek of black powder, and she pressed her fingers through it, whispering endearments that he did not hear, and listening to the terrible, grinding sobs that seemed to wrench his body to pieces. She could feel the heat of those tears soaking through the thin cloth and wetting her body, and she held him tighter, straining him against her, until at last they stopped. The racking shudders ceased, and presently he lifted his head and looked up into her face.

His eyes in the fading twilight held an odd, blind anger, and his arms lifted and pulled her down onto the grass. She felt his hands on the thin cotton of the sari, wrenching it away, and he hid his grimed and smoke-blackened face between her small firm breasts. Her skin was cool from the river, and smooth and sweet, and he kissed it with an open mouth, moving his harsh cheek and his aching head against it, holding her closer. Then his hands moved again, and for a fleeting moment the fear and the horror of her wedding night returned to Winter. But this was not Conway, drunken and bestial. This was Alex – Alex——

There was neither love nor tenderness in Alex's hands or his kisses. They were deeply and desperately physical, and she knew that for the moment her cool body meant no more to him than an anodyne to pain – a temporary forgetfulness and release from intolerable strain. But it was enough that she could give him that.

Conway was dead – they were all dead. All those people who had lived and laughed in the cantonments at Lunjore and at Delhi. Mrs Abuthnot, Colonel Abuthnot, Delia, Nissa, perhaps Ameera too. The whole world was breaking into pieces and dissolving in blood and tears and terror. But here in the quiet forest there were only herself and Alex – Alex's arms and his mouth and his need of her. Alex who was alive . . .

At long last his hold slackened, and he lay still. The sky darkened above them, turning from green to a violet-blue that was strewn with stars. The starlight and the thin moon made odd shapes out of the trees and the thickets and the tussocks of grass, and sometimes something rustled in the jungle or an owl hooted in the darkness. Once, very far away, a barking deer called a warning that a tiger was passing, and once a nilghai, the wild blue bull of the jungles, crashed through the dense undergrowth not a dozen yards away. But Alex slept the sleep of utter mental and physical exhaustion, and Winter held him in her arms and watched the stars and was not afraid of the night noises or of anything else.

She thought once, and fleetingly, of Lottie and Lou Cottar. They would think that she had lost her way or met with some accident, and Mrs Cottar would not dare to call her name or show a light, for fear that her failure to return might mean that there were men in the jungle hunting for fugitives. They would be frightened, but it could not be helped. Alex was asleep and she would not wake him even if she could.

His head was heavy on her breast and the weight of the arm that lay across her and pressed her down on the warm dry grass seemed to increase with every breath she drew, while her own arm beneath him had passed from numbness to prickling pain. But she did not move except to hold him closer, her cheek against his hair, and presently a breeze got up; a hot breath of wind that the river had cooled until it blew pleasantly through the jungle with a sleepy, soothing, rustling sound, dispersing the mosquitoes and night-flying insects and lulling her at last into a sleep as deep as Alex's own.

Even the screeching of an owl from a *sal* tree on the edge of the clearing did not wake them. But five miles and more away, beyond the jungle and the nullah, a jackal howled in the gardens of the Residency and woke the Commissioner of Lunjore.

The Commissioner returned slowly to consciousness and to the all too familiar waking sensations of an aching head, red-hot eyeballs and a tongue that felt too large for the dry mouth that contained it.

He lay still for a while, feeling the nausea rise in waves. His head was lying on something lumpy and stiff. Not a pillow . . . what was it? He tried to turn his head and found that he could not do so, not because the shooting pain that the attempt sent through his skull discouraged such a movement, but because his cheek appeared to be stuck fast to some dried and gummy substance.

There was a roaring noise in his ears and he discovered that his arm was lying across a body – a woman's body by the feel of it; frills and furbelows. Curls tickled his forehead and there was a smell of violets – Chrissie! Must have been drunker than he thought if he'd taken Chrissie to bed and couldn't remember it! Bed? Why, he was on the floor! Chrissie must have been drunk too – damned drunk. Must 'uv been a helluva party! What had happened to the others? He opened his eyes with an effort. Dammit, it was morning! – a pretty kettle of fish!

The room was full of a hot yellow glare that waxed and waned, wavered and grew bright again. Sun comin' up. He shut his eyes again and realized that he must move. Wouldn't do to be found in broad daylight huggin' Chrissie Wilkinson on the floor. He lifted his head with a violent effort, wrenching it free from whatever had held it, and had a brief glimpse of Chrissie Wilkinson's face and her tumbled over-bright curls before the pain of the sudden movement made him retch and retch again.

He vomited helplessly, aware, even through the agonizing waves of nausea, of the odd manner in which the hot sunlight beyond the windows wavered and flared. Presently the worst had passed and he lifted his head at last and propped open his aching eyes with his fingers. It began to dawn on him that it was not sunlight outside the window. It was not even daylight. It was night, and something was on fire. 'Servants' quarters,' thought the Commissioner. 'Blurry fools! – they c'n dam' well put it out themselves!' He stumbled to his feet and staggered across the room to the windows.

The servants' quarters had been smouldering for many hours, for the servants, having looted what they could, had run away, and a piece of glowing charcoal from an abandoned cooking fire had fallen out onto a roll of matting. The flames had spread slowly, and it was the sudden and unexpected night wind that had fanned them to a blaze so that they set alight the whole row of tinder-dry huts.

The Commissioner stared dully at the roaring flames. The glare hurt his eyes and he supposed that by this time half the place was aroused and that the fire would soon be under control. He turned back to Chrissie Wilkinson. He must wake her and send her home. Wouldn't do to have an open scandal. He noticed suddenly that he was not even in his own bedroom, but in his wife's. Where was Winter? Nice thing if she were to walk in on a scene like this! He doubted if she would stand for it. He staggered back across the room and dropped on his knees beside the silent figure on the floor.

'Gerrup, Chrissie. Wake up – party's over. There's a fire, and fellows will be comin' in. *Chrissie*!' He shook her. She felt very odd. Not warm and plump and soft as Chrissie had always been, but stiff – stiff and cold.

A shudder ran through the Commissioner's obese body and the shock seemed to clear some of the fog from his brain. He moved so that his shadow no longer fell on her, and saw then that she was dead. Not only dead, but appallingly injured. He put up a trembling hand to his face, feeling it and realizing that it was blood from those wounds that had dried and held his cheek to her breast. Had he killed her? He could not remember. He could not remember anything. Had he gone too far at last and murdered her in a drunken frenzy?

He whimpered her name, tugging at her cold body. 'Chrissie! – Chrissie! No . . . can't be true . . . I couldn't—— *Chrissie*!' He tried to stand and finding that he could not he crawled to the door on hands and knees. Every door and window in the house stood wide and the glare of the burning buildings filled the rooms with hot light. He saw the shambles in the hall and pulled himself upright.

There was a body lying across the door at his feet, its face upturned to him: Alex's servant, Alam Din. There was a broken sword in Alam Din's hand, for he had tried to hold the door against the howling mob of killers, and had accounted for three before he had himself been killed and the door that he had defended battered down. Their bodies still lay where they had fallen, for the mob had not even paused to remove its own dead. The Commissioner held tightly to the door jamb and after a long time, shivering as though with ague, he crept forward, supporting himself against the wall.

The house was deadly still, and except where the light of the burning buildings illuminated it, dark with an impenetrable darkness. A darkness that hid many things, as the flickering flames revealed others. The corpse of a child that had been cut almost in half by a blow from a sword lay just inside the dining-room door, and across its body, as though to protect it, lay its mother, Harriet Cameron.

Harriet Cameron – what was *she* doing here? The Commissioner stared down at her with glazed eyes; she never came to his parties; too much of a prude. Harriet Cameron . . . This was a dream – a ghastly nightmare from which he would awake. This was delirium tremens at last! He would never touch another drink – never. He would reform; lay off drugs and women and drink – turn over a new leaf. *God*! what was that! . . . a head without a body! Captain Wardle's head, grinning up at him from the stained carpet – white teeth gleaming in the fitful light, glazed staring eyeballs glinting – the headless trunk in its scarlet and gold uniform sprawled a yard beyond it . . .

The silent ruined rooms, the black shadows and the lighted spaces where the pulsating glow of the fire penetrated, were peopled by the dead. There was blood in every room, and bodies – and bodies. Stiff, cold bodies of women and children who had died with open screaming mouths and staring eyes, and whose mouths still seemed to scream silently while their dead eyes were fixed in horror. Elderly, faithful, loving ayahs who had thrown away their lives struggling to protect their small charges. Men, brown and white, whose faces still grinned with rage and the lust of killing.

Their staring eyes appeared to watch the Commissioner, and it seemed to him that they mouthed at him silently. He staggered out into the open to escape them, but they were there too. Of course this was a dream! That was why it was so quiet, why nothing moved except the wavering light and the shadows that wavered with it. But there were three things that he could hear quite clearly. The crackle of the fire, his own footsteps, and his own rasping, panting breath.

The parched grass of the lawns and the dead leaves crunched under his feet, and he stumbled over something that had once been Mrs Gardener-Smith. Her clothes had been stripped off her by looters, and the indecency of her ample body, dragged out from among the jasmine bushes among which she had striven to hide, struck him as wildly comic, and he went off into a shrill peal of laughter because the nightmare – or the brandy – should have conjured up so incongruous a picture as Mrs Gardener-Smith lying naked on his lawn.

But at the sound of that high, hysterical laughter something moved at last.

Three ungainly, slinking shapes: hyenas, who drawn by the smell of death had braved the vivid light, and who now galloped away across the open lawn to the refuge of the shadows.

That movement, and the sound of his own laughter, brought an icy sweat trickling down the Commissioner's body, and he fell on his knees beside the naked corpse and touched it with a shivering hand, gripping the cold flesh.

It was not a dream. It was real. This was all real. They were all dead. He staggered to his feet and stood swaying – listening. But the night and the garden and the darkened house were as silent as a new-made grave. There was only the sigh of the night wind and the crackle of the flames, and his own gasping breath. There was no one alive in all the world except himself – Conway Barton, Commissioner of Lunjore.

The appalling horror of that thought gripped him by the throat as though a hand had reached out of the darkness and clutched at him. The roof of one of the distant servants' quarters fell in with a sudden uprush of flame and a shower of sparks, and the glow began to fade. The light was dying out, and when it went he would be left alone in the dark – alone with the silent, stiffening, rotting dead and the slinking hyenas. He shouted aloud, screaming for Ismail, for Iman Bux, for Winter, for Alex; but only the echoes answered him.

The light flickered lower and he began to run, stumbling, howling, shrieking. He tripped over a body that lay huddled on its face before the yawning darkness of the gateway, fell, and felt his hand touch another that lay in the shadows; scrambled up again, and still screaming, ran out into the dark road that led through the silent, deserted cantonments.

The sky was paling to the first light of dawn when Winter awoke and felt Alex move and draw away from her.

After a moment or two she opened her eyes slowly and sleepily, aware, despite the rough grasses below her and the numbness of her arm, of a feeling of miraculous restfulness and physical well-being. Alex had risen and was standing beside her, his profile dark against the greying sky, and although it was as yet barely light enough to distinguish more than the outline of his face, she knew that he was frowning.

He was not looking at her, and she lay and watched him with an aching, possessive love as the light grew and deepened and his features and the forest about him ceased to be flat silhouettes and became three-dimensional, emerging from the surrounding greyness and taking on form and shape. As the sky brightened she saw that the sleeves and breast of his torn coat were black with dried blood, and the sight brought her suddenly to her feet, clutching at his arm:

'Alex! – you're wounded!'

Alex turned his head slowly and looked at her, and her hand dropped from his arm. He said: 'No. I'm all right.'

'But – but you – you're covered in blood!'

'It isn't mine,' said Alex in a flat and entirely expressionless voice. 'It's Niaz's. He's dead.'

He looked down at the stained, discoloured coat, and began to remove it, stripping it off slowly and with difficulty as though his muscles were stiff, and letting it fall to the ground. The blood had soaked through to his shirt, and seeing it, he frowned with a faint distaste and turned once more to look in the direction of the river. He said after a moment or two, and without turning his head: 'I'm sorry about last night.'

His voice did not express sorrow, or anything else – unless it was perhaps the same faint distaste that had shown in his face when he had looked down at his stained shirt – and Winter's heart contracted with the familiar ache of pain that she had felt so often when she looked at Alex. 'Are you, my darling?' she thought. 'Are you really? Don't be sorry, my dear love. Anything but that! . . . my love, my dear love.'

She wanted desperately to put her arms about him and to tell him that she loved him, and that nothing in all the terrible things that had happened or would happen mattered more than that. But she knew that she must not do so. He did not want to hear it, and he would not understand it.

She disentangled the length of blue cotton from among the grasses and re-wound it about her slender body. The movement brought life back to her numbed arm and wrenched a sobbing gasp of pain from her, and Alex heard the small sound and misinterpreted it. She saw him flinch, but he did not turn.

He said: 'I'm going down to the river. I shan't be very long. Stay here.'

He disappeared into the jungle, and Winter stood listening until she could not hear him any longer. She stooped then and picked up his discarded coat. He would need it, and she could soak the stains out. She shook the dried fragments of grass from it and as she did so something fell out of one of the pockets; a small folded square of paper. She picked it up and smoothed it out mechanically. It was her own note – the one she had written to him when she had returned from Lucknow, and which Yusaf had taken to him in camp. He had kept it. She stood looking at it for a long time and then she folded it again very carefully and replaced it.

It was growing lighter every moment and presently a bird began to twitter in the trees behind her. A hint of the terrible heat that the coming day would bring was already in the air, as though the unseen sun, still far below the rim of the horizon, had exhaled a fiery breath of warning. Winter knotted up her heavy tangled hair, and searched among the tall grass for the revolver and the bundle of linen. A jungle-cock began to cackle in the thickets and then once again, as on the previous evening, the stillness was broken by a babble of bird-song. A flight of parrots screamed out of the trees on their way to the river, and other jungle-cocks awoke and saluted the dawn.

Alex returned at long last. He had evidently bathed in the river, for he was clean again. The dirt and grime and powder stains were no longer on his face, and his hands and arms were free of dried blood. His hair was black and smooth from the water and he had washed out his shirt and trousers and put them on again. The saturated material clung to him wetly, moulding his slim, hard body, but it was already beginning to dry in the dry heat. He took the revolver and the bundle of clothing from Winter and said: 'What have you done with Lou Cottar and Lottie? What were you doing out here last night?'

'They're all right – at least – at least I think so,' said Winter, turning to follow him. 'I went to bathe in the river, and I lost my way coming back. It was getting dark——'

Alex appeared to know his way through these jungles, for despite the absence of paths and the fact that one tree or bamboo-brake or tangled thicket looked exactly like the next to Winter, he walked ahead of her unhesitatingly, until suddenly the dark entrance of the Hirren Minar was before them.

There was no sound from the ruined building, and he groped in the gloom and found that the rope ladder had been withdrawn. He said softly: 'Lou – are you all right?' and there was a swift movement above his head as though someone had been standing there with held breath, listening, and a voice said: '*Alex*!' The rope ladder dropped and two minutes later they were both in the upper room. Mrs Cottar said: 'What happened to you? I thought——' She leant against the wall and burst into tears.

Alex pushed aside the *chik* that she had hung across the open archway, and went out onto the flat roof outside. The sky was bright now, and the day was already breathlessly hot. The tall bamboos that concealed the Hirren Minar, towering to the level of the ruined dome, walled in all but a small part of the roof, leaving a narrow gap through which he could look out across the jungle and catch a glimpse of the river. He sat down on the crumbling parapet and stared at that small square of brightness, and presently the sun rose and lit the tree-tops, and the temperature leapt up as though the door of a gigantic furnace had been flung wide.

There were things that he had to think about. Things that must be thought about soon. But all at once he knew that he could not do so now. He could not think about anything at all. He had not eaten for over twenty-four hours, and for months past he had considered problems that were now of no further importance. He would give himself a day in which to get what rest he could. At least he was clean again, and that in itself seemed enough of an achievement for one day. He had not expected to be clean again. He had expected to die grimed and filthy and with his face stiffened and caked with dust and blood and sweat.

The problem of the three women in the room behind him would have to wait. They could not stay there indefinitely, but they could at least stay there for a day or two; perhaps longer. He noticed incuriously that the ruined roof which was normally a foot deep in dead leaves and the debris of dying bamboos had been swept clean. A man would not have bothered. The thought of the three women pressed like a heavy weight on his shoulders, and his mind rejected it, turning tiredly away.

Winter came out on to the roof behind him, and a ray of the morning sunlight, piercing through the heavy screen of bamboos, caught her in a brilliant shaft of light. Alex turned and surveyed her with a faint surprise as though she were someone he had never seen before. She was still wearing the blue cotton sari that she had worn last night. It was a scanty length of cloth, and it moulded the slender beauty of her body with a classic perfection. Her skin glowed gold in the golden sunlight and her black hair had blue lights in it, and he thought with an entire lack of emotion that she was the most beautiful thing he had ever seen – and a stranger.

The wary, withdrawn creature whom he had met at Ware; the sea-sick child in the cabin of the *Sirius*; the Condesa de los Aguilares; Mrs Conway Barton – they had all gone. The wariness and the withdrawal had gone too, and the great dark eyes were no longer unsure but quiet and untroubled. There was a serenity and a glow about her. Something that was almost happiness.

How can she look like that? thought Alex with a faint twinge of irritation. As if she were entirely content and there were no longer any problems that mattered. Had women no imagination? Had nothing of all that she had seen made her realize that her life from now on – all their lives – was only a matter of living for an hour or a day more, by luck and cunning and the grace of God?

Winter said: 'Breakfast is ready.'

The incongruity of the commonplace, matter-of-fact statement at that time and in that setting suddenly struck him, and he laughed for the first time in many days.

Alex lay flat on his stomach in a thicket at the edge of a glade in the jungle. He held one end of a thin cord in his hand and he was watching the leisurely approach of a peacock and his retinue of wives. The cord operated a primitive trap some twelve feet ahead of him which had, during the past fortnight, accounted for several jungle-fowl, two green pigeons, a pea-hen and an unwary porcupine. The porcupine, as a culinary problem, had proved insoluble, and after struggling with it for an hour or more, Winter had handed the charred and unsavoury remains to Alex for immediate burial.

The Hirren Minar was well stocked with salt and parched grain and a miscellaneous variety of the more durable stores, but they needed fresh food, and Alex did not dare fire a gun for he knew that the sound of a shot would carry far in the long, hot silent days. They had fish-hooks and lines, however, which had proved more than useful, and he had found that it was possible to trap birds.

Cooking was a difficulty, because they were afraid of showing smoke. In that still air it would have risen straight and betrayingly above the tree-tops, and there was no knowing who might see it. There were probably other fugitives in the jungles, and the hunt might well be out against those who had taken refuge there. So they cooked only after dark or before dawn, and in the lower room of the ruin, blocking the door with a home-made curtain of grass and bamboo to avoid showing a gleam of light. It was a hot and choking performance, but Winter and Lou Cottar managed it without complaint.

They had been in the Hirren Minar for over two weeks now, and already it seemed as though they had lived there for months – for years even. They had settled into a routine of living, occupying themselves with petty domestic details; living a curious dream-like life in the hot, silent, shadow-barred jungle. They might have been castaways on a desert island, surrounded by a thousand miles of empty sea, but the three women appeared to be contented enough. They never spoke of Lunjore or of anything that had happened there. At least, not before Alex. He did not know what they spoke of when he was not there.

Lottie's gentle, trance-like daze had survived that second escape from massacre, and though she talked continuously of Edward, her clouded brain accepted the simplest lie, and the presence of Winter and Alex convinced her that all was well. Life in India was so very different from life in England – it was not in the least what she had expected it to be. But one must be prepared to make allowances for foreign customs, and when Edward's manoeuvres were over they would be able to live in their own bungalow in Meerut again. She must be patient and not complain.

Lou Cottar, too, schooled herself to patience. At first it had been enough – and more than enough – to be alive and safe when so many were dead or living in dread and discomfort and danger. But as the days went by she began to take the security for granted, and ache to escape from the jungle and at least attempt to reach civilization. The British could not all be dead! That was nonsense. If only they could escape they would surely find that life elsewhere was going on much as before.

Lou had lived only for amusement, and for men; and she yearned for the society of her own kind again. For lights, noise, music, laughter – all the things that made life an entertaining affair. Josh would be in Calcutta, and she felt sure that Calcutta at least was still in British hands. She had never been particularly fond of her husband, and had regarded him with tolerance rather than affection; they had gone their own ways and had not interfered with each other. But Josh represented a way of life that suited Lou well enough. She took no interest in her own sex and had little use for them, and to live cooped up in the company of two young women with whom she had nothing in common was both tedious and irritating. But Lou possessed common sense and courage, and she knew that because of Lottie English they must take no chances. Lottie was no responsibility of hers, but that fact did not weigh with her. She had, surprisingly enough, begun to feel an odd fondness for the little creature. A feeling that verged on the maternal, though she would have scouted such an idea with scorn had it been presented to her by anyone else. Lottie frequently irritated her, but she knew that she could not abandon her – that none of them could.

If Alex had paid her some attention Lou might have felt more reconciled to the situation. She had always considered that Alex possessed more than his fair share of sexual attraction, and she had been interested in him both as a male and as a personality. But Alex did not see her. He did not see any of them, except as a responsibility and a collective millstone about his neck. Hampered by them, he was tied to the Hirren Minar until he could make arrangements to get them to safety – if there was any safety to be had anywhere in the country.

Outside the jungle that sheltered them and yet hemmed them in there must be so much to be done. So much that needed doing. Delhi to be retaken. Somewhere beyond the borders of Lunjore William would be doing the work of ten men: and John Nicholson too, of whom it had been said that single-handed he could cow an entire mutinous army corps into obedience. Henry Lawrence in Lucknow and John Lawrence in Peshawar. Herbert Edwardes, Alex Taylor, James Abbott; Hearsay, Grant, Campbell, Outram – a hundred others. None of them would be standing still, and they would need every pair of hands and every brain and heart they could muster to save the country from falling into anarchy. Yet he, Alex Randall, sat here idle, tied hand and foot by the necessity of protecting the lives of three women.

If he could only be rid of them! If he could only get them to safety he could reach Henry Lawrence, or the troops that must surely by now be marching to attack Delhi. And then there was his own district . . . But he could do nothing as yet. For the moment at least the women were safe, and he could not move them until he had more reliable news.

He had slept most of that first day at the Hirren Minar, and awakened to a ravenous hunger that had been only partially appeased by a mess of dried corn and a somewhat muddy-tasting fish that Lou Cottar (who had found the lines and fish-hooks) had caught in the course of the afternoon.

He had been unreasonably angry on discovering that Winter had cooked it over a fire that she had made in a corner of the stone chamber below, and had informed her tersely that she had shown a lamentable lack of intelligence, and that in future no fire would be lit by day. Winter had smiled warmly at him, rather in the manner of an adult humouring a cross and convalescent child, and had apologized with a lightness that had further infuriated Alex, since he took it to be an indication of the fact that she had no conception of the precariousness of their present position. He would have to take charge of them. Left to themselves they would be lost. He could not leave them to die.

He had left them to themselves the next night and all the following day, and had made no mention on his return of where he had been or what he had been doing. Winter, who knew him better than Lou Cottar did, had not even asked. Lou had asked, and had not received an answer. For Alex had gone back to the Residency.

There was a bundle of native clothing in the ruined dome of the Hirren Minar, and Lou Cottar, coming unexpectedly upon him as he set out – she had been down to the river – had taken him for a Pathan and been betrayed into a scream.

'Oh God, Alex, you frightened me! – I thought for a moment——'

Alex said: 'Does it change me so much?'

'Yes. I don't know why – it's only clothes. You look so much darker, and that hair makes a difference.'

'It's a mistake to wear false hair,' said Alex, pulling at the greasy locks that fell onto his shoulders beneath the *puggari* cloth, 'but it can't be helped.'

'You should grow a moustache and beard,' said Lou, 'then no one would know you.'

'I would, except for the fact that it happens to grow too damned light; a good deal lighter than my hair. And though one can get rid of it quickly enough, it takes a hell of a time to grow again when needed. I may not be back for some time. Don't show a light if you can help it.' He had turned away and disappeared into the jungle in the direction of the Lunjore road.

The Residency had been deserted except for the kites and the crows and the scavenging pariah dogs, and the sickly-sweet stench of corruption had hung over it in a cloud almost as tangible as the clouds of bloated flies that buzzed above the dead. But there was nothing to be learned there. Not even the names of those who had died, since very few were still recognizable.

Alex had nerved himself to search among them for some evidence as to who they had once been, but he had been forced to abandon it. His own bungalow was empty, and like the rest of the bungalows it had been systematically looted. There had been an attempt to set it on fire, but the flames had not taken hold. The office, however, was reasonably intact, for the mob had not been interested in files and papers and had not troubled to destroy them. It had, however, contained one unexpected object. The body of the Commissioner of Lunjore.

Conway Barton had been slumped on the floor between the inner door and the desk, and Alex had turned him over and found no wound upon him. He was wearing little but a gaily coloured dressing-gown and one slipper, and there was no clue as to what he could have been doing there, or how he had got there – whether by his own will or by force. But one thing at least was obvious; he had not been dead for as long as the bodies at the Residency. And from the appalled expression on his ridged face he would seem to have died of fear.

It would have taken too long, and been too dangerous, to dig a grave for that fat, bulky body, and Alex, having collected certain files and records of importance, had closed the door on it and left him.

There was little that remained among the debris of the Residency or his own bungalow that was of any use, but having hidden the documents from his office in the roof of the deserted stables, he had made a small bundle of various objects which he considered worth removing, and filled a torn haversack with fruit and corn from the trampled garden. He had seen few people in the cantonment area, and had kept out of sight himself, crouching behind walls or in the shelter of tamarisk scrub at any sound or movement.

Alex had not gone to the cantonments again, and he had not again used the roads by day. He went – when he went – by night, and returned at dawn to sleep through most of the day.

On the night following his return from the Residency he had gone to the village where his *shikari*, Kashmera, lived; walking through the crops by the light of a narrow moon. It had been a grave risk, for he was well known in the village. But it was a risk that had to be taken, since he could do nothing without news. The old *shikari* had come to the door of his hut and had known who it was even in the faint starlight, for he, as Niaz had been, was cat-eyed in the dark. He had turned to speak reassuringly to someone inside the hut and had followed Alex out into the night, and they had crouched among the shadows of a corn field for half an hour, whispering together.

Three days later it had been Amir Nath and his hawks whom Alex had met at sunset by the third milestone outside the cantonments. Sometimes it would be Kashmera, sometimes Amir Nath, and once it was a friend of Alex's from the city, Lalla Takur Dass, a bazaar letter-writer who lived in an alleyway near Ditta Mull's silk shop. And in this way he heard the news of the city and the villages and the surrounding districts.

It was not yet safe to move, they told him. The countryside was in a ferment, for there were bands of armed sepoys swaggering through the villages. They had caught a sahib and a memsahib hiding in the hut of a villager, and had not only slain them, but had slain also the man who had given them shelter, and all his family with him, as an example to others. It was they who were responsible for the continued panic. The villagers for the most part asked nothing more than to be left in peace to continue with their ploughing, sowing and reaping. It mattered little to them who governed the land provided the rains did not fail and the crops were good, the taxes were not unduly heavy and allowances made for bad years and poor harvests. Several of the local talukdars were taking an active part in the revolt, and the lower elements of the city could always be relied upon to create trouble. But others among the talukdars had remained quiet and were watching to see which way the cat would jump, as were many men in Lunjore.

'But if thy people do not take Delhi soon,' said Amir Nath, 'they too will join with the others. There is no news of that yet, but there is talk that all the sahib-*log* are not slain, as was at first believed, and that an army marches from Ambala to retake Delhi. If that be true, and Delhi be taken, then many who now waver will stay quiet. Remain thou quiet also, and in hiding, until the worst is past. There have been many sahibs and memsahibs, and *baba-log* (children) also, who being driven out of hiding by lack of food and water have been taken and slain, or sent as prisoners to those who be no friends of the Company's Raj. To move now were to run all heads into a noose, for there is no safety east or west, north or south. Oudh also has risen, and it is said that Lawrence Sahib and all the *Angrezi-log* in Lucknow will soon be slain, and that the *Jung-i-lat Sahib* (Commander-in-Chief) is dead at Ambala . . .'

None of the news was reassuring, and it was obviously unwise to exchange the comparative safety of the Hirren Minar for the dangers of a cross-country flight to some district that might well prove to be in a worse state than Lunjore. And there would appear to be few safe places to make for, if any of Alex's informants were to be believed.

The tales that they told were all of disaster to the British. The whole of Oudh was in a ferment. In Cawnpore General Wheeler was constructing an entrenchment for the defence of the garrison and the European population. Delhi was still in the hands of the insurgents, and there was no news from Meerut. There had been trouble in Agra, and it was rumoured that the troops had mutinied at Allahabad and massacred the British. Punctually to the given day the sepoys in Barelli and Shajehanpur had mutinied, and Khan Bahadur Khan, a pensioner of the Company, had been proclaimed Viceroy of Rohilkhand. He had celebrated his accession by ordering the slaughter of all the British who had been unable to escape from Barelli, and there had also been a brutal massacre of Europeans in Shahjehanpur.

Yes, there was news in plenty – and all of it bad. There was nothing to be done but to keep the women in hiding, and Alex chafed at the inaction and occupied himself with snaring birds.

Winter alone of the four occupants of the Hirren Minar had no need to pray for patience. She was, for perhaps the first time in her life, entirely content.

The heat did not affect her to the same degree as it affected Lottie and Lou Cottar, and the jungle and the river and the ancient, hidden ruin held a strange enchantment for her. They did not belong to the everyday world. They were something lost and forgotten and right outside reality. She shut her mind to the memory of all that had happened to her in Lunjore – to the heartbreak and bitter disillusionment that had awaited her there; to the long months of degradation and misery; to the horrors of the last day and to the thought of the worse things that might even now be happening in the world beyond the forest. She would not think of the past or the future. Only of the present. And the present was Alex.

It did not worry her that Alex hardly looked at her and rarely spoke to her, or that when he did it was generally with an unmistakable undercurrent of exasperation. She felt as though she had loved him all her life and knew everything about him, and ever since the night following their flight from Lunjore she had felt so completely a part of him that she could sometimes follow the processes of his thoughts as though they had been her own. Harsh experience had taught her to expect little of life, and now it contented her that Alex was alive and within reach of her, and that she could watch him and listen to his voice, and feel his presence even when she could not see him.

The only unpleasant times were when he would go out to get news from the villages. She had never asked where he went or whom he saw, but she was always frightened, with a sick shuddering fear, that he would not return. She would stay awake, pulling the makeshift but remarkably effective punkah that he had made from bamboo and dried grass so that Lottie could sleep in more comfort, and straining her ears to listen for the sounds of his return. Yet even these nights had their compensations, since it meant that he would sleep for part of the day, and then she could look at him without the need for concealment.

She noticed that he talked to Lottie far more than to either Lou or herself, and also that he had a special voice for Lottie. A voice that was gay and gentle and curiously reassuring. It could always reassure Lottie, and even to hear it was an assurance of safety to Winter.

Lottie and Lou Cottar, in spite of the appalling heat, still wore the dresses they had worn when they left Lunjore. Alex had brought back needles and thread from one of his night excursions, and they had mended them neatly. He had also, somewhat unexpectedly, brought a wine-coloured cotton sari with a deep blue border and a matching cotton bodice, such as the village women wore, for Winter.

Lottie and Lou Cottar could not be persuaded to wear such things. They had discarded their petticoats, stays and pantalettes, but they clung to what they considered a civilized garment as though it gave them some assurance that this was only a temporary interlude that would soon give place to normality. To have thought anything else would have been to lose a part of hope; to give up a plank of the raft which supported them in an uncharted sea.

'You're letting yourself go native, Winter,' snapped Lou Cottar one hot evening, in an unwonted outburst of irritation. She looked resentfully at the girl, and in the same moment thought how well the draped folds of the cheap sari became her, and how much more effective the silky, blue-black hair was when it swung in thick plaits almost to the knee, than when it was rolled up into the conventional heavy chignon.

Mrs Cottar had never considered little Mrs Barton to be particularly striking, but looking at her now she thought suddenly that she was beautiful; like something out of some Eastern fairy-tale – a princess from the *Thousand and One Nights*. Surprised at herself for the unexpected imagery of the thought, she said irritably: 'You are the only one of us who does not look out of place in this God-forsaken hole – and who doesn't seem to mind being here.'

'I don't,' said Winter dreamily.

Lou Cottar stared at her with an indignation that changed to sudden comprehension, and she said abruptly: 'You're in love with him, aren't you?'

Not so very long ago Winter would have considered such a question an unwarrantable impertinence in the worst possible taste, while to answer it honestly would have been unthinkable. But this was not the civilized world they had known. This was Eden. She smiled at Lou and said: 'Yes.'

'Is he in love with you?'

Winter thought of the letter that Alex carried in the inner pocket of his coat. But then he might not even know that he still had it. She shook her head, and Lou said tartly: 'Then he's a fool!'

'I think he has too much on his mind to bother about anything like that,' said Winter reflectively. 'Just now he can only think of me as a nuisance. I think he has always thought of me like that. A tiresome responsibility that he would like to be rid of if he could.'

'Not only you,' said Lou with a twisted smile. 'All of us. And I can't say that I blame him, because if it wasn't for us he could go. And if it wasn't for Lottie——'

She glanced towards the bed where Lottie lay asleep, and her thin features sharpened with anxiety. She said with suppressed violence: 'That damned baby! It's hanging over us all like – like the monsoon. Something that you know is coming and that can't be stopped. Not that I couldn't do with the monsoon and I suppose that will be here before we know where we are. But if only one could stop that baby! It's knowing that she has to have it and that there's no way out that gets on my nerves. What are we going to do if we can't get her away? We *must* get her away! How much longer has she got?'

'About six weeks I think,' said Winter doubtfully. 'Perhaps it's seven.'

'Six weeks! Oh God – and here we are doing nothing. *Nothing*! What in heaven's name are we going to do if she has it here? Do you know anything about babies?'

'No,' admitted Winter.

'Neither do I. Not a damned thing. I've never had any of my own and I've never been interested in women who did. They look frightful and become dead bores. We've got to get her to some civilized place where there is a doctor. Why doesn't Alex do something? We *must* get her away!'

Alex, lying under a canopy of leaves in the hot, dry jungle grass and watching the shadow of a *sal* tree draw out across the clearing, was making the same calculations and coming to the same conclusion.

It was a conclusion that he had come to days ago, but he could still see no safe way of translating thought into action, since the reports he received were all the same: it was inviting death to travel anywhere, for neither the roads nor the by-paths, the villages or the towns were safe. There were bands of *budmarshes*, looters and mutineers all over Rohilkhand and Oudh and throughout the North-West Province, and to remove from Lunjore would be to leave the frying-pan for the fire. Only the Punjab, if the reports were to be trusted, remained unaffected, but to reach it meant a long, difficult and dangerous journey, and one which Lottie was in no condition to undertake on foot. She would have to travel in some sort of conveyance, and that meant going by road and not across country. The thing was impossible as yet.

Alex remembered with a sinking of the heart certain words from the Epistle to the Thessalonians: '*. . . then sudden destruction cometh upon them, as travail upon a woman with child; and they shall not escape.*'

Six weeks . . . perhaps seven. But anything might have happened by then. Troops must be being hurried out from home or stopped on their way to China. Reinforcements must be coming. And once the tide had turned it would be possible to demand help from those who at present were watching the swing of the pendulum and unwilling to commit themselves one way or the other. For the moment Lottie was safer where she was.

'That damned baby!' thought Alex with an exasperation and anxiety that equalled Lou's. 'Why on earth do women have to——'

And then without warning a thought that had never occurred to him before struck him with the sudden violence of an unexpected blow over the heart. It wiped the problem of Lottie from his mind and substituted a far more frightening one, and he forgot about the peacocks and let them mince past him unheeded while he stared blindly across the clearing seeing only a slim figure in a faded blue cotton sari.

'No,' thought Alex desperately – 'no! It couldn't happen. It was only once——' He had not thought of Winter for days, except as one of three women who were, unavoidably and infuriatingly, his responsibility; and at the back of his mind there had lain an unjust and illogical anger because she had been the means of turning him aside from the course he had set for himself, and by so doing had been indirectly responsible for the death of Niaz. He did not want to think of her now, and with an abrupt movement he buried his head in his arms as though by doing so he could blot her out of his mind and from his conscience. 'Oh God, not this!' thought Alex as he had thought once before at Hazrat Bagh when she had cried in his arms because of a wild goose. 'Not this – not now. I can't stand it . . .'

The sudden movement caught the bright eye of a king crow who was balancing on a bough of the *sal* tree, and it cried a warning that sent the peacocks hurrying away through the jungle. But Alex lay still and did not move for a long time.

That night he took a graver risk than he had yet taken, and went into the city, riding a thin village pony that he had procured with the assistance of the apprehensive Kashmera. 'It is not safe!' urged Kashmera. 'The Huzoor is too well known in Lunjore.'

'There are few who will recognize me now,' said Alex, and it was perhaps true. His face was thinner and there were no longer any curves in it; only hollows and angles – and lines.

'Tie up the jaw as though it were wounded,' advised Kashmera. 'It is an old trick, but it serves.' He had fetched some rags from the hut, and Alex drew the blade of his knife slantwise in a shallow cut on one side of his chin, stained the cloth with it and bound it up roughly.

'That is better,' approved Kashmera. 'Perhaps after all thou wilt return. Leave the horse by the cane field. He will not stray.'

That night was the twelfth of June, but the news that Sir Henry Barnard had fought and won a battle at Badli-ki-serai on the road to Delhi, and that once again there were British on the Ridge, and Delhi itself besieged, had not yet reached Lunjore.

There was elation in the city, for the reports and rumours that had been received were all of successful risings and of Europeans and British garrisons murdered or besieged, and it lacked only ten days to the twenty-third of June – the centenary of the Battle of Plassey which an ex-clerk of the East India Company, Robert Clive, had fought with three thousand men against an army of sixty-eight thousand, and in winning it had won half India. The rule of the 'Company Sahib', said the prophecy, would last for a hundred years from the date of that battle, and now that day was near . . .

The talk of the bazaars only served to convince Alex that he still could not move the women. He had bought food and tied it in a corner of cloth, and ridden back in the bright moonlight with angry despair in his heart.

'Is there no news, Alex?' demanded Lou Cottar the next morning, following him out into the jungle and facing him among the hot shadows of the *sal* trees. 'You must have heard *something*. Even if it is bad news we would much rather know than be kept in the dark.'

'All the news is bad,' said Alex shortly. 'It's no good. We can't leave yet.'

Lou said: 'But we must go soon! Can't you see that if we don't, Lottie may——'

'Do you think I haven't thought of that?' interrupted Alex brusquely. 'Don't be a fool, Lou! At the moment there would appear to be nowhere to go to. She may have a bad time of it if she stays here, but she'll certainly die – and so will the rest of us – if we are mad enough to attempt a cross-country trip just now. The jungle at least will do us no harm.'

But he had spoken too soon, for the jungle that had seemed to befriend them suddenly showed its claws.

They had gone down to the river that evening, all four of them, as they did every evening, because it was cooler there and there were always clothes and cooking-pots to be washed and fishing-lines to tend. Winter had not seen the cobra until it lashed at her, hissing, as she bent to disentangle the edge of her sari that had caught on a thorn. Her foot touched the cold coils, and the fangs bit into her left arm just above the elbow.

Alex had been less than a yard away from her and he had swung round as she cried out, and had seen the snake slither across her path, and the two small punctures on the smooth tanned skin. The next second he had leapt at her and caught her; his fingers tight above the wound, forcing the blood down, and his mouth against it, sucking at it with all his strength.

Lou had come running and had beaten the grass with a stick, and then snatched up a petticoat that was to be washed and ripped at it frantically, tearing at it with her teeth. It tore at last and she wound a strip of it above Alex's straining hands and pulled it tight in a tourniquet.

Alex lifted his head and said hoarsely: 'Permanganate – on the ledge at the left back – quickly,' and Lou turned and ran, stumbling and tripping among the grass and thorn and creeper, while Lottie wrung her hands and wept.

Alex jerked the knife he carried from its sheath, and caught Winter to him, holding her hard against him so that she could not move, his hand a vice about her wrist. He said: 'It'll hurt. Don't move,' and cut the wound across deeply, twice.

He felt her teeth clench on the thin stuff of his shirt and her body twist to the pain, but she did not cry out and he dropped the knife into the grass. The blood poured down her arm and his in a red tide and he lifted her and carried her swiftly back to the Hirren Minar.

Lou Cottar met them a dozen yards from the entrance with the little tin of permanganate crystals clutched in her hand, and they had filled the wound with them, and had got Winter up the rope ladder. Alex had let the arm bleed and she had looked at it with a frown of pain and said in a dazed whisper: 'It will make such a mess on the floor.'

'We can clear it up,' said Alex with white-lipped brevity. 'Lou, for God's sake get back to Lottie!'

He had bound it up eventually and given her as much opium as he dared, and later, when Lou and Lottie had returned and he had realized that she would not die, he had gone out and been exceedingly sick behind the impenetrable thicket of bamboos.

Winter had run a high fever that first night and Alex had held her clutching hands while she twisted and turned and muttered unintelligibly, and Lou Cottar bathed her burning body with cool water. 'Is she going to die?' Lou had asked once. There had been a break in her voice, and her face had been barely more than a pale blur in the darkness beyond the line of moonlight that lay between the broken archways.

'No. She'll be all right in a few hours,' said Alex with more confidence than he felt. 'Give me that cloth and go and lie down, Lou. If you crack up too, I swear I'll go out and shoot myself!'

Lou had laughed on a sudden breath of relief and had obeyed him, and Alex had taken the slender fever-racked body into his arms and held it close, his cheek pressed to the burning forehead. The moonlit night had been breathlessly hot and Alex's own body was wet with sweat, but his hold seemed to soothe her, and after a while he felt her slacken and lie still in his arms, and knew that she was asleep at last and that the fever had broken.

'My love!' thought Alex, moving his mouth against the hot smooth skin and the damp waves of silky hair that were as dark as the darkness about him. 'My little love ...'

Quite suddenly the gnawing restlessness that had lived with him hourly during the last weeks fell away from him, and he no longer cared what became of anyone else – or of India – as long as Winter was safe. He could wait patiently now. She was no longer a burden and a responsibility, but part of his heart, as she had always been. What did it matter if they had to wait here in hiding for months – or years? 'Only after this,' thought Alex, 'I must not kiss you again or touch you again, because if I do I shall only take you again – I couldn't stop myself – and it may be months, or a year, before we can get away.'

He thought of Lottie and shivered. One day the news would be better. He had no doubts on that score, because what he had once told Kishan Prasad had been true. Even if every European in all India were killed, the British would send, if necessary, every man they had, to avenge them. It would not be so much the loss of territory or prestige that would bring them, and nerve them to fight with stubbornness and fury, but the murder of their women and children. They would not forgive that, or rest until they had avenged it.

One day, perhaps very soon – or if the mutiny was really widespread, perhaps later than he had thought – the British would be in control again and it would be safe to leave the jungle. They could get away then . . . get married. Barton was dead. It was only a question of waiting.

44

Winter had recovered quickly and suffered remarkably little ill-effect from the incident. The wound that Alex's knife had made had healed cleanly and given the minimum of trouble, and though the fever and loss of blood had kept her on her back and feeling absurdly weak for several days, she had soon been about again.

She saw very little of Alex after that, and suspected that he was deliberately avoiding her, but she knew that some tension in him had relaxed and that he was no longer impatient or irritable. She was aware, too, that he had developed a habit of watching her under his lashes. He would lie on the river bank in the evening while she and Lottie and Lou washed the clothes and cooking-pots, and she would look up and find his gaze on her, and feel as always that familiar contraction of the heart.

When the sun had set Alex would go off to set fishing-lines and traps while the three women bathed in the river, returning to eat the evening meal; and because he had taken to wearing nothing but a loin-cloth these days, his body was burnt as brown as his face and he could have passed anywhere for a Pathan. He had been out less for news than for food of late, and but for the relentless, exhausting heat the days passed peacefully enough.

Alex, like Winter, found the heat unpleasant but bearable. But to Lou, and more especially to Lottie, it was an interminable torture. They watched the skies daily for signs of the monsoon, and longed for rain; but though clouds would sometimes gather and they would hear thunder rumble along the horizon and see the heat-lightning flicker, no rain fell to temper the intolerable heat, and they lived for the early mornings and the late evenings when they could lie and soak in the coolness of the river.

Alex became afraid of the river, and he drove in stakes about the narrow curve of the little beach where they bathed, in case their continued use of it might attract the attention of a mugger, and that one day one of them might be dragged down by yellow-toothed jaws into deep water. But there was too much food in the river these days for the muggers to bother with live prey. The bodies of the British came down on the current, bloated and bobbing to the undertow, and once one had stranded by the little beach: a woman whose long hair had caught in the tree-roots so that her mangled corpse swung gently to and fro in the ripple as though she were swimming – or struggling.

Alex had sawn through her hair with his knife and pushed her off into the current, and the others, arriving five minutes later, had wondered why he was looking so unusually grim. He had not looked like that for some time past; he had looked relaxed and almost contented, and had taken to humming under his breath as he set fishing-lines or devised further methods of keeping the temperature of the Hirren Minar within bearable limits. But that night he had gone to the city again, and when he had returned at dawn his eyes were once again hot with restlessness. For it seemed that the tide was turning at last.

The British whom the boasters in Lunjore had declared were all dead or swept into the sea were encamped once more upon the Ridge before Delhi. The Guides had marched from Mardan and were now with the Delhi force, and Hodson Sahib, the '*Burra Lerai-wallah*' (great in battle), was also there, commanding a regiment of horse that he had raised.

They would of course be defeated – annihilated! – it was only a matter of time: but all the same there was a noticeable breath of uneasiness in the bazaars. It was disconcerting to find that the sahib-*log* were not all dead. And it was said, whispered one man to an awed group in the Sudder Bazaar, that Nikal Seyn himself was riding for Delhi! Nikal Seyn, the sound of whose horse's hooves could be heard, so men said, from Attock to the Khyber, and whom many declared to be a god, and no man. The speaker had shivered and thrown a quick backward look over his shoulder as he spoke.

'It won't be long now,' said Alex, his eyes blazing in the grey dawn light. 'We shall have to stick it out here a little longer, but the monsoon must break soon, and then it will be cooler. And when Delhi is taken we'll be able to get away. A good many of the waverers will come over to us then, and we shall be able to get help on the road.'

Another ten days; perhaps a fortnight – or a month. But what did it matter now that the end was in sight? They could afford to wait a week or two more.

'I suppose so,' said Lou, wiping the pouring perspiration from her face with the back of her hand. 'We shall have to wait. I see that. We've been lucky – luckier than so many others. Perhaps the luck will hold.'

But it did not hold.

That same evening Lottie had strayed away to pick jungle berries, not twenty yards from the river bank, and she had heard someone moving through the bushes and had turned, expecting Lou who had been fetching water.

But it was not Lou. It was a bearded turbanless native in torn and soiled clothing, who carried a heavy bundle upon one shoulder and bore on wrist and ankle the marks that are made by iron fetters.

She was not to know that this was one of the criminals who had been released by the mob from the city jail, or that he had subsequently murdered a Hindu merchant and his family, and escaped with the loot to the jungle. But Lottie was under no illusions as to his intentions.

He had stared at her unbelievingly, and then his lips had stretched into an evil grin. A memsahib – a *feringhi*! His eyes glittered and he dropped the bundle he carried and drew a stained sword from its sheath. He moved towards her quite slowly, crouching a little, the dry jungle grass rustling and crackling about him, and Lottie's mouth opened in a soundless scream. She made no attempt to turn and run, but stood frozen and still like a trapped rabbit, and she did not hear Lou coming up from the river. Neither did Bishul Singh, *dacoit*, for he could see nothing but the petrified face of the white woman before him and hear only the crackling of the undergrowth as he crept towards her.

Lou never moved from the Hirren Minar without a revolver, and she dropped the *chatti*, and as the man looked round, checked by the sudden sound, she pulled the gun from the sling she had made for it, and fired. The man jerked upright and his eyes and his mouth opened in a look of incredulous astonishment, and then he swayed, coughed, crumpled at the knees and fell sideways with blood pouring from his mouth.

'No!' screamed Lottie. 'No! No! *No*——!'

Alex had been reinforcing a bamboo ladder that he had made to replace the rope one that Lottie found it difficult to climb, and he had heard the shot and the screams, and dropped it and ran. He had taken one look at the man on the ground and at Lou who was holding the screaming Lottie, and said: 'Where's Winter?' And then Winter had run through the bushes, white-faced and panting, and he had gripped Lou's shoulders and shaken her and said: 'Were there any others?'

'No. I don't know,' said Lou jerkily. 'He was coming for Lottie with a sword. I shot him. Lottie – Lottie! – it's all right, dear, it's all right.'

Alex said: 'Get on, get back – all of you. He may not have been alone.'

But Lottie would not go. She had struggled and screamed, and Alex had turned and taken her from Lou and carried her back to the Hirren Minar, holding her with her face pressed hard against his shoulder to muffle her screams. He had put her on her feet for one moment at the foot of the ladder, and she had turned and fled back, and when he caught her she had fought him, writhing and twisting and clawing at him, her thin distorted body suddenly possessed of surprising strength, so that it had been all he could do to get her back into the upper room.

Alex said: 'Pull up the ladder, Winter. And close the entrance. Lou, give me the opium – and the brandy. It's all right, Lottie dear, you're safe now.'

But Lottie had screamed and shrieked and fought as she had screamed and fought at the Kashmir Gate at Delhi when she had seen a grinning bearded man leap at Edward with a sword, and had seen her husband fall, spurting blood from that terrible wound, and had been dragged away to be lowered over the battlements and fall into the dry ditch below. 'Let me go! – let me go! They're killing him! Edward – *Edward*!' screamed Lottie. And then quite suddenly she had gone slack in Alex's arms and they saw with unutterable relief that she had fainted.

Alex laid her down on the narrow camp bed, and letting down the rope ladder, ordered Winter to pull it up after him and went out into the twilight jungle.

He turned the dead man over, and recognizing him realized that he was probably on the run, and straightening up he stood still, listening for a long time, but could hear no sounds that suggested anyone moving through the jungle. Presently he made a cautious circuit of the immediate area but found no one, and returning to the corpse he dragged it to the river bank and pushed it off into deep water.

The bundle the man had dropped proved to be full of valuables. Silver coin, a large quantity of Indian jewellery, an assortment of bric-à-brac that could only have come from the looted bungalow of some European, and one object that told its own story: a woman's hand that had been hacked off for the sake of the rings it bore and which had presumably proved difficult to remove. Alex disposed of that gruesome and decomposed relic and carried the bundle back to the Hirren Minar. The money would come in very useful and he could only hope that Bishul Singh had not made an assignation with anyone to meet him on or near this spot. Judging from the value of the loot he thought it unlikely: it seemed more probable that the man had intended to keep it to himself.

There was an appalling smell of burnt feathers in the upper room of the Hirren Minar, and Alex climbed the ladder to find Lottie still unconscious and Lou and Winter, their faces no more than white blurs in the dusk, making desperate efforts to revive her.

'Leave her alone,' advised Alex. 'If she has remembered Delhi she is better off like that. We'd better light the lamp.'

They used the lamp as little as possible, partly to conserve their scanty stock of oil, but mostly because it necessitated covering the open archways with solid screens that Alex had made from bamboo canes, roots and dry grass, so that the light would not show. In the day-time, when the hot wind blew, they poured water on those screens, which helped to cool the room, but after sunset when the wind dropped the screens made it unbearably hot, and there was no breath of wind blowing tonight.

Winter went below to prepare the evening meal and Alex handed her a revolver without comment. He was still not entirely sure that the dead *dacoit* had been alone, and he did not know how far the sound of that shot and Lottie's screams would have carried.

Lou lit the small oil-lamp while Alex mixed brandy and opium with water. 'It may keep her quiet for a bit when she comes round,' he said, and pushed the brandy bottle at Lou: 'You'd better have some of that yourself. You look as though you need it.' They had been as sparing with the brandy as they had been with the oil, but Lou drank and felt grateful for the fiery liquid.

Lottie had not recovered consciousness for another hour, and when at last she had moaned and stirred they had been able to make her drink the opium brew without much difficulty. She had sat up, propped against Lou Cottar's shoulder, and had stared up at Lou's face and at Alex and Winter, with eyes that had lost the dazed sweetness that they had worn for so long.

She said at last: 'Edward is dead, isn't he? They killed him. I – I remember now. And they shot Mama – and – and Papa. Where is Sophie?'

'Sophie is safe, darling,' said Winter. 'She is in Cawnpore.'

'They killed Edward,' whispered Lottie. 'They – they cut him with their swords, and there was a man with a knife who——'

Winter said: 'Don't think of it, darling – don't.'

'How can you stop yourself thinking of a thing like that? I should have stayed with him but they wouldn't let me. I should have stayed with him——' She turned her head against Lou Cottar's shoulder and wept, and Alex got up and went out.

He had slept in the jungle that night, in the grass before the entrance of the Hirren Minar; but he had lain awake for a long time listening to the night noises and straining his ears for any sound that might be made by men. He could hear, intermittently, a murmur of voices from the upper chamber of the ruined building behind him, but it came at longer and longer intervals and at last there was silence.

There were clouds in the sky that night, but they held no promise of rain; only of hot winds and dust, and it seemed as though they intensified the heat, pressing it down onto the gasping earth so that it could not escape, as though they were a lid on a gigantic cauldron. They were gone when Alex awoke with the first light of dawn, and the sky was clear again. Clear with the hazy clearness that promised a day of grinding heat.

Alex went down to the river and lay in the water on the narrow ledge below the bank, watching the sky turn from pale green to saffron while the birds awoke in the thickets above him and a troop of monkeys came down to drink. He lay there for a long time, until the sun leapt from below the horizon and the burning day was in full flood across the pitiless sky and the parched jungle. It was only then, when the sun flared in the tree-tops, that he realized that none of the three women had come down to the river that morning. They were usually there well before sunrise, and he would leave the small beach to them and return to the Hirren Minar. But today they had not come.

He left the water reluctantly and felt it dry on his back almost before he had reached the top of the bank. Between the tree shadows the sun was like a raw flame on his shoulders as he walked back to the Hirren Minar, and he had reached the entrance when he heard that agonized moaning, and stopped.

He stood quite still for perhaps five minutes, knowing with despair and anger and pity what it meant. Then he turned away and sat down in a patch of shadow on a fallen block of stone that fronted the low stone ledge before the Hirren Minar. This at least was not his affair. There were two women with her.

Listening to the moans he wondered why the Almighty had thought fit to inflict on womankind such a lengthy and agonizing method of populating the earth. And why, in the name of Allah the Merciful and Compassionate, had this got to happen now?

He leaned back on the warm, time-worn stone and wondered just how much difference this was going to make to all of them. The problem of this unborn child had been hanging over them all ever since the day of their escape from the Residency: marching remorselessly towards them; unavoidable and inescapable. Wars and riots and mutinies, famine, disaster and the crash of dynasties – the processes of birth stopped for none of these things. Lottie would have to bear this child even though her husband, mother, father and half her friends were dead, and India awash with blood and anarchy. Except by dying, she could not escape it.

Probably just as well to get it over, thought Alex. After all it was a perfectly natural process. Nothing to make a fuss about. Happened half a million times a day and was a simpler matter than one would suppose. He had assisted at the arrival of Chytuc and helped a bitch who was in difficulties to produce her litter, and once he had sat up all night reading by the light of an oil-lamp a manual on midwifery, and receiving terse instructions from a doctor who had crippled himself in a fall from his horse while riding fifty miles to attend the wife of a typhoid-stricken surveyor in a lonely forest camp, who was about to give birth to her first child. It had proved a slow but comparatively simple affair. But the woman had been wide-hipped and healthy and not in any way comparable to the childish smallness and fragility of Lottie.

'What *are* those women doing to her?' thought Alex impatiently. He could hear Winter's voice and Lou's, and Lottie's agonizing moans going on and on. The moans rose to a scream that was more fear than pain, and suddenly he could bear it no longer. He leapt the stone ledge and was up the ladder and in the comparative coolness of the upper room.

Lottie was lying on the camp bed, fully dressed and clutching at the sides of it; her eyes wide with terror. Winter knelt beside her and Lou Cottar leant over her with a tin mug in her hand. They turned their heads towards him and on both their white faces was the same terror of the unknown that was on Lottie's, and Alex, seeing it, realized in that moment that not one of them had the least idea of the mechanics of birth.

The suffocating prudery of the age saw to it that the majority of young women were kept in complete ignorance of such matters, and neither Winter nor Lottie had even seen a cat having kittens, while Lou Cottar, who could certainly not be classed as either young or an innocent, had never had any children of her own and was entirely uninterested in the conversation and gossip of those who had. All three of them had only the haziest idea of what happened when a child was born, for the whole affair was shrouded in the deepest mystery and only referred to in whispers. It was, moreover, considered by many that the less a young mother knew about childbirth the less likely she would be to panic about it in advance, while once the birth had begun – well, there was nothing for it then but to endure it.

Alex could see all these things written clearly in the desperate, terrified faces of the three women, and a sudden fury of exasperation took him by the throat. He thrust Winter and Lou aside and said savagely: 'What in hell's name do you think you're doing? Come on – get her out of those clothes!' And saw again the same expression reflected on three faces. Even in this extremity they could feel it to be unspeakably shocking to remove Lottie's dress in his presence, and his exasperation mounted. He bent over Lottie and took her hands, feeling them turn and clutch frantically at his, and said: 'Listen to me, Lottie. You've got to think of your baby now and not of anything else. Forget that I'm a man – or anyone you know. Just try and do what I say. Will you do that?'

Lottie nodded, clinging to his hands, and he released them with difficulty and said shortly to Lou: 'Pull that fan and keep the flies off her. Have we got enough water in the place?'

'I – I think so,' said Lou. Her face was quite white and her assurance had suddenly forsaken her. Lou would have faced a howling mob with calm and courage, and she had not flinched in the face of danger. But Lottie's pain and fear were something that she could do nothing to relieve, and it left her feeling sickened and helpless.

'Well, make sure. And if we haven't, get it.' He turned to Winter, who had removed Lottie's clothing, and said: 'Get down there and heat some water. And here——' He reached for a clasp knife from the stone ledge and handed it to her. 'Boil that in some water – let it boil for five or ten minutes and then take it off and leave it in there.'

She turned without a word and descended the ladder and Lou said: 'The smoke——'

'We shall have to chance it.' He heard Lottie's moans rise once more to a scream and went to her swiftly, taking her hands again, and Winter heard him talking as she fetched wood and dry grass and lit the fire that they had never yet lit by day. He was telling Lottie about the child. What it was doing, and what her own body was doing to help it in its struggle for release, and what she must do to help them both. It sounded, suddenly, entirely natural and reasonable, and no longer some dark and mysterious and inexplicable process fraught with terror and uncertainty. His words evidently carried the same reassurance to Lottie, for her agonized moaning ceased.

'You can't avoid a certain amount of pain, dear,' said Alex, 'but there isn't anything to be frightened of, and it will be here soon.'

'*He,*' said Lottie. 'Not "it".'

Winter heard Alex laugh, and thought again: 'He has a special voice for Lottie. Dear Alex – darling Alex——!'

The long morning wore away, and the appalling heat filled every corner and crevice of the Hirren Minar as though it had been a tangible thing; a weight which could be lifted from the shoulders if only the body had possessed sufficient strength.

That day, when they needed it so badly, the hot wind failed and the air was as still as brass. Lou and Winter took it in turns to pull the bamboo punkah and to sponge and fan Lottie, while Alex sat by her, talking to her; pulling against her as she clung to his hands, dragging at them and screaming. The sweat ran down their faces and blinded their eyes, and Winter and Lou flinched and gasped at every scream, but Alex's voice remained steady and reassuring and Lottie's eyes clung desperately to his – as desperately as her hands.

Once Lou had dropped the wet cloth she had been holding and jumped to her feet, her eyes wide and staring in her white sweat-streaked face and her hands pressed frantically over her ears to keep out the sound of that terrible screaming. 'I can't bear it!' she gasped. 'I can't bear it——' She had started to run from the room and Alex had released one hand and caught her arm in a crushing grip, forcing her back. He had not spoken, but Lou had looked down into his face and experienced as violent a shock as though he had struck her. She stood staring at him, trembling and gasping, and then her tense muscles had slackened and the blood had rushed up into her face, and she said: 'I'm sorry.' Alex's fingers relaxed, and she had looked down dazedly at the marks they had left, and stumbling back to her place had picked up the cloth and continued to bathe Lottie's writhing body.

But before the morning was out Alex knew with a sick despair that he would not allow to show in his face that he was fighting a losing battle.

Lottie's meagre strength ebbed with the day, and Alex gave her brandy and cursed both man and nature for allowing any woman born with that narrowness of hip to conceive. He could not see how it was possible for the child to be born at all – let alone be born alive. And yet it was so nearly born. But the afternoon had gone, and Lottie's strength with it. She could do no more. He would have to do the rest himself. He looked at Lou and saw that her hands were shaking, and he turned his head and spoke over his shoulder to Winter: 'Hold her for me.'

Lottie's daughter was born just as the sun touched the level of the treetops; and long before the gold had left the sky Lottie was dead. She had survived the birth, and she might have lived if she had fought to do so; but she had neither the strength nor the desire to hold on to life.

She had spoken only once. Lou had washed the tiny, whimpering creature and laid it against Lottie's thin shoulder, and Lottie's sunken eyes had opened slowly and painfully and she had looked at it. A last ray from the sinking sun had pierced through the bamboo screen and touched its small head, and Lottie's bloodless lips had curled in the shadow of a smile.

'Red hair,' she whispered. 'Like Edward's. Take care of him, Lou.' And then she had died.

Lou had wept, but Winter had not cried for Lottie. Lottie was with Edward, and she had loved Edward so much. That tiny red-headed morsel of humanity, if it lived, might have comforted her, but it would never have made up to her for the loss of her Edward, or wiped out that picture of him dying cruelly before her eyes. She washed Lottie's light little body and dressed her again, and went out to the river before it became too dark to see, leaving Lou with the child.

Alex was sitting on a fallen block of stone among the jungle grass near the entrance to the Hirren Minar. He had his head in his hands, and in the dusk he had been almost invisible against the background of the bamboos that towered up behind him.

Winter stood watching him for a moment or two, and then she went to him and put her arms about him, and laid her cheek against his hair. He turned his head against her shoulder with a tired sigh and his arms came round her quite gently. He leant against her for a long time without moving or speaking, as though he were too tired to wish to do either, while the dusk deepened about them and the evening star shone bright in a soft green sky.

Alex stirred at last, moving his head so that his lips lay against the curve of her throat, and his arms tightened about her, drawing her close. And then a peacock screamed from beyond the bamboo-brake – a harsh, grating cry that seemed to echo the gasping screams that had rung in their ears all that hot agonizing afternoon – and she felt his body jerk almost as though he had been abruptly awakened from sleep. He pushed her away from him suddenly and violently, his hands coming up to grip her arms and wrench them away, and he stood up swiftly and said in a voice that was as hard and as rough as a steel file: 'No, I'm damned if I will! Not after today. I won't let that happen to you. I won't, do you hear. Go on – get back in there before I——' He bit the sentence off, swung round and disappeared into the dusk.

He had returned an hour later and fetched the heavy-bladed knife that was used for cutting through thick jungle, and gone out again. It had taken him the best part of the night to dig a grave that would be deep enough to protect Lottie's little body from marauding animals, but he had managed it at last.

They had buried her in the clear pearly light of the early morning, an hour before the sun rose, and Alex had said as much as he could remember of the service for the burial of the dead over her grave. He remembered a good deal of it, for India was a country where that service was used with depressing frequency. Afterwards he had gone off to bathe in the river at a spot higher up the bank, leaving the narrow beach by the tree to Winter and Lou, and had not returned until an hour after the sun had risen.

The upper room of the Hirren Minar was clean and swept and tidy, and yesterday and all the nerve-racking torture of those long, hot, agonizing hours seemed a year away. Winter had handed him food which she had kept hot for him in a covered cooking-pot among the embers of a fire, and he had eaten it and watched Lou who was feeding the baby with water in which she had boiled a little rice. She dipped a clean rag in the liquid and gave it to the tiny creature to suck, and there was a look on her face that Alex had not thought it possible for Lou Cottar to wear. A soft, absorbed wonder. He observed it with interest and a certain astonished amusement – Mrs Josh Cottar, of all people!

Lou said thoughtfully and with entire seriousness: 'You'll have to get me some milk. I wonder if we could keep a goat?'

Alex finished his meal and came over to look at the skinny, wrinkled little object with the fluff of reddish-gold down on its head that had cost Lottie her life, and looking at it he had a sudden warm feeling of achievement. He had not been able to save Lottie, but he had at least saved this minute scrap of new life from dying before it had lived, and all at once that seemed a thing as well worth doing as the saving of a province. He touched the tiny waving hand, and felt it close about his finger with the instinctive and unexpected tenacity of a sea anemone.

Alex laughed and said: 'You shall have your goat, Lou, if I have to steal it. What are you going to call her?'

'Amanda,' said Lou promptly.

'Good Lord! Why? Did Lottie——?'

'No,' said Lou. 'Lottie was sure it was going to be a boy. She never knew it wasn't. It's just that I think Amanda is a nice name for her. It means "worthy of love".'

Alex stroked the downy head with a forefinger and Lou looked up at him and smiled. 'Still three women on your hands, Alex.'

'Four,' said Alex with a grin. 'You've forgotten the goat. And I can clearly see that a goat is going to be more trouble than the rest of you put together.'

It was a prophecy that was to prove lamentably correct.

Alex had slept most of that day and had gone out at sunset. He had returned at dawn dragging an exceedingly vocal goat procured for him with suspicious ease by Kashmera, whom Alex suspected of having stolen it. The goat had been loath to accompany him, and he had been compelled to carry it for the first part of the way.

Lou and Winter had attempted to milk it, collectively and severally, and had been reduced first to desperation and then to helpless mirth in the process. Alex had refused to help. He said that he considered that he had discharged his part in the affair by procuring the animal, and that he was damned if he was going to turn *gopi.* They must learn to deal with it themselves.

They had done so, and the baby throve. It was astonishingly tenacious of life, and survived the untutored treatment to which it was subjected, as it had survived the horrors and hazards of that pregnancy and premature birth. The goat gave far more trouble. It evinced a desire to stray and could be trusted to eat its way through any and every rope. Alex constructed a strong door of thick bamboo poles to replace the flimsier curtain of grass over the entrance to the Hirren Minar, and they kept the goat in the lower chamber at night.

It had awakened them the second night by bleating plaintively and monotonously, and when at last it had ceased they had heard a rasping, scratching sound, and Alex, who had been sleeping on the open roof, had looked down over the ruined parapet and seen by the clear starlight and a waning moon the beautiful black-barred body of a tigress who crouched before the bamboo door, clawing at it with a taloned paw. The tigress had heard the movement above her and had looked up, her eyes glinting like green moons, and she had stared at him for a full minute before leaping away into the thickets.

Alex had strengthened the door, lashing a double layer of bamboo poles the thickness of his arm across and across it, and the next night the tigress had been back again. He heard the scrape of her claws, and lifting a lump of earth that he had taken the precaution to bring with him dropped it on her from above. There was a sharp and un-tigerlike yelp and she had bounded away into the jungle.

'Why didn't you drop something heavier?' demanded Lou, who had been an interested spectator.

'Because I have no desire to have a wounded tiger in this bit of the jungle,' said Alex. 'They are unpleasant things to have around.'

'But it will only be back tomorrow night.'

'Probably. But it won't get through that door. There's that baby of yours starting now. If it isn't one thing it's another. Who wouldn't be a bachelor?'

Lou had laughed and hurried back to feed the wailing child, and the next night they had been awakened at moonrise by a leopard snarling and tearing at the bamboo door. But apart from these disturbances the long, burning, breathless days were peaceful enough.

The jungle dried and shrivelled and turned brown about them, and the river shrank; but still the monsoon delayed. They never spoke of Lottie, as they never spoke of all those whom they had known in Lunjore, or of anything that had happened there. Their life went on as before, except that now there was the baby to look after in place of Lottie, and Lou had lost her restlessness.

Lou had never liked children. She had not wanted any of her own, or been in the least disappointed when none had been born to her; she had looked upon it as a blessing. But somewhere, unsuspected by anyone, least of all by herself, there must have lurked an unquenchable spark of the maternal instinct; and now, unexpectedly, it had sprung alight.

Perhaps Lottie, dying, had been able to sense its presence and its potential strength, for it was not to Alex or to Winter that she had spoken. She had said: 'Look after him, Lou,' and Lou had taken the child and looked at it with a sudden awe-struck and exultant sense of possession.

That sense of possession had grown stronger every day, and now she did not mind how long they stayed in the Hirren Minar. She was afraid of moving from it. They were safe here and they must not take any risks. She could even bear the intolerable heat better because the child seemed to take no harm from it, but she waited and panted and prayed for the rains. If only the rains would break!

'Alex, how much longer will it be?'

'God knows,' said Alex. 'Any day now.'

The news from the outside world, if it could be believed, was not encouraging. Sir Henry Lawrence had fought a disastrous action at Chinut and had been heavily defeated, and now he and the British in Lucknow were closely besieged in the Residency. General Wheeler and the Cawnpore garrison were reported to be at their last gasp in the torn and shattered and pitifully inadequate entrenchments that they had scratched up out of the earth, and where they had fought and died and held out under the glaring heat and the blizzard of shot and shell since the sixth of June. In Jhansi the Rani had urged on her people to revolt, and had offered terms to the Europeans who had taken refuge in the fort. The terms had been accepted, and they had surrendered – only to be seized, bound and slaughtered; men, women and children together. Not one had been spared in that cold-blooded butchery.

Mutiny had broken out in Allahabad where the sepoys had murdered their officers and massacred all Christians, and the only news that seemed to hold out hope was that the British still clung to the Ridge before Delhi, although their force was as yet more besieged than besieging.

'Wait yet awhile,' urged Kashmera, as he had urged so often before. 'Thou art safe in the jungle.'

But the jungle had finished with them, and it would not let them wait.

45

Alex had been setting a snare at the entrance to a small clearing some fifty yards from the Hirren Minar when he smelt smoke.

He had not been feeling at all well that day. His head ached and he thought angrily that Lou or Winter had disobeyed orders and lit an early fire. Then all at once he realized that the hot wind that was rustling the dry grass and dead leaves was blowing towards the Hirren Minar, and not away from it. There must be someone else in the jungle, and upwind of him. He left the snare and returned swiftly, pulling the grass back over the path that he had taken, and ordered the two women, who were about to leave for their evening bathe, to get back into the upper room.

'Pull up the ladder and keep a revolver handy,' said Alex peremptorily. 'And drag the slab over that hole. I'm going to have a look round. Don't move until I come back.'

He had disappeared and they had waited a long time, making no noise and listening to the interminable croon of the hot wind and the monotonous rustle and clank of the dry bamboos. Presently Winter had lifted her head and sniffed as Alex had done.

'Smoke! So that's why—— Lou, suppose it's some of the others? It might be. We can't have been the only ones to get away.'

'More likely charcoal-burners,' said Lou in a whisper. 'If it were men hunting for us they wouldn't warn us by lighting fires.'

Alex had returned half an hour later and called up to them that they could come down. He looked strained and uneasy. The smoke had come strongly on the wind, but the wind was dying now with the dying day, and soon it would be dark enough for him to verify his fears.

Lou, carrying the baby, had made straight for the river, but Winter had stopped and looked at Alex with anxious eyes: 'What is it? What are you afraid of? Is it men?'

'I hope so,' said Alex with an uneasy movement of his shoulders. 'We could probably deal with them – or avoid them.'

'Then what is it?'

Alex's eyes were searching the sky to the south-west. There had been clouds in the sky all day; dirty copper-coloured clouds which he had hoped might mean rain at last. But was there something more than clouds there? He said: 'I think the jungle is on fire somewhere over there. It may burn out, but—— Oh well, we shall soon know.'

The wind died and the smell of smoke died with it, but later, as the sky darkened, a pink wavering glow that was not the sunset grew steadily brighter until it drowned out the last of the daylight and spanned the horizon from north to south.

Alex watched it from the roof of the Hirren Minar. 'It may miss us,' he thought. 'Or it may burn out before it reaches us.' But he had little hope of it doing either. So little hope that he made a bundle of those few things that seemed to him urgently necessary, and carried them down to the river bank.

Presently the wind rose again, and now it brought with it not only the smell of smoke, but drifting ash. Soon there would be sparks, and the forest was tinder-dry from the scorching June days. He returned to find the two women standing on the open roof watching the sky, their faces clearly illumined by the distant glow. They turned together to face him, and once again, as on that day in the jungle when they had fled from Lunjore, their eyes were wide and strained but devoid of panic, and he knew that the anxiety in Lou's was not for herself, but only for the child she held.

Looking at them Alex was conscious of a confused mixture of emotions that included gratitude, relief, tenderness, a passionate admiration, and a disgust of himself because he had once considered them as nothing more than millstones round his neck and a tiresome responsibility of which he wished he could rid himself. He found that his voice was a little difficult to control and said with unnecessary curtness: 'Can either of you swim?'

'Yes,' said Winter, who had spent a few weeks every summer at Scarborough – Lady Julia considering the sea air good for growing girls.

'A little,' said Lou Cottar. 'But – but Amanda——'

Alex said: 'We'll have to make some sort of raft. Just in case. Get me all the ropes you can, Lou, and give that child some food. Light the lamp, Winter – and get a fire going below. We'll have to see what we're doing.' He disappeared down the ladder and they heard him hacking down the heavy bamboo door that he had built to protect the goat.

They worked with feverish haste, tearing down the split-cane *chiks* and using them to face that triple platform of bamboo, and carrying down the box that Lou had been using as a cradle. The door made an admirable raft, and Alex found himself feeling grateful to the goat for the first time since they had acquired it. The perspiration poured off them as they worked, for the heat of the fire added itself to the remorseless heat of the June night, and the wind blew that heat across them so that soon it hurt to breathe. The air was full of smoke now, and they could hear the crackle of the flames, while the light of the fire that Winter had lit in the stone room was no longer necessary, because the world about the Hirren Minar was as bright as though it were bathed in a red sunset.

Alex said: 'Bring anything that isn't too heavy and that you think is worth bringing. I can manage this; it doesn't weigh so much. We may have half an hour or so yet, but it isn't safe to bet on it. Be as quick as you can.'

He departed with the raft, and they went back up the ladder for the last time, and collecting all the food they could carry, took a last look about the queer stone chamber in which they had lived in such discomfort and found such strange happiness and content, and Winter smiled at it with sudden tears in her eyes, as though she were saying good-bye to a dear friend. Then she helped Lou down the ladder with the baby, and they were out in the jungle and Lou was hurrying towards the river while Winter followed her dragging the protesting goat.

They could not have found the way by night, familiar as it had become; but this was not night. This was daylight, and hotter than any day they had ever known. The fire was no longer a distant crackling chorus, but a steady roar, and the sky was a brilliant rose-pink pall of smoke shot through with sparks. A bird was singing gaily among the branches of a thorn bush as though it imagined that the dawn had broken, and the undergrowth was alive with movement. Peacocks, jungle-fowl, porcupine, a fox, three jackals and a chital hind ran past them, making for the river, and there was a crashing among the bushes as a bull nilghai thrust its way into a clearing, saw them, and backed away snorting.

If the wind had died the fire would not have reached them for several hours, but the wind drove the sparks ahead of the wall of flame, and where they fell they started new fires, so that the roaring blaze leapt forward with seven-league boots and ate up the miles with terrifying swiftness.

Alex was waiting for them on the little shelving strip of bank where they had bathed so often. The makeshift raft floated high and light in the water, and he was lashing the tin box to the centre of it. He took the baby from Lou and laid it in the box among an assortment of bundles, and stretched a strip of wet cloth above it as an added precaution against smoke and sparks. It was less easy to get the goat on board and safely tethered, but they managed it.

'You can't swim in that, Winter,' said Lou, hurriedly divesting herself of her dress. 'I'm sorry, Alex, but this is no time for modesty.'

Alex grinned at her and waded out as far as the steeply shelving bank allowed, while Winter, following Lou's example, removed her sari and rewound it, wrapping it around her in a straight strip so that it covered her from armpit to knee.

Crouching in the cool water under the shelter of the high bank the heat was not so intolerable, but the river looked appallingly wide – the far bank as though it were miles away. Lou remembered the muggers who haunted every Indian river, and shuddered. She said anxiously, looking back at the jungle: 'Don't let's go until we have to. It's still quite far away. It may miss us after all.'

Alex said: 'Not a chance, I'm afraid. Look over there. They know.'

Lou Cottar turned her head and looked. A herd of nilghai were plunging down the steep bank not twenty yards below them, and taking to the water to swim out steadily into the red-dyed river where the current took them down in a long, slanting line towards the far shore. A moment later there was a crash above them, and a wild boar, his tushes and his little pig eyes gleaming in the leaping light, slithered down the bank and without paying the smallest attention to them launched himself into deep water. And then suddenly there were animals all about them, so that the steep banks seemed alive with terrified forest creatures, and for a moment or two they forgot their own danger in the wonder of that sight.

A tawny, spotted shape leapt down the bank and crouched on the narrow ledge almost within reach of their hands, snarling with terror, its tail lashing wildly. But the leopard's green gaze passed them by, for his fear and his hate were not for them but for the fire behind him, and presently he too took to the water. From somewhere further up the bank they heard the unmistakable snarling roar of a tiger, and a troop of frantic monkeys leapt and howled in the tree above their heads. One of the monkeys, a mother clutching a skinny big-eyed baby, sprang down upon the raft and huddled against the bleating goat, chattering and grimacing.

'Come on,' said Alex. 'If we wait any longer we shall have a cargo-load of stowaways.' He found that he had to shout to make himself heard above the roar and crash, and that he felt oddly stupid and lightheaded: he would have liked to have sat down in the water and stayed where he was. He pulled himself together with an effort and said: 'Listen, Lou, I've rigged up a sort of tow rope and I'll go ahead with it. If you're not much of a swimmer, keep hold of the raft and keep upstream of it. Winter——' He turned to look at her and fought down the choking fear that threatened him; the fear of the current; of the man-eating muggers of the river – 'Winter, you push from behind. Give me as much help as you can, and – and don't for God's sake let go.'

He had made a rough-and-ready harness of rope, and with that across his shoulders he struck out from the bank and felt the current catch him and draw him and the raft downstream as a shower of sparks fell hissing into the river.

He did not glance back but swam on steadily, striving with everything in him to keep from being drawn too far down the stream, because the road and the shattered remains of the bridge lay only a mile away, and there would be men in the huddle of mud and wattle huts behind the toll-house on the Oudh bank where he and Niaz had tied up the occupants on the day they blew up the bridge. He could be certain, too, that the toll-keeper and his family from the Lunjore side would have procured a boat and crossed the river to join them when they saw the fire approaching. It would be dangerous to land anywhere near there, and he must not let the raft be swept too far downstream.

The oil-smooth surface of the water was filmed with ash and charred leaves and full of frantic swimming animals, many of whom clawed at the raft and held onto it, dragging sodden shivering little bodies onto the sheltering bamboos; squirrels, rats, mice and a bedraggled mongoose. There were pig and deer; sambhur, chital, kaka, blackbuck; nilghai, jackals, panthers, tigers, a scaly four-foot iguana and a solitary elephant with a broken tusk in the river that night, swimming as desperately as the four humans for the safety of the far bank.

It seemed to Alex as though they would never reach the other side. As though the river were endless. His head ached and his muscles seemed to have no strength in them, and there was a cramping pain in his stomach. The rope bit into his shoulders and caught across his throat and choked him, and he could feel the drag of the dead weight pulling to the pull of the current, for Lou could do little more than cling to it and keep afloat. And then quite suddenly there were sandbanks ahead of him as though they had lifted from the river, and the current no longer pulled at him, and he had reached the shallows.

All about him wet furry shapes were dragging themselves onto the warm white sand, licking their fur and shaking themselves before crawling or scuttling away towards the distant line of trees, and Alex freed himself from the rope harness and dragged the makeshift raft forward until it grounded.

He turned then at last, and saw that they were all there. The shivering goat, the baby lying placidly in its box, the monkey still clutching its round-eyed offspring, Lou Cottar on her knees, staring blindly ahead of her and breathing in deep gasps, and Winter lying full length in the shallows with her long hair cloaking her slim body in blackness and her chin on the edge of the raft. He walked over to her unsteadily and reached down a hand to pull her to her feet.

'I can't,' said Winter, and laughed up at him. 'I've got no clothes on.'

'I like you without your clothes on,' said Alex, and pulled her up into his arms and kissed her, holding her cool wet body close to him and tasting the water that ran into his mouth from their wet faces and their dripping hair. He held her for perhaps a minute, oblivious of Lou Cottar, and then released her gently, and putting her away from him, bent to untie the goat.

The monkey, abruptly taking fright, leapt from the raft and fled across the sand. And suddenly they were all laughing. Laughing helplessly from strain and overwhelming relief, and because they were still together and still alive. They stopped at last, and turned to look at the wall of flame that was the bank that they had left: and saw that they had left it only just in time, for hissing, burning branches were falling into the water and there was nothing but flame to the turn of the river that hid the broken bridge-head. The Hirren Minar must be somewhere in the centre of that furnace, and tomorrow there would be nothing but miles of black, smouldering desolation where yesterday there had been dense jungle.

A hot spark fell on Alex's bare arm and he winced and swung round suddenly to look at the line of trees behind them and beyond the long stretch of the sand. Lou Cottar, following his look, said with a catch in her voice: 'It can't reach as far as this!'

The flames could not leap that wide expanse of river, but the wind was carrying stray sparks across it, and the jungle everywhere was tinder dry. But they could not remain exposed to the brilliant light at the edge of the shallows. They would have to make for the trees.

Alex bent without a word, and untying the box from which Lou had removed the baby, filled it with the various things that they had brought with them, while Winter retrieved the wet folds of her sari from about her ankles, and dragging the goat followed them across the wide level of the sands to the shelter of the grass and the casuarina scrub that fringed it.

The long swim across the river had cooled them, but now they were hot again. Unbelievably hot. The air scorched their lungs with each breath that they drew, and the river and the wide sandbanks and the line of the jungle were lit with a bright pulsating glare as though it were a stage in the full blaze of footlights and gas-lamps. Every blade and leaf and twig of the jungle behind them stood out from its fellows, highlighted and black-shadowed, and here and there a floating spark would alight and wink and go out, or catch at a brittle powder-dry spear of grass and show a brief spurt of flame.

A tuft of pampas grass twenty yards from them caught alight and flared up, and Lou caught her breath in a harsh gasp, and snatching at the end of Winter's wet sari, dragged the end of it free and drew it across the child's face. She said desperately: 'It's almost dry already! We shall have to get back to the water. Alex——'

Winter saw Alex's face stiffen queerly and knew that he was visualizing taking to the river again and going down with the current – for how far? And for how long? They might have to go for miles, hemmed in between two walls of fire, with only that makeshift bamboo raft to hold to. Then suddenly and unexpectedly he gave a dry sob of relief, and holding out his hand, palm upwards, said: 'Rain!'

It was the monsoon at last.

Unbelievingly, incredulously, they turned their faces up to the furnace of the sky, the hot drifting ash and the falling sparks, and felt something warm and wet splashing upon their parched skins.

'Wait here,' said Alex. 'I'm going to get the raft.' He leapt down the bank and they saw him race across the sands as the first heavy, blessed drops began to fall. He upended it and shouldered it and presently he was back again, panting and breathless. 'Get in among the trees; under the thickest stuff you can find,' he said jerkily. They forced their way into the thicker jungle with the raindrops splashing onto their shoulders and the glare from the burning trees on the far bank lighting their way, and using the raft as a roof, wedged it at an angle to carry off the rain and make a rough shelter among the trees, stowing the bundles and the baby under it as the first slow drops turned to the full, drumming downpour of the monsoon.

They stood out in it, letting it pour over them as it roared out of the sky like some tidal wave such as the one that had overwhelmed lost Atlantis, drowning out the roar of the burning jungle. It was not rain as Winter had known rain. It was a solid wall of water falling on them and smothering out thought; and cool – and cool——

The glare diminished and died at last, and they were in wet darkness in the drumming, drenching rain. The thick jungle and the platform of bamboo and matting were an inadequate shelter against that torrential downpour, but they did not care. It had cooled the appalling heat and they could breathe again.

It was still raining when the dawn broke greyly over the drenched miles of blackened smoking wasteland, the pock-marked face of the river and the sodden jungle around them where the canes and the tall grass sagged under the weight of water.

Winter heard Alex stir, and opened her eyes to see him walk out into the pouring greyness. She sat up, pushing the wet hair back from her face and shoulders, and saw that Lou was still asleep, wearing nothing but the cotton chemise in which she had swum the river, and with her arm about the box in which the baby slept. They had propped up the lid with sticks last night so as to provide extra shelter for the baby and the various belongings that were wedged at one end of the box, and the baby, though presumably damp in the manner of babies, appeared to be otherwise dry.

Winter rose to her knees and wringing out her wet hair plaited it, and looked ruefully at her damp sari. But there was nowhere in the jungle that was dry. The warm rain drummed on the leaves, pouring off them in fountains and cascades and runnels, and the steady voice of the water drowned out all other sounds. There would be no need to bathe in the river today, thought Winter; and then realized with a sense of shock that it was not going to be so easy to reach the river from this bank, since to gain the brink would mean exposing themselves at the edge of a wide belt of open sand a long way from the safe shelter of the trees.

Struck by this thought she turned to rummage cautiously among the few articles they had brought with them from the Hirren Minar, and found a cooking-pot which she set to catch the water that was sluicing off the roof of their temporary shelter. The noise and the movement failed to wake Lou, who slept on while Winter instituted a search in the nearby jungle for any fuel dry enough to burn. Only yesterday the whole forest could have been lit with a single match, but this morning it was no easy matter to find a handful of grass and dead leaves with which to make a fire.

Presently the baby raised a feeble wail and the sound woke Lou, who sat up rubbing her eyes, and after a time came out and joined Winter. She looked up at the grey, weeping skies and round at the sodden jungle and said briskly: 'We shall have to build a hut.'

Winter looked at her and smiled, remembering Lou's previous restless desire to escape from the jungle, and contrasting it with her present and instant desire to construct a more permanent shelter so that she could remain safely in hiding during the coming months. Lou returned the smile. They could still smile in spite of all that had happened to them, and they were still smiling when Alex returned, pushing through the drenching undergrowth. But at the sight of his face their own faces were suddenly sober.

'What is it?' asked Lou sharply.

'That bloody goat!' said Alex forcefully.

Lou gave a choked cry and ran to the side of the shelter where they had tethered the goat, but there was nothing there but a chewed piece of rope, and the goat had gone. 'We must find it!' said Lou. 'We must! How am I to feed Amanda? It can't have gone far.' But the goat had gone for good.

'I can only hope that some wet and hungry tiger has made good use of it,' said Alex sourly. 'It will be a richly deserved end. Don't be silly, Lou! Give it some rice, or boil it some flour and water. No one is going to notice smoke today.'

'Will you stop calling her "*it*"!' snapped Lou in sudden and irrational fury.

Alex grinned. 'You're getting damned maternal, Lou. One day you'll persuade yourself that it – sorry, she – is your own child.'

'She is,' said Lou, and went to join Winter who was building a fire in a hollow tree that she had discovered some twenty yards from their shelter.

Alex looked after her with a half-smile that turned into a grimace of pain. He went into the shelter and found the small tin of opium pills and swallowed down a few of them with brandy. 'I cannot go sick now,' thought Alex dizzily. 'Not now——'

But no amount of brandy and opium could keep the fever at bay, and half an hour later Winter, bringing him hot food on a plate of leaves, found him lying under a tree a few yards from the shelter, his body jack-knifed with pain and his breathing harshly audible above the steady patter of the rain. His brown, sun-burned skin had an oddly grey tinge and seemed to be stretched too tightly over his cheek-bones, and there were dark patches under his closed eyes. Winter put the food down very carefully, surprised to find that her hands were steady when her heart was beating with such terrified swiftness. She laid a hand lightly on his forehead.

The harsh heat of it appalled her, and Alex opened his eyes and looked at her between narrowed lids. He seemed to have some difficulty in focusing her. His forehead creased in a scowl of pain and he said in a blurred, difficult voice: 'Be all right . . . only . . . dysentery. Tell Lou . . . keep that baby away . . . dangerous . . .'

There had followed a nightmare interval of days and nights – none of them could ever have said how many, it had seemed like a month and was probably no more than three days – in which Alex's body had been torn and burned and wasted with dysentery and raging fever, and it seemed to Winter that he could not live. She had not known the meaning of dysentery, for though it was a plague common to all India, any explanation of it, or of what a severe attack entailed, was not considered a suitable subject for the delicate susceptibilities of ladies. She had stayed with him day and night, doing everything that it was possible to do for him, endlessly and tirelessly; holding his head on her lap, forcing the brandy and opium that were the only medicines they possessed down his parched throat, feeding him with boiled rice and rice-water, listening to him rave when the fever mounted, and feeling every cramping pain as though it were a pain in her own body.

She slept only when exhaustion overtook her, and then with her hand on him so that she woke when he moved. She had never in all her short life seen an illness like this, or imagined it, and at times it seemed worse to her than the birth of Lottie's baby had been. But Alex held onto life, and it was, in the end, Lou who had betrayed them.

Lou knew something of dysentery, having experienced a mild attack of it herself and seen Josh suffer a worse one. She told Winter all that she could remember of the course of the illness and its treatment, and she had looked at Alex and said: 'I don't think it's only dysentery. I think he's got some sort of fever on top of it. Josh wasn't as bad as that. Unless – unless it's cholera.'

She had kept away for fear of carrying the infection to the baby. But the pouring rain, and the sudden breaks when the rain would stop and the sodden jungle steamed under the molten heat of the sun, had not suited the baby as the dry heat of the Hirren Minar had done. The baby wailed endlessly and heartbreakingly, and vomited up the rice-water and the thin gruel that Lou made with flour and coarse country sugar. And the supplies of even those commodities were running low.

'She will die without milk!' said Lou, wild-eyed and desperate. 'She must have proper food – she must!' She had walked up and down, clutching the wailing infant to her breast and said passionately: 'Why can't I feed her myself? Why aren't we made so that we could if we wanted to? She needs it, and I can't give her anything – *anything*!'

Winter did not hear her. She had been watching Alex's haggard burnt-out face and dry, cracked lips, and her mind and her heart were as desperate as Lou's. She did not even notice when Lou went away, and it was only when she found that there was no fire lit – for Lou had been dealing with all the cooking – and no food prepared, that she found that Lou and the baby had gone. And even then she imagined that they could not be far away.

The rain had stopped and the jungle that had been so brown and brittle only a few days ago was now a hot, humid greenhouse in which new grass and leaves and creepers and every variety of growing thing had sprung up overnight in lush abandon. The damp heat was less bearable than the dry heat had been, and Alex seemed to struggle for every breath he drew.

The sound of his laboured breathing tore at Winter's heart, and for the first time in the long weeks since she had run from the Lunjore Residency she turned her face away and wept: wept hopelessly and helplessly and silently; the hot tears running into the grass roots as swiftly as the raindrops that had poured down onto them the day before.

She did not know how long she lay there, face downwards on the steaming ground, and she did not hear Alex move; but his hand touched her and she lifted her head and saw that his eyes were open. There was a faint frown in them but they were entirely lucid and no longer clouded and unfocused or blind with pain. He spoke with a palpable effort and in a voice that was barely a whisper:

'What's the matter?'

Winter pushed back her hair and stared at him incredulously, the tears drying on her cheeks. He had not looked like that, or spoken sensibly, since the illness had struck him down. His frown deepened and he said: 'Why are you crying?' Winter brushed away the tears with the back of her hand and said unsteadily: 'I'm not – not now.'

She rose to her feet and stumbled away to light the fire and boil water, because Lou was still not back. And it had been the first time for days that she had not left him expecting to find that he was dead when she returned. She had made a brew of flour and rice-water and sugar, and stirred brandy into it and taken it back to him; and his eyes were still lucid.

He drank the decoction because he was too weak to refuse it, and lay still afterwards looking ahead of him under half-lowered lids. Presently he said: 'How long?'

'I – I don't know,' said Winter with a break in her voice. 'Days. Don't talk.'

'I shall be all right now,' said Alex in the same difficult whisper, and he had closed his eyes and gone to sleep with his head in her lap.

Winter had slept too; her head thrown back against the tree-trunk behind her; and when she heard voices and someone had shaken her she had thought it was Lou.

But it was not Lou. It was a party of men armed with *lathis* and in charge of a man who wore a rusty sword and carried an old-fashioned musket.

'These are not sahib-*log*!' said one of the men scornfully. 'They are but the *nauker-log* of the mem.'

But one of them had peered closer and said: 'Nay, they have *Angrezi* blood in them at least. We will take them. Up, thou!' The speaker stirred Alex with his foot and Winter had said furiously and in the vernacular: 'Let be! Canst thou not see that he is sick?'

The tone and the quality of the Hindustani she used gave the men pause, and they looked at her doubtfully. It occurred to them suddenly that this might after all be an Indian lady of good family. Her fingers tightened imperatively on Alex's shoulder, and he had obeyed the unspoken warning and remained silent. He could not have risen if he had tried. The man with the musket said uncertainly: 'Of what city art thou?'

'Of Lucknow,' said Winter without hesitation. 'Of the household of

Ameera Begum, wife of Walayat Shah, who is my cousin and lives in the Gulab Mahal by the mosque of Sayid Hussain. This man is of Persia, and my – my husband.'

The men observed her owl-eyed and consulted in whispers, and Winter heard the leader say: 'What matter? The order is for all to be sent to Pari. Send these also.'

They had rifled the contents of the shelter in which Lou and the baby had lived, removing the revolvers and the shotgun and anything else they could find, and ten minutes later they had moved off through the jungle taking Winter and Alex with them.

Alex, helped to his feet, had not been able to stand without support, let alone walk, and they had used the roof of the shelter to carry him on. It had taken them surprisingly little time to reach the road, and Winter realized that they must have been swept down by the current further than she had supposed on the night that they crossed the river. There had been a bullock-cart waiting on the road, and a curious crowd of villagers – and Lou Cottar. Lou, white-faced and haggard, and clutching the baby.

She had stared at Winter and Alex in horror and said hoarsely: 'I didn't mean . . . I didn't know this would happen. I thought I might find a village where I could get milk. And – and they did help me. They were kind. I didn't realize they would go back to see if there was anyone else. I only came by the sand because it was easier, and – and they followed the marks. I thought——'

Her voice choked and stopped and Winter said: 'It's all right, Lou.' And then they were thrust into the cart and jolted away down the long uneven road towards Pari.

It had been dark by the time the captives reached the little walled town near the jheel; the town that Alex and Niaz had skirted on that autumn night when they had ridden from Khanwai and crossed the bridge of boats, hidden under the sacks and the sugar-cane in the bullock-carts.

The cart that now carried Alex, Winter, Lou and Amanda creaked to a halt beside a gateway in a mud wall, and they were taken out and hustled across a dark courtyard and into a long, low-ceilinged room lit by a single guttering cresset. The two men who had carried Alex laid him on the floor and the door banged behind them. An iron bar clanged into place, and someone at the far end of the room stood up in the shadows beyond the circle of light and said hoarsely and incredulously: '*Winter*!'

Winter was on her knees beside Alex, and she looked up, startled; blinking a little in the dim light that seemed dazzling after the darkness outside. A face moved into the range of the lamp and stared down at her wide-eyed: a strange, haggard face, dirty and unshaven and with a blood-stained bandage tied about its head. She looked up at it for a long moment, puzzled and uncertain, before she recognized it, and then at first she did not believe it. For it was, incredibly, Carlyon who stood there. Carlyon, whom she had last seen on the verandah of the little dâk-bungalow beyond the ford on the road to Lunjore, and whom she had thought to be – if she had thought of him at all – several thousand miles away in England

There were other voices behind him, and other faces. Eight other faces; tired, worn, dirty . . . and British.

Carlyon said hoarsely: 'Winter – it is Winter, isn't it? What are you doing here? They said you'd all been killed.' His voice was as raw-edged and ragged as his clothes, and other faces that Winter knew separated themselves from the shadows: Captain Garrowby – Dr O'Dwyer – Mrs Hossack——

Mrs Hossack clutched at Lou Cottar and wept, and Captain Garrowby said: 'Mrs Barton! – Mrs Cottar! How did you . . . we thought you must all be dead. We thought that we were the only ones who had got away. Who is that with you?' He lifted the lamp and said: 'Good God, it's Randall——!'

'Only just,' said Alex in a whisper. 'Hullo, Garrowby. How did you . . . get out?'

There were *charpoys* in the room, six of them placed end to end along the walls, and Captain Garrowby and Carlyon had lifted Alex onto one of them, and he had lain there and listened to the story of another escape.

The Garrowbys, Dr O'Dwyer and his wife, and Mrs Hossack and

her four children had not gone to the Residency, and so had escaped the massacre. Mrs Hossack had intended to go, but had been delayed because Dr O'Dwyer had been at her bungalow to see her eldest child, a seven-year-old girl, who had been suffering from hot-weather fever. Captain Hossack, of Colonel Packer's Regiment, had been shot down on the parade-ground by his men, and his Indian orderly had ridden to warn Mrs Hossack to escape. The doctor, whose bungalow was next door, had run to fetch his wife and they had all entered the Hossacks' waiting carriage, intending to take refuge at the Residency. But the Garrowbys had stopped them. Captain Garrowby of the 93rd had been warned by his men, and he had ridden for his bungalow and bundled his wife into the trap and rounding the corner into the Residency road had seen an obviously hostile crowd collecting before the gates. He had turned the trap, deciding to make for the river, and had met the Hossacks' carriage. They had all made for the bridge and had crossed it at least two hours before Alex and Niaz had reached it.

Fearing to be stopped, they had said no word at the bridge of the panic in Lunjore. But at Pari they had been attacked by a mob which had included mutinous sepoys from the disbanded 7th Regiment. The coachman and Captain Garrowby's syce, who had been with them, had stood off the mob for a few minutes and paid for their loyalty with their lives. But in those few minutes the party had turned and driven back furiously the way they had come, and abandoning the carriage and trap had taken to the jungle and hidden there.

One of the Hossack children had been killed and Captain Garrowby and Mrs O'Dwyer had been wounded in the firing. Mrs O'Dwyer had died two days later. The rest had wandered in the jungles, living on roots and berries and first one and then another of the two elder Hossack children had died, and later Mrs Garrowby too had died of heat-stroke and exhaustion. Captain Garrowby and the doctor, with Mrs Hossack and her remaining child – a baby of six months – had been driven to ask help at a village on the outskirts of Pari, and the villagers had taken them in and treated them kindly. But three days earlier they had been put into a covered cart and brought to this house – they did not know why, nor how long they would remain there. They had been given food, and had not been ill-used, but the atmosphere and the attitude of their jailers was not reassuring.

The four other captives had arrived on the following day: Lord Carlyon, The Reverend Chester Dobbie, Mr Climpson and Miss Keir – the sole survivors of a party of fifteen Europeans who had hoped to escape from Oudh and had been attacked and massacred at a village five miles away. They too had been fugitives for many days before being captured and brought here.

Winter had paid no attention to the recital of escape and misery, for her eyes had looked past Carlyon to Dr O'Dwyer, and she had run to him and pulled him across the room to Alex, and after that she had only watched his face and listened to what he said. 'He'll do,' said Dr O'Dwyer reassuringly. And then a native woman had brought coarse food and a bowl of fresh milk, and Lou had fed the baby and told the story of the last weeks, and the voices and the faces and the heat of the low-ceilinged room had mixed and melted together and Winter had fallen asleep and had not stirred or wakened until the sun was high in the sky.

There was an enclosed courtyard on the far side of the room where the prisoners had spent the night, and the door leading out into it had been unlocked at sunrise.

The same native woman had brought food again for the captives, but she had refused to answer questions and had gone out to the far side of the courtyard to join a crowd of gapers who peered curiously at the *feringhis*, discussing them and speculating about them and chewing *pan*.

'What do you suppose they mean to do with us?' asked Lou uneasily, rocking the baby.

'Keep us as hostages, I think,' said the Reverend Dobbie, who thought no such thing but trusted that God would pardon him that comforting lie.

'Hostages for what?' inquired Lou.

Mr Climpson, a middle-aged Magistrate who had escaped from his burning bungalow with the assistance of a loyal servant, said: 'The local Talukdar has been wavering for some time. He cannot decide which side is going to win, and he seems to have given orders that any Europeans found in these parts were to be taken prisoner but not harmed. I think he means well enough, but he is getting nervous. The whole of Oudh is now in revolt, and since the Chinut affair the British position looks bad. I think that is why he has had any of us known to be in the district brought here.'

'Yes, yes,' said Mr Dobbie, nodding reassuringly at the women. 'I am sure that is right. He feels that we shall be safer here. That bar on the door may keep us in, but it also serves to keep others out.'

Carlyon, leaning against the jamb of the open door, surveyed him under drooping lids and wondered if the little man really believed that. Carlyon had heard the story of Jhansi and the public slaughter of the Europeans who had accepted the Rani's terms of surrender. That hapless garrison had been roped in three lines – children, women, and men – and bound and helpless they had been butchered in that order, so that the women had been forced to see their children die before their eyes, and the men to see both die in turn before their own end came.

He had heard too – the news had been told to Mr Climpson by the headman of the village where they had lain hidden before being brought to Pari – of the massacre of the Cawnpore garrison who had accepted the offer of surrender and safe-conduct by Dundu Pant, the Nana Sahib. If Mr Climpson's informant was to be believed, the exhausted survivors had been allowed to embark in boats that were to take them to Allahabad; but once the last man was on board the thatched roofs of the boats had been set alight by the boatmen, who then leapt out into the water as the watchers on the bank opened fire on the blazing, drifting targets. In this manner the last of the Cawnpore garrison had died, with the exception of some two hundred women and children – of whom there had been close on four hundred in the entrenchments on the fifth of June – who had struggled ashore and been taken captive.

In the light of these stories Carlyon was inclined to take a very different view of their situation from the ones advanced by either Mr Climpson or Mr Dobbie. It seemed to him far more likely that they were being kept alive in order to provide a Roman holiday for the mob when a suitable occasion should arise: the type of public spectacle that the hapless garrisons of Jhansi and Cawnpore had provided.

'I should have gone home,' thought Carlyon. 'I must have been mad.'

He had meant to go. He had returned to Delhi, raging because Winter had escaped him, and had heard later, through friends of the Abuthnots, of her marriage. But he had not gone home, which would have been the sensible thing to do. He still wanted her more than he had ever wanted anything in his life, and he could not bring himself to admit defeat and return to England. As long as he was in the same country there might still be some chance for him, but once he left it there was none. What did a few months, or a year, matter to him? He could afford to linger in India for as long as he chose, and he was convinced that a few months of marriage to this clod of a Commissioner would cure her of her romantic attachment. Then, when she moved to the hills (as she was sure to do) she would find Carlyon there ready to console her.

He knew in his more sober and reasonable moments that he was behaving in an un-adult and ridiculous manner. A manner which no one – least of all Lord Carlyon himself – would have thought Lord Carlyon capable of. Yet he had stayed. He had kept in touch with Mrs Gardener-Smith solely in order to obtain news of Winter, and on hearing that she intended to go to Simla in May he had arranged to spend the hot weather there, and had gone to Lucknow with the intention of travelling to Simla via Lunjore so that he could see this man Barton for himself. But while there he had been struck down by a severe attack of fever which had delayed him, and the tidal wave of the mutiny had swept him up into its hungry flood and brought him, after weeks of wandering and privation, to Pari – and to Winter.

Carlyon leant against the door and watched her now as she lay asleep. She must, he thought, have been very tired to sleep as deeply as that. Food had been brought hours ago and the courtyard was bright with sunlight. There was noise and talk and movement, but she had not stirred.

The three other women in their soiled bedraggled Western clothes looked haggard and shapeless and ugly with anxiety and exhaustion. But this relaxed, sleeping creature managed still to be beautiful, though it was a different beauty from that which had attracted his instant attention in the ballroom at Ware.

This was a woman, and no longer a girl. A woman thin-faced from strain and sleeping the sleep of utter exhaustion, but still as lovely a thing to look at as any man – even one as weary and desperate and as frightened as himself – could wish to see. In that hot, horrible room, surrounded by her fellow-captives in their stained and ragged clothes, she looked as colourful as a poppy growing on a rubbish dump, and merely to look at her was a refreshment to the eye and in some way served to lessen his fear and his despairing fury.

Carlyon had never known before what it meant to be afraid, but he knew now, and he had often wondered of late how much longer he could keep it from showing in his face. Were the others equally afraid? He supposed that they must be, since only the completely unimaginative could fail to be. It was curious, this value that all men placed upon an outward display of calm. He was more afraid – as probably every man in the room was – of showing fear than of the actual thing they feared, and the fight to keep from showing it was the hardest part of living through the dragging, tormenting days: harder than the uncertainty, the intolerable heat, the torn, sweat-soaked clothing and the coarse scanty food, or the memory of horrors seen and endured and the dread of worse to come.

It was an escape from that fear, and from ugliness and reality, to look at Winter lying asleep, the lovely curves of her body moulded by the thin folds of the wine-red sari whose deep blue border reflected in the blue lights in her hair. The smooth curve of the bare golden arm, the line of the long golden throat and the black sweep of the lashes that lay against her thin cheek were an assurance that the world still contained other things besides hate and terror and violence.

Carlyon became aware that he himself was being watched, and looking beyond Winter he encountered Captain Randall's grey, speculative gaze.

He would not, he thought, have recognized Randall if Garrowby had not addressed him by name. The man seemed to have shrunk to no more than skin stretched over bone, and the almost black sun-tan had an odd undertone of greenish-white. Close on a week's growth of beard blurred the outline of jaw and chin, and there were dark patches like bruises under his eyes. But the eyes themselves, with their thick black lashes that were almost as long as Winter's own, were as unmistakable as Winter's had been; and meeting them, Carlyon was conscious of a sudden flare of hostility and antagonism. That familiar antagonism that this man had aroused in him from the moment that he had first seen him in the drawing-room of the Abuthnots' bungalow in Delhi.

He had not known then why he should have disliked Randall so intensely; it was enough that he did. But he knew now. The reason lay stretched between them. A woman in a wine-coloured sari.

They had escaped from violent death by the narrowest of margins; they had lived as hunted animals and now they were herded together as captives; their countrymen everywhere were being pursued and slaughtered and defeated, and the Empire of 'John Company' was crumbling into ruin. They had seen sights that would haunt their sleep for as long as they lived – and they did not know if they might live as long as another day, or another hour. But for a moment they could forget it all and stare at each other with antipathy and cold anger; the greater issues giving place to an instinct as elementary and as animal as that which drives rival stags to fight in the spring.

Yet another bedraggled captive had come to swell the ranks of the prisoners that day, an elderly Eurasian clerk who had been found hiding in a village some five miles to the south. His tale differed little from the story of escape and flight, horror and hardship and final capture, that had been the lot of all of them. The villagers had helped him and sheltered him, but he like the others had been sent without explanation to Pari.

'It is not thee country people who are cruel,' said Mr Lapeuta in his soft sing-song voice: 'They are like us you know – veree ordinary people. It is thee towns-people and thee sepoys who are hot against us. I think that thee Talukdar of these parts, he will protect us if he can, but thee sepoys and thee maulvis they are putting pressure on him, threatening him. He will not kill us, but I think that he wishes to be rid of us because he is fearful of thee maulvis, who preach against us, and he would like to wash his hands of us all. If there is better news, then doubtless he will keep us here so that he can show how he has sheltered us, and gain much reward. But if thee news is bad, then I think he will send us away. That is what thee headman in whose village I hid told me.'

'Send us where? Why?' demanded Carlyon.

Mr Lapeuta glanced round cautiously, but the women were taking their turn in the primitive wash-room on the far side of the courtyard. Nevertheless he lowered his voice in deference to the code that his European blood enforced upon him, that women must not be alarmed but must be shielded from harsh truths and not be asked to face reality. 'I think,' said Mr Lapeuta, 'that he does not wish to have us killed in these parts. If he sends us away, even though he may know that it is to our deaths, he can then say, if thee British armies come, "I did all that I could, I protected them, but I became most fearful for their safety and so I sent them away to more powerful protectors; is it *my* fault that those others caused them to be killed?" Oah yess, that is what I much fear he will do.'

The accuracy of Mr Lapeuta's forecast was proved within three days. News from Lucknow trickled into Pari, and it was news that took the heart out of the captives, put heart into the rabble, and frightened the Talukdar into ridding himself, Pilate-wise, of the responsibility of the fugitive Europeans whom he was holding captive.

Sir Henry Lawrence was dead. He had died in the beleaguered Residency at Lucknow, and all over India men heard the news with a catch of the breath. Now that he had gone it would surely be only a matter of days before the Residency was captured, and its defenders massacred as the garrison of Cawnpore had been.

The Talukdar wavered no longer, but hastened to rid himself of the haggard band of British before they were murdered by the mob in circumstances that might involve him in trouble in the event (which now appeared less likely) of the Hell-born ultimately defeating the insurgents and regaining power.

He sent in more and better food, permitted the services of a barber and allowed the women facilities for the washing and mending of clothes. And having impressed his excellent intentions upon them he had them hurried by night into covered carts such as *purdah* women travel in, so that they might not be seen and dragged out on the way, and sent them off under guard.

They had not known where they were going, but the unexpectedly good treatment they had received after days of surly neglect had raised the hopes of the majority of the party. It did not raise Alex's hopes, or Mr Lapeuta's, for they had a better understanding of the native mind than their fellow-captives. That understanding enabled them to read the motives of the Talukdar of Pari with accuracy, and they had scant confidence in the future, or in the good intentions of those to whom they were being sent. Winter alone might be safe, thought Alex. Her dress and her command of the vernacular set her apart from the rest of the British captives, and this cousin in Lucknow might yet be able to save her. He drew what comfort he could from the thought.

In the hot jolting darkness of the cart he knew that he had only to move his hand to touch her. They had sent him in the cart with the women because he was still absurdly weak, and because, he suspected, Winter had demanded it. She had made friends with the native woman who had brought them food, and had coaxed her to bring more eggs and milk, and once even a chicken from which she had made broth for him and for the two children. He had lain on the string cot and listened to her talking and laughing with the native woman in the courtyard, and had thought, 'She will be safe if anyone is,' and had blessed the chance that had made her cousin to Ameera.

She had adopted a different attitude towards him during those few days at Pari, and he smiled in the darkness, thinking that no man could ever submit to having the things done for him that Winter had done, without losing some small part at least of his personal entity and independence to her. He knew that she was frightened for him in the same way as Lou was for the baby, and he knew, too, that neither of them had any fear at all for themselves, and therefore were not burdened, as the rest of them were, with the grinding necessity of hiding fear. Alex envied them that.

Even Mr Dobbie was afraid. He did not fear death, but owned to a horror of seeing others die by violence. 'It is the thought of having to see women and children killed that appals me,' Mr Dobbie had said, shuddering. 'I pray I may never have to witness that again. It is a terrible thing to see. One cannot forget it, however much one tries.'

Alex could not forget it either, and his stomach turned at the thought of what might yet be done to Winter and Lou. At what had been done to Alice Batterslea, and to the women whose unrecognizable corpses had strewn the grounds of the Residency at Lunjore. But he would not believe that it would come to that. He believed that Winter could not only save herself, but Lou as well. He had to believe it, and so he made himself believe it, and derived some comfort thereby. There was only one other spark of comfort to be found in the present situation, and that was that he was no longer responsible for their safety. The weight of that responsibility had been lifted from him at last, and he need no longer plan and contrive and lie awake worrying over problems connected with the feeding and protection of three women whose lives had largely depended upon him. He was as helpless now as they were – and as incapable of doing anything for them as the six other men who jolted along through the darkness in the second cart.

The thought of one of those men gave Alex a familiar twinge of anger. His dislike of Carlyon had been as instant and as instinctive as Carlyon's had been for him, but now he found himself unable to forget that he had once seen Winter in Carlyon's arms. The thought infuriated him; and the fact that it could do so at a time like this, when such purely personal considerations should surely seem insignificant and petty, exasperated him still further. Was there no escape from the emotional bonds that sex imposed upon mankind? It was ludicrous and humiliating at such a time, when they were all together in the same and sinking boat and none of them knew from day to day whether they would be unpleasantly dead before the next sun rose or set, that he should suffer tortures of jealousy because Carlyon had once kissed Winter. The fact that at the time he had done so, he, Alex, had actually considered that it would be a good thing if she were to marry Carlyon as an alternative to Conway Barton, did not occur to him.

He could not endure seeing Carlyon watch her by the hour. His own helpless and degrading weakness had not improved the situation or his temper, and he would have given anything to be back in the Hirren Minar, lying in the hot grass on the river bank setting fishing-lines while the three women washed clothes and cooking-pots in the twilight; though when he had been there he had fretted and agonized against the enforced inaction and had done nothing but think and plan how to get away.

Well, he had got away. They had all got away – even Lottie. And it occurred to him to wonder if, after all, Lottie might not be the only one to be envied.

* * *

The four days and nights that followed their departure from Pari were a horror that equalled anything that Winter and Lou had yet endured. The carts made slow progress, because the heavy rains had turned the roads into quagmires. The torrential downpour soaked through the inadequate covering and drenched the huddled occupants, and when the rain ceased the sun turned the hooded carts into a steam-bath in which the perspiration poured off them, soaking them afresh and less pleasantly, and the temperature rose until it became difficult to breathe.

They heard no news in those days, and did not know that on one of them the last survivors of the Cawnpore garrison had died, and with them, Sophie Abuthnot.

Little Sophie Abuthnot, as small and fair and fragile as Lottie had been, had survived both that ghastly siege in General Wheeler's pitifully inadequate entrenchments and the horrors of the massacre in the boats at the Sati Chauri Ghat, only to meet a more terrible fate. For the guns of the British advance could be heard at Cawnpore, and Nana Dundu Pant had heard in them the bitter knell of his hopes. All the evil fury and hate of which he was capable, and which Alex had seen in his face and heard in his voice in the vault beneath the ruins at Khanwai, had been let loose on the only victims that remained in his hands – the two hundred exhausted, hopeless, helpless women and children who were herded like animals in one small building, the *bibi-gurh*. He had listened to Havelock's guns and had given the order for their murder.

It had taken all day to kill them, for they had shrieked and dodged and twisted and striven to protect their children. But it had been done at last, and by nightfall the floor of the *bibi-gurh* was deep in blood and littered with the bodies of the dead and dying. When the new day dawned the butchers had dragged out the corpses and flung them into a well outside the house. Sophie had not been dead when they had thrown her down, but she had died under the weight of the dead. There had been several who were not yet dead, and one small child who was unharmed, and had lain all night, numb with terror, hiding under the corpses. The mob had laughed to see him run screaming round the well, and had caught him and swung his head against the stone work, and thrown him in. And half India shuddered in horror and drew back from the edge of the pit they had digged, for that massacre turned many men who would have fought the British to the bitter end to lay down their arms and return to their homes.

'There can be no blessing on such a deed,' said Ameera's husband Walayat Shah, who had hated the British and rejoiced at the news of the risings, and had himself taken part in attack after attack upon Sir Henry Lawrence's beleaguered garrison in the Lucknow Residency. But on the day that he heard the news of the murder of the women and children in the *bibi-gurh* at Cawnpore he had broken his sword in two and thrown away his musket, and come back to the Gulab Mahal and had not left it again.

'We cannot prevail,' said Walayat Shah. 'The *Jehad* is dead. Those who slew the women and the babes have slain it also. To slay in battle or in hot blood, that is well. And to kill men, if they be unbelievers, is to achieve Paradise. But to slaughter captive women who have suffered the harshness of war and sorrow, and been robbed thereby of all strength and will, is a deed to blacken the sun! I will fight no more against the *feringhis*, since God can no longer be upon our side.'

Alex had been taken from the cart in which the women travelled, at dawn on the first day. He had not come back, and presently the second cart had rumbled away. One of the escort told Winter surlily that he was to travel with the men, but she did not know if this were true or not, and when their own cart had started again, and without him, Mrs Hossack had given way to hysterics. 'Oh God,' screamed Mrs Hossack, 'they've killed him! They've killed them all! They never meant to send them with us. We're alone now – we're alone!'

Winter had felt the blood drain away from her heart. Was it true? Had they always meant to separate them – putting the men to death and allowing the women to live? Would she ever see Alex again? She had tried to force her way out and had been thrust roughly back again, and the cart had jolted forward on that long nightmare journey.

They were given little food and insufficient water, and Lou Cottar's face aged with every crawling hour. Mrs Hossack, cradling her small son, had wept and moaned with a hopeless and despairing monotony, and Miss Keir had suffered from bouts of sickness that added to the stench of the broiling, steaming cart. They had given the best of the food and almost all of the water to the two children, and Lou had made a paste of boiled rice and water and fed it to the baby with her finger-tip.

The scarcity of food had been bearable, but the lack of water in that terrible heat had been a torment that had only been partially relieved on the second day when Janet Keir began to shriek and rave and tear frantically at the side of the cart, and Winter had flown at the escort with a flood of words that she was not even aware that she knew. Daunted by this blazing-eyed virago who could curse them so efficiently in their own tongue, the men had produced at the next stopping-place not only water but milk; though little enough of either.

There had been no sign of the other cart again, and the terrible days had crawled past without their knowing whether the men were dead or not, or where they had gone. Winter nursed Lottie's baby when Lou fell at last into a brief exhausted sleep, and longed for the Hirren Minar as a lost soul might long for Paradise. But the Hirren Minar was only a scorched and blackened pile of stone standing gaunt and exposed among a waste of charred stumps and layers of sodden ash, and Lottie was dead and her grave lost among that desolation. And if this terrible journey lasted much longer

Lottie's baby would die too. Perhaps they would all die – perhaps Alex was already dead.

The sun was sinking again in a blaze of blood-red light that pierced through the chinks of the cart and its covering, but the darkness brought no relief. Winter's mouth was dry and her tongue swollen, her throat parched with thirst. Her head and her body ached with one vast throbbing ache that seemed to beat like a gong in her brain, and the heat was like an iron band about her neck, tightening slowly and inexorably so that soon she would not be able to breathe. The ugly scar that Alex's hunting knife had made on her arm burnt as though it were an open wound again, and the choking stench of the cart made her famished stomach cringe with nausea.

How many days had they been in the cart? How many times had the sun gone down? She could not remember. They had had no food that day, and they had been given water only once and in the early part of the morning. Even Mrs Hossack moaned no more, for her parched throat could produce no sound, and the children who had wailed weakly all day were silent. Miss Keir too had ceased to writhe and mutter and beg for water, and lay still at last. Was she dead? or was she only asleep like Lou – or was Lou dead too?

Winter became dimly aware that the cart was passing through crowded streets. Light and voices and noise pressed about it and somewhere guns were firing; guns and a ceaseless, distant crackle of musketry. There was a smell of cooked food. A pungent aromatic scent of *ghee* and dung-fires and *masala*; of roasting *chunna*, hot dust and decaying matter; of sandalwood and sewage and burning oil – the scent of an Indian bazaar.

The noises fell away and at last the cart stopped with a creaking jolt, and there were more voices. Rough voices, angry voices, shrill voices, whispering voices; and then the stout cloth that was bound over the end of the cart was unfastened, and the four dazed, semi-conscious women were dragged out to stumble and fall to the ground, their legs giving way under them.

There was a man with a drawn sword in his hand, shouting, and another man with a musket, and Winter thought numbly: 'They are going to kill us,' but it seemed a matter of supreme indifference. And then someone ran to her and lifted her, and the voices and the lights and the shouting men spun together in a circle and turned into darkness.

BOOK SIX

THE GULAB MAHAL

Winter awoke to find herself lying on a low bed in a strange room. It was still dark, but the greying sky beyond the window gave enough light to show the outline of the room.

She felt clean and cooler than she had felt for a very long time. It must have been raining again. She lifted her aching head with difficulty and saw the dark shape of an earthenware pitcher on the pale-coloured matting on the floor. The sight of it re-awoke her raging thirst and she groped for it, and lifting it drank, and drank again, as if she could never drink enough; and lay back and tried to think, and found that she could not . . .

She could think of nothing at all. A grey fog of utter hopelessness filled her mind, and she closed her eyes and lay still, feeling that greyness engulf her. Alex had gone – everything had gone. There was nothing to live for any more – not even Lottie.

The light brightened slowly, turning from the first pallid whisper of dawn to the clear glow that precedes the sunrise, and the silence gave place to familiar sounds; faint and few at first, but gathering in number and volume. A rustle and a twitter of birds and the hoarse cawing of a grey-headed plains crow. The chatter of a squirrel and the creak of a well-wheel. A conch blowing in a distant temple and a muezzin crying the call to prayer from the minaret of a mosque: '*Prayer is more than sleep – than sleep!*' Minas whistling and parrots talking, a ring-dove cooing softly and monotonously, and a distant murmur of voices.

The brightening light beat against her closed eyelids and the grey fog in her brain lifted and shredded away like mist drifting off the river in the early morning, and slowly and almost imperceptibly the pain in her heart lessened and peace took its place.

She felt but did not see the first dazzling rim of the sun lip the edge of the far horizon, but the glow behind her closed eyes brightened and she opened them on the same vision that she had seen once before when she had lain in the river by the Hirren Minar and had wished for death. The rose-pink sky and the formal patterns of leaves and flowers and birds. The vision that had once before drawn her back from despair, and the dream that had glowed before her mind's eye for so many cold years . . . the moon out of reach. But this time it was real. This was the Gulab Mahal——

She lay quite still, not stirring; barely breathing. Thinking confusedly that she was asleep – or dead. It could not be true. When at last she moved it was to stretch out a hand and touch the green parrot on the wall beside her.

Firishta – it was Firishta! The old, long-forgotten name from her childhood returned to her. So he was not a real bird after all. She had thought that they were real – the flowers and trees and birds who lived and moved against a rose-pink sky. They were not alive and they had never been alive. They were carved and moulded in painted and polished plaster. Why had she not remembered that? But it was still Firishta. And it was, incredibly, wonderfully, the Gulab Mahal.

She was safe at last. She had come home.

From somewhere in the distance there came the sound of gunfire, but she did not hear it. She rose and walked slowly about the room in a waking dream, running her hands over the dear familiar flower patterns, caressing the painted birds and beasts. She did not know that this was the room in which she had been born and in which Sabrina had died. She only knew that every foot of it was familiar and beloved. She saw the crescent-shaped shadow steal across the floor, and remembered it too, but did not fear it, as Sabrina had done, for it was linked with love.

She did not know how she had come there, or know that it was the Talukdar of Pari's determination to play safe that had been responsible. The Talukdar was a cautious man, and in the unlikely event of the British returning to power he did not wish it to be said that he had sent his captives to certain death. He must cover himself, and he remembered what his men had told him of the woman who was no *Angrezi* and who claimed kinship with the wife of Walayat Shah of Lucknow. He would send them to the care of Walayat Shah, and thus his hands would be clean. Walayat Shah might spare the woman if she were indeed blood-kin to his wife, and although he would undoubtedly hand over the remainder of the party to those who would make a public spectacle of their death, the woman at least would be able to testify that he, the Talukdar, had only acted for the best.

The heavy curtain over the doorway rustled and lifted, and Winter turned at the sound and saw that it was Ameera. They clung to each other and wept and did not speak for a long time, and then Ameera held her off at arm's length and looked at her.

'It is true then,' said Ameera. 'I thought it a dream. So thou hast come home at last – but in no auspicious hour. Dost thou know that I have spent the night upon my knees before my husband, begging for thy life and for the lives of those with thee? He would have turned all from the door, but Hamida was in the courtyard and she saw thee and ran to me. At first I did not believe; and then I knew that it could be no chance that brought thee here. This surely was written. For hadst thou come two days ago, or even one, I could not have saved thee. My husband was hot against thy people, and he hates them still and would rid himself of all whom the Talukdar of Pari sent hither. But because of the word that was brought from Cawnpore, he will hold his hand.'

So it was Sophie who had saved them – Sophie and all those women who had died in such fear and agony in the *bibi-gurh*. And if Sophie had known that the manner of her death would play a decisive part in saving Alex Randall's life, she would, being Sophie, have for her part been content to die.

For all the captives from Pari had arrived at the Gulab Mahal, though they had been brought for safety's sake by different roads. And all had been given shelter, because Walayat Shah, who had at first refused to take the responsibility of sheltering men whom he would gladly have seen dead, had listened to Ameera's pleading and remembered Cawnpore. He had had no thought of gaining from it, as the Talukdar had had. It did not occur to him that by giving them shelter he might claim immunity and reward from the Army that was known to have defeated the Nana Sahib's forces and retaken Cawnpore. He looked upon it, quite simply, as a penance laid upon him by God that he should risk his own life, and that of his sons and the whole household, in order to protect the lives of a weary handful of hated *feringhis*. He knew that if it should become known in the city that he was housing these people their lives, and probably his own, would not be worth a moment's purchase. Yet he took them in.

They were lodged in a secluded wing of the Rose Palace, adjoining the zenana quarters. Their rooms were hot and cramped, but the one on the ground floor, allotted to Lou, Mrs Hossack, Miss Keir and the two children gave onto a large private garden that was separated from the rest of the garden by a high wall, and was full of orange and loquat trees and a tangle of roses and jasmine. Six of the men shared a room immediately above it, and above that again, reached by a steep narrow stair, was an isolated square of roof, screened from the view of the zenana roofs by a wall and a pavilion that enclosed one end of it, where they had put Alex, who, as a sick man, it had been thought best to segregate from the others instead of having him share their cramped quarters. Walayat Shah having no desire to find all his unwelcome guests falling sick.

A split-cane *chik* hung over the open side of the little pavilion by day, and it was appallingly hot. But the gruelling heat of the day was compensated for by the coolness it afforded by night, and Alex lay there day after day on a narrow *charpoy*, listening by the hour to the firing as the siege of the Residency dragged on, and longing, as he had done in the first days at the Hirren Minar, to be gone – and for news.

Winter had been given Sabrina's room as by right, and she had begged that Lou might share it instead of being penned in the far smaller apartment on the ground floor with Mrs Hossack and Janet Keir. Three of the most trusted servants of the household had been put in charge of the *feringhis*, who had been given native dress to wear in place of their own ragged garments, and were not permitted to go even into the secluded garden except between sunset and dawn. They were kept in complete segregation from the other inhabitants of the Gulab Mahal, and they had little fault to find with this, since they lived in daily and hourly fear of discovery and death. They knew that it was not in Walayat Shah's power to protect them should their lives be demanded by the rebel leaders or the rabble of the bazaars, and they felt safer behind closed doors and in each others' company, despite the heat and the cramped quarters.

The continuous rattle of musketry, punctuated by the boom of guns, that all through the day and for a large part of every night came clearly to their ears, was both a continual reminder to them of the peril in which they stood, and that they were not the only British in Lucknow. They could hear the crash of exploding mines as the mutineers tunnelled towards the defences of the Residency and the stubborn beleaguered garrison ran out counter-mines and blew up their galleries; and whenever there was a lull in the firing they shuddered and waited and prayed for it to begin again, for fear that silence might mean that the Residency had fallen at last.

The garrison in the Residency had numbered barely a thousand combatant British and seven hundred loyal Indian troops when the crisis had arisen, and they were hampered by the presence of well over a thousand women, children and non-combatants, as well as by lack of adequate food, by sickness and appalling problems of sanitation and the disposal of the dead. The position they held had never been intended for purposes of defence. The hurriedly constructed and inadequate fortifications were flimsy in the extreme, and the forces surrounding it numbered twelve thousand fighting men, many of them British-trained sepoys, backed by the rabble of the city. It could not have withstood a single concerted assault that had been pressed home, but the mutineers possessed no leader of real ability. The attacks were never delivered in sufficient strength, and the siege dragged on.

Alex had made one unexpected friend in the Gulab Mahal. Dasim Ali, uncle of Wali Dad who had been Juanita's husband, and great-uncle of Ameera.

Dasim Ali, who had once admired the blonde Sabrina, was now an elderly gentleman whose beard was dyed scarlet with henna, and his shrewish wife Mumtaz was the senior lady of the pink palace. Mumtaz was as bitter against all *feringhis* as Walayat Shah, and disliked her husband's great-niece Ameera as much for her foreign blood as for her beauty. But Dasim Ali was a placid and pleasant person who harboured no bitterness towards anyone – except on occasions towards God, who had granted him no sons.

He had wandered up one evening to the roof-top where Alex lay, and had looked vaguely surprised at finding it tenanted by a sick man. He had not realized in the dusk that this was one of the *feringhis*, and would probably not have realized it even in the daylight. He had greeted Alex courteously, and when it had finally dawned upon him whom he was addressing, he had been pleased to be amused.

After that he paid frequent visits to Alex's roof-top, where they would play chess and discuss a multitude of subjects from a point of view that would not have occurred to the average Westerner. Dasim Ali would also bring Alex the news of the city and the progress of the siege, together with such scraps of news as trickled in from beyond the borders of Oudh.

Winter too made friends in the Gulab Mahal, and she was the only one who went freely to the women's quarters. Dressed in Ameera's clothes and wearing Ameera's jewels, with her blue-black hair in a heavy plait and her slim feet bare or in a pair of Ameera's flat, curl-toed slippers, she would have passed anywhere as an Indian woman of good family, or from the hills, where women's skins are fairer than they are in the hot plains. Even Dasim Ali's sour and shrewish wife ended by grudgingly accepting her presence, and had once even condescended to instruct her in the art of making a certain sticky sweetmeat of which the children of the Gulab Mahal were particularly fond.

Once again, after so many years, sitting on the zenana roof in the twilight, Winter heard the old familiar stories of her childhood told to those children, as Aziza Begum had once told them to her. And as she listened she heard too the ugly sound of gunfire from the beleaguered Residency, and was disturbed by conflicting emotions.

'Mrs Hossack says she wonders how I can endure to be friends with them, when their people are killing our people,' she confided to Alex, sitting on his roof-top one hot evening. She had carried up a strange brew made from herbs that Hamida had assured her was invaluable for those recovering from dysentery and fever, and having stood over him while he drank it under protest, had stayed talking to him in the twilight.

Mrs Hossack's observation had evidently worried her, for after an interval of silence she returned to it: 'It's not that I forget what is happening to my own people. I couldn't forget, even if I wanted to, while I can hear the firing and know that every time I hear it it may mean that someone in the Residency is dying. But – but that does not make any difference to the way I feel about Ameera and the others. Mrs Hossack says that it should. She hates them all. I know it is different for her. They – their people – killed her husband and one of her children, and two more died. But——'

She stopped, her brows puckered in a frown, unable to explain how it was that she could feel so friendly and at ease with these women while at the same time be tortured by hope and fear and a burning anxiety for all those of her own blood who were stubbornly defending themselves in the wreck of the Residency.

Alex said drily: 'It is considered a patriotic duty in time of war to hate every member of the nation one is fighting against, and we only remember the injunction to love our enemies and do good to those who hate us when those enemies are safely defeated.'

'But Mrs Hossack——' began Winter.

'Mrs Hossack, poor woman,' said Alex, 'will remember the death of her husband and children, and the cause of it, until the day she dies. What she will not remember is that thousands of the race who killed them have stood by us, and died for doing so. There are not only white people in the Residency, Winter. There are Indian troops too, and Indian servants, who could escape death and disease and starvation by deserting to their own people, but who are staying to help a handful of British to hold out, and who will be considered traitors to their own side and butchered without mercy if the Residency falls. There is no particular merit in fighting for your own skin when you know that it is fight or die, but there is considerable merit in being prepared to die when you know you can escape quite easily. Put at its lowest, there is a certain stubborn foolhardy heroism in that.'

Winter turned to look out over the trees and the roof-tops to the fantastic fretted silhouette of mosques and palaces, dark now against a darkening sky, and after a moment or two she said: 'What will happen in the end?'

'That depends on what you mean by the end.'

'When all this has ended. Will we hold it for always?'

'No,' said Alex, turning over on his back and looking up at a frieze of fruit bats flapping silently overhead on their way to the orchards and gardens of the villas that fringed the crowded city.

'Why? Why do you say that?'

Alex considered the question for a moment and then said reflectively: 'A hundred years ago this country was a collection of quarrelling, warring petty kingdoms, for ever at each other's throats. The Company – or Clive – put a stop to that, and we've been making a nation out of it ever since. We've done it in our own interests of course, because you can't mix profitable trading with continued uproar. But also because, as a nation, we cannot resist moving in and showing someone how to run his affairs when we see them being run damned badly. We regarded this country as being in a deplorable mess, and set out, fired by an entirely genuine and proselytizing zeal as much as the desire for profit, to put our neighbour's house in order and hand on what we consider to be the blessings of civilization. Which is why we have managed to combine conquest with a pleasant glow of self-righteousness. But once we have welded India into a more solid whole it will become increasingly difficult to hold on to it.'

'Is that a prophecy?' inquired Winter with a smile.

'No. It's common sense. It's too large a country. Bacon once wrote something to the effect that if a handful of people, with the greatest courage and policy in the world, grasped too large an extent of territory, it might hold for a time, but it would fail suddenly. He was right.'

'What about America?' demanded Winter.

'There weren't so many Americans in America,' said Alex lazily. 'All they'll have to do there is to exterminate the original owners or pen them up in smaller and smaller reservations. But India happened to be very well stocked with Indians.'

Winter got up and went to lean on the parapet, looking down on the garden below. The scent of dust and the sharp smell of wood-smoke rose through the hot, still air, and there were rockets going up into the darkening sky over the city, for it was the festival of Bakr Id. From somewhere in the zenana quarter a woman was singing to a sitar; the words clearly audible in the quiet evening – as clear as the crack of shots from the Residency . . .

'. . . *Wae nadani ki waqt-e-marg*
Yhi sabit hua
Khwab tha jo kuchh ki dekha jo
Suna afsani tha.'

Winter said: '*Nani* – Ameera's grandmother – used to sing that. "*Alas we were all ignorant and only at the time of our death was it proved that whatever we had seen was all a dream, and whatever we had heard was a short tale.*" It's a song that was sung long before Plassey was fought. This is such an old country——'

'No, it isn't,' said Alex. 'It's new. It's as new as – as Russia, if you like.'

Winter turned to smile at him in the dusk. 'Now you are just arguing for the sake of argument.'

'No, I'm not. Anything that has such tremendous possibilities and horizons is new. We are old. You can predict more or less what will happen to us. But you cannot predict what will happen to her. She has lain fallow for centuries – they still use the same methods of ploughing and irrigation that they used when we were wearing skins and living in caves. They've gone to seed. But seed if it's ploughed into the ground produces something new. Think of what they could do! We've started them off again – ploughed them in, if you like. They'll hate us for it, but they wouldn't have done anything for another hundred years or so if left to themselves. We've tried to go too quickly and force our way of life on them, but in a hundred years from now – or two hundred, or three – their history may show that Plassey wasn't an end or a defeat, but a beginning. Even this that is happening now was probably needed.'

Winter turned quickly from the parapet and came to stand at the foot of his bed. '*Needed*? Why, Alex? Why? You can't say that something as horrible and as cruel as this was needed! Mrs Hossack and that child of hers, and that child's grandchildren, will remember some of the things that have been done. And so will Ameera's children. They'll go on hating.'

'Perhaps,' said Alex. 'Though for ourselves we are poor haters and we have short memories. But I cannot believe that this revolt will not mean the end of the Company. I believe that the Crown will have to take over now, and if that happens it is going to mean an enormous stride forward as far as India is concerned. This may mean as much as Plassey. More!'

'And when we go?' asked Winter.

'When we go Hinduism will probably come into its own again, and if they aren't careful the country will drift back into an Eastern version of the Balkans – in which case Russia may well win the game after all! But one thing at least we can be certain of. All this that is happening now will not be regarded by them as a mutiny, but as a heroic War of Independence and Liberation. And because they are a young country they will deny their own atrocities and make political capital out of ours, and the truth – which is neither black nor white – will be lost. But I will have been dead a long time by then. And so will you! Here come the rest of the castaways. Unless it's old Dasim.'

There were footsteps and low voices on the narrow stairs that led up to the roof, and then Carlyon was there, scowling at the sight of Winter and Alex talking together, and Mr Dobbie and the others followed behind him, coming up to breathe the cooler air now that the light was fading.

Arthur Carlyon was a handsome man and the Mussulman garb he wore suited his tall, broad-shouldered figure. Alex lay and watched him as he stood by the parapet talking to Winter, their figures outlined sharply against a green sky in which the first stars floated palely, and disliked him with an intensity and thoroughness that he had not thought himself capable of. But Winter had lost her fear of Carlyon, and, if she had thought about it at all, had forgiven him.

What he had done, or tried to do, belonged to the shadowy past and was completely unimportant. They had all passed through too much, and a yawning, unbridgeable gulf seemed to divide them from the life they had led before the *Shaitan ka hawa* – the 'Devil's Wind' – had roared across India in the heat of May. Only the present was real; and even that possessed a dream-like unreality that was typified, thought Alex, by the two figures who stood against the darkening sky – an Eastern prince and princess; graceful, oriental, formalized. An illustration by a Persian court-painter to a story from the Arabian Nights – Prince Ahmed and the Fair Pari-Banou, who were, or had been, Baron Carlyon of Tetworth and Mrs Conway Barton.

Even Lou added no touch of reality to those days. The brittle, acid, fast-living, hard-drinking Mrs Josh Cottar of Lunjore had vanished without trace, and in her place was an anxious-eyed woman who looked ten or even twenty years older than that other Mrs Cottar, and who appeared to think of nothing but the welfare of a tiny, placid infant with a fuzz of red hair and round, solemn blue eyes.

'Lou,' said Alex crossly one evening, 'you are getting to be a dead bore over that baby. I have it on the best authority — O'Dwyer's – that she isn't smiling at you. It's wind.'

'Dr O'Dwyer doesn't know what he's talking about,' said Lou calmly. 'Of course she's smiling at me. She knows me.'

'So she ought to. You never leave the wretched child alone for five minutes. What is Josh going to say to this?'

'I don't know,' said Lou. And she might just as well have said 'I don't care'. 'There, Alex! – she *is* smiling.'

'Take it away,' said Alex irritably. 'It smells of sick. And so do you, Lou!'

He was abominably bad-tempered these days, and Winter put it down to the natural irritability of convalescence.

He had recovered to a reasonable extent, but he did not move from the pavilion on the roof, because the fever had an unpleasant habit of returning at unexpected intervals and he could not seem to get free of it. Also he preferred being left alone to being sent down to join the other men in a room on the lower floor. He considered that he saw quite enough of them as it was. They were allowed to come up to his roof on most evenings, since it was thought to be safer for them there than in the garden, and the women would usually join them for an hour or so.

There were only three women now – four, if one counted Lottie's daughter. Miss Keir had never recovered from that nightmare journey in the covered cart. Her mind had given way, and her health had already been seriously affected by the privations she had endured in the weeks before her arrival at Pari. She had lingered on for a few days and died one hot night within a week of their arrival at the Gulab Mahal, and Lou Cottar had moved down into Mrs Hossack's room in her place.

Lou had said that it was because Mrs Hossack was afraid of being alone, but Winter confided to Alex that she thought Lou had made the exchange because Mrs Hossack, as the mother of four, was a mine of information on the subject of babies, and could be relied upon to give helpful advice should any infantile crisis threaten Amanda.

Winter could not help feeling grateful for the exchange, though she had grown very fond of Lou and thought the baby a darling. But it was wonderful to have her room to herself again: her own room – Sabrina's room. To be able to sit there in peace and quiet. To talk to Ameera there, and to the other women and children who would visit her, without Lou, restless and uncomprehending, sitting silent while they talked and laughed. The nights too were doubly restful now that there was no baby to demand food and Lou's frequent and anxious attention.

'Lou of all people!' said Alex crossly. 'I should have said that she was as unmaternally minded as a goldfish, yet here she is, reduced to a state of crooning imbecility in a mere matter of weeks. I am beginning to think that I made a great mistake in assisting that infant to get born. It will be a lesson to me to mind my own business in future.'

He turned on his elbow to look at Winter, and said disagreeably: 'I don't see you making much fuss over the brat. Are you devoid of any maternal instincts, Mrs Barton?'

'No,' said Winter, giving the matter thought. 'But you see, it isn't my baby.'

'It isn't Lou's,' said Alex.

'Yes it is. Lottie gave it to her.'

'And I wonder,' said Alex unpleasantly, 'what Edward English's parents are going to say to that?'

It was a thought that frequently worried Lou. Supposing that Edward's parents demanded the child?

'They can't have her!' thought Lou. 'She's mine! They *couldn't* take her——'

She lay awake at night worrying about it, when she was not worrying about the child's health. Amanda's health need not have given her so much anxiety. The tiny creature throve and gained weight and ceased to wail and whimper. It was in fact a remarkably placid baby, and as babies go a very pretty one. Lou adored it.

'Has she been christened?' asked Mrs Hossack one day.

'*Christened*?' Lou looked up from bathing Amanda in a small metal basin. 'No, of course not. How could she be?'

'There's Mr Dobbie,' said Mrs Hossack. 'He's a clergyman so he could do it. She should be christened. It's safer.'

'Safer? What do you mean, *safer*?' demanded Lou impatiently.

'Supposing she should get ill, and die – you would not want her not to be saved,' said Mrs Hossack.

Lou had glared at her, clutching the child. 'She isn't going to die! What nonsense you talk, Ida!'

But the thought of having the child christened had taken possession of her. Not because she paid any attention to Mrs Hossack's lugubrious views, or that she believed that an unbaptized child would be refused admittance into Heaven. It was the thought of Edward English's parents that weighed with Lou. They might have their own ideas as to names. The child was going to be christened Amanda, and also Cottar. The surname of English would be hers by law.

Fired with this idea Lou had approached Mr Dobbie, who had instantly agreed to perform the ceremony. Lou had long ago cut up her petticoat and various other articles of underwear to make napkins and other necessities for the child, and now she made a christening robe from her pantalettes and saw nothing humorous in the action.

Amanda Cottar English was christened 'in the presence of this congregation' on Alex's roof in the late evening; Alex, Winter and Mrs Hossack standing as godparents. The ceremony brought a considerable portion of relief to Lou. It seemed to make Amanda more her own, and the claims of the misty and faraway Englishes – Lou was not aware that Edward had been orphaned for several years – faded and became less alarming.

But its repercussions were unexpected.

The fact that there was a clergyman available who was qualified to perform Holy Offices had dawned suddenly upon Lord Carlyon.

It was surprising that it had not done so before, for Mr Dobbie had held frequent services ever since their arrival. But it had not occurred to any of them that he could also officiate at other ceremonies of the Church. It did so now, and Carlyon had managed to get Winter to himself in the garden two evenings later.

It had rained heavily that day, but now the skies were clear and the garden smelt fresh and fragrant in the dusk. They had all gone out to walk under the orange trees because Alex had suffered a relapse and had been feverish all day, and Dr O'Dwyer had decreed that he must have quiet.

Moonlight had filled the garden with pale shadows before the last of the twilight had faded, and Carlyon had stood among the orange trees and once again asked Winter to marry him. Not at some future date when they could escape from this house and from Lucknow – if they should ever escape – but now, at once. Tonight or tomorrow. Dobbie could marry them . . .

'I haven't anything to offer you now. I'm just a penniless prisoner. But when we get away it will be different. Then I can——'

Winter put a hand on his arm, checking him. 'Don't! please don't.' Her voice was quick and distressed and her face in the soft moonlight was troubled. 'If – if I loved you it wouldn't matter if you could never give me anything but yourself. But I don't, and so I cannot marry you.'

'Why? Why not? You need someone to look after you; to protect you. I would take care of you. I love you – I can't live without you! What does it matter whether you love me now or not? You would one day. I could make you. Barton is dead. Give me the right to take care of you. Winter – Winter——'

He had caught her hand, and she drew back quickly: 'I am sorry. I cannot. Thank you for – for wanting to, but——' She seemed to think the words were inadequate, and stood before him twisting her hands together as though she were trying to think of something less hollowly polite and baldly negative. But the moonlight showed him that there was a sudden abstracted look in the wide, black-lashed eyes, and he was seized with an angry and wounding conviction that she was not thinking of him at all, but of something or someone else.

He reached out and caught her hand again, gripping it by the wrist in a hard grasp that she could not break, and said hoarsely: 'Is there anyone else? Is that why you won't marry me? It was Barton before – who is it now? Is it Randall? I've seen the way you look at him sometimes. You were in the jungle with him for weeks, weren't you.'

His rage boiled up until it seemed that it must choke him. Some part of his brain, standing coldly aloof – some part of the bored and cynical Arthur Carlyon of the London drawing-rooms – told him that he was making a vulgar, jealous and melodramatic scene; but he could not stop himself:

'It is Randall, isn't it? What is he to you? Are you his mistress? Do you spend your nights with him on that roof? Is that why you persuaded your black relatives to let him sleep up there instead of with us?'

He saw the shadowy reflection of a succession of emotions cross the face that the strengthening moonlight threw into sharp relief against the darkness of the orange trees: disgust, anger, contempt, and finally – and surprisingly – pity. As though she could understand the cruel pain that was responsible for that torrent of insult, and could sympathize with it. She stood quite still, waiting for him to finish, her eyes grave and steady. But it was the pity in them that hurt most and which drove him to the final stupidity.

He released her wrist and caught her swiftly into his arms as he had done once before in Delhi, and kissed her with angry violence. Kissed her mouth and eyes and throat again and again and as though he could not stop.

She had not struggled or cried out. Perhaps she had known that it would have done little good to do either. She had stood entirely still, enduring his bruising kisses as though she had been a lay figure without life or emotion, and her very immobility had brought him to his senses as nothing else could have done. He released her at last and stood back from her, breathing in hard gasps. She had not spoken, and after a moment she had turned and walked unhurriedly away between the orange trees of the walled garden, her pale-coloured Indian dress showing like a moth among the shadows, and the Indian jewellery she wore making a soft chinking sound that died away into the dusk.

Mrs Hossack, who was walking up and down with her small son in her arms, said: 'Mrs Barton, I wanted to ask you if——' But Winter had passed her without hearing her and had gone into the house and up the long narrow flight of stairs. She drew the muslin veil over her head and across her face as Ameera and the other women did on the rare occasions on which they moved outside the women's quarters, and passed along a narrow enclosed verandah and up the final flight of stairs that led to the roof where Alex lay.

The moonlight and the last touch of twilight made the open roof seem very bright after the dark passages and stairways, and the rain had cooled it so that it smelt pleasantly of washed stone.

Alex's bed had been dragged out into the open, presumably by Dr O'Dwyer. He was lying on it with his back to her, wearing only the scanty cotton loin-cloth that alone made the heat of the day bearable, and his body looked painfully thin and very brown against the pale-coloured *resai* that did duty as a mattress. He heard the chink of Winter's jewellery but he did not turn, and she came to stand beside him, looking down at him and wondering if he were asleep. After a moment or two, as she did not speak, he said ungraciously: 'Well, what is it?'

The irritation in his voice gave her a sudden qualm, and for a moment her resolution faltered. Her hands gripped together tightly and she took a deep breath and forced herself to speak calmly:

'Alex, will you marry me?'

Alex did not move for an appreciable time, and then he turned slowly and looked up at her. It seemed to him that there was a tight band made of some hot metal round his forehead, and he could not think at all clearly.

'What did you say?'

'I asked you if you would marry me,' said Winter steadily.

'Why?'

She sat down on the edge of the low bed and as she did so the muslin veil slipped back and off her shoulders, and the clear moonlight showed red marks on her throat. The hand she raised to catch at the veil was bruised too about the wrist with the plain prints of the brutal grip that had held it.

Alex reached out and caught her hand, holding it with thin hot fingers, and looked at those marks; and Winter, noticing them for the first time, jerked it quickly away.

Alex said thickly: 'Carlyon?'

'Yes. No. I mean – it doesn't matter.'

He sat up and found that it tightened the band about his head by several notches. It should surely be impossible to feel so ill and so angry at one and the same time? Separately perhaps, but not together. He said: 'Yes, I'll marry you. And what's more, I'll do it now. Go and tell Dobbie I want to see him. And wait a minute – give me some of that opium——'

Winter never knew what he had said to Mr Dobbie, but whatever it was it appeared to have persuaded Mr Dobbie to accede to the unexpected request for an immediate marriage. Lou knew, because Lou had come in search of Winter and had heard a murmur of voices from the roof. She had almost reached the top of the stairs when she had heard Alex say: 'Very well, then, I'll have her without. And you can take that on your conscience! It won't be on mine.'

Lou had turned round and come down again, looking thoughtful.

Winter had been married at night and by moonlight, as Sabrina had been. And like Sabrina, with no preparation at all and in a wedding-dress that did not even belong to her.

She would have worn Ameera's scarlet and gold wedding-dress with its wonderful fringed and tasselled head-veil, but out of deference to the doubtful and anxious Mr Dobbie she had worn instead a dress of heavy white silk, yellowed by the years and scented with the *neem* leaves and tobacco in which it had been kept, that had belonged to Ameera's mother, Juanita de Ballesteros.

There had been a lace mantilla too; once white but now as yellow as the silk and as fragile as the lace on the wedding-dress that had been Anne Marie's and which Sabrina had worn when she married Juanita's brother, Marcos, in the chapel of the Casa de los Pavos Reales twenty years ago. It had in fact been the self-same mantilla that her mother had worn on that night, though Winter did not know it.

The moon that looked down on that strange wedding looked down also on the ruined, looted, burned-out shell of the Casa de los Pavos Reales and the blackened, grass-grown paving stones of the terrace where Marcos and Sabrina had stood together on that other moonlight night to watch their guests ride away. But the scent of the orange-blossom and the lemon trees remained, and was as sweet on the hot air as it had been on that long-ago night.

The scent of orange-blossom rose too from the walled gardens of the Rose Palace, and reached the flat roof-top where Winter stood in Juanita's white dress and felt Alex's parched, fever-hot fingers push a heavy ring of beaten gold and silver onto the finger that had once worn Kishan Prasad's glowing emerald. The ring too had been one of Juanita's, a gift from her mother Anne Marie, for none of the Europeans had possessed such a thing – any trinkets they might have had having been either taken from them or parted with in exchange for food long ago.

Alex had worn Mussulman dress, borrowed for the occasion from Dasim Ali, and had only managed to keep on his feet with the assistance of opium and one of the pillars that divided his room from the roof. He had stood with his back to it, and had looked so entirely un-English in the moonlight that poor, worried Mr Dobbie had suffered yet another qualm.

Up to now it had been young Mrs Barton who had always seemed to Mr Dobbie to look like an Indian. He had never seen her wear anything but Indian dress, and he had never quite followed the intricacies of her relationship with the Indian woman – or women – in the Gulab Mahal. But tonight, wearing the long full-skirted stiff silk dress with its old-fashioned neck- and sleeve-line, her black hair drawn back and rolled in a heavy chignon at the back of her small head and the folds of the lace mantilla falling demurely about her, she looked like any young lady arriving to be married in one of the more fashionable London churches, and it seemed entirely wrong, thought Mr Dobbie unhappily, that he should be marrying her to a Mohammedan.

But to Winter there had been nothing strange about this wedding. It was the fulfilment of the promise that the Gulab Mahal had always stood for – that old Aziza Begum had given to her and Zobeida reaffirmed so often – that once she returned to it, all would be well.

She stood in the warm white moonlight and looked down at a ring that had once been Anne Marie's as once, long ago and on just such a night, Sabrina too had done. And like Sabrina she was suddenly aware of an uplifting sense of timelessness – as if all Time were one, and she would live for ever in the future in Alex's children and hers, as she lived in the past with Marcos and Sabrina; with Johnny and Louisa . . .

But her wedding had not ended peacefully as Sabrina's had done.

They had all been gathered there on the roof, their shadows black in the moonlight, and the fantastic skyline of the Lucknow palaces like a purple pattern at their backs: Lou Cottar and Mrs Hossack, Captain Garrowby, Dr O'Dwyer, Mr Climpson, Mr Lapeuta and Lord Carlyon. Even Ameera and Hamida had been there, standing in the darkness behind the lowered *chiks* that screened the interior of the pavilion from the roof, in deference to the fact that Ameera was in *purdah* and could not be seen by strange men.

The guests had come forward to offer congratulations and good wishes at the end of the brief ceremony, and Carlyon had confronted Winter and said in a deliberate drawl: 'Am I permitted the privilege of kissing the bride?'

Alex said: 'Not in future,' and hit him.

It had been luck more than strength or science, and rage more than luck, that had caused the blow to send Carlyon sprawling, for although Alex had recovered a good deal of his strength, the fever had once again drained an appreciable amount of it from him during the past twenty-four hours.

Carlyon had come to his feet, white with fury, and had returned the blow with a good deal more science and considerably more strength before the remainder of the wedding guests had rushed in to separate them. Alex had been unable to defend himself, because the well-meaning Mr Dobbie had leapt at him, catching his arm, and Winter had turned and clung to the other. Carlyon's clenched fist had taken him under the jaw and he had fallen between them as though he had been pole-axed, hitting the back of his head on an angle of the pillar as he fell, and had not recovered consciousness for some considerable time.

'*Men* !' said Lou furiously. 'As if we were not in enough trouble already! Now they'll try and kill each other as soon as they get the chance. You'd think there was enough fighting going on without—— Oh God! *Men* !'

Winter spent her second wedding night, as she had spent her first, in tears and terror. But this time it was on her bridegroom's behalf and not on her own.

Alex's own recollections of the night were hazy. His head hurt abominably, his jaw ached, his body burned with fever and his parched mouth was full of blood from a cut that his teeth had made in his tongue. Somebody periodically gave him water to drink and persuaded him to spit out the blood instead of swallowing it, and someone else – or the same person – put a pleasantly cool and aromatic-smelling compress on his forehead and changed it at intervals.

The fever had lessened towards morning, and he had fallen asleep at last and had not wakened until the sun was hot on the roof. And then it had been Lou who had been standing by one of the pillars in the pavilion, peering through the slats of the *chik* and listening to the crackle of rifle-fire and the boom of guns that had been silent during the past night but had begun again with the dawn.

She had turned when she heard Alex move, and said anxiously: 'It sounds like a big attack. Listen to that! Are they *never* going to be relieved? We were told that tale about Havelock taking Cawnpore days and days ago, and Cawnpore is less than forty miles away. *Why* aren't they here?'

Alex dragged himself up and went to stand beside her. They could see the smoke from the cannonade hanging like a haze above the roofs and the treetops that hid the Residency, and he listened, as Lou had listened, and presently said: 'How long have we been here? Three weeks? or is it four? It feels like months, and it must feel like years to them. Havelock *must* get through soon. Oh God, if only one could——'

He turned away with a groan, and subsiding again on the edge of the low *charpoy*, closed his eyes and leant his aching head against the wall behind it. After a minute or two he opened them again and frowned at Mrs Cottar:

'What are you doing here at this time of the morning, Lou? Got a sudden fit of the bore with that baby at last?'

'No,' said Lou. 'I promised your wife that if she'd go to sleep I'd see that you were all right.'

'My——?' said Alex, and stopped. 'Good God! Of course. Then I didn't dream the whole thing. I seem to remember hitting that bastard Carlyon—— Sorry, Lou, I apologize.'

'He hit you a good deal harder,' said Lou with a grin.

'Did he?' Alex put up a hand and felt his bruised and swollen jaw tenderly. 'Hmm. He must have done. I don't seem to remember that. I thought something hit me on the back of the head.'

'It did. This pillar.'

Alex lowered himself cautiously back onto the folded *resai* and said: 'That accounts for it. I feel as though I'd been run into by a siege gun. What happened to – my wife?'

'I rather think she spent the night bathing your fevered brow,' said Lou. 'She doesn't seem to have much luck with her bridegrooms. Conway was filthy drunk.'

She saw the sudden black scowl that replaced the frown of pain on Alex's forehead, and said abruptly: 'You brought her out to him, didn't you? What possessed you to let her marry him? *You* knew what he was like.'

Alex said: 'Shut up, Lou. If you want to play at being Miss Nightingale you can give me some water. If you want to talk you can go away.'

Lou brought him food and water and prepared to depart, but with her hand on the *chik* she stopped and turned back.

'Alex——'

'What is it now?' demanded Alex ungraciously.

'Lord Carlyon——' Lou hesitated and bit her lip.

'What about him?'

'You won't—— Alex, we're all in the same boat. You know as well as I do that someone may give us away any day, and then – and then it will be all over with us. We've got to stay together, and that man has got a bad temper and not much control over it.'

'I don't seem to have had much control over mine lately,' said Alex wryly.

'I know. But that's different. You wouldn't do anything that might jeopardize all of us just because you were in a rage. But he would. You don't know what a lot of nonsense he's been talking. About escaping from here.'

Alex turned his head and looked at her oddly, and she met the look and said with a twisted smile: 'Oh yes – I know you've thought of it too. We've all thought of it, if it comes to that. But we – the rest of us – have enough sense to see when we are well off and not do anything stupid. And we know that we don't need to escape. That we may be kept cooped up in two small rooms all day, but that it isn't to keep us prisoners. It's to keep us safe – and everyone else who lives in this house, for that matter! If we really wanted to go away, they'd be thankful to be rid of us. But Lord Carlyon won't believe that, and he doesn't understand more than half a dozen words of Hindustani. If he once got out of this place he'd be caught before he'd gone a hundred yards, and that might give us all away. So you see——'

Lou jerked restlessly at the edge of the *chik* and turned away to peer through it again, her back to Alex. He did not speak, and presently she said: 'He has only stayed quiet because of Winter. Because he's in love with her, and because we've told him – all of us – that it was safer for us to stay here than to take our chance outside; and safest of all for her because the Begum is her cousin. And he wouldn't leave unless he could take her with him. He asked her last night to marry him – did you know that? And then inside an hour she marries you instead, and he has to watch. And then you knock him down!'

Alex still said nothing and Lou turned and faced him, her eyes desperate. 'Alex, *please*! Don't quarrel with him. Keep out of his way. Don't goad him into doing anything that may jeopardize all of us. Promise me you'll leave him alone?'

Alex said: 'Provided he leaves my wife alone.'

'Of course he will, now. But you can't expect him not to speak to her, and if you're going to hit him every time he does——'

'My dear Lou,' interrupted Alex irritably, 'at the moment I couldn't successfully hit a fly. No, of course I will not start another brawl! I must have taken leave of my senses to start one last night. But if you imagine that I am going to apologize to the man, you are wrong. Get on back to your baby, there's a good girl. My head is splitting and I can see six of you. And just at present one is more than enough.'

Lou had gone and Alex had lain on his back all through the gruelling heat of the day, and had thought as coherently as the pain in his head and desperate anxiety over the fate of the Residency garrison would permit.

Lou did not realize that there were only two things that had kept him from leaving the Gulab Mahal as soon as he was capable of walking, and they were neither of them what she had supposed. The first was the fact that a sick man was a liability and not an asset, and until he could rid himself of this damnably recurrent fever, and the weakness that went with it, it was infinitely more sensible to stay where he was, since he was of little use to anyone in this condition. The second was Carlyon. Carlyon and Winter. Winter was safe enough (or as safe as she would be anywhere at this time) with the occupants of the Gulab Mahal. But she was not safe from Carlyon.

He realized the sense of Lou's request, for they were none of them safe with Carlyon. Carlyon had an ugly and unpredictable temper and was altogether too autocratic and egotistical a person to be relied upon to exercise patience and play a waiting game. He was also frightened, and that made him even less reliable. They were all frightened. Alex himself had woken more than once in a sweat of fear at the sound of a party of shouting roisterers passing on the far side of the high wall which enclosed the Gulab Mahal, imagining that they were a band of mutineers come to batter down the gates and demand that the *feringhis* should be given up to them. But neither he nor any of the others doubted that the inmates of the Gulab Mahal would keep them hidden; for their own sakes as much as to save the lives of their unwelcome guests, though there was always the danger of some servant betraying them for money or spite, or of the news leaking out through carelessness.

But Carlyon did not believe that. He knew little or nothing of India, and the little he knew had taught him to believe that all Indians were treacherous murderers, not one of whom was to be trusted. He refused to admit that the inmates of the Gulab Mahal were restricting his liberty, and that of the other Europeans in hiding, in order to save their lives. They were being kept prisoner, and would one day be handed over to provide a spectacle for the mob. Had not the fifty luckless captives in the dungeons of the King of Delhi – almost all of whom were women and children – been taken out and publicly slaughtered before a milling mass of spectators?

Carlyon had urged that they should attack the servants who cared for their needs, overpower the adult males in the house, seize any weapons they could find in the house, and thus provided with arms, money and food, escape to Cawnpore where Havelock and his army were known to be encamped. It was no great distance; less than forty miles. He had formulated other schemes, equally rash and impracticable, but had been persuaded that any such attempts must expose the women and the two children to too great a risk; and he would not escape alone and leave Winter. And now Winter, to escape him, had married Alex Randall.

She must have been very frightened of Carlyon to have taken such a drastic step, thought Alex, staring up at the flaking plaster of the ceiling while the heat danced upon the open roof outside. What had he done to her? Tried to rape her? Alex felt rage rise in him again at the thought and turned over and buried his face in his arms.

Lou was right. He must keep from quarrelling with the man. He had kept from doing it when they were in Delhi, and he could keep from doing it now. 'All in the same boat,' Lou had said. It was a leaky craft at best, and if two of its occupants started fighting in it they might well overturn it. As for Winter, now that she was his wife his name should be enough to protect her from any further insults from Carlyon. But he himself would have to continue to keep her at arm's length or they would be lost.

The fact that she was now his wife made no difference to that particular situation. It merely made it more difficult. They might be here, or on the run again, for months – perhaps a year. Or more than a year. The garbled stories and rumours that Dasim Ali brought him were always more of successful risings than of defeats, and it was difficult to gain any clear picture of what actually was happening in the outside world. If the whole of India was really in revolt it was going to take more than a few months of campaigning to reconquer it and restore order. Months, thought Alex, perhaps a year – perhaps longer . . . And he thought again of Lottie.

He could not forget Lottie. That appalling, agonizing day had burnt itself into his brain. Nature did not stand still for wars. Lottie's baby had not delayed its arrival because of murder and massacre; they had merely hastened it. It had had to be born, and prematurely at that. And in the process it had killed Lottie far more painfully than any shot fired from a carbine, or any stroke from a sword.

Had Alex kept away that day, and kept out of earshot as he had meant to do, leaving her to the women, he might have felt differently about it even though he would have returned to find her dead. Women did die in childbirth, too many of them. It was regrettable, but nothing – or very little it seemed – could be done about it.

But he had not kept away. He had stayed with Lottie instead, and he could not forget the torment she had endured before she died, or the fact that with proper medical care and attention, doctors, midwives, all the paraphernalia of modern medicine, she would probably have survived. But this was war. It was worse – civil war, rebellion, anarchy. There could be no safety anywhere for any woman in the country until it was over. He could not run the risk of watching Winter die as Lottie had died, and for the first time he was grateful for the ill-health that would provide him with an excuse to keep her at arm's length.

The gunfire had continued for the greater part of the day with a fury that told of a large-scale attack upon the Residency, and an hour before noon the thunderous explosion of a mine shook the Gulab Mahal and disturbed the birds who were sheltering from the heat in the trees of the garden, sending them flapping and cawing up into the hot air.

Alex could hear the boom of the guns and the crash of the shells with shuddering clarity, and the shimmering heat of the roof-top seemed to vibrate to the sound and strike at his body with the same savage regularity as the sound itself struck through his throbbing head.

Was it just another attack on the Residency – or was it Havelock at last? But it could not be Havelock. The city would have been in an uproar and there would have been fighting in the streets if the relieving force had arrived. This that he could hear was still fire that was being directed at and returned by the Residency . . .

'If only I could get away!' thought Alex. 'If only I could get news! How much longer can they hold out? How many of them are there left?' It was unbearable to lie there and listen to those sounds, knowing what they meant; knowing what it must be like inside the battered and beleaguered Residency; and to do nothing – nothing!

He had been brought a nauseous draught in the course of the afternoon by Rahim, the elderly, silent servant who looked after him. The Begum Sahiba had prepared it, said Rahim. Alex drank it to save argument, and it had relieved the pain in his head and eventually sent him to sleep. And so, for him, the day that marked the second serious assault on the Residency passed. And the flimsy defences still held.

But the hope of relief that the hard-pressed garrison had once expected hourly was receding. Havelock's army, which had crossed the border into Oudh in the last days of July and had subsequently fought and won two battles, had suffered heavy losses in the fighting, and finding their communications threatened by the Nana Sahib's forces, had fallen back on Mangalwar to wait for reinforcements. Twice in early August Havelock had advanced again towards Lucknow, only to be checked: the first time by an outbreak of cholera, and later by the mutiny of the Gwalior Contingent which had compelled him to secure his base and fall back on Cawnpore.

The news that the *feringhi* army was in retreat was received with wild rejoicings in Lucknow, and the position of the beleaguered garrison – and also of the handful of refugees in the Gulab Mahal – grew even more precarious. Many of the insurgents and a large proportion of the populace who had been daunted by the realization that an avenging army was almost within striking distance of the city, swung back to the wildest heights of optimism when it was learned that the enemy had not only been forced to retreat, but were no longer within the borders of Oudh.

The sound of desultory firing from the direction of the Residency became an integral part of life in the Gulab Mahal: as familiar as the cawing of the grey-headed crows, the liquid cooing of the doves or the creak and squeak of the well-wheel. It was, to the fugitives, a comforting sound, since it told them that the garrison was still holding out and that the Residency had not fallen . . .

There had been a third assault on the eighteenth of August (Alex had

worked out the date and scratched it with a nail on the wall of the pavilion) and they had waited, all of them, with a tension that seemed to make it difficult to breathe, for the sound of musketry-fire to start again after the silence that had followed the din of the assault. And hearing it they had felt their nerves and muscles go slack with relief, and had breathed as though escaping from near suffocation. Three days later they had heard the thunderous crash of exploding gunpowder, and Dasim Ali had told Alex that evening that it was the work of the garrison, who had at last succeeded in blowing up Johannes House, a stronghold of the mutineers beyond the perimeter of the defence, from which a deadly crossfire had been directed upon the Residency.

But the next day there had been another sound. The sound of gunfire from the south-east.

'By God – they're here!' cried Alex, running to the parapet of the roof in the drumming, drenching downpour of the monsoon rains and straining to listen while the water poured off him in a warm torrent.

It could only mean one thing: Havelock was marching on Lucknow again. And presently, as the downpour ceased and a hot wind began to blow, the sound of those guns came clearly through the humid, clean-washed air.

They had heard them at intervals all that day and for much of the following one, and it occurred to Walayat Shah for the first time that perhaps God had been at his side when he had agreed to shelter those bedraggled fugitives for the sake of the dead of Cawnpore, and that perhaps, because of it, he and his household would one day be saved from destruction. It was not a thought that pleased him, for had it not been for his horror of the treachery and the butchery of Cawnpore, he would have preferred to die fighting the *feringhis* rather than to accept any favour from their hands.

But they had heard Havelock's guns no more; nor any news of what had happened to his army. And August dragged out its slow length, and it was September. And still the dwindling, dying, fever-racked garrison in the Lucknow Residency held out, and still the torn rags of the Union Jack fluttered defiantly from the flagstaff that had been shot down and replaced so often, and at the cost of so many lives, on the topmost roof of the shattered Residency.

49

It seemed to the fugitives in the Gulab Mahal that they had lived in their hot, cramped quarters in the little pink stucco palace in Lucknow for a lifetime.

Day succeeded day with an appalling, crawling monotony, and nerves grew ragged and tempers flared. It needed very little to touch off a furious quarrel and an exchange of blows between the six men who passed the greater part of their time shut in together in one small hot room, where the floor space was largely taken up by the cheap string cots on which they sat or lay for most of the day-time, and on which they slept at night.

The lack of news from the outside world was the worst affliction they suffered. The heat was endurable because of the frequent downpours that roared off the roofs and gutters and drenched the gardens, cooling the hot stone and turning the dust to liquid mud where frogs croaked and winged ants hatched out in drove after fluttering, crawling drove.

The food was scanty, since there was little money to spare for the feeding of a band of Hell-doomed infidels, but it was enough, and the sanitary arrangements, though primitive, were adequate. Compared with thousands of their fellow-countrymen, they were living in comfort and safety. But not to know what was happening to the garrison in the Residency, to Havelock's forces, to the regiments on the Ridge before Delhi, to the rest of India and the Empire of 'John Company', made the long days longer and frayed their nerves to breaking-point.

They had discussed, endlessly, the possibility of escaping from Lucknow and trying to make contact with the relieving army, and one night three of them, Captain Garrowby, Dr O'Dwyer and Mr Climpson, had climbed out of the enclosed garden, scaled the outer wall by standing on each other's shoulders, and vanished into the maw of the city.

They had told their plan to no one, for they realized that a small party stood a better chance of escape than a large one, and they considered that Lapeuta and Dobbie, both elderly and frail, were better off where they were, while Alex was not only still subject to occasional bouts of fever, but naturally could not be asked to abandon his wife and leave her behind in a city that might well soon be taken by assault. As for Carlyon, they had had no intention of saddling themselves with a man who had done nothing to endear himself to any of them, and whose ignorance of the language and the country, combined with his uncertain temper, would make his company a hazard to all of them. They had therefore kept him in ignorance of their plans and had only, late in the evening, told Mr Lapeuta in order that their disappearance

might not panic the remaining fugitives into thinking that they had been done away with by any of the inmates of the Gulab Mahal.

Carlyon had stormed and raged when he had awoken the next morning to find that they had gone, for he realized it might mean weeks if not months more of this enforced confinement for himself. He knew that he could not get far alone, for apart from not being able to speak one word of Hindustani, he had no knowledge of the city or the country surrounding it, or even in which direction to go in order to reach the British force.

Lou and Mrs Hossack had been white with anxiety, Walayat Shah relieved, and Alex restless and either silent or curt to the point of rudeness.

But Captain Garrowby, Dr O'Dwyer and Mr Climpson had not gone far. They had kept together instead of taking the wiser course of separating, and they had lost their way in the maze of streets, so that dawn had found them still in the city. They had been stopped and questioned, and that afternoon they had been shot, and their bodies hung up by the heels for an encouragement to the mob.

Dasim Ali had brought Alex the news on the following evening. The men, he said, had been tortured first to make them tell where they had been hiding, because the state of their garments and their shoes suggested that they must have been sheltering in the city itself, and had not, as they claimed, reached it only that night. Moreover they had been captured trying to leave Lucknow and not to enter it.

They had died without divulging their hiding-place, but Dasim Ali's wife Mumtaz, and others of the Gulab Mahal, had been frightened and angry, and immediate precautions had been taken to see that none of the remaining *feringhis* jeopardized them by escaping. That the three men had not betrayed them under torture did not mean that one of the others might prove less courageous if caught and subjected to similar treatment, and any more *feringhis* found in the city might lead to a house-to-house search. The doors were locked now at night and the gardens patrolled, and what little liberty the fugitives had previously possessed was drastically curtailed.

To Lou and Mrs Hossack, made selfish by fear for the safety and well-being of two small children, the loss of Dr O'Dwyer meant more than the fact that all three men had been caught and killed. Privately, they considered it thoughtless in the extreme of Dr O'Dwyer to have even contemplated leaving: he should have thought of them first. They had no confidence whatsoever in the herbal brews and remedies of the native women in the Gulab Mahal; which was hardly surprising, for many of the medicines prescribed for illness were of a wildly improbable and entirely useless character; such as verses of the Koran written on scraps of paper in cheap bazaar ink and boiled in water – the water then being considered a sovereign specific for every form of illness. But Dr O'Dwyer had been a tower of strength when colic or convulsions or any other infant ailments had threatened Jimmy Hossack or Amanda Cottar English, and now that he had gone their anxieties were doubled.

Neither Lou nor Mrs Hossack would, at that time, have escaped from the Gulab Mahal if they could, and the death of the three men who had done so had only served to convince them that their greatest safety lay in staying where they were. But they hated the small, hot airless room that became an oven when the sun shone and grew damp patches of mould on the walls when the rains fell. They hated the invading armies of creeping, hopping or flying creatures which came in under the ill-fitting door or through the fretted stone that filled the narrow windows, and which could not be kept out. They hated the native dress they wore and the native food they ate, the monotony and the confinement. They quarrelled with regrettable frequency and got on each other's nerves to the point of desperation, and complained about each other to Winter.

Winter herself was far from happy in those days. She might never have been married to Alex, and she was often tempted to wonder if that brief ceremony on the moonlit roof had ever taken place, or if she had only dreamt it.

She still slept and spent the greater part of each day in her own gaily painted room, and Alex still lived in the little pavilion on the roof. She saw as little of him, or less, in these days, as she had when they had first come to the Gulab Mahal. His manner to her was much as it had always been, and he did not appear to think that the fact that she was now his wife necessitated any change in the monotonous routine of their days.

She wondered sometimes if she had been mistaken in thinking that Alex cared for her. Had he after all only thought of her as he had thought of that auburn-haired actress whom he had taken home one night from a party at the Lunjore Residency? Would he ever have married her if she had not made him? He had never made any attempt to touch her or kiss her since the night that he had kissed her at the edge of the river when they had fled from the fire, and she had been sure that he loved her. Had he only kissed her then from relief – because they were safe? The same relief that had made them all laugh together helplessly a moment later, despite the fact that they had been driven from the safe refuge of the Hirren Minar and were stranded in a strange jungle and within the hostile borders of Oudh?

Alex had recovered much of his former health, and the maddeningly recurrent bouts of fever left him at last. He was still painfully thin, but his skin no longer had that underlying and frightening tone of greyness, and his hair was crisp again instead of lying dull and lack-lustre. But Winter could not forget that he had been ill with fever on the night that she had asked him to marry her, or that he had been drugged with both fever and opium when he had actually done so. If he had been in full possession of his faculties, would he have consented to marry her? She began to wonder why he had ever agreed to do so, and if he had really not known what he was doing, and had subsequently regretted it.

It did not occur to her that Alex imagined that she had been frightened by Carlyon, and by some attack that Carlyon had made upon her, into taking the extreme step of asking him to marry her, for Carlyon's savage kisses had not frightened her in the least, and she had forgotten them long before the bruises they had left had faded. It had been Carlyon's disclosure that Mr Dobbie was as qualified to perform a marriage service as a christening that had sent her straight to Alex, and it is doubtful if anyone or anything could have frightened her to the point of doing such a thing. To ask a man to marry you was shameless and unheard of, and possible only in the case of the Queen of England, whom etiquette and protocol had compelled to propose marriage to the man of her choice instead of being in the gratifying position of hearing him propose to her.

Winter had had her own reasons for asking Alex to marry her instead of waiting in the hope that he might one day ask her himself, but she did not divulge them. Ameera and Hamida knew, and Lou guessed, but she did not ask any questions.

Winter did not even trouble to avoid Lord Carlyon. She saw very little of him, and that only in the company of the others on the roof-top by starlight or moonlight, or in the walled garden at dusk and before sunrise. She was seen in the gardens with less and less frequency at dawn, but Alex did not think to inquire why she alone so rarely took advantage of those cooler early hours under the trees, and supposed that she slept later. Recently, on the few occasions when she had joined them, he thought that she looked tired and strained and that there were shadows under her eyes. But it was difficult to tell in the grey first light of the morning. They all looked ill and weary by that light after the hot, restless nights.

Alex himself was silent and more short-tempered than ever these days. He knew that he was fit enough now to leave the Gulab Mahal without fear of being struck down by fever and weakness just when he needed his strength and his wits most. He knew that he should go and what he should do – as he had always known. And he was sure that Dasim Ali would help him to get safely away. But he could not bring himself to leave Winter while Carlyon was in this ugly, dangerous and unpredictable mood. He did not trust Carlyon, or the ability of any of the others to protect his wife. He told himself repeatedly that this was absurd, and that Ameera alone, or Lou, would see to it that she came to no harm. But would the efforts of either of them – or any or all of the others – keep Carlyon's passions in check as Alex's mere presence could do, because he was Winter's husband? The opposing strains tugged and dragged at Alex's mind and his emotions, and he hated himself for not going. And could not go.

Carlyon for his part no longer regarded Alex with dislike, but with active hatred and a corroding resentment which was not only on Winter's account, but because of the greater degree of freedom and, above all privacy, that Alex enjoyed.

To Carlyon the enforced and continual company of two such men as Lapeuta and Dobbie was as near unbearable as made no matter. He had nothing whatever in common with either of them, and he regarded them both, from a social standpoint, as being on the level of the servants' hall. Their views, their voices, their conversation and their mannerisms – in particular their soothing and somewhat nervous manner towards him, as though he were some fractious invalid to be humoured – frayed his nerves until there were times when he could have shrieked aloud. To be compelled to associate with them, to be locked up with them in one small room day after day and night after night, was, in his opinion, considerably worse than any solitary confinement would have been.

He did not know that Alex saw no more of Winter than he himself did, and imagined him to be enjoying a halcyon honeymoon while he, Carlyon, sweltered and raged and dragged himself through the long, weary, endless hours in the company of a tedious little Eurasian and a prosing parson who suffered from dyspepsia and prefaced and punctuated every platitude with a small dry cough.

And yet there was something that he did not understand about Winter and Randall. Something that did not quite square with that tormenting picture of a halcyon honeymoon. Winter did not look well, and she did not have the appearance of one who is happy. Neither, for that matter, did Randall. But then Randall had always had a trick of wiping all expression from his face when he wished, and it was difficult to know what he felt or thought. Neither he nor Winter seemed to have much to say to each other, and they might almost be thought to avoid each other's company, although they were never very far apart during those evenings in the walled garden or upon Randall's roof-top.

Carlyon knew that he would stand less than one chance in a hundred of winning free of Lucknow even if he should somehow manage to get out of the Gulab Mahal, yet he still spent the greater part of each day in brooding over and plotting escape. And then with the evening he would see Winter again, and know that he could not leave as long as she was there . . .

She appeared to feel no embarrassment in his presence and would talk to him as pleasantly as she talked to any of the others. It was only Randall whom she appeared to avoid. But then Randall was always there: always within sight of her, or within earshot, to remind Carlyon that she belonged to someone else.

He had at times wild, insane, ridiculous ideas of killing Randall so that she would have to turn to him, because there would be no one else; Lapeuta and Dobbie would be useless in any crisis. He had been a fool, as he had been once before. He had not learnt his lesson. He had frightened her, and she had protected herself in the only way she knew, by marrying Randall. But with Randall out of the way he could prove to her that she had nothing to fear from him, and then surely she might turn to him at last? – if only because there would be no one else for her to turn to.

In his calmer moments he knew that the idea was mad, but the heat and the discomfort and the deadly days were beginning to make him a little mad, and his temperament had never been created for endurance. He had seen Alex sitting on the coping of the well late one evening, and it had suddenly occurred to him how simple it would be to thrust him in. It could be done so easily in the dusk. One quick movement of the arm, and the man would fall backwards down the long dank slippery shaft and drown in the black water below.

Lou, who had been watching him, had read the thought in his face as clearly as though it had been written there in block capitals. And seen, too, the moment when it occurred to him that there was a rope and a well-wheel, and five other people who would hear the fall and the splash and who would not stand by and see a man drown. Carlyon had turned abruptly away to walk restlessly up and down the narrow paths, but Lou had not forgotten that look. She had warned Alex later that same night, and he had laughed at her.

'My dear Lou! You're letting your imagination run away with you. I agree that he would probably enjoy seeing me dead. I'm not sure that I wouldn't feel the same if I were in his shoes. But feeling like murdering someone and actually doing it are worlds apart. I should have been hung ten times over long before this if I had laid violent hands on all the people whom I have felt that I wouldn't mind hitting with a meat-axe.'

Lou said: 'I'd agree if I thought that he was entirely sane. But I don't think he is any more.'

Alex had merely shrugged his shoulders and dismissed the subject, and Lou had spoken to Winter, who had been frightened. She had begun to watch Carlyon instead of Alex, and both men had noticed the fact. Alex, who knew her, knew that she was frightened, and Carlyon, who did not, imagined that she was coming round to thinking more kindly of him, and the thought encouraged him in the belief that if only Randall could be got rid of she might yet turn to him.

There had been a fourth major assault on the Residency towards the end of the first week in September, and the refugees in the Gulab Mahal had listened to the sound of it with the same hope and dread with which they had listened to the din of the earlier assaults: but this one too had failed. Since then there had been nothing more than the usual desultory firing, broken occasionally by the boom of an exploding mine or an exchange of shells, and once more the siege had bogged down to a question of dogged endurance.

The weather was growing cooler and the heat was no longer a grinding torment but a discomfort that could be endured, and sometimes after a day of drenching rain the night air held a hint of chilliness; a promise of the cold weather to come.

Alex's roof was now pleasantly cool once the sun had set. It was high enough to catch the light breeze that awoke at sundown, and it became, because of this, a more popular gathering-place for his fellow-fugitives than the garden, for the breeze discouraged the mosquitoes and gnats and other winged pests which haunted the humid shade of the orange trees. They had all been there one evening after a strangely silent day on which there had been an eclipse of the sun.

The eclipse had lasted for three hours and had bathed the city in a weird brown-tinted gloom where the shadows lay pale and wan, and during that time the firing had ceased and men had stood silent in the streets to watch the shadow of the moon creep across the fiery disk until it had blotted it out. Even afterwards there had been little firing, and the day had seemed curiously quiet and heavy with tension.

Alex's bed had been dragged out into the open, and the three women were sitting on it, talking in undertones while the men walked idly to and fro, when Winter had seen the same expression on Carlyon's face that Lou had seen once before in the garden.

Alex had been sitting on the parapet, looking out towards the hidden Residency where the occasional gun-flashes showed behind the trees and the intervening buildings. There had been no one near him and Winter had seen Carlyon look at him and had known what Lou meant. Only this time Alex was not sitting on the coping of a well. This time there was a clear drop of thirty feet or more below him, and iron-hard earth instead of well water. Carlyon moved quietly towards him, and Winter rose swiftly and running after him caught his arm. He had swung round, his purpose entirely plain on his contorted face, and she had stood looking up at him, her fingers tight on his arm and her wide, frightened eyes holding his and trying to force him back into sanity by an effort of will.

Alex had heard the light running step and had turned too. He could not see Carlyon's face, but he could see Winter's, and also her clutching fingers on Carlyon's arm; and he was suddenly aware of what she had thought the man had been going to do. He remembered then what Lou had said, and he glanced down at the drop beneath him and felt his stomach contract and a cold sweat break out on his forehead. He stood up quite slowly and moved unhurriedly away, and Carlyon shivered as though he were awakening from a momentary trance. The tension went out of his muscles and the fixed stare from his eyes, and Winter's hand dropped from his arm.

She made some light and trivial remark on the subject of the eclipse without knowing what it was that she had said and without hearing his reply: and then Lou was standing beside Carlyon and had drawn him away, and Winter sat down very suddenly on the parapet where Alex had been sitting a moment ago.

Her knees were trembling and she had to clench her teeth hard to prevent them from chattering. There was a curious humming sound in her ears and she felt very cold. She did not hear Alex walk towards her, but a hand dropped on her shoulder and she knew without turning whose it was. He held her shoulder in a warm and comforting grip, and after a moment or two she lifted her own hand and laid it over his. She did not turn because her eyes were full of tears and she did not want Alex to see them, but the trembling of her body stilled, and presently Alex gave her a small reassuring shake and released her.

He was more careful after that, and he did not again approach too near to the edge of the roof when Carlyon was present. He saw even less of Winter than usual in the following week for she did not once appear in the garden in the early morning, and for three evenings running she did not join the others on the roof. He had asked Lou for the reason, and Lou had replied shortly that she was not feeling very well but that it was nothing to worry about, while Winter herself, taxed with it on her reappearance, had said lightly that the heat and an over-ripe *papiya* that she had eaten had been responsible.

Alex had accepted the explanation, and might have continued to do so for some considerable time if it had not been for an unexpected storm that had blown up out of a clear sky some four nights later.

He had been sleeping out on the open roof, and the first intimation he had received of the storm was when he was awakened by what appeared to be a tub of cold water emptied over him. This was not the warm rain of the hot weather, but the colder rain of autumn, and there was a wind behind the rain, driving it against him and chilling him to the bone. He was drenched almost before he was awake, and the roof appeared to be awash with water.

It had been awash often enough before during the monsoon, but then the rain had beaten straight down upon it, and he had slept under cover and not in the open. Tonight the wind blew the rain straight into the narrow porch-like pavilion where the *chiks* had been rolled up, so that it was as cold and wet as the open roof.

'This is where I catch pneumonia,' thought Alex exasperated, wrestling in the pitchy darkness to release the sodden *chiks*. He became aware of someone else on the roof, and Winter's voice calling his name through the lashing of the wind and the rain and the infuriating flapping of the *chiks*.

'Alex – Alex – where are you?'

'I'm here,' shouted Alex. 'What do you think you're doing? Get on back! Where are you?'

He groped for her in the blackness and caught a wet arm, and as he did so the brief, fiendish blast of wind that had driven the storm before it died out as quickly as it had arisen, and there was only the rain falling steadily onto the roof with a soft splashing sound as though it were falling into a lake.

Alex said furiously: 'Winter, are you mad? You'll be drenched. Get on back to your room!'

He heard her laugh a little shakily and she said: 'I'm drenched already. And I won't go down unless you come with me. You can't stay up here for the rest of the night. You'll only get ill again, and we've had enough trouble with you already.'

'You sound,' said Alex, 'regrettably like a nurse I used to have when I was about six. All right, I'll come. Be careful of those stairs. If we fall down them in the dark we shall break our necks.'

The room that had once been Sabrina's seemed hot after the coldness of the wet windy roof, and there was an oil-lamp burning. The flame wavered in the draught and the painted plaster trees and birds and flowers seemed to move with the moving light as though they had been alive, and the curve of the rose-coloured ceiling was full of soft shadows so that it was difficult to tell how high it was.

Alex took the cloth that Winter handed him and rubbed himself dry with it, removing his wet loin-cloth and appropriating a length of turquoise blue muslin – evidently a head-veil – to replace it. He sat down on the carved and painted bed and looked about the room, charmed by the gay, childish grace of the formalized patterns and the clear colours which, though rubbed and worn in many places, were still jewel-bright. And then he looked at his wife.

Her hair had been unbound for the night and she was wringing the water out of it and twisting it up out of the way in a heavy shining knot at the back of her head. Her arms were lifted, and the brief cotton sari she wore wrapped lightly about her was drenched with rain and clung wetly to her body, outlining and revealing every rounded curve of a figure that was no longer the reed-slim one he had known.

Winter finished knotting up her hair and said: 'There's another *resai* over there. Will you mind sleeping on the floor?'

He did not answer her and she turned to look at him, and saw that he knew. There was a white shade about his mouth and his eyes were wide and very bright, and she stood quite still, looking back at him gravely, her gaze steady and a little apprehensive.

After a long minute Alex spoke as though speaking were difficult. He said: 'Is it mine?'

'Yes.'

He held out a hand to her and she came to him as slowly as if she were walking in her sleep, and Alex reached up and drew her down into his arms and said in a voice that she had not known he possessed: 'Why didn't you tell me? Oh my love – my little love!' He laughed suddenly; a laugh that broke on a dry sob, and held her away from him so that he could look into her face.

'And to think,' said Alex, 'that I have been keeping my hands off you for weeks – for months! – because I was afraid of this.'

His hands stripped away the sodden sari and his fingers pressed through the heavy wet waves of hair, and then his mouth closed down on hers, blotting out thought.

50

They were allowed three days of unclouded happiness. Three days and nights of complete and unalloyed rapture and contentment, made the more sweet by being snatched out of the ugly mire of blood and fear and frenzy that fouled half India.

They had come into possession of a kingdom, and Sabrina's room was an enchanted garden a thousand miles removed from the harsh realities of the warring world outside. They had so much to talk of and to tell. So much to ask and to remember and to forget. And so much to give that needed no words for its expression.

They went up to the roof-top only after the others had gone, and lying in the crook of Alex's arm, counting the stars that shimmered and blinked and blazed in the tented velvet of the sky, Winter no longer heard the firing from the Residency or the night noises of the city, but only Alex's quiet breathing and the steady beat of his heart under her cheek.

She was entirely and completely happy with a happiness that many touch once but do not hold. At Ware she had longed for the Gulab Mahal as a child cries for the moon, and on so many nights and through so many years she had wished on a star. Now she did not need to wish for anything any more, because all that she could ever have wished for had been given to her – together with every star in the sky. She knew now that whatever happened, and however much pain or horror or parting the future might hold, she had touched every one of those stars and held the moon in her hand, and that if she died tomorrow she would die content.

They had seen little of anyone else during the three days that followed the night of the storm. Only Ameera and Hamida and Lou. Alex had not seen Ameera before, except as a veiled figure on the night of his wedding.

'But thou art the husband of my cousin now, so for a time I will forget that I am of India, and a Mussulman, and be of my mother's people, who keep no *purdah*,' said Ameera smiling at him.

Alex had looked from one face to the other and seen the similarity of the de Ballesteros blood, and had laughed and said: 'Thou art not of India only, Begum Sahiba. The West is there also.'

Ameera shook her head so that her earrings jingled. 'Nay, that is not so. There may come a time when it is possible for one person to be of both, but that time is not yet, and I do not think that my children's children will see it. Their children, perhaps. I shall be dead then, and shall not know. But those who are, as I am, of the East and of the West, must cleave only to one if they wish to avoid unhappiness. To stand with a foot in each is to be neither: and

I have chosen the East. It is only when the blood of one alone runs in the veins that those such as my cousin can be happy in both, for then there is no war, pulling both ways. Thy son too, when he is born, may love this land and its people as his mother does, and, I think, as thou dost also. But it will be for love alone, and not because of any tie of blood.'

Lou had come in search of Winter on that same day and had found Alex there. She had looked relieved and said: 'So you've told him, have you? I wondered how much longer you were going to be about it. Is it——' She bit the sentence off abruptly and blushed hotly for perhaps the first time in her adult life.

'No,' said Alex shortly, answering the unspoken question. 'It's mine.'

Lou drew a deep breath of relief. She said: 'I thought it might be, because you didn't come back that night and—— But I was afraid it was Con's and that was why she wouldn't tell you.'

Winter said: 'How long have you known, Lou?'

Lou laughed. 'Probably almost as long as you have. It wasn't difficult, living as we did.'

Alex said: 'I didn't know.'

'Oh, *you*!' said Lou, and left them.

They had not seen any of the others, and did not know that their absence had driven Carlyon to the ragged fringes of desperation and rage. While he had been able to see them – one or other of them – and to note the fact that their behaviour towards each other was almost that of strangers, he had been able to feed on the hope that Winter had perhaps only married the man as a way out of a difficult situation.

But now they had both removed from his sight, and they were somewhere together, and he could not endure it. Everything that had happened to him since his arrival in this appalling, barbaric, abomination of a country was Winter's fault. Winter's and Randall's! The discomfort and the tediousness that he had endured on the journey from Calcutta, and in Delhi. The rage of disappointment and the wound to his vanity and egotism. The sleepless nights and the gnawing, unsatisfied hunger for a woman who had escaped him. The illness and the heat and the horrors of the mutiny. The weeks of hiding in jungles and hovels, the fear that lived night and day at his elbow, and the long torture of confinement and inactivity; day after day after day of Lapeuta and Dobbie, and the all too brief daily sight of Winter – as lovely and disturbing and desirable as ever and always out of reach. Of Randall, always watching.

Winter and Randall! *They* were all right. They suffered no hardships and knew nothing of the tortures he endured. Hidden away somewhere and locked in each other's arms, durance and monotony and fear meant nothing to them. He himself was the only one who really suffered, and the others were all in league against him, ranged in the opposite camp: allies of the dark-skinned, sly-faced jailers who held him prisoner . . .

And then after three days Alex and Winter had come down to the garden again, and together, and even in the soft uncertain dusk Carlyon had been able to read Winter's face.

They could all read it, and the others had looked at her and smiled, because she was young and lovely and in love. She did not touch Alex or stay very near him. She did not need to. But even the dullest and least imaginative of minds could sense and almost see the bond of love and belonging that linked them, and as Carlyon watched her the rage of the last three days – and of all the days that had gone before – boiled up in him like a seething bubble of lava breaking through the thin crust of a volcano. The fumes of it rose to his brain so that he saw her through a red mist of rage as the sole author and architect of all his misfortunes.

She had been standing less than a yard away from him, her face clear in the pale moonlight, and he had leapt at her and caught her by the throat, shouting a torrent of accusations and obscenities, shaking her to and fro as his hands choked the breath from her in a strangling, agonizing, frenzied grip.

Alex had reached them first and had hit him between the eyes with all his strength, and he had released Winter and staggered back, and then come at Alex, screaming senseless, futile words.

They had overpowered him at last and dragged him, still struggling and shouting, back to the room he shared with Lapeuta and Dobbie, and Alex had carried Winter up to the painted room and held her in his arms while Ameera and Hamida put cold compresses on her bruised and swollen throat.

Later a message from Mr Lapeuta had been brought him by Rahim, and he had left her to the care of the women and gone up to the moonlit roof to find Mr Lapeuta waiting for him. Mr Lapeuta and Dasim Ali, who had both come on the same errand.

'It is not safe that that man remain longer in the Gulab Mahal,' said Dasim Ali. 'Who knows but that his shouts may have been heard by those outside the walls? He cried aloud, and in *Angrezi*, and while he remains he is a danger to us all. He must go.'

Alex's face whitened and the lines cut deeper about his mouth. Half an hour ago he would have killed Carlyon if he could, and even now he would not trust himself within range of the man. But to send him out of the Gulab Mahal meant sending him to his death as surely, and less mercifully, as though they had put a loaded pistol to his head and pulled the trigger.

The man could not be held responsible for that frenzied attack on Winter. He was mad – or very nearly so. Too mad to be trusted, and as Dasim Ali had said, a danger to every single inmate of the Gulab Mahal. But to send him to certain death in cold blood——

'We cannot do it,' said Alex at last. 'It were better to kill him here. It would be quicker. They tortured the others. He would be caught in an hour – less!'

'If he went alone, yes,' said Mr Lapeuta. 'But perhaps not if we go with him, Reverend Dobbie and myself. We have discussed this and we think it is possible. I, as you see, can pass veree easily as an Indian. Also I know Lucknow, and so does Reverend Dobbie. Lord Carlyon need not talk. We will tie a bandage over his eyes with much blood on it, and say that he has been injured in thee fighting; for his eyes are of a colour that is not usual in this country. We can lead him. We may be caught, as thee others were, but I think we have more chance than they, for Reverend Dobbie has dark eyes and speaks thee language with great fluency. It is worth trying, sir. To leave him here endangers all in this house, and he can endure no longer. This has come harder on such a man than on us, sir. He is I think a brave man, but not a patient one.'

Mr Lapeuta glanced at Dasim Ali and added: 'I had wished to see you so that you might approach this gentleman and ask his help and his permission. But he is here now, and he is in agreement with me.'

'"*The raft of the benevolent gets across*,"' murmured Dasim Ali, looking thoughtfully at Mr Lapeuta: 'It may even be that thou wilt all reach safety.'

And so they had gone. Their skins had been darkened with dye and they had been given food and a little money and what clothes they would need, and had been smuggled out by a small side door in the wall. They had taken, too, the clothes that they had worn when they arrived there, tied up in a ragged bundle.

'If we are stopped we can say that we stole them from thee dead in thee cantonments,' said Mr Lapeuta. 'But the old gentleman has said that there is news that thee army moves on Lucknow again, and if we can join them we do not wish to be shot by our own side.'

Alex had not seen them go, for he did not wish to see Carlyon again. He had gone back to Winter and held her and kissed her with a passionate intensity as though he were saying good-bye to her. And she had known then that he would go too.

It had rained again that night, but in the morning the skies were clear and the clean-washed air brought the sound of guns. Havelock's guns.

Alex had gone up to the roof in the dawn to listen. He had drawn away very gently from Winter, and thought that he had not awakened her, but she had felt that first movement and had not stopped him. When he had gone she had lain for a long time staring at the wall with unseeing eyes, and after a time she had turned on her face and wept quietly without sound or movement.

All that day the sound of Havelock's guns shivered through the hot sunlight, coming nearer and nearer until it seemed as though they could only be a few miles from the city. And as twilight fell the four who were left of the British in the Gulab Mahal gathered on the roof-top to watch and listen.

'We shall be able to get away!' said Mrs Hossack, her voice trembling in hysterical thankfulness and relief. 'We shall be safe at last – at *last*! When will they be here? Why don't they hurry!'

'They are fighting a battle,' said Alex. 'They will come as quickly as they can, but they won't get a walk-over. Listen! – they must be at the Alam Bagh!'

He leaned on the parapet, his breath coming short and his eyes blazing, straining to listen: knowing that men he knew would be fighting out there – pressing on with everything that was in them to the relief of the battered Residency whose indomitable garrison had held out stubbornly all through that terrible, burning summer, and by doing so had occupied and held in check an army which, but for their resistance, would have been free to turn and attack the Delhi Force and create havoc throughout the North-Western Provinces.

'We shall soon be safe!' sobbed Mrs Hossack. 'They *must* be here soon – perhaps tomorrow!'

But Winter did not speak, or Lou. Winter only watched Alex, oblivious of the guns. Absorbed in him as though he were the only person present: as though she were trying to imprint every line and angle and hollow of his face on her mind, and every tone and inflexion of his voice, so that she could keep them there sharp and distinct through the long days to come, and never forget them.

Lou was silent because now that deliverance seemed so near at hand she was suddenly frightened again. Not of possible hardships, but of the shadowy spectres of Amanda's grandparents who might claim the child. All at once she knew that she did not want to leave the Gulab Mahal, as she had not wanted to leave the Hirren Minar. She was safe here, she and Amanda. She clutched the small, solemn red-headed creature tighter in her arms and the baby set up a protesting wail.

Lou and Mrs Hossack had taken the children away and left the moonlit roof to Alex and Winter, and for a little while only, Alex had forgotten the thunder of the guns.

The wind shifted in the night, and in the morning the cannonade was less easy to hear, and that day it came no nearer. But on the following day the guns were no longer a mile or so outside the city, but firing from within the city limits as the Highlanders and the Sikhs and the British and Indian Cavalry and Infantry under Havelock's command fought their way through the streets.

The gates of the Gulab Mahal were barred and barricaded and every shutter closed and bolted, and none stirred outside while the city shook to the savage din of battle. And as the sun sank, the wind blowing from the direction of the Residency brought with it a new sound, faint but unmistakable. A roar of cheering.

'*They've got there* !' said Alex with a catch in his voice and a lunatic desire to cheer himself hoarse. 'Listen to that! They've got there!'

'They're safe,' said Lou, and wept.

They had got there at last. But the garrison of the Residency, though sure now of survival, had not been relieved after all. They had only been reinforced. The regiments who had fought their way through the streets had been too badly mauled, and their losses had been too great for them to be able to do more than join the exhausted defenders in the Residency and to stand siege there themselves.

The tumult in the city died down and the stench of death rose from the streets like a tangible cloud to foul the air. And once again the familiar rattle of musketry-fire, punctuated more frequently now by the boom of guns, sounded from the direction of the Residency.

Alex waited for several days, gleaning what news he could from Dasim Ali, and from Rahim who had been into the bazaars. But from what they told him there seemed to be little chance of the situation developing into more than another stalemate, if not a retreat. The garrison was hampered by an inordinate proportion of women and children whose safety could not be jeopardized, and now that Havelock and Outram, with the relieving force, were also penned up in the Residency it seemed more likely that they would have to remain where they were until they in turn were relieved, since to fight their way out with the women and children would be no easy task, and would mean abandoning Lucknow and that indefensible position that had, miraculously and courageously, been defended for so long. They would have to retreat not only from Lucknow but from Oudh, and it might be many months before another and stronger force could be marched to attack and take the city.

Alex had talked for a long time with old Dasim Ali on the last evening of September, and afterwards he had gone down to the painted room and to Winter.

The light of the oil-lamp played upon the rose-coloured walls and the painted plaster birds and flowers as it had on the first night that he had seen that room, and once again it seemed to him that the trees swayed and the birds moved, and that the shadows made a mist under the curved ceiling so that he could not tell how high it was.

Winter was combing out the long waves of her hair, and he sat on the low Indian bed, as he had done that first night, and watched her; and did not speak.

After a moment she laid down the comb and turned towards him. The light of the lamp behind her fell upon his face but left her own in shadow, and the soft wavering flame threw an aureole about her, glinting on the long ripples of her black hair and outlining her small head.

She looked at him in silence, as she had done once before in that room; seeing in his face what it was that he had come to say. And once again he held out a hand to her, and she came to him and put her arms about him, standing between his knees with his head against her heart as she had stood in the dusk outside the Hirren Minar on the day that Lottie had died. Now, as then, he held her quite gently, leaning against her, and presently he said: 'I can take you with me. There are troops at the Alam Bagh just outside the city. It will not be too difficult or too dangerous to get you there. You can pass as an Indian. And once you were there you would be safe. After that it would only mean reaching Cawnpore, and then by river to Allahabad and Calcutta. If Havelock is here it means the road must be open.'

Winter said: 'Would you come with me?' and knew the answer before she asked it.

She felt Alex's arms tighten about her. 'To the Alam Bagh, my darling. Perhaps to Cawnpore.'

'And after that?'

'I – you would be safe then.'

Winter put up one hand and stroked his dark hair, pressing her fingers through it; pressing his head against her so that he should not lift it and see that she was crying. She said softly and quite steadily: 'And you?'

Alex moved his head against her as though he were in pain. He said in a harsh, difficult voice: 'I must go back to Lunjore.'

He felt her flinch, and said as though she had spoken: 'I must, dear. I should never have left. There was so much that I could have done there – or tried to do. It – it is my work; my responsibility. It's my *own* district! And I ran away from it, because——'

'Because you were saddled with three women,' said Winter with a break in her voice. 'But you can't go back there now. Alex, you can't! They would only kill you. There wouldn't be anything you could do there alone – not now. You'd only be throwing your life away, and it isn't only yours – it's mine too. It's *mine*!'

Alex's arms were hard about her; he said: 'I know, my heart. But it isn't true that there is nothing that I could do there now. And – and there is more than an even chance that I shall be safe. There are several of the talukdars who I think would stand by me. Safdar Beg will lend me men; I got his revenues back for him and he was grateful for that. And Tará Chand – oh, a dozen others. There is no one to keep order there now. But once they see someone in authority again it will quiet them and bring back order and sanity; give them the assurance that there is still a stable Government and a law that does not depend on the will or the whim of any individual who happens to be temporarily in power. That is what they need; peace and quiet and that assurance. It wasn't the villages, or even the city, that created the trouble. It was the sepoys, and they will have gone now. If I go back now I can—— Dear heart, I must go back! Give me leave to go.'

Winter said: 'And if I will not? Would you still go?'

'I – I must. But I would go happier if I went with your leave.'

She said in a whisper, because she could not trust her voice not to break again: 'Go with it, my love,' and felt something that had been strained and taut relax in his mind more than in his body.

He leaned his weight against her as though he were very tired, and the tears that she had wished to hide from him ran down her cheeks to her throat so that they wet his face, and he felt them and tried to lift his head, but she held it closer and after a little while she said: 'When are you going?'

'Tonight. In an hour.'

She did not make any sound, but he felt the effort to control it shudder through her body, and knew what that effort had cost her. He said: 'Can you be ready by then?'

She did not answer him at once, but her hand relaxed its pressure against his head and began to stroke his hair again, quite gently, and presently she said: 'I am not going.'

He looked up then, quickly, and saw her face wet and sweet and calm above him. She smiled down at him, the soft, tremulous shadow of a smile, and laid her palm against the hard cheek that was wet with her own tears:

'Dear, I could not go. They would send me away to Calcutta. I should be at the other end of India. I shall be nearer to you here, and far safer than you will be. Ameera will take care of me, and I shall be among friends. I was born in this room, and I have thought about it and loved it all my life. Perhaps your child will be born in it too. I will wait here for you.'

Alex said: 'You don't understand, my heart. I can't let you stay. One day we shall attack this city, and take it. You don't know what that would mean, but I do. I have seen a city sacked. If you were here——'

Winter's hand moved from his cheek to his mouth, covering it so that he could not speak, and above it his eyes looked into hers steadily and for a long time. Then his lashes dropped and he kissed the warm palm that closed his mouth, and did not argue with her any more.

He had gone before midnight, slipping out by the narrow side door by which Carlyon and Lapeuta and Dobbie had left, and there had been only his wife and Dasim Ali to see him go.

Winter had stood pressed against the little iron-studded door and listened to the sound of his quick light footsteps dying out on the dusty road outside, and presently the night had swallowed up the sound, and old Dasim Ali had touched her on the arm and she had turned away.

She had cried again on the bed in the painted room after he had gone, and Ameera had comforted her. But in the morning it was the room that had comforted her most. She had woken to find it bright with the dawn, and as the sun rose and the familiar shadow crept across the floor and touched the bed on which she lay, peace and reassurance flowed back and filled her heart and her mind and her body. Nothing could hurt her while she was here. Alex would come back. She had only to wait.

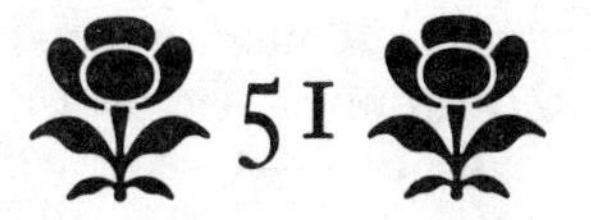

51

Three of them left. Winter, Lou and Mrs Hossack. And the two small children; Jimmy Hossack and Lottie's daughter Amanda.

Mrs Hossack had been horrified and indignant when she had heard the news of Alex's departure, and had expressed herself strongly on the subject to Lou Cottar.

'I cannot *understand* how Captain Randall could have brought himself to do such a thing. To desert his wife at a time like this. To escape himself and to leave her behind, alone and unprotected. Not to mention *us*. One would have thought that he would have remained here to protect us all.'

'From what?' inquired Lou shortly. 'We are perfectly safe here; and if a mob should break in, one man would not be much help.'

'Well, I consider it very shocking in him,' said Mrs Hossack, 'and I cannot conceive how he can have brought himself even to contemplate such a thing.'

'He has an odd idea that duty should come before personal inclination,' said Lou drily. 'He also has a peculiar sense of proportion and value, and imagines that three women, who are really as safe as they can hope to be, are of less importance than the welfare of his district.'

'Personally, I should have thought that the first duty of an Englishman was to protect women,' said Mrs Hossack indignantly.

'I'm sure you would. It is a pity that so many of them would seem to agree with you,' said Lou acidly, and turned her back on her.

Mrs Hossack had preserved an offended silence for at least half the day, but towards evening Jimmy Hossack had been fretful and refused his food, and had later become feverish. He had grown steadily worse and Mrs Hossack had been frantic.

'He is going to die!' wept Mrs Hossack hysterically, rocking herself to and fro and wringing her hands. 'I know he will die! . . . with no doctor . . . no proper food . . . no medicines – this dreadful, horrible house! Oh Jimmy – *Jimmy*!'

Lou had slapped her. It had proved an efficacious remedy as far as Mrs Hossack was concerned, and Jimmy Hossack had not died. But he had lost a great deal of weight and did not regain it, and his recovery was so slow as to be scarcely perceptible.

Jimmy's illness had frightened Lou almost as much as it had terrified his mother. What if Amanda were to get ill? – really ill? They must get away! They *must*. Alex had said that a road must be open from Cawnpore to Calcutta, and Josh would be in Calcutta. Josh would not object to her keeping Amanda. Josh had never objected to anything that Lou did. He would probably be amused at the idea, and might even one day come to look upon the child as being as much his own as she herself did. And she, Lou, had red hair too. If only the Englishes—— Oh, to hell with the Englishes! She must get Amanda to safety. What was the Army doing? What was Havelock doing?

But Havelock, whose command had now been taken over by Sir James Outram, was still besieged in the Residency that he had hoped to relieve. And October came and went, and the air was cool now; the gardens bright with flowers and the early mornings sharp and chilly.

The news that Delhi had been recaptured by the British had reached the Gulab Mahal two days after Alex had left. Delhi had been taken, but the price had been high, for Nicholson was dead. He had been shot trying to rally his men in the attack on the city, and all that could die of him had died nine days later – leaving behind an imperishable legend and the echoes of those hooves that could be heard from Attock to the Khyber. 'Nikal Seyn' was dead, and the men of the frontier who had fought at Delhi – Pathans, Multanis, Afghans – had wept above his grave, and many, who had cared nothing for the Raj and had given allegiance only to him, had gone back to their own country. *'There be many sahibs – but only one Nikal Seyn . . .'*

The year wore slowly on, and the ceaseless, familiar sound of musketry and gunfire from around the Residency still made a background to each day, and it was not until mid-November that once again the roar of guns and the din of battle rattled the rickety fabric of the Gulab Mahal as another British force fought its way towards a second relief of the Lucknow Residency, and once again the ugly tide of war surged through the narrow streets of the city.

Once again the gates of the pink palace were barred and barricaded; but fortune was with it, for it did not lie in the line of the advance, and the flood-tide of the street-fighting passed it by.

For a week gunfire and the crashing detonation of buildings being blown up shook Lucknow, but no one seemed to know how the battle went. The Residency had been relieved for the second time, but had Lucknow itself been captured by the British? None from the pink palace dared go out for news because the streets were not safe, and food ran short and there came a day when there was no milk for Amanda and Jimmy Hossack.

Havelock died in that month, and on the day after his death word had been whispered in the dusk at the barred gate of the Gulab Mahal that the *Jung-i-lat Sahib*, Sir Colin Campbell, was going to retreat from Lucknow and fall back once more upon Cawnpore, and that the evacuation would take place that very night, and in great secrecy. The women and children were to leave in carts and *dhoolis* at midnight while the city slept; stealing out under cover of darkness and making for the Alam Bagh, which was strongly held by the British.

Ameera had brought the news to Winter. 'My husband and Dasim Ali,' said Ameera, 'say that if it be thy wish, it can be arranged that thou and the two women with the children go also. There are *dhoolis* here, and men to carry them, and they will join with the other mem-*log* at a place that is known to them, and take thee to safety. But it must be decided swiftly, for already it is dark.'

Winter had smiled lovingly at her. 'I will tell the others. It may be that they will choose to go. But I will stay here – unless thou and thy husband wish me to be gone. And if that be so, then thou wilt have to send me away by force!'

'That we shall never do,' said Ameera, embracing her. 'Is this not the house in which thou wast born? Go and tell thy friends to make ready if they would go.'

They had gone.

Mrs Hossack had tried to persuade Winter to go with them, and even Lou had urged her to leave. 'I know you are safe here now,' said Lou, 'and that you will be happier here than in Allahabad or Calcutta, or wherever they send us. But it isn't safe to stay. Can't you see that even if they are retreating this time, they will come again? Lucknow will be taken in the end – it's got to be! And when it is, the fighting will be far worse – a hundred times worse – than it has been this time, or the time before. The place may be sacked. Anything may happen. You can't risk it, Winter. You have the child to think of.'

'It is Alex's child,' said Winter. 'Alex knew that Lucknow would be taken, but he did not make me leave. Don't you see, Lou, that even if I wished to go I could not? Everyone in this house has risked their lives to save ours. And when they took us in they had no idea of profiting from it. We owe them a debt; a very great one. If I stay here, and I am here when the attack comes, the fact that I am in this house may save it. I could not leave . . . Alex knew that.'

Lou had wasted no more words. She had, somewhat unexpectedly, kissed Winter; and even more unexpectedly, there had been tears in her eyes. They had smiled at each other with affection and respect, their hands holding tightly for a moment, and had kissed again, saying nothing because there was so much to say – and yet so little that need be said. And then Lou had gone. Lou, Amanda, Mrs Hossack, Jimmy.

The gate creaked shut behind them and the bars and bolts grated hurriedly back into place, and the shuffling footsteps of the *dhooli*-bearers faded and were swallowed up by the night as Alex's quick, light ones had been.

Sir Colin Campbell's army – Havelock's army – retreated from Lucknow, taking with them the women and children and all who remained of the gallant garrison who had held out so stubbornly and for so long, and leaving behind them the lonely dead and the empty shell of the Residency where a tattered Union Jack still fluttered in the dawn wind above the broken roof. And in the Gulab Mahal, the little pink stucco palace in Lucknow city, only Winter remained of the thirteen fugitives who had been taken in and given shelter on a hot night in July.

Once again the tide of war drew out of Lucknow leaving the ruin and the wreckage behind it, and there were no more sounds of the siege. Only the doves and the crows and the parrots again, and the chattering squirrels and the hum of the city from behind the high wall that shut in the Rose Palace.

There was firing still, but not from the Residency. It was further away now, from the Alam Bagh – the 'Garden of the World' – a walled and fortified royal garden some two miles outside Lucknow, where Sir Colin Campbell had left a force under General Outram to hold at least one outpost within sight of the city.

The Maulvi of Faizabad, the best of the generals that the mutineer armies had produced, attacked the British there, and cut their communications with Cawnpore. All through the succeeding months the Alam Bagh was attacked again and again, as the Residency had been. But unlike the Residency it was not a besieged garrison holding out against insuperable odds, but a strongpost that defied capture and waited for the day when it would act as the spearhead of the final advance upon Lucknow.

There was no word of Carlyon and the two men who had gone with him: or of Alex. But the bearers of the *dhoolis* had returned, saying that the memsahibs and their children had reached the Alam Bagh in safety, and had been sent forward with all the other mem-*log* to Cawnpore. So Lou and Mrs Hossack at least were safe, and Winter hoped that Lou would not find that escape had robbed her of Amanda. Lou deserved Amanda.

The year drew to its close, but the mutiny still raged. Men still fought and died, and in Lucknow the mutineers dug defences and built barricades in preparation for the attack that they knew could not be long delayed. For the make-believe Mogul, Bahadur Shah's, brief, soap-bubble dream of Empire had vanished with the fall of Delhi: Dundu Pant, the Nana Sahib, was a fugitive, and many of the strongholds that the insurgents had won were once more in British hands.

But within the faded, pink-washed walls of the Gulab Mahal the days passed peacefully, and Winter sank into the life of the Rose Palace and became part of it – as she had been part of it in the long-ago days when Juanita and Aziza Begum had been alive and Winter herself a small, black-haired child playing with the painted plaster birds in the room that had been Sabrina's.

The inmates of the palace frequently forgot that she was not one of them by birth, and she spoke and thought and dreamt in the vernacular as she had done as a child. She busied herself with the same household tasks, and was scolded by Mumtaz and instructed in the mysteries of drying and preserving fruits and spices, of making jasmine oil and soap made from powdered gram, or preparing *surma* – the black ore of antimony used for beautifying the eyes. There were few idle hours in the Gulab Mahal, and there was always Ameera, and Ameera's small sons to play with, and other and older children to fly kites with on the roof and to tell stories to, and their mothers to gossip and laugh with.

Twice a day, morning and evening, Winter would go alone to the roof-top where Alex had lived, and look out across the tree-tops and the lovely battered city, towards Lunjore.

'He is not dead,' she told Ameera. 'If he were I should feel it; here, in my heart.'

But there were times when she was not so sure; when terror would suddenly overtake her and she would think of him lying dead or dying in Lunjore – tortured or wounded or sick. And when those black times came upon her she would run to her own room, and the room, as it had always been, was a talisman and a charm that could reassure her and make her believe that all would be well. She had only to lay her hand on the gay, worn curves of Firishta, and stroke his plaster feathers, to feel calm flow back to her as though his touch were indeed magic. Alex would come back.

And then in January she had heard news of him at last. Old Dasim Ali, who had friends everywhere, had heard by a roundabout route that there was a Sahib again in Lunjore who had brought back order to the district. He had been protected by a bodyguard of men provided by a Sirdar who had reason to be grateful to him, and with this backing he had taken control of Lunjore, put down the malcontents and set up courts again with native magistrates and judges and native police, so that life was gradually returning to normal. The rumour gave no name, but Winter did not need one. She knew that it must be Alex, and that he had been right to go.

All through January the insurgents had kept up their attacks on the Alam Bagh, but in mid-January the Maulvi had been wounded and driven back. Their inability to carry the Alam Bagh by assault, and the defeats inflicted upon them, disheartened the rebels, and they began to quarrel among themselves, and many drifted away, returning to their own towns and villages. But many more stayed and continued to attack, fighting with ferocity and valour, and towards the end of February a last and desperate assault was launched against the garrison. The Royal Begum of Oudh had accompanied the rebel army in person, together with her Prime Minister and many of the great nobles of Oudh, riding in state on gorgeously caparisoned elephants.

Winter heard the opening of the cannonade in the early morning, and it shook the walls of the pink palace and sent the startled crows and pigeons cawing and whirling above the roofs of the city. But the roar of the guns meant no more to her than the cawing of the crows, for her pains had started before dawn and the guns were only a dim and disregarded background to the ordeal of birth.

It was not an easy birth, and there had been times when Ameera and Mumtaz Begum and Hamida, and others of the women who were continuously in and out of the painted room, had looked at each other in fear and anxiety.

But Winter remembered a long, hot, agonizing day in the Hirren Minar, and Alex's voice talking to Lottie – explaining, encouraging, soothing; and it was as if he spoke to her now as he had spoken then to Lottie; telling her not to be afraid. And she had not been afraid.

Through the waves of pain she could see the pink sunset sky that was the walls of her room; the dear enchanted trees and flowers that swayed in a secret breeze against that sky, and the birds and beasts that had watched her own birth and been her first playthings.

The sun had set and the moon had risen. Ameera had lit the oil-lamp, and her shadow and Hamida's and other shadows of women moved and leapt upon the walls, and the ceiling was lost in a rosy mist as it had been on the night when Alex had come down from the roof, and on the night that he had left her. And then suddenly she had thought that he was in the room, and had screamed to him by name – a scream that rang out through the open windows and across the silent garden and awoke the echo that lived within the high, encircling walls – 'Alex!' . . . *Alex!* . . . *Alex!* . . . And to the sound of that echo Alex's son was born.

It was March when the long-expected attack upon Lucknow began, and day after endless day the guns had roared in the city while the streets became battlegrounds and graveyards and charnel houses, and the dead littered every yard of the contested ground.

Colin Campbell's army – Highlanders, Sikhs, Punjabis, British and Indian regiments of Cavalry and Infantry, Peel's Naval Brigade and Jung Bahadur's Gurkhas from Nepal – had stormed the defences and flung themselves on the guns, fighting forward yard by yard through the red, reeking streets; through the storm of grape and canister and round shot and the choking smoke of burning houses; past fortified palaces and over the bodies of the grinning dead, driving the insurgents back from street to street, from building to building . . .

Curiously enough – or perhaps justly – it was Carlyon who was largely responsible for saving the Gulab Mahal from the sack and slaughter and destruction that overtook almost every house in that shattered city. Mr Lapeuta, Mr Dobbie and Lord Carlyon, Lou Cottar, Mrs Hossack and the children, had all reached safety. And they had told their stories, and told too of Captain Alex Randall's wife who had remained behind in the house and with the people who had sheltered them. And later, when the Delhi Column had joined Sir Colin Campbell's force and the army moved to the final attack upon Lucknow, Carlyon had used his considerable influence to urge that the Gulab Mahal should be granted as much protection as was possible in such circumstances. It had been promised him, and even in the frenzy of the fighting the promise had not been forgotten. With the terrible tumult of battle ebbing and surging like a furious sea through the city, rifle-butts had knocked on the barred door of the Gulab Mahal and men's voices had shouted above the clamour, demanding entrance.

Winter had gone down to them alone, wearing Juanita's white dress, not knowing who it might be. She had heard the British voices above the din and had opened the gate, tugging at the heavy bars and locks with her small hands – for the gateman had run away in terror – and had opened it at last to see the smoke-blackened, blood-streaked faces that filled the once quiet street.

They were men of the Highland Brigade and half a dozen mounted sowars of Hodson's Horse, and there was an officer with them. A man on horseback who laughed down at her and dismounted to take her hand. 'Do you remember me, Mrs Alex? I met you at Delhi – William Hodson.'

'Yes,' said Winter, looking up into the white, battle-grimed, laughing face of the man whom Alex had said would always be twenty paces ahead, and thinking that no one who had ever met him would be likely to forget him: 'I remember.'

'I cannot stay,' said Hodson. 'I came only to tell you that as far as possible this house will be protected. If you see Alex before I do, tell him that the astrologer in Amritsar was right! He will know what that means. But if we get these wretches on the run I may see him before you do.'

He sprang back into the saddle, saluted her, and wheeling his horse galloped away with his men behind him; his face as eager and his eyes as hot and bright and glittering as though he rode to meet a friend or a lover instead of the death that awaited him that day.

The Highlanders had stared at Winter open-mouthed, and had grinned at her. Friendly, amazed, half-shy smiles that had transformed them in an instant from furious, fighting animals with the red haze of killing on their faces, to kindly, ordinary men with wives and children and sweethearts of their own. Then the door had been barred again and an order signed by Sir Colin Campbell himself nailed to it, and while the fighting lasted a guard had stood at the gate and protected the Gulab Mahal from the looting and the frenzy of battle-crazed, blood-drunk troops until the worst of that delirium was past.

Food had become scarce again in the pink stucco palace while the fighting swayed to and fro through the city and none dared venture beyond the walls, and towards the end of the month, when the last resistance had been crushed and the terrible guns were silent, there was little food to be obtained in the broken, burnt-out bazaars, and the shattered city starved.

Winter grew very thin in those days – as did Ameera and Hamida, and many others not only in the pink palace but in all Lucknow. But the baby throve, and her anxiety was not on her son's account. It was, as it had always been, for Alex. For the fall of Lucknow had not brought peace to Oudh.

General Sir Colin Campbell, the Commander-in-Chief, had committed one of those incomprehensible tactical errors that mar the success of so many campaigns. He had prevented General Outram from cutting off the enemy's retreat, with the result that the greater part of the opposing army had escaped.

And old Dasim Ali, hearing that news, had shaken his head lugubriously and wagged his red beard. If only part of that army crossed into Lunjore, said Dasim Ali, it would go hard with Randall Sahib – if he were there, and still alive.

April brought with it once again a warning of the molten heat to come, and the small bare rooms of the Gulab Mahal seemed airless once more, and stifling. Food was still scarce and milk was still scarcer – but news was scarcest of all, and what there was of it was never reassuring.

The mutiny was being stamped out, and the savage reprisals that Alex had feared and predicted were accompanying that process – in the old and evil belief that only blood and savagery can repay and wipe out the stain of blood and savagery.

The British troops who had been rushed to the defence of the dying Empire of a 'Company of Merchants Trading to the East' expected no quarter and gave none. They went into battle, shouting as their battle-cry '*Remember Cawnpore! Remember Cawnpore!*' – and they remembered Cawnpore and killed without mercy and hung without mercy; condemning a man as often as not for the colour of his skin as from any proof of guilt.

But although it would be many months yet before peace was fully restored it was already plain that the prophecy that the rule of the Company would end a hundred years after Plassey was to be fulfilled. India had become too great a thing to be the private possession of a Trading Company. It would have to be taken over by the Crown; that long step forward that Alex had spoken of.

'We have not won back Hind,' said Walayat Shah, 'but it was the Company's Raj that we had hoped to pull down, and, *Shook'r Khooda*, we have succeeded in that! For now the Company's Raj will go, and their long reign of robbery and confiscation will be ended.'

Soon it would be May again, and the breathless, burning days that a year ago had seen the fuel catch fire would see it still burning fiercely, though with a dying flame, in Jhansi and Rohilkhand and Gwalior and Oudh. But there was still no news from Lunjore——

'Surely if her husband were alive he would send word?' said the women of the Gulab Mahal. 'It must be that he is dead.'

That thought was often clear on their faces and in their kind, troubled eyes, and one day it had been too clear to be borne, and Winter had answered it as though it had been spoken aloud:

'No! It is not true. He is not dead. He will come for me some day. I have only to wait . . .'

And she had snatched up her son and carried him up to Alex's roof-top although the sun had not yet set and the heat shimmered on the hot stonework, and had strained her eyes in the direction of Lunjore as though her love and longing could reach beyond the horizon and pierce the distance and the dust-clouds and heat-haze that hid it from her sight.

The withered leaves of the trees below her rattled drily under the fingers of a little hot wind that blew through the garden. A wind that must have blown over Lunjore. 'Some day,' thought Winter. 'One day . . .'

They were words that she had been saying all her life. She had said them as a child at Ware. 'Some day I shall go back to the Gulab Mahal——' And she had come back. Surely some day Alex would come back too.

The sun dipped down towards the horizon and bathed the shattered city in beauty, hiding its blackened, gaping scars, and Winter remembered what Hodson had said to her – Hodson whose star, as the astrologer in Amritsar had prophesied so many years ago, 'would arise and burn bright among much blood', and who had died in the battle for the city – '*I may see him before you do.*' Had he too spoken prophetically? Had he indeed met Alex?

Quite suddenly she could bear it no longer, and she turned and ran desperately, as she had run before, to the refuge of the painted room, sobbing and shuddering.

The reflected glow of the sunset filled it with a warm rosy light, touching the trees and the birds and the flowers into the same enchanted life that lamplight could give them, and the leaves and the petals welcomed her and the birds and the beasts nodded to her and Firishta watched her with a bright, friendly, reassuring eye.

She pushed the bed to one side and sank down on the matting with the child in her arms, and leaned her head against the cool carved plaster, pressing her cheek against the comforting curve of Firishta's round green head. Her eyes closed and gradually the helpless trembling of her body lessened as little by little the fear ebbed away from her.

The baby went to sleep in her lap and the glow faded from the room, taking the gay brightness from it and leaving it as cool and as softly colourful as an opal.

Outside the windows the birds were settling down to rest with noisy chatterings and cawings and a flutter of wings among the orange trees, and beyond the far wall of the garden the dome of the little whitewashed mosque with its iron emblem of the crescent moon cut a lilac pattern against the evening sky.

The hum of the city rose up about the Gulab Mahal, washing around it; and through it and above it Winter could hear all the familiar, friendly sounds of the house. The distant chatter of shrill feminine voices, children laughing, a baby crying, the aged gateman clearing his throat and coughing asthmatically, a clatter of cooking-pots and the creak of the well-wheel. The sounds mingled and mixed with the no less dear and familiar scents of water sprinkled on parched ground, of the spicy smell of Eastern cooking and the smoke of dung-fires, the scent of warm dust and sun-soaked stone.

The sounds and the scents seemed to weave a web about the painted room, isolating it in safety, and Winter drew a long slow sigh and felt the last of the shuddering fear leave her.

'Some day,' she said, whispering the words against Firishta's green head. 'One day——'

There were footsteps and a murmur of voices in the passage beyond the doorway, and then someone lifted the heavy curtain that hung before it, and she opened her eyes and looked up. And it was Alex.

GLOSSARY

Angrezi British; English
Angrezi-log British people
Ayah child's nurse

Bairagi Hindu holy man
Bakri goat
Begum Mohammedan lady
Belait England
Beshak assuredly
Bhil grave dug by the Thugs for their victims
Bhoosa straw
Bibi-gurh women's house
Bourka one-piece head-to-heels cloak, with small square of coarse net to see through
Budmarsh rascal; bad man
Bund irrigation bank
Bunnia shopkeeper
Burra-lat-Sahib Great-lord-Sahib (Governor-General)
Butchas 'young ones' (children)

Charpoy Indian bedstead (usually string or webbing)
Chatti large earthenware water-pot
Chik sunblind made of split cane
Chirag small earthenware oil-lamp, used in festivals
Chowkidar night-watchman
Chuddah sheet or shawl
Chunam a fine, polished plaster
Chunna roasted gram (a form of grain)
Chuppatti thin flat cake of unleavened bread
Chupprassi peon

Dacoits robbers
Daffadar sergeant (cavalry)
Dâk mail; post
Dâk-bungalow posting-house; rest-house
Dâk-ghari horse-drawn vehicle carrying mail
Dazi tailor
Deputtah head-scarf
Dhobi washer of clothes; laundryman
Dhooli litter; palanquin
Durbar public audience; levee

Ekka light two-wheeled trap

Fakir religious mendicant
Feringhi foreigner

Ghari any horse-drawn vehicle
Ghee clarified butter
Gopi milkmaid
Gurra earthenware water-pot

Havildar sergeant (infantry)
Hookah water-pipe for smoking tobacco
Howdah seat carried on back of elephant
Huzoor Your Honour

Ilaqa district

Jaghirdar landowner
Jehad holy war
Jemadar junior Indian officer promoted from the ranks (cavalry or infantry)
Jezail long-barrelled musket
Jheel shallow, marshy lake
Juggra trouble; quarrel
Jung-i-lat Sahib Commander-in-Chief

Kala hirren blackbuck
Khansamah cook
Khidmatgar waiter at table
Khussee short-handled axe, carried by Thugs
Koss two miles
Koti house
Kotwal headman
Kutcha makeshift

Lance naik lance corporal
Lathi long, heavy staff, usually made from bamboo
Lotah small brass water-pot
Lughais Thugs who were responsible for the burial of the dead

Machan small platform built in a tree
Mahout elephant driver
Maidan parade-ground
Manji boatman
Maro! Strike! or Kill!
Masala spice
Maulvi title of a Mohammedan priest
Mem-log white women
Mullah Mohammedan priest
Munshi teacher, writer

Nani grandmother (diminutive)
Nauker-log servants (literally, 'servant-people')

Nautch-girl dancing-girl
Nullah ravine or dry water-course

Padishah ruler
Pan betel-nut rolled in a bayleaf and chewed
Parao camping-site
Piara darling
Puggari turban
Pulton infantry regiment
Punkah length of matting or heavy material pulled by a rope to make a breeze
Purdah seclusion of women (literally, 'curtain')
Pushtu the language of the Pathans

Resai quilt
Rissala cavalry (regiment)
Ruth domed purdah cart, drawn by bullocks

Sadhu Hindu holy man
Sahib-log white people
Saht-bai literally, 'seven brothers': small brown birds which go about in groups, usually of seven
Sepoy infantry soldier
Serai caravan hostel
Shabash! Bravo!
Shadi wedding; marriage
Shahin peregrine falcon
Shamianah large tent; marquee
Shikar hunting and shooting
Shikari hunter, finder of game
Sirdar Indian officer of high rank
Sowar cavalry trooper
Subadar chief Indian officer of company of sepoys
Syce groom

Taklief trouble
Talukdar large landholder
Terai a tract of land running along the foot of the Himalayas north of the Ganges
Tulwar curved sword

Zemindar farmer
Zenana woman's quarter